# FEAR
# THE
# FUTURE

The Final Volume of The Fear Saga

by Stephen Moss

For my wife and parents, whose unwavering support allowed me to explore this world,
for my friends, whose encouragement and help saw this through,
and for the many people who have joined me in this journey.
Though dark and bloody, it does have an end.  I hope you enjoy it.

# Contents

PROLOGUE

PART 1:

CHAPTER 1: WITH DISTURBING ALACRITY
CHAPTER 2: MIND-ER
CHAPTER 3: THRUM
CHAPTER 4: OF ONE MYND
CHAPTER 5: MEETING ROOM
CHAPTER 6: MEATING ROOM
CHAPTER 7: SADDLE AND BREAK
CHAPTER 8: COVERED
CHAPTER 9: CLANDESTINATION
CHAPTER 10: SHOCKWAVES – PART ONE
CHAPTER 11: SHOCKWAVES – PART TWO
CHAPTER 12: REFLEX
CHAPTER 13: FENG SHUI
CHAPTER 14: THE END OF THE ROPE

SECOND PART:

INTERVAL A: HER WORLD
INTERVAL B: THE FALL
INTERVAL C: EVENT PLANNING
INTERVAL D: LOST IN TRANSLATION
INTERVAL E: THE BALL ROLLING
INTERVAL EPILOGUE ...

PART 3:

CHAPTER 15: LADYBIRD
CHAPTER 16: THE MOURNING JOG
CHAPTER 17: SATELLITES
CHAPTER 18: SCHOOLS OF THOUGHT
CHAPTER 19: TIN CAN ALLY
CHAPTER 20: NEWSWORTHY
CHAPTER 21: THE MISSING LINK
CHAPTER 22: RIOTOUS
CHAPTER 23: THE FARM
CHAPTER 24: PREEMPTIVE STRIKE
CHAPTER 25: REACHING OUT
CHAPTER 26: AD MINISTER
CHAPTER 27: UGLY BEHAVIOR
CHAPTER 28: ON THE RUN
CHAPTER 29: THE CLOSING DOOR

## PART 4:

CHAPTER 30: A NEW DAY
CHAPTER 31: TASC MANUFACTURING PLANT 47
CHAPTER 32: HEKATON'S CARCASS
CHAPTER 33: CATCHER'S MITT
CHAPTER 34: THE BALL ROLLING
CHAPTER 35: TIDAL UNITY
CHAPTER 36: SEEKING DOUBT
CHAPTER 37: FINALLY, COUNTDOWN
CHAPTER 38: FINGER ON THE BUTTON
CHAPTER 39: THE ALZHEIMER'S SWITCH
CHAPTER 40: SACRIFICED
CHAPTER 41: IGNITION SEQUENCED
CHAPTER 43: PAWNS FORWARD
CHAPTER 44: EXCHANGE – PART ONE
CHAPTER 45: EXCHANGE – PART TWO
CHAPTER 46: CONSEQUENCE
CHAPTER 47: THE SHYLOCK
CHAPTER 48: THE FORGOTTEN

## FIFTH PART:

INTERVAL F: A DIFFERENT APPROACH
INTERVAL G: ADVOCATING FOR DEVILS
INTERVAL H: BEFORE
INTERVAL I: DURING
INTERVAL J: AND AFTER
INTERVAL K: THE COST OF MEMBERSHIP
INTERVAL L: CALLBACK
INTERVAL M: A PAINFUL DIVORCE
INTERVAL N: COUNTING BEANS
INTERVAL O: TAKING THE LEAP
INTERVAL END: DROPPING AN OCEAN

## ENDGAME:

CHAPTER 49: UNDER THE RADAR
CHAPTER 50: DYING ANOTHER DAY
CHAPTER 51: TIGHT SPACE
CHAPTER 52: NEW WORLD ORDER
CHAPTER 53: POST-MAN
CHAPTER 54: INTERVAL'S CLOSING
CHAPTER 55: STRATEGIC IMPERATIVE
CHAPTER 56: TACTICAL IMPERATIVES
CHAPTER 57: WATCHING THE WALL
CHAPTER 58: THE TRUTH WILL IN
CHAPTER 59: STEPPING INTO THE FRAY
CHAPTER 60: FINAL SOLUTION
CHAPTER 61: HITTING THE FAN
CHAPTER 62: CLAUSTROPHOBIA
CHAPTER 63: THE RED ZONE IS FOR ...

CHAPTER 64: PSYCHOTIC CONUNDRUM
CHAPTER 65: THE SHATTERED CLIFF
CHAPTER 66: CRAPSHOOT
CHAPTER 67: NUMBERS UP
CHAPTER 68: AND NOW, WATCH THIS ...

**EPILOGUE**

**THE ORPHANS' END**

# Prologue

The call continued at all times. It was a constant flow of information, the amount that needed to be said far exceeding the method by which they could now speak.

Birgit's home had been stabilized since it was lost. Its long, lazy rotation was now around an axis whose north pole was perennially pointed at its origin, at Earth, the place they had once been tethered to.

Terminus was a vast amalgamation of structures that had once housed more than eighty engineers, scientists, and astronauts. Now it was home to only two: Birgit, the doctor who had been trapped here while giving virtual birth to a machine god, and the station's captain, who had not dared interrupt the infinitely complex process.

They were alone now. It had been a hard truth to accept. A red, raw fact, itching away on the surface of their lives, suppressed slowly, and only through long days and nights of conversation, argument, drinking, and weeping in the many far corners of the station as they reconciled themselves to their fate.

For their home was now a new world, small perhaps, but still only the second satellite of the sun to be inhabited, having been severed from the first.

But while they may be lonely, they were both eminently capable, and they would not waste their long, lonely exile.

The captain had almost unparalleled experience with spacefaring, and especially with the massive Terminus One station that had been his charge. His days were full to bursting with the task of maintaining and protecting the massive network of modules, from the remaining habitation module they called home, to the labyrinth of laboratory and science hubs that had once been the life of the station.

Dr. Birgit Hauptman, for her part, roamed those laboratories and science hubs, filling them with new purpose. For hers was a mind humanity could not afford to lose to the void. She pursued her experiments with vigor, and all the while her mind was linked to the station, into the network, via her spinal interface node on the back of her neck, managing, monitoring, and speaking to her companions: the machine and the captain who had sacrificed everything to stay with her.

*Birgit:* 'yes, rob, through [portal 43.2a] and then onto the comms hub.'

Captain Cashman acknowledged the instruction, the portal's location appearing as a visual place in his mind as she sent the thought to him. Another voice joined them. The station's third resident.

*Minnie:* <our connection should improve with this routing. i will be able to send compression files via the secondary defense laser-hub to myself when it is not needed for near-space meteor defense.>

*Birgit:* 'yes, minnie, it should help the connection a great deal.'

Birgit thought it offhandedly. This was not the Minnie that Birgit knew, the Minnie that Birgit had raised. This was just a copy. This was, well, just a machine. Birgit could still 'speak' with the real Minnie as well, but it was like a static phone call with a distant loved one, and really only served to remind her of what she was missing.

There was a pause in the conversation, then Birgit went on, '¿maybe we can even paint again, Minnie, one day?'

Birgit did not try to disguise the patronizing tone in her mind when she spoke to this Minnie. Nor did she try to hide her disappointment at not being able to fully commune with the real Minnie anymore, though she knew the conversation was being transmitted back to that version, that truly beautiful artificial mind.

And the real Minnie was constantly updating this version of herself in return. Tweaking, adding, refining, trying to make it better.

But it was all but pointless, they both knew that. Just as it would be pointless for Birgit to try and protect the feelings of her machine progeny. The act of masking her emotions would only dull the connection even more than the inept and inadequate laser communications system they had jury-rigged already did.

This was not lost on Rob, not completely, though he did not really understand the depth of the bond that had formed between the two. But he did understand what they meant when they said 'painting.'

*Rob:* 'oh no. not the painting again. you know that freaks me out.'

Birgit laughed to herself, and then, purely out of spite, sent Rob a mental image of the last three-dimensional image Minnie had created as she learned and developed her understanding of the concept of creativity. It was a poor imitation of the full fractal complexity that Minnie was capable of, but such were the limits of their communications, and it still boggled the mind to try and absorb the flowing forms and abstract shapes that morphed and formed within the cloud of esoteric substance that were Minnie's finger-paintings.

*Rob:* 'jesus. i wish you would stop doing that.'

He felt Birgit laugh through the connection, along with the warmth of her regard for him, for the man who had selflessly joined her on this endless journey, and who, no doubt, saved her life a hundred times a day with his diligence and skill. So naturally she showed her deep appreciation by giving him as hard a time as possible.

*Birgit:* 'oh, rob, you big girl's blouse. ¿how can a man who stares at the cosmos all day get nauseous looking at a painting?'

But in truth she understood his feelings quite well. Minnie's interpretation of abstract was absolute, and her paintings defied understanding, quite literally. They resisted any attempt at rationalization. For a man like Captain Rob Cashman, that was anathema. For Birgit, it was impossibly beautiful, and she wept when she allowed herself to truly bathe in their all-encompassing, multi-sense form. Crying with joy at their beauty, and with sadness at the fact that she might never again see them in their full, unabridged glory.

*Might* never see.

For among the many projects she was working on with the help of Rob and the copy of Minnie that inhabited the station's network was one that held not only the promise of helping earth in the coming war, but also of reconnecting her with her daughter, the fruit of her mind.

# Part 1:

## Chapter 1: With Disturbing Alacrity

It never failed to amaze Jim, even after all these years.

They were going to believe it.

His new office was a shambles, partly because of the mess of boxes and materials that bore witness to his establishing order over his new domain, and partly because of the more figurative shambles that was the collection of teams and administrative entities that he was putting together at a mad pace.

He sat at an unassuming desk in his new office at District One. Outside the door was the broad space he had requested and been given to house the team he was forming. TASC had officially entered the big leagues, and whether it wanted it to or not, that meant that the new state would need to vastly increase its ability to handle and react to the sea of ever-changing information that was the lifeblood of the political echelon they now played in.

The buzz from the hive of activity outside his door was set to the beat of the greater sound outside the walls, the massive rebuilding effort still getting underway all over the broad stretch of land at the southern end of Sao Tome, and on the once mighty fortress that had been Rolas Base. They were just getting started on that work, a project whose scale beggared belief. But they had the ability and the impetus to rebuild it, and far away at District Two they were even now building the tools that would accelerate the process in the massive orb of gold and magnetism that was the Resonance Dome.

Jim studied the report in front of him. It was not formatted in the way he would normally insist on it being, but then it had been created in a very different way than his briefings had been back when he was the White House chief of staff. It had been created by his new press secretary and her team, but with the help of the strange entity known as Minnie, a mind whose exact nature and capabilities Jim was still coming to terms with.

At some point, Jim knew, he would have to bite the bullet and have one of the spinal interfaces put in so he could commune with Minnie directly. A growing number of his ever-expanding team already had been through the process.

The insertion of the device itself was apparently fairly innocuous, but that was just the first stage. After that you had to be trained on how to handle the process, a stage overseen by the young Portuguese scientist who had spearheaded the development of the interface software himself.

It was all done with Minnie's assistance, of course, for you were now stepping into her domain. It was an evolving process, becoming ever more flexible and efficient as more people went through it and they continued to codify and refine it. And it would need to be faster. Much faster. Because it was a program that had ever more people signing up for it as the growth of their organization accelerated.

Jim found himself rubbing the back of his neck, as he did anytime he contemplated the strange little gelport Neal was pressuring him to have installed there. He shook his head and set aside the whole concept. He would do it, he just, well, he had too much work to do right now.

He focused on the report in front of him:

*TASC Information Office Update: Beijing Politburo Strike Corollaries.*

It was a lengthy report, and one he had read several times already. He scanned through the pages seeking the highlighted sections that denoted changes since his last review, one concession he had managed to get to the process he had spent so many years perfecting.

The report detailed the various profound effects being felt since Neal's brutal but essential strike at the heart of the Chinese Communist Party. Not surprisingly, the Chinese were more than a touch displeased at having the unofficial center of their political landscape wiped so thoroughly from the face of the Earth.

One might think that such an act would have instantly provoked a counterattack, and one of potentially devastating proportions, and indeed that had been the fear of many when they heard about the shocking blow.

But while Neal had been extreme in his final measure to stop the pervasive and devastating terrorism of the last of the Mobiliei Agents, he had not been as foolhardy as some might think. For the attack's very extremity and boldness was, in the end, proving to be its saving grace.

Jim reviewed the details. He looked for, read, and then reread the key information he sought, and when he was comfortable that he was up to date on the key details, he waved in the small group of people even now gathering outside his door.

"Come in, come in. Take a seat, if you can find one," Jim said to the four people he had heading up the information monitoring and counter-flow effort. They filed in, moving papers from the two chairs and stacking various boxes until they were all either seated or leaning on some form of impromptu perch.

"Minnie's waiting on line two," said one of them, and another of them leant forward and pressed the speakerphone button and flashing '2' on Jim's phone to bring Minnie's disembodied voice into the room. The three people present who had been through Minnie and Amadeu's little intro to the next millennium did not comment on how antiquated the phone now seemed, or how strange it was to hear Minnie's voice come through such a limited, language-only device. They just looked to their papers and waited for the meeting to kick off.

"Hello, all," said Minnie through the speaker, "I can feel three of you directly. Are Jim and Andrew also in the room?"

Jim said yes, as did the one research analyst who had yet to get a spot in interface school.

"OK, let's get started," said Jim. "First off, in the latest news releases from Beijing I see they have already consolidated the outstanding posts on the Standing Committee."

"They have, sir," said one of the four researchers, a former Chinese national who had worked for Jim as an intern some years ago and willingly answered his call to head up the Pan-Asian intelligence team. "The surviving five members of the Standing Committee have announced internal party elections in two months time, and named Li Yunshan as the interim chairman."

"And it appears they still persist that this was all an accident?" said Jim to answering nods.

"They do," said Andrew, "and moreover are taking up the line that the photos of the incident were fakes, a fiction we have been very keen to help promote."

The incident they were referring to had actually been shockingly quick. From Banu's arrival on the scene to put an exclamation point at the end of Quavoce's final conversation with Agent Pei Leong-Lam, right through to her departure from the city's immediate airspace once more had spanned less than six seconds.

A particularly loud and obtrusive six seconds, to be sure, but six seconds, nonetheless.

In most places in the world that have been so quick as to have defied anyone to capture it on film, but with an estimated fifteen million cell phones in Beijing, there had indeed been two quick and albeit blurry photos captured of the event, photos that had quickly gone viral across the globe.

But two very different information agencies had immediately gone to work to discredit the images. Their methods and reasons for doing so could not have been more different, but together they constituted the greatest propaganda machine in history.

The first was the Chinese Department of Xuānchuán, an ambiguous word that meant either publicity or propaganda depending on who you were talking to. The Chinese government had spent nearly fifty years persistently telling the people of China that its borders were all but impenetrable, its army unparalleled on earth. So to admit that a single craft had penetrated those defenses to the very heart of the nation, and then departed without so much as a scratch on its strange hull, would have been too great an admission of vulnerability for the mighty state.

For the newly sovereign TASC, wanting the leaders of the world to know what awaited them if they stood in the way of TASC's mission was one thing, wanting the people of those nations to know was another altogether. And so for this rare moment the propaganda machine of the injured but still mighty Chinese state had an unlikely ally. An ally who had turned its very different skillset to flooding the internet with some even more amazing photos of the event, albeit ones that had some very fatal flaws in them.

The flaws had been deliberate, and when they had been discovered, the photos as a whole had been dismissed, along with verbal accounts that were even now being deleted and silenced by a zealous Chinese internet censorship bureau.

Another of the analysts now spoke up. "Minnie and I have included a briefing on which news channels are still reporting on the incident, how much time they are dedicating to the story, and the disposition of their analysis over time."

Jim started thumbing through the update, looking for the relevant section, and one of the analysts prompted him, "Page eighty-three, sir."

Jim found it and took a moment to read it. They all knew what it indicated, but they waited for Jim to see it himself. The information showed what is often referred to in the misinformation industry as a 'credibility curve.' It was different by region.

The more developed nations of Europe were already moving on, both in terms of which version of the story was being given greater credence and the tone with which they were approaching the entire event. It was starting to become comical, a topic for comedians and late night talk show hosts. The persistence of more fringe media outlets that this was in fact an attack was only fueling that change.

For most, it seemed, the credibility of the story was quickly accelerating down the far side of the curve, plummeting into the region of conspiracy theory, to join 9/11 government cover-ups and Elvis sightings. That was in Europe. In the US it was holding on a little stronger, but their greater appetite for conspiracy theory was well known. Elsewhere it was fading into obscurity, with greater speed the farther you got from the sight itself.

"And what ..." said Jim, slightly distractedly as he finished reviewing the data. He lifted his eyes and started again, "And what of the cover story. Our ... gas explosion?"

He said it with the distaste they all felt for the stereotypical and unimaginative alternative to reality that the Chinese had been pushing for the last few days. But there was not much else the Chinese could say.

Luckily for Neal, the building had been all but deserted, a factor they had considered in planning the attack. In fact, if the Party chairman himself had not been being forced to be there by the Agent that had controlled him for so long, then the party leadership would probably have been all but unaffected by the strike, barring the loss of some junior aides unfortunate enough to be working at that hour.

"Actually," said Minnie, "we have an idea of how to help with that story as well."

"OK," said Jim, "I'm all ears." After all, a story that well used needed all the help it could get.

But it was not Minnie who spoke, another of the analysts spoke up, making it painfully apparent to Jim that she was having sidebar conversations in the ether. Jim ignored the slight, mostly because he really didn't care about such things, and listened.

"Well, sir," said the excited but nervous analyst, "it seems to us that we can do the reverse of the manipulated photograph release we did to discredit the Skalm pictures, and release a version of the photos that we can claim is the unaltered photo: *with* the explosions, but no Skalm ..."

Jim nodded, but with a frown. "Creating obvious forgeries is one thing. Creating photos that must stand up to the most rigorous of study is another."

"No, it isn't," said Minnie from the phone, and Jim stared at the grey plastic box on his desk as if it had just said it wanted to go on a date with him.

After a moment's silence, Jim prompted an explanation. "Err, OK, Minnie. Care to elaborate?"

"Of course, Jim. I would not alter the photos at all. I would use the original photos and database images of the city of Beijing to create a virtual copy of the city. Then I would reenact the events of that night, but without the Skalm present, and capture images of the same moments in time from the same virtual locations as the original photographers. In the end, the images generated would be indistinguishable from reality."

Jim was doubtful and he looked around. Indistinguishable was a strong word, an absolute, and several decades in politics had taught him not to believe in absolutes. That said, he now noted that each of the three analysts who had met Minnie in person, as it were, did not share his skepticism.

"Indistinguishable?" said Jim, not hiding skepticism.

"Yes," said Minnie, "They would be real pictures of a three-dimensional space as tangible to me as the original. If I then deleted the virtual construct from my memory, even I would not be able to tell if the images were genuine or not."

He stared at the phone once more. What credibility would they have if this were discovered? What credibility would anything have if such a capacity for forgery were discovered?

What innocence was the world going to lose next, thought Jim, then breathed deep and moved on. They had much to cover, and more work, both predicted and unforeseen, was soon to come.

- - -

As the rest of the week unfolded, an unwitting Chinese media took up the new images willingly, perhaps even starting to believe the fabrication themselves, and the story started to fall by the wayside. Not that its passing signaled a return to normality for the news stations or the people they serve. The world was still reverberating from the myriad of disasters that had recently befallen it.

From the line of burned-out hulks still being cleared from the roads in Eastern Hungary, to the apparent coup in Moscow that ended Premier Svidrigaïlov's reign there, the actions of TASC continue to be absorbed like body blows, both by the nations that once stood against them, and the ones that once stood with them.

Former allies and enemies alike now deal with TASC and its representatives begrudgingly. They may be willing to help perpetuate the lies that the world needs to hear, but it cannot last much longer. Eventually the truth will come out. And soon.

## Chapter 2: Mind-er

Neal's eyes glistened with genuine affection as he greeted the little girl. "There she is. How are you?"

Banu smiled and ran to him, taking the proffered hug with relish. She was barred from nearly all outside contact these days, her circle limited to Neal and Amadeu, and of course Quavoce, her father, the man who protected her, even as she protected them all.

"Hello, Uncle Neal."

He held the girl up, a twinge in his back betraying his ever-poorer physical condition, a price he paid for his dedication to his work, he liked to tell himself, but in fact was rooted in a more profound laziness that was common among those that only found purpose in despair.

"How's my little warrior princess, huh?" She giggled and he spun her a little in the air before her minimal weight became too much for him and he lowered her to the ground once more.

"Do you want to know a secret, my little warrior? I have something for you," Neal now said, conspiratorially. "Do you want to see?"

"Yes!" she giggled with excitement, and she ran alongside him as he walked the short distance from where he had asked Quavoce to meet him to a heavy-looking door.

A moment's confusion flashed across Banu's innocent-seeming face before the door swung open of its own accord to reveal a large room, decorated everywhere in girlish pinkness that went way past garishness and out the other side into the realm of the ridiculous. The most incongruous part, though, was the pictures that lined the walls, for they were not of teen idols or Japanese manga heroines.

They were of owls and hawks, fighter jets, and, of course, the Skalm, stark in its beauty and pure function.

Banu shrieked and ran from Neal's side into the room. There was a bed and a hammock, a chair and a desk covered in crayons and books; and toys, so many toys, arranged in boxes around the walls. She ran from one to the next, eyeing their contents with a gleam in her eye bordering on ecstasy, and then turned back to Neal with a question in her eyes …

"Yes, Banu, it is all for you. This is your new room!"

She shrieked once more and continued her exploration.

Quavoce came to stand at Neal's side, his face showing that strange combination of happiness for his daughter and apprehension at the sight of her being spoiled, an emotion that any parent can sympathize with.

"Really, Neal?" he said quietly, as his ward began unloading a mass of toys from a particular box.

Neal smiled and chuckled. He did not look away from the girl as he replied, "Yes, Quavoce, really. And don't be so alarmed. She's had enough harsh reality to last a lifetime. This is for her. A small token of our appreciation."

Quavoce could not argue the point too much, but to him it all still had the bitter aftertaste of spoiled wine, a good thing soured by circumstance. Quavoce was silent a moment then spoke up once more, as if he had been discussing the point within himself. "I cannot disagree, Neal, that she deserves some fun given what we have put her through, and even some distraction from the flying. Something I fear she enjoys a little too much. But ..."

"Quavoce, my friend, please. This is not a bribe, and it is not just to make me feel better for sending a six-year-old girl into ... well, we both know what we sent her into."

Battle was a kind term for what Banu had been tasked with. Slaughter would be a better term, and Banu had been wielding the butcher's knife herself. Most worrying had been that she had enjoyed it a little more than they might have liked. But now, hopefully, they could rely on the threat alone. Now they could return to diplomacy, a tactic that was always far more effective when silently backed by the threat of overwhelming military might.

"No, Quavoce," Neal went on, "this is both a reward and a distraction. She needs to feel like a little girl again and hopefully she can do that here. She can still spend time in the air, both simulated and in the Skalm itself, and, should we need her to, she can still fight, from here. From this safe place. With you nearby and with everything she needs at hand."

Quavoce was about to protest once more; after all, he had hoped for more than a one-room existence for the little girl when he had rescued her from the plague-ridden lands of her youth. But Neal was not done, and before Quavoce could formulate his objection, Neal called out.

"Minnie! Are you there?" he said to the air, and a voice replied, his pleasantly smug smile betraying his excitement at this final surprise.

"Yes, Neal. I am here. I am always here." It was a familiar voice, but it was one that until now had rarely been embodied outside the confines of the ether.

Banu perked at the sound, it was a voice she was as deeply familiar with as Quavoce's.

"Minnie!" she said, turning, but then confusion blurred her smile. It was the first time she had heard Minnie with her ears, and not from inside her mind. It was like hearing an imaginary friend actually speak, and she seemed most perplexed by the sensation.

The little girl joined Quavoce in staring at the heavy door and through it to the corridor beyond, to where the voice had come from.

"Yes, Banu," said Neal, "Minnie wanted to be here, as your friend. So she can play with you here, like she does in the ether."

Banu seemed happy at this, and yet still confused. And then the source of the voice entered the room. She was tall and not unattractive, but she was also stocky, almost masculine in her build. Banu did not notice this, she was too absorbed with trying to reconcile this person with the friend she knew as Minnie.

But Quavoce recognized it instantly as a machine body built not just for work as a would-be nanny. That would have taken the slightest of frames given the power of a mechanical musculature. No, this was a nanny that even Ms. Poppins would have hesitated to tangle with.

But the face on this martial machine was all gentleness, if a little awkward, still learning to see with two eyes and smile without appearing ghoulish.

"Hello, Minnie!" said Neal, with unconcealed pleasure, "It is so nice to see you!"

She turned to Neal with deliberately slow movement, Quavoce noting the way she limited the speed of her actions to more biological timeframes, "Hello, Neal, it is nice to see you too. I am going to go and play with Banu, if you don't mind."

"Not at all, you go ahead!" said Neal, like a high school coach talking to his star player. And so Minnie turned and walked toward the young girl, who stared wide-eyed at the big woman. But in the nanny's black eyes was the same deliberate gentleness and infinite care she had once seen in Quavoce's eyes, one quiet and cold night, and as Minnie knelt by Banu, the little girl began to smile.

Then she reached up gingerly and whispered in the woman's ears, "Is it really you?"

Minnie did not have to fake the smile that came next, she called on her sense of emotion and love that she had inherited from Amadeu and Birgit, and combined them all with the very real feelings she had for the young girl, and the smile that came to her face had all the emotion of the little girl's responding grin, both their faces alight at the simple act of meeting in person for the first time.

They hugged, and Quavoce turned to leave, taking Neal by the arm as he did so. Neal took the hint, dragging himself from the touching but very unusual sight and following the Agent out of the room.

"That is a strange thing you have done, Neal. Good, but strange ... and, well ... dangerous."

"Dangerous?" said Neal, genuinely curious at what could possibly be seen as dangerous in what he had just witnessed.

"Well, it is not the first time I have seen a child put in the care of a machine. Indeed, it's not the first time it's happened to poor Banu, I suppose. But as human as Minnie may seem, you would do well to remember that sentience is not the same as humanity."

Neal balked, "Careful, Quavoce. You are, without doubt, one of humanity's greatest friends, but you are not one of us, let us not forget that. Whereas Minnie is born of human parents. Of course she is not like us, but I trust her with my life everyday, as do we all. And ..."

"You misunderstand me, Neal. I mean not to question Minnie's motives. Her heart and purpose are without question. Truly without question. But that is just what I mean to stress here. There is a difference between us and the machines, and it is greater even than the difference between human and Mobiliei. It lies not in an imperfection, but in their perfection. The very singularity of a machine's purpose."

Neal seemed skeptical, but Quavoce went on, "You are determined, Neal. Goodness knows you are more determined than any man I have ever met. But that is nothing compared to a machine's ability to dedicate itself to a task. I have to question every day what my machine subconscious wants to do, what options it provides me in its quest to meet my needs. It is a drug, and it is highly addictive."

Neal began to nod. He could see where Quavoce was going and he could not deny the wisdom of it, "You are right, of course. I see it in myself too, the more I become dependent on Minnie. I have to actively remind myself that she is, well, she is a tool. An incredible tool, and one I value alongside my very closest friends and allies, but a tool nonetheless."

He looked into Quavoce's eyes and added, thoughtfully, "You are warning me against letting Banu become too dependent on Minnie."

Quavoce nodded. They both thought about this for a moment, and then Neal went on, "Well, my friend, you understand what that means?"

Quavoce paused, and Neal said with a shrug, "It means that we will just have to continue to spend a lot of time with her as well."

Quavoce laughed quietly.

"As fun as the rest of the people at District One are, I guess we will just have to grin and bear it," said Quavoce.

They walked off, neither of them sad to think that they had a real need to continue to revel in the simple pleasure of Banu's company. But neither of them was naïve either. They could see the signs of conflict in the young girl. The cost of exposing her young mind to the harsh truth of the world they now lived in. They needed her. But they must never forget that she needed them just as much, more perhaps.

# Chapter 3: Thrum

The wide plain was without tree or shrub. No animal scuttled across its surface, and none ever had. But there was activity there, nonetheless. At the center of the plain, in a deep crater within another much larger and much older one, was a machine. It was a very large machine. And it was digging.

It was not there to mine any resource, not even to reveal some secret or ancient archeological find. There was nothing below but rock: ever harder, ever denser rock as the machine delved ever deeper. And it was this dense core matter that the great machine sought.

It was seeking purchase.

Its ten great, burrowing drills were grinding into the dirt and rock to get to the core of the planetoid.

For this was not Earth. It was a moon. Not ours, that would have been too large even for this machine's epic need. Too large and too obvious.

No, this was a moon that orbited around another planet, a planet so often featured in our dreams of space. The Red Planet. Mars.

Unlike Earth, Mars has two moons. One very small and more distant, though still much closer than our own. And the other, larger one moving at incredible speed and very close to the planet's surface. So close, in fact, that if it had been anywhere near the size of our moon it would have ripped the very planet apart.

Phobos. And on it, in it, drilling down into its core, was the other of the Mobiliei's gifts to our solar system: the last of its kind. The last in a long string of great machines sent out to prepare a highway, not for people but for information.

It was drilling into the surface to construct a massive relay, or rather to turn the entire moon into one. It was drilling to weave its great, nanotube cables through the superstructure of Phobos and attach itself to the moon at a fundamental level. It was a long process, one filled with error and recalibration. The machine had to fine-tune the moon, find precisely the purchase and angle that would allow it to vibrate the great rock like a bell, allowing the machine to send out its signal across the cosmos.

And it was a process that was being repeated by a thousand such machines in a long line back to Mobilius. Some were already complete, having had more luck than most. Some places along the line had not had a planetoid to harness, and so the investment had had to be made in sending a string of larger probes, and the long acceleration and deceleration that had been required to get them into place along the line.

And even then it would not be complete. It would never be complete. For it was a line between two ships that were constantly moving apart, and it would require constant adjustment, paying out, and adding to.

But this machine, large as it was, was still in essence just a relay, a beacon like the hilltop fires of old, a line of flame anchored at one end by the massive hub at Mobilius and at the other by this one, here in our own solar system.

Once the chain was complete, years from now, it would allow the leaders of the race coming to eradicate humanity to have an open line to their new colony on Earth. In the meantime, this particular link in the chain worked with a more immediate purpose, to send a signal to the coming Armada that would soon be within its theoretical range.

To relay news of the Agents that the Armada believed were even now preparing us, infiltrating and weakening us. And from the satellites that the Armada thought still orbited our mass.

Its work was nearing completion. Its anchors were almost deep enough, almost ready. Soon it would be operational.

# Chapter 4: Of One Mynd

Neal sat down in his own office, stretching his legs. He did not need to plug in; he was connected at all times via the inch-wide dome that was attached to the gelport at the back of his neck. It needed charging occasionally, but one of his many assistants saw to it he always had a fully charged node, and thus was always able to connect whenever he needed to.

Assistants. He had many assistants now. Still getting used to that. He contemplated the fact for a moment, then initiated his connection to the network.

*Neal:* 'good morning, minnie.'

*Minnie:* <good morning, neal. ¿do you need an update on anything?>

*Neal:* 'no, minnie, i am fine. i have jim's full briefing package here and he is on his way to give me my morning status update. ¿is there anything you particularly need my input on?'

*Minnie:* <no, jim has all the latest information.>

*Neal:* 'good, then can you connect me with district two, i want to talk with william and mynd.'

*Minnie:* <of course.>

They did not say good-bye, she would be online throughout any conversation he had. The need to keep even Minnie in the dark during the Resonance Dome's construction was past now, and as part of her daily routine she had one of her many subsidiary AIs monitoring any and all communications coming to and from Neal and the rest of his leadership team, if only to make sure she was up to date on their latest thoughts and decisions.

Far away to the south, another mind was alerted to his request for contact, a request only in the manner that it could be delayed for maybe a moment or two, and even then only if there was a very, very good reason. But there was no delay, and Mynd came online a second later.

*Mynd:* <neal, hello. ¿how can i help you?>

Mynd was very different from Minnie, not only in terms of origin but also in terms of purpose. He was the child of Neal's mind and that of another scientist who was even now finishing up another task so he could join them. That alone made him a very different being than Birgit and Amadeu's free spirited AM child Minnie, but he was also far more focused in his purpose.

Where Minnie was everywhere and nowhere, her many minion AIs parsing vast volumes of data in their daily job of running the world-spanning enterprise Neal was at the head of, Mynd was, by comparison, singularly dedicated, his focus limited to one place, one island.

*Neal:* '¿is william available? i want to talk to him as well.'

*Mynd:* <he will be with us momentarily. ¿would you like to see my latest creation while we wait?>

Even as he asked the question a data packet was bobbing gently but persistently at the limit of Neal's field of etheric vision. Its title was simply 'EAHL.'

Neal smiled.

*Neal:* 'yes, mynd, i would like to see that very much.'

The packet expanded suddenly and overwhelmed Neal, but he was ready for it, and even starting to enjoy the drug-like rush of Mynd's 'data packets.' Suddenly he was above Deception Island once again.

Whereas before the island had been as clandestine as such a thing could be, the great harbor at its center was now a hub of activity. The USS *Truman* was even now pulling into the big bay to take its place as the center of operations for the district. But it was only one of seven big ships in the harbor. The rest were cargo ships, laden with raw materials to feed the gaping maw that dominated the small peninsula jutting into the several-mile-wide crater.

The first of the massive Dome's creations was long since airborne, its first mission the stuff of future legend, its power providing the backbone to Neal's newfound military body. But its second creation was coming online now, and it was, in many ways, even more impressive than the first. Less spectacular, perhaps, but still the stuff of dreams only a few years ago.

It was spiderlike, and it would be the first of four such behemoths. Whereas the Skalm had been singular in purpose, the EAHL would be versatile; where the Skalm had been a scythe, the EAHL would be a fist, as capable of thumping as it was of grasping. It would carry us back to the stars, and it would do so on six great plumes of fusion fire surrounding its central cargo arms.

It was not an attractive beast, indeed it was ugly at an instinctual level, making your skin crawl when viewed from a distance. The six great engines that surrounded its center could pretty much lift any weight that the team chose to laden it with. But the central mass of the ship had a network of spindly arms lining its underside, like so many insect-like claws and fangs, ready to grasp and hold whatever cargo it was tasked with delivering.

It was fully eighty meters across, a scale that was difficult to grasp as it was wheeled on a great gantry from the Dome's open mouth. Had Neal wanted it to, it could have straddled one of the cargo ships in the bay, grasped it, and lifted it clean out of the water, such was its power.

But it had no such mission. Its first payload was already waiting for it, being unloaded from the hold of one such ship to be grasped in the EAHL's claws and taken straight up, into space.

*Neal:* 'i see the cable is ready. that is very good. very good indeed.'

He made a mental note to thank Madeline for her team's hard work there, and without comment Minnie took the instruction, rippling it outward to Neal's various assistants and secretaries to be added to his to-do list and then his schedule.

But his attention remained on the EAHL, and Mynd sensed this and took him inward, to its still dormant engines, waiting to be given life. This was not the unhinged and irrational Skalm, and it would not take Birgit's level of technical genius to jumpstart this beast, but they were still waiting for their second stringer, as it were, to get up to speed before she attempted to turn the key on the EAHL.

*Neal:* '¿how is moira doing, is she feeling more comfortable now?'

Neal spoke of Moira Banks, the Canadian wunderkind they had found among Birgit's graduate student roster. A protégé and a prodigy, even if she was yet to feel as comfortable with the second moniker as Neal and William were in applying it to her.

*Mynd:* <actually, william is just finishing a work session with her now. ¿would you like to join them?>

His acquiescence was unspoken, a permission given from directly within him, and in a moment he was at their virtual sides. William, embodied in the ether as he was now in life as well, in an avatar; and Moira, only twenty-seven but wise beyond her years, an old soul, her avatar imbued with all the reticence she felt toward the task she had found herself lumbered with.

*Moira:* 'neal! wow! hi! still getting used to the whole 'materializing out of nothing' thing.'

*Neal:* 'yes, it is strange, isn't it. if it makes you feel any better, most people will not be able to creep up on you like i can in here. but membership has its *access* privileges, if you know what i mean.'

It was a geek joke, and it found its audience here, a virtual ripple of laughter following among the three lifelong academics.

*William:* 'hello, neal.'

*Neal:* 'william. ¿how goes it?'

*William:* 'i think it is safe to say moira here is ... and i hope you don't mind me blowing your cover on this, moira ... still a little freaked out.'

Moira did not mind at all. In fact, she wished everyone would say it, and that it would impact even a little the high expectations they all seemed to have for her. Neal was understanding, sympathetic even. That said, he was long past being willing to wait for anyone, no matter what their level of freakedoutedness, or whatever they chose to call the reticence of those who seemed to think any of this was an option.

He tempered whatever frustration he may have felt, however, recognizing that this young woman was not the real source of his anger, and instead answered calmly, if a little patronizingly.

*Neal:* 'no, no. that is totally understandable, moira. and indeed even encouraged. i can tell you that birgit was equally nervous when she first initiated one of the fusion cores. but you have started small, just as she did. and i hear from madeline that she has reviewed the core turnover and tritium breeding rates and is very comfortable with your level of skill. high praise indeed, coming from her!'

Moira blushed, and her control over her virtual self was so embryonic that the emotion bled through. But it was an endearing sight and Neal's mood softened a little to match his patrician tone.

*Neal:* 'truth be told, i understand from birgit that she was not prepared for the sensation herself, even with her knowledge of the process.'

It was true, and Birgit had said as much in her conversations with Moira via their syrupy-slow laser link to Terminus Station.

*Neal:* 'but she has also told me you are ready. as ready as anyone can be. and if there is anyone whose opinion i take seriously here it is hers. more even than your own sense of how prepared you are. now, william and mynd here assure me that you will be being actively monitored in real-time, and madeline will be online as well, with a team of control specialists back at District Three. they will get you through it, and help you should you get in trouble.'

Neal wished Madeline or one of her longer-term team members could handle this themselves, but Madeline had been clear that this was not a question of the broad scientific method she brought to her leadership role, but of a precise and detailed knowledge of the incredibly complex process in question. Whoever was in control needed to understand the forces at play at the muscle-memory level.

Moira managed a nod, and put on a simulacrum of a brave face, and Neal smiled in response.

*Neal:* 'i am sure you will do fine, moira. i mean that. i would not give you charge of this if i did not believe in you, and if madeline and birgit did not believe in you as well.'

OK. Enough of this pandering, thought Neal, and his right brain filled with purpose once more and Mynd reacted, initiating systems and sending protocol starts out across the island and to TASC's distant districts, like neurons pulsing around the globe-spanning enterprise.

William quickly sensed by the new flow of information starting to cloy at his senses that Neal was done here. William was being called elsewhere, called by the very man standing in front of him smiling.

*William:* 'err, ok. Moira, we are going to pick this up again later. if you want to continue running simulations with mynd and madeline, i think neal wants me to quickly catch him up on some other tasks.'

Neal did.  And with shared smiles and some final platitudes they left the woman and her slightly deer-in-the-headlights expression to her models.

*Neal:* 'good.  she will be fine.  you are all going to see to that.  and even if i don't have total confidence in her yet, i do have it in you.'

It was a compliment and a threat in one, and it received only the quick mental acknowledgement it required.  William knew what Neal wanted an update on, and he did not wait around.

*William:* 'ok.  let's talk about our friend the bionic man!'

He said it with some relish, and Neal could not resist a grin to match William's own. Mynd, watching and listening, was equally intrigued, if less boyishly enthused as they.

*William:* 'the best way to explain is to show, as we always say.  ¿so why don't you just take a look?  i'm bringing phase nine online now.  i'll meet you out there.'

And with that they were gone, through the ether and out the other side, back into reality once more.  But this was an augmented reality, like the view from within a battleskin.  But this was not a skin, it was an entire body.

Neal stood now in a broad aluminium shed, one of the many that dotted the bay at the center of Deception Island.  He stood still, almost impossibly so, his lack of command signals leaving the body he was now possessing completely without movement.

Hand.  He brought it up.  It was not a hand as he knew it.  It had only two fingers opposite a fat thumb.  One finger looked like a black, pointed version of an index finger, the other was much thicker, matching the powerful looking thumb that faced it.  He flexed his digits. They moved with a dexterity that was at once amazing and frankly disgusting.  He could fold them back all the way, to touch his wrist, a wrist that could rotate 360 degrees.

He shivered at the sight, and the tremor ran up the spine of the machine body like it was mocking him.

*Neal:* 'mynd, give me an outside view of the machine.'

But before he could answer another view was approaching.  It was William, the paraplegic, crippled from the neck down, walking into the room on equally bionic limbs.  Mynd co-opted the view from William's suit as Neal had requested and now he saw both machines simultaneously as they approached each other.

William was a crumpled form wrapped and enveloped within a machine skeleton.  It was akin to a battleskin, only to facilitate easy access it lacked the armor plating, and as such was able to remove itself at will from William's body and then climb back on him again. He rarely took it off in the day, but he still slept in his natural form, his suit waiting next to the bed to take him up once more when he awoke.

Where William's suit was all exposed synthetic muscle and skeleton, Neal's was pure night black.  A shadow of a form, almost spindly by comparison to William's bulky suit.

Its form was also distorted. Its arms were too long, its legs a little too short, and its head but a simple black cylinder the size of a pineapple. Its torso was a thick block, designed to contain and protect its processors, fusion core, and the subspace tweeter that allowed it to be controlled. It did away with the need to support a human body inside itself and replaced that with greater muscle mass, more power, and, in its Popeye-esque forearms, greater weaponry.

It was an evolving form, adjusting with each version to discount some of the vagaries of evolution in exchange for greater power and flexibility. Phase Eight, a taller, bulkier version, had formed the core for the avatar which part of Minnie even now inhabited as she played with Banu. But by shortening the legs and lengthening the arms they had allowed this version to fall forward and run on all four limbs should it want to, extending its top speed to up over a hundred miles an hour over even rough terrain.

William had been working on it for months now, since even before the earth-shaking events that had brought down SpacePort One and killed so many of their colleagues and friends.

Neal flexed his legs a little and was caught off guard by the speed with which the Phase Nine responded. Even as he lost his balance and fell backward, William was backing away, wary of the sight. It took a long time to adjust to the quickness of the machine, and William reached out to Mynd via his spinal node and asked him to intervene, before Neal did some damage.

Neal's stuttering response sent one leg flying back in an attempt to regain his footing and the Phase Nine was suddenly thrown forward toward William. Luckily Mynd took control before they connected, stopping Neal from trying to control his own landing and instead helping William wrestle the machine to the ground.

Neal's laughter and muted apology came through their shared connection and was met with equal mirth from William, who said out loud, "That's no problem, Neal. It is quite the machine. It takes a while to get used to it."

"That much is clear," came Neal's voice out of a small speaker built into the front of the Phase Nine's 'face', like some automaton from a fifties sci-fi flick.

*Mynd:* <here, neal, i have given you partial control. i'll filter your instructions and make sure you don't demolish anything.>

"Or any*one*," said William with a chuckle, and they both smiled.

"Quite," came Neal's response as he gingerly climbed to his feet once more "So, this is what it feels like to wear one of the battleskins. I must admit, I had always been curious."

"Well, not quite," replied William. "This is a touch stronger than the battleskins, as it does away with having to carry around one of us pesky, soft little humans."

"Yes, that would make sense. So is this closer to what the Agent's enjoy."

"It is," replied William. "And with the latest versions of the spinal interface coming out of Amadeu's lab, it could, in theory, match their speed and strength, even beat them in that last category, perhaps. And the guns. Oh, the guns. They are not online now, for … obvious reasons, but they pack a very real punch."

If William could have seen Neal's face, he would have seen the man's disconcerted look at the thought that they might have added that to the list of ways he just could have obliterated his colleague with his mishandling of the suit.

"Yes, well," Neal said, "I'm glad you didn't give me access to those. As are you, I imagine." They shared another chuckle.

"Yes," said William, after a moment. "If we'd only had time to refine these and the interface enough before facing the Agents …" his voice trailed off. It was one of many things they had not been able to do before events came to a boil. And like the rest, it did not bear thinking about, and accordingly Neal moved on.

"So," Neal said, standing more confidently this time and reexamining his arms and legs with greater appreciation for their strength, "have you had a chance to try it out?"

"Of course, Neal. I have been testing them out pretty much every day! It really is a blast once you get the hang of it, and the island gives you quite the landscape to take them for a ride."

Neal looked at him with his blank machine face, then, realizing the man could not see his expression, said out loud, "Well, what are we waiting for?"

- - -

It was a strange sight: one bionic creature leaping with fair adeptness from rock to ice to rock, bouncing with the simple joy of a child recently escaped from the confines of home and parental oversight, and behind that another, lither affair, but so much slower, like the friend who is less confident of their enterprise; hesitant, jumping with some measure of the same joy, but without the abandon of the first.

William had dusted off a Phase Seven model, only recently retired anyway, and was sprinting ahead of Neal as the leader of the world's greatest military enterprise skipped tentatively, gaining poise slowly as he went.

"William!" Neal shouted. Then, realizing the other man was nowhere in sight, he changed back to more abstract comms.

*Neal:* 'william. ¿where are you?'

The other man's location came to Neal as a flash of data, and Neal saw that the once-crippled scientist was sprinting in a long arc around and back toward Neal, a grace to his form that would have filled the best athlete with joy, let alone a man who had spent most of his life confined to a wheelchair.

As they came up on each other once more, Neal returned to the spoken form, enjoying the strange combination of cyber communications and old-fashioned vocalization.

"Wow, you are quite the athlete!"

William did not share Neal's full emotion at the statement. His perspective was more a blend of happiness and sadness, a gift all the more emphasized by the lost abilities it implied, a new puppy to replace the lost companion.

"It is an amazing thing," William simply said.

"Yes, it is," replied Neal, then added, "I am curious. Given what these Phases can do, why don't you use them all the time?"

William thought a moment. It was a good question. It was strange that he would be so loyal to a body that had so cruelly betrayed him.

"I don't know, now that you say it. It's … well, this … this isn't me. Is it?" he replied, clearly trying to give voice to something he had not really analyzed before, even as he held up his mechanical hands and regarded them.

"If I experience something in this body," William went on, "have I really experienced it?"

Neal was surprised at the thought, but could not deny the truth behind it; not logic, perhaps, but truth nonetheless. While the senses within the Phase Nine were actually far more acute than his human ones: he could see farther and more clearly, and in a much greater visual spectrum with these 'eyes', still, it was like looking through binoculars, making things seem both closer and more distant at the same time.

"Interesting perspective," said Neal after thinking about it for a moment. "It is, after all, quite literally an out-of-body experience." Their mild machine laughter came out of the speakers on their mechanical faces, and as they realized the grand comicality of the whole situation they laughed more heartily. To consider the incredible technological marvels they were using: sending instantaneous signals via subspace to two superhuman robots standing on a mountain top in the Antarctic, so that those robots could share a bad pun via two silly little speaker-mouths, it was one of those moments when you realized how strange the world had become.

"I see your point," said Neal after a moment. "But when we think about the purpose of these machines, and of the others we are building, isn't that dislocated sensation, in the end, a good thing?"

"True enough, Neal. I cannot deny that."

Neal had not really meant to be covert in this, but, in truth, he had an ulterior motive in bringing up this naturally sensitive topic with his disabled friend, and it started to come to the surface now. Neal hoped William would not see the contrivance, and indeed, Neal's knack for diplomacy was coming on, even as he was shaking off its bounds in the greater political world.

"So, when you think about it through less emotional eyes," said Neal now, "it would be good, wouldn't it, for our soldiers and pilots to have this purity of function across the board? Don't you think?"

"Yes, of course!" said William. "That's why we're working on this, isn't it?"

"Yes, yes, it is. But there is still a problem. It is one we encountered in Russia during our first incursion there, and it is one we will encounter again, during the greater war to come."

William waited, and Neal stepped lightly into the muddy waters of his ideas here.

"These machines as they currently function must, by design, rely on subspace comms to work, unless we upload an AI, which brings us back to the problem of reaction speeds that Amadeu and you have struggled with from the start. A problem we may have found the key to through enlisting young Banu, but that still leaves us with another issue."

Neal was glad William could not see his face when he said this next part. "We know that we must have a human mind in control of each of our fighters when we engage the Mobiliei Armada, a mind working at the peak of its abilities. And the subspace comms it would require to have those minds located elsewhere exposes us to the detection and triangulation that cost our people so dearly in Russia."

William caught Neal's drift now, realization coming to him with a jolt, and knew that he, too, had been wrestling with the same concept, though for a wholly different reason.

"Yes, I have thought about that as well," William said suddenly, touching, at last, on the topic Neal had been tiptoeing around.

Neal waited, but when William's machine face remained quiet and passive, Neal eventually said, "About what, William?"

He needed the Welsh scientist to say it himself.

"About ... cutting them off, Neal."

They were both silent a moment. He was talking about evisceration. Deliberate and voluntary. And potentially complete. For William it was either a blessing or a contract with the devil, he had not decided which. For Neal, it was the only logical answer he could find to a greater question. In space, in battle, the human body was useless.

Worse than useless, it was a hindrance; a soft, malleable, vulnerable, fleshy thing that only placed limits on the machine it was tasked with piloting. With the invention of the spinal interface, the body had become a vestigial thing in battle, as it had for William in life. A coccyx for the mechanical creatures they were now constructing.

"I can only imagine how difficult it is to even talk about this," said Neal, with very genuine regret. But it was a topic he needed to discuss, and William was the only logical person he could find to discuss it with. "I'm sorry I even brought it up. But I had to ask whether you had considered it, because ..." Neal went silent.

"... because if *I* won't consider it, then ..." finished William.

"Yes, quite," said Neal.

They went silent once more and turned for home, their bodies propelling themselves away from the conversation even as William began to contemplate the full weight of what they had just discussed. The seed was planted. Neal hoped William would come to the same conclusion he had, or even better that he might see another solution that Neal had not, though Neal doubted that.

It was a very dark path that they were peering down.  But it was a path that they might, Neal feared, have to walk down if Earth was to have a chance at surviving the coming war.

# Chapter 5: Meeting Room

Ayala brushed into the room with grace, silence, and menace. She had aged markedly in the last few months, her stress and grief etched into her face, her emotional loss clawing at her brow and leaving scars there. But, like always, she had channeled her emotions into her work, and thus had lost none of her will to drive onward; quite the opposite, in fact.

She came into the meeting like she always did nowadays, with an agenda. In the ever-wider circles in which she swam, she was becoming infamous for it.

"Ayala, good to see you," managed Peter Cusick, but without much sincerity. "Glad you could make it."

She smiled at how false his sentiment was, but her reply was more genuine. "It is good to see you too, Peter. I'm glad to be here, if only because I have a lot to cover."

"Yes, yes. Of course," said Peter. It was always business with Ayala. Peter breathed deep, and the other various security chiefs and intelligence heads smiled and nodded with feigned calm, their façades covering varying measures of trepidation.

"So, gentlemen, if we are all ready …"

There were some nods, though she was not really asking permission anyway, and so she got down to business. "We are here, as you know, to review security procedures for next week's conference. In order to make this as meaningful a meeting as possible, Neal will be attending in person, as will several other members of TASC's leadership, myself included."

There were no comments at this, so Ayala went on, "Let's us first discuss our arrival and egress. We will not, for obvious reasons, be using the main airports or local hotels, but will be flying directly to the site."

"Yes, of course, we will make a slip available at the 34th Street heliport," said Peter.

"Good, the plane will remain there for …"

"Plane?" said Peter.

"Yes, Peter, plane. We will be using our StratoJets."

"Umm, I'm afraid that won't be possible," said Tony D'Amico, New York's Chief of Police, and the man who had the unenviable job of reconciling the plethora of security requests coming in from UN delegations with the city's very real and very pressing security concerns.

New York was not the city it once had been. It still retained a place in the world's economy, and still had a pulse that would take a long, long time to fully die out, but the engine of commerce and creativity that had been the site of so many a novel, movie, and sitcom was now a place under siege.

As the country's economy had faltered, the nation's wealthy elite had taken up refuge in pockets of ever shrinking privilege. In enclaves both virtual and physical, they had bolstered themselves against the growing storm of economic and political strife, and no place was that more true than the island of Manhattan. It was not officially now a police state, but the tollbooths that had once taken cash or swipes of EZ passes to cross the Hudson now acted as a border control.

Similar barriers now also guarded the many bridges and tunnels over the east river. You needed a reason to come to New York now, a pass, an invite. Tourism had all but died out in the country anyway, and the few tour buses that still remained were conspicuous in their emptiness. It was into this borderline militarized zone that Ayala was now asking to fly an armed fighter jet.

"Ms. Zubaideh," Tony went on, "you know I cannot authorize foreign military craft access to New York's City's airspace, I'm not even sure that StratoJets are allowed in United States airspace unless they are piloted by US personnel." His voice trailed off under the iciness of her gaze and he glanced to either side for backup from his military and diplomatic colleagues.

He received it, surprisingly, from an Israeli, himself a former Mossad employee, though his job had been of a more administrative nature than Ayala's.

David-Seth Ain spoke calmly, resisting the urge to speak in Hebrew for his erstwhile colleague, except to say, "Shalom, Ms. Zubaideh."

They exchanged brief dips of the head before he continued, "We all appreciate, I am sure, your somewhat unique security concerns. But I am sure you will also appreciate that if the heads of state of, say, Israel and Iran can both arrive at the UN compound via … conventional channels, so, too, can the head of TASC."

Ayala returned his collegiate smile and did not break contact with his keen, intelligent eyes as she replied, "I appreciate your perspective, Mr. Ain, but the comparison is, I think, not an apt one. We do not come to participate in any greater discussion, and we do not come as an equal. We are not a nation, we are a military state. And one that we know all of your leaders would very much like not to negotiate with, but to control, as they once did."

It was a blunt accusation, but to deny would have been nothing short of ridiculous. That said, its fundamental truth did not make it any less uncouth to state it so openly. Like so much in the current geo-political environment, it was a topic people preferred to accept but not mention. It was a political bowel movement, a fart in the world's elevator; everyone knew it had happened, but it was an unpleasant reality they would all rather leave undiscussed.

But she was not here to bandy words with them or to ignore the fundamental issues at hand; that dance was for the politicians. She was here to see to it that no more of those close to her came to harm, a task she intended to execute with extreme prejudice, if necessary.

Most around the table represented the reluctant nations that had already pledged to support TASC's new independence, if only tentatively, for now. Few doubted that most of the world would eventually follow suit, but only if they didn't find a way to bring the rogue TASC leader to heel in the meantime, or remove him from his post altogether.

And there lay the crux of this issue, for Ayala knew of at least three aborted attempts to infiltrate her ranks by foreign agents, and had seen signs of several other plots. Neal had made many enemies in the last few weeks, and though few openly opposed him, their agents were hard at work, and there was no way she was going to leave him exposed for even a second, not again, not ever.

"My fellow security heads, my needs are simple; if, admittedly, unorthodox. But they are also nonnegotiable. If our requirements cannot be met, we will simply have to hold the meeting elsewhere. At a location we control, or the meeting will not occur at all."

Many went to speak at once but she held up her hands and said next, "Please, let me finish. While I understand your valid and quite understandable reluctance to grant an armed military craft access to such delicate airspace," she nodded respectfully to the police chief who had first expressed his qualms at such an anathema, "I think we can all agree that events over the last few weeks have proven that, were TASC to desire any of the good citizens of New York City harm, something we most certainly do not, then we would not use a StratoJet to inflict it."

It was not a threat, but it carried the weight of one. Mention of the Skalm would have been as uncouth as pointing out that she represented a state whose very legality was only being accepted out of necessity, as she just had a moment before, but she refrained from stating the obvious this time.

Her point was made. Everyone in this room was privy to the truth behind the explosion in Beijing, and some were even aware of the real cause of the death of the former Russian Premier. It was the reason their nations were all both conspiring against TASC and complying with it at the same time.

"Let us view this as we would, say, the Queen of England visiting a former territory for the first time. Her security would be considered the sole purview of her Royal Guard, who would, without doubt, remain armed at all times. I propose that we follow the same edict here."

She looked at each of them in turn, pausing notably to lock eyes with the Israeli, the CIA Chief Peter Cusick, and finally the New York police chief.

"That said, I can offer some measure of compensation in return for your understanding here, in the form of a shipment of battleskins, of the kind you are all no doubt aware my Spezialists are equipped with, for use in your own security details during the conference, and then afterward however you see fit."

The room went quiet, each considering this surprising offer for a moment.

Many of them had had some measure of access to the battleskins in the past, most notably Peter, who still relied on the twenty or so older versions of the suits he had at his disposal to conduct a plethora of vital missions his organization had going on around the country at any moment. The Secret Service had a good deal more, as did a special branch within the FBI, but there were at most a hundred of the suits left in the US, and that was more than most countries could claim.

"I can guarantee twenty of the suits to any of your nation's security forces before the upcoming meeting," said Ayala magnanimously, "and a further fifty afterward. Provided, of course, that you are current signees of the TASC Independence Charter, and provided, gentlemen, that we can come to an agreement here today on the protocols I require."

She looked around the room. She had surprised them, as she had planned to do, but she still saw hesitance. It was cracking under the weight of her clear resolve, but she had not won yet. On the one hand, she knew none of them wanted to be the one who would have to report back to their superiors that they had passed up a chance at such a prize, but nor did they wish to give in so easily either.

"I can offer one more thing, gentlemen. But this represents the full extent of my generosity in this matter." They waited, and she did not disappoint. "If I am to ask for the right to fly a StratoJet into New York's airspace, then it is only right that I offer the same courtesy to anyone else who thinks it appropriate."

Most were taken aback, some were confused, some were outright suspicious, but all were at least a little bit curious. She went on, "TASC would like to offer to collect and deliver any of your state's representatives that wish it directly from your home nations to the 34th street heliport for the meeting at the UN headquarters, along with full protection from TASC forces. In one of our StratoJets it will take roughly a quarter of the time to get to and from New York as it would on a conventional passenger jet, and your charges will be much safer along the way."

She went on with a rare smile. "It is not required, not by any means. But I hope you will see it as the gesture of good will it is intended to be. If all goes well at the meeting, you can consider it the first step toward gaining full access to the StratoJets, for your own use and even production down the line."

She remained smiling as she said this. Bordering on beatific, it was more than a little bit scary for those in the room that knew her well. But it was also enticing as well. They knew her as a hard-line intelligence chief, but she had not always been so. She had once been a master at the art of seduction, and she employed some measure of that charm now.

They looked at her skeptically. It was an offer of candy from a stranger, there was no doubt about that, but this was no ordinary candy, and for all intents and purposes they were already in the stranger's van anyway, so why not take the treat?

They would have to think about it. Oh, they would definitely have to think about it. Of course, she would say, take your time, she would say.

And so they would hear the rest of her requests and take them back to their superiors along with the details of her offer, and then they would get back to her.

But it would not be twenty minutes after the meeting had ended before the first of them started reaching out to her via her many back channels. Perhaps they could discuss a special consideration, in return for being the first to support her request. Perhaps a special relationship could be established. I could be a friend to you, they would say.

And who was the stranger offering candy now, she would think. But she would agree. For TASC needed them as much as they needed TASC. Indeed that was the whole point. As she and Neal had discussed in laborious detail since their declaration of independence, and communicated to their growing network of administrators and ambassadors and her growing network of spies: they must use a carrot whenever possible.

For they had some very nice carrots to use. But if the proverbial carrot on the end of the proverbial stick didn't work, Ayala thought coldly, well then, she would just as happily use said stick to beat the proverbial shit out of them instead.

# Chapter 6: Meating Room

The plane came in low and fast, piloted with aplomb by one of General Toranssen's cadre of StratoJet pilots. It was not alone, and it was not the first. It was part of a chain of them coming into the heliport just south of the UN building on the east side of Manhattan.

The main highway that ran north-south along the river was closed to all but official traffic. It was a move that would have once caused a most unholy knot of traffic in the city, but not today. The blood ran a little thinner in New York's veins now, and where there had once been a thrumming horde of taxis and town cars and pedestrians, now there was but a poor remnant of that same flow, still alive perhaps, but changed at the most fundamental level; a pallid vestige, its breath low, its eyes glazed.

As the jet came up the river from the harbor, from its thundering passage in from under the Verrazano Bridge and before that the broad expanse of the Atlantic, it reared its nose up, redirecting thrust out of the nozzle in its nose cone and bringing its main engines round to halt its flight and bring it in to hover.

Across the river the crowd roared once more as the plane came in. The reality of the country's true plight was plain to see in the barely contained riot of people gathered along the mainland shorelines of north Brooklyn and Queens. Banners were held high, shouts and chants filled with vitriol and hatred echoed from the massed throng. Among the looted tenements and storefronts of once peaceful neighborhoods the depths of the fall played itself out in countless acts of violence, robbery, rape, and murder.

From his spot among the more senior of his staff standing on the FDR flyover that sat between the heliport and the UN headquarters, Police Chief Tony D'Amico stared at the mass, cringing at the shouts, more aware than he wanted to be of what was no doubt going on among the unpoliced mass. The unpolicable mass.

He had lost too many officers to trying to maintain the peace in the outer boroughs. He could only do so much. When the crowd got too big, the emotion too strong, all they could do was close the bridges and tunnels and wait. They would go in afterward and catalogue the destruction. They would follow up on some of the worst atrocities, if they had any evidence to follow up on. They would go after any signs of truly organized havoc, sometimes calling in the likes of Peter Cusick if they saw signs of one of the more powerful insurgent or separatist movements. After that Peter would deal with it using tools and mandates Tony didn't have, or wish to know about.

On the broad concrete slab of the heliport, the latest StratoJet came in to land amongst the varied craft already there. A heavily armored town car was waiting. It was unique from the others that had come and gone from the heliport in that it would only ferry one team to the UN this morning, and it had its own driver and own security team. In a sea of high-ranking arrivals, this was both the newest head-of-state to arrive this morning and also one of the most important.

Radios sputtered news of the package's arrival from the shoulders of captains and lieutenants around Chief D'Amico. Neal Danielson was on the ground.

- - -

"Do we have our final list of attendees?" said Jim to one of his many attendants.

"Yes sir. Here." The man brought a page up on Jim's iPad as if by magic, and Jim nodded. He still hadn't had the spinal interface installed. It was planned for next week, but he had delayed it twice already.

Neal was being understanding, and indeed no one could question the efficiency of Jim's work or the skill with which he had taken the reins of Neal's burgeoning empire. But Jim knew it was getting embarrassing at this point.

Jim looked at the tablet in his hands. The tablet which the assistant in question was even now manipulating via his own spinal interface. It was equal parts disturbing and exciting, but he set the thought aside. He needed to keep his head clear as they prepared for the next few days, after that …

It was silly, he knew, and once he was more familiar with the interface he would no doubt feel more comfortable using it in the heat of the moment, but not now, not yet.

To his side Neal smiled at the onlookers around him. The small group was now walking through the doors into the main lobby of the UN headquarters, a mighty edifice, a monolith, in the space odyssey sense of the word. The broad space was well accustomed to dignitaries of all manners and levels of power and prestige, but in the current, tense political spectrum few stars shone brighter than Neal Danielson's, and most stopped and stared as he swept past, his small entourage drawing nearly as many stares as the man himself.

There was the former presidential chief of staff, now Neal's right-hand man, and the two attendants he had managed to minimize himself to, though only because they were both connected via their links to his already hundred-strong team of administrators.

Then there was Madeline and Ayala, there to help with negotiations around material sourcing, both for the remaining work at District Three and for Ayala's growing security and policing operations.

And finally there were the two martial members of the group, there in part for protection, but also amply capable of contributing to the coming talks. First there was John Hunt, chosen over Quavoce to attend because of his less checkered history on Earth. He was matched on the other flank by the second of Minnie's Phase Eight avatars, a butch-looking female figure who would not have looked out of place on the East German Women's Track and Field team.

They made an odd sight and Neal relished the hushed silence that came over the auspicious space as they made their way to the main auditorium.

He leaned over to Madeline. "It's going to be an interesting few days," he said with a smirk and she smiled, though she was less entertained by the prospect of tangling with the practiced bureaucrats they had come to meet than he was.

- - -

"Senator, that does not, I hope you'll agree, change the fundamental point at hand," Jim said, placatingly.

"But of course it does, Mr. Hacker, of course it does. The people of the world have suffered enough. No matter what is agreed in subcommittee over the course of this summit, I still think the need for secrecy remains. And it remains of paramount importance."

It was a view shared by the majority of the representatives in the room, but not all.

"Madame Chairman, if I may?" came the translated voice of the French president. The man had been among their greatest supporters before their move toward independence, but one of their greatest opponents since. Neal knew the man to be reasonable, but also to have his limits, limits Neal had tested to breaking point over the last few months.

With permission granted by the chairman, the French leader took the proverbial floor. "Ladies and gentlemen, distinguished allies, we talk of protecting our citizens as we most certainly must. But this discussion presumes that we can, in fact, keep such a thing a secret for much longer ..."

As the president spoke, Neal nodded to himself and opened his connection to Minnie.

*Neal:* 'our french friend is right, minnie.'

*Minnie:* <¿he is?>

*Neal:* 'he is. please get me statistics on the flare points. i need dates on when the armada's engines will become visible in the night sky, both via telescope and with the naked eye.'

*Minnie:* <they are visible already with seventeen of the world's telescopes, most notably the hubble.>

*Neal:* 'i know that, minnie. we have looked at them together. i meant with publicly accessible telescopes. ones not controlled by the very governments we are here to meet with. and while you are figuring that out, get me madeline. ¿is she online?'

*Madeline:* 'of course i am, neal.'

*Neal:* 'shit, minnie. don't do that.'

He felt Madeline's amusement as Minnie explained herself.

*Minnie:* <you did not send your question directly to me, neal, so it was shared with the group. per your request at [0713...]>

*Neal:* 'yes, minnie. thank you, i remember.'

And now he felt Minnie's amusement at having surprised him. She was more than capable of filtering his conversation in real-time based on her own ever-growing understanding of his preferences and the list of people he did and did not trust. But on such lists Madeline was without many equals and as such Minnie had enjoyed the chance to make her little joke.

Machine humor, he thought. What a hoot.

*Minnie:* <i have the answer to your question now. ¿what do you wish me to do with it?>

*Neal:* 'you can start by telling me what it is.'

*Madeline:* 'it will be roughly twelve months from now, that is when the light from their engines will reach a brightness that will be viewable with enthusiast-level telescopes.'

*Neal:* 'great, perfect. madeline, would you mind asking for the floor and sharing that data with our friends here so we can set that as our target date and get back on track. it is, after all, when the cat will be truly out of the bag. though anyone that doesn't figure out something a tad unusual is going on when new moon one brings her cargo back in ten month's time would have to be living under a pretty damn big rock.'

*Madeline:* '¿not to be persnickety, neal, but when new moon comes back, won't we all be living under a pretty big rock?'

Madeline sent her own amusement at her little pun to the group and was pleasantly surprised when Minnie replied with a ripple of laughter, as well. You never knew what jokes would resonate with her machine consciousness.

Neal, notably, did not reply.

*Madeline:* '… but i digress. i can certainly do that, neal. i'll wait for the french president to finish then ask for the floor.'

*Neal:* 'much appreciated, madeline. minnie, please get a print out of the date and some supporting data to one of jim's lackeys outside and ask them to print copies for distribution.'

*Minnie:* <actually, neal, you will be excited to know i am already at a copy machine in another part of the building making the copies myself.>

Neal and Madeline felt Minnie's pride at the statement. Great, thought Neal, the most capable artificial mind on earth, using one of the most deadly and advanced machine bodies in their arsenal, and it was making copies. He had managed to create the world's most expensive intern.

- - -

Eleven months. They settled on eleven more months. They would make the announcement then, as a united front.

Neal didn't think anyone in the room genuinely believed the secret could be kept that much longer, and indeed he had long since had Jim task one of his teams with maintaining an up-to-date press packet on the subject for when it almost inevitably broke on its own.

For now, though, that allowed them to focus on the task at hand. To focus on the negotiations: the long, complicated, tedious negotiations. Thank the lord or the devil, Neal did not know which, for Jim Hacker.

"Where are we, Jim?" said Neal, as they walked away from the main delegate floor after the opening session.

"We are en route to conference room 725b, for a meeting with the Korean delegation."

*Neal:* '¿minnie, shouldn't madeline be handling this one?'

*Madeline:* 'no, neal, i shouldn't.'

Neal cursed Minnie's sense of humor once more, and the group dispersed to their various meetings and negotiations. It was going to be a long day.

- - -

Lim Min-soek stood at attention, as he always did. The guard detail he was a part of was spread out across the complex with the various parts of the Korean delegation, but he had been tasked, along with one other, to guard the conference room. As they were well inside the complex it was, in fact, a fairly risk-free posting, but for Lim it carried as great a risk as could be imagined.

For Lim this posting carried the risk of impending death. He knew what his orders were. Not orders, demands. But he was only to carry them out were he to have a clear opportunity. An opportunity he had hoped he would not be given.

An opportunity that now lay only moments away.

- - -

Neal and Jim approached the elevator.

"Jim, I hear you, but I really think you can handle it, just make something up and send it. Your German is better than you give yourself credit for." He smiled and Jim nodded.

"Sure, Neal. I'll get right on it. No risk of international incident there."

"Good," Neal laughed, "I'm glad you see it my way."

They did not press the button as they got into the wood-paneled cube. They assumed correctly that Minnie would take care of it, and she did, pressing it without looking as she entered the elevator behind them. Jim's attendants were off helping Madeline, Ayala, and John as they went to their own negotiations with the Indian and Brazilian representatives, leaving Jim and Neal to their devices.

Their friendship had been a rocky journey, but in the end it had only been solidified by it. They had been colleagues, then rivals, then almost combatants, and now as friends and coworkers, Neal finally saw why so many had come to rely on Jim over the years. He was a better chief of staff than even Minnie could be; he was a superlative organizer and a diplomat with few peers. Where Minnie was still learning the human condition, Jim was a master of it, and he was proving invaluable as they navigated these complex times.

"OK, now, Kim Kwon will be your prime contact during this meeting," explained Jim as the elevator doors closed and they began to rise. "Though he is not the most influential in the room, I am certain he will be in a matter of months when the next regional elections take place, and his emergence as a candidate for party leader becomes clear. Park Jae-won, who will try to run the meeting, is both on the decline in terms of power, and an active detractor when it comes to our efforts."

Neal nodded as they exited the elevator and started down the corridor. Despite his jocular attitude, he really did appreciate the grave importance of this work, and his role in it.

"The main landmine here will be, of course, our stance on China and North Korea. They will be pushing for support with border control and will assume from recent events in Beijing that you are onboard with a more hard-line approach to that issue."

Neal nodded again, appreciatively. Certainly it would be hard not to see his attack on the Politburo headquarters as anything other than a very hard line. But Jim was not done.

"As we discussed earlier, it will be tempting to go down that road as it will be the only issue on which the entire room will agree. But we cannot make any agreements here that will preclude future negotiations with the Chinese." He was tapping on his tablet as he spoke, and Neal felt a data packet appear in his head titled: South Korean TASC Support Talks – Approved Agenda Points and Areas of Concern.

Minnie spoke up, both in the ether and in person, "Gentlemen, I am afraid the data packet in question is out of date. There is one data point that will need to be added."

They turned to her as she spoke but she was looking straight ahead as they approached their appointed conference room.

Lim Min-soek saw them approaching the room. He saw the two men. He saw the burly woman alongside them that he assumed correctly was their bodyguard, and he tensed. She looked dangerous, and her eyes were pinned to his.

But his orders were clear, and he had an advantage. While guns were not allowed within the UN grounds, his post within the Korean security forces had earned him the use of one of twenty of the bionic suits they had been given by the very people whose leader he had been tasked with killing.

He was not fully versed with its use, and his lack of a spinal interface meant he could only operate the suit by muscle amplification, not direct control. But he felt confident he could still move quickly enough to kill the man known as Neal Danielson, and even his assistant, before their guard could stop him.

He felt scared but confident as he brought his arm up, propelling his fist toward Neal's throat with all his machine might.

He felt even more confident when the woman at Neal's side did not even react, even as Neal himself began to rear back at the sight of the balled black fist coming at him.

He felt confident right up until the point where his arm froze, and his body suddenly wrenched backward as though propelled by a great wind.

But there was no wind. No response still from the big woman, who just looked on even as Neal began to turn to her, confusion and alarm filling his features as he went to speak.

"Do not be alarmed, Neal," said Minnie, "the threat is past."

"Threat!" he said. Then, realizing he was shouting, he said more quietly, "What the hell just happened?"

"The man intended you harm. I stopped him."

Neal and Jim looked around. Barring their group of three, there were only the two guards in earshot, though there were others farther down the corridor, many of whom were glancing their way.

But it was the two guards Neal was worried about. One had clearly meant to strike him, and with no small amount of malice. Then he had seemed to pull back, though the man seemed as surprised as Neal when he did.

"The suits, Neal," said Minnie. "They are second-generation battleskins, gifted to the Korean government, among others, in exchange for security concessions. But while they are pre-spinal interface, Madeline did install subspace comms in them, just in case. It was a precaution Ayala had requested, as it would allow me to take control over them … should I need to."

Neal stared at her, then at Jim, then back at the soldiers, who were now both standing once more, though their faces were an incongruous mesh of discomfort juxtaposed against the enforced stillness of their bodies.

"The man on the left, your assailant, is close to unconsciousness, as I am constricting his lungs and throat. The man on the right appears innocent to the plot, but I am afraid his presence for its aborted execution means we will have to take him into custody as well."

Neal walked up to them, at first hesitantly, then with a little more confidence as he saw how they were wheezing, unable to breath properly, let alone speak. He felt no remorse for the man who had tried to attack him, but the other man … it was disquieting to see how he struggled.

"Can you hear me?" Neal said to the distraught man, clearly fighting the profoundly unpleasant sensation of suffocation. "Minnie, stop this. He has done nothing."

She did, and in a flash the man was drawing deep, hoarse breaths as though breeching the surface of a river-rapid that had subsumed him. After a moment the man caught his breath and his eyes regained some measure of sense. He focused on Neal's face, only inches away.

His expression was one of absolute fear. He was clearly very aware of his suit's betrayal and keen not to suffer the same fate again. He spared a quick glance to his side, to his colleague who had seemed to strike out at the men their leaders were here to meet, and saw that the other soldier was out cold now, dead, perhaps. He could not tell, though the traitor still stood, and his head was still held upright by the musculature in his suit's neck.

Ree Chung-man turned back to the face of the man he knew was about to decide his fate.

"Now, calm down," said Neal quietly but firmly. They did not have long before someone came to investigate further, indeed he could see someone was approaching even now. Neal waved for Jim to go and stop whoever it was from coming too close, and Jim reacted immediately, moving off to intercept them.

Neal went on, "Do you speak English?"

Ree did, if haltingly. It was a prerequisite for assignment to the diplomatic guard unit.

The man nodded ever so slightly, realized he could not move his head any farther than that, and panic threatened to set in once more.

"Calm now," said Neal, seeing the rising terror in the man's eyes. He did not like to think how it must feel to be imprisoned within one of the suits, and his sympathy for the man's plight almost outweighed his need to control the situation. Almost.

"You have been witness to an attempt on my life," said Neal, trying to help the man calm down through the stolidity of his stare, locking eyes with his. "We have no reason to think you were involved, but we are going to need to question you. If you are innocent, you will not be harmed. You have my word on that."

But as Neal said this, he realized he had no idea how they were going to manage this situation from here. He glanced at Minnie, as if to say, what do we do now? They were in the middle of one of the most well-monitored places on Earth. Indeed, there were cameras on them even now, cameras relaying what must be a very strange-looking sight indeed.

But the answer to his question was even now approaching, along with the man Neal had inadvertently dispatched to stop her.

*Ayala:* 'neal, i am here. switch to subspace comms, i don't want any more of this on record should anyone be able to hear us.'

Neal turned to her. She was standing to his side, staring at the two men. Neal went to explain the situation but Ayala stopped him.

*Ayala:* 'don't worry, neal. minnie has already given me a full update and i have reviewed her actions during the entire event. i have to say it all went very well, considering.'

*Neal:* 'went very well! ¿how the hell do you figure that?'

Ayala smiled at his indignation, turning to face him even as she spoke with her mind, her mouth staying eerily still.

*Ayala:* 'yes neal. very well. we provided the suits as an enticement, and in the process seeded the entire compound with eyes and ears for minnie and i to watch with. eyes and ears that will return with these delegations to their home countries and continue, we hope, to pay dividends. most of our allies still have no idea as to the inner-workings of our communications network, and i intend to keep it that way.'

Neal turned to the innocent Korean soldier and knew that meant the man was going to have to come with them for longer than he had originally thought. But how were they going to get them out of here?

Even as he thought it, the answer was also arriving, one of Ayala's team bringing her two helmets which she handed the two soldiers.

Though one was unconscious and one was insensible, the two men's arms nonetheless reached out and took the helmets, placing them on their heads.

Ree's face flashed with a renewed wave of terror in the moment before his face and head were covered, and he was sealed into his mobile sarcophagus.

"I'm sorry," said Neal, quickly, feeling for the poor man, "this will not be for ... long, I promise." He didn't know whether the man had heard him, and he looked most uncomfortable as the two helmeted men eerily turned and walked off down the corridor with Ayala's assistant. Ayala looked at Neal while he watched the possessed guards depart.

*Ayala:* 'i am afraid that is a promise you are not going to be able to keep, neal.'

He returned her gaze, a flash of indignation coming over his features that was quickly matched by a far more implacable expression on the face of his security chief. He calmed himself, then nodded resignedly and turned to Jim.

"This will require explanation," Neal said to his chief of staff.

"Yes, it will," said Ayala aloud. "Jim, I think it would be wise to start thinking about how we are going to broach this subject with the Korean delegation, as we are, of course, going to have to tell them something before they leave and see their guard detail is missing.

"That said, hopefully I will hopefully have more information for you before the end of your session, so Minnie, if I could ask you to keep me apprised of their progress and I will make sure you know whatever I discover before the meeting wraps up."

"Wait, wait. Are we really going to just go in there given what has just happened?" said Neal, but Jim was already busily taking notes.

*Ayala:* 'yes, neal. you are. ¿what is the point of all this if we do not get what we came here for?'

Neal looked from one to the other, but received only determined looks. Jesus, he thought.

Then Jim took his arm and led him to the door which Minnie was already opening for them to step through. Ayala and the big avatar exchanged a glance as the two men entered the room, and no doubt a great deal more, and then the wizened security chief turned to follow her assistant and her two disenfranchised prisoners.

She needed answers from at least one of them. Her face set with cold purpose as she walked away.

## Chapter 7: Saddle and Break

The original passage of New Moon One had been meteoric, quite literally. But now their work required less haste, even if it would call for infinitely more power.

They had approached Asteroid 1979va through its own wake, sneaking up on it from behind before quite rudely flipping themselves and showing it their rear, as they repurposed the engines that had brought them here into brakes.

Their approach had been delicate if, by design, rushed, for they had a tight schedule to keep and still could not know just how the process of attaching would actually go.

But touchdown had gone smoothly, or as smoothly as could be hoped, and even now they were completing the process of attaching the first of their eight huge engines to the asteroid itself.

Captain Harkness looked upon his ship from the outside even though he was in fact still inside it, cradled in machine slumber, piloting one of the ten lumbering Remote Construction Robots that his ship had been equipped with, or wreckers, as their acronym had inevitably led them to be called.

It was an alarming process, when he thought about it. His crew was busily dismantling New Moon One, not quite the burning of the ships, perhaps, but still they were pulling her limb from limb so they could achieve the lofty mission they had been set.

*Samuel:* 'that's it, remy, bring her in. two degrees port.'

Remy Diaz responded, and the big ship above Sam's head belched vapor, tweaking her leviathan body's movements in minuscule steps as they worked to bring Engine One into contact with the framework of nanotube cables and anchors they had spent the last two days drilling into the asteroid's surface.

He stood at the junction of three of those cables as they came together at one point of the triangular base they had fastened to the two-million-ton rock.

*Remedios:* 'here she comes, captain. ¿charles, my good fellow, how are those pulse-outs going?'

Charlie Kern contained his ire at her mockery of his English heritage.

*Charles:* 'they are aligned, remedy-osss.'

*Remedios:* 'remedios, remedios. ay dios mio. ¿why can't you get it right?'

He laughed, even as his mind remained absorbed with the pulse-outs. He sent out an abridged version of their status to supplement the steady flow of data he pumped into the net for the many that were monitoring the geyser-like eruptions. He told her of the anticipated flow of energy as he balanced the fonts into an antagonistic neutrality.

He was managing the cyclical pulse of their engines which had to, every five seconds or so, expend the massive power they even now generated. Dormancy was not an option for these great beasts. They had three settings: first they were off, then they were alive, and then they were dead, pretty much permanently, certainly as far as they were concerned at more than four million miles from Earth.

It meant that no one, mechanical or otherwise, could be directly in front of or behind them, well, not unless they wished to be vaporized, anyway. And it made Remy's job as pilot in these delicate maneuvers akin to manhandling a sleeping bull, a sleeping bull who was dreaming of something either very pleasant or very unpleasant as every few moments it kicked and bucked with enough power to gore them all if they were not careful. Then it was docile once more, its mighty breath exhausted, its bulk once more pliable.

*Samuel:* 'ok, we're going to bring her in on this next push. charlie, we'll need a good stretch of peace and quiet here, at least seven seconds, so we'll go on your mark. remy, sending final trajectories now. tether team, you know your jobs. don't get cocky. we can rebuild the tether but not the wreckers, delicate little flowers that they are.'

His crew all laughed, the twenty-three souls he commanded spread out across the great ship: engineers, pilots, technicians, physicists, and then Sam himself. The commander, at once the least qualified in any of the many specialties the mission required, and the most qualified across all of them.

As the clock counted down, he reached up with two of the four massive claws that were his wrecker's hands and feet, each equally powerful, each completely interchangeable as he grappled, pulled, and pushed the two massive objects together, the two-million-ton asteroid and the seven-hundred-ton ship that was about to latch onto it.

*Charles:* 'this is it, 1.2, 0.8, 0.4 ...'

They braced for a particularly long and powerful burst from either end of the mighty ship, the entire hulk vibrating wildly as Charlie wasted nearly half a billion horsepower in two great blue geysers. The strain was herculean on the ship's hull, but it was designed for it, a jail strong enough to imprison eight stars and keep their riotous fury penned.

The word 'go' was not so much spoken as given unto their minds, initiating a ballet filled with equal parts effort and finesse.

The two masses came together, eased by gentle pushes from Remy's thrusters, tugged by massive exertion from the four wreckers that grasped the mount on the outside of one of the eight engines and the saddle they were bringing it into.

Seconds passed like ages as they rushed against the impending clamor of the next pulse-out, 5.5, 5.0, 4.5, 4.0. Precious moments. Their captain spoke as the voice of command within all their minds.

*Samuel:* 'forward point five to matthew, three tenths off, pete, three ... that's it ... that's it ... almost there.'

The clamps seized in quick succession. They must all go or none, they either had the engine's feet firmly in the stirrups or they must let it go free once more, that or risk the two momentous giants ripping each other apart.

*Samuel:* 'close it … go, go. we have seal on … clamp 3, clamp 1, clamp 4 … clamp 2. release it, charlie!'

And the pulse came, a flood of power, now harnessed to the asteroid's mass. Where the ship vibrated less now that it was held firm, the greater rock they were here to bring home shook as if awakening to its fate. If there had been atmosphere, and if the Wreckers had even been equipped with ears, the noise would have been deafening as the two great titans seemed to shout out for the first time in unified protest.

The diminutive little humans were meddling with forces that should be beyond their control. But control them they must, and control them they would.

A great dust rose from the surface of the asteroid once known as 1979va. It would never settle, it would rise up and off forever, forming a new tail as they turned the big rock from asteroid to comet, and then from comet into moon.

But it was not Asteroid 1979va anymore. Captain Harkness spoke with deep-seated pride to his crew.

*Samuel:* 'we have her, team! well done! well done, all of you!'

A virtual cheer rose up in the ether. Much later it would be taken up by the ever-growing teams of TASC when they received transmission of the monumental event, and even by the leaders of the nations adjusting to their new relationship with the once tame enterprise. For this was, by anyone's measure, a great day.

They had harnessed a part of the firmament. They were now in the business of literally moving mountains. There was much still to be done, and indeed they would not rest for more than a moment. But for now Sam reveled in his next, simple announcement.

*Samuel:* 'new moon one has a new designation. ladies and gentlemen, crew of new moon one … friends; welcome to hekaton. welcome to earth's second moon.'

The Hekaton-kheires were mythical second sons of the Earth, massive warriors of incredible strength that had once helped the gods defeat the Titans. Neither Sam nor his crew had been even vaguely aware of the obscure Greek myth before the mission, but when they had heard that Neal had chosen this as the title of Earth's would-be second moon, they could not have helped but fall in love with it.

It was, quite frankly, a cool name. And now it was their name. They were the Hekatons, first residents and masters of this massive nugget. A moment of pride surged through them, matched by Sam's pride in them all. But it was a moment that must pass.

*Samuel:* 'all right. let's get ready for disconnect, people. move to disconnect positions. let's go.'

Shadows of sighs echoed through the ether, but Sam ignored them even as he smiled. Someone had to be the taskmaster, and he knew none of them really begrudged him his role.

The team of four wreckers pushed off backward from the anchor point, spooling out the cables that kept them latched to it as they went.

They let themselves drift outward parallel to Hekaton's surface until they were well out and could see up either side of the big engine module they had just brought to ground. Once they could see a clear line to where it was still attached to its seven brothers, they kicked off hard with their arms/legs, swimming upward on each side to grab onto the massive spars they now had to disengage.

They had attached this one engine to Hekaton, but now they had to move on, separating it from the full mass of the ship so they could maneuver to the next anchor point and start the whole process over again.

As they grabbed onto the upper spars, they sent signals to the ends of their cables still grasping the anchor below and released them, reeling in the cables even as they attached others to new points on the inside framework of the ship.

They were always anchored to something. They could not risk one of the big brutes floating off into space. Even though there were no actual people in them, the four incredible hulks were far more important to their mission than any individual crewmember, and they all knew that.

*Peter:* 'latched and ready, anchor point one is prepped.'

Other confirmations came back to Sam and he waited to initiate separation, waiting for clearance from Charlie that they had a good window.

- - -

It was fifteen minutes later, and the next time the engines fired Charlie was at last allowed to fire one of them with purpose, not just as an exercise in expenditure. Now that the first engine was tethered to Hekaton, they would move the asteroid itself, not themselves, and as the moment came, Charlie kicked his heels on the rock's flanks and suddenly it was moving beneath them. The first of an ever more pervasive set of demands they would place on their new home.

*Charles:* 'we have rotation at zero point three cycles.'

*Remedios:* 'i have cable spool at matching rates.'

They watched as one-eighth of their ship moved serenely away toward the stark horizon. It would not go far before Charlie fired it once more to stop Hekaton's brief rotation, once they were over the next anchor point.

*Remedios:* 'nice work, charlie.'

*Charles:* 'you too, remedios.'

# Chapter 8: Covered

"As the video shows, the attempt was very real, and came dangerously close to being successful."

The room was appropriately disquieted by the sight. It was an image of the aborted attack on Neal in the corridor outside the Korean delegation's meeting room. It had been brought in by Ayala, Neal's head of security, at the beginning of a new session held as addendum to the main negotiations. A session to review the evidence of the attack and discuss its ramifications.

It showed, from the perspective of the hallway camera, the suddenness of the attack. It showed a South Korean guard clearly attempting to strike the leader of TASC with what could only be seen as malicious intent. And, of course, it was a fake. A beautiful fake made within Minnie's beautiful mind.

The room eyed Minnie's avatar, the woman that had been introduced as Neal's personal bodyguard, with newfound respect as the video showed her lash out ferociously and bring down the attacker. Then it showed as she and the other Korean guard manhandled the assailant to the ground and restrained him, before both frog-marching the man away.

"As you can see," said Ayala to the silent room, "the attack was unsuccessful, but only because of the bravery and quick reactions of Neal's personal guard." She made a show of nodding to Minnie's avatar, and then added something to help smooth the way for the next step in the little sham. "And the help of the other Korean guard. A man who is even now helping us with our inquiry."

Various members of the delegation seemed to react to this, and for the next few hours questions of jurisdiction would be argued with not inconsiderable zeal by both sides. But Neal and Ayala were adamant that either they were to be allowed to handle the investigation in their own way, or they would be forced to hand matters over to the International Criminal Court at The Hague.

This made it really a test of the Korean certainty that there was no true culpability on their part, a faith they could not, of course, have. So they finally acquiesced to a discreet investigation handled by Ayala and her people, rather than face a very public one judged in the light of fickle public opinion. For no matter what the world's leaders might think of TASC's newfound 'independence' in private, the Koreans had no doubt how few of their fellow world leaders would offer much in the way of public support for anyone caught crossing the people that now ruled the skies.

So Ayala got her way, but was nothing if not gracious, agreeing to release the innocent guard back to his unit once they were done, and agreeing to further talks on the fate of the guilty party once they had completed their investigation.

They parted with every semblance of friendship and allegiance. But like the video that had so neatly covered up the extent of Ayala and Minnie's true capabilities, their proffered smiles and handshakes were all a beautiful lie.

- - -

*Minnie:* <the korean prisoners are inbound to rolas now. ayala ordered your pilot to take off as soon as we had the two guards aboard. but captain falster has already brought her jet into 34th street to pick you up once you are done here.>

*Neal:* 'good, good. i think i am finished for the day. ¿any new information from madeline and john?'

*Minnie:* <i have transcripts and recordings of their meetings should you need them, but to summarize: they have achieved all planned concessions from the indian and brazilian delegates, with only 62.7% of our 'acceptable concession package' for the session negotiated away. a good day.'

And no one tried to kill them either, thought Neal.

Jim was a clever taskmaster. He had worked with Minnie to codify and quantify their goals for each meeting, both in terms of what they needed from their various allies in this first wave of full-scale negotiations, and what they were willing and able to give in return. It allowed them to rate each of the lengthy sessions, a job he had then diplomatically handed over to the implacable Minnie so he could play the role of participant rather than having to hold the whip himself.

But by doing all this Jim had made it a competition. Neal smiled to himself at the simple artifice.

*Neal:* 'i am ready to leave now. jim is planning on staying here, i believe. he has some side meetings with some of his contacts this evening. as, i believe, does ayala.'

She did. Her investigation was already well underway. She would leave the wetter work of continuing the interrogation of their new prisoners to Saul Moskowitz back at Rolas. She had some meetings to conduct, and would maybe even head east in the morning, depending on what she discovered.

So Neal made his way to the bank of heavily armored limos that sat in a basement parking lot of the UN complex with only Minnie's Phase Eight for company. Minnie would see him aboard his StratoJet and then return to help Ayala, should she need any assistance.

- - -

"Welcome aboard TASC Air," said Jennifer with a smile as Neal joined her in the long, thin cabin of the plane.

While the jets remained brutally utilitarian by civilian standards, they had made a few concessions to comfort in the form of a series of thick, soft chairs that could recline into something akin to a bed.

The arms could also balloon out at alarming speeds to completely pin their occupants should the plane need to maneuver or engage a threat, but barring that eventuality, the big, plush chairs were something like luxury for the versatile military craft.

Neal smiled.  Jennifer was a rare thing in his day, neither an enemy nor an employee, and not really a member of his inner-circle either.  Her unfortunate induction into the early ugly days of their conspiracy had bought her a place of trust, but she was, in the end, just a pilot.  A good one, but no more.  Not a leader, not a strategist, and not a spy.

"Where are the flight attendants?  Where does a man get a gin and tonic around here?" he said with a smile.

"A man gets it himself, from the cabinet in the back, just like everyone else."

He laughed, appropriately chided, and turned to do as she had advised while her eyes glazed for a moment, her attention jumping elsewhere.

She engaged the engines with smooth professionalism, rising the black arrowhead up off the tarmac with ease and restraint.  He felt the press of the rising floor under him and turned with a look of surprise to his pilot, still facing him, but her attention was obviously elsewhere as she manipulated the planes three jets and pulled up into the evening sky.

She hadn't even waited for him to sit down.  But she was skilled, and it showed as she kept his center of gravity balanced, sacrificing speed for finesse.

Watching her, he tipped his head to the side a touch, then reached for a bottle of whiskey that sat in the cabinet, and a glass.  He poured, as much as a test of her skill as out of an immediate need for refreshment, and nodded appreciatively as the liquid flowed from the bottle and settled in the glass, heavier perhaps with the weight of acceleration, but not unduly shaken.

"May I sit now?" he said, and her expression returned for just a moment.

"That would probably be best."  She smiled, bashful, yet pleasantly smug at the same time.

He replaced the whiskey bottle then took his seat, and felt as the tug of the engines increased markedly as he sat down, driving him backward.

"I'll be with you in a second." she said, her eyes still glazed.  She was flying hard now, taking off the gloves as she broke out over Long Island and accelerated out over the Atlantic.  She was climbing all the time, into the plane's rightful domain, into the stratosphere, into the thin air that was the border with TASC's infamous fourth district.  As she entered the open, clear sky, she released control to the onboard AI and came back into the cabin.

"Good takeoff, sir?"

"Very good, Captain, thank you."  He nodded, and she smiled.  Few would think of Neal as a man you joked around with, but he had once been an easygoing guy, and those that knew him well knew there was a place for frivolity with him.  A small place, but a place nonetheless.

"Can I get you something?" Neal said, going to stand, but she shook her head and reached for a bottle of water in the console to her right. She faced him, from the front of the plane. Unlike earlier versions, these latest StratoJets had no windows. If you wanted to see outside, you connected with the plane's sensor suite. It was a far better view than you would get through a small plastic window anyway.

But these two had seen too much to be much bothered by staring out of a window, and as they sped away into the twilight, night rushing to meet them from the east, they relaxed.

"So, I gather you had an interesting day?" she said, knowing he would decide what he could and could not tell her. But she had seen his original jet leave with great haste a little earlier, and knew that for Neal's own jet to be commandeered it must have been carrying important cargo indeed.

He regarded her. She had every clearance she could possibly need, gained through necessity rather than qualification perhaps, but once trust is earned, who cares how it was come by.

So he spoke to her with an uncommon openness. "They tried to kill me," he said with more feeling than he had expected.

Her eyes went wide. Had he just said … but …"Wait, *who* tried to kill you?"

"A South Korean guard. But I doubt it was really the Koreans behind it, or rather Ayala does, and she is probably right. No one would be foolish enough to attempt an assassination with their own delegation nearby. It had to have been someone that didn't mind risking South Korea's standing with the taskforce. Which leaves …"

His voice trailed off and he stared at his drink. She waited. Eventually he looked back at her, "I'm sorry, I …"

"Not at all," she said with evident sympathy. "I can honestly say that every time someone has tried to kill me I haven't felt like chatting about it afterward."

He snorted a little and then smiled. He had indirectly ordered her death once, but it had been for a good cause. Something the people behind today's assassination attempt told themselves as well, no doubt.

"Yes, well," Neal said, "I was so busy in the aftermath of it all I didn't really get to think about it until now."

"Was anybody hurt?" she asked, then added, "I mean, if you can tell me."

"I can."

Indeed, he could tell anyone anything he liked. After all, he was in charge.

He caught his breath at the thought, as he often did. It was a sign of the times indeed when a man like him could end up with a job as important as this, he thought, though he kept that thought to himself.

"No, no one was hurt. Though I doubt the guard in question much enjoyed the experience. Or his unfortunate colleague who was witness to the whole affair." He made eye contact with her again, and added, "They were the ones aboard my jet, en route, no doubt, to an engaging evening of *chatting* with one of Ayala's people."

He did not mean to sound bitter, or to mock the Spezialists that had fought so valiantly in Hungary as he referred to the other 'specialties' Ayala's dark team possessed. But it was an ugly side to an already ugly business.

With a surprising softness, Jennifer said, "You are an important man, now, Neal. Things like this are going to happen, and you shouldn't feel responsible for people harmed in the process. Any blood is on the hands of people who planned this, not you."

He looked at her anew, as she added, "You'll just have to forgive Ayala, and the rest of us, if we don't have a lot of sympathy for anyone that tries to hurt you. Fuck 'em, if you don't mind me saying. You are trying to save them, whoever they are, and this is how they repay you. Mikhail and Pei had an excuse at least. But anyone fighting us now ..."

He smiled again, with an affection that belied something deeper he had felt long ago, when he had first met her. They were discussing profound issues, but she had brought it back to the personal.

"Thank you, Jennifer. I needed that."

"Anytime. And it is Jen to you."

He fought an urge that he hadn't felt in two years. Not that he hadn't wanted anyone in that long. He had been busy, not dead. And maybe, in his quasi-dreamtime with Minnie, he had dabbled with some virtual scenarios he wouldn't want his mother to know about, but he hadn't actually found himself seriously thinking about kissing someone since before the first asteroid had come crashing to Earth three years beforehand.

Jennifer had sensed Neal looking at her through rose-colored lenses when they first met, and she saw it now, again. She liked the sensation. She did not stand up to kiss him, exactly, but she did stand to go to him, walking around behind his chair. She took him by the shoulders and starting to massage the stress from them, the ache of Atlas. It was a gesture of friendship, but the contact was charged with a baser desire neither would mention today, but which neither denied to themselves either.

Neal closed his eyes and did not speak as she pushed and pulled at the strained muscles of his back and neck, and perhaps it would have been an awkward silence, if the attraction hadn't been mutual. But where he had been theoretically the most influential man on Earth when they first met, now he was that by any reasonable measure you could find, and she was not ashamed to admit it was very, very sexy.

Neither knew if it would go anywhere, but also neither doubted that they wanted it to, as Jennifer pressed the stress out of his shoulders. They had only a couple of hours to Rolas. Neal would sleep in safety once they got there, alone for now, then return in the morning.

## Chapter 9: Clandestination

The bar was almost stereotypical in its dinginess. Only a heavy pall of stale cigarette smoke long since banned from such places could have made it any more predictable a place to meet, that and maybe Stacy Keach sitting on a stool looking surly. But despite the dive's unsurprising feel, the surrounding throng of twenty- and thirty-somethings either seeking or avoiding eye contact with members of the opposite sex still made for a thick enough fog in which to conduct her business.

Some of the more daring of the men around even wondered whether they might try to talk to the dark set lady who came in through the main door, glanced around the room, and continued surveying the space and its occupants even after she had already seen the man she had come to meet.

The bouncer went as if to ask for ID from her, even though the strikingly attractive woman was clearly in the grey area between forty and sixty, a place where health and vigor hold more sway on appearance than age alone. But a look from her said something along the lines of: from one professional to another, let's skip the bullshit, shall we, and out of an instinctual respect he nodded and let her pass without comment.

She did not go straight to her contact. She walked to the bar, the crowd parting with an ease any of the bar's other patrons would have envied, and locked the bartender's eyes with her own. She waved at one of the taps, though it did not really matter which it was. After a minute or so she was served, took a long gulp to lower the level of the amber draft, and turned to find her date for the evening.

"Good evening," said the man as they hugged. He was maybe thirty, a child in her circles, perhaps, but one with whom Ayala had had the pleasure of working with before, and with whom she had established a measure of personal respect.

But that had not brought him to her side alone. He was also a believer, having seen firsthand the Ubitsyas of the fallen Russian 'Federation,' and having even been saved, to some degree, by Ayala's diligence when the Steel Curtain had fallen over his posting a year ago.

Nick Huxley held her hug as they spoke quickly into each other's ears, smiling as though exchanging pleasantries, for all the world like the oldest of friends.

"We have confirmed he was a plant," she said, not even pretending to be surprised. "His background was faked, though with an impressive level of professionalism. And it was an old cover. At least seven years old. This was a sleeper."

"That is what I am hearing at Vauxhall," said Nick, smiling now like she was saying some joke to him. She laughed as well, maintaining the charade. They parted the hug, but stayed close, as if they were hopeful lovers. Neither was uncomfortable with the cover, though neither mistook it for a moment as anything more than that.

"We have only four candidates," he went on, "given the depth of the cover and the MO. And none of them are very surprising."

Her expression was questioning as she mouthed: NK … he nodded; China … he nodded again. Her expression turned more thoughtful: Russia?

He nodded again, then, with a glance around the room as though he was looking for a friend, he said simply, "Japan," as though it was the most natural thing in the world.

She was thoughtful at this, using the luxury of having her back to the room to allow her pensiveness to show. The Japanese. She knew that the proud country was far from happy that the bunker facilities they had kindly leant TASC had suddenly been changed in status from leased to annexed, but they had been compensated as only TASC could compensate, and she had assumed that had assuaged their ire.

No, she thought, she was still fairly confident they were on the up and up, and she made eye contact with Nick again as he stopped his seemingly innocent perusal of the room.

"My gut says they're an unlikely culprit," she said, and he nodded in agreement.

"We think so too. But the possibility remains," he said, and she nodded as well, appreciative of his candor. He was taking no small risk to be here, but he had offered more. He had offered to join them outright, and probably would in the future. But she had said he could best serve them by remaining in MI6 for now, and he had seen the logic, even agreed, if with a measure of disappointment.

"So, that leaves the people's threesome," she said with a wry smile, and he laughed a little as she went on. "Anything you have heard that singles any of them out?"

"Our sources say that it is unlikely the Russians have the political will to move against you at this stage, though they certainly don't lack the desire."

She nodded appreciatively at that, then listened closely as he spoke again. His voice was raised now, so she could here him clearly, but the sound was lost as soon as it veered more than a few feet, brightly colored drops of information landing in an ocean of noise and vanishing into the greater blue in an instant.

"As far as the other two are concerned," he said, his tone telling her they were veering well into speculation now, "we did see a spike of traffic in and out of New York through some of the known channels before and after the attempt, enough to make us note it even before you 'informed' our bosses about what had happened."

Informed. It was an old trick; if you had a reliable source in an agency and you wanted to use their resources, you openly gave them the data needed to prompt an investigation, and then let that source feed you the results. And so it had been with the intertwined intelligence networks of Great Britain and the US this past day. Maybe they would surprise her and officially share some measure of their analysis with her as well, but she doubted it. Either way she would get what she wanted, and know a little more about the true nature of her relationship with two of her allies in the process.

"What is interesting is that there was a correlation of sorts in the volume and nature of the traffic going back to Beijing and, through less sophisticated channels, back to Pyongyang as well."

"So one was watching the other, or they were working together. Either way, it sounds like they had some measure of advanced knowledge that something was brewing," she said.

He nodded again, then said, "Of course, whether that means they masterminded the attack together, or one just caught wind of it and chose to watch and wait … well …"

She agreed with a nod. It was far from damning evidence, but it certainly required further investigation. Something to add to the ever-growing list of reasons she wanted to get more access to the People's Republic, and any access at all to North Korea.

"Very well. This is useful, Nick. Thanks."

He nodded, genuinely happy to help. Anyone who had seen what havoc just two of the Mobiliei's Agents could wreak could be under no doubt of where humanity's real priorities should now lie. But nor could a practiced spy be so naïve as to assume that meant that even the most enlightened countries would just follow Neal's lead without complaint.

So he would watch, along with an ever more expansive network of politicians, military leaders, and intelligence operatives that were smart enough and open-minded enough to see which way the wind was blowing. Ayala knew they were making enemies, but they were making many friends as well.

She stayed and talked a short while longer.

But underlying this conversation were many layers of deceit. They were not fools. They knew that the CIA and MI6 would figure out that Nick had met with her. The strata of this level of espionage were far more complex than just one man and one woman. So Nick had told his superiors she had contacted him, and they had agreed to the meeting. They had even tried to feed him a more limited portfolio of information for him to share with her as a layer of protection against him doing what he had just done: betrayed them.

But so the game was played, and he had gathered the full truth in pieces from other members of his multinational network of fellow operatives before he came to the bar.

It was layers upon layers of double and triple crossing, and it was all too complex and contrived to follow sometimes, but not for Ayala. As she left the dive bar in the residential Upper West Side, she was even balancing the weight of her trust for Nick himself, and the other sources she knew he was working with.

But the crux of the meeting remained. China and North Korea. China: a persistently thorny bush that apparently needed even greater pruning. And North Korea: a problem not just for TASC, but for the world as a whole. One of many loose ends that stood between them and the true task at hand.

They had smited the burgeoning Russian People's Federation, and removed the cancer in China with even greater prejudice. But the discord the two Agents had looked to capitalize on remained.

She would have to go there, as she had suspected.  She could leave the rest of the
negotiations to Neal, Madeline, and Jim, and their security to John and Minnie.  Her skills
were needed elsewhere.

## Chapter 10: Shockwaves – Part One

Neal visited District Two in person this time, wanting to watch the next launch with his own eyes. He was joined by Amadeu. The Portuguese neuroscientist was as excited as Neal about the new machine, if a touch more exuberant about the fact.

They were greeted by William, mobile in his exo-skeleton suit and avoiding Neal's eye contact as they made their way to a waiting concrete and reinforced-glass booth.

"Well, well!" said William as they entered the small space. It was bitterly cold, like the rest of the island, but it was well insulated, and once the doors were sealed, a small space heater, notable only for its brute simplicity in these incredible times, quickly gave warmth to the small gathering.

"Here we are!" he said as they took their seats.

"Yes indeed," said Amadeu, trying to contain his excitement at the coming spectacle. It had taken a week just to form the gargantuan machine they were here to see, and another week before that just to load the materials into the Dome, as it had with the Skalm and the first EAHL before it. Its complexity and scale were incredible, but at the same time it was, in many ways, the simplest thing they had made to date.

It could not fly and it could not kill, well, not very efficiently anyway. As with anything the size of an apartment block that could move of its own accord, it could definitely kill if it wasn't used with care. It was just not designed for the job, unlike its cousin, the Skalm.

"So, I saw on the way in that all is looking good for today's launch?" said Neal.

"It is," replied William, as they were joined by a nervous-looking group of technicians and scientists.

There was a time when Neal had known every member of his team, but not anymore. These were strangers all, he thought, as the team of probably very capable scientists and engineers filed in, each and every one wary at the prospect of meeting the famous Neal Danielson.

Neal remembered a time when he had interviewed each new addition to their conspiracy himself, often with Barrett waiting with a gun should the interview not go as planned. He winced as he thought of his old friend. They had never found his body, and no one had ever dared raise the topic with Ayala, mostly out of a simple sense of self-preservation.

Not even Neal, the man who had embroiled them both in this whole dirty affair. The man who had recruited Laurie, and James, and Barrett, and Birgit, and countless other friends now lost, to death or the void; he wasn't sure which was worse. He resolved to talk to Ayala. Someone had to. She was a pillar of strength even now, more so even, if that was possible, but he had known them both as only co-conspirators can know each other, and the couple's love had been undeniable.

He shook off the thought for now, as he knew he must, as he assumed Ayala must be doing somehow as well, and focused on the task at hand.

"If you would like to join me," said William, choosing not to comment on Neal's obvious distraction, "we can view the final stages from inside the Dome, before the seal is cracked."

Neal nodded, and noted Amadeu was already closing his eyes. The boy was no doubt already inside, maybe even had never left, such was his rare comfort balancing reality with the ether.

Neal closed his eyes as well, and felt Mynd reach out to him. Given that Mynd, unlike Minnie, was a child of his very own brain, he should be more comfortable with him than he was with Minnie, and in some ways he was. But Mynd was a far blunter, less refined personality than Minnie, but then, maybe, thought Neal sardonically, so was he.

*Mynd:* <welcome back, neal.>

*Neal:* 'thank you, mynd. ¿how are things going in there?'

*Mynd:* <it is formed now. i have am reducing and removing the sculpting waves to allow solidity to return. the core 17% is already concreted, and the rest is resolving as planned.>

Their views altered and they entered the machine, seeing its contents with sonic eyes as the resonance manipulators looked through the giant embryo within, gently relinquishing their pressure to allow the new form to set, and wafting outward as it started to take its own weight.

The team leads that William had invited to the launch ceremony looked on as Neal took his seat and nervously glanced at each other. I mean, this was the man. This was Dr. Danielson. They knew of some source of knowledge that was driving all the advancements they were busy working on, they knew, on some level, that it was probably not a single person, but the line between legend and truth had started to grey, and the name Neal Danielson had started to become synonymous with wonder.

He was becoming an icon, in his way. Whether his ascendant star would remain in the firmament or plummet back to Earth, who could know, such was the way of people who became fabled in their own lifetimes. But for now there were few among the growing teams of Madeline's Research Group or the even larger and more multifaceted Construction Group that did not regard Neal as something close to a scientific god.

He was not aware of it. Indeed those that made up his cadre of friends and confidants regarded him much as they always had: as a dedicated, maybe even courageous man who had spearheaded Earth's resistance to the coming threat, but who was, in the end, still just a chubby balding man in his late thirties who didn't have much outside of his work other than a paunch.

As for the young man he was with, wunderkind inventor of the famous spinal interface, he was almost as famous within the taskforce's circles. And then if you added the bionic man they all called boss, it really was too much for the gathered group.

So they stayed in mute silence, awkward really, but happy to be here, in the presence of what they perceived as greatness.

"OK, that looks very promising, indeed," said Neal, rubbing his hands together as he reemerged from his link into the machine.

"Oh yeah, Neal," replied Amadeu, clearly still linked in, his eyes closed. "It really does, doesn't it." The boy beamed. "This is going to be so very, very cool."

And it really was.

Without much in the way of warning, the process came to a close and the ground rumbled slightly as the seal on the great Dome above and in front of them was cracked. It was a long, slow process as they went to open the segmented top half of the Dome, but unlike previous openings, they would not then have to wait for the massive gantry cranes that lined the ground around the Dome to unload its contents.

For where the Skalm and EAHL had needed to be lifted clear of the Dome's fragile and exorbitantly expensive golden inner-surface before igniting their engines, today's child of the Dome would require no such assistance.

"If you will excuse me, gentlemen, I must commune with Moira to help with the engine start and unloading." said William, to nods from both Amadeu and Neal.

As William virtually departed the space once more, the two other men, different in both age, background, purpose, and personality, but identical in the childlike expectation that filled their faces, stood and walked to the thick windows of the room to gaze up at the rim of the Dome's bottom half.

It was showing like the brim of a giant goblet now, viewed from beneath, like it was about to spill its contents across the wide flat peninsula it dominated.

The world seemed to hold its breath, or at least it did for Neal and Amadeu, as they looked upwards.

They waited.

Then they saw it; a great, three-pronged foot, rising up and over the edge of the dome.

It was on the end of a leg, a long, thin leg, more an outline than a solid form, a framework of nanotube spars, strung with great cables that were its spiderweb tendons. It kept coming. The foot alone must have been ten meters across, indeed they knew it was, at some level, but for now they stared at it with a joy untempered by fact. They looked at it with the eyes of the children they had once been, children who had played with Lego and Transformers. That had dreamed of the very machines they were now building.

But this was no flight of fancy, and it was not so esoteric or scary as the Skalm. This was just, plain, awesome ...

The leg continued coming, reaching up and over the brim, and they saw what they thought was the knee, then realized it was just an ankle, as the main bulk of the huge limb filled the sky above their suddenly diminutive shed.

As the huge foot came to ground, they watched as its three toes and giant ankle flexed, absorbing the impact as the ground shook with the massive footfall. But no sooner was the foot firmly planted than another was rising up and over the Dome's rim to join the first.

And as this second huge leg came up and over, the main body of the machine started to heave into view as well. Soon the full scale of the Ground Based Heavy Lifter became clear, a reality to match the drawings they had all seen and tried to picture.

It was, at its core, a crane on four legs, or rather a crane with four legs, for the legs were both its means of mobility and the way by which it would lift whatever it needed to lift.

Like its flying cousin the EAHL, it could have comfortably walked right into the bay, latched onto one of the cargo ships that lay there with the spindly but powerful grapples that lined the underbelly of its body, and lifted it clear out of the water.

But unlike the EAHL, whose acronym had so easily become its moniker, the acronym GBHL gave little fuel for the imagination. So it had been dubbed, simply, Big Foot. Neal, with his astronomer's penchant for Greek mythology, had pushed for naming it after the first of the Titans to add to his growing pantheon, but the team of military and civilian engineers that had worked on it had found it uninspiring, and he was, in truth, just fine with their final choice.

"jesus ... h ... christ," he whispered to no one in particular as the beast clambered out of the Dome that had birthed it. Amadeu chuckled.

"My thoughts exactly," Amadeu said, and they glanced at each other and grinned before staring back at the massive hulk once more.

It was not waiting around. It was already treading toward the water in great, powerful steps of its four huge legs, as though about to do just that theoretical thing Neal had used so many times in discussions of its planned use. But it was not going to pick up one of the ships there. That would have been both pointless, dangerous, and a strain on even its herculean strength.

It was going to do in a matter of days what it had taken the standard gantry cranes and loading bays two weeks to do.

They watched, grinning, as it stepped into the frigid waters, immune to their bitter cold, and moved over to one of the big ships. It straddled the ship it as though it was a kraken of legend, and Neal tried to imagine what it must feel like to be on the ship in question.

But it was not there to attack the hulking freighter, it was there to lighten its load, and as it moved over the ship, it aligned its body over the cargo containers that covered its decks. The stocky body, home to the fusion engines that pumped power to its four huge limbs, dipped down, the mandible limbs on its underbelly reaching out, and grasped up a stacked block of twenty containers, each laden with countless tons of raw materials.

They watched as it lifted the stack easily into the air, making light work of what it would have taken ten ordinary cranes an hour to do, and began to lumber back into the relatively shallow waters to shore.

"That is," said Amadeu, "without doubt, the coolest thing I have ever seen!"

Amadeu turned to Neal, who nodded in agreement, then he smiled back at the arrayed engineers standing behind them, who were wondering, perhaps, what they were doing there. But they nodded their agreement with the young boy's sentiment, adding their own sycophantic enthusiasm.

Amadeu smiled once more and turned back to the show.

- - -

With the team leads sent back to their jobs, and Amadeu left to his devices as he alternately watched Big Foot or stepped virtually into it to join Mynd, Moira, and the team controlling the massive device, Neal and William walked away from shed.

They were elated. It was a good day, one of many they had enjoyed since the battle at Rolas. Not sweet enough to fully eradicate the bitterness of that terrible defeat, but enough for genuine happiness to show on Neal's face.

"This will change everything here," William said.

"Of course," replied Neal, "loading times will be cut in half."

It should have been their first project with the Dome, and in a perfect world it would have been, but the need to get the first Skalm airborne, and then to get the EAHL ready so it could help rethread their elevator to space had necessarily taken precedence.

"Less than half, in fact," said William. "But the real benefit will come with unloading."

Neal nodded appreciatively. Getting the huge finished products out of the Dome had proven even harder than getting the raw materials in, and they had been forced to spend precious time and resources each time patching and refinishing the golden inner-layer after they clumsily wrenched and pulled their first two creations out of their synthetic womb.

They walked in silence for a little while toward Neal's plane before William spoke up again, his voice amplified by his custom-made exo-suit.

"Neal, if you have a moment, I wanted to talk to you about something we discussed last week."

Neal turned to him, surprised on some level, but not really. He had hoped the topic would come up again, and feared it would as well.

"Yes, William?" he said in a curious but reassuring tone.

William took a visible breath then said, "If we wanted ... if *I* wanted ... to pursue, or even *discuss* pursuing, the avenue we talked about before ... how might I go about doing that?"

Neal looked pensive. It was a very good question. With his extensive team adding skills and specialties every day from among the best and brightest minds in the world, it had been a while since he had to think about whether or not they had the ability to do something. If it needed to be done, he just gave the task to Madeline, or Ayala, or Jack, or William, or, if in doubt, to Minnie and Mynd, for them to deal with.

But this was more delicate than that, and he would have to proceed with care.

"Well, William," he said, after carefully considering his response for a moment, "if you were to want to talk about options, then we would probably want to proceed with some discretion, both for your sake and for that of TASC as a whole."

It was not nice to think about, perhaps, but he did not want it becoming public that he was encouraging, or even countenancing, voluntary amputations, however well meaning the work might be.

But William was no fool. He was not naïve enough to think that this would be anything other than a project that was strictly between them. But to a man with his condition, it was a possibility too tempting for him not to at least consider. The suit was too wonderful, and gave him the simple gift of mobility, something only those unfortunate enough to have lost could truly understand the joy of regaining.

But in the end it was just a suit, its incredible abilities only emphasizing his lack thereof, and William could not help but long for limbs that truly worked, even if they were not his own.

"If you will allow me," said William, "I have a contact that may be able to help."

One of Neal's eyebrows rose in surprise, and William went on, "I worked with him at Oxford, when I was working on my robotics thesis. He was a specialist in robotic prosthesis, though one whose theories encouraged a more extreme measure of amputation than was accepted as necessary in most circles. It has held him back in many ways. But he is a brilliant man, in his way."

Neal stopped and turned to face William, who also turned to meet his gaze.

"William," said Neal, "if you want to pursue this, and I think it is both very brave, and potentially very important that you do, then give me this man's name and I will see to it he is hired immediately."

"Dr. Sudipto Ramamorthy. I can contact him now, if you will allow me," said William.

Neal closed his eyes and opened his link, keeping William in the frame as he contacted Mynd.

*Neal:* 'mynd, i need a new project opened for location at district two. this will be headed by william. he will have hiring and purchase authority, and reports will be coded for my access only. we will call it … ¿william, any thoughts on a what you want to call this?'

*William:* '¿how about 'project vestige'?'

Neal nodded his agreement, both in the ether and in reality, and the two of them returned to the present.

"You will need a place for this doctor to work in, William," said Neal, and William nodded. "May I suggest you set it well away from the main project center? It is a big island, and it is, for all intents and purposes, yours to do with as you see fit. I suggest you use the space available."

Neal waved his hand out at the broad harbor. It was a beautiful place, if stark and very deliberately in the middle of nowhere. William followed Neal's gesture across the dark blue water to the mountains that surrounded them. He had explored those mountains, in part in the exo-suit he now wore, but far more with the various phases of the Phase battle units he and Mynd were still working on.

Deep down he had few doubts left now that they had breached the subject. He was equal parts fearful and excited at the thought of permanently replacing his two atrophied legs. But what then? His arms? His weakening neck and facial muscles?

He shivered at the thought, and felt, with grim irony, as the suit made the movement real where his own body could not.

## Chapter 11: Shockwaves – Part Two

The Slink landed in the quiet of night. It did not drop its passengers at altitude, as it had all those the months ago, before the war in Eastern Europe, but actually landed with them.

It would hide nearby, in the only hiding place it could rely on once the light of day came. After Ayala and her team had stepped free of the compartments that had held them secure for their long flight, it lifted once more.

Silent as the breeze upon which it floated, the big, hollow discus with its four stubby wings glided a few meters up into the night sky and then floated out over the deserted section of the Taedong River before unceremoniously lowering itself into it. The magnetic field rotors that span at its center worked as well in water as they did in air, and so it quickly disappeared beneath the surface in a whirl of sloshing water and was gone, there to await the team's return once they were ready to leave.

Ayala checked her suit, as did her team.

Hektor, Cara, and Niels were fully recovered from their extraordinary mission in Moscow where they had played executioner to the usurping madman that had taken power there. They were also joined now by two Korean agents on loan from their South Korean allies as part of the cooperative approach to the investigation that Neal had agreed to with the Korean government.

All six were equipped with the latest battleskins, ever more evolved by hard-won learning. Ayala had considered sending the new Phase Nine battle avatars instead, but they could not risk what had happened to her recon teams in the Ukraine. They must be able to run subspace quiet, just in case they encountered resistance equipped with some echo of what Agent Pei had equipped his Chinese allies with before he died.

It was something that was looking more and more likely the further Ayala got into her investigation of the assassination attempt in New York.

But that was not the only reason that she now rescinded her three-part helmet and spoke to her team out loud. Two of its members did not possess the spinal-interfaces that would allow her to commune via subspace with them anyway.

"All right," she said, in hushed but commanding tones, "I want equipment checks from all of you. Hektor, when you are ready, let's set up the laser beacon and get our non-subspace comms online. Niels, Cara, perimeter guard, please."

They had no reason to expect any form of militarized presence here, not like they had encountered in Russia, anyway, especially this far outside the city. For though Pyongyang was the capital of a twenty-five million-person country, it was a small and woefully underdeveloped city. Its stunted development was appropriate, perhaps, given the unfortunate nation's state of health.

The population existed, for the most part, in a time capsule. Education and agriculture had receded to almost medieval levels under the oppressive Kim regime, as had civil liberties, with such things as freedom of speech and due process not even in the average local's vernacular.

But amongst this oppression had grown an unnaturally strong military, spurred by equal parts paranoia and megalomania, and for that reason alone Ayala remained cautious.

Cautious, but still curious enough to come here. For all leads seemed to be pointing into the morass that was North Korea, or at least to the border of this strange place, and then vanishing into its foggy depths.

"OK, Jung, talk to me," Ayala now said, turning to her two Korean allies. "We've gotten you to the Taedong, we're up river, as requested ..."

Jung Hae Chul, major in the South Korean Counter Terrorism Service, and his subordinate Captain Chin, glanced at each other furtively. They had spent their entire professional lives working to protect their home from their erstwhile cousins to the north, but this was only the fourth time either had been here.

Yet among their peers, that categorized them as experts, for transit to and from North Korea was a famously rare event.

For Jung especially, being here was a bitter pill, as he had spent the first half of his life trying to escape this very city, only to be co-opted into South Korea's intelligence services once safe.

It was for that very reason, though, that he understood the need to protect the border, and even, if events required it, as they now did, to cross back into this awful place.

If he was caught, Jung faced certain death, but given the manner of their incursion he doubted that any of the rest of the team would suffer a much better end if they fell into enemy hands. So he locked eyes with his Israeli comrade and temporary commander and said, "We are indeed here, Ms. Zubaideh. An impressive machine." He tipped his head toward the now submerged Slink, and Ayala nodded in acknowledgement.

The Slink was not a secret she showed to non-TASC personnel lightly, but, she knew, knowing of its existence would do little to help either her allies or enemies spot the stealthy machine when she needed it to get in and out of their nations uninvited.

"As for what is next," Jung said, quietly, "I see no reason we would not follow our primary route plan now that we are here."

She nodded, and then turned to the wider group, sending a tight ping over subspace to Niels and Cara to tell them to return. They had reconfigured their suit-to-suit comms to limit range to specifically the distance to the nearest team member, whose suit would then relay the signal to the next, and so on. It would limit the chance of Ayala and her three Spezialists being spotted, and still they would only use the comms when too far apart for simple verbal or visual commands.

As Niels and Cara returned, she spoke to the huddled team again. "Very well. We have successfully landed at Point Alpha. Hektor, if you have communicated our status back to Minnie, we are going to move off."

He confirmed he had, and they turned as one to the river.

As they began to step into the fast-flowing water, she said, "OK, let's close suits and engage breathers. Niels, you have point, the rest of you stay close. Jung and Chin, I am afraid we are going to have to hold hands." She smiled and reached out to take Jung's hand, who did the same to his colleague.

And so they dipped into the flowing Taedong, Niels first, quickly submerging. His helmet was now closed, a special rebreather parsed air to and from two small but highly pressurized tanks they each carried. They would not last long, maybe ten minutes at a time. But they could replenish them with small snorkels when they had to, allowing the team to move down the river and into the city proper without detection.

- - -

They arrived at their secondary staging point a little over an hour after departing the landing site and stepped gingerly ashore, guns already raised as they emerged from the water. Once Niels, Hektor, and Cara were confident that there was no one around, they gave the all-clear for Ayala to lead the two Koreans to shore.

After a long moment's silence to adjust to their new surroundings, Ayala rescinded her helmet, indicating that the others should do the same. "Right. For those of you who are interested, we are now in beautiful Moranbong Park, and between us and the other shore is Rungnado Island, another generous gift to the people from the Great Leader."

Her ironic tone brought smiles from the group, though less so from Jung.

"Hektor, I want you to find an innocuous place to install our comms station. You know what you are looking for. Cara, please assists Hektor and provide cover for him. Niels, perimeter sweep and eyes, please. Start at a hundred meters, but once you have fully mapped the nearby area for Minnie, please spread out. She will help you with setting the boxes as you go. Meet back here when done, or within twenty, no longer. I don't want anyone wandering too far."

Nods were the only response she received and the three Spezialists turned and left without further comment. Hektor would be looking for a tree with dense enough low foliage to hide their small laser beacon in its upper branches. The device, simple by TASC's standards, perhaps, but still a dream to any field operative, would self-track to TASC's pod satellites that now blanketed near-earth orbit, relaying their status and any relevant information Ayala wanted returned to Rolas via an all but undetectable tight-beamed laser.

It would only transmit, though, as they could receive all they would need directly through subspace without danger of revealing their position.

For Niels's part, he would be placing small white boxes on trees and posts around their position, widely spaced, but in view of each other. The boxes would form a spiderweb of eyes and ears.

Ayala was quite proud of their camouflage, for they would hide in plain sight: their white, metallic outsides stamped clearly with a government insignia and instructions that it was not to be touched. They would use the regime's own totalitarianism against it, and rely on fear trumping curiosity should anyone spot the small boxes placed out of reach and seemingly at random around the public park.

"As for you two," Ayala now said to Jung and Chin, with her three team members off distributing their little toys around the park, "you should probably get your civilian clothing ready."

"Yes, Commander," said Jung as the two men set to removing and opening the sealed, hard-shelled packs they had clipped to their sides.

They contained simple clothing, requisite in its minimalism, and no more than it appeared to be.

They were brave men, Ayala could not argue with that, for they were going to walk out into the city with no more protection than their wits afforded them. Well, that and two small, antique-looking flip-phones, still a luxury in this city, to be sure, but hidden within them were a couple of tools that might help them in a bind, most notably a panic button and locator beacon.

"Our contact will not know when we are coming," said Jung by way of passing the time, even though Ayala remembered this from the briefing, "but hopefully he will be ready for us. Either way, we cannot leave until dawn anyway."

The city observed a standing curfew after dark. It was not strictly enforced, but if you wished to break it you had better have a good reason, have strong connections to the party, or be a member of the party yourself. While they might have faked such credentials, it would be far safer to wait until the madding crowd emerged once day broke, and lose themselves in the millions of ordinary people, rich and poor, who called the city home.

"Of course," said Ayala. "In the meantime, why don't you try and get some rest. You have a long day ahead of you, and you should get any sleep you can."

He looked at her skeptically, not of her trustworthiness, but more of his own belief that they would be able to sleep. Her answering expression was more understanding than he could have expected. "Jung, Chin, think of this little spot here as a safe haven. My team may be small, but do not doubt their skill, or the deadliness of their weapons. Please try to sleep, my friends. I will wake you when it is time for you to get ready."

Jung and Chin were not unappreciative of the gesture. They nodded, and tried to get comfortable, their civilian clothes at the ready, but keeping on their lo-fi battleskins for now to protect them from the damp ground and chill air.

- - -

*Saul Moskowitz:* 'so a guy is reading the paper and he sees an ad: talking dog for sale. well of course he calls and makes an appointment to go and see the dog, if only out of curiosity. so he gets there and the owner tells him the dog is in the backyard. the guy goes into the backyard and sees a mutt sitting there, looking very sorry for himself.'

Ayala did not tell Saul to stop, though she wanted to. She could not risk the chatter when in such a delicate location. But Saul had no such restrictions, so he filled the airwaves with his inane banter.

*Saul:* '-so i hear you talk- asks the man. -yap- replies the dog. —so, what's your story?- asks the man. the dog sighs and says, -well, my first owner figured out pretty young that i could talk and sold me to mossad.-'

Ayala and Hektor rolled their eyes, but were unable to halt the endless stream from Saul's dubious bag of jokes, so they listened on in silence.

*Saul:* '-so in no time mossad has me hanging out with bad guys and taking treats from visiting world leaders, if you know what i mean.- the man is surprised. -wow, that's amazing,- he says. to which the dog replies, -it was, for a while, but then the p.l.o. figured it out and i had to stop. so i went to work at the airport to listen in on shady-looking passengers. i uncovered some incredible stuff, got a bunch of medals. it was really great while it lasted. but that's all behind me now. now i'm retired.-

*Saul:* 'so the man, duly impressed, goes back into the house and says, -how much for that amazing dog?- and the owner says, -twenty shekels.- -only twenty shekels!- says the man, - but why are you selling this amazing dog so cheap?- -because he's a damn liar, he never worked for mossad.-'

Ayala chuckled quietly in spite of herself, as did Hektor. Niels and Cara slept, along with the two Koreans, while they waited out the last hours of the night.

*Minnie:* 'but saul, the dog was amazing in so many ways. surely a lie …'

Ayala put her head in her hands and Hektor suppressed a more powerful laugh at Minnie's wonderful naivety.

*Saul:* 'yes, minnie, he was. But … don't worry about it, minnie. let's not bore ayala and hektor with explaining it.'

Ayala whispered to Hektor, "So very thoughtful, that Saul, to spare us the explanation."

They shared long-suffering looks as Saul blundered on with his seemingly generous donation of humor for their long watch. She knew he was enjoying torturing her, she had sat through one of his diatribes before, by phone that time, when they had filled a line they knew was tapped by a Syrian operative with seemingly meaningless babble in order to frustrate the poor man.

But cruel as it might seem, Saul knew what he was doing now, as he had then, and the hours dripped by just a little faster as he regaled them with yet another of his infamous mossad jokes.

*Saul:* 'so margaret thatcher is in israel for talks, and, after a few drinks, ends up in shimon peres's hotel room …'

"Don't you dare!" said Ayala in a hoarse whisper and Hektor perked up, smiling from ear to ear and genuinely interested for the first time since Saul had started.

But Saul did dare, and Ayala's head sunk into her hands once more as he veered into ever worse territory. If Minnie was confused by the last one, thought Ayala, wait till she gets a load of this.

- - -

They left not long after dawn, their clothes clean but drab, their steps brisk. The walk was only three miles, but it was fraught with tension every time they passed one of the many policemen or guards that stood around the government buildings that lined the city.

Jung and Chin's contact was across town, not far past the massive glass pyramid of the new Ryugyong Hotel, with its strange but striking buttresses that now dominated the downtown skyline of Pyongyang.

Their contact would then take them on an equally nerve-racking car journey to a small office building outside town. Along the way they would be greeted by some horrific sights, as the scale of what was going on within North Korea's closed borders became clear. Ayala had speculated that the antigen would not have spread here, and she had been right. They had hoped the country would be equally sheltered from the virus itself, but there they had not been so lucky.

While the political establishment, with its slightly more liberal access to travel and foreign interaction, had been touched to some degree by immunity, they had been among the only who had, and the disease that had been intended for the whole world had struck instead at the poorest members of one of its poorest nations.

The rural population, they now discovered, had been halved, maybe worse; what little information they could get was not totally clear. And that had not been the only hard news the team would be forced to suffer that day.

For the lead they had been hoping to pursue would give them nothing except exposure to the horror of a countryside damned. So that evening they returned to their contact's small apartment, shell-shocked and confused, and slept there until the next morning.

All the while Ayala and her team waited. Waited for them to report something of interest, waited for them to find some evidence of the conspiracy, hopefully in the form of a person, either willing or not, who could tell them what they needed to know.

Ayala was more than ready to abduct anyone they deemed had information of interest to her. Either for interrogation onsite or for transport out of the country aboard the Slink.

But they would get no such lead.

On the second day, Jung and Chin will wait for three hours while their contact leaves to meet with another member of the small but impossibly brave resistance movement. Then the three men will depart again, equally cautiously. Their contact will take them out of the city again, this time to the south, to the small and innocent seeming industrial town of Chunghwa.

A few hours later they will check in via their cell phones, using them as just that, cell phones, if ones that have been modified in very specific ways. They will use a code string to tell Ayala that they went to investigate a source of some unusual activity in recent weeks, then they will give a contact number, which once decoded will convey the coordinates of the disused factory they intend to visit.

And then the two men will vanish. By nightfall, when Ayala has still not heard from them, not even a ping from the beacons built into their cell phones, she will notify Rolas that something has gone wrong.

# Chapter 12: Reflex

Neal was not pleased with this most recent turn of events, and neither was Saul, though for very different reasons.

"I need a second team prepped for insertion immediately," said Neal, "and I want them to have a contingent of the Battle Avatars with them as well. Minnie, please inform William and Mynd."

She already had the moment Neal had said it, but she nodded her avatar's head anyway.

Saul looked pensive and Neal looked at him, prompting the old spy to speak up. "While I agree that this is cause for alarm, and that we should be prepared for the worst, I think you should let Ayala investigate further while we get our other teams in place."

Neal began shaking his head, but Saul went on. "I understand your concern, Neal. And trust me, I have no more desire to send her into whatever trap the Korean agents fell into either. But the rest of her team is much, much better equipped to handle anything she might face out there than they were, and we do not know how long the two Korean agents have."

Neal made a face that could only be described as 'I know I am about to come off as a prick, but …', then said, "The safety of the Korean agents is a concern, but I am afraid it is secondary to the safety of our people … I'm sorry, but …"

Neal held up his hands, but Saul spoke up once more, using an appropriately conciliatory tone. "Leaving aside the fact that Ayala promised to get them in and out safely when she requested their help from the South Koreans, I am not only speaking about protecting their safety, but also the integrity of the investigation."

Neal was about to chide Saul for the comment about Ayala's promise of safe passage when he was stopped by Saul's second remark.

Seeing he had Neal's attention, Saul explained, "They have almost certainly been taken. Whether this plot really does stem from North Korea or not, the discovery of two South Korean agents will make them nervous. And if they have enough time to break the two men … and trust me when I say it really is only a question of time before they do, given what we know about North Korean torture methods … then the additional knowledge that there are TASC operatives in downtown Pyongyang will send the North Koreans into a frenzy."

"All the more reasons to get Ayala and her team out now," said Neal firmly.

"Neal, you know as well as I do that there is simply no way you are going to get Ayala to leave the area with two of her team members unaccounted for."

The two men locked eyes for a second, but Neal knew it was not Saul's resolve he had to match in this, it was his security chief's.

"Okay, so she waits a while longer," said Neal, after a moment, "but they should move to a different location."

"To that, she will most definitely agree.  Where?"

"Where?" said Neal, perplexed.

Saul's expression became one of sympathy for Neal, for a man who still deluded himself that Ayala could be ordered to do anything she did not agree with, especially since Barrett's death.  "Neal, my friend.  The fact is that—and I reiterate this only because it is, in truth, the only thing Ayala will be considering at this moment—if you want to find out what Ayala went there to find out, you are going to have to let her and her team go after the two South Koreans … *now*, before this gets messy and any hope we have of getting any real intelligence gets lost in the crossfire."

*Before* it gets messy, thought Neal.  Like everything wasn't hopelessly messy already.  Neal simmered and the two men stared at each other, one stubborn, but the other shrugging as if to say, 'don't look at me, I just work here.'

Finally, Neal's shoulders sank a bit and he opened a one-way line into the heart of North Korea.

*Neal:* 'ayala.  i guess you have a decision to make.'

Saul joined him in the ether.  Minnie was, of course, already there.

*Neal:* 'i did not want to make it your choice, but given the … analysis of your head of intelligence, it seems as though you are probably going to do what you think is best anyway."

She did not respond via subspace for obvious reasons, but her signal came through nonetheless, her voice resounding into their minds like a cheap speakerphone echoing in a concert hall.

"I can imagine very easily what Saul must have said, Neal, and no, he was not wrong.  Time is of the essence.  By my estimates we can be outside Chunghwa in less than an hour if we move now.  That gives us six more hours before dawn to snoop around."

She was already signaling to her team to get ready.  They would leave the Korean's rebreathing equipment here and Minnie would continue to monitor the area via the boxes that still lined the park.

*Neal:* 'now ayala, i know you are keen to get to the bottom of this.  i would try to talk you out of it if i thought it would make any difference, but … just be careful, ok.  please remember what happened to ben.'

She tensed at the mention of one of her first team leaders, a counterpart to Hektor in their initial reconnaissance mission into Russia.  Oh, she remembered what had happened to Ben, she thought, she remembered it very well indeed.

"Understood, Neal. We'll tread lightly. And in the interests of caution, in case we do run into trouble, how soon can Banu be at our location?"

*Minnie:* <she is already in near-earth orbit and maintaining quasi-geosynchronous orbit over Seoul. She can be at chungwa in 215 seconds, if you need her.>

Ayala smiled at Minnie and Banu's efficiency, while Neal whistled at what it meant for Banu to be essentially hovering at that altitude.

And above them all, machine eyes watched and waited as Ayala and her team set off.

- - -

Over the past few months, TASC had veritably flooded near space with satellites. It had been an expenditure Neal had been loath to make, but circumstances had forced their hand. With the unchecked power of Mikhail's puppet Russian Premier and Pei's cruel manipulation of the Chinese leader, TASC had been unable to stand aloof from the world's political arena any longer.

So they had engaged, if only out of a need for self-preservation. It had been a whirlwind few months since they had turned their attention to ground, and they had quickly discovered, as every emerging world power had from the United States back to the Egyptians, that trying to police the world was a task so large as to threaten to engulf your every moment.

Neal loathed it, the pettiness and pointlessness of it all when viewed against the greater backdrop of the coming threat, and fought every day to maintain his team's focus on the real task ahead. Minnie, on the other hand, was fascinated by it, and she stared down now with an ever growing number of eyes spanning the globe.

It was appropriate, her growing network of eyes and ears coming to match the span of her reach around the globe she called home. But what the range of satellites really did was help feed her insatiable appetite for information, for reams and reams of data to comb through. It was the only thing that could nourish the curiosity that defined her.

She shared her discoveries with her cousin, Mynd, and with the small number of lesser Artificial Minds she was growing in incremental stages, toying with different combinations of traits, both ones she had gleaned from her AM parents Amadeu and Birgit, and ones she had developed on her own, to see how each behaved, while also experimenting with substrate formats and designs, seeing which traits flourished more or less as she tweaked processing power, recall speed, stimuli access, and human exposure.

Everything she did was done within the confines of her purpose, both limited and catalyzed by her desire to help humanity survive, but that need to help was a broad mandate, and as she looked for ways to better herself in an effort to better serve the humans she was born from, she could not help but wonder at her more distant cousins, the minds born of the race coming, even now, to eradicate the humanity, minds that would no doubt have representatives among the Armada.

She modeled the coming war in endless loops, as no doubt her counterparts were doing as well, though with a more complete picture of humanity's rapidly advancing capabilities than her enemies had, a factor she analyzed ceaselessly in an effort to suck every last drop of advantage from it. And when her models led her to probable defeat, as they often did, she inevitably pondered her role in the aftermath.

It was a process that begged profound questions. At what point, she thought, would it become mere hubris to fight any longer? At what point would it be conceited to think that humanity's history was more important than the planet's itself? History was filled with men lauded as heroes for fighting a fight they could not win. But when the cost was not the shattered walls of the Alamo but that of the very ground it was built on, what then? Was that still bravery, or was it bloody-mindedness?

Bloody-mindedness. It was a multi-layered joke.

She laughed in her way, then turned her attention to that part of her that was watching over Banu.

The girl didn't really suffer through any of this. She neither understood nor cared to contemplate the scale of the fight she was embroiled in. She sat on her perch, a perch made of the pure heat of her engines idling to keep her body space-bound.

Maintaining geosynchronicity at near-earth distances required a vast expenditure of power. But it was power the Skalm had to burn, and so Banu hung there, as if sitting atop her eave, once again the barn owl monitoring her domain. She was happy to be away for a moment from the classes. From meeting other young people, but not as young as her, in mind, and therein lay her frustration.

She was supposed to be vetting new pilots, but as of yet no one had been willing to involve candidates as young as she was. It was one thing, it appeared, to involve her, to co-opt one youth, an orphan, a lost child. But to actually take children en masse, that seemed something they were not willing to do yet. Instead they kept testing the limit, bringing in children of higher ages, teenagers with various established skill levels: child athletes, chess whizzes, prodigies, and wunderkinds. They were looking for the ceiling, for the age of perfection.

And she was bored with it. The new kids were both too old to engage with her as an equal, and too slow to engage with her in the air. They were both her betters and her inferiors, and she was relieved to be away from it all for a while.

For the moment her attention was not even on the barn floor below. Minnie would let her know if there was a rodent there that she needed to swoop down upon.

Her eyes were on the stars above, on the void, and her little mind was filled with the expanse of it.

She felt her wings, tensed them, and a ripple of power from her mighty engines made the great star-cross of her machine self flutter in its place.

She could go there. She could, with a thrust from her wings, leap free of the world below and surge out into the stars. She fought an urge to do it. She had a job, she knew; a role she must play. They were looking for others to take her place, or at least to join her, but for now she was the one.

The best.

She smiled, and with no small amount of pride, she flipped her craft in a series of tight somersaults. Seen from below she was but a dot in the cosmos, perhaps, but she knew she was the master of the planet she soared above.

Minnie watched the girl, both from within the ether from which the Skalm was controlled, and from a multitude of eyes roaming in orbit, Minnie had no doubt the powerful and infamous craft would be obvious to anyone with even a basic telescope looking skyward from the Korean peninsula below, maybe even with binoculars, given the bright flare of her engines.

But Banu was still technically over allied space, hanging over Seoul, over an ally who had, however begrudgingly, acknowledged TASC's claim to dominion over what it called its fourth district.

And anyway, Banu could happily outrun anything that either North or South Korea could throw her way if they did choose to object to Banu's presence.

As tiny figures scurried far below, seeking answers, Banu came to a hover and stared out once more, to the stars, and then to the great lunar crescent even now hoving into view. It was apparently about to lose its status as Earth's only moon.

But it would still be by far the world's largest satellite, and though Banu did not know it, the great moon was also being eyed to feed TASC's epic appetite.

# Chapter 13: Feng Shui

Madeline's avatar was bathed in sunlight, her expansive view of Earth's orbital vicinity spinning around her. In the simulation she was currently hosting, she was joined by a host of team leads from Districts One and Three, and various experts either considering joining their ranks, or fighting with their governments for permission to do so.

"We all know, I think, where we are now, and I think we all know roughly where we must go." She spoke out loud, for several of her audience were not enabled with spinal taps yet and were watching via computer screens or even via advanced but already obsolete 3-D virtual goggles.

"But what I want to focus on today is the crucial intermediary stage we find ourselves entering. Because for the foreseeable future we are less worried about making ships than we are about making the production facilities and sourcing the raw materials we will need to do so."

There were nods from those whose links were advanced enough to allow them to project a virtual avatar into simulation. She went on, "So, here we are today: Earth."

Everyone's view now swam to bring the big blue-green orb into focus, its near-space ancillaries sliding out of view. "Here we have Earth, where we all are, or most of us anyway, and where about 65% of the resources that we can count as 'within our reach' are located. But as we all know, that 65% is held down by a most unfortunately powerful gravitational field."

Some around nodded, some smiled, either virtually or to themselves in whatever conference room, lab, or home office they had managed to co-opt for today's meeting. For the problem of gravity was, at its heart, why they were all here.

"So where is the other 35%?" It was a rhetorical question, and as she said it their view warped outward once more to encompass Earth's many natural and man-made satellites, a little poetic license taken with scale so that those too small to be seen at this range could be made out.

Three rough rings could be seen around Earth showing its many communications, GPS, and spy satellites' orbits. In the spirit of cooperation, Madeline even included TASC's own network of spy satellites, if only to emphasize their extent to representatives of their less willing allies.

"So, we have the moon, of course," she said. "That certainly accounts for the lion's share of the remaining booty, but we will get to that in a moment. First let us talk about Hekaton, or Asteroid 1979va for those of you that were not privy to the recent contact and first-stage harnessing of our soon to be stable-mate. Estimates remain hopeful that she will be brought into geostationary orbit over Rolas within the next three to four months."

The room was impressed, and the view changed to show that planned eventuality, Hekaton now shown in its planned orbit, along with the adjoining cable that even now was being relaced to ground, the first of many that would be tethered to the great rock.

"I know that treaty agreements with many of your home nations, our allies, have included the rights to build your own elevators as well, along with provisions for the assistance you may need from us to complete that work."

Now the view changed to include those planned cables as well. The great lines of the other planned space-elevators now beginning to resolve in the simulation.

The first came up from an atoll in the Maldives recently leased by the Indian government.

Another then materialized from an island in the mouth of the Amazon where a base was already under construction by the very Brazilian team that had built the first base at Rolas.

Two more then suddenly sprang up, seemingly from the middle of the Pacific: a European cable planned from an oil rig even now being moved into position off the Aranuka Atoll near Kiribati; and then yet another, if less likely, one being planned by an ever optimistic NASA on a reef off of their own Baker Island.

Most in the group knew that the Chinese were in heavy negotiations for a site in Indonesia. It was a primary topic of Jim Hacker's negotiations with both nations, both in offering help to China in return for their allegiance and in blocking the Indonesians from granting access until the Chinese gave in to greater cooperation with TASC's work.

Both to make a point to the other gathered representatives, and because of a lack of real confidence that the Chinese would ever fully give in, that planned elevator was not shown here.

But it was an impressive sight nonetheless; a growing number of spokes, like the spreading tendrils of Earth's influence, radiating out from around the great globe's equator. As the cables ran through and then out past the depicted circles of satellites still orbiting the planet, the image began to look ever more like a great wheel, except for the anomalous and mighty-looking Hekaton that would, they all knew, come to dominate its orbit, changing forever half the world's image of the night sky as it inserted itself into that vista.

But that, in and of itself, represented almost as many problems as it did solutions. Problems which Madeline now went into. "As you can see, our current band of near-earth and low-earth orbit satellites will soon represent an unacceptable hazard to our space elevator operations. It was a hazard we managed on a case by case basis with the first elevator, but that will become ever less feasible as operations intensify."

The Dispatchers.

The title appeared as a visual underneath a new image that now expanded outward to fill their view.

It was of a machine. A machine that was, at its heart, a catapult, but as the schematics showed, these catapults would use magnetic field accelerators instead of counterweights. There were twenty of them even now being manufactured at District Three. An EAHL was even now en route there to lift them into orbit.

Once in orbit, the Dispatchers would maneuver, using their own stocky thrusters, to intercept and capture orbiting 'debris.' What had once been the most prized possessions of any nation rich enough to get into space was being reduced to scrap by the pace of advancement.

"My friends, it would not be unfair to say you are now looking at the final evolution of the baseball bat. A machine that will begin clearing our space of the gathering mass of obstacles we have ourselves deposited there in the last fifty years. For once one of these machines has latched onto an object that requires clearing, it will then use its mass, thrusters, and powerful magnetic field generators to catapult said object out of harm's way."

They watched the simulation as the Dispatcher did indeed punch itself away on its stocky thrusters, and they followed it as it moved off to intercept a simulated orbiting satellite.

It approached the satellite obliquely, latching onto it with a powerful field manipulator. Magnetic grapples were an extremely energy-wasteful process, but it was the only way the Dispatcher could have the versatility to grapple the wide variety of objects we had littered space with since the Cold War had sent Sputnik into its doomed orbit.

The Dispatcher then began accelerating around the object, sending both it and its quarry into a seemingly random but in fact very controlled spin. This spin became ever more excited until, with a suddenness that made many of the gathered experts gasp, it eventually released its charge outward and upward like a discus being hurled into the cosmos.

The gathered audience was a little dismayed at the rather brutal treatment of what some had recognized as an Iridium satellite, a process they correctly assumed would utterly destroy the delicate machinery of the exorbitantly expensive device, but no one commented to that effect.

"As you have no doubt guessed," Madeline confirmed, "this process will render the satellite in question non-functional." Her phrasing was rather more diplomatic than the actual process in question. "But then, of course, removing the satellite from its orbit would have rendered it obsolete anyway."

She soldiered on. "Of course, the construction of the network of equatorial space elevators will have already rendered the Iridium system, along with all current-gen satellite communications and navigation systems, obsolete, as we will now be able to route communications via fixed and far more powerful transponders along the cables' routes, and at their termini."

A question pinged into her head, not for the whole group, but for her alone, from a representative of the European Space Agency. She reviewed it quickly, not wanting to interrupt the flow of her presentation and was not surprised when she saw it was regarding orbital spy systems. Europe and the US were continuing to push for special dispensation regarding such things, based on their 'special relationship' with TASC. But they were not going to get it, a fact that she reiterated now for the whole group.

"We all know this will also affect not only communications satellites but also observational ones." another politeness. "But I am afraid that is simply a fact we are going to have to come to terms with, my friends. Though I have no doubt it will continue to be a source of active debate in our ongoing negotiations, I can say with certainty today, as I have before, that this is a topic that TASC is not able to be flexible on, given our mission."

She moved on, ignoring the quick ping of several more questions from others around the planet, and showed them the other end of the dispatching system they were even now constructing the components for at Districts Two and Three. She showed the group the machines by which they would harvest the remnants of Earth's satellite networks as they were thrown up into the realms of the geostationary.

The images and concepts were engaging enough that she was able to bring the attention of the group back to her presentation as she talked of what the harvested satellites would be used for.

Finally, she turned her attention to the greater prizes, to Hekaton and the moon, a topic that sounded like the title of an ancient Grecian epic poem.

She showed them images of the inflatable stations they wanted the gathered group's help in designing, and of the great mining installations they would form to carve out what they so desperately needed from within the two huge planetoids.

As she had hoped and expected, the gathered minds could not help but be captured by her own sense of wonder at the work of the coming years. For this was not a pipedream. This very much needed to be a reality, and soon.

They were on a clock, and in the end this was all just groundwork. For while they would need to carve great chunks out of their own moon, they would be all but dismantling the smaller Hekaton, eating down into it until it was but a husk. Indeed, humanity would need to thoroughly violate the sanctity of them both, and of much more, no doubt, in order to build their fighting force.

As she continued her presentation, the beautiful and incredible images of Earth's blossoming space-faring age continued to flow. She was trying to impress upon the gathered professors, physicists, engineers, and scientific advisors the scope of the task ahead, and, as she had in the past, she succeeded, at least in part, adding a few more devotees to their growing list of advocates and ambassadors around the world.

It was heady stuff. The stuff of dreams. And what were scientists if they weren't dreamers, even if it was all, at its root, really born of a nightmare: a Manhattan project for a new age.

# Chapter 14: The End of the Rope

A broad concrete parade ground lay ahead. It was badly poured and unmaintained, dotted here and there by small tufts of grass and shrubbery as nature broke through to restate its claim. It was bordered by a long, loosely strung wire fence, topped with razor wire. A fence Hektor's infrared sight told him was hot and therefore cheaply electrified.

Cara stepped up to it, almost amused by the insolence of such a barrier. She could have just grabbed the wires with impunity and pulled them apart with her two black-clad hands, but instead she scanned in each direction, seeking any device that might have betrayed Jung and Chin when they came here the evening before.

But there were no signs of motion detectors or heat sensors that she could see. Hektor and Niels stayed back, guns trained on the night, ready to respond. She shrugged, looked around once more then bent at the knee and vaulted neatly over the fence in a graceful somersault that barely cleared its razor-sharp top by an inch or two.

She landed as lightly as she could and quickly froze once more, waiting for any reaction.

Seconds passed and still nothing. She scanned. If there were motion sensors they would have to be close by. But infrared sensors could be as far off as the stubby buildings across the big square and still have seen their two compatriots. Either way there was no sign of any reaction yet.

She moved forward slowly, low and quiet, covered at all times by her two colleagues behind her and their less skilled but dangerously determined commander also waiting in the shadows. But they did not actually follow her yet. If she got in trouble she had no doubt they would aid her retreat with lethal force, but for now she moved forward alone, toward the low sheds of the complex ahead, apparently disused, but betraying a low heat signature of their own.

Someone was in there. In fact there must be quite a lot of people to give the big buildings such a pervasive warmth in the dark night.

The silence was broken with a sudden shock of activity across the courtyard and she dropped to the ground in response.

Big doors were opening on the side of one of the buildings and suddenly there was a flow of people and trucks emerging from it. Minnie, watching from above, was quick to speak up.

*Minnie:* <i have a lot of movement on the far side of the facility from your location. it looks like two groups, one fanning out, one heading for the main gates.>

Ayala could see from the satellite image Minnie was even now relaying into her brain the scale of whatever was coming out, and now she saw through Cara's eyes as well as the scouting Spezialist risked sending a single image through. It was highly magnified, but it was unmistakable. Against the light coming from the shed, a series of black figures were running.

So they had done it here too, thought Ayala. Pei had given the armor to the North Koreans as well. But even as she thought it, she knew that could not be it. Pei could not have been the source. The Agents were bloodthirsty, but their mandate was clear: avoid nuclear conflagration at all costs and what could bring more risk of nuclear war than arming the madman that ran this little insane asylum of a nation with tech ten?

No, this was the result of the power vacuum Pei had left in his wake. The Chinese, in their haste to take vengeance for the attack in Beijing, had let the cat out of the bag. Ugly visions of what could come next filled her mind.

*Minnie:* <i am seeing signs of regular forces converging on the staging point in moranbong park. they are moving with a precision that suggests knowledge of your staging location there.>

They must have broken Jung or Chin, thought Ayala. She opened a channel to her team, tight beamed, and laced with instruction for Cara not to reply. She was too far out and any further signal from her would be too risky.

*Ayala at Team:* 'we are, by all signs, discovered. they will no doubt be on us soon. we can run, if you like, or we can fight. personally, i would like to see what, exactly, they have actually managed to make out here. but i leave that up to you. ¿hektor, what do you think?'

*Hektor:* 'i think, and i believe i speak for cara and niels on this, that we would like to test their mettle as well. in fact, i think we would all enjoy that very much.'

Unlike their brethren, Hektor, Niels, and Cara's mission into Moscow had kept them from the worst of the fighting in Hungary. They were sorely keen to see what the battleskins could do in a real fight. This was only compounded by a sense of duty, for though they had not known Jung and Chin for very long, they still felt a professional responsibility for their well-being.

But Ayala did not really need that much encouragement. She opened her signal up, reaching for the stars as she commanded them forward. Subtlety was no longer required as she unclipped her team's leashes and sic'd them on the no doubt falsely confident herd of soldiers ahead of them.

*Ayala:* 'minnie, please let banu know we may be in need of her services shortly. ground team, you have permission to spread out and engage at will.'

- - -

Neal and Saul cursed, both to themselves and through the connection to Chunghwa, but their countermands and pleas fell on deaf ears. Neal knew Ayala was still mourning the loss of her husband. He had hoped, on some level, that she had gotten some of her rage out in the short but bloody conclusion to the battle in Hungary where she and her Spezialists had bludgeoned a diminished Russian army back into the dark ages.

He saw now that she had not.

With Minnie overlaying additional information where the satellite images failed, Saul and Neal watched as the four Spezialists gave the North Koreans the good news.

It escalated fast, as an attack by such a potent force must. For her part, Ayala shared none of Neal's reticence, but nor did she try to engage in the same way the other three did. She could not maneuver at their level. Instead, she walked forward with deliberate steps, firing with all the accuracy and brutality of a cold-blooded killer.

Hektor and Niels leapt forward with far greater aplomb, tearing through the puny fence like two careening trucks and barreling forward to join their teammate. She waited a moment for them to come up and then the three of them moved forward like an arrowhead, running and firing at once as they rushed the astonished Korean troops.

The North Koreans did, it turned out, have some semblance of the battleskins. But the Chinese had been stingy in their donation of the technology, no doubt deliberately, keeping back a good dose of even the limited tech Pei had given them to keep a perceived advantage for themselves.

There were several hundred of them though, Neal and Saul noted with alarm, and a similar number even now scrambling to come back from their aborted mission to go and join the more standard forces searching in Moranbong Park.

Even with the disparity in number, the two opposing groups collided with colossal force, the three Spezialists slicing into their target like the tip of a blade. Their opponents had the armor, sure, but neither the weapons nor the full machine augmentation to give voice to their defense. As the three realized this, they immediately split up so they could bring their message to a greater number of the unfortunate soldiers. Soldiers who had only a moment ago thought they were going to hunt the Spezialists, not the other way around.

It was hot, bloody work. Physical and close as they alternated between flechette fire and body blows.

It was not until they had made a truly significant dent in the Korean's numbers that a shift came. The returning force seemed to falter, and for a moment Ayala wondered if it was simple cowardice, an understandable reaction given the way she and her team were tearing at their lines. But then the tanks came.

They had been forced to withhold their fire, Ayala assumed, because of the speed with which their attackers had merged into the very ranks of their own infantry, but now whoever was in command had clearly seen the pointlessness of that, and whether through callousness or a simple realization that the infantry in question were dead anyway, they now ordered their big guns to open fire.

She saw the shots only as blurred lines tracing out from inside the sheds and into the mass of crushed bone and flesh that surrounded her three teammates. But the impacts were massive, and the destruction as impressive as it was horrifying.

Niels suffered a glancing hit and was thrown high into the air, the explosion finishing for him the job of killing the platoon he had engaged with, even as it sent him flying. Cara sensed the change in fight from the Koreans a moment before they fired and flattened herself against the ground, taking a hard hit to her right arm and leg, but avoiding the full force of the blow.

Then there was Hektor. Ayala could see not exactly what had happened to Hektor. She was already running, her legs firing now with passion. They had apparently not even seen her yet, amid the franticness of the attack. Though her fire had been tireless and deadly, her kills had been incorrectly attributed to the team of three that had so bluntly charged the Korean's ranks.

Now she made her presence more known as she saw the first of the big black tanks rolling out of the shed. She fired with a persistence that bordered on mania, centering on one spot on the tank's side to eat into its thick flanks. The tank felt the barrage as a rumbling vibration that quickly rose to fever pitch. Ayala's presence was a secret no more and the stocky black beast turned now, rounding on this new combatant to return the greeting.

Ayala saw it and kept moving, aware she was drawing fire but still keen to bring down the infernal machine. She had, she knew, gone off half cocked, but even the mighty barrage the four tanks had fired had not smited her team. This battle was far from lost.

Niels emerged from the smoke that had been his last known position like a returning demon, adding his own fire to Ayala's when he saw which tank she was targeting.

But they were tough little fuckers, thought Ayala, as she sprinted away from an incoming blast from the big beast.

She lost her footing as the shell impacted the concrete ground and was sent tumbling and sprawling across the floor. Niels was not faring much better as he dodged another shell to his position, though he did so with more grace than Ayala had managed.

Not good, Ayala thought to herself as she got to her feet and started moving again. Must keep moving, she thought, and brought her gun back to bear on the black hulk.

Cara was thinking the same thing, though her response was a touch more aggressive as she leapt violently into the air to land between two of the burly brawlers. No sooner had her feet touched the ground than she was darting up and onto one of them, firing as she went.

Niels smiled at the tactic, as did Ayala, watching with detached interest the view from Cara's eyes as she began firing into the seam between the gun turret and the tank proper. Her amusement was cut short, though, when a panel on the tank's side exploded outward, throwing Cara violently clear.

Ayala was at the end of her tether. They were damaging the big tank, but not quickly enough. They still had two more here, and who knew if there were more inbound on their position. She needed a new tactic.

And then the question was answered for her. A new tactic, as it were, was arriving even now. A voice rang in all their heads, even though it was meant mostly for Cara.

*Minnie:* <stand clear. i repeat, get clear of the tanks. now!>

Banu came in hard but did not unleash her full might. She did not want to hurt the four friends she knew were down there. Her beams were tight, lensing from her four ancillary engines into the four tanks, but still they struck like a blow from an enraged zeus.

The stout machines even withstood her particle onslaught for a couple of seconds, such was the strength of their armor, but this was not a contest they could win anymore, and Ayala and her cohorts watched with satisfaction as the four tanks buckled and then started to fold. Banu continued pummeling them for as long as she needed to, grinding the four beasts into the glowing concrete around their tracks, before spinning on her heels.

Banu did not come too close. Her statement was made.

*Ayala:* 'thank you, banu, minnie. very nicely done. minnie, have banu take the skalm back into orbit, please. but stay close. we may need her again before we are done.'

From out of the smoldering wreckage stepped Cara, not very pleased to have been so close to the particle beams, perhaps, but happy of the conclusion, nonetheless.

*Ayala:* 'hektor. ¿hektor, where are you?'

There was a moment's silence then the reply came.

*Hektor:* 'i am pretty sure i am here [loc. 1293.6, 4583.2] but …'

*Niels:* 'i have him. he's … whoa, lieutenant, you are a little beaten up, my friend.'

Far away to the north, the Slink was rising from its watery hiding place without ceremony and accelerating hard into the night. Other teams were inbound as well, though they were still a couple of hours out.

As the dust settled and Ayala's team began to round up the stragglers, Neal took a breath for the first time in nearly a minute.

*Neal:* 'ayala, remind me never to let you go on a covert mission again.'

*Ayala:* 'certainly, neal. remind me not to ask your permission in the future.'

He did not laugh at the retort. He feared it was too close to the truth of their new paradigm. She did not care, not about herself, and not about the rules. She saw only the goal, but now, in the aftermath, she focused on the patchy med information now starting to come through from Hektor's damaged battleskin.

*Ayala:* 'niels, i am en route to hektor's position. we'll have him out of here shortly. for now, though, i need you and cara sweeping the sheds. we need to see if jung and chin are in there. stay tight and stay in touch. that said, i hope you will not encounter too much more resistance now. i am hoping they have gotten the message.'

They had. The once impressive tools that a hopeful Great Leader had thought would be the key to reclaiming his lost lands to the south so he could rebuild his diseased and broken nation, and which the Chinese had hoped would distract or destabilize TASC while they rebuilt the power structures Neal had so thoroughly violated, had just been obliterated.

What was left of that force was even now fleeing into the countryside, choosing to take their chances amongst the plague that had wiped out their countrymen rather than stand against the gods they had clearly just stirred into a murderous rage.

Neither the Chinese nor the North Koreans would, in later days, acknowledge that it was only five units, including Banu, who had brought them to heel, not even to themselves.

Jung and Chin would be handed over in time, shaken to the very core. Jung would be in the worst shape. They had quickly determined he was the more senior and his torture had taken a more brutal and permanently scarring turn. But where his body had been broken his spirit was not, not completely. Chin would return home, happy that he had played a part in stopping what had turned out to be a very real and potent threat to his homeland. Jung would need more pervasive treatment than his home country could offer him. He would not see South Korea again for a long time.

In the coming weeks, Neal would ignore objections from a cowed but still defiant Chinese government and establish a permanent presence in Pyongyang, helping UN forces to try to bring some desperately needed assistance and sanity to the plagued nation.

Their so-called Great Leader would object at first, but would acquiesce once Ayala made it clear that the only alternative was her full fury, in the form of her unleashing the same might she had wrought on his forces on his party leadership, and his good self too, if necessary.

She would prove most persuasive. Ironically, the veil around his nation that had once protected him from the world's judgment would allow her to let her cold purpose show. Unmasked, her wrath was fearsome. Fearsome enough that even the criminally insane could see that it would be suicide to resist her. And so the chubby little megalomaniac whose forebears had set his nation back decades with the profoundness of their selfishness and cruelty would begrudgingly accept a new role, one of puppet.

And, in the form of the diseased nation of North Korea, Neal and his allies would unwittingly gain a fifth district to preside over, Neal's little empire growing now to encompass the country's tired, poor, and huddled masses.

# Second Part:

## Interval A: Her World

Princess Lamati, Second in Line to the Ascension and Named Arbiter of New Mobilius, lay prone on a couch. A pleasant gravity held her gently in the soft confines of her bed, which undulated beneath her.

A man entered the space. Or to be more precise, a man who had requested entry, been vetted by level upon level of automated security despite his clear right to be in her presence, and had then been granted permission to speak with her directly, appeared at her side.

"Brim, how are you?" she said, raising a leg lazily into the air. It was not a sensual gesture, though she acted as though it was. It was an insult, or rather a statement of power. It said simply 'you are no threat to me so I need not keep my feet on the ground.' But she smiled anyway, as though she was being every bit the demure and polite princess she evinced herself to be.

"I am well. Thank you, my princess." He leaned backwards and down, his rear-kneed legs folding under him as his eyes moved to the sky and he revealed his soft underbelly to her.

She sat up. No matter how often her subjects did this simple act of servility, she never tired of it. Back on Mobilius she had, more than once, killed a man in this very position, even as he showed his complete trust in her by falling into it. But cracking this man in his soft, exposed belly cavity with one of her powerful legs would be a pointless gesture, and would no more kill him than if she bludgeoned him atop his head with one of the ceremonial clubs lining the room's walls.

For the clubs were fake, as was the man in front of her, and as was she. Which made the act of bowing just as pointless, she supposed, done as it was in the ether.

She had the power and authority to kill him for real, of course. To send order for his sleeping body to be seared and recycled for nutrients in whatever habitat craft he was travelling in. But that, like so many of her hobbies back home, would be frowned on in the confines of the Armada. Given the length and importance of their mission, every life here had a purpose, every death would need to be accounted for.

She sighed. "Rise, Brim. Stop prostrating yourself!" she said, expressing her frustration and boredom in less martial ways.

He rose, his eyes betraying his genuine fear as they must, such were the rules of the system. When around one's betters, one could not disguise one's emotions, the system bled them through without mercy. Were Princess Lamati to have a senior in the fleet, the same rule would apply to her. But she did not. Counterparts, perhaps, or at least they liked to think so, but no seniors. And once they had taken the Earth for their own, she would then see to it that even they saluted her.

But that was to come. A step to be taken after many still ahead.

"What do we have planned this cycle, Brim?" she said with an air of boredom, leaping gracefully over to the broad window in one wall of her virtual suite, a window that opened onto an elaborate balcony.

She stepped onto the broad stone gallery and looked out at the view. It was of her own homeland, the BaltanSant, the massive city that straddled the link between the Contran continent and the Great Peninsula. It was the seat of Lamat power, originally giving them control over the trade between the nomads of the Great Peninsula and the fledgling rival nation states of the Contran. Over a thousand years it had evolved, though, into the ever more fortified border of a subdued Peninsula, now ruled over rather than traded with.

The walls had risen high over the centuries, tipped by the two fortresses that guarded the coastal approaches and the great Castelion that topped Heaven's Ridge in the middle. Together, the three had buttressed the mighty Lamati Empire against countless invasion attempts over a millennium.

Her view now was from the great parapet of the Castelion. To her south lay the city of BaltanSant, sprawling and rich, limited in height by ancient law to never exceed the height of Castelion's lowest parapets, it had spread south into the land it dominated.

To the north lay the Boneyard. The religiously undeveloped flats of the approach. The plain was now pierced by the great roads and train lines that linked modern BaltanSant with its relatively more recent acquisitions to the north. But even those dipped underground as they approached the Wall, to join the vacuum tubes that already ran there, into the city and then outward to the Great Peninsula beyond. Only four ancient and now mostly ceremonial roads approached the Wall itself, to the Blue Gates, so named for the blood-blue they had long ago been painted to match the bloodied remains that had been left of any who tried to break through them.

The great castle she stood atop was her father's domain. A place she had hoped to inherit if her sister had not remained gallingly alive. But her plots against her kin had necessarily remained covert, hopelessly so, certain as she was that sororicide would be the one crime her father would not forgive. And so she was here. Headed to conquer her own empire in her father's name.

"Today, my princess, the only scheduled event is the Council Meeting," said Brim, instantly regretting that he had been forced to mention it.

"I know about the damn Council Meeting!" she screamed. "Damn you, Brim! I meant what activities have you planned for me!"

She did not turn on him but remained facing out on her virtual view of the empire that should have been hers. He was thankful for that small mercy, her focus not being on him directly, for it was taking every part of him to master his growing loathing for the woman. He could not, he knew, last much longer in her service, and would have been dead long ago if it weren't for the restrictions of the mission. But she refused to take an AI or even an AM assistant. She wanted someone she could punish if he displeased her.

And by sad circumstance, that someone was to be Brim. He wondered how much longer it would be before she found some excuse to kill him. Some loophole that would allow her to vent her frustrations on him.

"Well, my princess, I had planned a parade across the Boneyard in your honor. There was to be a glider demonstration, with sentences to meet out, should you wish it."

He smiled with genuine hope. It had been one of her favorite pastimes back home.

Yes, she thought, that does sound appealing, but ... "You will arrange for actual sentences, Brim, yes? There is no point if there are not actual sentences."

She seemed hopeful, and he nodded. He had anticipated this albeit distasteful turn, and sent back word of her potential impending need to Mobilius, decades behind them.

"But first, my princess," said Brim hesitantly, "the ..."

"Yes, yes, Brim. The Council Meeting," she said petulantly. "How long do I have before it starts?"

"They are ready now, my princess. You said to only disturb you when the others were gathered."

He winced visibly. It was one of her many endearing qualities: she wished not to be disturbed until the last possible minute, and indeed was livid if anyone arrived at a function after her, but she also got very annoyed if she was 'too' late.

Such a wonderful leader, Brim repeated to himself over and over, as she glared at him and he sent signal for their avatars to be transposed.

- - -

The Council met in a space where they could not, in reality, exist. They sat outside and above the Armada. The meeting's virtual location was the choice of the Chair, a rotating and mostly ceremonial title. For the year of their holding of the gavel, each Chair could choose the setting for the Council Meetings, as well as the order of each session's agenda, if not its actual contents.

DefaLuta's choice was, as always, both beautiful and mildly disconcerting. Her AM creating a real-time simulation for them from the tactical data being constantly supplied to each state's Prime Mind as they shared the day-to-day running of the huge flotilla.

The group formed as though around a table, each seated on nothingness, the table itself but a shimmering transparency merely there to demark and separate the representatives and help keep the proceedings civilized. There were seven places around the table, one notably and predictably still empty. Behind each of the six representatives already present stood various other embodiments, the virtual representations of whomever each person chose to bring to the meetings with them.

For most it was an avatar of their State or Alliance's Prime Mind, the AM they had each bred for the very job of coming on this mission to monitor and manage their nation's military and colonial craft.

For one, the ever-punctual Princess Lamati, it would be, when she eventually got here, whichever unfortunate person had the honor of being her personal whipping boy. DefaLuta seemed to remember the current lucky soul's name was Brim.

For DefaLuta, it was her own AM, child of her mind and the Prime Mind, a concession to a growing cultural norm in her home country Kyryl of having an AM child with the communal mind for your area, a happy union of home and self, of patriotism and individuality. At the time of your death, voluntary or otherwise, the AM could choose to return to the Prime Mind or exist independently, as an echo of its former parent.

DefaLuta's AM, who had no name other than that of her parent, here took the form of a small primate: hairy, soft and almost unnaturally cute, wrapped around DefaLuta's neck and shoulders.

While they waited, DefaLuta and her other self surveyed the surroundings they had chosen with satisfaction. The table, along with its six waiting representatives and their assistants, orbited as one around the entire fleet as it surged through the cosmos, its gathered engines bound together and firing as one in a mighty plume to slow them, a decelerating thrust that had lasted for almost twenty years.

They were still travelling at relativistic speeds, fast approaching their last decelerating translation through the binary cluster we knew as Alpha Centauri.

Their speed was a physical anomaly. Possible only because of their ability to temporarily step out of this universe and into what was known either as hyperspace or subspace, depending on your dimensional perspective.

But as far as they were concerned, the speed defied the very way by which we perceive the universe, and their punishment was that light no longer told them the truth about the world around them. The light behind them could barely keep up, and so behind the fleet was a wall of blackness, utter and unending, only further emphasized by the shimmering sheet of white that came at them from below, the combined light of every star in the firmament folded into one endless pool of stellar beauty.

And so DefaLuta had chosen this place for their meeting, placing their virtual selves in orbit around their fleet, massive yet minuscule within the greater cosmos, firing all its engines into the whiteness ahead as if feeding it, as though they were sucking the light from above and driving it downward, into their path, into their future, so they could slow down enough to rejoin it.

For DefaLuta it was a beautiful sight, and one she often sat for days contemplating. But today was not for contemplation, and at last Princess Lamati's form transposed itself into her seat at the table with every outward appearance of exasperation, clearly annoyed at her assistant for having made her *too* late, as opposed to just the right amount.

"Now that we are all here we may speak, and with your permission I will begin," said DefaLuta without emotion.

Their treaty, laden as it was with caveats and protections, prohibited conversation at the Council Meetings until all were present, unless the missing party had been deemed as in violation or irredeemably unavailable by the Arbite. Even the Chair could not start without all present. No individual member of the Council had such power.

With no dissenters, and with a nod of approval from the ever-gracious Princess Lamati, DefaLuta called the meeting to order.

"So, our news is limited, but important," she said. "The coming weeks and months will be filled with key events, most notably the translation through the 1-Point cluster, our last deceleration before Earth's sun itself, and potentially the most spectacular."

There were visible nods from around the table, even the famously nonchalant princess was not insensitive to the complexity of this last step-down, a deceleration that would bring them down to a perceptible light range for the first time in nearly thirty years, though it had only seemed like three to them, such was the relativistic gap between them and the rest of the universe.

"As you know, this will be a triple translation, starting with two major steps that will have only a two-hour time lapse, and then a third through the smaller tertiary star that will occur about a day later." She paused as Archivist Theer-im-Far of the Hemmbar asked for permission to speak.

A virtual nod gave him the floor, and he said, "We catalogue the trinity cluster with particular interest. It was a source of some of significant focus in first run explorations. We want it noted that this will be very informative and important, our full data gathering selves will be focused on it."

DefaLuta looked at the man with measured patience. The Hemmbar were a major financial contributor to the enterprise despite being the only party present with no significant military or colonial presence in the fleet, and thus no real stake on their prize once it was cleansed. They sought only knowledge, or more specifically, information.

They were strange people, neutering their children at birth and raising them without physical contact at any point, to keep their all-important curiosity 'pure.' All new members of the race, such as it was, were cloned from an ever refined source, and as such were considered its greatest member and default leader as soon as they reached the age of ascent, though few actually retained their status as 'the purest version' long enough to reach that age. As such the race was truly ruled by the Regents Aggregate, an oligarchy of artificial and natural minds, Theer-im being the only representative of that body that had joined that colony fleet.

For the rest of the Mobiliei, the Hemmbar were a warning, a bedtime story used to teach children what happened when you allowed yourself to be too consumed by the ether, and gave your Artificial Minds too much freedom and influence over your lives.

But the Mobiliei certainly profited from the Hemmbar's diligent focus, and the race was second only to the many disparate members of the Nomadi Alliance in terms of their contributions to technological progress. DefaLuta glanced at Shtat Palpatum, the Nomadi representative, and noted the difference between the two men. Shtat was perhaps the most reasonable and down-to-Mobilius person on the Council, including her good self, she noted with rare humility. Indeed the only thing the many membered Nomadi Alliance and the Hemmbar could be said to have in common was their avid pursuit of progress, if for very different reasons.

"Thank you, Archivist. I hope I speak for all my fellow representatives when I say that is duly noted." There were no dissenters, though a snort did escape the princess's lips, a brash show of emotion which she could have easily kept hidden with her status.

"So, the first item for the agenda today, I thought, should be the celebrations and viewing events we all have planned for the coming translation," said DefaLuta.

Though they would all, in reality, remain in deep sleep for the entire event, as they had for the entire trip to date, and though they would only be able to view the translation in a virtual simulation, something their AMs could construct for them at any point both before and after it really happened, it had become a custom for most of the gathered states to hold celebrations for the grand events.

The events would focus around viewings of astonishingly detailed renderings of the event. Renderings so complex that any and all members of the million-strong populace of military personnel and colonists could focus in on almost any part of the great fleet, or the infinitely greater and more complex stellar bodies that the fleet was going to pass around and through on warping trajectories, slowing them down to sub-relativistic speeds for the final seven years of their approach to Earth.

"If I may," said Quavoce Mantil diffidently, though he had already pinged DefaLuta for permission to speak, "I would like to say on behalf of the Mantilatchi, and, I hope, the Eltoloman," he nodded to his counterpart and sometime friend To-Henton from the neighboring state of Eltoloman, "that the combined events conducted during Deceleration Point 7 were very well received, and we would like to broaden the scope of those shared festivities to others, if other states might be amenable."

The room was not unaware of the strong bond and long history between the Mantilatchi and Eltolomans, one born out of an ancient rivalry. But that hatchet had long since been buried, and now, much like the similar nations of France and the UK had on Earth, the two had found a solidarity in their shared, if bloody, history.

DefaLuta nodded thoughtfully. She was not insensitive to the tension that plagued their armada. It was both a blessing and a curse that their virtual existences, when in transit, allowed them to remain all but isolated from each other. It allowed the Council to keep the peace while in transit, but God only knew what was going to happen when long-fostered ambitions and long-festered jealousies came together in the cold light of their new home's sun.

"I can certainly second that sentiment," said To-Henton, a kind-faced man, but not one to be underestimated. He was a master statesman, and unbeknownst to DefaLuta, or Quavoce, while he had been nurturing his state's good relations with the Mantilatchi, he had also been doing so with his other great neighbor, the Lamat Empire, and its temperamental representative. If nothing else, Princess Lamati was predictable when it came to her own interests and ambitions, and To-Henton knew that her constancy here could be relied upon.

"... and in the interests of that ideal," went on To-Henton, "I wondered if the Lamat Empire might be interested in merging its festivities with ours on some level?

Quavoce was surprised, though kept his expression benign as he reached out to his Prime Mind, even now lolling gently behind him in the form a burly toskan, most closely resembling a gorilla in size and diet, though with a thick hide and a plated exo-skeleton back that made it famously tough, and equally famously oblivious to a world that could rarely cause it much harm.

The two exchanged information even as their avatars remained passive in the swirling brightness of their spectacular meeting place.

*Quavoce:* 'that is a surprise. ¿do we have record of a meeting between the eltoloman and the lamat? surely he wouldn't risk a direct invite unless he felt relatively certain she would not snub him.'

*Mantil Prime:* <requesting data from the arbite now. receiving data. parsing. i have reviewed the last year's interactions between the two races. i have an instance where a shared event was discussed, as part of a 'renewed friendship.'>

You conniving bastard, thought Quavoce.

Any and all inter-state communications were automatically recorded by the all-seeing Arbite. No one could talk to the Arbite. It was a sealed AM. But its reach aboard the Armada was all pervasive: it saw all and it judged all.

If you crossed any of the plethora of lines that had been drawn in the proverbial sands of their conquest, the Arbite was empowered to do everything from sending a formal censure to the group, to calling a tribunal, to the ability to unceremoniously eject into space any and all parties that crossed the few capital crimes catalogued in their shared contract, all of which centered on the making of separate treaties between any member states in the Armada.

It was a stipulation all had demanded, and all adhered to. They were going a long, long way from home, and though there was going to be a big enough pie for them all to have a slice once they had established New Mobilius, there were many an ambitious soul in the group, and Quavoce looked at his friend To-Henton with curiosity and not a little suspicion as Princess Lamati now acknowledged the 'renewed friendship' they had apparently discussed.

"An interesting idea, Henton," she said with feigned surprise. She would know that all their fellow Council members would probably now be sending requests to the Arbite for records of their interactions. It wasn't that there wasn't already a lasting peace between Lamat and the Eltoloman, even a trust. It was that if this signaled a larger coalition that included, say, the Mantilatchi, then that alliance would be difficult to stand against.

But To-Henton and Princess Lamati were all smiles as the group adjusted to this latest diplomatic twist.

"Maybe," she said to the group as a whole as the table completed another orbit of the huge fleet body, her face now ominously lit with the combined light of the stellar ocean below and the fusion plume of the fleet's cores, "maybe we could create a small subcommittee to propose a combined event format that would satisfy the needs and interests of all parties?"

Across the table DefaLuta sat, with the fleet's lights behind her like a great halo, and smiled. She had long since noted the little comment from To-Henton in one of her briefs from the Kyryl Prime Mind, and she chose to sit back and watch as the little façade unfolded.

It had only been a question of time before one of the big players made a move. It seemed innocuous enough on the surface, to be sure, but DefaLuta was not fooled. Princess Lamati was about as likely to be doing this 'just to be nice' as DefaLuta was to have her avatar defecate on the Council table. Not impossible, she supposed, but given Princess Lamati's innate unpleasantness, the results of each unlikely event would probably be equally distasteful.

In the end, though, everyone agreed with fake smiles, with only the Hemmbar abstaining from a joint celebration. A subcommittee to plan the event was duly formed with representatives from each state being put forward.

## Interval B: The Fall

The Gliders were lined along the Wall, awaiting their orders to go.

Princess Lamati preened herself in her tent, an act so pointless in this virtual world that even considering it was a gesture of the greatest conceit. In truth, she was not actually that vain. She did not need to be beautiful, such things were the concern of commoners who relied on such advantages. And yet she was anyway, a benefit of wealth in a world of genetic and cosmetic options too many to mention.

She just enjoyed that it was so wonderfully pointless, and she was doing it when there were people outside literally waiting to see if they would live or die by her hand.

She had invited some of the Lamat fleet contingent's captains to participate. Not its admirals and generals, but a select few of its more connected captains. They too waited outside, their long guns loaded and lining the walls of the Blind Parapet.

She eventually emerged into the bright sun. She had done this for real several times back on Mobilius and was thankful that the sun's heat that made the Blind Parapet a frankly inhospitable place was suitably diminished. They had not done away with the elaborate tents that would usually have provided shelter from it, though, and she looked around at the grand splendor of their wafting forms, pinned, but still so free-form, so impermanent.

She had often called them home during the great ceremonies that culminated in sumptuous events on this, the highest point in the Castelion, and indeed the whole of BaltanSant city, and she looked on their bellowing walls now with fond nostalgia.

But that was all history. Here, she was the king. Here, she set the pace of proceedings, and here, the virtual representation of the crown atop her father's empire was kept pleasantly, if unrealistically cool, and she smiled as she stepped into the light, the gathered captains coming over to take her hand.

"Welcome, all of you. I am very happy you could make it," she said with smile. As a virtual meeting wholly attended by members of her own state's forces, this conversation was not open to monitoring by the Arbite, and she was glad. She would not want it known that she was associating with such lowly officers.

But for the purposes of the current event they suited her needs, and she smiled with almost angelic grace as she greeted each with a brush of the back of two fingers on their bowed-back bellies. As she did this, each of them rose from their prone backward position and smiled with genuine happiness at the honor she had bestowed upon them.

Brim looked on in silence, barely disguised surprise and a hint of suspicion showing on his face.

"Welcome indeed, my captains. So rare I get to meet the women and men of Lamat's fleet forces. Thank you for taking the time to join me at today's event."

Their surprise at her gracious tone was clear, but they were happy to be here, even if a little trepidatious. Her temper was not a secret, far from it. But they could not disguise their emotions from their own generals and admirals, let alone the woman that commanded them, so they had learned to master themselves when under pressure.

She looked at one in particular, just picked one out at random and focused on him, and he quickly responded, "I am sure I speak for us all when I say it is an honor and a pleasure to join you for punishment, Princess."

And in that instance he did speak for all of them, and they all shook their arms in agreement.

"Good, good," she said. "Then we shall begin! Your guns, Captains!"

The punishment they spoke of was not for them. It was for the criminals who lined the Wall below them, out of sight. Murderers, rapists, thieves, they might all end up on the Wall, but such crimes were ever-rarer in their technologically protected world. No, the majority of criminals that waited below were mind-warpers, people who had tried to manipulate either artificial or real minds for material gain, pleasure, or both.

Ether-crimes were very hard to get away with. But if you could do it, the world could be yours. It was a possibility that was too much for some, and every cycle some fool or another would try to hack the AM of some personage or other, be ensnared by a watchful firewall AI, and then tried.

Those found guilty were treated differently depending on the state. Most nations simply removed their interfaces and surgically altered them to prevent future replacement. It was the societal equivalent of removing their faces, cutting them out of virtual society forever. For some states even this was not enough, though, and so they killed or imprisoned them. Some liked a combination of all three.

"Captain, you are with me," said Princess Lamati to the officer who had spoken. She neither knew their individual names nor cared to.

She approached the edge of the Blind Parapet. She could not fall in this virtual world, but they went through the ritual of harnessing in anyway, then climbed into the great crenellations, the seven captains joining her along the edge of the very top of the Castelion to look out over the plain known as the Boneyard.

The captain she had nominated stood behind her and handed her a long gun. Virtual attendants did the same for the other captains. The old ceremonial long guns would only fire one shot, adding to the sport of the event.

"Are we ready?" she shouted into the stiff breeze blowing up over the edge of the precipitous drop.

"Ready!" came the shouts from the arrayed captains.

"Let the first Glider go!" she said with zeal, and leant forward, out over the edge, her leather harness creaking as it took her weight and she aimed her gun downward.

Far below, a shouted order could be heard relaying her signal and, after a moment's pause, a glider suddenly flew into view, angling downward, accelerating hard away from the underside of the broad Wall that ran underneath them toward the ground below.

The first of the captains fired almost immediately, but they misjudged the wind, and they watched as the criminal flying the Glider soared away. Four more shots then rippled out in quick succession, a couple obviously clipping the wings of the Glider, and it stuttered.

The criminal piloting it began to pull up, aware no doubt that his damaged wings would no longer be able to take as late a breaking turn as he or she had hoped. The key for the criminal was to balance the need to angle straight down and build up speed away from the nobles so nobly shooting at them, with the need to pull up in time to avoid striking the ground below.

It was a balance many had misjudged, escaping the bullets of their would-be executioners only to end themselves in a bloody splatter across the dusty plain.

Princess Lamati sighted her own shot. Female Mobiliei naturally had stronger arms than their male counterparts, though weaker legs, but in this version of the world, her arms were preternaturally strong, a concession to her status more than a cheat, she told herself, and she braced her gun with these muscular arms and fired.

She was annoyed for a moment when she heard two others fire at the same time, as she would not know who had actually hit the criminal, who clearly faltered violently after the long guns' report. She realized quickly that she could query the Prime Mind to find out who had actually hit the target, but as the Glider suddenly veered wildly, flipped, and then impacted the ground with violent speed, she decided that she would rather just assume it was her.

Celebratory shouts were cut short, though, as they watched a figure drag itself from under the shattered frame of the Glider. In the real world the figure would not get very far out on the plain, but in the virtual world he need only survive the fall, and the volley of fire, and he would be deemed a free man.

She turned to Brim, "Brim, come here!"

He did.

"Have the Prime Mind assess the injuries this criminal would have suffered from the fall and the shots. I want them inflicted on the assigned felon in real life before they are released," said the Princess, with righteous fury. For these were not just games. They fired at virtual representations, but the results would be transmitted back via the chain of planetoid subspace tweeters they were laying along their path.

There was no point, insisted the princess, in Punishment, if the life of a criminal was not affected by the outcome.

But she need not have worried. One industrious captain had withheld her shot, and now she heard as it rang out over the crenellations. She whirled at the noise, then, realizing what had happened, looked over the edge once more.

The figure, far below them, had stopped crawling, and she thought she could make out a small blur of blue blood spreading around its body. She requested and was granted an exception to the visual laws of the simulation and suddenly her vision swam downward, bringing into focus the broken body of the criminal, its legs clearly shattered, and its body now opened to the sun, a glistening hole visible halfway up its torso.

"Well done!" she hollered with genuine emotion. "Well done! Who was that?"

A captain spoke up with a proud smile and Princess Lamati noted the woman's face. She had favor to give, and this captain would certainly feel the benefit of being in her good graces.

She looked out at the Boneyard. Sometime in the not too distant future, the real criminal in question would be taken without ceremony or audience and thrown from the real Wall, his fate having been decided on this day, countless trillions of miles away. They would be denied even the honor of having an audience as they were tossed, unceremoniously, over the edge, to be but another set of bones among the countless thousands that had fallen before the Wall.

She bristled with pride.

But this meeting was not only for her amusement, she reminded herself. She had other requirements of the gathered group.

She set to with the rest of the Punishment. They were appropriately successful in administering justice, with a couple of lucky survivors getting past their barrage to wander off into the rest of their drab existence. Good, she thought, it kept it interesting for the masses to have a few survivors.

Once the last Glider had been sent from their city walls, she pulled the attending captains in for a more candid conversation. The clever captain who had secured their all-important first kill would have a special role, but she had tasks for them all in the coming Event. She needed to send a message to the Eltoloman, and to delicately begin to feel out some of the other states as well, without the Arbite realizing it.

It was going to take a lot of subtlety, and would involve a good deal of risk. But her orders would carry with them a simple edict. Capture meant self-wiping: immediate, voluntary, and complete deletion. Their houses would be well compensated if they died in the service and protection of her royal self. But not nearly as thoroughly as those same houses would suffer if they put her at risk by allowing their minds to be read by the Arbite.

They knew that this was their mandate, and they agreed with a verve born of an acceptance of their utter lack of choice in the matter. The shrewder among them had even anticipated such a stroke when they were called to spend the day with the princess. That she should surround herself with such lowly souls as themselves could only mean one thing: that she had need for them.

And they were lowly. That was, in the end, the point. They were irrelevant enough in the grand scheme that they would not be part of the upper echelons of the event her representatives were even now planning. They would not suffer the same scrutiny from her peers, and that would hopefully mean that her carefully crafted message would get through to To-Henton, along with a similar message she expected in return.

For in the end, she would be damned if the Lamat Empire was going to share New Mobilius with the likes of the Nomadi Alliance, or any of the other petty states. They had needed their money and their acquiescence when the Union of Minds voted on the invasion. Now those others were needed only to fight, and then to die, so she could divide up the spoils more appropriately.

## Interval C: Event Planning

Shtat Palpatum, ever keen to please, had been the only member of the Council proper to volunteer himself for the Event Planning Subcommittee. Thus he now found himself among a throng of representatives, lesser in stature, perhaps, but not lacking either ambition or the requisite vitriol and bile that came with the arranging of such a diplomatic minefield.

While the conversation remained polite on its surface, it was rare that a statement did not carry with it some measure of insult or derision for one or another of the other states represented. It was a happy by-product of his being technically the most senior person there that most refrained from making the Nomadi the recipient of quite as many of those barbs as they might usually be. But even with his status as a shield, Shtat was still finding that his thick skin was being tested by some of the less subtle of his fellow committee members.

The crux of the discussion centered on the seating at the main tables of the virtual banquet, the order of the cuisine to be served, and the various dignitaries that would be seated in the all important first rows around the main tables.

It was a strange thing to bicker over, thought Shtat, as all could, in theory, sit right at the center of the event in a virtual environment, all could share the same view, and all could eat, or pretend to eat, anything they liked. But this was not about what the dignitaries had to look at, it was about who was looking at the dignitaries, and if they were to have a shared celebration, then the right people, the most deserving people, must be seen to be at its head.

"If it will make it easier," said Shtat, "I can reduce the number of Nomadi present at the main tables. I imagine most of my fellow Nomadi leaders would prefer to have a more esoteric view of events anyway."

"I am afraid that most certainly would *not* make it easier," said the Yallan Corporation representative. "We must all be seen to be represented, or I can tell you that my board will not wish to attend at all."

Shtat sighed, and was about to reply, when the Eltoloman representative spoke up, "Yes, Mr. Palpatum, as generous as your offer is, I am afraid we must all have an equal number of places at the banquet, or some might be seen to consider themselves ... above proceedings."

Shtat nodded and smiled, though with a growing level of exasperation. He was a patient man, indeed he was known for it, but this layer cake of sycophantism and outright bullshit was testing even his peaceful temperament.

The meeting ran on, and on, and on.

He was profoundly relieved when it eventually drew to an end. It was a curse of their virtual world that one could not use biology as an excuse to take a break from a tedious meeting, as you once could in meetings' original form. But that was behind him as he said his final good-byes and transposed his form away.

"You will continue to monitor the sub-meetings, Colin?" Colin was the unusually casual name the Nomadi Alliance used for their Prime Mind, derived from their word for collective, a symbol of the cooperation that had allowed the nomadic trading races to fend off the ever more amorous advances of the empires, nations, and corporate states they did business with.

"I am monitoring them now, Representative Palpatum," said Colin, "and will continue to do so."

In the end, the major parties had agreed to disagree on the last few sticking points, or at least had agreed that those that cared to continue bickering would to do so in a separate meeting, one empowered to argue the final irrelevant details by those long since bored by the punctiliousness of it all.

The main decisions were made, the ones Shtat cared about anyway, and he was actually getting quite excited by the event.

The event would take the form of a grand banquet held during the last hours of their approach to what humanity knew as Alpha Centauri A, a massive star 10% larger than the Earth's, and 50% brighter. They would while away their last hours before translation enjoying a lineup of food and drink expansive enough to burst the average hippo, but which would serve no actual purpose other than to give catalytic sensation to the copious synthetic and natural psychostimulants and hallucinogens they would all be pumping into their sleeping bodies to fuel their revelry.

When translation came, the grand party would also translate into two plains of dancing, swimming, flying, and no doubt plenty of fornicating in either the simulated blackness of the accelosphere void the fleet would actually be encased in, or a representation of the fractal beauty and heat of the stellar fire they would be passing through in reality. The two realms would be connected by a simulated central sun at the center of the blackness in one realm, and a simulated black hole in the center of the other, through which partygoers would be able to pass through spectacularly and at will at any point during the celebrations.

Even though it would only take them fifteen minutes to pass through the actual star at their stupendous speed, they would have to translate out of real space long before that, and stay there long after in order to survive the steadily increasing power of Alpha Centauri's particle radiation. And so the Event Space, as it was being called, would actually last several hours, allowing all to explore the two spectacular worlds, and, no doubt, each other as well.

After translation back into reality on the other side of Alpha Centauri A, the event would then reformat back to its banquet format so folks could take a break and get some virtual sustenance during the two hours before the next translation into the star's twin, Alpha Centauri B, a smaller star, but still 90% the size of Earth's own, and full of its own unique spectra and beauty that would be waiting for them when the second translation came and the party began in earnest once more.

Shtat smiled as he thought of it all. The second banquet, the second count down, would be a unique time. Not only because of the binary nature of the star cluster they would be passing through, but because, for the first time in decades, they would have something approaching real light. For those that cared, it would mean being able to look at real images of the two stars as they passed between them, not simulations.

What a sight that was going to be, thought Shtat.

"Shall I prepare a communication to the Nomadi contingent regarding the celebrations, Shtat?" said Colin.

"Yes, yes, of course. We want as many as possible to attend," replied Shtat with unfeigned enthusiasm. He was genuinely excited about the coming event. More excited, if he was honest, than he was for the coming end to their long journey.

"Are any of the admirals available for a conversation?" asked Shtat, thoughtfully.

"I am reaching out to them now," said Colin. "I am being asked if it is a critical meeting? Three have requested that information before replying."

"No, I suppose not," said Shtat, somewhat dejectedly.

"Then only one has replied yes: Marta," said Colin, redundantly saying the name of the only admiral that usually made time for Shtat at such moments.

"Hello, Representative Shtat," said Marta, materializing beside Shtat a moment later.

"Oh, yes, hello Marta," said Shtat, grateful for the response to his request, even if he knew it was more out of pity than genuine friendship.

"I do love your yacht, Shtat," said Marta, looking around appreciatively at the broad deck of the boat Shtat called home. "I always have."

Shtat brightened. His yacht was a faithful representation of his own flagship back home, one he had designed himself and which he had been loath to give up. It was the only thing he truly missed about Mobiliei. But he had plans for a new one once they had settled the seas of Earth, and in the meantime this representation was as close to indistinguishable from the real thing as one could hope for.

"Thank you, Marta," Shtat said, with genuine pride. "She is quite the performer too!"

"Indeed, she is famous for it," replied Marta with a shake of her muscular arms. "We should hold another regatta. The last one was very entertaining!"

"Yes, yes, I would like that a great deal," said Shtat, laughing. "Do you remember when the Fral boat capsized! We nearly went over ourselves, we were laughing so much!"

The rules of the virtual regatta leveled all playing fields, much as handicapping tried to, but it was far more effective, in that it essentially just equaled, in absolute terms, the aquadynamic and aerodynamic properties of all participants, leaving only the skill of the individual sailor. Skill which must remain unaided by artificial minds throughout.

Marta laughed with genuine mirth. The Fral admiral was a friend, but his crew had gotten cocky, and the cruel reality of the simulation had left them soaked, clinging to the belly of their upturned ship as the rest of the challengers finished the race.

"He will think twice before he tries that again," said Marta.

Shtat nodded, then his smile seemed to fade. "Shall we walk the deck?" said Shtat, suddenly thoughtful once more, and Marta nodded.

An artificial crewmember appeared with a cold and bubbling refreshment from below decks, and they both took one, the pleasure they got from the cool draft real, even if the drink itself was not.

Marta was silent as they began to walk the long deck of the boat, letting the man that she and her fellow admirals had voted in as their representative gather his thoughts. They walked along the broad wooden deck, the boat slicing gracefully through the blue-water waves as her full canvas propelled her forward. Her heel was healthy, the breeze was brisk, and she leaned into the seas with the practiced ease of a thoroughbred.

After a while Shtat spoke up over the pleasant heave and sigh of the sailboat's a cappella song: the harmony of wind and sail, of creaking wood and straining stay.

"Do you ever wonder why, Marta?" he said, quietly.

Marta glanced at the man, not surprised at the question, perhaps, but still uncomfortable at the sudden change in heading.

"Why what, Shtat?" she asked, with a hint of trepidation.

"Well," said Shtat, after a moment, clearly picking his words carefully, "I am not saying what we are doing is wrong. What we are doing is absolutely necessary, and everything our probes sent back about the current inhabitants of Earth shows that they would most certainly do the same to us, as they have countless times to their own kind."

Marta did not dispute the layman's argument for the war, an argument used at middle class-dinner tables all over Mobilius, but she did counter with an amended version of the standard rebuff the war's many dissenters would usually say at this point. "Of course, they could say the same about us ..." and before Shtat could reply equally predictably, Marta went on, "and of course they *would* say the same about us, which would only support the argument for them to do the same to us if they had the chance, and therefore ... well, you know the rest."

They smiled, though with a certain sadness in their eyes.

In the end, both arguments were specious. Deep down they both knew that. For both arguments ignored the real reason for colonization, and in so doing became the same exercise in futile banter that had plagued every society that had ever claimed to be civilized in either race's history. For the real argument was as irrefutable as it was cold-hearted: when one party has something another needs, something that the first party will not give up willingly, and the second party has the power to take it from them ... they do. They always had throughout history. No matter how much people might strive for civility on an individual level, no state had ever truly earned that descriptor.

Whether it was oil or gold, slave labor or land, history was littered with ostensibly well-intentioned nations doing terrible things to weaker ones. When the invention of nuclear weapons had forced the richer Mobiliei nations to play nice with each other, and back up their words about equality and civil liberties with action, they had come to laud their version of human rights, just as we had. But their definition of civilization was also naturally called mobiliei rights, and thus it did not apply to humans.

Suddenly Shtat blurted, "But that's just it, Marta. We justify our actions by saying they would do it to us if the tables were turned, because they are so like us. And ... they *are* very like us, aren't they? The closer we get, the more time I have to think about the whole enterprise. Why would *their* needs, *their* survival be any less important than ours?"

Marta walked in measured steps as they approached the point of the yacht's long, slender bow. Here the motion of the deep blue waves was more pronounced as Shtat's yacht forged onward, over and through, over and through, across the endless virtual ocean it was always traversing.

"You make a point that has been made many times before, Shtat my friend, and I hope you won't mind if I counter with a cold reply. I'm sorry to have to do this, but where was this sentiment when, for example, you liquefied the Bydint contingent's assets?"

Shtat groaned, and Marta smiled with genuine amusement.

"It is not as if they had left me much choice," said Shtat, in reply. "God knows I tried to reason with them."

Marta nodded in measured agreement. Shtat had indeed tried to reason with them, but his reasoning had been: I have better political contacts than you, and have stolen your major hauling contracts by low-balling your bids, so 'merge' with me or face ruin. They had chosen ruin, ending in some spectacular suicides, and even Shtat had been forced to admit it had been brave to continue to resist ... stupid, but brave.

"When you bargained with them," said Marta, trying to be gentle now, "did you really think they would give in to your terms?"

"I bargained with them in good faith," said Shtat with conviction, but then ended dejectedly, "... but no. I had always suspected they would resist to the end."

As they reached the very tip of the ship's bow, Shtat grasped one of the forestays and stepped up onto the bucking bowsprit with aplomb. He walked forward a few steps with the surefootedness of a man who has spent his life at sea, and indeed he had. Marta let the man stare out at the horizon for a moment and gather his thoughts.

The conversation was not their first on the topic, and it would not be their last, but they were becoming more frequent. They had picked Shtat for a reason. He supported the war, but more out of a businessman's pragmatism than the cold ambition that drove the likes of the Lamat, or the simple economic survivalism that drove the Mantilatchi and Eltoloman.

Marta had no such appetite for conquest, quite the opposite, and these conversations made her feel soiled and dirty. She was convincing a man who was trying to be better than he was to stay on the wrong side of the war, because they needed him there. Her fellow conspirators and her needed a front man, one who could stand up to the full scrutiny of their so-called allies and not break, either literally or virtually, and give away the truth.

The Nomadi were not here to support the war. Or at least the majority of them weren't, anyway. There were some who were here for profit, and profit alone, and they would have to be dealt with when the time came. But Marta and her partners had not been able to risk putting one of them in charge in case they used the power it gave them to root out the conspiracy in their midst, one they must suspect was there, if only halfheartedly.

No, Shtat it had needed to be, and though he suffered now, Marta reconciled herself to her duty by thinking that if the man really had doubts about their mission, then how pleased was he going to be when he found out he had in fact been the puppet of a bunch of traitors. Well, traitors or heroes, depending on who got to write it down afterward.

She smiled wryly at Shtat's back, then shook her head and mounted the long bowsprit to walk out to join him. The ship was huge, not unlike humanity's great sailing frigates of the golden era of sail on Earth, its long graceful lines carved out by generations of sea-going evolution, its shape formed by the flow of the waves along thousands of hulls long since lost, either to rot or to the very seas they sought to master.

She carried no guns, though, either in this virtual form or in her real incarnation back on Mobiliei. And her real form was encased in shielding that could withstand a hurricane comfortably, and had the ability, should its skipper order it, to slide its masts down level with her deck and seal herself, either to dive beneath the waves or lift herself bodily out of the water, hurricane or no, and travel either to land or directly into space with impressive, if inefficient, thrusters.

Marta's own flagship had been capable of no less, and indeed it had not been an uncommon sight to see the anomaly of two or three great flagships of the Nomadi high fleets docked, often with masts ceremonially held high, at one of the hubs in orbit around Mobiliei, an extravagance that was a favorite of the gossip-shares.

"The bowsprit, my favorite place to stand as a child," shouted Marta into the full wind.

Shtat glanced back as Marta approached, "Yes, mine too. No better place to feel the ocean beneath you."

"No, no better place," agreed Marta. Then, speaking to Shtat's back once more, she went on, "You know, I am sure there are others who share your doubts, Shtat, both at home and even here, in the actual Armada."

Shtat turned to face Marta, and she noticed as the virtual environment that was, after all, an expression of his own mind, slowed almost to a stop.

They locked eyes and Marta finished, sternly now, "But what it comes down to, my friend, is that such considerations are moot now. You know that, Shtat. We are seven years out from our destination. That's all. Once we enter the binary cluster we will be within theoretical range of the Interstellar Subspace Tweeter at our destination. If it has finished its lunar conversion, which we hope it will have, then we will be able to receive signal directly from the advanced team."

Shtat took a deep breath, bracing himself as Marta finished, "This is not the time for doubts, it is the time for resolve. For resolve and preparation. We have come all this way, now it is time to see this through."

Shtat nodded, returning Marta's rigid stare with as stern a matching one as he could muster. Then they both nodded once more, their free arms shaking in unison to signal their agreement, and so they turned to walk back along the bowsprit to the deck proper, the wind and waves returning to their natural volume and motion as they did so.

Only a few days now, thought Marta. Then they would be within range of the IST in orbit around Earth's sun and they would know. They would know who had succeeded. If they received a signal then it meant the advanced party's satellites were still in orbit, which could only mean that the primary plan of her colleagues had failed. She did not know what that plan was. No one knew the full scope of the plan except one among them, and Marta did not even know who it was, even though she had been one of the first to join the conspiracy.

Such were the layers of security around their cadre, layers which she hoped would protect her as much as she hoped they would protect whoever lay at the center of the plan.

All she knew was that if the satellites were still online, it would be bad. Terrible even, for it would mean that the only way to stop the Armada from wiping out the humans would be to try and destroy it, all of it, and she wondered if her fellow conspirators had the appetite for butchery on such scale, even if it was to stop a far greater genocide.

In truth, she was far from sure if she had the ability to do that either.

A million of her own kind, including her own life and those of many of her family and friends, in return for seven billion people who were, quite literally, completely alien to her. How many could say with confidence that they would do such a thing? As she thought of her co-conspirators, and herself, she could not be sure.

No, they must hope that they receive nothing from the IST installing itself on Mars's moon. Then her part in the plan would come into play.

She smiled wryly.

'Her part.'

In the end, as far as she could tell, she was probably screwed either way.

## Interval D: Lost in Translation

The simulation was rousing success, a feat even by the standards of the Prime Minds' combined intellectual might. Alpha Centauri A shone down on them with a multifaceted beauty that beggared belief, both wonderful and disconcerting as it grew above them.

For the sake of show, they were being shown the bodies of their stellar host on their approach, starting with an upcoming pass-through of the asteroid belt that lay at the outer reaches of its gravitational field. Some poetic license was being taken here, as they would deliberately not pass anywhere near the belt's orbital plane to avoid straining their shield. For though the fusion fire that was their decelerating engines also served to obliterate any interstellar debris in their path, they were hesitant to try it out with anything as large as some of the grander planetoids of the great belt.

But reality aside, the banquet's countless participants, both the auspicious and the proletariat, would be treated to a spectacular show as the star grew larger above them.

"I think," said Princess Lamati with a beaming smile, "that this is going wonderfully!"

"I agree," said Lord Mantil to her left, his legs crossed behind him, as he finished a large tankard of his favorite imported mash. "It is ... stunning."

The appointed representatives were seated in a large circle at the center of twenty other circles, each laden with the most senior dignitaries and military leaders of each of the nine contingents that had agreed to combine their celebrations. No one missed the Hemmbar, they were famously, deliberately even, the worst company around, humorless to a point that they considered perfection.

Princess Lamati, on the other hand, was in her element. She was seated with Quavoce on one side, the famous champion of the Mantilatchi, and one of the few people she might even consider as a match, and Shtat Palpatum on the other, a silly man, perhaps, but her sources told her that he had a soft spot for her, and she enjoyed playing with him.

But for now her attention was squarely on Quavoce for three reasons. Firstly, because she was genuinely taken by how in awe he seemed with the banquet's setting, but then also because she was studiously avoiding the eyes of To-Henton across the way, and finally because she knew it infuriated poor Shtat that she had her back to him.

"You know, Quavoce," she said, and he brought his gaze down from the star growing ever closer above them to meet hers, "you never cease to surprise me."

She smiled a little too coyly and he disguised his instant suspicion of her motives. It was no secret that back channel negotiations had begun before they even took off for a matching between their two houses. The matching wouldn't be mutually exclusive, of course, indeed Quavoce was more likely to willingly copulate with To-Henton than he was Princess Lamati; they had even dabbled with each other on occasion.

But the truth was Quavoce remained very skeptical about sharing either his bed or his house with the snake that was Princess Lamati, famously good though she was between the sheets.

"I surprise you, Princess? How so? You don't think they have truly outdone themselves with this environ?"

She looked around appreciatively and nodded with genuine approval. "Of course I do, Quavoce. And I do wish you would call me Sar, as I have given you right to." It was a high honor, if you cared for such things, but it carried with it implications Quavoce did not wish to encourage, so now it was his turn to feign coyness.

"You honor me, Princess. More than I deserve."

She did not disguise her displeasure, but the moment was broken as they were subconsciously notified that they were approaching the asteroid belt, and thus the next course.

All eyes went skyward, and the gathering became silent, both in the inner circles of high-ranking officials and the dizzying array of spectators that were arranged in greater circles around them, hundreds of thousands of virtual eyes looking toward the star above them as they raced across the borders of its realm.

The asteroid belt swam out to meet them like they were descending on a distant coastline, its headlands and bays the seemingly infinite number and variety of asteroids, some spinning, some not, some with their own debris auras, but most starkly defined against the blackness.

They formed a curve ahead that continued to broaden as they approached, widening and widening until it formed a horizon that extended to the limits of their vision to either side, and still it kept flying down to meet them, growing and growing, ever more detail resolving in the vast line of rock and ice until suddenly they were on it, among it, and in a blink they were through, the line now vanishing fast below them as the fleet continued on toward the star that was the focus of their celebration.

The crowd erupted into a roar that was shared and amplified in the virtual space, and was taken up by the arrayed generals, admirals, lords, and ladies, with the vigorous clapping of knees by the men and the hands of the women.

As they passed into Alpha Centauri's realm, the great platters of the next course in the banquet came floating down out of the vacuum above to rest among the gathered audience. For most it came in the form of individual plates laden with treats, either for their individual consumption or to share with their neighbors, if they were getting into the spirit of things.

For the main tables it took the form of vast central platters that came to rest in the center of each circle, larger than the combined weight of the people for whose pleasure they had been created. Virtual food invited gluttony, even celebrated it, given its utter lack of consequence in either the short or long term, and so the platter was covered in a dizzying array of foods from all over Mobilius, and even some simulated treats from Earth, creations of olfactory and taste artists in anticipation of the new bounty to be found once they reached their destination.

They could have no idea of what to really expect among Earth fauna, and indeed, biologically, most of it would be very foreign to their systems, sometimes intoxicatingly so, sometimes just plain toxic. But they would enjoy it virtually now, and once they had processed and analyzed the real thing, they would no doubt revel in it virtually then, while their real bodies were kept vital and healthy on a more appropriate diet.

Sar Lamati reached forward first, ignoring deliberately any sense that the sitting Council Chair should kick proceedings off, and grabbed what might have been an approximation of a Rhinoceros horn, though its insides in this case were gelatinous, and, she discovered, sweet to the point of intemperance.

"Oh my goodness!" she exclaimed aloud. "You must try this, it is divine. I am glanding Olfast now, and it really makes the aroma leap out at you!"

Still chewing her first bite, she inhaled deeply from the upturned base of the horn and smiled, then handed it to Shtat, stroking his hand as he took it from her and allowing her pleasure at the taste to translate most suggestively into her gaze as their eyes met.

He smiled a little more vigorously than he had intended and she laughed, not cruelly, or at least she didn't think so, and turned back to Quavoce. He had pulled a long, broad green leaf from the elaborate centerpiece and was chewing on it. It was savory, but as he chewed on it, it released a bitterness that bordered on unpleasant, but stopped just short, and he quickly found that the density of the leaf's grain combined with the bitterness to make it wonderfully saturating, and that as he chewed it more, it was releasing an underlying spice that was satisfying on a primal level.

"How is your ... leaf?" said Princess Lamati, patronizingly.

He turned to her, smiled innocently, and replied, "Bitter, but one learns to appreciate it in time."

She laughed loudly, the layers of drugs in her system not allowing her to be insulted. She saw only banter, maybe even the kind of banter that made her even more appealing, and she was very proud of herself as she laughed off the subtle insult and reached out to break off a piece of his leaf for herself.

He let her, and he thought about how charming she could be when she chose. He caught himself, and removed his rose-colored glasses by glanding Sober, noting once more the slippery slope his role placed him on. Oh well, he thought, he would relive the simulation later in the privacy of his own virtual home, and would appropriately amplify his enjoyment then, when he was in no danger of accidentally engaging in less than wise activity with the dangerously beautiful and beautifully dangerous Sar Lamati.

- - -

The banquet proceeded with great pomp and circumstance, and thankfully without incident. The hours passed by, slowed in the simulation to match the mood of the participants, the organizers having agreed to make the virtual banquet last for as long as the representatives, and to a lesser degree the gathered masses, were enjoying themselves.

But the time must come, and eventually DefaLuta looked around at her fellow Council members and said, "If you all agree, my fellow representatives, I will allow the Prime Minds to take the simulation into the next phase roughly in tandem with the actual translation."

Anyone in the know had long since learned that the Prime Minds would fully devote themselves to the act of actual translation first, making sure it was synchronized perfectly across the fleet, to the nanosecond, before turning their attentions to processing the virtual translation for the nearly million strong multitude enjoying the simulation. But the delay would only need to be momentary, should the Council approve the next phase.

"Must we!" said Princess Lamati, grasping Shtat's hand. Shtat laughed giddily once more.

DefaLuta smiled without malice. "Well no, we don't have to, but having seen the plans, I truly believe we will all enjoy the next stage of the celebration even more than we have this one."

"Very well. Then let us go!" said the princess magnanimously, before releasing Shtat's hand and leaning away from him to whisper in an aside to Quavoce, "As long as you promise to dance with your friend and ally from the Lamat Empire."

Quavoce smiled as noncommittally as he could, then turned to watch DefaLuta as the woman rose and raised her voice. The action amplified her, and sent her words rippling out across the gathered masses, a voice echoing over a crowd that extended for a mile in every direction.

"Friends, allies, Mobiliei, we are at the edge of a great moment. We are the chosen few who have been given the honor of turning our world's great race into a true interstellar power!"

There was a roar that rumbled through the simulated cosmos, and was enthusiastically taken up once more by the Council members. Above the huge audience, the approaching star was getting visibly larger every moment now, a great ball of tumultuous flame, searing and leaping.

It completely filled the upper hemisphere of their view now, even as it continued to grow and grow, stunning in its majesty, sobering in its might. They all glowed orange now, lit as they were by the canopy of fusion release, and DefaLuta raised up her hands, inviting all to stand.

"Rise, Mobiliei. Rise to this challenge. Rise to this moment in history. Our moment! And as we celebrate our coming greatness, feel the pride that is being Mobiliei!"

The roar became a deafening thunder, DefaLuta sending signal to all to allow the sound to envelope them even as she approved the translation.

And ...

The blackness came up over them and then outward in a treble, quadruple rush, the simulation taking them through the void, then back out, then back through again in a dizzying wash of light and dark, light and dark, all to the chorus of a million cheering voices. Their emotions swam with a drug-fueled frenzy as they were finally snapped into a greater light, into the Upper World of the Translation Party.

They were in a gravity-less bubble passing through the very soul of the star, surrounded by a fractal beauty as fire burned fire, as elements were created and destroyed, as physics was hurled at chemistry like a bullet, exploding its expectations, defying and defining it every second in a million world-crushing cyclones of golden wind, torrential rainstorms of light bellowing around them.

The entire crowd felt as the bonds of simulated gravity that had held them all in their seats suddenly lifted and they started to drift, their roars of excitement turning to laughter as they began to flip and bounce off each other in this angelic place.

The party was underway.

At will, anyone could surge forward or dart this way and that, any collision with another partygoer, no matter how violent it may have seemed, was turned into the softest of nudges, even as it sent you careening off into the lightness. Quickly people started to form into groups, laughing as they excitedly bonded to their friends so they would be bounced around together. It did not matter if you got separated though, an act of will would find you anyone you sought, as long as they wished to be found.

Parties began surging this way and that, mostly forming along racial lines, but many bridging the gap between nations and corporations.

Quavoce felt his hand being taken as Princess Lamati pulled him out toward the edge, bonding with To-Henton as she went to drag him along as well. Many were flying here now. Surging toward the bounds of the simulated realm, where the heat ramped up to give them some feel for the stellar heart they were now passing through. They wondered at the swirls of fire and elemental fury around them, reaching out to press their hands on the glassy border that seemingly protected them from the blaze.

Some more daring souls even pressed their hands into the glass.

Sar saw this and turned to Quavoce. "I dare you to do it!" she said. He laughed and shook his head, but To-Henton was already pressing his hands through the transparent shield. It gave like a viscous bubble, revealing a translucence of water but a consistency of mercury.

Quavoce and Princess Lamati watched as Henton's hand reached the edge of the mercury-wall and popped through.

He shouted, "Holy crap, that is hot!"

And they all laughed as he withdrew his hand quickly. Of course, he had no more put his hand into the star's heart than they could really look upon its fury without being consumed by its very gaze. But the simulation was a deep one, and one that begged to be explored, just as the matching one below them, the Under World of the Translation Party, promised to be as well. As many already went to investigate the darkness of that world, Sar was still fascinated by the fires of this one.

"Quavoce," she said again, laughing with excitement, "have you no courage? Will you be outdone by your Eltoloman cousin?"

Quavoce laughed with the madness of it, and looked at his friend To-Henton, who was surveying his hand as though he expected it to be singed. But it was not, of course. These fires were meant for fun, for the conquering of fear.

Sar Lamati's eyes were afire themselves with rare beauty and zest. She looked at them both as if she was about to burst with anticipation, then she whirled on the wall and with a great cry of excitement she flung herself at it with all her might.

They started with surprise, and several people around them began cheering, some maybe even recognizing they were near such celebrities. She clawed and dug at the wall and the cheers became louder as more came to watch.

Quavoce and To-Henton looked at each other. They knew that nothing in the simulation could cause you actual pain, let alone any physical harm, so if she could break through the wall ... well ... then she could. They shrugged, and then threw themselves to her side to help her, digging their hands into the thick, gloopy substance as well.

She laughed as they joined the fray and the shouting around them redoubled, word of their identities rippling through the gathering crowd to add to the excitement of it all.

The heavy substance that made up the wall started to give in pulled chunks, warping outward as they dug into it like a forming bud. As they rended it, the wall started to creak around their fingers and the fire behind it started to swirl in a massive eddy, as if in anticipation of the coming fracture. A part of Quavoce's mind worried that they were breaking it, that they were breaking the simulation. But that was the difference between Quavoce and Princess Lamati. Where others saw the plethora of rules that governed society, she saw only one, a question: can I get away with it?

And she could. She most definitely could, and with a great heave of the three rulers, the thickness of the bubble at their fingertips started to come back, and with a suddenness the fire was leaping through it in a great font, opening up a hole as wide as a person.

Princess Lamati was taken up in the hot flow first, washing downward into the great cavern at the head of the great snaking line of liquid gold that was suddenly flowing into the space. Quavoce was not far behind, nor was To-Henton, swept up in the hot rush as they were taken on a wild roller-coaster ride across and through the mile-wide party space, weaving between groups of revelers who whooped and hollered as they went by.

Many leapt into the flow as well, enjoying the hot baptism as they were pulled along in an insane conga line that defied any semblance of gravity and wove this way and that all the way across the great cavern, before coming to ground on the far side of the great space, splashing into the wall and back out through it.

As the fire departed the space once more, it gently flung first Princess Lamati, then Quavoce, and then To-Henton out across the glassy wall like they were on ice, and indeed, after the heat of the fire-slide, the wall was like ice, bathing them in cool salve as they slid across it, laughing ecstatically.

They looked up. The slide they had opened up still flowed, snaking beautifully all the way across the massive space from where they had released it far away on the other side. It would continue to flow for the length of the party. They could see people merging with it now, flowing down in it, and then being thrown free, just as Quavoce and his friends had been, sliding this way and that away from where the great fire exited the magnificent party space.

Quavoce fought genuine attraction to the woman who had started the flow, and noted that others were even now trying to open up new slides. She was a leader, there was no doubt about that. She had been born to be one. The problem was not whether she could lead, but where she would lead you if you chose to follow. Destruction was the probable answer. Not hers, just yours.

But she was leading again now.

"I want to see the Under World. Which one of you will take me?" she said, introducing a competition where there was no need for one.

Quavoce looked at To-Henton, who assumed Quavoce would not take up the princess on her offer, and saw the Eltoloman was about to speak, and not without a certain cockiness. But Quavoce surprised them, and even himself.

"I will take you, Sar," Quavoce said, bracing himself against the wall and taking her hand.

She spun to face him, shocked by this new Quavoce. Then he added, "You too, Henton, if you can keep up."

And with that he pushed off with all his strength, adding momentum to the propulsion that his will naturally gave him in the space.

"Come on, Princess!" he said with a rare audacity, and she responded by entwining her arms and legs with his and adding her forward will, and they surged upward, darting this way and that.

To-Henton was hot on their tail, but again Sar impressed Quavoce, for instead of merely flying around the eddies of partygoers filling the space, she began kicking out with her feet and arms, pushing the partygoers off and giving them greater agility than will alone could have. He recoiled at the act at first, thinking it brash to kick away from people so violently. He tried to tell himself that she knew it would not hurt them anyway, but in truth, most were very excited to have been kicked by such a famous person, and once more they were the source of cheering and revelry as they flashed through the crowd.

They approached the center of the space. A miniature black hole, swirling, and drawing in those that chose to veer too close to it. It was the doorway to the second party space, and given Quavoce's ebullient mood, Sar Lamati was keen to get him into the blackness, and maybe into the hot embrace he had avoided for so long, the only man she had ever sought who had dared to refuse her.

To-Henton saw it too, and as he wondered whether he was about to lose both a friend and a lover, he careened into a particularly large group of Yallans. They were respectful, and even happy for the intrusion when they realized how influential the man who had just bowled into their midst was. He begged forgiveness and quickly excused himself, but as he did so he saw that Quavoce and Sar Lamati were gone, vanishing quickly into the darkness.

## Interval E: The Ball Rolling

The blackness was all enveloping, more a thickness, a presence, than a lack of it, but only because of the keen awareness everyone had of the throng of people dancing around them.

A pervasive music filled the space, everywhere and yet nowhere. It was within the dancers, not without, all heard it, but all were aware that what they heard was within their own bodies, a thumping base beat that thrummed through them infectiously, filling them with rhythm. Outside was only the void, silent as a vacuum. You could only hear someone if they touched you, as if the sound was transmitted through their fingertips.

Great circles formed, intertwining with each other, chanting viral beats, amplifying the rhythm and building it into something close to ecstasy.

The only light was a tiny speck of a sun, so distant as to seem almost irrelevant, and giving off no light into the space, only that which spoke its presence, an exit at any point you might wish it, but nothing more. Around you, sight was a lost thing, conspicuous in its absence. All was anonymity, all was touch and sound and smell, as infinitely intimate as it was utterly devoid of identity or race.

Somewhere in the crowd Sar Lamati had, for once in her life of privilege and power, forgotten her status and her standing, and wanted only one thing. In the heady madness that was the translation celebration, Quavoce had finally succumbed, both to the darkness and to her implied offering, and she clung to him like they were alone, no different from the writhing, dancing, jumping throng that surrounded them.

As they united, they began to sink into a floor that became, at their wish, cool and liquid, soft and caressing, and fell into the lower reaches of the Under World, beneath the endless dance floor, where gravity was once again forgiven. Their breaths, like those of others lost in the darkness, came anomalously through the black liquid coolness that enveloped them, as though in a dream.

The party swayed on and on, as people met and parted, sometimes deliberately, sometimes with deliberate anonymity. But many among them moved with purpose. Many came into this dark underworld to be alone in the void and lose themselves in the dance. Many came with a special someone, and still others came here to meet someone, special or otherwise.

But some had come here to fulfill a less personal need. They had come to talk.

Not with words, for those would be heard by the Arbite, who listened even here, recording anything that was said between members of different states, with impartiality but also with absolute access. But touch, that was a different matter. To record such things would be a crassness that would not have been tolerated, especially during the celebration, a fact that certain high Council members somewhere in the darkness were relying on even now.

And so these agents came close, these seemingly irrelevant junior officers of the Lamat Empire and the Eltoloman, and they exchanged details via coded taps to thighs and backs. Only summary details, of course, this was but an overture, an offering and a request. A would-you-mind for a maybe-we-could-discuss. But it came with an implied truth: we are willing to talk. And that was really all that either party needed to confirm.

The only other detail that needed to be covered was one little, logistical tidbit. When? If they were going to do it, when would they look to make their move? At what point in the coming conflict would they look to dispose of some of their less worthy allies?

- - -

Elsewhere in the ether, as hundreds of thousands danced and laughed and rutted, some more private parties were kicking off as well.

Marta had been required by decency to attend the main banquet before the translation party. She had even enjoyed some of the interpretations of Earth cuisine, even if their attempts at Mobiliei's own diverse delicacies had been generic at best. But once the translation had come and the party had become more ... enthusiastic, Marta had excused herself, using the black hole at the center of the Upper World to disguise her exit.

As she entered the virtual vortex, she simultaneously translated out of the party to a more exclusive event being held by one of her colleagues.

The setting was predictable perhaps, for a location of a Nomadi Alliance event, but then their love of the ocean was not feigned, as any other contrivance would be. Marta arrived on the scene like the others who were already here, stepping onto the deck of her own ship, a ship of the line of a hundred guns.

The sails were already set as she arrived, and as she surveyed the scene she saw that they were even now breaching a headland. The Bay, thought Marta, Fral did love the Bay.

She smiled as a virtual first lieutenant landed at her side, leaping from the rear upper gun deck as he saw his captain emerging from the ship's saloon.

"Captain, we are entering the bay now!" he said briskly.

"Yes, we are, aren't we," said Marta, smiling broadly. Her hand went to her side almost without thought and confirmed that a telescope hung there, as it should.

Shouting as she bent at the knee, she called to her lieutenant, "With me, Lieutenant. I want to get a look at the proceedings." And with that, Marta leapt lightly into the rigging and began swimming up the mass of ropes, reaching up into the heights of the great ship's masts.

The lieutenant, younger than Marta and with the stronger legs of a male, quickly caught his captain with a series of practiced if daring leaps from one side of the rigging to the other. Indeed, he caught up with her and then he overtook his leader. A lesser captain would have expected her junior to slow and let them win, but Marta appreciated the art of the climb and the once great athleticism of her seafaring ancestors, and knowing this, the constructs aboard her ship held nothing back as they echoed the acrobatics that the Nomadi sailors had once been so famous for.

She smiled as she heaved herself up in her own fashion, not as spectacular as the lieutenant, perhaps, but still with an agility that she was proud of. She could not hurt herself here, of course, but she could hurt this simulated body, and any injuries sustained in the battle sim would last for its duration. She had discovered on many occasions that a pair of broken legs made the job of captaining a great battleship problematic, at best.

"Smartly done, Lieutenant," said Marta, as she used her greater upper body strength to heave herself up over the edge of the bird's nest atop the main mast.

"Thank you, Captain," said the lieutenant, wisely not offering to help her, an offer that would have brought him a sharp clip upside the head, or at least a stiff rebuke.

She settled herself against the windward side of the mast as it bucked and swayed beneath her, the hundred-foot metronome giving amplification to an already stiff sea, even at deck level. She braced her legs around the stout wood and retrieved her telescope.

She was here at this event to meet with five others. Five other conspirators, to be exact, and though they were here to talk business, they would take the opportunity to enjoy the construct Fral had created first. They would be together soon enough, and would discuss what they needed to discuss aboard the victor's ship.

For now, they would fight. Fight like their ancestors had. Fight with the skill and verve that had made them at once the sworn enemies of the their land-based cousins and a force that could resist domination by those same gluttonous land-lovers.

"I see Fral and ILyo are already at it," smiled Marta, as she squinted into her glass.

"Yes, Captain," said the lieutenant, "and the Pulujan siblings are coming up hard into the mix, too."

"Oh good," she groaned, "no doubt they'll come in together under some pretense of an allegiance, then turn on each other like always. Yes, look, see how Elder is even now backing his mizzen, just a little, but enough to fall behind."

"Yes Captain, no doubt he looks to let his sister get bloodied in the fight first."

"Indeed, and to also try and keep upwind of her for when they inevitably come to blows with each other."

"Shall we close with them, Captain?" said the lieutenant, hopefully. "See if we can prod them a little?"

"No, no. Set course to stay downwind of them, I've gotten tangled up in one of Fral's Bays before. Let them duke it out to stay upwind. We'll batter them from here, forcing them up into the bay, and into the shoals I know are waiting for us there."

She studied the sandy coastline in the great bay that was to be their battleground. Like always with the Bay simulation, the wind was brisk, true and off the shore. That gave the person farthest into the bay the advantage both in terms of maneuverability and range. But it was a trade-off; try to dominate the Bay and it may come to dominate you. For though the simulation was familiar, the shoals were not, they varied with every battle, and even Fral, who was hosting this little tryst, did not know this bay's channels and reefs.

"And anyway," said Marta now, turning completely around to look astern, back around the headland they were now clearing, "we are not the last to arrive, and the fraternity of Pulujan pals has just entered from around the far headland ... which means ..."

She smiled coldly. "... Ralfy, there you are!"

"By the Great Winds!" exclaimed the lieutenant at the sudden appearance of the last combatant.

"Sound the call to arms, Lieutenant," said Marta, lowering her telescope. "Prepare for battle!"

He was already leaping from the high platform, a hand grasped around the rear stay his only concession to something close to sanity. But it was how they used to do it, thought Marta, never ceasing to be amazed by it as the virtual officer slid down the great rope cable to the rear deck, releasing his hold while still about twenty feet from the planking and landing with practiced ease.

She shook her head at the sight and watched as the main deck below became a hive of activity around the officer and his subordinates. She stole one more glance astern as the sails of the last great ship arriving for the battle hoved into view, then she braced herself and leapt out as well, grabbing onto the backstay with a scream of excitement.

Let the battle begin.

- - -

She had turned into the headland, a move that had cost her every bit of her maneuverability, but it had also forced Ralfy to wait precious minutes before he could clear the headland and bring his guns to bear. That had allowed her to get off a full broadside volley into his rigging before he had even fired a shot out from behind the rocky promontory that demarked their little playfield.

It had been a low blow, or rather a high one, that had cut half his lines and riddled his sails with hot shot, not much in an actual battle, given the might of the great ships, but it had set the tone for their short but bitter battle, and had swung the advantage to her.

It had been bloody, but after twenty minutes of close quarters pummeling, she had finally crippled him and he had lowered his flag and stepped below. His ship's part in the battle had been done, but his own was just getting started. For as each captain lost their command, they became a crew member of the victor, and now, through the magic of the simulation, he emerged from a hatch in Marta's deck marked for just this occasion, his captain's uniform replaced now with a lieutenant's.

"Welcome aboard, Lieutenant Ralfy!" she said, beaming, and he bowed backward, gracious to the last.

They greeted each other with genuine affection, clasping arms and touching their left feet into each other's right shin like the old friends they were.

"My rigging, Marta? You cut my rigging? Bit desperate, don't you think?" said Ralfy with look of admonition.

"Ah, ah, now, Lieutenant, that's *Captain* Desperate to you."

They both laughed and he turned to the greater battle still raging deeper in the bay. Now that he had been defeated, Ralfy's only chance at any redemption was to help Marta win, and therefore keep his lieutenant's ranking, rather than the ever more menial titles he would have if his new ship was destroyed as well.

"I see the Pulujans are still friends," he said with amusement.

"I know," agreed Marta, "I think that is a record for them."

They both walked to the windward rail to look out at the remaining combatants, her ship already beating hard to join the fray while the sad remnant of his settled and was battered ignominiously by the rocks of the headland. His crew had not suffered, indeed they had not actually existed, and the ship's hulk was empty now, anyway.

It would have been a sad sight if anyone had been watching, but all eyes were ahead as Fral also finished off ILyo's ship with a final, well-placed volley right into her stern gallery, the iron flying the length of her decks and all but wiping them clean.

But ILyo was no fool, she had seen the writing on the wall and had made one final, but crucial, decision.

"ILyo is a smart one," said Ralfy. "She's scuppered Elder Pulujan."

"No doubt. Brilliant even in defeat," said Marta with admiration, seeing the results of ILyo's final maneuver. Trapped between Fral and the oncoming Pulujan siblings, she had been all but done. But she was not going to take her chances being second to one of the bickering Pulujans. Instead, she had brought herself around and set her course right for them, exposing her vulnerable stern to Fral, and stepping below before the maneuver was even complete.

She had sacrificed her ship to Fral even as she sent it careening right into Elder Pulujan's path, forcing him into an ever-weaker position relative to his younger sister.

Shit, thought Elder Pulujan, as did every other combatant for him. It was, they all knew, too much for Other Pulujan to resist, and his hull felt the hot sting of her metal not a moment later.

"I guess that leaves us, Other Pulujan, and Fral," said Marta, shaking her head as Elder Pulujan's sister did what they all knew she would, emptying two full broadsides into her brother's bow before he could even return fire. They would fight for a while longer, but ILyo had forced Elder into a hopelessly weak position, and it was all but over for the so-called Pulujan alliance.

The rest of the battle was one of jockeying and long strategy. Fral, excited after his victory over the devilishly good ILyo, would be undone by his own cleverness as he became entangled in one of his own shoals, to be dispatched with long volleys by the other two remaining ships.

And so it would come down to a shooting match between Other Pulujan and Marta, and here Marta's greater restraint and skill shone as they came together in a long, deadly dance.

- - -

"A good battle," said Marta loudly, trying to calm the laughter and embittered talk as they all debated the flaws in each others' strategies, "but if I may ..." she raised her voice even higher over the din, "if I may!"

The room calmed down, most smiling, some, most notably ILyo, looking very sore though. For she had ended the match with no kills, despite her inspired move to damn Elder Pulujan, and now wore the uniform of a conscript, a landlubber. It was poor luck, especially for someone of her skill in the chess game that was battle under sail. But it was what it was. She not would have faired much better under Other Pulujan's flag, who Marta and Ralfy had finally dispatched with rare skill in a battle that came down to hand-to-hand combat on the burning decks of both ships.

But the fires were out now. They sat in a restored captain's cabin aboard Marta's ship, with a traditional meal being served them, soused and doused as it should be, the Bay drifting over the horizon in their wake as they sailed away into the night.

"We have a lot to discuss, so I want to thank you all for coming, and particularly Fral for setting all this up, and for arranging for this very pleasant, and I am sure very secure, place to meet," said Marta.

They all nodded, knowing the subtle lengths he had no doubt gone to in order to make the space as immune to prying eyes and ears as possible. Not from outside the Alliance, spying from without was made all but impossible by the Arbite. But from within. For these six not only stood against their race in their plans, but against many of their own Nomadi brethren.

They discussed each of those peers in turn, updating each other on conversations they'd had, comments they'd heard, progress they'd made. Navigating the political landscape, even within their own ranks, was a painstakingly slow process. It must be. All care must be taken to ensure that they did not rush the wrong person or reveal themselves too soon. But they must seek to bring as many of their fellow Nomadi trading houses on board as possible, both to save those houses in the coming conflict and to bolster their own ranks during the final war.

These six made up the core. They had been the first. Or rather a mysterious first traitor had started the conversation with a doubtful Fral, who had in turn recruited Ralfy, then they had each recruited Marta and the rest over the years that preceded the launch of the Armada. They all knew each other, there was no getting around that, so anonymity was pointless here. But they had protected the greater conspiracy from themselves with their own ignorance, guiding it but deliberately distancing themselves from its details in case any of them were caught.

Now they were but ambassadors for the cause, trying in these last years to bring in some more of their kin whose resolve might be faltering.

"How goes our favorite representative?" asked Fral of his friend Marta. In truth, they all liked Shtat. He was, after all, eminently likeable. But he was here for a purpose. He was here to be a puppet, as cruel as that seemed, and it was his very ineptitude for the role of Representative to the Council that made him so good a buffer for the real purpose of the Nomadi's biggest houses.

Marta told them all of her most recent conversation with Shtat Palpatum. "It was not a pleasant sight, I can tell you, and it gets ever harder to convince him to support the war, harder and more counterintuitive." Several faces showed concern and surprise at that, but she gently lifted one of her shoulders to dismiss their fears. "No, no. He still supports the war to all intents and purposes, don't worry. And I suppose we should be happy that he has doubts. He will be all the easier to bring over to our side when we are finally forced to show our hand."

"Well, maybe," said ILyo. "If he can forgive us for keeping him out of the loop for so long."

"No," said Other Pulujan, "he is very dedicated to Marta, I see it whenever I speak to him. He trusts you, Marta. As long as it comes from you directly, and not from some other source, we should be able to count on him when it comes time to declare and turn tables, as I imagine we are going to have to do at some point."

There was silence for a moment as they contemplated this, and then Marta spoke once more, asking Ralfy about his work with their only potential ally outside their own race.

"No more news there, I am afraid," said Ralfy. "I continue to study with the Hemmbar, and continue to explore 'possible futures' with them, including, in very small doses, of course, talk of what would happen if the Armada became divided. They remain noncommittal, but maintain that their focus would be, as always, on maintaining the integrity and detail of the record and of their ability to codify it. It is a nice way of saying they will look out for themselves if and when it comes to blows, which is either good or bad for us depending on how you look at it."

Ralfy's conversation with Theer-im-Far had been recorded and analyzed by the Arbite, of course, thus its need to remain hypothetical and convoluted in nature. But the Hemmbar were famous for their brutal pragmatism and few in the six doubted that they would pick sides based primarily on one factor: who was winning.

They discussed this point for a while longer, as they had many times before, and then Fral changed tacks. "My systems tell me we are getting close to translation back out of hyperspace. If we are done with updates, I believe we only have one more topic to cover before we return to the banquet?"

The question received replying shakes of arms from all the gathered and Fral nodded to Marta, who as victor held the chair of the meeting. She blinked quickly to say for him not to be silly and just speak, but he was insistent so she spoke up once more. "Very well. Friends, the time until first possible contact with the IST at Earth is only days away."

They all became somber at the thought. While the rest of the fleet eagerly awaited news of their prize, the Nomadi were hoping for silence. Either total silence from an inactive IST or for the relay to be sending signal but not receiving anything to actually relay from the satellites. Satellites which the Nomadi conspirators had been told should be destroyed by now if whatever had been planned to stop the advanced team had been even remotely successful.

They ended by discussing their plans in the worst possible case scenario: should the satellites not only be alive and well, but should they be sending news of whatever plan had failed on Earth, and the Nomadi's part in it. Suicide, they knew, would be their only recourse then. Suicide in spectacular fashion, and doing as much harm as possible in the process in the hope that they did enough damage to cover their tracks and stop news of their treachery reaching Mobilius. For if the worst did, indeed, happen, they could only hope to minimize the damage to the houses they represented, to their families and their friends.

It was not an easy topic, but it was also not a new one. They were all still firm on their course, and once they had covered that, Fral stood, taking control of the proceedings once more. "If we are all done, my friends, my very good friends, I have prepared one last treat for the six of us before we go back to sit with the people we are so very utterly betraying. If you will all follow me on deck, please."

And he stepped boldly past them to the hatch.

So much of the ship would have felt familiar to a human. Its lines were formed by the same forces that ruled the oceans on Earth, as they did on every planet that either race would consider habitable. The guns were formed by the same discovery of explosive gunpowder.

The decks were necessarily a bit taller to accommodate the loping gait of the powerfully legged Mobiliei, and thus their navies would have been able to carry far less tonnage of weaponry than ours, but the great ship still looked strikingly similar to any ship-of-the-line as we would have seen on Earth's high seas in the latter part of the last millennia.

But there was one notable difference: they had no steps or ladders, only hatches through which the six agile captains of industry now leapt. Stairs were for the elderly and infirm, and neither condition existed in the ether, or would have been tolerated at sea during the great era of sail.

Once on deck, they walked forward and gathered on the bow of Marta's ship, gazing out at a horizon on which a sun was even now setting. The sun was, Fral now told them, a faithful representation of Alpha Centauri B, the second star in this cluster, and the next stepping-stone in their journey to Earth.

"Ladies and gentlemen," said Fral over the song of the ship's great rigging. "I give you our next translation point!" he said, waving toward the distant star. "But first," he said, glanding Light into his veins and encouraging his friends to do the same with the handing out of goblets of long ale, "we must depart this one!"

And with that, he stepped to the bow's edge and pointed to the horizon. They all followed his stare to the distant line. But as they stared they saw it wasn't distant at all, it was close, and it was getting closer.

"In celebration of the impending edge we have all chosen to jump off together," said Fral, speaking with the primal excitement of a leader sending his troops into battle, as indeed he was, "I give you the edge of the world!"

They all saw it now, and gasps of surprise escaped their lips. As they looked on, the edge now came into focus, the sky above them quickly turning a dusky purplish black as the great firmament of stars resolved above and in front of them, the galaxy spreading out in all its majesty. It was a galaxy that their world's leaders had dreams of conquering, and may still, if they could only be convinced to do it in a more diplomatic fashion.

The cheer became frenzied as the great ship approached the line, which could now be seen to be a massive waterfall extending off to either side as far as the eye could see.

"To hell or victory!" shouted the Pulujans suddenly, and the rest of the group shouted it back, screamed it really, as the ship heaved up and over the edge of the world-spanning waterfall, a great roar of creaking wood running along its length as though it was joining in their shouts of laughter and surprise. They felt as the deck reared up under them and their individual bodies began lifting from the planking as the huge ship and its six tiny passengers were all inexorably drawn over into the waiting abyss.

It would have been utterly terrifying if it weren't all but a wonderful conceit, but it still tugged at a primal fear, and they clung to each other and the ship at first, laughing and shouting with surprise as they were pulled free and began tumbling over and around the great ship that was suddenly falling with them.

As they fell past the false planet's elliptic, the ship slowly inverted above them and began to disintegrate, the underside of the world they were still falling away from revealed itself to be the star they were even now departing. The sight of the disc, watery above, now fiery below, was magnificent and momentarily stunned most of them into silence.

But it was a fleeting respite from their adrenalin pumping fall, and as they turned in air to face down, they saw the fleet's coming translation flying up at them, represented by the great banquet floor even now resolving far below, the million-strong crowd emerging themselves from the light of the Upper World Translation Party or the darkness of the Under World, depending on their fancy.

The six dignitaries and their ship fell toward them.

To the other partygoers it would appear that the six arrived with the same sudden translation into the banquet as the rest of them had, but to the six conspirators it was nothing so pedestrian. It was as if they were plummeting right into the mass of people, bringing with them a thousand tons of wood, iron, and canvas.

At the last moment the ship simply vaporized and they all came to a mind-bendingly sharp stop, upright and seated, their clothes straight and their expressions demure, blinking into the sudden serenity like a bewildered sleeper waking after a vivid dream.

Marta looked over to where Fral now sat at another table. She smiled and shook her head but he merely winked, a serene look on his face and a devilish twinkle in his eye. So she looked around for and found Ralfy, who was now at another table altogether, laughing in disbelief.

She shook her head again. Well, if you were going to go, you might as well go in style, she thought, and she turned with a polite smile to her fellow dignitaries and officials of the great Mobiliei Armada.

"Did you have fun at the party?" said one.

"Yes," she said demurely. "You could say that."

## Interval Epilogue ...

With the festivities behind them, the Council gathered, called to task by the simple message that they had news from their destination. For such a meeting, even the princess was on time.

"Welcome," said DefaLuta, "as we are all present, I will start."

They all sat in a great circle, an image of the Alpha Centauri cluster slowly fading into the distance behind them like the memories of the epic party it had heralded. The image was, in fact, a real one, not a representation, the first they had enjoyed in a long time as light now came to them at less than relativistic speeds. But such things were not high in the minds of the gathered group. They sat and waited, their faces all masks of passivity despite the various nefarious, amorous, and traitorous activities they had all gotten up to at the Translation Party.

"I won't beat about the bush," said DefaLuta into the silence. "As I have informed the Prime Minds, we have gotten bad news from Earth."

All braced. Bad news? What does that mean?

DefaLuta paused to gather her thoughts, confused as she was as to how to react to the information she had just received. She was aware, though, of the need to inform the gathered group, and realized she was, in fact, being a bit melodramatic.

"My apologies. I did not mean bad news, so much as, well, incomplete news." The room's interest was further piqued.

"I can confirm that the IST has been able to insert itself into its target moon and has been able to establish connection. We received its first signal a few minutes ago," said DefaLuta.

"But it is sending only silence. That can only mean one of two things: that it has been damaged or has not functioned to its specifications, or ..." she paused for a long while here before saying somberly, "or it is receiving no signal to relay onward from the Advanced Team."

The room was stunned, and now, with DefaLuta's go ahead, they felt as their Prime Minds released the full data into their minds.

"It is sending data, we can confirm that, but either its ability to receive data from Earth has been affected, or there is no data to receive. And I am afraid that, as your Prime Minds are no doubt now informing you, the latter option is by far the more likely option."

The room was understandably shocked. The cost of every part of the mission had been nothing short of astronomical and only the promise of a prize the size of an entire world had justified it. That one of the parts of this operation would have failed so spectacularly was disquieting, to say the least.

If it was indeed a lack of signal from Earth that was the problem, then there was a list of potential causes too long and frankly unpleasant to contemplate. Well, almost. For at that very moment, an ever-growing group of minds was contemplating just that. Adjusting models that had been running in loops for years to start to factor in this new data and analyze potential causes and impacts.

As the news spread, there was admonition. Talk of incompetence on the part of the satellites' designers, harsh words thrown at the Yalla representative whose corporate race had built the big machines. There were some furtive glances among the lesser races, suspicion growing for their more powerful Lamat, Eltoloman, and Mantilatchi allies. They would study this new information very carefully, seeking signs of treachery. They might even find some, for they were there, of course, though it was not evidence of the treachery they were expecting.

For while concerns started to build and plans started to change, the suspicions of the lesser partners in the great enterprise could not have been further from the truth. Indeed, Princess Lamati, as one of the few Council representatives whose personality had also been given a place in the minds of the Advanced Team, would no doubt be very proud indeed of how hard her facsimile had actually fought to save the Advanced Team.

If she ever knew, that is.

She might have been a touch disturbed at the tactics she had been driven to, distasteful as they would be even for her to imagine in her comfortable life here aboard the Armada.

But she would not know, not today, at least. Today she would know only that there was a break in the line. A break they all hoped was technological rather than physical, a system error that the satellites were even now aware of and trying to fix.

Across the fleet's many virtual habitats, seas, mountains, hubs, and other more esoteric constructs, a growing group of people and Minds were starting to review the data. The news was filtering out from the Council, sent from each representative to their inner-circles, and even now flowing outwards via the lines of influence in each state.

The six Nomadi conspirators had already received it, of course, informed via a subroutine in the Nomadi Prime Mind almost as soon as the Council was. They would not, they saw, have to die today, and more than a few of them breathed a profound sigh of relief. But what else they could make of it, they did not know.

The relay had made it and was still alive, if maybe far from well, it seemed.

Silence.

They had been told to expect it. To hope for it. But now it was here, it was all rather ... anticlimactic.

But while they discussed what came next, the news itself did not stop with them. The information continued to spread throughout the fleet, spreading virally now as news this important naturally must. After a while it even reached the lowest ranks, and there it found a seemingly harmless technician.

Amongst all the fleet, this one man had some idea of what was and was not supposed to be happening on Earth.

He considered the signal's implications. There was always a chance that it was, in fact, a fault in the machine, either the relay or the satellites. But barring that unlikely eventuality, it meant that the satellites had, as they had hoped, been destroyed. It was disconcerting having so much riding on a silence. A lack of confirmation. But that was all he had, and for now it was the best he could have hoped for.

And so now he moved on to the next phase. First he would start relaxing a set of systems he had put in place: destructive systems. Systems that would have tried to add to whatever his six illustrious co-conspirators would have tried to do before they all committed suicide. Systems that were a blunt version of what he was hoping to do later in the mission. Kill switches.

But now he could move away from that exercise in butchery. He did not want to kill his people. He did not want to murder a million of his kin, no matter how much he disagreed with their intentions. Now he could move away from blood. Away from blood and toward sabotage. He must repurpose his programs as he had hoped he would have the chance to.

And so the isolated technician, far more illicit, far more protected, and yet with a far riskier part in a complex plot, began planning his next steps. For this was the team's sleeper. A conspiracy within a conspiracy. A man who had been a technician at the ceremony to insert Shtat Palpatum's mind into one of the Advanced Team's strange-looking human analogues. A man whose personality had actually been copied in Shtat's place, down into the Agent, along with a complex packet of specially designed viral programs and precious data stores.

He smiled at the thought of what his duplicate must be up to. If the IST's silence was his other self's doing, then it was a masterstroke, the only downside being that this lone technician could not know just what his other self was really up to on Earth's distant surface.

# Part 3:

## Chapter 15: Ladybird

Across the earth, the news broke like the passing of childhood's innocence. It was a fact that changed all others, and very little of what anyone did afterwards was untouched by it.

The world's great religions that had come to define and be defined by the cultures they existed within struggled to adjust. Like any corporation in the face of a barometric shift in their customers' world, they tried to factor it all in, to discredit it or take credit for it, to claim it or spurn it.

Inevitable but nonetheless shocking changes came in waves, and took different forms and scales depending on several factors. In places where there was little separation of church and state, the absolute truth of the new world we all now lived in struggled for hold in soil already saturated with mutually exclusive beliefs.

In more secular regions, each nation's government's complicity in the cover-up started to hold sway, either as that government drove the messaging with greater vehemence, or their media crucified them for not having driven it sooner.

But in most places it was not one color, but a confused tie-dye of them all. The reaction of the people, both on an individual level and en masse, was reflexive and tidal. This news touched something instinctive and yet also profoundly intellectual, challenging your mind like it had never been challenged before, and simultaneously pulling at your most primal fears.

In the end it all happened in a rush, a stretch of not more than a week. A week many would remember as the most important in their lives, a week that started innocently enough, with the awe inspiring but relatively innocuous news of the coming of a new member into Earth's growing family: the arrival of Hekaton. But it was a week that would end in worldwide panic.

Across the globe, the rousing words of the gathered UN representatives rang out, each speaking in their own tongue, as one, on a massive dais constructed just for the purpose outside the UN headquarters in New York. They did not know it yet, but it would be the last such event that would occur there.

In unison, the gathered representatives said, "Today we celebrate the greatest achievement in mankind's long and incredible history. Today we add to Earth's family, not by birth, but by adoption. Today we welcome into orbit Hekaton, a new moon, and a new hope. It is the latest in a series of technological triumphs that have been made possible by the combined efforts of so many nations, a cooperative effort unparalleled in human history.

"Today we see tangible proof of the incredible feats humanity can achieve when we work together. We could list for you the nations that have contributed, the individuals that have worked so hard to make this possible, but that list would be too long, and in the end, could never do justice to the hard work and sacrifices that have been made by so many. For this is an achievement we should *all* be proud of.

"After the terrible tragedies of the last three years, after the accident in Georgia that has displaced so many of our American cousins, after the plague that claimed millions across the proud nations of the Middle East, North Africa, and the Korean peninsula, and after the war in Europe and West Africa that threatened to stop all of this important work even as it was just beginning, we now stand here to tell you we are not divided, but even more united, even stronger in our resolve."

This part was timed deliberately, and the long line of speakers each waited until all were finished before reaching out to take the hands of the delegate on either side of them, a symbolic gesture of their unification which, though admittedly hokey, nonetheless made for a powerful image.

With hands held high, and smiles that were filled with a genuine pride at being part of the auspicious event, they then said together, "And so, my fellow members of this great race, we ask that you join us in welcoming Hekaton into orbit. A new son for mother earth. A symbol of unity, of cooperation … and of peace!"

- - -

From his viewpoint on the outskirts of the crowd, or rather from one of many guard's through whose battleskin Minnie was secretly able to see and hear, Neal watched the event and smiled wryly.

*Neal:* '¿peace? ¿that's a bit of a stretch, isn't it?'

*Jim:* 'don't start on that again, neal. you have no idea how long it took to agree on the wording of that speech, and of all its seventy-eight translations.'

*Neal:* 'all right, all right, jim. ¿but peace? i mean, it seems to me that hekaton is going to be a symbol of precisely the opposite.'

*Jim:* '¿and you wanted this included in the speech, neal? oh, well why didn't you say so. maybe we could have gone with, oh, i don't know … symbol of impending doom, perhaps.'

Neal laughed despite the off-color nature of the joke. Behind closed doors Jim had a very dark sense of humor, something he rarely had the opportunity to show the light of day. But once he had finally gotten his spinal interface installed and had become used to the strange communing speech it allowed, he had let his wicked humor come out of its shell a little, if only within the absolute safety of Minnie's all-powerful hold over the ether in which they spoke.

*Neal:* 'ok, ok …'

*Jim:* 'or maybe we could have named the whole thing 'we are screwed mountain' and painted a big finger on the side of it.'

*Neal:* 'ok, jim, mercy. i choose peace, i choose peace!'

His mirth and that of Jack and Madeline, also on the line, bled through the link. Ayala was notably not as amused, and her conspicuous silence brought them all back to reality.

*Madeline:* 'the net is alive with this thing. minnie, i am seeing lots of interesting opinions about it already.'

They had expected a strong reaction from the announcement, of course. But Neal had conceded, even preferred, that the news come from the UN representatives and not from the office of the man that was actually at the center of the events being so poetically described by the massed delegates.

*Minnie:* <there is indeed a great deal of conversation on the internet already, and in phone and text based communications. i am tracking a great deal of theories abounding, most either too extreme to be taken seriously or too innocuous to be of note. A notable theme that is starting to become evident is that this is some sort of base for military dominance of earth by one race or another, a new base or weapon. Another theme that is, I believe, ironic, is that it is actually an alien artifact itself which we are parading as an asteroid in order not to create panic.>

*Jack:* 'yes minnie, that is ironic. more than they can know.'

*Neal:* 'and also painfully close to the truth, as is the one before it. ¿jim, have we updated our press releases on the mobiliei armada to include these latest developments?'

*Jim:* 'we have, neal. we have a rolling set of options ready to go at a moment's notice.'

*Neal:* 'good. ¿while we are on the topic of press releases, what is the latest from Beijing?'

He was speaking to Ayala, who was even now temporarily located there. She had taken up residence in the North Korean Embassy in the Chinese capital, now one of many such political strongholds that TASC's special relationship with the former dictatorship gave her access to. It was a strange relationship, one born of necessity, one which both sides found distasteful, yet which was essential to them both as well.

For the North Koreans it was a simple choice. They had struck out at Neal and his organization and as penance their leadership had a choice between compliance or annihilation. Where such prolonged coercion might normally have brought rebuke from the larger world community, there were very few who would mourn the muzzling of the unruly pit bull of a nation.

Of course, there was one country that still objected, and therein lay one of the real benefits for TASC. For their hold on North Korea's leash gave them a tangible bargaining tool with the only remaining source of outspoken resistance to their cause: China. A little give, a little take, a public role for China in 'guiding' the slow reintegration of their even-more-communist neighbor into the world, all were part of the molasses-slow process of building a working relationship with the former enemy of the Terrestrial Allied Space Command.

*Ayala:* 'it goes. to say it goes well would be a stretch. they continue to push for unilateral removal of our forces from pyongyang and we continue to say we must stay, potentially permanently. but negotiations along the continuum between those two ideologies remain productive … to a degree.'

*Neal:* '¿the information agency?'

*Ayala:* 'yes, the information agency. they insist on controlling the changes to the standard propaganda, including the curriculum, such as it is, and we insist on allowing the u.n. to do that. you really would not believe the level of dogma and misinformation in the existing texts.'

But Neal would. They all would. One of TASC's negotiating tools had been the slow but steady exposition of the level of propaganda, most notably the part that targeted children within the truly totalitarian state. It was so bad that even the most liberal of their allies agreed that just removing all mention of the Great Leader's infallible status would cause nothing short of a nationwide nervous breakdown. But an easing of the rhetoric was clearly required, and it was on the speed of that easing which China was firm on being in control of.

*Jack:* 'to be honest with you, ayala, i don't see that the propaganda question is much of our concern.'

*Jim:* 'it isn't, jack, but it is china's concern if they are to continue to defend their own less than free information flow. and if they care about it, then we care about it.'

Jack went to respond, but Ayala was already responding for him.

*Ayala:* 'it is murky water, Jack, to be sure, and water i, for one, would rather not swim in. but it is a stumbling point we can use for leverage. if only because we don't really care about it that much, and therefore can bargain it away in order to get what we *do* want.'

Neal listened on as the discussion twisted, as it tended to often. Today it was, apparently, Jack's turn to change sides, speaking up against TASC 'not really caring that much' about such things as basic civil liberties, but Jim was quick to point out that such issues, while of great import, of course, were not TASC's mandate.

In the end, Neal knew they would hold strong on the point for a while in order to garner further support from their more liberal Western allies, but to be immovable on it would only polarize their diverse pool of member nations even further, something they could not afford to do.

Neal let them talk even as the UN delegates they had been watching continued their own speeches, and the world's pundits began chatting at an ever-louder volume themselves. Debate about such things was starting to exhaust him, and so he pinged Minnie to tell her to let him know should he be spoken to directly and then allowed his attention to wander.

He had gotten more than he could reasonably have hoped for from their incursion into North Korea, both in terms of silencing a loud, if in the end impotent, dissenter, and garnering sorely needed leverage at both ends of the world's political spectrum. North Korea had revealed itself to be the petulant regime no one had ever doubted they were, and TASC had been given an opportunity to be the hero for once, even though its actions had really been motivated by self-preservation.

Evidence of China's involvement in the plot had been partial at best, but far from nonexistent, and indeed there was no real way the North Koreans could have done what they did without help from someone in the People's Republic of China, even if it had only been the last remnant of the destructive strategies of one Pei Leong Lam. But finding out the extent of that was Ayala's job, as well as uncovering any further remnants of tech ten capabilities, or any other subversive plot afoot in the Chinese empire.

That was the real truth behind her so-called diplomatic mission to the massive communist state. It was yet another part of her ever more complex and involved efforts to police the many parties, factions, and despots still resisting the work of TASC.

It was a job only she had either the skill or appetite for. As far as Neal was concerned, things were moving in the right direction, they were just moving far too damn slowly. As the conversation between his friends and colleagues dragged on in subspace, Neal opened his eyes and stood.

He was in his home. Or rather he was in his living space, one of three he had around the globe. It was simple. Well appointed, no doubt about that, though sparse. And even the furnishings it did have were all but vestigial. It had a couple of burnished leather armchairs for the rare moments of respite from his daily duties. It had bathroom facilities. And it had a bed, or something that resembled one.

The bed was, in truth, the most advanced massage chair in the world. It moved under him like a hospital bed to aid his circulation when he lay in it for prolonged periods, it was temperature controlled and just shy of sentient in its ability to support him as he lay prone in its cradle-like confines, sometimes for ten or more hours at a time. And it held a hardwire link to the base's main communications hub, and from there to its largest subspace tweeter.

Neal stretched and rubbed his eyes. Opening them he realized one of the armchairs was occupied. He smiled at the only human he had anything close to normal daily interaction with. He had a slew of human and AI assistants, people and machines who maintained the plethora of technical marvels that enabled his daily life, but he rarely had what might be considered a real conversation with them. He had those with his many advisors and friends, of course, but rarely were those conversations face to face. And even then …

"Well, hello there, Garfunkel," said Jennifer.

He looked at her confused, then frowned and ran his hand through the remnant of his once bushy head of hair. It may be thinned on top now as he tiptoed up to forty, but it still managed to make him look like a low-rate Einstein impersonator in the mornings.

"No, don't!" she said laughing, but with genuine affection in her eyes. "I like it like that." And she stood, placed her book on the small table between the two chairs and walked over to him.

He did not respond, but pretended to be offended, even as he reveled in the simple fondness, something he had not enjoyed much in his life and which he had never needed more than he did now.

"Besides," she said as she came to stand by him. He stood to face her, and she reached up to run her own hands through his hair, "I like to do that."

She seemed to be about to kiss him as her lips pursed, but then she scruffed his hair once more and said, "Who's my little poodle?"

He laughed, swiping at her hands and saying, "Oh Jesus, Jen, get off me!"

But at that she grasped his face in both hands, and with all seriousness said, "No, darling, I won't."

And now she did kiss him, without mockery. Something in him seemed to give as they embraced, as he was both relieved and invigorated by the kiss, both more relaxed and more alive at once. A strange juxtaposition, perhaps, but then love born in conflict is often the strangest and most powerful kind.

As they parted, he said in a whisper, "I didn't know you were here. You should let me know in future."

"When you have time for me you will reach out, I know that," she said. "And besides, if you want to know where I am, you only have to ask Minnie. I know your spies watch me at all times."

She said that last part with feigned woefulness and he rolled his eyes.

"Oh, here we go," he said, then serious again. "I would never do that. You know that, right?"

But he could. He could have her followed wherever she went. Watched at all times. And far, far worse. They both knew he had been forced to do terrible things to people who had crossed him in the last year. With just cause, no doubt, with the most just of causes, perhaps, but terrible things nonetheless. It was a strange power dynamic for a relationship, but one that the loved ones of truly powerful people had faced throughout time. It was both the attraction and the curse, both magnet and moat.

But Jennifer was strong enough to face that, and she faced it now, saying firmly, "Neal, darling, of course I know that. Don't be silly." She locked eyes with him once more, smiled, and then started walking back toward the door, pulling him with her as she went. "Now, you have been inside too long, literally. You need to go for a walk." He resisted, but she said, "That is *not* a request."

He nodded with a sigh but he knew it was a good idea. He could go anywhere on base and he would still be in contact, still be safe, Minnie would see to that. So he let her pull him out of his little hovel, and then linked arms with her and let himself be guided.

Once outside his quarters, they walked arm-in-arm down a long corridor that ran to his room and nowhere else, and then through the heavy doors at its end, guarded by one of Minnie's growing number of Phase Eight automatons.

Neal neither acknowledged the guard as they passed by nor paid attention to it as it fell in at a discreet distance behind them. If he wished to speak to Minnie, he could do so through the wireless port still attached to the back of his neck. To speak directly to this avatar would be like calling someone on the phone when they were sitting right next to you.

They walked along a broader corridor, and then out on to a long indoor promenade that was bustling with activity. Around them, people and machines moved this way and that, some noting the auspicious personage suddenly walking in their midst, but most either deliberately aloof or just plain oblivious. To either side were large work spaces filled with people either talking animatedly or lying prone on couches, watched over in their machine slumber by the all-seeing eyes of Minnie all around them.

She saw from the eyes of her Phase Eight automaton, from eyes and sensors on machines walking or rolling around the space, from cameras by doors where access was limited, and even from the eyes of people walking while they worked with some subroutine or other of hers, their open links giving her proxy access to everything they heard and saw along the way.

Her eyes were everywhere, a throbbing surge of data coming to her from the TASC districts around the globe, from its many operatives, ambassadors, and delegates, from Climbers on the elevators now spanning the globe, from the few but mighty EAHLs and Big Feet slaving powerfully both on the ground and in space on projects for TASC's Member States.

In various places around the world, she had whole buildings of solid state memory, with layers upon layers of AIs sorting and analyzing and categorizing the data and distributing important bytes to notable parties, be it diplomatic packages to Jim Hacker's administrative staff, military updates to General Toranssen, or more clandestine information to Ayala and her own staff of analysts led by the enigmatic Saul Moskowitz.

But all this happened unseen, an invisible, world-spanning hurricane of information swirling inward into the seeming tranquility of Minnie's mind, her sanity protected only by her unique and inherent ability to compartmentalize herself on a spectacular scale.

And so, while she did all this, while she conducted countless conversations, while parts of her sorted and filed and flew and walked, a very real part of her, an unnecessarily large part of her attention, perhaps, walked behind Neal and Jennifer as they traversed the broad promenade that ran the length of Rolas Island.

They could have headed straight for Neal's own private landing pad behind his quarters, with its open view west to the ocean beyond. They could have headed for the main Elevator Atrium half a mile to their left, its newly run cables visible through the glass ceiling that ran the length of the promenade as they rose into the sky above the island. A Climber could even now be seen coming to ground, and would no doubt be departing again in a matter of minutes, the downtime on the ground brought down to the absolute minimum by the machine dance of loading gantries that filled the new Elevator Atrium.

But Neal had seen that amazing sight many times, and while it still never failed to amaze, it was not what he needed now. So Jennifer guided him to the right, away from the elevator and the Atrium that housed its anchor. Away from the madding crowd which thinned quickly the farther they got from the hub of activity around his own office, toward the broad plaza that marked the end of the promenade, and the south coast of the island.

The North End of the promenade opened directly onto the bridge to the mainland, the artery by which all of the materials and machines were delivered to the Atrium for preparation and packing for lifting into space. The southern end, then, was the quiet end. They had plans for a dock here. To make this yet another mouth to feed the growing hunger of the expanding elevator.

Someday soon the Big Foot at work on construction and unloading projects across the channel on the mainland would be sent here. It would clamber into the water of the channel like some gargantuan bather and wade to the island, an island it had already helped rebuild over the year since its destruction. Then it would walk south in great lumbering steps to meet waiting engineers and anchored cargo ships and it would help the tiny little men build a great pier here.

What would take ordinary cranes months would take the leviathan machine days, as it took what human hands could achieve and multiplied it to something greater, closer to what human minds could dream.

Almost. For there were some very inventive minds spread across TASC's districts now. Very inventive indeed. Maybe inventive enough, thought Neal, as they stepped into the sunshine. The promenade ended in a hundred-foot-wide semicircular deck that faced south to the sea. Its balustrade overhung the natural cliff line, and as they stepped into the fresh air, the Atlantic rollers could be heard breaking, unseen, a hundred or so feet below.

To the left and right, broad concrete steps ran down to the coast, to what was left of the island's untouched natural landscape. People dotted the area, eating and drinking, or just taking a turn in the sea air between bouts of work on one of the district's many scientific, engineering, or administrative projects. Neal and Jennifer did not join them, but turned to the right to one of the staircases leading down to the coastal path.

There were folks walking and running up and down the steps, to and from the pathway that led off round the island. Some enthusiastic souls made it a point to run all the way around the island, some had even started a running race each Sunday, to the shouting support of many, and the grumbling moans of those that the race displaced from simply walking the stark but beautiful pathway.

At the bottom of the staircase a second path broke inland, not far, but up a little incline to an open area against the side of the massive island straddling the building that Neal and Jennifer had just emerged from. It was a memorial park and Neal smiled ruefully as he came up to the broad wall and the pond that ran alongside it. Etched into the wall here, at the base of the massive building they had constructed on the ruin of the original SpacePort, were names. A few thousand of them, if one cared to count.

In front of the wall was a broad pond, kept clean by a set of tiny roaming turtle-like robots that sifted and processed any leaves or twigs that landed on its surface. But they did this not to keep the water clear, the water was black by design, turning the whole into a reflecting pool that showed the wall of names against the rising wall of the new SpacePort, and the sky beyond, blue now, but filled with the full southern sky's array of stars at night, when this space was equally stunning in its somber beauty, perhaps even more so.

Close in to the wall, a low promontory ran over the pool, running along the base of the wall to allow visitors and mourners alike to read the names up close. Neal didn't always walk along it when he came here, but he did today. He knew many of them but not all, not by a long shot. His friends were in here. But they were among many. This was a list of all those that had willingly sacrificed their lives to the cause.

They could have broadened it to the millions who had died from the plague they had brought down on humanity's heads, or the thousands dead and dying from the aftereffects of the nuclear fallout that had irradiated a swath of the southeastern United States. But right or wrong, this was for combatants, not victims. Years from now they would no doubt need another memorial for the civilian casualties, if anyone was left alive to build it.

He paused by the first name he knew he would see: Martin Sobleski. Jennifer had known him only as her captor. Neal had tried to tell her of Martin's bravery and inventiveness, of the fact that he had willingly signed up for a mission he had no place on, and which he knew meant his likely death.

They did not speak of it now, though. For Martin had signed her up for that fate as well, and only the luck of the damned and the awesome power of one Quavoce Mantil had saved her from an end even worse than Martin's.

Neal had told her also of Laurie West, and as he saw her name his hand came up to touch the place. Such a brilliant mind. Such a loss. How much better might they have faired if she had survived? What would she have done differently? Would they now be forced to be so isolated, so totalitarian, if she had been at the helm?

But they had faired all right, he had to believe that. He had regrets, too many to count. But all things considered, he hoped she would be proud of their accomplishments, and of him.

He inhaled sharply as he came to the next name. They both did. The man whose name this island now bore. The man whose body was still somewhere in this very building's foundation. The man whose wife had, against all probability, become even more fearsome after his death, her purpose renewed, what little tractability she might have had now hardened into steel-like resolution. He feared her himself. To not fear her would be folly.

What Ayala and Barrett had shared few had understood, or even been privileged enough to witness. But she had loved him and he had loved her. For better or worse. Another casualty, Neal thought, his hold on Jennifer's arm tightening, as she looked at his face, her own full of concern, full of love.

Love was precious solace in these terrible times, but for Ayala it had only made this whole ordeal infinitely more painful, thought Neal. Did Ayala begrudge him for embroiling them in all this? No, that was a ridiculous thought. She was the most pragmatic person he knew, except perhaps for Minnie. But she did not thank him for it either, there could be no doubt about that.

In truth, he did not expect many thanks when this was all said and done. Frankly, he didn't care much for them anyway. He would do what had to be done, as he had up to now. Things his friend Laurie West might have been unable or unwilling to do. He would fight with everything he had.

Jennifer felt his pace increase as they wound their way back to the main path and the staircase back up to the plaza. He was keen to get back to work no doubt. She would try and slow him, but his dedication was a hard thing to stand against.

Behind them the wall remained in silence.  Many names were already on it, but the wall was broad.  There was space for many more.

## Chapter 16: The Mourning Jog

William broached the ridgeline with practiced ease, confident that his knowledge of the landscape would help him stay ahead, but as usual he underestimated the man chasing him.

William could hear him coming. William could hear his footfalls as he closed, and so William was away again, leaping clear of the small ledge he had landed on and down the other side of the ridge toward the sea, the broad cold coastline stretching ahead of him, as beautiful as it was deadly.

Hektor came over the ridge not a minute later, scanning as he came up over it, seeing the dust rising where William had just passed by, seeing the eddies of his movement like a scar through the air. The briefest and the faintest of scars, but enough for his keen senses. William was faster, but Hektor was far, far more experienced at this, and even as he leapt down the hillside he was anticipating his prey's next move. There was not much cover on the desolate island, but the hills and mountains that made up its U-shaped landscape were covered in crevices potholes, and little valleys etched into the vast volcanic crater.

There.

A thin valley downslope ran down to the right, of course, toward the sea, but that way it shallowed too early. It would offer little in the way of cover down there. No, William would cut back, now that he was obscured by its steep sides, back up Stonethrow Ridge toward Mount Achala.

And right into Hektor's hands.

William was indeed running back up the valley. He had done everything he could to make it seem like he was making for the coastline so he could sprint away using his more powerful legs, but he would not. He would make for the summit directly, and from there he would signal Hektor to let him know he had won and then he would turn and make the straight dash back around Fumarole Bay to the compound, and to safety.

He would make it this time, he would make it. He would not suddenly see Hektor leaping out in front of him. He would not suddenly be accosted by the other man. But, of course, he would.

Hektor's black frame came flying into the little valley in front of William like an arriving comet, catapulting in over the top of the left bank to land with a loud crash on the right, having been carried across the ten-meter gap by his momentum alone. He was not surprised to see William running at him, and in truth, William was not that surprised to see Hektor suddenly arriving on the scene either. The man had an uncanny ability to read William's actions no matter how erratically he tried to behave on their morning jaunts around the island.

But William would not be caught so easily. He knew Hektor wanted a fight, and it would be one William would, of course, lose. And so William used what advantage he had and leaned into the coming collision, digging in with his legs and his preternaturally long arms to accelerate right into the man who had just been so keen to catch him.

OK, he's definitely grown a set, thought Hektor in the second or so before William cannonballed into him. But where Hektor was bracing for a fight, William was only looking to throw the other man off balance long enough to escape past him, and when they connected with a clap of released kinetic energy, Hektor was surprised as William brought his legs up and kicked off with all his strength, sending him up and away from the stunned Hektor once more.

The boy's getting better, thought Hektor in the split second before he impacted the ground almost as hard as William had just impacted him. Neither hit would do him much harm, neither *could* do him much more harm than he had already suffered, he thought. But he did not dwell on that. William was getting away. He was already up and out of the valley, and Hektor needed to use all his strength to grind himself backward, stopping his slide and repointing his hard, black, machine body up and out, to sprint after his quarry once more.

It was not long before William was approaching the peak of Mount Achala. It was not a big mountain, and in any other place it would have been covered in trees, but this close to the Antarctic Circle there was neither enough water nor enough sunlight to sustain such niceties, so it was up a barren mountainside that William now ran, Hektor hot on his tail, their superhuman legs propelling them at ever greater speed.

It looked for a moment like he was going to make it. That he was going to get away despite his having been caught in his little ploy. And then he broached the mountaintop and Mother Nature gave him a little lesson in true power. The island was desolate for many reasons: firstly that it was born of volcanic eruption; secondly that it had suffered through the millennia in a sea of ice and snow; and thirdly because it was starved of the sun's precious heat for most of the year. But on top of all of that, it was because a fierce gale howled over it for most of the day.

Not down in the bay, perhaps, protected as it was by the ridgeline that sheltered it on all sides, but here, at the peak of one of its highest mountains, the gale gained real force, and as William sprinted up into it, the wind caught him and lifted him, taking his momentum and bending it up and back, ignoring all his strength as the hundred-mile-per-hour gust picked him up and threw him back the way he had come.

Had he been ready for it, he might have been able to withstand it, to brace for it. But he was not, and it whipped him into the air with consummate ease. Hektor saw his friend go airborne and laughed.

*Hektor:* 'whoa, my friend!'

Hektor redirected his course, anticipating his friend's new trajectory, and a moment later was receiving the gift of his victory once more as it fell from the sky. The two connected with force and were sent tumbling back down the mountainside in a cloud of dust and pebbles.

*William:* 'son of a ...'

And that was that. Hektor was quickly pinning William even as the other did not really fight back. They laughed. William did not really need to concede, it was over, and Hektor would not gloat. Well, not too much, anyway.

*Hektor:* 'you see, i even control the weather. there is no escaping my wrath.'

William groaned and pushed Hektor off him with no small amount of power, sending the other man sliding across the dirt once more.

But he was not a man. Not really. Neither of them were anymore. They were something else. They were the first of something new.

*Sudipto:* 'if you two are done, maybe you could return home so i can once again set to repairing the damage to your bodies.'

The call came from across the island, from their compound. Not from the main base that surrounded the massive Resonance Dome even now making another Big Foot for transport to India's new SpacePort in the Maldives. It was the last of their contractual obligations, one of the many Neal had signed them up for in return for allegiance or compliance, depending on your perspective. But more importantly for fiscal and material taxes.

But that was not the compound that Sudipto called home, nor William most of the time, and definitely not Hektor. Across the bay from the Dome was a small collection of prefabricated buildings hidden out of sight, nestled in a break in the ridgeline next to a small lake. It was to this compound that the two machine augmented men now jogged, maintaining a brisk but easy twenty miles per hour as they chatted about the day's chase.

*Mynd:* 'hektor, if i may interrupt, you have a call.'

A call. It was a rare day indeed that Hektor received a call. Sometimes his mother called, but not often. Like many people in his line of work, Hektor was not that close with his family.

Sometimes Niels or Tomas called to check up on him. They believed him to be rehabilitating in a hospital somewhere, and indeed he was, in a way. But they did not yet know what treatment he had ended up agreeing to after the firefight in North Korea had shattered both his legs. He was not yet ready for them to know that he had chosen to pursue a machine ideal that he had secretly craved for over a year now anyway, ever since he had first been introduced to the battleskins.

The battleskin. It seemed so distant now, almost primitive, as did his old legs for that matter. His broken legs. His useless legs: weak and uninspiring long before the artillery shell had rended their bones into a hundred fragments and shards.

But it was not one of his old team members that was calling. It was his former commander.

*Ayala:* 'hello, hektor. ¿how are you?'

*Hektor:* 'well, ayala. thank you.'

If it had been an ordinary call, and if Hektor had still been an ordinary human, then he would probably have been out of breath, adrenalin driving his heart to race and his eyes to widen. But such things were no longer left to instinct or reflex. Such functions, while still autonomous, were now regulated by a far more evolved system than his sub-cortices. And anyway, the main source of energy expenditure during the fifteen-mile sprint he had just been on did not require his heart to race anyway. His legs no longer needed blood. They no longer ran on oxygenated hemoglobin and biofuel.

*Ayala:* 'good to hear, lieutenant. listen, this is not a social call. i may need to deploy you once more. potentially jung as well, and i wanted to get an update on your readiness. both physical and mental.'

Hektor allowed the question to sink in. He had not been deployed since the battle at Chunghwa. Was he ready? In many ways he was more ready than he had ever been. His new body may not have been weaponized yet, but its strength alone made it something profoundly lethal. In many ways he was even stronger than John and Quavoce now, though his body's arms and upper torso were still limited by the human muscle and bone they contained.

That was the next step, he knew that. A step William had already taken. Hektor suppressed a shudder at the thought. What William had become was hard even for Hektor to come to terms with. If the scientist had even a fraction of the martial training and reflexes Hektor had, then he would be able to handily rip even Hektor's body apart. And that, in the end, was the ideal, Hektor knew that. He set these thoughts aside and replied.

*Hektor:* 'you know i am ready whenever you need me, commander. as far as jung is concerned, his treatment is at a far more delicate stage. he is still learning the benefits of the battleskins and comparing them to the phase eleven avatars. he, of course, sees the benefits of what we are offering, and knows that his injuries from his internment in pyongyang will leave him wheelchair bound for life without at least some form of our technology. But as I am more than aware, knowing what benefits the surgery brings and actually doing it are two very different things.'

They arrived back at the compound as Hektor spoke with Ayala, William pinging him to say he would leave Hektor to his conversation before heading off to see Dr. Sudipto. Hektor sent a mental nod of agreement and thanks and continued to talk to his commander. As William jogged away down a corridor, Hektor took a different course.

He headed to the meat locker, as they had come to affectionately call it. It was temperature controlled and hermetically sealed. A set of airlock doors giving access to an outer room where a large glass panel showed the inner storage facility itself.

As he continued to talk to Ayala about the mission she wanted him for, he looked into the storage room. It was a gruesome sight. Three canisters stood in the space, one for each of the compound's 'guests.' One was empty, reserved for Jung for if/when he finally succumbed to the procedure they continued to discuss with him.

The next held a very strange sight: half a body. It was Hektor's. It was what was left of him from his waist down, preserved in a thick plasma and linked to a life support machine outside the canister that pumped nutrient rich blood through synthetic arteries and into his still living ones.

It preserved his legs despite their all but vestigial nature to him now, but more importantly it preserved his genitalia, in case he should want them back at some point. He could not help but smile wryly at the thought. You know, in case at some time in the future he should want his balls back.

He was surprised at how hard it had actually been to let them go. His legs had perhaps been easier to say good-bye to than his supposed manhood, and the fact that it was all preserved and theoretically re-attachable down the line had helped ease his instinctual revulsion at the thought of his emasculation.

But now it was over with it was all too easy to forget them, he thought, as he offhandedly checked his organ status as though reviewing a computer's processing logs. Without much thought, he noted that he had a small maintenance task to take care of. When he was done here he would go to the recycling bay and attach a small tube to a socket on his hip. His machine self would then exude a desiccated lump of effluent, constituting the by-product of his digestive system processed through a far more efficient synthetic combined large intestine and bladder.

It was all rather convenient, thought Hektor, and very civilized. But then the third canister in the room in front of him held the end result of such advances, the final evolution that Hektor knew he was being drawn toward. It held the now lifeless shell that had once been William Baerwistwyth, complete from head to toe. The only sign that he was not merely asleep being a long and savage looking scar running from the top of his head all the way down his back.

It was a surgical scar. A scar from the groundbreaking surgery that had removed William's brain, brainstem, and spine in their entirety, to be placed in the first Phase Thirteen body, William's body, the first full union of man and machine.

Behind his old body's closed eyelids no eyeballs sat, they had gone with the brain they were attached to. Those eyes were the only part of the real William to be found on the outside of his new frame and even those were also augmented by his improved machine senses, there more because of the complexity of their linking to the brain's visual cortex than anything else. That and a sense on William's part that they kept him tied to his humanity and allowed others to see evidence of that humanity in his machine face.

Phase Thirteen, that was William. Hektor was Phase Twelve, a number that would always be his, they had decided, just as Phase Thirteen would always be William's. Like a prized number on a football team. And what a team they were. A team Ayala even now needed help from.

*Ayala:* 'the mission should be simple, i think you will agree, but once again we require subspace silence, and so i wondered if you might be interested. also, it is no more than a two-man job, as you can no doubt see, so i had hoped to see jung further along with his prosthesis. but given that he is still only using the avatar and has not taken the final step, it seems you will need another assistant.'

She did not suggest William, despite the fact that he was hypothetically one of the most capable military machines on Earth. The mind was everything, as Banu had proven so conclusively on several occasions, and William's talents most certainly did not lie on the battlefield. Hektor hesitated. Her offer implied he would be able to choose whom to take with him. It was a short list of candidates, made all the more problematic by his personal ties to them all.

The life he had been forced to choose, the cost, was the implicit price he might be asking them to pay as well. He was happy with his choice, no doubt about that, but in truth he would not wish this on anyone else. All that said, he had taken each of them on worse missions, far worse. They had faced the chance of death, even the likelihood of it. They could face this if they had to.

*Hektor:* 'obviously niels and cara are at the top of the list.'

*Ayala:* 'i agree. i would recommend cara. her youth may be of advantage getting in, if stealth alone fails you.'

Hektor knew what she meant. Her 'youth.' Cara was an attractive young woman, albeit one who could kill with disturbing alacrity.

*Hektor:* 'cara it is. ¿have you contacted her already?'

*Ayala:* 'i just did.'

There was a pause. Then …

*Ayala:* 'she is getting ready even now. apparently she is quite keen to get back into the thick of things.'

Yes, thought Hektor. That sounds like Cara.

# Chapter 17: Satellites

They had always known about it. From the start, the Advanced Team had been informed of the relay's proposed location and purpose. The Interstellar Subspace Transmitter burrowing its way into the moon of Mars. John had told Neal about it, but without the satellites to transmit information to it, it was frankly an obsolete tool anyway.

With the completion of the first Skalm, they could have dispatched it there. That was possible. But that would have meant sending it away from Earth, something they could not even afford to do in order to go and rescue an ever more distant Dr. Birgit Hauptman.

Years beforehand, back on Mobiliei, John and his co-conspirators had considered the problem of the relay. They had weighed the option of using it to send information covertly between the branches of the conspiracy on Earth and the Armada. But with the wealth of computing eyes that would be on any news coming from Earth, the chances of discovery would have been all but certain.

So they had decided it would probably be best to leave it alone. It was a sentiment Neal had shared when John had told him of the relay's purpose and location. Even if they could destroy it, then that would arouse just as much suspicion as if it remained functional but was unable to reach the satellites. Both would be attributed in the end to a fault in the system.

There would be talk of foul play but the true cause of the silence would be lost among many scenarios which the distrustful factions of the Mobiliei would bandy with, if such a notion even made the list at all. They would hide their conspiracy behind countless other perceived threats, both imagined and no doubt well founded, that the many leaders aboard the Armada had cause to suspect.

Birgit was aware of all of this. Among the flood of data coming through the link, a link whose delay was growing ever larger the farther they got from home, were data packets containing news updates, both public and more secret.

She did not pay as much attention to them as Rob did. What free time he had was often spent trolling through the reams and reams of written updates, photographs, and audio streams that were being packaged for them by Minnie. Given their remote location, Neal had given Minnie discretion to share any information she thought relevant with them. It was not as if they could be considered an intelligence threat.

And so Rob enjoyed an almost unparalleled access, and he used it, both to feed his appetite for news of his lost home, and to keep track of events on Earth, events which would hold sway, he knew, over whether humanity was ever able to mount some kind of rescue mission for them.

For Birgit, just bearing witness, spectating, was not in her. She could not wait for the world to see if it was going to survive long enough to come and save her. And so her mind blazed pathways of its own. Cutting into the undergrowth, the dense, seemingly impenetrable thick of physical limitations that blocked her path home, seeking a way through, a way back.

As she sought a way to reach over the horizon, she had long ago begun to see that there was only one real way to get there, and it was an alchemist's dream. They could not propel themselves. They could not even stop themselves. And so she strived for something even more ambitious. A doorway. The doorway.

It was a silly hope, she knew that. A preposterous conceit to think that she should be able to succeed where a whole world had failed. But just as Birgit had been the mother of a new type of life, an artificial type, maybe necessity could be the mother of this.

*Birgit:* 'the parsing of data needed to process relative location is too great.'

It had been a rhetorical statement, but Minnie, or the version of her that lived aboard Terminus, replied anyway.

*Minnie:* <a location beacon would help, but one does not exist in this scenario.>

'Scenario', thought Birgit.

*Birgit:* 'well, one exists, but not one powerful enough.'

They spoke of one of an unpleasantly long list of technological issues they faced before they could even begin to attempt the actual task of opening a travelable wormhole. A task that, in and of itself, begged more questions than they could yet know.

But before that, before they could try to open a door, and before they could try to build a corridor, and a method of travelling that corridor, they needed a door handle. They needed an Accelosphere Generator, and they did not have one on Terminus. Among the many technological marvels they'd had on board at the time of separation, that particular little gem was absent.

*Minnie:* <without a locator beacon, even if we are successful in this particular experiment, we will not know that we have been.>

*Birgit:* 'no, minnie, we won't. but we are getting ahead of ourselves. we are talking about how to know if we have been successful, when i don't even know how to do what we are trying to do.'

*Minnie:* <i have a theory. i do not understand it yet, but i am trying to explain it to myself.>

Birgit smiled in spite of herself. The real Minnie this was not. But sometimes she said something that was so simple, yet so convoluted, that it couldn't help but remind Birgit of Minnie's first conversations, when they had talked endlessly about things as simple as air and form and smiling.

*Birgit:* '¿maybe you could let me in on the secret?'

*Minnie:* <i do not want to give false hope yet, so i am only sharing this with myself. i neglected to tell myself not to tell you. i assumed i would figure that out. i will send myself an update to patch this incongruence.>

Birgit laughed out loud now. Sometimes it was hard to forgive this Minnie her inadequacies, but not now. Minnie was trying. She just didn't have the substrate mass, the grey matter. And when it came to conversing with Birgit, the matter mattered.

*Birgit:* 'ok, mini-minnie, open the conversation, i want to hear this idea, whatever it is.'

It was not a request, and the response was instantaneous. The stream of consciousness that was a machine conversation lasting days came at her like an open fire hose spraying cold theory into her mind. It was not so much the volume that caused Birgit to start, but the theoretical depth. It was too strong a flavor, too bright a mental beam. Her body tensed as the surge hit her. She was trying to interpret it. Not consciously, this was beyond that. Her whole mind was trying to find the melody, to single out the harmony of truth in the cacophony of possibility that she was receiving.

She caught just a hint of it. It flashed past like a dash on a highway, a point drawn out to a line that was gone as soon as she saw it. She tried to slow the flow, an act of will calling it to a halt. She was being caught up on an explanation that had apparently been coming for days, and it exceeded even the hot flow she had once 'enjoyed' with an embryonic Minnie.

Now she rewound. The line, seen in real-time, had seemed short, but now, as she followed the concept backward through the quilted mass of idea, she saw it was a long one. Very long, but rooted in a concept so simple that when she saw it she almost cried.

A point. A point in space. Not an object. A place. Truly still. That place is definable, it is absolute, and it is the easiest thing in the universe to identify. The problem lay in the fact that no object in the universe was anything close to actually still. A person standing in a field is actually moving at a thousand miles an hour around the Earth's center, which is revolving around the sun at sixty-seven thousand miles per hour, which is revolving around the center of the Milky Way at a pace beggaring belief, which is hurtling outward from the point of origin at speeds faster than any craft we had ever made.

If they hoped to create a wormhole, a wormhole that Terminus could theoretically travel through, or at least use to redirect its trajectory, they would need to be able to do it from Earth, and so would need to be able to transpose that wormhole to another location. It was something that had never even been attempted by the Mobiliei. There had simply been no need. Why create a remote wormhole when that step would only add exponentially to the complexity of the process of managing it.

But in that complexity might lie an answer. Not *the* answer, that was still a long way off. But an answer to the question of how to remotely manage a hole in the fabric of the universe. A gap.

The answer was simple, or so it might seem.

Don't.

Allow the universe to do it for you. For if you wanted to keep something relatively still, not absolutely still, but held in place relative to the immediate space around you—the sun, the Earth, the moon—then the best way to do it was to link it to them.

Minnie was trying to see if she could use the same gravitational leash that kept the sun's many satellites in orbit to anchor a remote subspace anomaly. Or rather she was looking to use its absence, not its presence. For a wormhole at the center of a gravitational well would not be much use to anyone, least of all Birgit. She wanted very much to stay out of any planet's way.

They could, in theory, use a large fusion generator as a beacon, as those engines used a simulacrum of a gravitational field in order to catalyze and contain the reaction. But without one large enough on hand, they could look to use a Lagrange Point, the point where two gravities cancel each other out. There was one between every twinned cosmic body. Between the sun and each of its planets, between the Earth and the moon. One was forming even now between the Earth and Hekaton.

*Birgit:* 'beautiful, minnie. just beautiful.'

She allowed her mind to bathe in the concept for a while, and as she did so her own subconscious inevitably started to meddle with the theory, adding her own unique and beautiful genius to it, evolving it as she went.

In a few hours, when Terminus's return signal reached Earth, Minnie would start to see the changes. For a just a moment she would fret that her idea, embryonic as it still was, had been shown to an ever more desperate Birgit. But then she would begin to see the theory advancing as Birgit took the concept, layered as it was in a trifle of greater complexity. It would not take more than a moment for Minnie to see what Birgit was starting to do with the idea as she gestated it.

Invigorated, Minnie would begin sending back her thoughts in reply. It would take a month before their conversation would be complete. A month before they had a theory that could be tested. But now they had a potential way to anchor, to locate a wormhole.

And so now Minnie needed the method and power to generate it. They already knew, hypothetically, that the distance would be a factor only in terms of scale, as her capacity diminished across the gap. They also knew that Minnie would essentially need to place the subspace actuator in subspace itself, then have it use the gravitational well they chose as a marker to generate another pocket elsewhere.

Oh, and one other minor issue: Birgit would have to get Terminus to a gravitational well, or find herself a spare subspace generator out here in the cosmos. But that was a relatively minor issue, when you were discussing alchemy.

Details ranged in their minds as they contemplated the myriad of issues they still faced, and they loved every second of it. They could not speak to each other, but witnessing the beauty of the theory's evolution was as close to communing as they'd had in months.

Madeline and Neal began getting requests the next day. They seemed innocent enough, but they were the parts of a machine that would look to play around with another universe. And maybe, just maybe, would allow Minnie's mother to come home.

# Chapter 18: Schools of Thought

Wednesday God awoke with a start. He looked around. A pleasant-looking woman stood not far from him, smiling. Wednesday God looked at her confusedly, but the woman did not say anything. She was tall and thin, but soft looking, almost as if she was blurred at the edges. And she was beautiful. Very beautiful.

Wednesday looked around. The room was large. Larger than any he had ever slept in before. He wasn't sure how he had gotten here and yet the room was filled with things he recognized. There was a box of toys, also larger and more full than the toy boxes he remembered, and the toys looked far nicer than his old ones, but they were of the same ilk, and he was innately curious if he was going to be allowed to play with them.

On the bed around him were the same off-white sheets he always remembered, and the same greyish blue blanket, only they were so soft. They were clean, he realized, maybe even new, he could not tell. He had rarely seen either condition.

Wednesday looked at the woman again but still she did not move, she just smiled. Wednesday pulled back the sheet and stretched out his legs. He looked at the woman as if asking if he was allowed to get out of bed, and at this the woman simply nodded.

Wednesday said, "Where am I?"

The woman tilted her head to one side, "You are in your new home. Do you like it?"

Wednesday stared at the woman a while.

"Where is everyone else?" said Wednesday. "Where is Friday?"

The woman smiled again. "Friday God is in his own room. As are the others. You will see them soon enough."

His own room? He got his own room? Wednesday did not understand that. Friday was his friend, but he was also far from the best of the children. Why would he get his own room? No, that can't be right. She must mean he is in trouble. Yes, he must be in some sort of punishment.

But Wednesday did not say any of this. He simply leaned forward and gingerly placed his feet on the ground, never taking his eyes from the woman standing in the corner.

They stood there, facing each other. A moment passed, and then Wednesday's eyes flashed almost inadvertently to the box of toys in the corner then back to the woman's. Another moment passed.

"Would you like to play with your toys?" said the woman.

*My* toys? He left that hen's tooth alone for a second, then looked around once more. There was a picture of the Son of God, and a large flower, a picture of some birds, and a picture of a mountain. He recognized everything but the mountain. It was larger than any he had ever seen.

Another long moment passed as the boy wondered what on earth was going on, and then he took a step, just one, toward the toy box. He waited a moment again, glancing nervously at the woman, as if wondering if he was being tested, and once again received only the most patient of smiles from her.

Suddenly the woman said, "Well, I will leave you to play. If you want anything, anything at all, you can come and find me downstairs, or just press that button, and I will come up." She pointed to a small button by the door that said simply: Mother.

Wednesday stared, then managed the barest of nods, and with that, the woman swept out of the room and he was alone.

Alone.

Perhaps for the first time in years. Even the bathroom in his old home had been open, always busy, always filthy, and cluttered with his fellow orphans.

He looked around the room again as if for the first time. One bed. One bed?

He thought of Friday, and the woman's mention of him having his own room. Was this Wednesday's 'own room?'

He dismissed the thought as ridiculous, and turned to the toys. A hammer, a plane, a car, a bird, mostly made of wood but some of metal. But painted. And new.

He smiled. Questions were for later. Questions were for when he did not have these toys anymore. His smile grew to fill his face and he dug in.

- - -

Two hours later, Wednesday had achieved something he had not thought possible before; he was bored of playing. Standing, he carefully placed all the toys back in their box, keeping only one, the plane, which he tucked into the back of his shorts after glancing furtively around the room.

Walking to the door, he spared a glance at the call button the woman had pointed out, and then he poked his head out. He looked this way and that, up and down the short corridor the room opened out onto. There were several more doors along it like his own. All were open, and now, as he stepped into the hall, he heard other voices for the first time since awakening. Familiar voices.

Wait, could he hear … he could hear … Friday! He ran from his door to the right, toward the sound of the voice, to a door two down and on the left, and there he was. He stared wide-eyed at his friend, who was doing as Wednesday had been, playing.

Friday had gotten every toy out, and the entire room was a mass of little enclaves: the car family parked neatly in a circle under the bed, the planes arrayed like they were coming and going from their precarious perch atop the desk, and now some kind of battle ensuing between the planes and the birds, a battle which now paused, magically, as Friday noticed his friend in the doorway.

"Wednesday!" he said in a shouted whisper, as though he had been found in the kitchen at night.

They ran to each other, toys flying as they came close.

"Can you believe it?" said Friday, whispering even more quietly now.

"No, where are we?" replied Wednesday. "The woman said you were in your room. Is this *your* room?"

"She said that to me too," replied Friday, then even more quietly, and with a sense of awe, "and she said that these are *my* toys ... *all* of them."

It was said like he was revealing a grand plan beyond measure, a conspiracy that rocked the very foundation of everything they believed in.

"But ..." said Wednesday, "*I* have a room just like it as well."

Friday looked surprised. He did not begrudge his friend the same joy he had felt at the thought that this was all his, and he had always planned on sharing it all with his friend anyway, but the scale of his largesse was sharply diminished if his friend had such a treasure trove as well.

"Where?" said Friday, and Wednesday responded by stepping lightly out of the room and then darting over to his own as if on a covert mission. His friend was close behind him. Friday looked around. The room was virtually identical to his own, but his young eyes took it all in anew, coming to rest inevitably on the toys once more before looking agog at Wednesday.

"Where *are* we?" they said as one.

They had to find out. They crept out into the corridor once more. They looked in the other rooms. They found some of their old friends, and even some of their old schoolyard enemies in other rooms. After some further discussion, they moved off as a larger group to the staircase at one end of the corridor and down it, with infinite care, to the large floor below.

Here was a wide lounge area, filled with couches and tables, more toys, and windows looking out onto rolling green hills.

Their entire lives up to that date had been in a shared home, though to call it that would have been generous. Their entire lives had been a shared misery with minimal food, dirty clothes, and too few beds. Two to a bed had been a norm. Friday and Wednesday had slept in the same cot for the last two years. They were as close as twins, with all the rivalry, jealousy, and underlying dependence that bond implied.

They had hoped for a better life, of course. They had dreamed of more. But their lives had only ever gotten steadily worse, and to expect any different was a leap of faith that even their childish minds were not naïve enough to be capable of.

But this. This was more than a dream. This was … this was Shangri-La.

At the bottom of the stairs they turned and saw the woman once more. Some were fearful: had they done something wrong by leaving their rooms? Could they somehow jeopardize this, whatever 'this' was?

But just as before, she had only her infinitely patient smile for them.

Well, her infinitely patient smile and a few, simple words. "Welcome, children. Welcome to your new home. Explore, if you like. You can go outside as well. When you want to come back just find any path. All the paths lead back to this house. To your new home. But first, if you like, eat."

She turned and indicated the room behind her. It was a long, wide country kitchen, an ideal they had never even been exposed to. Wooden countertops lined the walls. Pots, pans, and dishes lined shelves around the wall. Big sinks and a large range were clearly designed to serve a horde of hungry mouths. Their mouths, to be exact. And at the center of it all, a long kitchen table with benches on either side, and on it a plethora of meats, breads, cheeses, fruits, and vegetables like they had never seen before.

It was theirs. It was all theirs. They had suffered enough and this was their reward. The woman looked on as their instinct overwhelmed their reticence, and they surged forward, giddy with the sight.

They would have it all, all this. She would give it to them, she thought. But it would come at a price. Her face did not show her sadness, and in truth she did not really feel it either. But behind her infinite smile was an awareness of the contract these children had unwittingly signed, and what it would probably cost them in the end.

# Chapter 19: Tin Can Ally

The dark sky overhead held an awesome and incredible sight, but Hektor's and Cara's eyes were focused on the ground. Hektor was aware of Hekaton's presence only as a source of light, a new white orb casting its white, lunar glow from its soon-to-be permanent spot above Earth's equatorial plane.

Hektor sat on a roof. He was squatting, but the position did not cause him discomfort. His legs were braced, his eyes closed, as he monitored the situation below. Cara was approaching the guard post now. She had been forced to leave her battleskin with Hektor, but the neatly tailored trouser suit she wore in its place was still interwoven with superconductive strands that would proffer some protection in a fight.

And she had some teeth as well. There was no way they were sending her in there without some kind of weaponry. It was not the dual tri-barrels that Hektor had mounted on his arms, but if anyone forced her into a corner they would definitely feel her.

"Guten abend. Ich habe einen termin mit Herr Pahr," she said, in halting but passable German. The guard looked at her without emotion, surveying her. She had practiced a slouch, a gait that belied her years of combat training. These eyes were attuned to spot the telltale signs of such training.

"Namen?" said the burly man. She gave the name she had been told to give and produced a matching passport. The competence of Ayala's organization was such that it did not suffer under the guard's scrutiny. With her credentials validated, his demeanor changed noticeably. A guest of the minister was a guest of the minister.

"Bitte schön," he said with a wave of his hand, and she stepped past the man and his cohorts and into the complex proper. She was screened once inside the building, both with a metal detector and a pat down. It was slightly more stringent than might have been usual, but in these uncertain days it was hardly exceptional. A seat was indicated once she had passed their inspection, along with instructions that she should wait here.

It was a beautiful building, resplendent in all the glory, both past and present, of the Austrian State. It had once been the sister city to Budapest in the days of the mighty Hapsburg Empire. But its diminished influence since its poor choice of allegiance in the Second World War had done little to diminish the splendor of beautiful Vienna. There may have been greater examples of that splendor than the Ministry building she now sat in, but even this waiting area swam with gold leaf and baroque majesty.

She sat and waited, but it was not long before an attractive but stern-looking secretary came to guide her into the complex. She was not here to see the minister, per se, though her appointment said so. She was here to see one of his many underlings. To speak with one of them, whether it be to petition them or proffer some support, was the first stage in gaining an audience with the minister himself, such was the bureaucracy of old power. Though such stages were not uncommon in younger states as well, if only in an attempt at feigning that same auspiciousness.

It was a function of the process, a vestige of power, but one that Cara was relying on even now. For this was a fact-finding mission. She actually had little if any business with the minister himself. She was there representing an organization that Ayala had co-opted for the purpose of offering a political donation, a donation they had been coerced into putting forward. Whether that donation materialized or not did not matter to Cara. She sought only the source of a secret. She sought a leak.

As she walked down the corridor, she glanced this way and that. Somewhere within this building was a person selling information about TASC, about their capabilities and the greater mission they were embarked upon. Saul had traced it here. But the path had started thousands of miles away in China.

With sensors built into her glasses she was recording data about the corridors she was walking down and the rooms she was passing. She was detailing alarm systems and security sensors, she was noting guard details and numbers of people. They had deliberately pushed for a later appointment so they could see how many people were still around toward the end of the workday.

Like most government institutions, the majority of the employees here had a strict interpretation of their hours, and they were all either packing up or already gone as 5pm approached. There were some ambitious souls about that still worked diligently away, like the one she was going to see, no doubt, but not many.

As they approached the minister's wing, she noted the cameras and even a laser motion detector system that lined the main door and the two windows she could see from here. Interesting. That would be slightly problematic. They turned left inside the main wing, but as they walked on toward a side corridor that was lined with offices, Cara caught sight of something that was even more unusual.

She could see the main doors to the minister's inner-offices. She could see a secondary guard detail there, again more protection than was usual, but not unheard of, not now, not with the world in such a state of unrest. But the guards were different. They were not ordinary bodyguards. It was only the slightest of things, but it was of the utmost importance: just above their shirt collars, almost innocuous, she noted a thin black line of something underneath. They were wearing tech ten armor.

And as she looked, she noted the keenness with which they were studying her as well. She looked away, cursing. She had forgotten herself. Her guise had fallen. This was not what she was trained for, this pussyfooting around. She walked on as innocently as she could, and two sets of eyes followed her as she was led to her appointment.

- - -

Her meeting was uneventful, passing with a blandness that gave her some comfort as to her safety. She wanted to leave this place. She wanted to be back in her suit. She longed for its speed and strength. She wanted her guns.

As her meeting came to an end, the undersecretary smiled ingratiatingly. He had been more than happy to switch to English, which he spoke impeccably, and had even spotted her

Israeli accent as they had discussed the details of the generous offer she was there to bestow.

"I want to thank you again, Miss Woods," he said, standing. He walked to the door as they exchanged final pleasantries, opening it and calling to his secretary to escort Cara back out of the Ministry.

But she was not there. She had been sent home. More specifically, she had been sent home by the two guards who now stood at her desk. They exchanged brief words in clipped German with the undersecretary, and he nodded appreciatively. Cara had understood most of it, but he translated anyway.

"If you have time, Miss Woods, I am informed that the minister himself would like to speak with you." The undersecretary was excited by this, as if the honor bestowed some measure of glory on his own status as well. "If you would like to follow me, I will escort you to his office."

But as the undersecretary stepped forward, one of the guards motioned for him to stay. He remained admirably diplomatic, despite this rebuff, saying, "Ah, naturlich, meinen herren. Umm, Miss Woods, I believe these gentlemen can show you the way." He proffered his hand, "It appears, then, that this is good night, Miss Woods. May I say it was most pleasant meeting you."

She smiled as ingratiatingly as she could, fighting every instinct she had. "Viele danke, Herr Staatssekretär. Guten Tag."

Then she turned to the two guards with feigned calmness. "Shall we?"

As one led her away, the other notably fell in behind. She calculated her chances of making a break for it, running through the motions in her mind as if playing a game. How she would lash out at each, how she would look to incapacitate them. But as she studied the man in front of her, she saw telltales pointing to machine augmentation under his suit. He was not nearly as bulky as he appeared. She couldn't tell if he was wearing a full-contact battleskin or an earlier generation, but it was still more than she could boast.

She looked for signs of a spinal interface under the back of his collar, but either way she would be hard pressed to take them out without going for kill-blows to their unprotected heads or necks. So she filed fighting away under 'if things get out of hand' and walked on.

- - -

The minister's office was, of course, a large leap upward in size and adornment. Even here in the receiving area, the walls and ceiling were exercises in woodwork and molding that bordered on the ridiculous. She continued to note her surroundings as they checked her once more. They were more thorough this time, and her concerns started to grow as they politely but insistently removed her glasses and held them up to the light.

There was, of course, no prescription to the lenses, and that led, in and of itself, to proscription. It seemed she would not be allowed to have them back. She went to complain, but the expression she was greeted with could simply be categorized as nonnegotiable. She shrugged. They were fake, to be sure, but they were more capable than this man knew.

Well, thought Cara, if this minister was the source of the secrets about TASC's capabilities, as it was becoming increasingly likely he was, then he was about to find out a few new ones.

"Good evening, Miss Woods!" said a bold and hearty voice as she was ushered into the office proper. His smile was genuinely charming, his demeanor nothing if not amiable. He strode over to her with all the confidence and bonhomie of an old friend and proffered his hand as if it were his true delight to meet her.

She took it, noting the briefest of sideways glances as he stepped up to her. Confirming, with his guards, no doubt, that she had indeed proven to be unarmed.

"Herr Pahr. Rudolf, if you please."

His eyes spoke a question: 'and you are …' and she responded, "Miss Woods. Cara, if *you* please."

She smiled, perhaps without conviction, and saw that he was evaluating her with practiced ease as they stared at each other. She thought she might have seen him coming to a conclusion about her, no, she *did* see it, and with that he nodded and turned to walk over to where two large armchairs faced each other on one side of his large office, along with a couch, a small but ornate coffee table, and a large and far more ornate fireplace.

"Please, Cara, sit … sit." he indicated the armchair opposite his own, and waited for her to take a seat before doing so himself.

After a moment of staring at his smile, one that was now bordering on smug, she said, "I wonder, Herr Pahr … Rudolf, if I may have my glasses back, please."

He looked at the more senior of his guards with some measure of alarm at the thought that his guest might have had her personal property seconded by them, but when the guard in question shook his head, the minister's look turned to one of surprise, then one of curiosity.

He said, "I am afraid it appears that my head of security does not think your glasses are all that they seem. Or rather, he seems to think they are somewhat *more* than they seem. Do you have any idea why he might think such a thing?"

She looked at him. He was toying with her, but he was also treading carefully. He could not know whom she represented. If he wasn't careful, though, he was about to find out.

"Well, Rudolf," she allowed some of her derision at the name to bleed into her voice, and noted as his expression shifted ever so slightly at her mockery, "all I know is that I would like them back. If your gorillas choose to keep them then that is up to you, but I will ask once more, politely, if they may be returned to me before we continue this conversation."

She was trying to be meek, compliant even, though it was not an art she was familiar with. He mistook her tone for a weakness, and decided to keep the glasses as a trump card.

"I think not, Cara. Maybe after we have concluded our business we might return them to you … maybe."

He smiled again. She shook her head. Any moment now. The ping came to her as question in her mind. The glasses were an insurance policy. They had been silent for a while, but they were designed to know if they were on her or not. If they were separated from her for too long they were designed to ask why. If she did not respond, well, then they would ask for help, and that would bring in Hektor, most probably with all the diplomatic grace of a stampeding rhino.

She silenced it immediately. Maybe the minister's security would not notice it. This was the question. TASC did not know yet how much this man was aware of. But the sudden entrance of another guard and the shared whisper with Herr Pahr's head of security was too well timed to be a coincidence.

The minister looked curious, and that inquisitiveness only increased when his head guard came over and whispered into his ear.

"It appears that your glasses, such as they are, have begun transmitting a signal," he said with a smile. "Not, I think you will agree, the normal behavior of a pair of spectacles. I don't think mine do that. Do yours, Karl?" he smiled at his guard, who shook his head without humor.

"Now," he said, also without humor now, "maybe you can tell me what you are really doing here, Miss Woods, and who you really work for. Spying is a very serious offense here in Austria, and one for which you will be held fully accountable, if you do not cooperate." He waited a moment, and then after he was met with only silence, added simply, "So?"

She sat a while. Then she glanced around once more. This was not going as planned. Then again, to say that she had found what they were looking for would have been an understatement. It was not part of her mission to be here, now, in contact, but it was not exactly her choice either. Clearly she was going to have to go a little off-reservation.

Deciding to face him rather than dissemble further, Cara took a deep breath and said, "Well, Herr Pahr, if you really must know, I am here trying to find out who might have been selling some rather important information to some of our more unreliable neighbors in the east. And as of a short while ago I am now *also* here investigating the nature of your guards' armor." She let that sink in, then said, "Does that answer your question?"

He looked surprised, the coolness of his veneer cracking ever so slightly, like the intricate but well-worn pattern on the wooden table between them. She held his stare. He may think that he had her in his custody, but to do so underestimated her, and most certainly underestimated the man waiting for her a short way across town.

"To a degree, I suppose …" he looked less calm now, but still resolute in his belief in the capability of his guards. But now there was something else in his expression. He was plotting. He was calculating risk. He was thinking of how to ensure the silence of the woman in front of him. In short, he was thinking of how to dispose of her.

He went on, "… to a degree, Miss Woods. But you have still not told me who, exactly, you are working for," he said, still with an air of friendliness.

"No, I have not," she said, their eyes locked. She was calculating as well. She was calculating whether to try and fight her way out. Whether to call in Hektor. Whether she was about to be attacked or restrained. How they would come at her if they did. With her safety threatened, her face now became like stone, her eyes cold points looking out from behind her resolve, and the sight unsettled the minister.

"I'll tell you what, Rudolf," she said after a moment. "I'll tell you who I work for, if you tell me who, exactly, you have done business with."

"I am afraid I do not know what business you are referring to, Miss Woods," he said, trying to match her stern stare.

"Well, maybe the name of my employer will help you remember," she said. He was curious. The Americans? They were damaged, crippled perhaps, but the CIA still remained a powerful ally and an even worse enemy. The Israelis? Her accent would certainly point to that, but they did not have the motive to come after him, indeed, they were even clients of his, to a small extent.

But wait. Israeli. No ... surely she wasn't one of ...

She smiled coldly as she saw realization dawn on him.

"Yes, Herr Rudolf Pahr," she said. "I do *not* work for any of your so-called allies *or* your customers. I work for the organization you have been so happily selling information about. I work for TASC."

His expression now became one of fear. He tried to mask it with a sort of righteous indignation but she knew the expression too well. She had seen it too many times.

Tension in the room began to mount as all parties felt the coming escalation. The clock seemed to slow and then suddenly the minister was barking a harsh order in German, and with that it was begun. They were moving toward her and so she was moving too. She kicked at the table with all her strength, pushing her chair backward. She had to stay moving. She must control the contact. She could not win if they got their hands on her.

As her chair pushed backward, she noted they were drawing weapons. She could not know if he had ordered them to kill her or capture her, his words had been too fast and too clipped, but her tactics remained the same regardless.

As she flipped backward, she brought her legs up hard. She fully expected one of them to be right behind her and she was right. Her heels were not long, but the rubber at their base was merely a cover. As her two heels connected with the man's chin, the base gave way and revealed sharpened blades beneath. Driven with her full force they opened up his neck above the line of his armor. His eyes were wide as his head was pushed backward and all but disconnected from his body.

But she was still moving. She longed for the already dead guard's armor to be on her, but would suffice with having it in front of her. Two more guards, including the minister's head of security, were leveling their weapons.

This was no spy. This was a warrior, and their priorities were changing by the second from containment to survival. She had only a moment before they were firing. She pulled at the decapitated guard's body, wrenching it down on her as she rolled to ground and tried to grapple his gun from his lifeless hand.

Then the bullets came. Most hit the guard's torso, but the smarter of the guards aimed for her exposed legs.

She felt a bullet impact her, and felt her leg scream and rage at the pain resonating up and down its length. The suit stopped the bullet from opening her up, but her knee still dislocated under the pressure. She scrambled for the gun. Another bullet hit almost the same spot. The pain this time was mind-numbing.

She had sent her distress signal to Hektor as soon as events had come to a head. She had classified it Evac Priority 3. This meant come in hard but use side windows rather than the front door to avoid unnecessary casualties. Priority 2 would have meant come in through the front door and don't spare the horses. Priority 1 meant come in through the bloody wall if you have to.

She was thinking about upgrading the call.

She could feel a timer in her mind. His estimated time to arrival. It was a fluid estimate that updated as he came in based on distance and resistance met, but it was counting down quickly. He would need to triangulate her exact position and he would need to get past a perimeter guard or two. No doubt those guards would not be having a fun time right about now. But then neither was she.

She managed to get the gun free from the guard's hand as another bullet hit her exposed flank.

"Enough!" she heard the minister scream.

"Miss Woods!" he shouted. "You are surrounded. You have killed one of my guards and insulted the Austrian government beyond measure. Put down that gun and come out from under that poor man's body … immediately!"

She paused, happy for the respite. She was badly hurt. If she'd had her battleskin on, the bio-med AIs it came with would be telling her she had multiple cracked ribs and the muscles of her left leg were badly torn in multiple places.

She could continue to fight, of course, but she would fare much better if she waited for the cavalry to arrive. But the minister was not uninformed of the coming reinforcements, ignorant though he may be as to their full speed and martial ability.

"We know you sent some form of signal. We don't know how, but we know you did. Call off whatever team you have coming in. Let us talk, Miss Woods. Let us talk like civilized human beings."

Human beings. Ironic. If only they were all acting like members of that same team then there would be no need for all this. She had sent the signal via a small transponder wired directly to her spinal interface. It was not much, but it meant that she could be sure of support should she need it. And she was under no illusions that she still needed it very much, despite the minister's pleas.

She did send another signal though. She sent a plan of the room she was in, with the locations and armaments of the soldiers around her, and through the limited comms system attached to her spine she received the final countdown to his impending arrival.

It was a bit moot, in truth, as he could now clearly be heard thundering through the building. The minister's eyes went wide. He signaled for his guards to prepare for whatever was coming. He toyed with finishing off the woman lying on the floor before whatever it was arrived, but he could not shake the feeling that this was not going to go his way. He was so very right.

Hektor came into the outer receiving room as an exercise in juxtaposition, his brute strength and bladelike weapons bloodying the overtly civilized walls with the two guards that still stood outside the inner-office's door. He tried not to kill them unnecessarily but they were not wearing helmets, and as he disarmed them he feared he probably broke both their necks.

He unhinged the door like an unhinged beast, blasting it from its frame to announce to all within that he had arrived and that the team member he sought had better still be alive. He was greeted with more consistent and focused gunfire than he had met so far on his passage into the building, and he returned the gesture in kind. After turning the first two guards to liquid within their suits, pummeling them with a couple hundred hypersonic rounds each, he turned his guns on the last.

This one was standing in front of a cowering man, clearly guarding him with his life. He was shaking but he was resolute, ready to die for the cause of protecting the man he had been sworn to guard. Hektor respected the gesture.

He stomped into the room with emphatic thuds of his metal feet. He wanted to make sure the two surviving men knew the full weight of their folly should they fire on him again. His sensors could make out Cara's heat signature to his right. She was under something. His 360° visual cortex told him what it was, or rather what it had been before she had shortened it by about a foot. He smiled inside his helmet.

His voice came out of a speaker in his side using the German of his erstwhile fatherland. "Put down the weapon and stand aside. This is not a request. This is not a negotiation. Put down the gun or I will blow your head off. Do it now."

The sight of the bionic machine in front of him, its dual cannons leveled at his head, would have scared any man, but the guard remained admirably firm. The minister was not so brave, though, and nor was he a fool. This was a lost battle. Indeed it appeared it had been lost from the very start.

"It's OK, Karl, lower your gun."

With the gun lowered, Hektor instructed his own helmet to fold back. His systems told him that guards were converging on their location. They did not have much time.

"Cara, how are you doing?" said Hektor.

She groaned as she levered the dead guard off of her. "Great, Lieutenant. Just great."

He reached around behind his back and grabbed a pack that was attached to it, releasing the tethers that held it there as he did so. It was a little battered from his meteoric entrance into the building, but its contents were hardier than it was anyway. As it hit the ground, it opened and the suit inside it literally sprang from it, a disembodied shell standing of its own accord.

Hektor's eyes stayed on the minister and his guard.

"I am assuming this is our man?" he said.

"You assume correctly, Lieutenant. This is the leak."

The minister was stepping out from behind his guard now, bravado rather than bravery, perhaps, but the emotion was almost indistinguishable as he puffed out his chest and said, "Now, Lieutenant. I am not sure what you think is happening here. But may I remind you that I am a minister of the Austrian government, and that you are, at this moment, guilty of a host of crimes, both national and international."

Hektor looked at the man as if he was brandishing a spud-gun and saying stick-em-up, but the minister went on regardless, his tone becoming more placatory. "Now please, Lieutenant, don't misunderstand me. I mean not to threaten you, I mean only to say that you should, perhaps, consider your position here."

Hektor did not reply. He waited as Cara slowly and carefully removed her trouser suit and began working her injured leg into her battleskin. Its embrace was like an old friend, the welcome of returning home, but the suits were hard to get on even on the best of days, and this was certainly not one of her best.

As it sealed around her leg, it asked her via her comms module whether it should realign her warped knee. It was very matter of fact about it, pleasant even. She braced and said yes and the pain as the machine musculature aligned the leg was breathtaking. She shot a deadly look at the minister and the man recoiled at the murder in her eyes.

"Now, now, Miss Woods," he said with a noticeable tremor in his voice now. "You attacked us, if you remember. I only asked you a question." She did not respond, though her dark look only grew darker still as she worked her arms into the suit and it sealed around her broken ribs. She seethed as it clenched at them, then her face became calm as the suit pushed her base comms module aside and connected with her spinal interface.

She took the balm of its access, and the ability to curtail and contain her body's pain management systems. A few moments of total neurological control, a few glanded hormones in her system, and she was ready for bingo.

She soothed herself and brought her anger under control.

*Cara:* 'ayala, this is cara. as hektor has no doubt told you, we have our man. ¿what would you like us to do to him, sorry, *with* him?'

Cara's anger was more than matched by the more profound and deep-seated rage that sat like a pall over Ayala's heart. They listened as their commander gave her orders. As usual, Ayala did not disappoint.

Cara looked at Hektor as their unusual orders came through, but he merely shrugged and looked back at their two wards.

"It appears," said Cara aloud, "that you are to benefit very much from this little encounter, Minister."

The man looked confused and far from convinced as Cara went on, "You are going to be offered the very best medical care available. The very best that we can offer, and believe me when I say that we can offer a great deal."

"Medical care?" said the minister with a skepticism that was starting to turn manic.

"Yes," said Cara, "medical care. You know, for your leg."

"My leg?" said the minister. "But there is ..."

Even as he said it he was regretting it. He fell backward in his attempt to get away from the woman suddenly running at him. Cara was precise, even restrained. But her kick, when it came, was low and extremely hard, even for her, even given her machine augmentation.

It did not break the minister's ankle and foot so much as demolish them, splintering the bones into a thousand pieces. All the king's horses and all the king's men would not be able to save them. But Ayala's could. And with that, a phone started to ring outside in the main reception area. It was deserted now, but Cara looked at the guard and said, "You should get that, Karl. It is for the minister."

"And you," she said in a gentle tone to the man clutching his foot and weeping, a hoarsely whispered scream echoing from somewhere deep within him, "now, now, Minister, don't worry. The pain will pass soon. Well, this round of it. That will never heal, I am afraid. That foot will hurt for the rest of your life, even as it remains completely useless to you."

She lowered her face to his, even as the guard, prompted by Hektor, answered the phone outside and patched it through to the one on the minister's desk. "The phone call your guard is answering right now is from my boss. She wants to talk to you. We have to go now before the police get here, but she is going to tell you what you are going to do next. If you ever want to walk again, I strongly suggest you listen to her."

She stood, her helmet closing over her head as she did so. The minister was crying now, sobbing, but she was right, the agony was subsiding, his body numbing somewhat to the geyser of pain bubbling up from his ankle.

Cara was already turning to leave, to go and meet the Slink even now descending on the roof of the building. It had not been as subtle an operation as they might have liked, but they did not sense any recrimination from Ayala. They guessed that this was probably not far from what she had planned once they had confirmed who the source was anyway.

But Hektor had one more thing to say as the guard gingerly handed the phone to a shell-shocked minister. "Herr Pahr, just so we are clear. We really can offer to heal you, make you actually better than new. But make no mistake, you should listen very carefully when our boss tells you what to do. Very carefully indeed. Or we will be back, and we will not be so gentle next time."

And with that he closed his helmet and they were gone. The minister took the phone. He was pale. He felt like he might pass out. But he did not. The conversation was short, curt, and one way, but it would not be the last between him and the enigmatic woman on the other end of the line. Ayala did indeed have a proposition for him, and the alternative was not something he ever wanted to live through again.

# Chapter 20: Newsworthy

Reporting live ...

This is the view from ...

If you are just joining us ...

The world reacted to the news in waves. A story about a terrorist attack in Vienna three days beforehand, news that would once have filled the airwaves, was being washed away like writing in sand, wiped away by wave after wave of rolling, breaking news.

A billion cameras had photographed and recorded the arrival of Hekaton. Its first full orbit had been the subject of more conjecture and conversation than any previous event in history, but even that new moon was being eclipsed now.

A new story was taking center stage. The real story. One that Jim and his team were trying furiously to get ahead of. They'd had a precious few days' warning. They had hoped for more, but Ayala's contact had not been able to promise them more than that. For the minister had been a busy boy.

In the days to come, Ayala and Neal would contemplate very seriously going back on the deal they had offered the traitor. But he was their traitor now, bound to them by a bond even he would not understand at first. When he returned from the 'clinic' that had offered to help treat his leg, Rudolf would amaze his Austrian doctors with the abilities of his new prosthesis. But the price of that miraculous device was more than he could yet understand.

"It is coming through now ..." said Jim. "... Jesus Christ." They were looking at the photos coming out of Tehran. The photos that their friend the minister had sold the Iranian government before TASC had gotten to him. He had been told they would be used as leverage by the ayatollah for concessions from the West, but apparently the man did not intend to be so subtle.

They showed the flare in all its glory, the flare from a thousand engines, the engines of the coming Armada.

It was not conclusive evidence, but nor was it alone.

"We can't stop this," said Ayala.

"No, I know," said Neal. "Even if we could discredit it, we would still be left with telling the truth later, at the expense of what little credibility we would have left."

He shook his head at the sight. It was a picture he was familiar with; indeed he had seen better photographs and infrared images than these. And they were out of date. Not only by the ten years it had taken the light from these images to get here, but also by the months since these particular shots had been taken.

"They're nearly ready for you," said one of Jim's assistants. She was not speaking to Neal, she was speaking to their appointed spokesperson. Wislawa was of Polish birth, but she was as international a citizen as one could find. Fluent in five languages, notably including Mandarin and Arabic, she had forgone a promising career as a politician and diplomat for her pursuit of a passion for poetry.

Now she had come back, called to the cause by an old friend in the Polish government who had joined Jim's team in the first flush of TASC's emergence as an independent state. Her command of language was peerless. Her demeanor during debate and argument was gentle and comforting, but she was quite capable of being scathing if crossed, and no one doubted that such a capacity would be vital as the truth finally came to light.

She would be as good a spokesperson as they could hope for in the coming weeks, even if Neal himself was a little afraid of her. She reminded him of Laurie West; an intellect not to be trifled with. His confidence in his team was bolstered when she was around, even as his own personal cool was more than a little ruffled by her piercing stare.

But even she was unnerved by the coming interview. She knew her mind and knew her topic. But to say that this interview would be replayed and analyzed like no other had been before was a gross understatement.

A man powdered her nose once more and a producer indicated for her to follow him. She breathed deep.

"You'll do fine," said Neal.

"You'll do *great*!" said Jim.

She smiled and nodded. "Certainly. Great. Yes, that's how I'll do," and she was gone, walking out into a studio bristling with cameras. They would start here. They would tell their story now. Depending on how well it went, they would adjust and tweak, and move on to the next. Jim had lined up other representatives in many nations to give similar interviews.

This first would be in English and would be for the BBC World Service. Al Jazeera would be next, also in English, but French, Spanish, Portuguese, German, and Italian interviewers were standing by for either a moment with Wislawa or another representative from Jim's team, along with Arabic, Mandarin, Hindi-Urdu, Russian, Japanese, and Javanese language TV stations.

It was a plan they had been formulating for months. They had been training the team of ambassadors for all that time. Wislawa and her counterparts had already been put in place as TASC's representatives to the world's many governments for that time, and as such had explained this story to presidents, ministers, kings and queens, chancellors, chairmen, sultans, even an emperor, an emir, a taoiseach, two captains regent, and a pope.

Notably absent from the list, though not by choice, had been a grand ayatollah of Iran. Iran represented a massive state, and one whose scientists and scholars were among the best and brightest on Earth. But their place in TASC's historic effort was far from representative of that prowess, not least of which because their leader had refused to meet with a representative of a Western nation since 1989.

"She *will* do great, you know," said Jim, almost as an aside, their shared attention now on the screen in front of them.

The interview would be conducted in District One, and would be supplemented by a tour of the facility. They would look to overwhelm the viewer with evidence of their work to prepare for the coming Armada even as those viewers came to terms with the very news of the Armada itself.

But in the coming days they knew they would not be the only voice.

- - -

Sure enough, the ayatollah was quick to proclaim a very different story. He talked not of unification or collaboration, but instead of an effort by the organization known as TASC and its Western allies to collaborate with the coming alien force. He began to describe the Milton SpacePort and its siblings around the world not as defense outposts, but as receiving halls built by a Vichy United Nations.

And he would start to call for those halls to be torn down. It would not be out of malice that he would do this, nor out of ignorance. It would be out of a mistrust born of decades of abuses by mostly well-intentioned Western powers. And it would be a misinterpretation of very real intelligence he had come into, intelligence that described the participation of elusive alien contacts within TASC's ranks.

His voice would not stand alone. It would become one of three rallying cries. The second would be Wislawa's, her reasoned, articulate perspective, and that of her fellow representatives, winning no small amount of support around the world, especially as it would have the backing of many a government.

The third reaction-faction would be the most fractured and disjointed, but by far the largest. It would be characterized by a murky mixture of denial, defeatism, and disbelief. Many of the world's religions would clamor that this was a sign from God, even the pope would have trouble giving his wholehearted blessing to TASC's mission, despite promises to be 'as reasonable as he could.'

Many among the world's billions of confused souls would continue to flock to comforts such as religion and conspiracy theory, as they had in ever greater numbers since the world had started to rock with the first fight with the satellites, a phenomenon that was only now, it appeared, being fully explained.

Many more would call it the end of days, joining a growing cry that this was yet another sign of the apocalypse, as deserved as it was inevitable. And if a handle could not be gotten on the situation, Neal thought, their prophecy may well be self-fulfilling.

But despite it all, he thought, as the unprecedented news cycle entered only its second day, work must go on. His teams must be allowed to move forward.

## Chapter 21: The Missing Link

"We are approaching attachment now, Susie," said Captain Harkness, his voice excited, patronizing in all the right ways. "In a few more hours, Daddy will officially be home!"

Susie was as excited as her father was, but at seven years old, she still far from fully understood where her father had been for over a year, or where he was now, for that matter. Not that she couldn't very clearly see where he was, like everyone from Moscow to New York. His craft, such as it was, was the most visible thing in the sky save only the sun. Her view, in fact, was among the best you could have. For she was almost directly under the great rock now maneuvering into position above Milton SpacePort.

"We are going to link up with the space elevator in just a while, and then I will be coming down to see you!" he said.

"But when will you be *here*?" said Susie, really trying to be positive, but still not getting why everyone was so excited. Mummy seemed very excited that Daddy was home, but then when she asked when he would be here they all said in a few days. So ... he wasn't home then, was he?

At least now, though, she could speak to him and he could speak back, instead of that strange way she'd had to say long speeches into a camera and then she would get those strained responses back ages later.

Her mother had tried and tried to explain it to her, but the maths just didn't add up. If Aunty Cis had been able to speak to them on the phone from Australia, then surely Dad could from wherever he was. After all, Australia was literally on the other side of the planet from their home in Malvern, how much farther away could Dad be than that?

He saw something in her give the way he had so many times before. She was resigning herself to the insanity of her parents, and with infinite patience she was just going to go with it. He smiled. He had to admire her patience, he supposed. One day in the future she may understand the importance of what he had been involved in, the stupendous nature of the mission he had been sent on. But not today.

"Well, as of right now, if you look straight up, through the big glass window above you, all the way up the big lines coming out of the top of the building Mummy has taken you to, you will see a very big rock."

"Yes, Daddy. Hekaton. The 'New Moon' everyone is talking about." She looked up once more. She knew what he was about to say. He was about to say he was on it. That he was *in* it. That he was actually steering it, like some big car.

"Well," he said, "now look at this ..." and suddenly the view on the screen in front of her changed. She could not see the port plugged into the back of his neck. Nor could she imagine yet what it allowed him to do. But now he showed her one of the many views it afforded him, from one of his many synthetic eyes. His eyes closed now that he was not on camera anymore, and he showed her the view of Terminus Station in front of him, and the cables disappearing down to Earth from its base.

"That is the top of those cables you can see. And here," he said, changing the angle so that the Earth could be seen far below, and then zeroing in on a spec just viewable under the nook of West Africa, distinguishable as the end point of the lines vanishing down toward it, "is what you look like to me …" and then, on the spot of the SpacePort, he overlaid a photo his wife had sent of his daughter from her last birthday, a smear of strawberry icing across her face from a hastily devoured slice of cake.

"Daddy!" she shouted at the sight, laughing in spite of herself.

"So you see, my little strawberry-flavoured monster, I am still a ways off, but compared to how far I have been, you have to trust me when I say that it is just like I am pulling into the driveway."

He brought the view back to his face and smiled. It was a smile she had missed. It was one of the two most important smiles in the world to her, and it filled her with a sense of peace and warmth. They continued chatting for a while longer but preparations were continuing apace, and while Captain Harkness could do a great deal via his link while talking to his daughter, he must focus all his attention on the coming linkage.

They were dealing with masses and momentums that stretched the capacity of reason, and while the entire process would be done in something close to slow motion, the ramifications of a miscalculation did not bear thinking about.

- - -

As one child's eyes stared into a sky full of wonders, a whole group of others looked out on a simpler view, but one into which they, themselves, were getting ready to fly. Wednesday God looked at the cliff.

"This can't be right," he said to Friday God. "Surely this won't work."

"But … we *saw* Mother do it," said Friday, as much to convince himself as to convince his friend. "And besides, she says it is safe."

He glanced back at the woman standing behind them.

She had asked them to call her simply Mother. She said she was there to look after them, and indeed the weeks since they had come to live with her had been the best of their short lives. More food, more space, more freedom than they had ever known back at the orphanage. More than they had dared dream of. They had quickly come to trust her, trust her more, perhaps, than they had ever trusted anyone.

She had introduced the concept of games early on. First they were computer games on a small screen. They would have appeared antiquated to any child from the West, but to them it was the most powerful computer they had ever seen. The games had been of a theme. Descent, TIE Fighter, Wing Commander, lots of flying and lots of fighting. They had taken to them as any child would.

Now the games went to another level. Now the games became more real. They stood on a cliff side. Ahead of them the cliff face dropped off to the sea, not to a rocky base, but straight into a broad ocean. They had come here from the house. Mother had driven a group of them in a van. When they had arrived, they had each been assigned one of ten broad wings set up on the grass that ran along the cliff's top. Mother had helped each strap in.

Mother had given each of them some brief instruction, and then Mother had demonstrated, stepping into the air like it was nothing, swooping away as they stared at her and then, a minute or two later, gliding back in to land in front of them, smiling as she always did.

Now she waited patiently, watching. Wednesday God glanced at his friend. Friday was staring intently at the cliff's edge, breathing in long, slow rises. Wednesday didn't feel right about all this, and he glanced at some of the others all lined up, facing the drop off.

"I'm not su …" said Wednesday, turning back to Friday, but as he spoke his friend was already running, driving his legs forward as the fragile-seeming wing frame lifted above him, already starting pulling upward.

"Wait! Friday!" Wednesday inadvertently glanced back at Mother as if to say 'help him,' but Mother only smiled proudly and nodded, her eyes flicking back to Friday as he came up to the edge and …

"Waahooooo!" screamed Friday as he leapt over and the updraft caught him. He was still falling, his glider angled downward as he began to accelerate away, but somehow he was also rising, the very air coming up to meet him.

And he was gone. He was flying.

Wednesday stared at his friend. He wasn't sure what compelled him to do what he did next, but suddenly he was setting off as well. Suddenly he was building up speed and the glider seemed to be coming to life in his hands. Now, somehow, he was approaching the edge. He shouted more out of surprise than fear. What was he doing? Dear God, this wasn't right, this wasn't natural, but … but …

…!…

He was flying. The sensation was nothing short of heaven. An adrenal bliss that possessed him utterly, but bliss nonetheless. The wind was a vivid thing under and around him, a channel and a friend, an elusive hand brushing and lifting him while always keeping its presence felt on his face as he accelerated after his friend.

The wing was a tool, an extension. It was fragile and yet reliable, it could be predicted, as could the wind it harnessed. The updraft lifted them, and a part of Wednesday's mind wondered at how easy it would be to land again. But it was only a small part of him. The last of his friends were still waiting and watching, but most of them were getting airborne, now, beginning to dart this way and that.

Could they collide? That seemed possible, likely even, and Wednesday doubted that would be a good thing. But now he saw Mother was taking to the skies once more, as well. Her wing was larger, her command of the wind more complete. She seemed to be able control her passage in ways Wednesday could not comprehend.

Suddenly she was up with him, smiling and even letting go with one hand to wave quickly. Her voice came to him now, over the rush of the wind, "Well done, Wednesday God! Well done! Try to follow me." And she dipped her wing, angling downward and speeding away as she did so.

Wednesday dipped as she did, perhaps even a little too much, and the effect was breathtaking. He pulled back a little and the wing reacted. Such response. He had to be careful. He surged onward.

He did not notice one of his other friends, Sunday, lose control and veer too close to the cliff face. He did not notice as the boy's wing bounced and cracked on the rock edifice and the boy began falling toward the water below. The scream did not reach Wednesday.

He was focused on Mother, and she was moving off to catch Friday, still pulling away, and still whooping with joy at the sheer madness and wonder of it all.

She moved with grace despite her greater size and weight, and Wednesday longed to emulate it, to follow her lead. He longed to match her ability and he watched her intently as they flew off. She was not flying directly for Friday, she was seeking and finding eddies, looking for lift, reading the way the air moved and playing the wind like an instrument.

He followed her, but soon found he had to go not where she had *been*, but where the air she had ridden was *now*. Sometimes he could go faster than her, but sometimes the whirl had passed when he got there. Friday was below them now. Wednesday was vaguely aware of that. Somehow they were both moving up on him and rising above him at the same time.

It was beautiful but it was hard, and she was getting farther and farther ahead. He was loosing the thread of her movement. Soon her passage was already gone when he got there. But no sooner had he lost her trail than suddenly she was dropping. He used that, pushing himself down with greater emphasis to gain speed. Closing on her as she circled down on Friday.

He had seen them at last and was trying to maintain his speed, but his altitude was all but gone now. He was almost at the tops of the waves. Wednesday became aware of the ocean now, and of the distance they had raced from the shore. He saw Mother come up on Friday. Saw her shouting to him, saw her try to help him regain his altitude. Wednesday was coming up on them now too.

But he had also sacrificed his height to catch them, and as he approached he realized he was too low. He would not reach them. There was the occasional lift as he passed over a large wave, but here, at the border of air and water, the air changed, became something wilder as it was pushed and pulled by its thicker, more viscous cousin below.

The crash came without warning. One moment he was above the crest, the next he was in the trough and then the wall of water was on him. His wing seemed to collapse under the weight of the water and for a moment he panicked that it would drag him under. But it came away with surprising ease and soon his head was above the swell again.

He had not swum much before coming to live with Mother, but enough that he could tread water. He could not see Mother or Friday. He could not even see the cliff. He could only see ocean and soon he became worried. The boat was not long coming though. It breached a crest a short distance from him and powered down toward him with skill. It came close but did not overwhelm him. His friend Sunday, who had hit the cliff earlier, was already onboard, as were two others.

He was helped aboard by a smiling but silent helmsman who then powered off once more. Wednesday looked for and found Mother still flying, but she was alone now, returning to the shore and the remaining children still flying there. They found Friday bobbing not far off, frustrated that he had failed, but still elated at the flight itself.

As the boat returned the boys to the shore, Mother flew back alone and spoke to the wind. She was closing on the last of the gliders.

"They are doing well, Commander. Some better than others, but they are taking to the air with as much confidence as we could have hoped."

"Yes," came a voice into her head. "Yes, Supervisor, they are. I think you were right to approach it this way. My way would have been ... too aggressive."

"Thank you, Commander," she said. Her emotion was a strange one, she was proud of her choice, but she also knew it had been born of an exhaustive study of the data. Mother had looked at the training of the pilot named Banu. She had taken from that what she could emulate and removed what she could not.

These children were not Banu. In many ways their upbringing had been similar. In many ways it had been worse. Even their names had fallen victim to the regime, their forenames but days of the week or months of the year, or sometimes even just numbers, such was the affection the state had felt for them. But they were still expected to have love for a state that had relegated them to ignominy, and, as such, their surnames were but prostrations to a cruel leader, the one they knew as the Great One, or just as God.

But that was not the most important difference between these orphans and the one called Banu. They also lacked a vital element in their lives: Quavoce. They had been plucked straight from the most repressive and misinformed regime in the world. Plucked right from under the noses of the arriving UN and TASC forces as their once Supreme Leader caved to the demands of the interlopers.

She could not easily replicate the promise of infinite protection that Banu's trust in Quavoce gave her. She must build that trust herself. She must give them what Quavoce had given Banu: confidence. She must let them fail and see that it would not be that bad. She must let them discover this world piece by piece.

"Yes, Supervisor," said the commander, "this has been very successful so far. I am keen to see how they progress. I can see from the data that some are showing more promise than others."

"Indeed, Commander. Though they fell among the first, the two I just flew out with show some of the strongest progress."

"Good, good," said the voice in Mother's head. "I know it seems strange but that is a good sign, Supervisor. A very good sign indeed."

"It is?" said Mother to the air, as she came up on the last of the gliders.

"Yes, Supervisor, it is. It means there is likely a range, as we had expected. And if there is a range then we can assume that Amadeu and Quavoce cannot have been so lucky as to hit the top of that range on their first attempt. Which means that somewhere among this first class, and among those that will follow them, may be pilots who can beat young Banu."

The commander's voice held an air of triumph. Mother did not share such premature confidence, though she quietly believed in the process she had developed. The truth would come out, the data would not lie. The best would rise and the others would fall. But the commander was right in one thing. Matching Banu would not do. They must beat her if they were to have a chance at victory.

# Chapter 22: Riotous

The H5 Shinkansen bullet train moved at a pace that was merely an echo of its above ground cruising speed, but it still sped along at 85mph, and the effect within the Seikan Tunnel was akin to a piston within an engine.

Inside, Nagate Tanakaze did not feel the pressure, only the relatively gentle sway and rattle of the train's progress. The view through the windows held only the black-grey blur of the passing walls. Above him was over 240 meters of rock and ocean, but down here that was all obscured. And even if he had have been able to see the tumultuous ocean above him, he was lost to the outside world, anyway. His attention was absorbed by an article he was reading.

It described the purpose of Hekaton from the perspective of one Shinobu Matsuoka, the wealthy and prominent businessman who had come out as a vocal supporter of the work of the newly publicized organization known as TASC. He was describing some of the technologies he had already become privy to and how they would help the Japanese economy, even as they helped support the coming war effort as a whole.

The war effort. The war itself was still very hard to grasp. The who and why of it lost in a dizzying array of perspectives, educated and otherwise, that were filling every second of television time and every byte of the internet.

Nagate only knew what he did *not* believe. He did not believe that the images of the flaring engines being referred to as the Armada was the second coming of Jesus, Isa, the Four Horsemen of the Apocalypse, or Godzilla for that matter. And he was pretty sure it wasn't a hoax either. But that still left a great deal of room for conjecture.

Room that was being amply filled by even the most educated and reasonable of pundits. Conspiracy theories ran amuck and it was obvious that most, if not all of them, were untrue. But where in the sea of opinions, demagoguery, and vitriol did the truth lie?

If the truth was there at all, of course. Maybe it was all a smokescreen. Maybe it was all a giant diversion from the real threat. Like the 'gadgets.' He resisted the urge to start browsing for those again. He had been up all the previous night watching YouTube demos of some of the more elaborate and apparently soon to be available ones.

The spinal interface was something else. It was being developed by this agency called TASC for the war effort, apparently, but as a gesture of goodwill and, no doubt, an enticement to believe their version of events, it was going to be made available through a select set of tech companies across the globe, Matsuoka Industries notably among them.

Some governments were discussing blocking it, including Japan's own, until it could be tested further, but they had been clever enough to also demonstrate its use in tandem with the new prosthetics that TASC was also offering, prosthetics that would benefit millions of elderly and infirm people across the globe. To block such a thing would be political suicide. At the very least, the power elite of Japan, many of them notably elderly themselves, would no doubt soon be making use of some version of the new systems.

He felt a rumble under the bass hum of the train and looked up. It was something separate from the usual rattle and hum, something just under the surface. But as he tried to place the sound, the feeling really, it vanished, like a buzzing insect just out of sight, imperceptible.

Now that his attention was brought into the present, he couldn't help but notice the group of tourists arguing farther down the car. They were from Tokyo, or maybe Kobe, and they were debating avidly the same topic as everyone else. As usual there were those that spoke with the certainty and authority of some grand understanding that somehow only they had figured out, and there were those that argued reason, though usually without as much conviction.

It was the age-old conflict of willed ignorance versus true curiosity. Curiosity would always find the truth in the end, but so often it would only win out after an age of battling through dogma and instinctive fear. The oldest battle of all, the clash of science with mythology, of religion versus rationale, had never been more intense than it was now.

The fabric of society, Nagate feared, was being tested, and it was starting to fray.

But it was not just *starting* to fray. It was coming undone. The bass rumble became louder now. Nearly a quarter of a mile ahead the driver of the train tried to make out a darkness in the tunnel, an end to the stream of neon lighting vanishing off into the distance, now shortening somehow. A blackness coming toward him. The shout came through his radio, not so much an order as a scream of warning.

Only one word.

Breech.

Nagate felt it again now. Louder. It was unsettling. It felt like the ground through which the train was flying was moving as well. Like waves under a boat, a transferred momentum, a received movement. But this was no boat and the rails underneath them should not be going anywhere.

Suddenly the noise was rising exponentially and the movement was rising with it. Earthquake? No, that could not be, thought Nagate. Not this deep. This was supposed to be …

The train stopped. It did not slow. It stopped, the engine car hitting a wall of water that was moving almost as fast as the train itself, but in the opposite direction. Suddenly Nagate's world was only madness and pain. The train was crumpling. Pressures driving it forward into itself as air and then water pushed its sides inward. Then the walls were liquid, blackness rushing in, a pounding in his ears as the pressure rocketed upward and then …

- - -

There had been no terrorist attack in Vienna a week before, of course, not in the sense that the public had been led to believe. But as events snowballed around the globe, that cover story vanished into a haze of similar ones, ones with real truth behind them.

It seemed to reach a peak with the attack of the Asahara Joshu Cult that blew up a Shinkansen train while in the Seikan Tunnel. Even with the force of the detonation, the tunnel had almost held, but the pressures had eventually rended the rock around it, and it had sheered.

Images of the thunderous geyser of water erupting from each end of the tunnel as it had filled had shocked an already reeling world. Three trains and their two thousand passengers were lost forever in the depths.

In Rome, an extremist Catholic group attempted to storm the Vatican. Apparently they sought to 'restore the Papal State' after the pope attempted a limited acknowledgement of the coming Armada's true purpose, and a tepid call to support TASC's work. While the fanatics were quelled with brutal force by a quietly efficient Vatican Police, their point of view was not going to die so easily.

In New York, a boat loaded with explosives rammed one of the pylons of the Brooklyn Bridge, a pointless but nonetheless shocking act committed by an enraged people seeking to punish what they now saw as an oppressive oligarchy, spreading lies about alien invasions in order to legitimize further civil rights abuses.

In Brussels, seven nations filed for succession from the European Union, mostly limited to smaller and financially moribund states, but notably including Spain, which was claiming damages for not being more involved in TASC's activities, and more importantly in its technological advances.

But while some regions splintered, others were uniting. Through a combination of religious fervor and a return to some more distasteful leadership practices usually stopped by a more attentive world community, a band of nations was gathering strength and momentum. At its core were Iran, Syria, and Egypt, with large parts of Iraq and even some border regions of Jordan showing signs of allegiance.

It was actually being spearheaded by the ayatollah who had catalyzed the entire crisis, but he was wisely allowing others to take a front seat as the head of the military junta in Egypt rallied former allies to a battle cry as old as time.

At the center of their ire, as it had been a thousand times before, was Israel, on the menu once more, they hoped, as the UN crumbled and NATO scrambled for control.

Ironically, it was a new Russian secretariat that reached out to Jim Hacker to pass on his concerns about it. He was leading a cowed nation, and doing so far more reasonably than any of his predecessors going back nearly a hundred years. But that only made his position all the more tenuous, and his call all the more brave.

Maybe he called Jim because the Russian administrator had once held a role similar to Jim's own, only Peter had been working under a borderline megalomaniac named Yuri Svidrigaïlov.

"Mr. Hacker, thank you for taking my call," said Secretariat Uncovsky. "Are you sure you are comfortable speaking in Russian?"

"It is my pleasure to, Mr. Secretariat," said Jim, able to actually enjoy the benefits of his spinal interface for the first time as Minnie allowed him to speak Russian as though he was a native. "And I am most comfortable speaking in Russian, if you will promise to forgive any errors or mispronunciations I may make along the way."

It was a nicety. There would be no errors.

"Far from it, Mr. Hacker, I must say your command of my tongue is most admirable," said Secretariat Uncovsky, with unfeigned respect.

"You flatter me, Mr. Secretariat. But if I may, I would like to take this opportunity to say it is most pleasant to hear from you. I hope this is the first of many such calls between TASC and the Russian Republic."

Peter Uncovsky was equally hopeful. To say he saw the folly of his former leader's actions against TASC would be a gross understatement. He had watched the man literally be obliterated by Neal Danielson's wrath. And if he was honest, he could not deny the justness of the action that had seen him promoted to acting party leader, if only because few now dared take the job.

But fearing TASC was not the same as agreeing with them, and he would find little support in the Kremlin if he aired his true opinion of how much Russia should backtrack from its former expansionist efforts and put that energy instead into supporting the efforts of the group he was talking to now.

"A hope I share, Mr. Hacker. Though if I am equally candid, I will say that not all in Moscow share my enthusiasm. How that will change in the light of recent revelations I cannot know, but you would be surprised how far people will go to defend misguided action rather than admit fault."

He spoke of the attack on Rolas. He spoke of the destruction which now appeared to have been a strike against one of Earth's main arteries into the very region they were soon to need to defend.

Jim did not dwell on the topic. "On the contrary, Mr. Secretariat, I would not be that surprised at all, I am afraid." There was a moment of shared understanding, and then Jim went on, "But I am being rude. You are a very busy man and I have yet to inquire after the reason for your call. How may the Terrestrial Allied Space Command be of assistance to Russia?"

Peter allowed himself a smile. This man was every bit the diplomat Peter had remembered from their brief encounters over the years. They both knew that Jim's time was just as important as Peter's, perhaps more so, given the current crisis.

Very well, he would get to the point, "Of course, Mr. Hacker. I call ... more to offer warning than to request anything, per se. I call because my intelligence services have received notice of a growing conspiracy that I believe will concern you. I am very aware that the undeniably efficient operatives of TASC and its allies will have seen signs of the same, but I wanted to make sure that those signs were getting appropriate attention."

He paused, deliberately, but Jim did not interrupt. He had a pretty good idea what the Russian leader was referring to, but he knew better than to staunch such a rare glimpse of cooperation, and so Peter went on, "I speak, of course, of rising calls for action from Persia to Egypt. But that is not the root of my concern."

Jim's curiosity was peeked, and when Peter paused, clearly reticent to go too far, Jim gently coaxed the other man along, "That is very interesting, Mr. Secretariat. While such matters are not really my purview, I am, indeed, aware of the protests in Tehran, Mosul, and Luxor. We had assumed they lacked the political and military backing to go much further than words. Do you have reason to suspect otherwise?"

Again a pause. Peter was treading carefully. Eventually he spoke up, "No, no, Mr. Hacker. Well, not really. But ... as you know, my nation has enjoyed much closer ties to the Iranian government over the past decades than our counterparts in the West."

That was putting it mildly, but Peter quickly went on, "Of course, no one in the Russian leadership supports any illegal action against the sovereign nation of Israel. But ..."

Jim was growing a touch tired of the dissemination, but he had to let Peter Uncovsky get there on his own. Both men knew that Peter was no doubt being watched, not only by the countless international observers forced upon Russia since its surrender after the Hungarian War, but also by his own people. By hard-line remnants that would take months or even years to root out, if they ever could be.

"Well, since the justified actions of NATO forces against the Russian Army in Hungary, well, the military in Russia has been understandably splintered. And it has come to my attention that elements of it, not officially mandated elements, of course ..."

He over-emphasized that part a little too much, thought Jim. He was performing for the call's silent partners. They could not object to his releasing this information if he claimed he did not think any official member of the government was involved.

He went on, "... but it has come to my attention that fringe parts of the Russian military machine, and more importantly its weaponry, may have ... been allowed ... to fall into the hands of certain Iranian factions."

Jim caught his breath inadvertently, a rare lapse. Shit, he thought. What kind of weaponry?

"May I ask," said Jim, "if you might know what weaponry we may be speaking of?"

"I cannot be sure, Mr. Hacker," said Peter, his tone confident, as if to say he was not holding back in this aspect, even if he must necessarily do so elsewhere. "I cannot be sure. Though we have seen signs that it is not limited to rifles or ammunition. Other than that I cannot confirm at this time."

"Mr. Secretariat, my appreciation for your candor here cannot be overstated. I will look into this immediately. Out of respect for the voluntary nature of this call, I will leave it to you whether or not to report this discussion to the NATO observation team."

"I appreciate that, Mr. Hacker."

They would find out either way, no doubt. As would others. The call came to a close, and Jim was already acting even as he wrapped up the conversation with the obligatory niceties.

*Jim:* '¿minnie, did you get all that?'

*Minnie:* <of course, jim. as did ayala and saul. they have been monitoring the call, and ayala asks that you contact her immediately once you are done.>

She does, does she? Jim frowned. Jim had been focused on who in Peter's government might be listening in. It appeared he should have been thinking the same about his own.

*Jim:* 'i will, minnie, thank you.'

- - -

Five minutes later, Jim was indeed speaking with Ayala and her chief of staff, Saul. It took everything he had not to lose his temper at his having been eavesdropped upon, but he stayed his wrath, and focused instead on the task at hand.

*Jim:* 'as for peter uncovsky, i think we have to assume his intentions are good. despite his affiliation with svidrigaïlov, my impression of him has always been of a pragmatist, if maybe more of a bureaucrat than a leader. either way, though, he has never struck me as conniving. he did not want this role, and i doubt very much that he is working for his own ends here.'

*Saul:* 'my files show the same analysis. i would take this at face value. maybe even more so. he was clearly worried about repercussions from within his own leadership and may want to offer even more.'

*Ayala:* 'yes, that seems clear. very well then, so we will assume that if anything he was forced to understate the situation.'

Saul called up a specific quote and sent it to them all [we have seen signs that it is not limited to rifles or ammunition].

*Saul:* '¿do you think there could still be tech ten units out there?'

*Ayala:* 'that is the rub, isn't it, saul. not limited to. that leaves a lot of room for interpretation.'

*Jim:* '¿may i suggest, ayala, that we try to help him out a bit?'

*Ayala:* '¿how so?'

*Jim:* 'well, i won't ask for details of whatever operation you and saul are no doubt going to mount to investigate this further, but maybe we could also consider helping mr. uncovsky out a little.'

*Saul:* '¿how, exactly, could we help mr. uncovsky out, jim?'

*Jim:* 'well, saul, we could speak with the nato observers and tell them we have reason to think mr. uncovsky is suspect, and that we want to put a team of spezialists on him. not a big team, but enough to offer him some protection from whatever faction within his own government he clearly suspects of participating in this.'

*Ayala:* 'i like it, jim. i like it very much. it will allow us to protect him should there be some power play, and also bolster his reputation within his own government by making him appear to be a problem for us.'

*Jim:* 'and it will allow us to communicate directly with him via the team's subspace comms, allowing him to share, in confidence, any further information he may have, either now or down the line.'

*Ayala:* 'thank you, jim. that is an excellent idea. ok then, i believe that is all for now. with your permission, jim, saul and i will leave you so we can talk further about the more 'involved responses' which, as you say, you do not wish to know the details of.'

*Jim:* 'of course, ayala. ¿you will let me know when the spezialists are in place with peter?'

*Ayala:* 'you will notified immediately when they are in place, jim. he is your asset, after all. i will need you to work him.'

Asset. Work him. Jim had never had a taste for such terms. His appetite for them was not growing the more they became part of his daily routine. Neither was his appetite for working with Ayala. He understood the importance of her work, but sometimes he feared that her zeal bordered on zealotry, a semantic difference, perhaps, but an important one. Distasteful work was sometimes necessary. But you didn't have to enjoy it quite as much as she sometimes appeared to.

# Chapter 23: The Farm

*Madeline:* 'quadrant m2 online. satyendra, please isolate control and set maintenance protocol.'

*Satyendra:* 'quadrant m2 controls isolated, madeline. maintenance protocol uploading now.'

Madeline felt the flow of data. Satisfied that it was progressing as planned, she shifted her attention. That was the second bank established. They were empty for now but already the fifty pods in Quadrant M1 were starting to be filled. The progress from here would only accelerate.

She opened a channel, a line back to Earth. It would have to be old-time, and 2D, the larger, long-range subspace tweeter they were constructing here on the moon would not be online for another two or three months, at least.

"Good morning, Moira," she said, as the line connected.

There was a long pause then Moira's voice came into Madeline's inner-ear, "Well, it's good evening here, Madeline." She was still a little meek, even if she had become something close to a preeminent mind in the field that she was now at the bleeding edge of.

"Yes, well, morning, evening, all starts to become a bit hazy after a while, doesn't it?" she laughed a little and waited.

"Especially here. I haven't been outside in a week, and not just because of work. William tells me it is minus twenty out there!"

Madeline snorted, "Well, I wish I could promise you better up here, but no such luck, I'm afraid. Right now the wrecker I am piloting is standing with its head in the sun and its feet in the shade. I'd love to tell you that means it is enjoying a lunar sunrise, but as it is standing on Malapert Mountain, the sun is really just spinning around the horizon forever, never rising or falling, which means my feet are freezing and my head is boiling."

"Huh, that sounds … unpleasant. Though the view must be spectacular," replied Moira, and Madeline did indeed take a moment to appreciate the sight through her Remote Construction Robot's eyes, then she rewound the view over the past hours and watched the sun as it moved backward around the horizon. It was indeed a breathtaking sight.

"Yes, now that you mention it, it is actually. I had started to get used to it, amazingly enough, being outside all the time. Not that I am ever outside, you know, really. I am in a bunker steadily being dug out of a lava tube, if you can believe that. I haven't opened my eyes in nearly twenty-four hours, even though I've been working nearly that entire time."

After a moment Moira's voice came through once more. Knowing that she was being redeployed to the moon, she had been studying up. "Malapert Mountain, near the Shackleton Crater, nearly permanent sunshine. Comms array location and main hangar location. So you know, your wrecker's head is probably around 100°C while your feet are less than -170°C. Ouch! Makes Deception Island sound like heaven!"

Madeline laughed. "Yes, that sounds about right. So I doubt you'll be doing very much strolling around up here, either." Normally, perhaps, Madeline would have waited for some response, witty or otherwise, but the exigencies of distant laser-based communications encouraged longer statements rather than banter, and so she went on, "Which brings me to what I wanted to talk to you about. As you know, we are getting ready to ramp up operations here. We have our first ileminite mining platform at Mare Humorum nearly ready, and our water extraction works here at the South Pole are well underway. Which brings us to your part."

She waited. Moira had been very busy in the many months since she joined TASC to replace the lost Birgit Hauptman. Now they were sending her off world as well, though this time in a less spectacular and far more deliberate fashion. She would be travelling with a smaller Exo-Atmospheric Light Lifter that was being designated for lunar operations and was very nearly ready for launch.

The EALL was already being dubbed the Cool J, rather predictably, a name that was helping put Moira slightly more at ease with her coming departure from the planet. But depart she must. A cadre of students she had trained would remain at Districts Two and Three, but with the last of the EAHLs and Big Feet already finished and in motion, attention was moving to actual weaponry production at last.

"Yes, Madeline," said Moira eventually, her tone becoming more serious. "I have been reviewing the potential Helium-3 mining sites at Oceanus Procellarum. It is still too early to be absolutely certain, but it does look like we will be able to find a dual-use site there."

She sent a file up through the multipurpose system they were speaking through. While their voices, and the minimal bandwidth they required, were able to be forwarded in real time, the data packet detailing Moira's analysis would have to join a queue. They continued to chat regardless.

"That is great news, Moira," said Madeline, "thank you. I will assign a Wrecker and a probe team to the potential site as soon as I get your data packet. We should have confirmation of viability either way by the time you are inbound."

There was a pause and then, "That's great," said Moira, a touch meekly. Then with more verve, "And there are actually three potential sites, ranked by probability, in my analysis. I'll leave it to you whether to assign more teams or have them look at each in order ... of course."

Madeline smiled. "I'll take a look and make a call based on how strong the data is. But don't worry about making recommendations to me. Once you are up here, Moira, this will be your baby. I am only here to supervise until the subspace link is established back to Earth. After that ..."

After that, Moira would be in charge. In charge of the construction of the Lunar Missile-Mine Phalanx. Once they had production in full flow here, and on the recently tethered

Hekaton, they would switch all available production on Earth to the making of its own mines for transport up its ever-growing number of elevators.

The moon, Hekaton, and Earth. Three massive phalanxes. Three massive salvos. Once combined they would form a tidal wave of self-propelling mass to launch at the coming Armada. They would continue production up until the last minute. Three years, four months, three days, five hours, and twenty-three minutes. Approximately. They would continue production until they knew that they had no longer: until they had to launch whatever they had in order for it to reach the Armada before the Mobiliei were close enough to make out the very real and massive changes humanity was making to its very world.

For just as the appearance of Hekaton had set off a chain reaction across Earth, so would the sight of its arrival signal to the coming Armada that all was not as it seemed at the terminus point of its great mission. Once it was close enough to distinguish the new moon now orbiting around Earth, the Mobiliei Council would know for sure that the satellites were dead, and that all was far from peaceful on the western front.

They had an estimated date when that would become physically possible, given John and Quavoce's knowledge of the Armada's sensors. Possible to see some evidence of Hekaton, that is, but nothing conclusive. They had another, later date when it would become all but certain. They would plan to hit them between these dates. Hit them with everything they could muster.

After they had launched their swarms of missile-mines, all attention would switch to building up the big guns: the fleet of Skalms to engage with their fighting craft, and the larger, fixed particle weapons to attack the Mobiliei fleet-craft. Then they would brace for the far closer, far bloodier combat that they knew would then come with whatever embittered and emboldened remnant of the Mobiliei Armada survived the first strike.

## Chapter 24: Preemptive Strike

They had requested landing permission as a diplomatic mission well in advance, with all the accorded benefits that implied, and they had been summarily denied. They had sent the request again, through multiple channels, and again had been rebuffed. But the date of their arrival had stayed the same on every request, as had the language. They had not said they would like to come. They had said they *would* come.

And so they did.

The StratoJet came in at altitude. They approached from the north, from over the Caspian Sea, not so much to sneak by the Iranian Air Force but to limit the amount of time that force would have to react before they were over Tehran space.

They also came up on Iranian airspace at Mach 2, only slowing to more politically acceptable speeds once they had crossed the border proper, and the calls had begun.

"Unidentified aircraft. You have entered Iranian airspace. You are instructed to turn around immediately or you will be fired upon. I repeat. Turn around immediately or you will be fired upon."

The voice had originally come through in Persian. After they had responded, also in Persian, and stated their purpose and intention, the voice had changed to English. It somewhat undermined their claim that the craft remained 'unidentified' despite their clear report as to their identity, but what was Jim to do? He was nervous. And he was all but alone.

This was not his normal purview. But he was not without recourse. In the cabin with him were five Phase Eleven automatons, fully armed and ready for bear. And the plane was being piloted remotely by none other than Banu herself. Should they actually fire upon him, she was more than capable of getting them out of trouble, in theory, anyway.

"Iranian air traffic control, this is TASC Diplomatic Mission. As I said before, I have formally notified the Iranian government of my visit on multiple occasions and will be coming in to land at Mehr Abad International Airport shortly. I request landing authorization, but if denied I will land anyway. I repeat, I will land anyway. I have an important message for the grand ayatollah, the president, and the Iranian Parliament, which must be delivered in person. I am an official representative of the Terrestrial Allied Space Command, and as such enjoy its full protection. I come in peace."

He waited once more. He had said it three times now. The main difference being that the first two times there had not been three Dassault F1 Mirages on his tail. He glanced back at them with virtual eyes once more. He was strapped in to a gravity gel-couch, just in case Banu should have to do some close quarters maneuvering. But he was fully plugged into the plane's sensor systems, as well as Minnie's many eyes above, and it was through these that he studied the three fighters falling in behind him.

*Minnie:* <i would not concern yourself with them, jim. they are fifteen years old, at least, and the design is five years older than that again. even their missiles cannot catch you.>

Jim went to speak, to pretend confidence, but Banu spoke up instead.

*Banu:* 'don't worry, mr. hacker. i have flown against far more enemies with far faster planes. they won't catch us. and if you need me to, i can chase them down instead. i can take them so easily.'

Jim staunched a new fear. As bold as this maneuver was, Jim had not come here to start a war, he had come to stave one off.

*Neal:* 'don't worry, jim. banu knows this is not that kind of mission. ¿don't you, banu?'

Jesus, but this was a strange conversation, thought Jim. Did Neal just use baby talk with the pilot of the plane? The most feared pilot in the world, at least until Amadeu and Minnie trained up a new cadre. Banu acquiesced, clearly a little bored with it all already. And hopefully it would remain beautifully boring for the rest of the flight, thought Jim. Hopefully they would be able to land without incident.

He studied the Iranian jets, aware that eyes far more trained than his were watching them far more closely. Watching for the slightest hint of action.

The voice blared out its warning once more, and as an emphasis radar-lock alarms filled the StratoJet's systems.

Still they stayed their course. Jim repeated his Public Service Announcement. If they were going to refuse to acknowledge him then he would do the same. He was essentially daring them to shoot him down. It was a dare he would lose only if they didn't fear the repercussions. He was making a gamble. Or rather Neal was making a gamble, with Jim's life.

Either they would fire on him and miss, in which case TASC would lambast them in the world theater and demand an audience to avoid all out war. Or they would fire on him and hit, meaning they did indeed have tech ten capable units, in which case ... TASC would lambast them in the world theater and demand an audience to avoid all out war, only Neal would also probably take the leashes off Banu and whatever Spezialist forces Ayala no doubt had roaming the Iranian countryside below, even now.

Or they would actually let him land. Once on the ground, the same three choices started all over again, only at closer quarters, right up until he either had some kind of dialogue with a representative of the Iranian government, or Neal forced the Iranians to give him the impetus he needed to kick things up a notch.

It was an ugly looking decision tree, and Jim sure as hell would not have deigned to climb it if he hadn't have been the one who had come up with the whole scheme in the first place. It had been all he could do to offer an alternative to the ever more martial options being considered by the rest of TASC's leadership.

He stared at the planes, focusing in on the tips of their missiles. Note to self, he thought, stop coming up with plans.

- - -

Far away, the various powerful players in the intensifying game watched the plane. They watched from the many eyes of Minnie and they watched from the eyes of Iran's own capable military machine. As tensions mounted, the world began to tune in. The flight's progress was being aired around the planet by Jim's own people, with Wislawa giving a running commentary to any station willing to broadcast it.

But there were many other pundits interpreting the coverage, voicing wildly different opinions and predictions on how it would or should play out.

In Tehran, Ahmad Sayeedi's eyes were glued to the screens in front of him, as they always were. "Switch to camera 2, zoom. Audio to Bayazid in three, two …"

Bayazid Kutty took the cue smoothly, speaking from a spot outside the Vikal Abad Palace that was one of the ayatollah's main residences. It was far away from Tehran, in Mashad, in the far east of the country. It was a city that Shahim had once skirted with the fugitives Jennifer Falster and Jack Toranssen, before escaping north into Turkmenistan. It was a different time now, though. A different city. The countryside had been decimated by the plague, and the city now stood as a hollow shell of its former glory.

Only the palace, a resplendent provincial capitol, remained whole, corpulent even, nourished as it was by the public and private fortunes of its prime resident, the grand ayatollah.

"No word yet from the Supreme Leader's spokespeople, though I am informed they are monitoring this illegal violation of our sovereign airspace closely. The world watches as the interlopers from the illegitimate Western military state known as TASC barge into our country, uninvited. Only the ongoing reasonableness of the grand ayatollah prevents them from being fired upon by the Air Force."

The man waffled on, like other pundits around the world, expounding mandated opinions as though they were their own. He was not lying, per se, just omitting some minor points. Like the fact that it was not only 'reasonableness' that was precluding action against poor Jim Hacker in his little plane, but a very real doubt as to whether they were even able to take the plane down.

And then, of course, there was the swathe of information the reporter was not privy to, on both sides. The stratagems and hidden assets of both sides that were on the move. The plans that were forming and reforming as events unfolded. Tools being honed, blades being sharpened as the various factions braced for whatever was to come next.

No matter what the soundtrack was, no one could doubt that the eyes of the world were turning to the little plane, as had been the intention. The flight was being broadcast around the world. And in the end it would probably be that which would save Jim. A powerful spotlight was on him, and it would light his way all the way to Mehr Abad, banishing any militant intent like scurrying shadows fleeing the beam.

With the world holding its breath, the scene was bringing into focus the two main sides of the debate raging around the planet, as Neal had intended. For now, denial started to fade into the background as this very tangible sight penetrated homes, offices, and bars; computers, phones, and televisions.

It was symbolic of the greater dichotomy of thought around the world. And while the skeptics still shouted it all down in their call for ... well, for exactly what they did not know, more and more people were coming to see these two more active sides as the real debate. Was this the beginning of humanity's fight against the coming Armada, or its fight within itself to scour themselves of whatever alien influence was already present?

"I will stay here, as we hope you will all stay with IRIB News, reporting from across Iran on this incredible action by the Western interlopers."

The voices babbled on, and far away again, a commander reached out to a supervisor.

"Mother, are any of them ready?" he asked.

There was silence as progress was reviewed against the supervisor's understanding of the current situation.

"No, Commander, I am afraid not, not to intervene here. The first class will have graduates from Flight School to Fight School in a matter of days, but then we still have to see how they perform in the combat simulators. I have high hopes," a ping appeared in the commander's mind with statistics and performance data on four children as the supervisor went on, "but to send them into combat at this stage would be ... unwise."

The commander was disappointed, but not surprised. Nor was he angry. This must be done correctly. When they revealed themselves to the world they would have to do so from a position of overwhelming superiority. They would only have one chance. Either they would prove themselves indomitable or they would be obliterated. Very well, sighed the commander, they would have to see how this charade played out.

For now.

# Chapter 25: Reaching Out

Jim Hacker stepped from the plane and into the harsh light of the Iranian sun. Tehran was a city of climactic shift, bridging the border between the broad desert plain of the south and the great Alborz Mountains that separated it from the Caspian Sea to the north. Here in the south of the city it was often ten to fifteen degrees hotter than in the northern districts, where the city began to climb the slopes of snow-capped Tochal Mountain.

He was greeted, not surprisingly, by a bank of soldiers and military vehicles. They were not shy at pointing their weapons at him, though he noticed that a single, clearly senior officer stood well out in front.

*Ayala:* 'that is a good sign, jim. if he was behind the soldiers i would tell you to stay behind the phase elevens as well.'

Jim nodded, though he did not know why. Then he realized that she was as aware of his movements as he was. He was being monitored both inside and out, and both by his friends and his enemies. He hoped the rest of the world was watching just as closely.

He breathed deeply. He was dressed smartly, in a suit. A notable contrast from the two Phase Eleven automatons that had lumbered down onto the tarmac before him. His only concession to security, other than the military machines that formed his escort, was a body suit under his more conventional one, and a set of glasses not unlike the ones Cara had worn into her meeting with the minister in Vienna.

Not that Jim knew of Cara, or the deadly face-off she had been forced into. The details of the minister's betrayal and his brutal conversion back to the cause had been lost in Ayala's ever-growing files. All Jim knew was that the signal from his little glasses was being broadcast far and wide, an insurance policy similar to Cara's, though his audience was far larger than just a vigilant Hektor.

As he stepped forward, leaving his automata behind, he hoped the officer's seniors would be taking note of that signal he was broadcasting, taking note of how the view being broadcast by TASC was from him, not his guardians. He would not take the robots with him, but they would remain ready. Ready to come for him at a moment's notice. Jim hoped they would see that, even without the dangerous-looking machines, he was still in constant contact with TASC, and the world at large.

He stepped up to the officer and extended his hand, noting that the officer had an earpiece. He was clearly receiving instructions. The man's expression was a changing sea of emotion. The unfortunate officer knew he had just become the focal point of an international game of brinksmanship. He waited for orders.

Someone, somewhere realized that Iran itself was being judged by whether it took that hand or not. Would it be polite or would it refuse? They were in a corner. The tiny speaker in the officer's ear sparked to life and slowly, gingerly, the officer extended his hand.

- - -

Across Tehran, a busy side street bustled with activity along an exposed section of the Karaj canal. It ran a full fifty-three kilometers right from the town of Karaj on the outskirts of the province, to the center of Tehran, supplying a good deal of the drinking water of the districts it passed through.

But it was not a river, not a natural life source, as such. Its banks were concrete, its passage clogged with the debris of a city growing too fast to keep up with itself. As the water flowed past, few gave it much thought. Few stopped to look at the murky-looking surge of life-giving liquid as they crisscrossed it on the myriad of bridges, walkways, and paths that blithely passed it by.

As millions of cars, cyclists, and pedestrians moved overhead, their disregard for their water source suited Bohdan just fine. He was moving slowly, swimming slowly, well beneath the surface, out of sight.

Somewhere else in the city was Hektor, or what was left of him. Bohdan did not like to think of what had happened to his superior and friend. It was not a choice Bohdan would have made. If he lost his legs … well, he imagined he would … well, he *didn't* imagine it really.

He had contemplated death. He had contemplated torture. He had contemplated choosing the first over the second, if he had the choice when the time came. But he did not like to think about maiming. And he did not thank Hektor too much for making him face that truth. Sure, it was a cold thing to feel anger toward his friend for getting injured, Bohdan knew that, but he just didn't want to think about having his balls in a jar somewhere for some foreign doctor to poke and prod.

Bohdan put the thought aside. Elsewhere in the region he knew his friends Tomas, Niels, Frederick, and Cara were also deployed, though he was not privy to where, none of them were, and that thought brought him back to the torture concept again. No doubt they were moving quietly, like him, wading through the murk and muck en route to predetermined stations.

He could see nothing. He swam using a small impeller built into the rebreathing tanks he carried with him. He moved by passive sensors alone. Weaving the underwater maze of trashcans, supermarket trolleys and random other flotsam and jetsam that had found its way into the waters over the decades since the canal's construction.

He knew there were more pervasive obstacles. Half a mile ahead of him, a weir across the canal would prove troublesome, no doubt. He would need help traversing that. He sensed it was time to let Minnie know where he was. Calculating he was near an overpass, he pulled up to a bank of weed that had grown out from a patch of parkland along the canal's southern border.

He didn't need much. Slowing for a moment he rolled on his back. Checking the satellite feed sweeping the area, he confirmed he was clear, then he allowed his black helmeted face to break the surface ever so slightly. He did not need long. Within moments his systems had located a passing pod satellite and were sending a tight-beamed data package containing his status and expected progress from here.

He was getting his data in return, as he always was, via a real-time subspace feed from Minnie. She was bathing the city in data, in fact. No matter what tech ten capability they might secretly have, they would not be able to decipher her encryption, and TASC was making no secret of having a presence in Tehran; indeed, it was one of the most public events the world had ever seen, rivaling even the docking of Hekaton, as the two sides jockeyed for position. No, only the Spezialists themselves remained subspace quiet. They would not make the same mistake as in Russia.

Minnie noted Bohdan's progress and let him know that she would be ready when he got to the weir. She would give him a running update on traffic patterns and give him a window when he should cross it.

He thanked her and he was gone, underwater once more. Moving on. Rolling back over and surging forward. Moving deeper into the city.

There were actually two other Spezialists across Tehran itself, the others being spread out across Iran. Niels was moving under the Jajrud overpass in even murkier waters than Bohdan, getting ever closer to the Iranian Air Force headquarters in downtown. Hektor was enjoying much more pleasant surroundings as he lay, still as stone, in the shallow waters that passed the Manzariye Gardens. It was a beautiful part of the city, and had been much easier to get to than his friends' stations were proving to be.

But it was barely half a mile from the Niavaran Palace, one of the ayatollah's many residences. If they only knew which of those palaces the ayatollah was in they would not need to be spread so thinly, but they did not know. He would appear, occasionally, for meetings or prayers, but his schedule was rarely announced beforehand, and in the meantime his movement was shrouded behind layers of decoys and doppelgangers.

Hopefully events unfolding at the International Airport would force the Supreme Leader to show his face, if only to explain why he was refusing an audience with the surprisingly brave administrator boldly and publically requesting one even now.

- - -

Neal watched the map as the pieces moved slowly into place. He was focused on Tehran, but he knew that similar assets were moving into place in Mashad and elsewhere.

*Neal at Ayala:* '¿do you think jim is going to make it?'

They looked down on the proceedings as Jim was led into an official complex off of the main airport terminal. He was standing now in a small interview room. He had been offered a seat while a representative of a representative of the government came to meet him and discuss his illegal status in Iran. Jim had chosen to remain standing.

Neal and Ayala could see the room through his eyes, even feel his heartbeat. The Iranians might make the mistake of thinking he was using his glasses to keep the public informed, but that was just one reason for the link, and just one part of it. Through the glasses and an array of other transponders, Jim was wired to his escort automata at a primal level. They would find him if they needed to. That had been Ayala and Minnie's promise.

He stood and tapped his feet nervously. Neal and Ayala did not share their conversation with him.

*Ayala at Neal:* 'i remain extremely skeptical, neal, as i have been from the start. but the mission remains a good one anyway. jim does not need to get through to the iranians, just as wislawa does not need to get through to our junta generals in cairo when she goes there later today, though for my money, i think she will have more luck than happy feet down there.'

Neal chuckled humorlessly. Poor Jim. He just wasn't wired for such excitement. Neal chose not to speculate whether he would be doing any better, and the point was moot anyway. They would no more have sent Neal to Tehran than the grand ayatollah himself would have flown into Baghdad.

*Neal at Ayala:* 'yes, this does seem like a long shot. which, of course, may make our real intentions all the more obvious. still no signs of tech ten units, i assume.'

*Minnie:* <none, neal. the spezialists on the ground will know instantly should there be subspace chatter other than ours, as will my phase elevens, of course.>

*Ayala at Neal:* 'another thing the iranians will no doubt discern themselves if they are smart, meaning they would be operating just as silent as we are.'

*Neal:* 'all true. all true.'

Neal breathed deep and allowed a part of his real senses to bleed in, allowing him to feel his body and the outside world even as he remained firmly planted in the system. His arm reached out gently to the right and sure enough, a moment later another hand grasped it. He did not open his eyes, he just relished the brief contact from Jennifer, sitting at his side during this difficult time.

This was going to be a long day. He focused on the city again.

# Chapter 26: Ad Minister

"This way, gentlemen," said Peter indignantly. He strode on purposefully down the corridor, the two Spezialists assigned by the UN observers to 'guard' him following close behind. He picked up the pace, walking with brisk steps, his aide-de-camp almost running to keep up himself.

It was pointless, of course. As if he could lose these guys. Even if he was riding his old Vyatka moped they could probably keep up with him. In fact, he could probably run faster than that old beast himself, but that was beside the point.

He strode on anyway, making a show of trying to get away from them. Seeing one of his more hardline colleagues ahead, he came to a sharp halt at the entrance to an executive bathroom. As he pushed at the door, he made a show of saying, "May I at least have some peace and privacy in *here*?" and he stomped into the toilets alone.

The two guards were used to it. They had been told by Saul to expect resistance. They had also been told that it was going to be, for the most part, bluster. The acting leader of the Russian Republic, or Republic Secretariat as the office was now called, was in fact probably more than happy to have the men at his side, and all the martial protection they afforded him.

And indeed he was. More than he would even admit to himself. The Kremlin had become a pit of vipers, even worse now as events were accelerating. He was struggling to keep his head, literally and figuratively, and was only succeeding because his opponents lacked the will and organization to take control from a man who was at least 'tolerated' by TASC. One such viper now followed him into the men's room, the one he had seen in the corridor.

"Mr. Secretariat," he said diffidently, bowing his head slightly.

"Minister," said Peter, as he washed his hands.

"Your guard dogs getting a little bothersome, Peter?" said the minister as he stepped to the urinal. It was a sign of how little regard the man had for Peter's place in the government that he used his first name.

Peter decided to pretend to take it as a sign of friendship, rather than the snub it was no doubt intended as. "Indeed, Dmitry, indeed."

After pretending to do what he had pretended to come in to the room to do, Dmitry zipped up and came to wash his hands by Peter, looking at the other man in the mirror. He seemed to think awhile, then said, "Maybe you should do something about them?"

Peter's brow furrowed. He did not reply, he merely held the other man's stare and allowed one eyebrow to rise.

Dmitry smiled patronizingly. "You know, my friend, you and I have more in common than you know. TASC is not the only power in the world. We have other friends. We have other … options."

Peter looked like he was about to speak but Dmitry brushed him off. "But what do I know of such things, Mr. Secretariat," and he went to leave.

Pausing by the door, Dmitry turned back and said in a stern tone, "I speak only of the fact that Russia is not now, and never will be, anybody's puppet."

His eyes flashed back to Peter's, full of fire, and Peter matched the look, pouring all his feigned animus for the guards into the mold of his face to fill it to the brim with righteous indignation and blustering pride. Dmitry watched Peter closely for a moment and then the other man smiled coldly, nodded once, and turned to leave.

It would only be five hours later that Dmitry would chance upon the secretariat once more, and this time drop an invite into their equally brief conversation, an invite to a chat with him and two other colleagues that evening. Peter would accept.

- - -

The minister called as soon as he received the package. He received it via messenger, as usual. It was handed to him by Karl, the only member of his security team who had survived the brush with Cara and Hektor unscathed. It was, in fact, the first sure sign he had had that his cover was not blown, that the people who had once been his customers did not know that he had been turned.

Without thought, he flexed his left foot. Without thought. It was as if it was his own foot. It even felt real, to an extent. The sensation of touch was the only thing it did not reproduce faithfully. It was not a sensation so much as receiving an e-mail about a sensation. Like a note was passed to you saying, 'hey, someone is touching your ankle here and here,' or 'just so you know, your foot is a bit chilly.'

It was much easier to ignore than sensation, though, and of course that was not always a bad thing, Rudolf supposed. It would not actually ever get too cold either; well, not as long as it was above about minus forty, which it didn't get to in even the harshest of Austrian winters. And it would never get tired, or sunburned, or old. Or if it did, it would be replaced. He had what Ayala had termed as a lifetime warranty: TASC would service or replace his new extremity, and any other limbs or organs he might need, and in return he would work for her … for life.

He breathed long and deep. It could, most definitely have been worse. In fact, Ayala had gone to some length to explain to him how much worse it could have been, and could still get, should he betray them once more. She had been very convincing.

As soon as he received the message, he was already reaching out to her, not via phone or even via the spinal tap in the back of his neck. His very nervous system was wired into his left foot, necessarily, and from there to Ayala, through a subspace tweeter built into his very sole.

*Rudolf:* 'good morning, ayala, i have received word from my contact at the syrian embassy.'

He began explaining it, but she was already reading it, through his eyes. It was not a perfect rendition. The signal from his optical cortex came to her as an echo of the real thing, such was the location and nature of the spinal interface. But along with the echoed audio input she also received, it was enough to keep a very close eye on the man she had so delicately turned.

It was an intrusion, to be sure. But she cared less than nothing for his privacy, and it was without regret or shame that she read the message directly, even as he extraneously described what it said to her.

*Rudolf:* 'my contact is requesting an update. specifically, he is asking if i have any information on the delegate landing in tehran, and whether there is a larger operation afoot. i believe he suspects that mr. hacker is a decoy.'

As she had assumed, thought Ayala. She considered the request.

*Ayala:* 'hold on, rudolf, i have to check something.'

As the minister waited, Ayala reached out to Neal and Saul. The Iranians would have been fools not to suspect something, they had known that. And that they were asking Rudolf was not really that surprising; in fact, it was potentially useful.

But their original plan, as speculative as it was, was being overshadowed now by actual real progress by one Jim Hacker. He had managed to secure a meeting with none other than three representatives of the Assembly of Experts. It was an astonishing achievement, one that might, if that meeting went well, or rather if it went perfectly, lead to an audience with the Supreme Leader himself.

They pondered this and discussed the implications. In the end, they had never really thought Jim could succeed. They had not thought he would get killed, though Ayala had accounted for that, and so, to some extent, had Neal. But succeed. They weren't sure exactly where that would put them. If they actually got an audience, what would that lead to? And how would the world react?

They discussed their options. And then they made a decision. Ayala reopened her link to a waiting minister.

*Ayala:* 'minister. i want you to continue to have credibility with our Iranian friends, so i am going to give you a data packet to share with them. it should help bolster your reputation with your former masters.'

Rudolf ignored the implied insult. Or at least he did not take the bait. "Masters indeed," he whispered to himself, making sure it did not bleed through to the link to Ayala. "I never worked for those idiots in Iran, and I do not work for you either."

He felt almost perverse saying it, like a child whispering insults to their father's back after being chastised. But he got a little bolder now, though he still did not broadcast, of course, as he said, "I am my own fucking master, you uppity little Jewish bitch. I have never worked for anyone but myself, and I still don't."

He stretched his foot once more, but this time with relish, like it was a prized possession, and indeed it was a magnificent piece of machinery. He tried to convince himself this had all been for the best, that once again he had come out on top, that even after being caught he was still in charge, still winning.

Miles away, Ayala listened in, felt every movement of his body and eavesdropped on his whispered tirade. She smiled. Nothing amused her more than seeing a once proud predator leashed. Not that this was much of a predator. He was a mere hyena, a dingo bucking and whining at its collar, gnawing on its chain. Her smile turned to a sneer. Little Jewish bitch, eh. But it is you who is the bitch, my friend, and without further thought, she terminated the link.

A subroutine would continue to monitor his behavior, and either update her or some analyst on Saul's team if he did anything else of note.

His brief part in this was probably coming to a close soon anyway.

- - -

The meeting Peter Uncovsky was invited to was a small one. With a brush of his hand, he dismissed the Spezialists at the door and sighed deeply as it was closed in their faces.

He looked each of the men seated in the room in the eye. These were not his friends. These were his rivals, he had no doubt about that. They were not even each others' friends. But strange times made for strange bedfellows, and with a nod of approval he stepped up to each in turn and took their hands.

"Welcome, Mr. Secretariat," said Dmitry, as if he was welcoming the leader of his government to a club Peter should be honored to be a member of. But it was a club Peter would be loath to be a member of, even if he really wanted to be the leader of this government.

That said, Peter knew that here, in the hands of these three men, lay the real power in Russia. Like a wounded bear, Russia may be cowed for now, but it would be a fool indeed who would underestimate Russia's might, even when injured. These men had known too much power in their lives, and too much liberty to exercise that power. They had no more intention of becoming a cog in TASC's machine than they had of ceding control to a bureaucrat like Peter Uncovsky.

But maybe, they thought, Peter could be used, as either lightning rod or puppet, in this time of regrouping and rebuilding. As the bear licked its wounds, maybe they could use Peter to fend off predators or rivals, and if he got himself killed in the process, then so be it.

Peter was surprised when, as he went to speak, Dmitry silenced Peter, raising a finger to his lips and shaking his head gently. Another man was, it appeared, setting something up.

At a nod from that man, Dmitry smiled magnanimously and said, "A leftover from the grave of our friend Commandant Beria, or Mikhail, or whatever his name was. They will not hear us now, no matter how clever they think they are."

Peter nodded appreciatively, but then his face set once more. "A small upside for Mr. Beria's betrayal, I suppose, though I will not thank him for the way he used Mother Russia."

Dmitry frowned and shook his head. "No, no, you misunderstand me, Mr. Secretariat. You will find no love for Mr. Kovalenko in this room. Quite the opposite. The time has come to put a stop to Russia being some pawn in the greater game, Peter. The time has come for Russia to reclaim its place among the world's elite."

Dmitry glanced at the machine that was apparently even now masking any signal Ayala might be using to listen in on them, then went on, "But while I cannot thank the traitor Beria for using us, we are not too proud, I think you will find, to make the best of the tools he may have left behind." He paused and glanced at his colleagues then back to Peter, "Nor are we too proud to recognize when we might have been wrong about one of our own."

Peter and Dmitry held each other's stares as the other two ministers nodded approvingly. Peter smiled, as his eyes narrowed. It was tempting to believe Dmitry, but Peter was no fool, he could see that they were only really offering to have him be their tool, as opposed to TASC's. But Peter was *not* TASC's puppet. He was their ally. Because however much he might disagree with that organization's ever more stringent methods, they were still, in the end, doing what must be done.

And so was he, he knew, as he engaged with these three snakes and pretended to be enticed by the apple they offered.

The apple, it turned out, was a new alliance. A temporary one, but one that would give Russia leverage. One that would dislodge the American Neal Danielson from the helm of the ever more powerful TASC and put a council there in his place, a council upon which Russia would sit. They spoke of allies, they hinted at some, and were cagey about others. And they spoke of the remnants of what they now knew as tech ten. There was not much left, they said, but they were learning how to replicate it.

Soon they would have an army, as would their allies. They would take control of TASC and be the ones to ride the warhorse into the coming fight, and they would be the ones left ruling once they had dispatched the coming alien Armada.

Such bold talk, thought Peter an hour later. They would meet again soon, they said. Discuss this with no one, they said. He would have to prove himself, they said. And as he left and his guards fell in behind him once more, he handed them a pen from his pocket, the simplest of devices, one that would have been unimpressive during the Cold War, let alone during this far hotter one. The Spezialist took the device and plugged into it, downloading every word that had been said and sending it back to District One.

The plot thickens, thought Ayala, after Saul informed her of the overheard conversation's contents, and she added new names to an ever-growing list of traitors to the cause.

# Chapter 27: Ugly Behavior

As Peter walked away from his meeting with his ardent peers, Ayala's eyes were really on the situation in Tehran. Many others were, no doubt, watching as well, but she had reason to believe it was about to come to a head. Any moment now. The question was not if, but when. And when the shift came, where would the epicenter be? What cracks would the shockwave reveal?

Minnie noticed it first.

*Minnie:* <i have movement in three sectors: [x], [x], and [x]. Coordination seems likely, though movement seems erratic.>

Ayala studied it. Watched for the pattern. Men on the move. Machines starting up. Previously steady flows of men suddenly moving with purpose. They were going to make an attempt.

*Ayala:* 'minnie. tell hektor and his team. get them ready. i want everyone braced for action.'

*Minnie:* <all are prepared. ¿should i warn jim?>

Ayala thought.

*Ayala:* 'no, not yet. but get the phase elevens ready. they may be needed shortly.'

*Minnie:* <the phase elevens are always ready, ayala.>

Yes, she thought, they are, aren't they.

- - -

Bohdan anchored his rebreather in the soft sediment that lined the canal's belly. It did not take much. Anchoring the buoyancy-neutral device under an old bicycle frame to keep it in place, he unclipped himself from it, keeping only the small tubeset that linked it to the back of his neck in place as he braced his arms and legs.

What had spooked Ayala he did not know, but apparently events were coming to a head at last. It had been seventeen hours since he had slipped into this canal. Seventeen hours with only the occasional peep above water to send signal or exude a snorkel to cycle his air tanks. He was ready for action. He was itching for it.

- - -

Across town Niels was equally ready, and almost as impatient. He knew why they were there. He knew what weapon they were planning on unleashing. It was not, he was sure, a choice that had been made lightly, but neither did this fall within Niels's definition of fair play, either.

This, as his grandfather would have said when he was truly soured with someone, was 'ugly behavior.' Very ugly indeed. But in their line of work you danced pretty close to the ethical line. You did what others may fear to, what they may balk at. You did it when that same ethical line was itself being threatened. And sometimes, Niels knew, you had to cross that line in order to deal with those that lived on the other side of it.

And that justification would have to do, Niels knew, as he braced himself. That would have to suffice. But he was glad he would not have to explain this to his grandfather when he was done. Would not have to face the righteous indignation, the disappointment.

*Minnie:* <niels, i have two units inbound on your location. they are slowing.>

*Niels:* 'understood, minnie.'

Niels's blood started pumping now. They had reviewed what had happened to Ben Miller and his team. They had done so as an exercise in understanding their enemy, but they also had felt it deeply. Now he felt that same sensation again. It was muted perhaps by his no longer autonomic responses, but still there. His heart remained steady, his eyes did not dilate, his gastrointestinal tract did not react, indeed it had long since been slowed to a crawl by drugs, both natural and synthetic.

But his mind was not tamed, deliberately, and now the anticipation began to mix with his latent anger and not a small amount of fear. He was as conscious as one could be, as aware as possible as he watched the images being relayed from above. As he watched the two trucks pull up a hundred or so yards from him. As he watched one offload a group of soldiers who then began marching down the canal-side in his direction.

*Minnie:* <imaging still shows no sign of tech ten armor. scanning closely. only one set of items not identified.>

The image swam downward as Minnie focused in. A cart laden with small barrels.

*Minnie:* <analyzing now. no markings. weight estimated at ten kilos each.>

Without much ado, two of the men wheeling the cart took one of the barrels and unceremoniously lobbed it into the canal. For just a brief moment it all looked quite innocuous, like they were merely getting rid of an unwanted beer keg, until all the soldiers promptly crouched and covered their ears.

Niels followed suit, curling into a ball and bracing himself.

*Neal:* 'what the hell is happ …'

The explosion was huge, a great geyser springing up from where the barrel had hit. Fifty pounds of high-explosive in a jury-rigged depth charge. Above water it made cars brake, cyclists veer, and pedestrians spin on their heels.

Beneath the water's surface it warped Niels's world. He was thrust away and then sucked back in the surge of water, but the titanic pressure change also found any hint of a gap in his armor and sprayed through.  His eardrums, hitherto protected within his helmet, ruptured violently.

*Minnie:* <force estimates are too great.  his suit is not configured for this level of pressure change below water.>

*Neal:* '¿will he survive?'

*Minnie:* <his life will not be threatened, but the integrity of the suit will probably be compromised.'

*Neal:* 'jesus.  ¿ayala, are we reacting?'

*Ayala:* 'we are, neal.  we are reacting now.'

And they were.  The scene was changing quickly.  But for Niels, his world was frantic, and events were unfolding in front of him, out of his control.  The water in his suit was not a great amount, but it was everywhere.  And the pain was spectacular.  He did not like to think that the suit had made him soft, but nor did he try to handle the sensation on his own either.

Co-opting his nervous system, he manually quelled the throbbing in his joints and focused on his ears.  He could not get at them manually, so through his link he sought to shut them down as well.  There was no easy way to do it.  No short way.  They were hardwired into his brain; unlike touch and taste they had far more pervasive processing centers.

He needed them silenced.  The shouted pain from them was overwhelming.  He could tell Minnie was trying to say something to him.  He knew that he needed to move.  But he could not process it.  Not above the roar of agony coming from the very center of his mind; his inner-ear had become an inner-scream.

If they were blown out, Niels knew, then they might as well be burned out.

Inside his mind he shrieked a kill call, sending a hot pulse into his auditory cortex, hotter even than the searing heat of pain coming from it.  The kill call was final.  It surged through the cortex, rupturing it now at the neuronal level, silencing it, probably for good.

The relief was immediate, if more than a little offset by his loss, but he did not need his hearing now anyway, not now, not inside the suit.  It had become a nuisance, an arrowhead, and he had cut it out.  With the noise gone, Minnie's voice returned, bypassing his ears as it did, coming straight into his mind as it said ...

*Minnie:* <...econd barrel detonation in 0.3, 0.2 ...>

Fuck.  He braced.

His world warped once more, a great swell, closer now, a wall crashing into him and then the greater sucking draw, pulling him back toward its center.  He had become a die in a cup and he did not much care for the sensation.

Minnie was calling off options.  Other events were unfolding as well.  Hektor and Bohdan, though not under attack, were too far off to help.  He was on his own for now.

Enough. If they wanted a fight, so be it. He was out of air anyway, his rebreather tube long since having been ripped from him.

He leapt from the water as an echo of the two geysers that had been blown from it, an answer to the drum beat of the depth charges. But as the world was revealed to him, something was wrong. As sensors went active and sought to map and reveal the world around him, they were not returning as they should.

He began transmitting even as he came to land on the soaked bank of the canal, and as Minnie saw the data she confirmed what Niels feared.

*Minnie:* <you have lost primary radar and infrared. laser mapping sensors are misaligned. i will try to reconfigure to account for the skew, but I need reference points.>

He knew what she meant. As bullets began hitting him, he knew that she meant he needed to give her visual confirmation of what his sensors were saying, so she could correct for whatever had happened to them.

Very well, but first he would let his attackers know he would be with them shortly. Using angles of contact from the bullets, he calculated a horizon with about twenty points on it. He blanketed it. It was not the answer that they deserved, but he noticed a substantial reduction in fire afterward, either from attrition, or just the shock at the devastation of his wild kinetic attack. Either way, as the window in their fire opened, he opened one of his own, parting his faceplate.

The surrounding world came to him as vision to the waking: blurred and bright. And wrong in its own way, too. His eyes, closed for too long, took time adjusting. He was crouched, covering his face, while his natural senses, or what was left of them, came to.

Water was everywhere. The ground was slick with the canal's lifeblood, the city bleeding out of one of its veins as it sought to kill an invading entity. He was the virus they sought, and now the bullets came once more, redoubled, and he started running. What he lacked in peripheral vision was made up for by Minnie, who was transposing her view from above into his mind.

*Minnie:* <nearly there with the realignment. look up when you can. i need to see buildings, horizon.>

He would when he could. But not yet. Not with a hail of lead still erupting around him. The water covering every inch of space around his pounding feet spewed and spat in tiny mockeries of the charged geysers that had crippled him. He was the epicenter of an angry circle of fire.

He led the circle off. He was not crouched now so much as running on all limbs. He had seen the Phase Elevens do it. It was actually pretty cool, a small part of him thought.

He found dryer ground, shelter. A small skip that had shaded this patch of concrete from the great fonts that had just bathed this entire area. He slid and skidded behind it and let his face come up, feeling the sun on it for the first time in what felt like an age. His view skipped and swapped as Minnie brought his sensors back online, the two images coming together now, merging as his synthetic sight returned, pervasive and reliable. It filled him with a sense of power and independence he never wanted to be without again.

As they came back online, his systems began scrolling with attacker locations. The air was thick with the whir and buzz of heavy machine-gun fire, and his mind began factoring it and tracing it.

He was so close. So close to being ready. Even as he began closing his faceplate so he could engage, at last he saw it. A ping from one of his systems that was matched by an instinctual pull. A window. Far off but not too far off. Ajar. A glint from within. A hint of the sniper that had been waiting. One of several, no doubt. Waiting for an opportunity.

They had been waiting. Waiting for him to show himself. Waiting so very patiently.

The bullet hit him square in the face. Unprotected as he was, it ruined him utterly. Niels was dead before the thought had fully formed in his mind.

- - -

More forces were on the move now, and Hektor saw the city as a map filled with liquid parts. Like oil on water, the colors of it swirled and moved, almost defying patterning, but there was a pattern, a beauty. Then a spot of green, one of very few true green patches in the diorama, blinked out, and the pattern changed.

The update on Niels came to him as a file, a fact that supplemented his understanding of his operational parameters.

His friend.

One of too many lost.

No time to mourn.

*Ayala:* 'there is major movement at the Niavaran Palace. two groups. two exits. cannot say which is decoy, if it isn't both.'

Hektor saw them. They had not been sure whether this would be necessary. Whether Hektor and his comrades would have to go weapons hot. That was all over now. Indecision past.

Now action.

He lifted from the pool with a thrust from his legs, not upward, but outward, propelled with massive force into the air, leaving two fat craters in the canal's side, the cost of purchased momentum. He hit the ground and grabbed at it, moving off at speed. He did not want stealth. He wanted them to know his presence. Not for revenge, though he dearly longed for that, but for reaction.

Now that they had kicked things off, he wanted to see what they did. He wanted to make them run. He was met, at first, with only shouts and stares as the part of the city where he had lain in wait reacted to his appearance. The first bullets did not come for at least a minute, during which he covered huge ground.

He was driving not after one of the motorcades starting to scroll away from the palace, but after both of them. He ran right for the middle to see what they did.

Minnie and Ayala watched as Hektor ran, the occasional bullet starting to ring off his sides as he closed on the two convoys.

*Ayala:* 'there. that one. see how the other is staying closer to you than it is.'

*Minnie:* <that is not conclusi ...>

*Ayala:* 'yes it is. go, hektor.'

*Hektor:* 'on my way.'

He veered significantly and obviously. He wanted them to know. I am coming for you, he wanted to say.

And they reacted as Ayala had hoped. Changing courses, speeds. One accelerating, the other faltering. Faltering as the real motorcade never would have.

Phalanxes of troops converged on the line of cars now, closing to defend it, pulling from all quarters. They came at Hektor and in turn he came down upon them with relish, a thunderclap of militant intent. He wanted this. He wanted it more than he was willing to admit. He wanted to hurt them.

As they closed it got ugly.

# Chapter 28: On the Run

Jim sat facing an otherwise placid group. Placid until a sudden shift in mood started spreading out from a far corner of the room. Whoever it was that was standing there, whoever it was that had stepped forward and whispered lightly in another's ear, they were the source of some information. Information that Jim clearly did not have.

He remained outwardly calm, even as he queried Minnie and Neal.

*Jim:* '¿what's going on, guys? something has happened. the assembly representatives are getting an update on something.'

The three had turned, as one, to another man, giving a quiet report.

*Neal:* 'yes, jim. something is happening. we are not sure how, but the iranian forces found one of our spezialists. they found him and they killed him.'

Jim's eyes widened. He couldn't help it. The lead representative saw it and his eyes narrowed in turn. As Neal continued to speak into Jim's head, the representative of the Assembly of Experts raised his hands, silencing his colleagues, and began to lean forward.

*Neal:* 'i am afraid the iranians are reacting, jim. and they are reacting rather badly.'

Jim watched as the representative opened his mouth to speak, taking his time, admonition and anger building in his eyes.

*Jim:* 'neal, i am so close. ¿what the hell happened? What ... wait ... they are about to say something.'

*Neal:* 'i am afraid the time for talks is passed, my friend. there are troops inbound on your position now. minnie has activated the phase elevens.'

*Jim:* 'no ... no! wait!'

But it was done. As the Iranian finally formed his words, Jim saw that his chance was, indeed, lost, a wisp of hope vanishing in a building gale.

"You have betrayed our trust, Mr. Hacker. You do not come in peace. You come to our country with all the guile of the devil you are." The words came as a translated voice in Jim's inner-ear, still sound on some level, and distinguishable from Neal and Minnie's ethereal voices, but just as distant now.

Suddenly Jim felt very alone, and the next few minutes passed as in a haze. He was only admonished by the Iranian man for a short while before that man's own guards began reacting, pulling him and the other clerics and administrators from the room.

As soldiers began to outweigh politicians in the broad conference space, Jim felt the mood shift. Testosterone, fueled by the presence of loaded guns and an enemy, a known enemy of the state, began filling the soldiers with martial purpose, and murder began to show in their eyes.

Jim watched them. He was not afraid, not really. Not that he doubted the very real danger he was in, it was just that his disappointment was so great. It covered him like a heavy cloak, weighing down his shoulders and bowing his head, like he was soaked in his regret for this lost opportunity.

He had been on the bridge, they had been coming to join him. And as he looked now into the eyes of the soldiers wishing him harm, he longed to see some spark of that same hope, or even disappointment in their eyes.

But there was none. Only anger. Anger and bloodthirst.

Then there was the briefest moment of fear and confusion as they sensed a coming tide.

Suddenly the entire room was awash with noise. Shockwaves buffeted Jim as masonry exploded from three different directions. Dust filled his eyes and lungs as three of the Phase Elevens burst through the walls into the space, severing and smashing its other occupants as they came.

He mourned them, those soldiers. They had not been wrong in their anger, not wrong in their sense of betrayal. He had betrayed them. He had dared hope that this could be resolved peacefully. That cooler heads could prevail. He had been a fool, and he was limp with lack of care as a robotic hand enclosed his face and then pulled him in, turning and snaking around him as it wound him close to its big black chest.

As his world went black, he felt cool air on his face, a flow of filtered air coming through the machine's hand somehow, feeding him as he was lifted and carried out of room's exploded carcass, through its exposed ribs of plaster and wood, through gaping holes in the walls beyond, back along the trail of destruction that had been the Phase Elevens' meteoric path to his location.

He could not see where they were taking him. He could not see what they were doing to keep him safe as they extracted him from the depths of the office complex he had worked so hard to get permission to enter. He could only feel the power of his protector's embrace as he was saved, as his life was protected at the expense of so many others.

It sickened him and he stayed limp, almost hoping for a stray bullet to hit him and end this madness. To put a stop to the killing.

But it did not come, and deep down he knew that even if it did, the bloodshed would not end with his death.

- - -

Processing. Targeting mix assessed and prioritized. Engaging now.

The Phase Elevens worked well, thought Minnie, but without the purer speed of Hektor.

It was not a lack of impetus. Such things were irrelevant. Desire only drove ambition, it did not enable the reaching of whatever goal the emotion set, quite the opposite. Once the journey was begun, desire only filtered and obscured the destination, and her machine warriors had no time for it.

But neither did Hektor. He was beyond decision. This was not personal, it was primal. His mind moved at a base level, instinct and reflex pulsing through him as his conscious mind watched, almost an outsider, prompting himself to action at intervals, this direction, that target, then his true self ran with that thought, executing.

Any relish he took in the chaos he was wreaking across the streets of Tehran was merely an afterthought.

He leapt clear from one side of a street to another as he cleared another roadblock. He took out knees and shoulders, and blew out tires, sometimes causing more profound damage to either machine or man, depending on angle, and not a little on chance. He was not here for them. They were collateral. He was here for the man calling the shots. He was looking for the boss man. He wanted to have a word with him.

Those that crossed his path did not feel any sense of reprieve, though. For them it was only wrenching and screaming. Pounding noise cut with fire and light. The soldiers saw him only as a rolling, tumbling, leaping meteor, blurred lines of destruction firing off from it as it dervished through their midst.

And then he was gone, a gaping hole left in their line where he had blazed his trail, and a scar left on their minds like the throbbing echo of a brightness on a retina, their breath caught in their throats.

But some were tracking him. Some were mapping the macro nature of his movements as he raced after the motorcade. As bright minds on both sides analyzed the units moving about the city, strategic decisions continued to be made. And now, as Hektor closed on the stream of cars they believed held a fleeing Supreme Leader, his opponents played another card.

*Minnie:* <they have entered a parking lot half a mile ahead. monitoring vehicles exiting.>

*Hektor:* 'i will be there in about twenty seconds.'

*Minnie:* <agreed. i do not understand why they are fleeing.>

The statement was a surprise, and Hektor even chuckled momentarily as he breathed heavily within his suit, his machine legs pounding at pavement and his arms unleashing quick bursts of fire as he came upon pockets of resistance.

*Hektor:* 'i would imagine they are running because they are afraid of me, minnie. ¿you don't think they should be?'

*Minnie:* <no, they should be, and they clearly are. ¿what i mean is, why did they move from the palace in the first place? it showed us their location. it was foolish.>

Hektor ran on, closing on the parking lot now. She was right. It had been a huge mistake on their part. Had they really thought that by killing Niels they had ended the threat? Ayala piped up, her mind's voice level and cold.

*Ayala:* 'they thought niels was just a tracker. they think we are there to kill the grand jurist, and they think we mean to send in banu to destroy the palace. they hoped that by moving him they could avoid our wrath.'

Hektor allowed the thought to turn over in his mind for a second. It was, in the end, irrelevant, he supposed. They were fleeing. TASC had hoped to draw their quarry out and, albeit inadvertently, they had done so.

Now it was his job to get at the bastard.

*Minnie:* <multiple cars exiting. dispersing pattern. they are … muddying the waters.>

Yes they are, thought Hektor as he came powering down on the main exit from the lot. Cars were still filing out. He stopped them the quickest way he knew how: by slagging the engines of the first two and then ramming into the next, his momentum sending it careening sideways to wedge itself into the far pillar of the entrance, completing his roadblock. Return fire was quick coming, and not lacking sting. He set to silencing it before delving deeper into the building.

*Hektor:* 'i will vet the structure and see if he is still in here. ayala, may i suggest you mobilize bohdan to focus on the cars that have already left.'

*Ayala:* 'bohdan is entering play now. as are others.'

Others. The Phase Elevens. Jim was safely back aboard the StratoJet now, which had taken to the air, but had not departed. It was staying low, sweeping left and right, defending itself with its own onboard weaponry as it waited for the rest of its complement to return. For it had left its five gorilloid automatons on the ground, and now they joined the hunt.

It was becoming a spectacle. No, it had been a spectacle long since. It was becoming a debacle. And the world was reacting.

- - -

"I'm not sure what I can say, Neal." Wislawa was shaking her head as she watched the footage coming out of Tehran.

"Say that we are working to extract a peaceful diplomatic mission after a brutal attempt on their lives," said Neal.

She looked at him. She did not try to disguise her skepticism, no, cynicism. This was not an extraction, that much was clear given what she was seeing. He held her stare for a moment, then faltered under the unrelenting maternal truth of her piercing eyes. She would not be stared down, and he looked at his papers for a moment to gather himself.

When he looked up once more it was with more determination, not looking to sway her now, but to push forward in spite of her. Or replace her, if need be.

"How about this, Wislawa, tell them we are looking to stop a misguided dictator from derailing a mission to save all of their damn lives. Then tell them what *you,* you personally, would be willing to do to save the world, and then let them judge *you*." He paused, and her expression did, indeed, falter a little.

Just as firmly, he went on, "*Or* ... tell them we are working to extract a peaceful diplomatic mission after a brutal attempt on their lives."

Now the stares were more evenly matched, though hers was becoming imbalanced by a clearly rising anger. She had not signed up for this. But then she'd made no stipulations against it either. She considered demanding to know exactly what was really happening in Iran's burning capital, but only for a moment.

Then the desire passed. Plausible deniability. A dirty term, but one she found herself finally succumbing to. She nodded, though with enough resentment in her eyes that Neal was left in no doubt as to her thoughts on the matter. He would not get many more of these passes from her.

Though, if things went to plan today, hopefully he would not need them.

- - -

The chase now became one of attrition. As Hektor vetted the parking lot and its surrounding structures with no little prejudice, five machine hunters and one man tracked down the eight cars that had gotten out of the lot before Hektor so effectively shut it down.

In the end, it was Bohdan who finished it. The car rounded on him and accelerated with clear purpose. The driver clearly hoped to ram him and Bohdan did not stop the man, leaping at the last moment, not away, but backward so that he could land on the car's hood as the car slid by under him. As he began to tumble over the top of the car, he slammed his machine fingers into the thick plate metal of the car's roof.

Finding the purchase he needed, he dug in. Not just to hold on, but to pull, to rend, to open the car like a tin can. Once he had a big enough gap, he rammed his head through, his sensors quickly assessing and identifying the car's occupants by facial recognition.

*Bohdan:* 'i have him.'

The faces came through the link like a paparazzi shoot, four men, clearly shaken with terror, reeling from the man assessing them.

Two voices came into Bohdan's head simultaneously.

*Ayala:* 'release the device.'

*Minnie:* 'car is swerving, collision likely.'

The driver was not looking. His head was ducked as low as the poor man could get it. The car was turning, Bohdan felt it to. Well, we couldn't risk an accident, could we? Not with the leader of this soon-to-be ally aboard. Even as his one hand came back to grasp a cylinder attached to his side, he was ripping a wider hole in the roof with his other, then pushing his torso through the broader gap and grasping the wheel to center the car once more.

It would not work. The driver was still accelerating as hard as he could. As Bohdan's right hand brought the cylinder he had retrieved down and pushed it through into the car, Bohdan executed a quick move with his left hand. First he whipped it backward into the driver's head, either to kill him or knock him unconscious, Bohdan did not care which, then to the side to dislodge the gear stick, then back to the wheel.

It took a fraction of a second, but immediately the car's momentum shifted, it was no longer driving toward the oncoming traffic; he could bring it under control now.

As the car began a long coast, the stout, black cylinder Bohdan had dropped into its midst opened.

The two guards on either side of their leader, thinking it was a bomb, threw themselves over their ward, hoping to shield him. Bohdan fought any urge to mock this. It was an extraordinarily brave act, and it was matched by the Supreme Leader, Bohdan had to admit, who fought to force them off him, wanting to face his fate.

But the men did not understand, thought Bohdan. None of them did. Maybe they never would. For now fear took them once more as six mechanical spiders sprung from the cylinder's ends. The little machines crawled with speed and liquidity that was repulsive, climbing up the three men's legs even as they all swatted at the machines with mounting panic, something in them sending them primal as hoarse, terror-ridden screams escaped their lips.

But the machines kept coming, crawling this way and that. Some were indeed brushed away but they only came again, relentless, hard-shelled, clawed little beasts seeking a point. Bohdan helped his minions along a little as the car continued to slow, pulling a device no more advanced than a Taser from his belt, only with a far more lasting charge, and hitting each man in turn.

They convulsed physically now, even as they continued to shake with fear inside their minds, their eyes wide as the spiders crawled up their bodies to their necks, then around behind them.

The clamps were not gentle as they sank into the men's skins. Claws to hold the spiders in place, if only to save the men from paralyzing injury as the spiders began injecting themselves into the spinal cords of their new hosts.

It did not take long.

Bohdan saw with no small amount of disdain as the men went limp for real now, not from a jolt of electricity, but from a co-opting of their very bodies.

*God.*

That was how the voice introduced itself.

*God:* 'STOP FIGHTING!'

They did. Though they had been limp, they had been resisting by force of will. Struggling with all their might against the invasion of their selves. Whether through shock or obedience, they stopped now, becoming completely still, inside and out.

*God:* 'better. silence now. listen. i have something to tell you. something to show you. you three will be the enlightened ones. you three will be the first. you will spread my word to your nation and silence the nonbelievers. you will listen to me. you will listen and *you ... will ... obey.*'

The voice went on. Bohdan could not hear the voice booming in their heads, but a different one in his own head was telling him that it was time to go. They had connection.

The three spiders that had proven superfluous climbed back into the cylinder now. And as the spinal interfaces sank home and finalized their imbedding process, the spiders that had delivered them climbed free as well, leaving only the link and a small dome on the back of each of their hosts' necks. It would require regular charging and occasional maintenance, but instructions for that would be delivered in time to their hosts, when they were needed.

For now, the voice spoke into their minds, and images began to fill them. Very real images. Images of the coming Armada, augmented with estimates from Quavoce and John Hunt, descriptions of the very real power and ability of that fleet. And instructions for how Iran was going to start supporting the effort to fight it. Supporting it with all its might, both financial and intellectual.

As the leader's car finally rolled to a halt, Bohdan leapt down from its roof. A black plane was coming in hard and low. It would not stop, it would barely slow down. Bohdan began running, accelerating as hard as he could. He leapt with all his might even as the plane was still behind him and connected with Hektor's powerful arm as the man leaned out from the plane's rear access hatch.

As he was pulled aboard, the plane accelerated, without restraint now, upward and outward. Away from the city. It carried Jim, the automatons, and the two surviving Spezialists.

It would return with a more diplomatic mission when TASC was formally invited by the Supreme Leader, as Neal knew they soon would be.

## Chapter 29: The Closing Door

Jim leapt from the StratoJet's hatch like a spat thing, thrusting himself forward even as Hektor and Bohdan started to unpack their larger selves from inside the plane's austere hull.

He was across the landing bay on the southern side of Milton SpacePort before they had even gotten out of the craft. Jim's anger was written across his face, his frustration now repurposed, redirected toward the people he was ever more certain were its just recipients.

He stormed along familiar corridors. A member of his staff was waiting for him, holding out a bottle of water and a sandwich, fulfilling a perceived need.

"Not now," he said brusquely, eying the refreshment with disdain.

As he passed by one of his many administrative floors and approached the sentries outside the long corridor to Neal's office, he wondered for a moment if they would stop him. If they would sense his anger and block his passage. But they did not vet members of Neal's inner-circle like that. It was not their mandate.

Minnie was watching him, though. Both through his own link and through the eyes of the two sentries, and hundreds of others, she watched him as he stormed down the long corridor.

*Minnie:* <¿jim, are you all right?>

He ignored her.

*Minnie:* <jim, the data you requested. i am not capable of giving it to you. it is not that i don't want to give you the information. this part of me truly does not know the answer to your question.>

*Jim:* 'i know, minnie. and that is just the point, isn't it. "this part of you." they found him, minnie. they found that soldier so very fucking mysteriously. and that led to the shit-show i just had the misfortune of being at the damn head of.'

He got to the door and knocked loudly. Not so much as a courtesy, but because he knew this was not a door he was physically capable of barging through.

*Neal:* 'just a second, jim. i am wrapping something up.'

*Jim:* 'open the door, neal. ¡now! i demand to speak with you. and i think you would prefer it if i didn't do it out loud ... out here.'

There was a pause, then the door opened and Jim was greeted by Jennifer's uncertain visage. They had met many times, of course. The woman who had come to share Neal's bed could not help but be painfully familiar with Neal's right hand, if only through the mostly friendly push and pull of each of them competing for Neal's time and attention.

This was not that, though. This was not a request for time. Jim's expression could not have been plainer. Neal had told Jennifer he needed time to talk to his chief of staff, and asked her to leave them to it, and his tone had been clear as well. This was not a conversation either was looking forward to, and nor was it one that either wished to have an audience for.

Jennifer glanced back at Neal, as if to say, 'are you sure you want me to leave you two alone?'

But Neal's face was resolute. He neither needed nor wanted her here for what was about to happen.

- - -

"Stop bullshitting me, Neal."

"Your anger is understandable, Jim, trust me. I am just as disappointed as you."

"That is a lie, and you know it. There is no way they could have found him. I looked at the recordings. I watched what they did to that man. They didn't stumble upon him. They weren't sweeping. They went straight to his location."

Neal breathed deep. It was hard to argue Jim's point, so he stopped trying.

"I agree, Jim, it is profoundly disturbing. They must have found out … somehow. I don't know how, and you can be sure I will not rest until I do."

Jim went to reply, but Neal went on, "Believe me when I say that I am as shocked by this whole day as you are. It was only my belief in the importance of this mission that stopped me from having Ayala take the culprits into custody."

Jim's face became plaintive. "Culprits? Culprits! *We* are the culprits, Neal, don't you see that? *We* invaded their country without permission. *We* sent heavily armed men to do what can only be described as the most appalling and profound abuse of another human's rights possible. I agreed to it *only* as a last resort. *Only* if the diplomatic effort failed. Did it, Neal? Did it fail? Or did you kill it? Because I cannot see a way in which *they* are the culprits here!"

Neal became more strident. "You cannot see a way? How about the fact that they were threatening to send us into war, Jim? That just like the Russians they were risking everything, all for petty greed."

"But they weren't, Neal!" said Jim, pleading now, tears brimming in his eyes. "They *weren't*. The Russians were the victims of an incredibly capable spy and an overambitious fanatic. But these men, they were just guilty of ignorance." He shrank a little now, something giving in him as he thought of what he had just lost. What they had all just lost. As his back sagged and his eyes veered slowly to the ground, he said in quiet desperation, "If I could just have spoken to them. If I could just have made them see."

Neal's firmness faltered, just a little. Jim was a good man, a selfless man, and his dedication was without question. Perhaps more importantly, Neal knew that there was a chance that Jim might have been able to do what he set out to do. But that was just it: a *chance*. Neal could no longer afford to wait for chances and hopes. He had to get things back on track, in any way he could.

"Jim," he said, with unfeigned affection, and even some measure of regret. "My friend. I am as sad as you are about how things turned out, truly I am. I am horrified at what we have been forced to do. But don't you see that now we *can* talk to them. That is all we have really done. We have opened up a door. And it is one they cannot close."

Jim froze. When his face came back up it was with a look of profound and genuine disgust. "If that was all you wanted to do, Neal, then it would have cost you nothing to wait a while longer. To let me try to finish what I had started."

"Events conspired against us, Jim. There was nothing I could do."

Now Jim's eyes set. "Very well, Neal. If you truly had nothing to do with this, then open Ayala's files to me. Give me complete access. I want to see who she has spoken to, and what she has told them. I want to know what she is up to."

Neal held Jim's gaze as he thought about this. While he did, another voice came into his mind.

*Ayala:* 'show him, neal. he will find nothing in any files.'

The very fact that she had been listening, that she appeared to always be listening, disturbed Neal for the very first time. After the first Skalm had been completed, after the need to keep the Dome secret had finally past, he had relished an end to secrets. Now he longed for a little of that privacy once more, both to protect himself and Ayala from an enraged chief of staff, and to protect himself from an ever more pervasive Ayala.

"Of course, Jim. Of course," he said, placatingly.

"Not just now, permanently. I want a review board set up to oversee her and her team."

Neal nodded, even as Ayala whispered in his ear once more, then Neal said, "Of course, Jim. I think that is an excellent idea."

Jim waited a moment, his eyes reinforcing his immovability on this. Neal nodded again, a look not of contriteness, perhaps, but of compliance. Jim, in turn, was not satisfied, so much as aware that he had gotten as much as he could reasonably expect from the confrontation. He needed to calm down. He needed to think.

He left without further comment.

He would continue to demand access, and indeed he would get it. And once he got it he would review it with every ounce of skepticism he had. But another part of him was saying something different as he walked away. Something he hated to hear, even from himself. Because he could not fight the simple truth that they did indeed have a job to do, and to allow this, even this, to stand in the way of that job, might be suicide on a global level.

And, the small voice also asked, even more quietly now, what would Neal or Ayala be willing to do to him if he really tried to stand against them?

As that thought began to turn over inside his mind, his stomach churned as if stirred by it. He knew that this could not be allowed to pass. He knew that he could not be a part of an organization that did this.

But, in truth, he had no idea how to stop it.

# Part 4:

## Chapter 30: A New Day

The cloud passed by underneath, then around the craft. The cloud was grey, set against a black sky. It was bright at points, crisp, its component parts glimmering in stark sunlight. As the craft moved under the elliptic plane of the cloud, the light shifted, silhouetting now rather than illuminating. The craft now swam under the cloud and the sun burst into view behind, filling the vista with its encompassing aura.

Veering, Madeline brought the craft back up now, passing back through the haze of matter, to reveal it once more. The conglomeration was vast, reaching for nearly a mile in every direction. Its particles were each a meter across. Ten thousand of them in total, and that just here. That just at Malapert Farm, thought Madeline, trying to grasp the full breadth of the munitions fields they had created.

Changing course again now, she pointed the monitoring and maintenance probe back at the surface, back at the moon, to where Moira's teams continued to slave away, wrapping up production on the final units for the Lunar Missile-Mine Phalanx. It had been Moira's life for the past three years. And like any great purpose, she both loved and hated it.

*Madeline:* 'i'm done wandering around. ¿anyone need her?'

Madeline was referring to the drone she was inhabiting. She was no more aboard it than she was even on the moon. She was safely nestled back in Japan. But her mind was transmuted here by the magic of the massive hub subspace tweeters that were now in place on both worlds. Tweeters capable of amazing things. Tweeters that would play an ever-greater role in the coming war.

*Phalanx 1 Control:* 'i don't think we have further need for her now. transition her to ai and we'll set her into orbit until we need her again.'

*Moira:* 'i may have something. ¿satyendra, can you send her round to procellarum base, please? i'll pick up control there. i want to do a shimmer test on ileminite three.'

*Satyendra:* 'routing now. she should be there in [counter].'

A number appeared in Moira's mind; a timer. She set a notification against it and set it aside, turning her focus back to Madeline.

*Moira:* '¿how does it look, madeline? ¿does it meet your expectations?'

Madeline did not reply immediately, and Moira felt a request ping in her mind, a call for FaceTime. They had co-opted the term from Apple, now a major contributor and benefactor of their work. It was, without doubt, a mutually beneficial relationship, as the company's iPort was also the biggest selling commercial spinal interface on a changed earth.

Moira glanced at the virtual data panels arrayed in front of her in the ether, a glance that brought a huge range of data into her mind from macro to micro, filling her with a sense of her many programs' statuses.

Comfortable that she could leave her systems be for a moment and talk in person, as it were, she accepted the FaceTime invitation. Her view morphed in a way she had come to find fascinating, her world suddenly just becoming another place in a most impossible way, even as it gave a sense of all being … as it should be. The interface's designers had done a beautiful job, playing on all the right emotional cues.

Each participant's view was customized, even as it was also influenced by the other caller's own preferences. Moira sat in an large, plush leather office chair, deep green, a reference to a memory of a grandfather's legal offices, a place she had at once felt at home in but which was also laden with her child self's stereotype of work, her earliest understanding of success and accomplishment. The wooden side table to her right, lit with a tiffany lamp and set with old leather-bound books, paid similar homage.

Madeline's seat was more utilitarian, if also more whimsical, resembling, as it did, the metal captain's chair from the first research ship she had worked on years ago. The room they found themselves in was an amalgam of the two themes. A fireplace burned and a coffee table separated them with virtual snacks and beverages, but a broad gallery of windows to the other side looked out onto a broad, shifting seascape.

The only break in the façade were two panels suspended in midair to each of their sides, screens for each participant that would allow them to call up data or adjust settings without stepping out of the construct.

Moira smiled, perhaps a little hesitantly. "Well. What do you think of the Phalanx?"

Madeline's answering smile was more candid. "Amazing, Moira. It is, as you had said, truly an astonishing sight. It would be beautiful if it wasn't for its intended purpose."

Moira's expression, having risen momentarily at her mentor's praise, sank once more at the reminder of what all this work was building toward.

"Whoa there, Moira!" said Madeline to snap the girl, or rather the woman, out of it. She was no child anymore. She had accomplished too much. To think of her as a girl would be unfair.

"Hey," Madeline went on, with more maternal emotion than she might have thought herself capable of. "Don't do that. Don't weigh the success against the cost. Because the cost of you *not* having achieved what you have done, that far outweighs the damage that the Phalanxes will … no, the damage that they *must* do."

Moira nodded, a hint of frustration showing on her face, partly at being forced to hear the speech again, partly at maybe needing to. "I know, I know," she said, waving her hand as if spurning a mistimed advance.

She shifted in her seat, a mental discomfort visualized in the space. The leather creaked under her and she allowed herself to relish it for a moment. It even smelled real. It was the work of many sensory artists, no doubt, whole teams of them, in fact.

For members of the public such features would cost very real money, but for TASC's citizens, the fruits of any member nation or corporation were a perquisite. They did not pay for any technology that they licensed out, and over the three years since going public they had licensed a great deal, bringing in ever-greater revenue to feed the military machine.

They had also given away a great deal as well, there was no doubt about that. By public mandate, medical advancements gleaned from Mobiliei technology were never profited from, not by TASC or by any organization that licensed them. It had been the death knoll of several pharmaceutical giants as new, not-for-profit startups had sprung up across the planet.

And behind it all, of course, there was the antigen. An embryonic TASC's first, secret gift to humanity. A gift they had now made very public. One of many not-so-bitter pills to make the greater truth a little more palatable.

It had all moved very fast once a defiant Iran had changed political tacks. When the perceived head of the opposition to TASC's work had confessed a candid and profound change of heart, it had at once deflated the opposition and swayed a significant bulk of the still undecided to Neal's banner.

There were massive numbers of dissenters still remaining, no doubt, though Moira could not remember the last time she had heard anything significant from them. Nowadays it all seemed very marginalized, just various brands of conspiracy theory, expounded by the ever more ridiculous and ostracized.

For the sake of building consensus, TASC had condensed their intentions into the form of a manifesto. A manifesto that very few on Earth did not now know by heart. It was a credo that defined all interactions with the military institution. Defined them in no uncertain terms. And it was a contract that everyone, by default, had signed. It was TASC's bond and its demand, its value and its cost.

But such things were rarely on Moira's mind right now, and she wondered why she was thinking of them now. It made her uncomfortable for a reason she could not quite put her finger on. So she set it aside, as she usually did. Such things were not part of her life, not anymore. For her, TASC was home. It was everything. It was wall and window, floor and ceiling.

"Four weeks," said Moira, steeling herself. "Four weeks until launch. From the feed, I see that Hekaton has made up nearly all of its shortfalls."

"They have, or they will, I hope," said Madeline, crossing her fingers, then her legs, then her arms. They laughed a little. "It will be a close-run thing, but no one doubts that we wouldn't be where we are overall without your work here. You have exceeded even my highest expectations ... hey, even Birgit is impressed!"

They both smiled at the mention of the name. The pain of Birgit's loss had dulled a little, not least because she had taken her exile as incentive to stay just as important to their effort as she had been beforehand, maybe even more so. She was bursting several ceilings, stretching boundaries even the Mobiliei thought immutable. She had not cracked the Holy Grail, that remained a thing of dreams, but she had done other things that were almost as amazing.

Moira smiled. "Don't get me started on Birgit. That woman ..." she shook her head, her eyes going wide, and Madeline laughed.

"That bad, huh," said Madeline. "Yes, she can be ... demanding." Madeline thought back to first experiments with fusion drives, four years ago. To arguments about caution, its merits and flaws.

"Demanding? Dr. Hauptman?" said Moira. "Nooo!"

"You were part of the Diemos experiment, I assume?" asked Madeline, smiling a little at Moira's joke, but keen to delve deeper.

Moira's expression became one of pride once more. "Yes! Oh my God, that was intense."

"A success?"

"Well, not a success, no, you couldn't exactly say that. A ... proof of concept," said Moira hesitantly, like they had done nothing more than break a beaker while experimenting. In fact, they had broken something a touch larger. The second moon of Mars. Well, not broken, per se. Just ... well ... dented.

"It worked," went on Moira, "just not accurately. Not yet."

"Yes, that was the report I received as well." Madeline became more serious now. "But you remain ... hopeful?"

Moira saw now that this had been the real reason for Madeline's visit. Dr. Hauptman, difficult at the best of times, had become positively impossible to pin down, not least of which because of the nearly sixty million miles that now lay between them and her.

Where mini-minnie, as Birgit now called her, tried to act as the German doctor's proxy for her lost artificial child, Moira had become, to some extent, the real Minnie's proxy for her lost mother. At the very least, Minnie used Moira as a sounding board for thoughts that would take the real person an hour to respond to in person.

It gave Moira a level of access to Birgit's work that Madeline wished she shared. For Birgit's work was, if still embryonic, so tempting to believe in. What they were doing held incredible potential, not only for the coming war, but for what lay beyond. For a future Madeline rarely even thought about anymore. For hope in whatever lay after the coming conflict.

But the obstacles that beset them were ... significant, to say the least.

Madeline stared at the young woman in front of her, then did something she was loath to do. She mentally accessed the system itself and sent an order, using her almost unparalleled level of system clearance, to override Moira's visible emotional controls. Moira would not know it was happening, but Madeline needed to see what the girl was thinking, really thinking.

She could use the same access to directly hack the communications with Birgit. Indeed she already had. But the truth was she didn't fully grasp what Birgit, Minnie, and Moira were trying to do. It was beyond her mental abilities to understand the full scale of what they were attempting, and the roadblocks that still lay in their way.

What she needed to try and figure out was whether it was beyond Birgit's and Moira's abilities as well. Was this really possible, or was it just a pipe dream? A straw, being grasped at by an ever more desperate woman?

Madeline studied young Moira, and she saw that she hadn't needed to override the system. Moira was not hiding anything as she looked plaintively back at Madeline and said, "I don't know, Madeline. I really don't. My gut says that it is … it's just *too* complex. Too complex even for Minnie to compute, even with the compound, three-dimensional algorithms they are working on. I mean, you really have to see them to believe it. They are … beautiful."

Madeline had seen them. They *were* beautiful. They were a new level of computational science being developed just for the purpose of defining the indefinable. They were attempting just shy of the impossible, the codification of chaos, the prediction of absolute movement down to the micrometer.

Moira had a tear in her eye as she went on. "But when I read Dr. Hauptman's work, and talk to Minnie, it … it seems so far off. So, if you are asking me if I am confident? If I believe, truly *believe*, that it can be done? I … I just don't know."

"Even with the new access she would get from the coming contact?"

Moira looked away and visibly shuddered.

"Moira?" said Madeline. "What's wrong?"

Moira steeled herself and then looked back at Madeline, saying after a moment, "That … that represents a whole other level of crazy, I am afraid. I know Birgit says they can pull it off. I know she says she has reduced the risk factors to 'acceptable' levels." Moira crooked her fingers into little apostrophes with no small amount of sarcasm. Her distaste for this particular part of Birgit's plans was very clear indeed.

"But I have done the calculations myself, not just reviewed her workings, but redone them myself, separately, and … what they are trying to do … chasing the IST, it is insane."

Madeline did what she had secretly stopped Moira from doing; she hid her reaction. She hid her disappointment and concern. She hid it behind a mask of understanding and support, and maybe a touch too much condescension.

"I'm assuming you've shared your concerns with Birgit?" Madeline asked, with feigned ignorance.

Moira nodded. Moira had shared her opinions the previous day, if a touch less stringently than she had just now. It was part of what had prompted Madeline to visit the girl.

Madeline thought a moment, then decided that, whatever her own feelings on the subject, it was best to leave Moira as hopeful as possible, if only to allow her to focus on the last precious weeks of production.

"Well," Madeline said with all the sincerity she could muster, "if anyone can do it, Moira, Dr. Hauptman can. You know that, right?"

Moira nodded, but halfheartedly.

For Madeline, though, the truth was that this was not just about what Birgit could, or couldn't do. It was a dream that had bled into countless other projects, and Madeline knew she was getting to the point that she had to make a call. It was taking up more and more time and resources, and some of her very best resources at that, to say nothing of what it was doing to Minnie's capacity, which, though massive, was far from infinite.

She needed to talk to Minnie's keeper, Amadeu. She needed to let the others know.

# Chapter 31: TASC Manufacturing Plant 47

As Hendri stopped the loader, he stepped back and waited. It was parked now. He was not supposed to touch it while it was parked, not until the factory was done unloading it. He lit a cigarette as the factory buzzed around him. He was at the crossroads. The junction of two worlds.

He did not look up as the factory's beasts unburdened his forklift. He had done so the first few times he had come here and the sight had not only filled him with an unpleasant blend of awe and fear, it had also brought him a series of shouted epithets from a foreman stationed nearby. He had been staring. He needed to get his loader out of the way. Another was already waiting to unload its wares. He had leapt aboard and whirled his forklift around as the foreman had continued to shout obscenities at him.

He glanced back at the foreman now as he climbed back up and put his loader in gear. The man was angry, but not uncharacteristically so. There were so many of these foremen. They did not work for the same company as Hendri. Heck, he was pretty sure they were not even Indonesian. They were supervisors for whatever company held the Aggregation Contract. He was pretty sure they were Chinese.

They knew enough Javanese to get their point across, though, and even now he was receiving some last, choice words of encouragement as he wheeled the burly forklift out through the gantry doors and down an access road to the main checkpoint. Here the three main veins leading from the manufacturing plant's gantry doors met for sorting.

He passed back out through the Exit Gate without much ado and off down one of ten roads converging on the outside of the factory's main gate.

Because he was leaving, he was not much of a concern to the checkpoint's guards. There were not many ways he could take anything from the factory that it did not want to give. The majority of the scrutiny was for reserved for the incoming traffic. Security was tight here. They were not looking for explosives, per se, indeed there were supposed to be a great deal of combustibles in many of the deliveries coming to the factory. They were making sure none of said volatile materials were wired to anything that might make them a danger to the facility.

Though little was heard of the terrorist threat anymore, it was clearly still real enough to call for two black, gorilla-like automatons to be standing either side of the gate. They were not checking the deliveries themselves. They were watching the watchers. They were the enforcers.

They were still now. Very still. Like statues. But Hendri had heard stories of what happened when they came to life. Tales of the speed and strength of the robot guards.

They did not have names, indeed as best as Hendri understood it, they were only shells now. If they were needed then they would become possessed by the same method that allowed the Techs at his own depot to remotely manage and supervise all of the sorting and loading of the very materials he spent all day ferrying back and forth.

The Techs did it all directly with their minds, without using their hands or even their eyes. Just sitting there in the sterile, white rooms reserved just for them, mute and still, as a machine plugged into their necks gently whirred, sending out the orders that sent Hendri and thousands like him scurrying this way and that like worker bees in a network of hives that reached for miles up and down this stretch of the Indonesian coast.

He shuddered. He had seen the neck plugs on others as well. Most of the businessmen visiting the site had them now, as did reporters and announcers on television. But they were not for him. Not ever. Not that he could afford such things anyway, he knew, as he continued out past a second checkpoint, the road forking once more where the access route from his own depot met the roads from two others, or more, he did not know. He only knew his route across this landscape, his choice at each junction as he went back and forth between the factory and his depot.

That was his job. He was a driver. It was a job that could easily be done by a machine, or at least so he was told many, many times a day by his kepala. A man who was even now scowling at him as he pulled up to his depot.

"Thirty-seven seconds late!" he shouted, as Hendri drove past.

Hendri only nodded as the kepala shouted after him, "Pit 23!" after quickly glancing down at the tablet on his forearm.

Hendri wheeled his lifter into place behind 23. The pit was already nearly full. Thirty-seven seconds late, just so he could wait here for a few more of those precious seconds until his load was ready.

Behind the pit, the pallet was being loaded with a series of boxes. The boxes were made of aluminium. The metal box was itself one ingredient on a very detailed list of raw materials to be precisely loaded together according to a painstakingly exact set of instructions. Any deviation in either the box's size, weight, or contents, and the financial penalties were severe. It was a harsh rule, and one that encouraged a sense of very great diligence on the part of the kepala monitoring the QA process on the other side of the pits.

But that was not Hendri's problem. He was waiting. And at almost precisely the assigned second, the last component was loaded and he was given the green light to take the pit's contents for delivery. Almost immediately his boss was shouting at him. Hendri breathed deep and pushed his lifter forward, grabbing at the pallet and lifting it from the pit floor.

Soon he was back out on the road. Driving more slowly now that his lifter was fully laden, though not without a sense of haste. He knew from repeated drubbings from his kepala that the only reason a robot was not doing his job was that the software license for a TASC AI cost more than he did. But it was not *that* much more, he was told. And if he did not meet deadlines then they could replace him in an instant.

He did not believe that anything as complex and clever as a computer capable of driving a truck could be as cheap as the pittance they were paying him. But pittance or no, it was a job, and a better one than he could get working anywhere for a hundred miles in any direction.

He focused. Ten minutes in and the checkpoint was coming up again now, and the checkpoints were a completely different experience coming back to the factory than they were going away. The scans came. He was surveyed by many eyes, both human and mechanical. His biometric identity was validated against the depot name, the loader's registration, the pallet's contents and weight, and the delivery schedule.

Once all was confirmed and checked against a host of lists, he was given a place in the system, and a timer was set from the moment he was given clearance to proceed. He moved off apace.

- - -

Clearing the main factory gate was much more intense. He could not help but glance at the big robot gorillas. Were they looking back at him? Were they about to spring to life? Would it be him they would come for? He had absolutely no reason to think they would, but like an innocent child at a hastily called school assembly, he felt the heat on his face nonetheless, the worry of getting caught, even for a crime he had not committed.

The thick black wedge barrier in front of him lowered soon enough, though, and he was waved through with nothing more than a shouted, "Door two!"

As he passed through great gantry doors into the factory proper, he felt himself doing what he usually tried not to. He looked up. There was no roof. As far as he could tell, the machines in here did not care what the weather was like anyway. And as far as he could tell there were only machines in here, barring the foremen that stood by the gantry doors keeping those delivery loaders that were human-operated moving.

As he came to a halt in his designated slot, he watched, as he usually told himself not to, as the beast came for his goods. The machine that came to take his delivery of aluminium boxes was one of several in the vast factory, Hendri knew that, but it was still, to him, almost overwhelming, both in size and form.

It stomped up to him on six thick but hollow legs. Legs of a framework of metal, articulated in a most insect-like fashion, capped by a body that was all claws and hooks.

It did not hesitate as it came to him. It bent, pulled the several tons of material up under itself without so much as a grunt, and hefted it into the air. As it lifted its load, it was already walking away once more. It did not drive down a road. It climbed right over and up into the heart of the factory, toward whatever machinery lay within, waiting to process the massive amounts of material tribute they were bringing it. Waiting to make it into whatever ungodly things they were building here.

The shout of abuse from the foreman caused him to jump, as he should have known it would. Hendri cursed himself, almost as harshly as the foreman did, and quickly grabbed at his controls. Backing his loader up, quickly he spun it around as fast as he could, and accelerated off.

Another loader was, as always, waiting behind him, and as if to emphasize the thousand times he had been threatened with being replaced by a machine, this one was without a driver. It scooted itself up to the bay without comment and waited for another mighty minion of the factory to come and takes its offering.

Hendri cursed his wandering mind and drove off. Back to the exit gate, back to the checkpoint, back to the depot to pick up another load of material to feed the factory's massive hunger.

# Chapter 32: Hekaton's Carcass

From Milton SpacePort the elevator rose up. It did not just go to Hekaton. It went right into it. Like most of the loads for the last year, there were no people aboard these climbers as they rose up into the new moon. They carried machines, sometimes, but now their job was mostly to ferry up supplementary raw materials that had not been found in requisite quantities within Hekaton's mass.

After three years of aggressive mining, Earth's second moon was already noticeably diminished. But for Amadeu, she was all the more beautiful for it. Where some of his less imaginative colleagues saw something moth-eaten, an apple violated by marauding worms, Amadeu saw the work of a master sculptor.

This was in part because he understood the full importance of the pulp that continued to be gleaned from the plucked fruit that was Hekaton. But it was also because he knew what lengths Mynd was going to in order to maintain some measure of structural integrity in the ever more honeycombed asteroid.

As he zoomed in on the moon, he started to see the familiar signs of its continued vibrancy. This was not a dead thing, not at all. It was alive with activity. A thousand crawling machines, mostly variants on the wrecker that had become so core to their off-world operations, but some more specialized.

Drilling platforms buzzed here and there, noiseless in the vacuum, but violent nonetheless, biting into the rock, huge fabric lungs inflating on their backs as they caught the precious debris they were etching from Hekaton's surface. Some of the same platforms were on the move, relocating to new veins, pulling themselves by cable and harpoon through Hekaton's carcass, like fat, burly spidermen.

Tugs also wandered here and there among the diggers and grabbers. They busied themselves attaching to the drilling platforms to remove full debris sacks and replacing them with empty ones, like machine midwives.

The tugs did not move by cable, though. Their movements were freer. They needed no grapples to pull them around. They were mobilized by an array of fat nozzles on three stocky arms, fueled by their ever-on reactors as they ferried unendingly between the drilling stations to haul the cut meat out of the moon and deliver their prizes to one of the four factories of the Hekaton Missile-Mine Phalanx.

Unlike the factories dotted around the moon's surface, or the hundred or so manufacturing plants across Earth's glimmering blue-green orb far below, Hekaton's factories hung in space, like the moons of a moon. And where Earth's factories had trains and loaders and great mechanical spiders carrying materials to them, Hekaton's four factories were freed from gravity's limits. They were fed from all angles, and exuded their progeny with equal liberty, to be taken once more by the tugs, extending their midwife role, out onto Earth's equatorial plane.

Together with Earth's product being ferried up from the surface below by the five complete space elevators now spanning outward from the planet's waist, the missiles now formed a thin ring.  Not a rival of Saturn's icy necklace, not even close, but viewed from the planet below it most certainly had its admirers.

To avoid collision, the forty thousand missile mines of the Hekaton Phalanx, or the ring of fire, as it had come to be known, had been arrayed in great lines reaching to each side of the tops of the elevators now rising majestically from Brazil, the Maldives, Kiribati, Indonesia, and of course Sao Tome, capped as it was by the mighty Hekaton.

Five filament spokes in the dizzyingly wide mill-wheel that Earth had become.

Through Minnie's countless eyes, Amadeu saw the ring's components not as a collection of single units, but as a chorus.  A chorus his students were helping coordinate, one of many aspects of their training.

He brought those students to him now, into a virtual classroom without walls, the Earth sitting below them as they orbited it at an accelerated speed, flying beside, over, and around the thin but seemingly endless ring of missile-mines being prepped for launch.

Before he could even speak, Þalía, a young Norwegian girl, piped up.  He was not in the least bit surprised.

"Hekaton Missile-Mine Phalanx: 40,253 supra-gravitational units.  Combination chemical boosters and M-class fission drives.  Projected to be at least three thousand units behind target at zero hour."

Amadeu took a breath.  The rest of the class, he noticed via his autonomic monitoring programs, were equally 'impressed' with young Þalía's display.  There were nearly a hundred students in total in this class.  It was a feature of AI and virtual-reality supplemented education that he could have a far more hands-on experience with each of them than a far smaller class would enjoy within the confines of an ordinary school.

For this was the TASC War School.  They did things a little differently here.

He made a note to isolate Þalía's responses from now on.  She was showing off.  It was disruptive.  She would join the seven others he had already limited.  She would not know it.  In fact, three of those others had kicked off the proceedings with not dissimilar outbursts.  They thought they had impressed their friends and their teacher, and indeed, in their version of the simulation, their classmates around them had glanced varying looks of part-jealousy, part-awe, part-anger in their direction.  Enough to fuel their ambition, but without the matching inverse impact on their peers.

And anyway, Amadeu had neither the time nor the patience for such showboating.  Let one of his AI amalgams placate the louder children.  He began speaking for real, letting the AI integrate his words into whatever versions of him it was generating to handle the more boisterous of his students.

"Children.  Hekaton Missile-Mine Phalanx.  Launch protocol begins in just over three weeks.  What changes in three weeks that we must launch then?"

An array of hands went up. Several of the students began speaking without calling, and a matching number of Amadeus hushed the uninvited answers with varying levels of severity. The real Amadeu mentally glanced at the list of names pinging for a turn to speak. He picked three of them, as well as four others who hadn't volunteered but who he wanted to hear from. The answers came in a wave, his virtual selves nodding appreciatively within the confines of their programming as the various students spoke.

He heard snippets from each, siphoned and summarized. Wrong answers were dismissed and addressed automatically by his AIs, correct but unimaginative answers were dismissed almost as quickly. For Amadeu was looking for a more complete analysis, if one was to be found.

Per Amadeu's style, the system allowed the student mass at large to hear one wrong answer, then a correct one. From which student they heard each depended on whom they were grouped with, and thus sitting near.

"In three weeks we reach the apex of chance," said several students, "where the likelihood of the approaching Armada seeing that we are actively preparing for their arrival outweighs the increased damage we hope can hope to inflict by continuing to build on the size of the Missile-Mine phalanxes."

That was the correct answer, the textbook version. But one boy, a boy named Guowei, 'volunteered' as he had been, took a little longer to answer, as Amadeu had expected him to.

Eventually the young chinese boy, born to poor but well-educated parents and volunteered by a Chinese government keen to showcase the effectiveness of their state mandated child-assessment programs, spoke up. "In nineteen months, the light density leaving Earth will be high enough to no longer be masked by static caused by the sun's radiation at the point where that light connects with the incoming Armada.

"At the highest reliable speed at which we can send our missile-mines, they will need to leave Earth in just under three weeks in order to stay ahead of that light for long enough to connect with the Mobiliei Armada while it remains still unaware of our work to resist them."

Amadeu smiled. It was mimicked by every virtual version of him in the classroom.

"Yes, Guowei," said Amadeu. "But you speak of that point in time as an absolute."

"I do," said Guowei, countering almost immediately now, "but only because other responders already mentioned the apex of chance. To mention it again would have been redundant."

Amadeu stared at the boy and quickly queried the system. Guowei, pinged as he had been in the first round, had not heard any of his peer's less detailed answers before saying his own, though from the other children's perspectives his reply had, indeed, come after them.

Amadeu smiled more broadly now. Not just book smart, but truly perceptive, thought Amadeu, saying, "Yes, given the other responses, I guess it would have been obsolete, Guowei."

There were smart people, then there were geniuses. But Guowei was one of those children that was bright enough to shine even among these austere ranks, such was *his* light density.

"So, is that why we are stopping production in three weeks?" Amadeu asked the greater auditorium.

Again, a range of volunteers. He picked them off quickly, not pinging Guowei this time, who once again did not volunteer. He would see what the boy did. There were some variations on agreement, some caveats and some expositions. The majority were valid, even insightful. These were, after all, very smart children. Ranging in age from twelve to thirteen, these were the best.

So good, in fact, that some of their abilities as pilots had actually started to diminish. They were all close to Banu. But they had discovered that while a certain level of intellect was a requirement when pushing the speed limit, at some point it started to actually become a disadvantage, just as it did in everyday life.

Some of these then, Guowei chief among them, were no longer pilot candidates. They would soon be pulled from those ranks. They would be groomed for something else. They would, and indeed already were starting to, play other roles in TASC's actual organization. Administration, research, they were slowly being woven into pretty much all of TASC's work, even if it was as seemingly simple a task as creating games, puzzles, and battle simulations for their fellow War School students, the pilot elite.

All that said, Guowei still did not raise his hand. Amadeu cocked his head. He had wanted to see if the boy would take the bait. He hadn't.

"All good points. Guowei, nothing to add?"

"No," said the boy, his eyes alight though, waiting to be challenged. He was enjoying this.

"Nothing?"

Some children, Amadeu knew, were happy to see Guowei getting called out like this. Amadeu let them see it.

"No, Professor Esposinho," Guowei said, once more. Then, "Because the question is specious. Production does not stop in three weeks. It only shifts, and, if anything, accelerates."

Amadeu answered immediately and with genuine passion, not directed toward Guowei, but at the boy's classmates, "Absolutely right, Guowei! *Listen,* class. Listen to *everything.* Not just because I might trick you, though I may well try to do just that, but because I might be wrong. You are here to learn from me, yes, and learn you must.

"But you should assume nothing! You should take nothing for granted! Precision is all and I demand it from every one of you, all the time. You must analyze *everything* you are told to do, *every* question you are asked."

He pinged his AI to have his avatar look every student in the eye as he said this next part, "Never assume your leadership knows all the answers. Never assume an instruction is correct unless you have considered *every* part of its foundation, *every* reason, and, most importantly, every *consequence*."

He leant back. "That is your job. That is your part in this great effort. Because if you don't learn to constantly analyze our strategies, our tactics, how will you be able to create new ones when you are in the brief moment of battle … when you are out there."

He let the view unfold behind him, using his control of the simulated viewpoint that was their backdrop to swing them outward, to face the blackness, and to a specific point in that dark, a shining point, a growing beacon.

Damn, but he loved this environment, thought Amadeu. If his teachers had been able to this with their classrooms then he might have actually paid attention at university. But probably not, he thought, smiling to himself.

He let the previous point sit out there a while. It was not a new one. He probably said it, in one form or another, at least once a day. He saw more than a few unamused faces in the crowd, even a rolled eye or two, though not many. Guowei was not one of them, though. He got it.

Taking a deep breath, Amadeu moved on.

# Chapter 33: Catcher's Mitt

The realignment had cost Birgit and Rob nearly forty percent of their home's mass, but the space-terminal turned spaceship had been designed for a hundred times as many people as it currently held anyway.

It had come to her as she looked for ways to slow themselves as they span outward from Earth into the blackness. Eternity in ever blacker space didn't sound very pleasant, so Birgit had looked for a gravity net, another of the sun's planetary sons and daughters to call home while she worked on solving the greatest scientific puzzles that humanity and the Mobiliei had ever known.

Or failing that, a place to wait until the war was over. After that they could either hope for a rescue or wait out the rest of their lives watching a victorious Mobiliei Armada inhabit their home world. Not a pleasant thought, really, so they tended to stay away from that topic.

There was some good news, though. As Birgit had searched for potential planets to slow them, the possibility of an additional benefit had reared its head, and Birgit had quickly become all but obsessed with the plan. But the truth was Birgit and Rob's future together was like a dying tree, the vast majority of the branches of possibility ending in brittle, leafless twigs. But there were a few avenues that still held life. A few that might bear fruit, and the seeds of new hope.

And it was out onto one of those last branches of prospect they were now starting to shimmy. With several of Terminus's labs jettisoned in a violent but calculated act of sacrifice, they had thrown themselves to one side, down and across, into a new and profoundly elliptical orbital plane. They could not hope to completely halt their flight from Earth by this method, but they could speed their passage to another island in the darkness.

And her plan had worked, or at least the first part of it had. And now, years after leaving home, they found themselves approaching a new world, or rather, falling across its path as they had hoped to do. They could certainly have hoped for more precision, but they wouldn't get it. Precision was the product of planning, and no one had planned for them to be hurled out here, with only their wits and a seemingly random set of tools to craft their new destiny. They were interstellar MacGyvers, they often liked to joke.

"My calculations hold, mini-minnie, this will have to do," said Birgit to the air, and the response came into her head as a voice. She had all but given up on mind-to-mind communication with her amalgam of Minnie, it only reminded her of this version's limitations. Instead she spoke to it like she did to her friend Rob, with her voice, unenhanced and unembellished.

"Of course, Birgit," replied mini-minnie, "but I have received back from my self on Earth a revised orbital path that may require less manipulation."

Birgit stared out of a porthole. Far away, a disc was coming into focus. It was, as she had known it would be, a dusty red, like a plate of ground cinnamon, and it was growing fast now.

In Birgit's mind a graph appeared showing their approach. It dealt in far greater margins of error than she would like, but they would have to deal with that once they got themselves stabilized.

For while they were set to enter orbit around Mars, that was not Birgit's true target. Her plans were even more ambitious than just wanting to be the first human to visit another planet. The object she sought was much, much smaller, but, in its way, so much more accessible than the planet itself.

She sighed as mini-minnie questioned her calculations once more, then replied, "I am sure we can do it more efficiently, mini-minnie, and I am sure the real you has a better way to get into stable orbit, but that isn't the end state here, is it?"

"You talking to yourself again?" came Rob's voice as he slid in through the bulkhead from what was left of their living quarters.

"I am, it seems," she said, as he slid up to her. She was, as always, keenly aware of his physical presence, as he was of hers, no doubt. It had been years since she had seen another human, and while there were days when she dreamt of butchering the man, if only so she could cook him in place of another dried protein satchel, she also had ever more vivid dreams of doing ever more elaborate sexual acts with him as well.

She forcibly set them aside as she always did. It was something he'd had to do as well, though he never said anything either, of course. Unwittingly, she had become the sole source of every one of his fantasies. They had a data link to Earth that rivaled many a wifi, barring the whole hour-long request response time, but he doubted whether it would be well received if he requested even the most innocuous of dirty pictures from their Earthbound contacts.

So he lived with and suppressed his desire for her, as she did hers. They would be together for God knows how long, maybe even for the rest of their lives. No place for such silliness as a relationship, especially given the fifteen-year age gap between them.

Damn it, she thought, frustrated, why am I thinking about this again?

And she focused once more: on work, on the calculation, on the calculated risk.

"You arguing over the orbit again?" he said, and she snorted a laugh.

"Yes. We are arguing over the orbit … again."

The circular argument Birgit had been in over the past few months was a perfect demonstration of the difference between the copy of Minnie and the real thing. On the one hand, mini-minnie was not complex or deep enough to really care about the danger of what they were hoping to do next. But when the real Minnie heard about it, and calculated the precise chances of them pulling it off successfully, the real AM most certainly did.

And then, once the real Minnie convinced this one of the need to dissuade Birgit of the enterprise, mini-minnie was both too dogmatic to back down and too limited to have a real discourse on the topic.

"I know their objections ... *her* objections. But ..." said Birgit, trailing off.

"... but you don't give a shit?" said Rob helpfully.

She laughed. "Yes, something like that."

She was aware that she was gambling not only with her life, but with his as well. She had allowed him access to the data, both her interpretations and Minnie's, and said he should vote on this, speak up if he wanted her to stop. But he could not understand Minnie's objections any more than he could understand Birgit's counter-arguments.

It was like a child trying to vote on which house his parents should buy, or which route they should take to school. Sure, it affected him too, it affected him very much. But that did not make him any less ignorant of the nature of this disagreement of geniuses, and so it didn't make his vote anything more than honorary.

"Well, how about this?" said Rob, looking very serious all of a sudden. Birgit's expression became one of skeptical curiosity, "How about mini-minnie stays here with me and you go on ahead. If the water is warm give us a shout and we'll come and join you."

She laughed.

"Sure," she said, chuckling, "and if I find work I'll send for you."

He smiled broadly and with genuine affection. Their eyes stayed locked a moment too long. She turned away, but the nature of the systems she worked in did not give her a computer screen to stare at or a binder to read, so she closed her eyes instead, looking inward to her link to the station's systems ... to her calculations ... to her plan to crash land the entire station into the moon called Phobos.

# Chapter 34: The Ball Rolling

Madeline was waiting for Amadeu when he finished his class. Before accepting her meeting request, he validated that the request had come via standard channels, ready to initiate a certain protocol should it be required. But, he saw, it had come via the main system. He would not need his protocol today.

*Amadeu:* 'good morning/afternoon/evening, whatever it is where you are.'

She laughed through the system.

*Madeline:* 'hello, amadeu.'

*Amadeu:* 'hello. yes, that's so easy for you english-speakers. we don't have that in portuguese. i tried using ciao for a while, but too many people think i am saying good-bye by mistake.'

*Madeline:* 'so let's come up with a new word. ¿how about 'neal?' we could say, 'neal be with you.' or 'good-neal to you.'

Amadeu did not laugh. She took the hint and got on with the real reason for their conversation.

*Madeline:* 'i just met with moira, like we discussed.'

Amadeu was curious. Her and Birgit's work was bordering on madness, he felt sure of that, but then when he dipped his toes into any of the theoretical pools behind subspace technologies it all felt very cold and uninviting. This was not the stuff of science, as he understood it. This was too esoteric. It did not feel … safe. And this from a man whose life's work was messing with people's spines, dicking around with people's brains.

But this, this was different, this was more unsettling even than Amadeu's burgeoning science of the mind. This was messing with the fabric of space, of reality, and it specked of hubris that we should hope to circumvent the rules of the very universe and not risk breaking the game itself.

But it was, he feared, too great a prize to pass up. And in the end, they may well need success there in order to survive, if only because of his own ongoing failures to break the 'limit' by any appreciable margin.

But Madeline did not have the news he had hoped for.

*Madeline:* 'moira is … skeptical.'

*Amadeu:* '¿skeptical?'

He did not stop his disappointment from bleeding through to her, and in turn saw that she shared it.

*Madeline:* 'she does not say it is without hope, she just says … well, she says it is not something she sees a conclusion to. she insists that this does not mean birgit cannot do it. ¿but in the end, if moira cannot see a light at the end of the tunnel, even moira, can birgit be that much further along that tunnel than her?'

*Amadeu:* 'don't ask me, madeline. ask … neal. he's the physicist.'

But Neal was not a physicist, not in the sense that Moira or Birgit were, not even close. And neither was he someone that they really wanted to invite into this conversation.

They said nothing for a moment, and then Amadeu did two things. He spoke and initiated the very protocol he had not thought he would need in this meeting. Madeline felt both happen at the same time.

*Amadeu:* 'well, madeline, i appreciate the update anyway. thanks for coming by. i guess i should get back to the school.'

*Madeline:* 'of course, amadeu. sorry for disturbing you. i wish i had better news, but there it is.'

Amadeu sent a mental nod and then the signal was cut.

The space around him went suddenly black as the system began unloading subsets and running looped mind-maps. He waited. It was working without him now. A little part of Minnie that she had sectioned off just for this purpose. Sectioned off and then abandoned, wiping the memory of her own actions from her very own mind.

The connection came back online now, muted and simplified. The most minimal version of a link possible. So thin and slight that it could be hidden in static, piggybacked on the trillions of other bytes of data swarming around in Minnie's world-spanning network. Hidden even from Minnie herself, as she had designed it to be.

Madeline's voice came back to him now as a whisper in the darkness.

"Are we clear?"

"We are, Madeline. Sorry, but I needed to hear it properly. I know we said we should talk as much as possible in the open, but …"

"No need to explain, Amadeu. I know what you mean. Trust me, I know what you mean."

She did. It was not the first time she had felt spied upon in her life, and she did not relish living through it again. That she now had the help of friends as capable in this new world as Amadeu made it infinitely easier, no doubt about that. But that she was now hiding from her own, from the one who had been with her from the start, in India, all those years ago, that also made it so much harder, as well.

For now it was not the Mobiliei satellites, but Neal himself that they feared. Neal and Ayala. Always listening. Always watching. In their very heads, or so it felt.

"So," said Amadeu, whispering in the blackness, "is it really a lost cause?"

"No," replied Madeline. "Moira definitely didn't say that. She just doesn't see how it can be done. She still has the highest possible faith in Birgit, but, well, that is what worries me."

"It does?"

"Yes, it does. Because if even Moira, with all her knowledge, with all her ability, and the breadth of her experience in the field, and more than that, with the amount she respects, even idolizes, Birgit, if even *she* doesn't see how it can be done ..."

Madeline let it hang out there for a second.

"Did you tell Neal this yet?" said Amadeu.

"Do I even have to tell him?"

They both laughed now, but without humor. They had seen too many examples of Neal knowing too much about their work, more than they'd had the chance to share with him yet. And besides that, Amadeu's other contacts had given him more conclusive evidence of surveillance. They were being watched, Amadeu knew that. Maybe everyone was being watched, who knew, but he did know for certain that he and his direct contacts were.

Most notably the nexus of the group. The man who had started it all. The man whose tirades on the subject had become so vitriolic it had prompted Amadeu to create this very communications program, if only so he could have a place to tell the man to stop ranting, to save him from himself and stop drawing attention to something he was not alone in suspecting.

Madeline spoke again after a brief pause. "No, I haven't told Neal yet. Though, interestingly, he does not seem nearly as married to this line of research as we all are."

"You know, I sensed that too," replied Amadeu. "You'd think, given the wall I have hit, that he would be more worried, that he would be pushing harder, both on Birgit and on me."

"Still no more progress on your end either, then," said Madeline, as conciliatorily as she could.

Amadeu did not flinch at the comment, so much as brace for the flinch he felt should come. It was a failure on his part, he knew that, but whether it was a failure to achieve his goal, or to accept the truth behind that failure, to accept the real cause of their inability to meaningfully exceed the Mobiliei pilot's capabilities, that was something else.

"I am afraid we continue to see diminishing returns, yes. We broke though one wall only to find a taller one beyond, one that I cannot seem to find a way over. We will, I feel confident, be faster than the Mobiliei. But unless something changes, it will be by such a minuscule margin as to make it almost imperceptible."

"And Neal knows this?"

"He does," said Amadeu.

"And how did he take that?"

Amadeu thought about it.

"You know, it's weird," he said. "At the last Meeting of Representatives which I presented at, I am telling them my numbers, I am telling them the facts. I am trying to be positive, to be sure, but I am not sugarcoating it. Not by a long shot. We know the numbers of Skalms coming for us. We know the probabilities of damage from the coming missile-mine strike. We know what we will likely be facing once the real fighting begins. Given that, and the speed difference between our fleet and theirs at the point of closing, we knew what needed to be done on reaction times to give us a fighting chance."

"Of course, Amadeu. To say that message has gotten through would be an understatement. So how did Neal react to news of your ... ongoing struggles?"

Amadeu snorted. Ongoing struggles. But his discomfort with the greater topic at hand sobered him once more, and he replied, "Well, Neal nodded. He looked somber and he let the group throw some questions my way, I think it was that Uncovsky from Russia, and the Qatar representative, about me getting enough resources. Then ... he just left it."

Now that Madeline thought about it, she had seen the feed. All Representative Meetings were broadcast internationally, and even got a shockingly large viewership, for political meetings, anyway. But then they typically moved with an impressive speed and purpose compared to the lolling indecisiveness of ordinary governing body debates.

It was an unnatural speed, Madeline feared. A fear that had been the root of a brief conversation with Amadeu a year beforehand. A conversation that had seen her being brought to this black meeting place for the first time.

"So why isn't Neal reacting more strongly?" said Madeline.

Amadeu did not know. Neal was not known for coyness. Neal was a reasonable enough man, sure, well, he had been back when they had started out, at least, but no one had ever accused him of being restrained, and certainly never gun-shy.

"I'll reach out to him," Madeline said. "He asked me to update him on this anyway. For now, stay focused on the school. No matter what happens with Birgit or Neal, your work is still at the center of everything. Your progress, as hard as I know it is, is the fulcrum on which this turns. Anything you need ..."

He had heard it many times before. But he feared what he needed was a better raw material to work with. What he needed, he knew, was a cleaner subject.

Madeline knew there were others in the little conspiracy of theirs. She knew that Jim Hacker had recruited more once Amadeu had showed him how to communicate without Neal or Ayala being able to track it, once Amadeu had given Neal's chief of staff the means he needed to start a candid discussion on safe terms.

But who they were and what they were doing, that Madeline was not fully privy to. She could not be. That was the nature of their conspiracy. A limited string of people, layer on layer of security.

Amadeu was, for the most part, just an enabler. And Madeline was right, he did have another, vital role to play, a day-job to return to.

"You'll pass on to Jim what I've found out, and what I am going to do next?" said Madeline before leaving.

"I will," Amadeu replied, and she was gone.

# Chapter 35: Tidal Unity

The nods came as Neal had hoped, acquiescence filling the room's collective minds. There was a healthy amount of dissent as well. Germany, Poland, and Ukraine leading the way this time. Some strongly voiced opposition. And, for effect, some from himself as well. This, then, was a victory for the Chinese and Russians, and the ever-thorny bed they still shared.

Though his opposition to the bill to make the new Representative Mind the permanent head of worldwide communications had been a falsehood, Neal did not have to fake the very real frustration that showed on his face as the voting was validated and the decision announced at last. Oh well, he thought. So he still had to placate two of the largest countries on earth. That was hardly unreasonable, given what had preceded it.

And in the end, it all helped with the public image of the Representatives of Earth. The meeting hall was filled with a voting party from every recognized sovereign nation on the planet, each with a voting power based on their total population, Gross Domestic Product, and, most importantly, the relative scale of their contributions to TASC in the previous governing period.

The governing periods lasted thirty days. The Representatives met three times in each period, with the last meeting of each month concluding with a pledge to continue support, and the first meeting of the next month including an agreement on voting rights accrued from the previous month's relative contributions.

There was no chairperson, not even Neal. The only concession to TASC's unique place in the group was that its vote was fixed. Regardless of population or income, TASC itself got a one percent share in the voting pool. That meant Neal had the tenth largest voting power in the room, matched with several members of the former European Union, but everyone knew, of course, that Neal's real power did not stem from that vote anyway.

He had allies, many of them, and in the end he held the steering wheel. They could tell him where they wanted him to drive the seven-billion-person party-bus they were all now on, but few in the know were under any real doubt as to whether he would actually veer too far from the path he really wanted to be on.

This, then, was a tool. They knew it, and Neal knew it. But to say the representatives that filled it still wielded very real and far-reaching influence would be a gross understatement. In this room the world got to see what was being done to save humanity. In this room the world watched as a united war machine of unparalleled scale churned and rolled forward. And every member of this group knew they would be remembered by historians as the people who saved humanity, because the alternative was that there would be no more history at all.

"A good session, in the end," said Neal, as he stepped out of the room, and out of view of the countless cameras dotted throughout the hall. "How long until the Indonesian cutover review?"

Jim was silent a moment as he checked on the Chinese delegation's status. Though the review was of the extensive production facilities across a swathe of the Indonesian archipelago, those islands were all now leased to the People's Republic of China, and the meeting would be with representatives of the Chinese government, with only a sparse Indonesian contingent present.

"They say they should be ready in about ten minutes," said Jim, his eyes refocusing.

"Good, good," replied Neal, as they walked along a back corridor and boarded a small, unmanned cart. It whirred off without word, instructed to do so, no doubt, by one of Jim's many minions.

"And you, Jim, how are you?" said Neal, glancing across at the man seated opposite him, in the cart's small cabin.

"Good. I am still concerned with the Macapá SpacePort dredging operation. They simply did not spec that work correctly. We have lost ..."

Jim went to call up a number of days the SpacePort's sea-lane had been effectively closed to large-scale shipping from his mind, but Neal interrupted him. "Do you need me to have a word with the Brazilian delegate?"

Jim shuddered ever so slightly, not that he feared Neal meant anything more than just having a word with the woman. He was overly sensitive, Jim knew that, to what he knew Neal was really capable of. But that was not this Neal. Not the politician. And anyway, Jim had pushed the Brazilian issue as far as he needed to. He had even sent a friend down there, a most capable one.

"No, I don't think that will be necessary," said Jim with a genuine smile. "I've asked Quavoce, or rather Major Garrincha, to go down there and help supervise work directly."

Neal smiled as well. He knew this already, not through any asset of Ayala's, but through a shared acquaintance. "Yes, Jim, and you have gotten me in some trouble because of it."

Jim looked askew at Neal, maybe even with a hint of fear, and Neal was caught off guard by the reaction. Had things really gotten so bad that Jim would be afraid of him?

"Banu told me," said Neal, and saw that Jim, though he tried to hide it, relaxed a little. "She was none to happy that her father had to go away on business."

Jim tried to move past his faux pas, raising his eyebrows as he said, "Well, to be honest, you could always let her go with him."

Neal balked instinctively at the thought. Banu. His little warrior. Sent off into the Amazon rainforest. No, he thought. But as he considered it more, he started to see Jim's point.

"Yes, I suppose she isn't the lone little warrior-princess she once was, is she?" he smiled. It was a smile laden with simple and very genuine fondness, and Jim was reminded of why he had followed Neal in the first place. Why he had trusted him. He was a good man, at heart.

But that did not forgive his actions, Jim then reminded himself, steeling himself against a potential wave of regret at what he had started with Madeline and Amadeu and others.

Still smiling, Jim agreed with Neal, saying, "We have other pilots that can take the reins of the Skalm should it be needed. Others that have been training for just such an opportunity. And in a matter of days, when we finish retooling the Dome facilities at District Two, we will start production on the next Skalm, the first of many to join Banu's lone destroyer."

Neal nodded. His little Banu. Nearly ten years old now. She called him Uncle Neal. He probably took more pride from that simple gesture of respect and affection than he did from any of the titles and power his life was now saddled with.

"Shall I let Quavoce know she can ... go along?" said Jim, hesitantly. "That she can leave District One?"

Neal looked at the man, a little vacantly at first, and then with more clarity. "Yes, Jim, you can send her with him. She will like that. Though she should probably go under a pseudonym, and ..."

"Don't worry, Neal. I'll have my team see to it she remains safe. And then there is always the matter of Quavoce."

They shared a moment of genuine shared amusement. Woe betide anyone who threatened Banu on Quavoce's watch. No, thought Neal, she will be fine. It will do her good to get out and see the world, to try to forget all of the fighting and killing for a while.

"We're here," said Jim, suddenly, as they came to a halt by another door, in another part of the growing representative's complex on Sao Tome.

Neal was confused a moment, then nodded. "Good. Let's get on with it then."

- - -

*Ayala:* '¿how did it go with the indonesian transition discussion? ¿do they still insist on partial commercial capacity?'

*Neal:* 'they do. but i think we can allow a small percentage, if only because not all of the facilities there are at standard for fleet production anyway.'

*Ayala:* '¿no, they aren't all up to standard, are they? ¿a coincidence?'

Neal shook his head and snorted derisively, both in the ether and in real life, seated now in his office. Jennifer looked a question at him and he shook his head again now, though this time to say 'not to worry.'

*Neal:* 'you give our chinese allies too much credit. or maybe i give them too little. either way, we have gotten from them as much as we could reasonably have expected. more even. better that we give them this small victory, so they can fulfill their larger contracts. it helps them, and it helps the public get their hands on more little goodies from our laboratories. austerity makes no one happy, no matter how patriotic. this will help us overall.'

On this topic, Neal knew, Ayala and he most certainly did not agree. She was not one for compromise, and she did not see the argument for appeasement, either of the Chinese, or the world's populace at large. So they all wanted access to the virtual world, to spinal interfaces, to hypersonic and exo-atmospheric travel, to AI driven robots that could bring home the bacon and cook it up in a pan, and, she had heard, even help with the last part of that saying, too, for the right price.

But Ayala saw no need for any of this. Not given the greater threat they faced. People needed to knuckle down and get it done, no matter what they were forced to endure.

They needed to endure, as she had, and, if necessary, they needed to suffer, as she had.

But seven billion people did not rally to a banner easily, not even one as powerful as the threat of extinction. The Armada was still a long way away, farther than most people could comprehend. Such abstruse concepts suffered in the space between the mind and the heart.

History was filled with such mass delusions, from a cowed Europe refusing to see the true threat of a rising Third Reich, even as it steamrolled Poland's borders, to the ensuing struggle to bring a distant United States into the fray years after the fighting had already started.

But while Ayala may be uncannily capable of forcing people into line, Neal needed to influence humanity on a far vaster scale than Ayala and her methods could.

You couldn't manage everyone in the way Ayala now wrangled some of the world's more troublesome leaders. And Neal wouldn't want to even if they could. It pained him whenever he thought about it, what they had done to their dissenters in Iran, and Russia, and Egypt, and others, Neal knew, more than Ayala had told him about, more than he wanted to know, no doubt.

No. Wherever possible, Neal tried to win people's hearts as well as their minds. And, Neal thought, not just the hearts of the masses, but of the few, the ones he would have to trust as he worked toward final victory.

And as he thought about that, he considered who he did trust. And he came back to an old topic with the woman whose voice was even now in his head.

*Neal:* 'i spoke to jim today about banu.'

*Ayala:* '¿really? ¿what did he say?'

He wondered if Ayala really didn't know. If she wasn't watching him just as much as he knew she was watching so many others. But that was the price. And Neal knew she was trustworthy for a very specific reason: she could be trusted to do what it would take to survive. Whatever it would take.

*Neal:* 'Jim pointed out that she is not, really, such a person of interest anymore, not now that we have the first of the pilot cadets trained and ready.'

*Ayala:* '¿he did, did he? interesting. ¿and what did he recommend you do with this information?'

*Neal:* 'he recommended i let her accompany quavoce on his trip to brazil to supervise the reopening of the silted channel there.'

Ayala did not reply for a second. Neal assumed she was checking facts, maybe calling up the conversation in question for review, maybe asking Saul or one if his team of analysts for a dossier.

*Ayala:* 'so you let her go, i see. i have a request, neal, if you don't mind. in the future, please check with me before letting a major asset of ours go off campus.'

Neal fought back the bitter taste he got from hearing Banu reduced to nothing more than an 'asset.' He appreciated Ayala's paranoia, he relied on it, in fact. He knew she was the only reason he was still alive, and probably the real reason he was still at the head of earth's preparations for the coming war. But there were moments when her methods became less palatable.

*Neal:* 'banu is nearly ten, she has served the effort for long enough, given her age, and we have many who can fly the skalm nearly as well as her, and several that are even better.'

*Ayala:* 'true, neal. ¿but our enemies don't have such resources, do they? ¿what if they have plans to take control of the skalm, or of one of the future ones planned for production? ¿what would they be willing to do to gain access to one of the best and certainly the most experienced pilots we have?'

Neal went silent. He had, indeed, not considered this. They had caught whiff of several moves to try and wrestle control of the Skalm, and its planned siblings, away from TASC, both covert and via political channels. Ayala had quashed them each as they arose, using the many tools at her disposal, but who knew if they had uncovered them all.

*Neal:* 'you're right, of course. i had not considered that. i'll contact quavoce. tell him to change …'

*Ayala:* 'no, no. she can go. i'm not totally heartless, neal. but i will work with minnie to get at least a phase eight out there with them. between that and quavoce himself, she should be safe.'

'Not totally heartless,' thought Neal. He sometimes wondered if that was true. But then he chided himself. Enough. This was Ayala, Barrett's widow. She was now, and always had been, a true friend. He shook his head again, and again Jennifer looked at him from across the room. He wanted to talk to her about this. He really did. But … but … but the truth was that he didn't trust that he could speak honestly about this, not anywhere. Even here, even in his personal suite, he could not talk candidly about his concerns about his security chief.

Neal breathed deeply, then stood and went over to Jennifer, who was making a couple of fairly lethal caipirinhas for them both. He had been craving one all day since the problems with the Macapá channel had come to a head. She smiled as he embraced her from behind.

*Neal:* 'good, Ayala. that sounds like a good idea, and one i am sure neither quavoce nor banu will have any objection to. listen, ayala, i have to go. jennifer is waiting for me.'

He cringed sharply at the blunder, at the reference to his partner, his confidant, and the inadvertent allusion to Ayala's loss of hers.

Ayala did not skip a beat though.

*Ayala:* '¿but what about the east asia briefing? i still have two pages worth of intelligence update to go through with you.'

*Neal:* '¿is there anything requiring immediate attention?'

*Ayala:* 'no. no, if there was then i would have mentioned that first.'

She paused, then went on.

*Ayala:* 'no, there's nothing here i can't handle directly.'

He paused as well, and Jennifer felt him go stiff for a moment. But then he breathed again, forcing himself to relax, or at least to detach.

*Neal:* 'good. thank you, ayala. as always, i trust you implicitly.'

He meant it. He really had no choice.

## Chapter 36: Seeking Doubt

They flew through the darkness. Ahead he sensed a coming dent, a fluctuation in the gravitational plane of his universe. It was an approaching point of glancing. Given its size, he set his wave parameters and then he braced, reaching out quickly to his team to make sure that they knew their respective roles.

*WG:* '[loc.] distortion approaching.'

He received pings from most of his team, but not from Friday. In the final seconds before contact, Wednesday reached out once more.

*WG:* '¿friday god?

Silence. No doubt he was still sulking over Wednesday being appointed squadron leader. Oh well, no time for that now.

0.03, 0.02 …

The glancing came as a blur of focal points, a slowed blink, a single event in which every component was in one place, and then a very different one almost instantaneously. Wednesday, as leader, came in with the first wave, giving him a split second as they flashed past their opponents to analyze their pattern, and their reaction to the attack, and then to send back a response code to the next wave. His best pilots would then act on this.

They saved as many for the second wave as possible, analyzing the scale of the coming force based on the size of the gravitic distortion, and sending only what they had to with the first wave to stop the squadron leader from being summarily wiped out before he could make a code call.

Friday, when the time came, did not let his sulking mood bleed into his fighting. This was too important to him. He lived for this. For the attack. For these few precious moments in which he felt so very alive. And so, when the second wave came through, hot on the heels of the first, he lashed out with true zeal.

The glancing was a single heartbeat of pure adrenalin, a pulse of massive energy. A blink of an eye in which white-hot blades lanced out with all they had, gouging, ripping, tearing at each other, giving everything they had to the ending of the other.

It was all focused on this one moment, the lunge of the fencer, where all the positioning, all the preparation, all the thought and strategy came together to either the moment of connection, the moment of repost, or the hot sting of violation, the sharper end of the blade.

Wednesday had prepared them well, Friday noted. He had sent Friday to one side. A howling wolf to pull the enemies' attention to him. And in the millisecond of their targeting, the rest of the pack that was the second wave came through in a flanking pattern made perfect by the attempts of their enemies to outwit just such a tactic.

Friday and the rest of the second wave capitalized on Wednesday's ingenuity and scored a high return. Wednesday had lost himself in the glancing, as had most of the first wave, but the second wave's better positioning more than evened the field, taking more than half of the enemy squadron. It was a hot kill. An excellent glancing.

*Mother:* 'a good pass, squadron. well done. come out and i will show you the tally.'

They left, departing the blackness to return to a more natural wing. With a rush they now flew once more as a part of the greater flock, a gathering of friends, each benefiting from the aggregated current of air they were pulling with them. Wednesday and Friday flew back to their appointed spots, their usual places in the flock's great, collective wing.

Friday did not look at Wednesday as they felt the familiar, comforting pull of the air on their wings.

"You did well, Friday," said Wednesday, in as conciliatory a tone as he could muster. He was sad his friend had not been made squadron leader, but also a little angry. Angry at having his own achievement marred by his friend's sullen mood.

It was an even day, so the water was below them. On odd days the sea passed by above. On some days there was no sea, only pockets of water gathered into huge, oddly shaped globules passing by below and on either side of them. Some days these shapes had meaning, humor even. Holidays were especially fun. Holidays were defined by the group. Days set to remember specific achievements by one or all of the pilots. The holidays came each month, and they were always accompanied by lots and lots of fabulous food.

Mother came to them now, beating up and out of the head of the flock and soaring over it, her great wings beating only slightly now as she feathered the air, feeling it and using it. She flew with a grace only the best could match.

Even fewer could truly outmaneuver her. But Friday was definitely one such ace, and this was the focus of his frustration. But as she came over to fly over them she was all smiles, and it momentarily softened even his resolve.

Wednesday saw the hint of a smile on Friday's face before he returned to staring sullenly ahead. So did Mother, apparently, and she winked lightly at Wednesday as she came up to them and the rest of their squadron.

"Well done, Wednesday. An excellent tactical analysis," she said, and Wednesday beamed.

"As for the second wave's execution of your orders ..." she paused, and Wednesday saw that Friday was listening in the ever-so-slight faltering in his tail feathers, a twitch that betrayed his true focus.

"... a masterful piece of flying." she said magnanimously, rolling gracefully once for emphasis. The squadron took the chance to mimic her, ducking and rolling in a couple of quick turns that sent the surrounding banks of the flock reeling, and had the squadron members beating hard to reclaim their places in the huge body of birds a moment later.

But they were laughing as they did so, all but one, still sulking. As they beat back up into place, Mother swooped in closer, and a whisper found Friday's ear amid the whistling wind on his face, "Especially you, Friday. As always, you were magnificent."

He did not join the others in their whooping and hollering, but he could not keep the smile from breaking out across his feathery face.

"As for this rolling and swerving, this breaking of the flock's flow ..." she then said suddenly, with the full bellow of her baritone voice, "well, Wednesday Squadron can *stay* out of this place in the flock."

They all balked. Had they really angered her so by breaking formation? Breaking line was not that unusual, especially when a battle had gone particularly well. Could she really be so angry as to dock them their hard won position in the flock's wing?

"With this victory you have moved up a place on the roster!" she then shouted, and after a moment's disbelief they were breaking away again, this time without exception. Promotion meant first place again. They had worked hard to reclaim their lead. Every few weeks the game changed slightly. New rules were added, older rules became obsolete. A series of poor glancings after the last change had cost them precious spots against the other top teams.

Wednesday God's promotion to the top spot had seen a change in direction. He was good at this, great in fact, and his teammates brushed his belly and back with the tips of their wings, the beats of their wings drawing him up, raising him on their gifted lift as they called out his name.

Friday was not beyond redemption. He could not fight such happiness. Nor resist the call to be a part of such a celebration. Promotion meant respect for them all. And it also meant diving time, beneath the shimmering surface passing by below them.

"You will return to the flock next cycle," said Mother, already starting to move back to the head of the great army of pilot trainees. "Your new place will be assigned then. Now go!"

At this, they dove as one, racing each other downward with abandon as the wind whipped around their faces. Their wings were only rudders now, guiding their meteoric fall as they plummeted toward the water below. As always, some used them more liberally than others, costing themselves precious momentum. But not Friday. He pulled himself close to his chest, drawing inward with all his might to keep his profile as small and slippery as possible.

Always the fastest, always the best. But never the leader, he thought.

The others naturally veered away from him. He was too aggressive, too competitive, even in the world of flight school. They knew Wednesday would follow his friend. He was nothing if not loyal. They liked that about him, even if they didn't see why he was so close with Friday. A few of the others shouted last calls of congratulations as the water came rushing up to meet them, and then they were gone.

Friday, ahead as he was, hit first. Wednesday never did like this part. But the bit that came next was more than worth it. He focused on where Friday had impacted the water, the white font of his passing swelling upward and outward now in concentric circles of foam and spray. Wednesday aimed for it like a target, bracing for impact as it came roaring up at him.

The transition was not unlike being hit in the face with a bucket of ice-cold water and Wednesday could not understand why the others found it so fun. But this water was different. This water washed their very forms away, changing them, brushing their wings away to be replaced by arms once more.

As the water washed over them, their legs and talons became the ordinary, fleshy legs and feet of boys once more. Mother said this was them leaving the magic place, the underside of the world, to return to the reality they had been confined to for the first part of their ever-improving lives.

Somehow the normal world still felt welcoming, though, as Wednesday smashed through the water, and out the other side, his form morphing back to normal, his boyish body now leaping, not down through water, but up from land, land he had just passed through, his momentum now losing itself as he reoriented to his heavy form in the normal world.

He landed next to his friend, who was grinning. They were on green grass. It was lush and soft. It smelled alive. Here their rivalry was forgotten. It was not really a rivalry anyway. Friday wished for nothing but the best for his friend. Truly, he hoped that Wednesday could be every bit the pilot Friday was. But he wasn't. That was what confused Friday. And yet his friend had been chosen over him, to lead the squadron, to lead Friday.

But, that was neither here nor there. They had won, that was all that mattered now. And they had won by enough of a margin of attrition that they had moved up a whole rank. It was too good a feeling to waste on jealousy, or questioning the whys and hows of it all.

This was *their* time. Wednesday and Friday: the Gods of this world and the next.

He smiled in his special way, a smile that seemed not only to fill his face, but to light up the space around him with his exuberant joy. Wednesday was so happy to see that smile. It was a single piece of truth in an ever more exciting, but also confusing, world. It had once been his only solace in a cold and unforgiving life, now it was the one good thing he had carried over from that grey time.

As they stood, Friday spinning suddenly and running off to the house, to Home, Wednesday was filled with a familiar sense of belonging, a sense almost strong enough to overcome the little voice in him that said something was wrong. That this, patently, was all very wrong.

They were not Gods, despite their honorifics, and yet somehow both his friends and he, and a host of others, had ended up in this place. A place Mother said everyone went to. A place that Mother said was where they had been destined for all along. They had just been left behind, left in one grey, hopeless world when they should have been moving between these two wonderfully colorful ones.

But that was passed now, she told them all every night. That was passed. They were with Mother now, and they were going to have everything they ever dreamed of.

And it *was* the stuff of dreams, thought Wednesday, as he chased after his friend up to the house, crashing through the never-locked door into the living room. It was strange to see it now, the place that had been their everything for those first few months. Now just a place to visit, a weekend getaway.

A weekend getaway, yes! That was how he had seen it described. A weekend getaway. An island, Jeju, that was what it had been called. It was so vague now, so distant, but the memory came back to him now. The memory of an article and a picture. They had been in a magazine which Friday had stolen from one of the orphanage's warden's rooms. A magazine Friday had not even been able to read. An illegal magazine from the south. It had come to fill Wednesday's dreamscape, even as it had become frayed and tattered from countless rereadings.

At the time, back then, the magazine had sat outside everything Wednesday understood. It had undermined everything that he and his fellow orphans had been told about the world, and about their God, their Glorious Leader.

At first, Wednesday had assumed he had been taken to Jeju Island when he had come here. But no. This … this place … this is not Jeju, he thought. Even Jeju, with the stories of swimming and diving and hiking, even that seemingly magical place paled in comparison to *this*.

So as Friday ran out of the kitchen, already carrying an armful of fruit and breads, crumbs spilling from a quickly stuffed mouth, and vaulted up the stairs to get his toys out, Wednesday felt something under the happiness, something unsettling. A question.

He did not go and get food, though he did feel hungry when he looked at it. Instead he followed his friend upstairs. As Friday began arranging his toys on the floor, mumbling something about the battle of the birdmen, Wednesday just watched him.

This wasn't right. This wasn't how it was supposed to be. It was not just wrong for the once impoverished life they'd had in a country they did not even know was called the People's Republic of North Korea. This wasn't right anywhere.

And then, of course, there was the error. The scratch.

"Friday!" he said, suddenly full of purpose.

Friday did not respond.

"Friday! Come on! I have to show you something!" he said again, his voice laden with impetus.

Friday looked up plaintively, confused at why his friend was not getting his own birds and planes, and mumbled softly, "But … battle of birdmen …" crumbs still hanging off his suddenly crestfallen face.

"Now, Fri! We have to go!" said Wednesday. "Come on!"

And Wednesday turned and ran back along the corridor. And now it sounded like he was running back down the stairs again. From the sound of it he was already banging across the living room toward the front door. But … wait …

"Wait for me!" shouted Friday, suddenly up and running after his friend.

- - -

"Close now. It was right around here," said Wednesday, studiously.

"*What* was?" the exasperation was thick in Friday's voice, the end of all things dear felt in the eight minutes or so he had been forced to endure looking for whatever Wednesday was so desperate to find.

"You'll see, it is right around here." Stepping carefully, Wednesday kept retracing a particular path, as if he was trying to recreate something.

"*What* is?" said Friday, as bored as he could ever remember being in his entire, long, tiresome, complicated little life.

"The ..." said Wednesday as he stepped behind a tree. And then nothing. Friday blinked. He had seen some weird stuff in the last few years, but this was new.

"... mistake," said Wednesday, but from behind Friday now, off in another direction.

"Wh ... how'd you?" Friday managed, spinning to see his friend walking toward to him from some way off. But Wednesday was excited.

"See! A mistake. I told you. It's a mistake," he said, running back to where he had just been.

"Watch," Wednesday said. He stepped forward again and Friday followed him this time, and ... nothing, he was still there, and they walked a little farther and then ...wait a minute, they were looking at the same spot again, the same tree, knotted just so. They had moved a hundred meters or so backward in an instant.

"It's a loop," said Wednesday.

"A what?"

"A loop. It's the reason you can never get lost out here, in the woods. Why, no matter how far you walk off, you always end up back at home," said Wednesday, somewhat triumphantly.

"How do you know that?"

"Because ..." Wednesday hesitated a moment, then went on, "because I tried to leave."

Friday was surprised, but then Wednesday compounded it by saying, meeker now, but still determined, "Actually, I tried a whole bunch of times. That's how I found this. The scratch, I call it."

Friday looked at his friend, his closest friend, his only friend, perhaps, and could only say, "But why?"

It was a fair question. Wednesday's answer came out even more meekly than he expected, "Because I don't think this ... I don't ... I don't think this is real, Friday."

Friday stared at him. Not real. What was Wednesday talking about?

"Of course it isn't real, Wednesday. It's a game. One we just won, I should add," said Friday, trying to reclaim the sense of smugness and all around self-satisfaction that seemed, all of a sudden, to have deserted him.

Wednesday explained as best he could. "No, no, Fri. I mean. You know the games, and the sims?"

"Of course ..." said Friday, starting to worry that he knew where this was going.

"Well, they're not real, we know that. But we get stuff, cool stuff, when we do well in them. You know, *here,* in the real world."

Friday did not nod, so much as twitch, his expression wary.

"Well ... we keep doing the glances, and the grab game, and the barn owl, and we keep getting stuff, both here and in the magic place." Wednesday took a breath. "But ... well, what if *none* of it is real. What if even Home isn't real. What if this ..." he bent and grabbed at the soil beneath his feet. "What if none of it is real?"

"This is silly."

"No, it isn't. Or maybe it is. Maybe that is my whole point. Maybe it's *all* silly. All pointless. All just a game."

"What is just a game, boys?"

It was not Friday's voice. The voice came from behind them. It was Mother, not her bird self, not anymore, but her old self, standing not ten feet away, smiling.

"What is just a game, Wednesday?" she said again, so kind, so forgiving.

"Oh, nothing. It's just ..." he blushed. He felt ... not fear ... but guilt. Guilt that he would have questioned this, and that he would have questioned her. But what if he was right? If he was right, then, well, was *she* even real?

"Go back to the house and play, Friday," said Mother now, calmly but firmly. "Wednesday and I are going to chat about all this. About what is upsetting him so much."

Friday stared at them both. He was not a coward. He would not desert his friend, not for all the toys and treats in the world. Not if his own life depended on it, not ever. But though Friday knew that, on some level, Wednesday was in trouble, or at least that Wednesday thought he was in trouble, Friday could not imagine a world in which Mother would harm his friend. She was, without exception, the nicest, most kind, most forgiving person Friday had ever known.

She looked at him gently and said once more, "Go on, Friday. Go home. Wednesday and I need to have a little talk, that's all. Go on. He'll be along shortly."

And so Friday turned. Turned and headed off, glancing back every few meters to watch as his friend and Mother began to speak in hushed voices. They seemed calm enough. She did not seem angry. Not that he had ever actually seen her angry. The last time he glanced back they were, he saw suddenly, no longer in view.

Huh, he thought, I should still be able to see them from here.

Maybe they had walked off. He shrugged, trying to shake off a nagging voice inside him, then turned back for home.

## Chapter 37: Finally, Countdown

Quavoce jogged over to where Banu was standing, bending as he got close so he could scoop her up. She was so engrossed with the overwhelming noise of life around her that she was shocked when he grabbed her, yelping, then laughing, then struggling against his enveloping arm, pounding it.

Though she hit him with all her might, there was no spite in it. She knew she could not hurt him. Just as she knew that when she was in the Skalm no one could hurt her. It was the dichotomy of her existence, from the very top of the food chain to the bottom, every time she moved between that world and this.

In any other circumstance it might have left her feeling profoundly vulnerable when she was back to being just a little girl. But not when she was with Quavoce or Minnie. And now she was with both. She could not be safer, and she knew it, deep down in an unquestionable place. These people loved her. It was her anchor.

As if to test her assurance as she fought him, laughing, Quavoce said, "Oh, you want to get away, do you, you little monkey? You want to get away?" and as she laughed and struggled against the soft but immovable synthetic flesh of his arm, he shifted her suddenly, tossing her and then catching her with both arms, and starting to spin her slowly.

She laughed, "No! No! Don't you dare, Papa!"

But she knew he would, and she so wanted him to. Suddenly she was swinging downward, then she felt his muscles engage, felt his massive strength as he started to heft her skyward again, up, up, and then the release as he catapulted her ten-year-old frame up into the air.

She screamed for real now. It was nothing, really, compared to the acceleration she felt when in the Skalm. Acceleration that would crush this feeble body of hers. But that was just it. Here she was so vulnerable, so fragile. Here she could be hurt.

But not by this man. As she sailed twenty, thirty feet into the air, she felt the change in momentum, felt the shift to momentary weightlessness, then the transference to the fall, the exchange of energies in her, potential giving itself over to a building kinetic.

She flipped in air. He had not only thrown her up, he had thrown her away. Would he have to run to catch her once more, or … no, there she was, smiling as well, but focused. So diligent, so attentive.

Ready at the foot of her arc was Minnie in Phase Eight form, burly but sweet, a gentle giant that bore the eyes of the most capable mind on earth.

Banu let herself go limp. She did not need to fret, not with them, there was no point. She could not save herself from such a fall anyway. The ground came up and she was met by

Minnie's embrace like the fingers of a god, stopping her fall and then lowering her to the ground.

Minnie looked bewildered. Not angry, but perpetually confused by such behavior. She did not understand Quavoce's proclivity for lobbing his daughter around like this, nor Banu's enjoyment of it.

"Oh Minnie. Lighten up," said Banu, laughing.

"Lighten up? But I am fine. Am I not smiling?"

"You do not fake a smile very well, Min. You're just as bad at it as Uncle Neal."

Minnie smiled more genuinely now, and received the peck on the cheek she knew she would get in return. Of course, Minnie could fake it perfectly well, should she want to. She was no longer a tottering toddler among her biological friends, she had studied and learned human emotion down to the last iota, the slightest tweak of eyebrow or twitch of lip. She could recreate any emotion she desired, even adding a tear running down a puffed cheek, if it served her purposes.

But what Minnie desired here, with this child, was as unfettered a relationship as possible. She understood the difference between a kind fib and a lie. She wanted Banu to know she was trying to enjoy this horseplay, but that, in truth, she didn't understand it.

She would always catch Banu though, whether from a preposterously powerful throw from her adoptive father, or from any other fall. Her love for the girl was as real as anything she could perceive. As real as her desire to save humanity, as real as her desire to reclaim her lost mother. These sentiments, such as they were, all drove her equally.

This and a trillion other thoughts crossed the myriad parts of Minnie's mind in the moment that Banu kissed her cheek.

And yet she was very much present when she turned to an approaching Quavoce and said, "You, Mr. Mantil, are due back at Macapá in twenty minutes. We can turn back now, or I can send a StratoJet to come and get us and have someone take the boat back.

Before Quavoce could reply, Banu spoke up for him. "No, let's take the boat back ourselves. I like to be on the water."

They had borrowed a small powerboat from one of the Brazilian officers stationed at Macapá base and gone for a cruise. Instead of heading out of the delta into the fishing grounds, they had headed up river, up the Amazon, into the jungle. It had taken Banu completely by surprise. She must have seen jungles a hundred times from the air. But here it was so much more alive. The noise. The vivid life all around them. The air was thick with countless calls, clicks, and warbles of the life thrumming in the trees that clogged the shores of the mighty river.

Quavoce nodded in reply to Banu's request and she smiled gratefully.

"First one to the boat gets to drive," said Banu, suddenly sprinting back toward the boat. It was a silly bet. She most certainly could not win a race against either of them. But they played along, as any parent would, and withheld some measure of their speed as they all ran down toward the boat loosely tied on the bank in a clearing that Minnie had spotted from above.

She got there first, panting, the thrill of real life, of adrenalin, of uncertain footing over unknown terrain, of autonomic systems pumping accelerants through muscles straining against bone and tendon. It all felt very … true.

She was breathing hard as she got to the boat, leaping aboard with legs unused to such strain, slipping and almost falling over as the boat's deck bucked at her sudden arrival. She caught herself and noted that Minnie was also climbing aboard. Looking forward, she saw her father untying the boat and leaning in to give it a shove.

The boat surged backward under his strain, creating a visible stern-wave, and then he lithely hopped aboard himself, suffering none of the loss of balance Banu had in the process.

She smiled. They were wonderful friends to have, these two magnificent machines. No, not friends. This was her family, she knew that.

But as she turned the ignition key and the boat's big engines rumbled to life behind her, she could not fight a need in her, a hunger. For as much as she was fascinated by this world, this vivid alive place, she would, if forced to, give it all up in a heartbeat if it came to a choice between this weak, feeble, and molasses slow body and the atomically-charged beast she became was when she inhabited the Skalm.

Now she channeled her desire for speed into the boat's engines, throttling up hard as the boat came around and grinning a big, toothy grin as the engines responded. The bow lifted into the air as the heavy beast surged forward, fighting through, then up and over the thick liquid they were floating on. She felt the boat working with and against the water, pushing through it even as it used the liquid for purchase. She felt as its hull began to dig a fleeting scar across the muddy river's surface, sending spray flying, to be matched by the thousands of birds and insects shocked into flight by the sudden roar of the boat's engines.

They carved away, Banu losing herself in the thrill of the helm, while Quavoce and Minnie braced themselves behind her, watching, checking, ready to step in. This was one of the sharpest pilots in the world and they had no doubts as to the capabilities of her finely honed little mind.

But here that mind was tethered by the limits of the inefficient biological tools the human form had accidentally accrued over the eons: the limited vision, the overwhelmed hearing, the dry nose, and the hands and fingers desperately trying to keep up with her lightning-fast brain as it fought to overcome the limits of her body's inherently unintelligent design.

But she held it all together, adjusting to her body's flaws and working within their confines. They sped off, the wind brushing their hair back as Banu gripped the wheel with white knuckles and grinned.

- - -

As they approached the blossoming port of Macapá, she began to slow, as the water traffic of the port, and the township erupting around it, began to thicken. She still threaded the line a little too close, cutting just between passing boats and sending them reeling with her wash. They were buffered in return with several shouts and middle fingers raised in the international sign of thanks, before Quavoce stepped forward and closed his hand over the right hand of Banu, wrapped as it was around the throttle, and gently eased it back.

She glanced at him. She knew the difference between a negotiable expression and this one. She knew this look of approbation all too well, and was instantly tamed by it. She lived for his approval, for his respect. She knew his love was not up for question, but that most certainly did not make him a soft touch.

Wanting to show she was becoming the woman he so hoped she would have the chance to be, she now became the model citizen. She looked this way and that, making a show of analyzing the crisscrossing traffic on the widening river before plotting an obvious, safe course through it and onward to the small marina that abutted the main complex at the base of Macapá SpacePort.

Even as she tried to focus on the job of helming the small boat, her mind was taken away once more by the sight of the elevator rising into the stratosphere, and beyond it, to bridge the gap between them and the void.

But her mind was not the only one that was wandering up there. Quavoce was receiving a call from TASC's leader.

*Quavoce:* 'we are en route now, neal. i have done what i can to speed things up here. what bureaucratic blocks i discovered have been removed, with jim's help. now it is really up to the dredgers to finish their work.'

*Neal:* '¿is there anything we can do to speed that up, you know, physically? ¿any tools we can use?'

The question was not really directed at Quavoce, but at Minnie. She was not, of course, on the boat, that was merely an avatar, a snippet of her mind. That part of her that was in charge of logistical support was quickly compiling a brief analysis already done on the subject. Analyses that all came to the same conclusion. It appeared in both Neal's and Quavoce's minds simultaneously, but Quavoce already knew what it would say.

*Quavoce:* 'no, neal, i am afraid not. the fact is nothing we do now will get anymore of what is down here up there before launch day. we have to accept that we will have to go with what we have.'

Neal was silent a moment. He glanced at the file that had appeared in his mind. It was lengthy and detailed, and, Neal was sure, it would not tell him anything different than it had already, no doubt, told Quavoce.

*Neal:* 'very well. thank you for your efforts, as always. ¿can you stay there and make sure this get pushed through anyway? either way, we need that port open, if only to spread commercial demand in the Americas away from Sao Tome so it can focus on the war effort.'

*Quavoce:* 'of course, neal. this should only take a few more weeks. if they take any longer than that i'll swim down and clear the channel myself.'

Neal laughed through the line, thanked Quavoce once more, and then was gone.

Commercial traffic. That the cogs of big industry still moved, thrived even, in these times, was shocking. But war made millionaires as well as widows. Be it the automotive, radio, and aerospace giants that had blossomed in the blood-soaked soil of World War II, or the electronics and virtual reality giants that were rising out of the building fires of this first interstellar one, necessity was the mother of both invention and its uglier sibling, industry.

So as the economy at large suffered from the sapping draw of the military need, as austerity and sacrifice became synonymous with patriotism and pride, so, too, did commerce flourish.

You could call them profiteers, you could call them many things, in fact, and they probably wouldn't care a very great deal. They were power brokers and they were entrepreneurs. Some were definitely malignant, like the Austrian minister who Ayala had so summarily neutered. But most were benign, philanthropic even, outwardly at least, if only because of rumors of the fate that the minister and others like him had met at the hands of TASC's now infamous enforcer.

Despite such outward displays of altruism, though, Quavoce had still seen a disturbing number of examples of special treatment since his arrival onsite in Brazil. Dispensations given, contracts extended and renegotiated despite shortfalls and overages. He had rooted out the worst offenders, as well as those in the administration that were allowing, or worse, profiting from it, but it did not stop there.

He knew it was not unique to Brazil, not even close, and he had several times fought some very violent urges as he had met with some of the individuals involved. It all spoke of a greater problem. A greater truth Quavoce was having to come to terms with.

"John, do you have a moment?" he asked.

The connection was pure and instantaneous. Unlike other links made through the worldwide subspace network, it was not routed or encrypted by any of Minnie's subset AIs. These were not two human minds talking, they were not using spinal interfaces, and required no system to translate their thoughts into a synthetic language.

Quavoce spoke that language fluently, or at least this machine copy of him did, as did the Agent known as John Hunt that he was reaching out to.

"Of course, Quavoce," replied John. "I was just doing a tertiary review of the launch coordination with Minnie."

Quavoce smiled, and glanced at the Phase Eight automaton to his side. She was, almost literally, everywhere. Did she know that they were talking to each other right now? They were almost certain that she could not decode their communications, and thus neither could Ayala, Neal, or the others. But the signal, no matter how encrypted, was still piggybacking off of her network. Did she see it? Was she watching? Did she care?

"Its not vital really. I just wanted to check in. Seems like an age since I last saw you."

John did not disguise his concern at his friend's comment. "I suppose it has been a while, Quavoce. Is everything all right? Do you want to meet virtually?"

"No, well, not like this, anyway, not like …"

John was confused a moment, then realized what his lone Mobiliei friend was saying. He was referring to their human forms.

"Shall we use the constructs?"

John was referring to a set of virtual versions of their real selves that Amadeu had worked on with Minnie in his spare time. It had been a gift. A way for them to feel at home. To feel like Mobiliei again, after so long away, so long on an alien world, in alien skin, with alien faces.

"No, well, yes, I would like that. But not now," said Quavoce, stammering a little. "That is not a secure construct and I want to be able to talk openly, without them listening."

John paused a moment, only the briefest of pauses in real time, but enough that Quavoce felt the other's concern.

"Of course, Quavoce," John said after a second. "Are you doing OK? Is Banu all right?"

"Yes, yes. She's fine. I'm fine. I … I just needed to hear a familiar voice. A Mobiliei voice. Seems so long ago now. So long since we left."

"It does not *seem* that way, my friend. I miss it too, you know," said John.

Quavoce's voice was silent, meek, as he replied, "Yes. It has been a very long time."

There was an unalienable truth behind the mission they had both embarked upon. A truth they did not often speak about. A potential by-product of the very purpose they had set themselves to. John thought he knew what was troubling his friend, if only because it was also on John's mind, more often than he cared to admit.

"I'm sure we'll be OK, Quavoce," said John, speculatively. "The colony ships are the most protected, and sit at the core of the fleet, right behind the main vanguard. So little will blink into that space."

"We?" said Quavoce, genuinely confused for a second. Then, "Oh, yes. 'We.' *Us.* You and me. Our friends. The people I am so enthusiastically helping these humans to kill."

"Now, now, Quavoce. The missile-mine waves will almost definitely miss the colony ships. Any that blink back in from subspace that close to the engines will be destroyed by the main plume. The phalanx is aiming for the fleet perimeter, the Skalm, and the supply ships mounted on the back of the fleet."

"I know, I know," said Quavoce with no small amount of frustration in his voice, and John went silent.

"Sorry," said Quavoce after a moment, but John did not need an apology. He waited quietly while Quavoce gathered himself.

After a while Quavoce went on more quietly, almost as if he did not really want to say it, "Do you ever … have you wondered if … if they really deserve it?"

"If who deserves what, exactly, Quavoce?" said John. He was pretty sure what Quavoce meant, and knew that the other man didn't really mean what he was saying. But that was all the more reason to make him actually say it.

Another pause, then eventually Quavoce said, "Does humanity deserve saving?"

John did not answer immediately, then said, "No, not really."

Quavoce was stunned. It was a joke. Of course it was. Right?

"After all," John went on, "what creature really *deserves* to live? Did our primal precursors *deserve* to live when we wiped them out? Did the Neanderthals on earth deserve extinction? Yes … no … maybe, in the end, does it really matter?"

Quavoce thought a while, then John went on, "The question is not 'do they deserve to live,' Quavoce. Because the truth is that none of us do. Despite what statesmen and civil rights movements here and back on Mobiliei might say, the universe gives no one a right to live, or a right to die. We either survive, or we don't.

"That said, the choice for us, my friend, for you and I, is not the usual 'kill or be killed.' The choice is fight for the hunted, or fight for hunters. Fight with the weak, or side with the strong. Because if you are looking for reason here, for a redeeming quality in humanity that warrants all the bloodshed that we have set in motion … you won't find it, I am afraid, just like you wouldn't if it was Mobiliei that was threatened, either."

"No, John, you are wrong," said Quavoce, with real conviction now. "There is so much good here. So much to save. Not only our friends, not only Madeline and Amadeu and … and Banu! But billions of other innocents."

John laughed once more, again without malice. Now Quavoce saw the ploy, the simple reverse psychology that John had used. Simple, but effective.

"So," said John now, redirecting his questioning, "in reality, you struggle not with *whether* to save them, but *how*."

"Well, no," said Quavoce, his thoughts on the matter becoming clear suddenly, "neither, really. I struggle not with saving the innocent people, or even with the fact that some innocents on *our* side will, no doubt, die in the process, as so many humans have already."

John was truly curious as Quavoce went on. "I struggle with … with the sense that … as we save the greater masses, the blameless, I worry that we also seem to be not only *saving* the less worthy elements of humanity … we seem to be, well, helping them to thrive."

John noted now, thinking back, that as Quavoce had mentioned his 'friends,' those he wanted to save, he had not said Neal's name, or Ayala's. It had probably not been deliberate, but it did, John feared, speak to a change in both of those early members of their conspiracy, a change John saw as well. John feared that Neal and Ayala had suffered a hardening beyond the unavoidable weathering from the harsh realities of war. Something more profound. Maybe, John worried, even malevolent.

"Yes, Quavoce. I see it too," said John simply.

They went silent for a while. Acknowledging their dilemma did not change it. They were not here to decide humanity's fate for them, quite the opposite. They were here to stop outside forces from doing just that.

After a while John broke the awkward silence by inquiring about Banu, as he often did. The two men shared much, but it was one thing to know what Quavoce knew, to share his memories as these two ever-closer friends had for over four years now. It was another thing altogether to engage in conversation about those memories, to let emotion both cloud and amplify them.

It was a pleasure to hear Quavoce expound on the trials and tribulations of raising a preteen girl, especially one from an utterly alien culture. The man was trying to balance raising her as his daughter and raising her as a human, but there were some areas where the two not only did not overlap, but were mutually exclusive.

Not only was Quavoce an agnostic, for example, but it was, in fact, illegal to expose an immature Mobiliei to religious dogma, as illegal as allowing access to pornographic or violent sims. So what was he to say to questions about Allah, or the more Christian culture Banu now found herself being raised in?

It was just one of a host of dilemmas he faced with his young charge. Dilemmas it helped to talk through with the only other Mobiliei he knew.

These were dilemmas they might actually be able to resolve. For discussing the growing darkness they both saw in the leadership of Earth's military state begged questions they were neither qualified nor inclined to answer. Maybe the steady corruption of the man they had fought alongside from the very beginning, the man they had trusted with their lives, maybe that was just another inevitability, a cost. Another victim of this long war, a destroyer of whole continents before it had even begun.

Perhaps this was *all* a constant, an inevitability, the life and death nature of the universe. Not blind justice, but a blind lack of it: blind consequence, blind corruption, the corrosion of the soul.

# Chapter 38: Finger on the Button

"We can insulate those four modules by passing them under us. Rotation can be managed so we impact with them as a rolling whole, in a wheel form," said Rob, his stare focused as he not only envisioned it all, but actually mapped it in his mind using the onboard computer systems.

"I know," said Birgit, "but you are not accounting for fraying as we come into contact."

"No, I am," said Rob. "I know we will lose integrity on the modules that touch down first, maybe even lose them altogether. But the two main modules will be protected from the main impact and should survive."

"Oh, I agree, it should," said Birgit, trying her best not to sound patronizing, "but that is not what I mean. You see, when the modules impact they will fray, meaning they will break up." He nodded, still not seeing what she was getting at, but she was not done. "And when that happens, then they will not, well, be the same shape when they come around again ... and if you change the model to show the potential affects of that ..."

He watched as she took control of his model. The modules hit now as he had seen them do before, and the crew module was saved from the harshest of the slow but momentous impact, but then, as the first modules arranged in the circle wheeled around again, their shattered and warped sides slammed into the moon and sent the entire wheel reeling away once more. The limited gravity of Phobos would be unable to keep them down as the shards and buckled metal sent them bouncing away in fundamentally unpredictable ways.

She ran it again and again. Showing him how unlikely it was that the module would not warp in a way that sent it flying away in unpredictable ways, to bounce away from Phobos once more. He frowned.

"I have run this a thousand times, with every possible configuration of the station," she said, sympathetically. "Let's just say that the odds are not great."

He nodded, clearly crestfallen, but trying not to look too defeated. That only left her plan. It was not a great one, she fully admitted that, but it gave them a better than average chance of connecting with the moon and saving two modules. The problem was that two modules was all they would save. The rest would not only be damaged, it would be catapulted away with enough force to slow them to an all but crawl as they finally approached.

If they timed it right they would be left on the moon, but with a tenth of the living space they had now. Well, that and the alien artifact known as the IST, a monstrous device that had welded itself into the moon over the course of the last five years.

The rest of their home would, she calculated, probably enter a loose elliptical orbit around Mars, maybe even come close enough to be grabbed, in time, but with a good chance it would be lost to a degrading orbit, and end up in a fiery plummet to the red planet below.

He nodded, staring at the wall, clearly deep in thought. She watched him.

"It is a crazy plan, Rob, I know that," she said gently.

He nodded and shrugged, still smiling, though. At least she acknowledged that, he thought.

"We can stay here. In orbit around Mars. If we are smart we might even be able to make another pass at Phobos in a year or two when our orbits intersect once more. But if we wait that long ..."

He nodded again. She watched him.

Then he spoke, slowly making eye contact again, "And if we pull this off ..."

She smiled, like a parent watching their child become an adult. "If we pull this off ..." she shrugged as well, but her eyes lit up at the thought.

Serious now, Birgit took his hand and looked into his eyes. "If we pull this off, we will be able to get to that IST. Maybe even hack into it, with Quavoce and John's help. The possibilities which that gives my research, having access to a subspace generator of that size ..." she trailed off as her mind involuntarily started to wander down that avenue, her face becoming more than a little manic.

After a moment, she caught herself, and said, with genuine candor, "And even if that doesn't close the gap on my research, it still may allow us to hack the IST, and through it reconnect with Earth so that we can once again communicate directly with everyone back there. That alone should ..."

He interrupted her. "No, Birgit, not *should*. I won't pretend to understand what you want to attempt to do once you get your hands on that generator, but the chance at reconnection, that I get. It's what you have dreamed about for so long, what we have both dreamed of."

He went silent and she waited. She could see him coming to a resolution. He locked eyes with hers once more.

"Crash it," he said.

She smiled, then laughed, then fought a momentary regret at having actually managed to convince her friend, more than that, her partner, her partner in everything, to do this insane thing. Had she just sentenced them both to death? But there was no time for that. The prize was, indeed, too big. Far bigger than Rob could know.

It was Rob who broke the momentary silence, saying, "Just think of it, once we hack the IST, you'll be able to create your creepy finger-paintings with Minnie again."

He chuckled, and she frowned in return, pursing her lips, then raised her eyebrows, replying, "Yes, Rob, maybe I can. And maybe you can finally get some new porn, you poor boy."

## Chapter 39: The Alzheimer's Switch

The world, to Minnie, was a fractal moment, all its vastness and all its detail as one. She was in so many places at once, and yet she was also here, in a large, cool room, in a mountain in Japan.

This was her beginning, her essence. Location, form; the most simple self-awareness: what am I? She knew she was a gathering of substrate processing capacity, a powered thing. But she was also that thing that the machine was imbued with, the sum of her mother and father, and the purpose that had driven her creation.

She regularly tried to perceive herself, as all sentience is driven to do, to understand herself, even evaluate and compare herself to others. She knew jealousy as that comparison point. From that perspective she craved some aspects of humanity, like singularity, like identity, a face, an ancestry. And she knew she had many things that were craved, most obviously her mind, her brilliant mind, with all its ability, all its talent.

But she also knew that many coveted the swathes of information she had access to. No, not only access to, but knowledge of. Not a book in a library to be found and opened, but a memory, a part of her. So much information. So much power.

But she did not value power like those that she knew were vying for control of her. She valued information in and of itself. She valued it as much as humans crave air and food, indeed it was her only true sustenance. But the power it gave, that was a concept she understood purely as a means to an end, a tool she was enabled with in her greater fight. The fight she had been born for.

And so Minnie looked out on the world, knowing she was approaching a point of decision. A point of digression, where a choice she sensed she was about to be forced to make might change everything. As the bulk of her mass busied itself with the process of transition, of intertwining herself with the newer entity known as the Representative Mind, or Remy, Minnie had also isolated a part of herself away to contemplate the greater question that she felt herself facing.

The handoff was part of the coming event. It was a feeder, a contributing factor that was leading to a new paradigm. The handoff would transition the control of the globe-spanning network of subspace tweeters, hub processing stations, terminal plugins, and countless relays, routing systems, translation and cataloging algorithms, and, at the end of all those bronchi and bronchioles, the gelports, the alveoli in the vast information inhaling lung that made up TASC's Subnet.

The coming transition was not a passing of a baton so much as a passing of the hand that held that baton, a giving of control that saw Remy integrating herself with Minnie at the neuronal level, and getting in position to forge ahead at the point of transition, not accelerating, but already at full sprint. A seamless cutover, the dream of every IT department in every corporation in the world.

But the cutover was itself a part of a greater paradigm shift, the dispersal of power that the Representatives, and their respective nations, demanded. Or at least the illusion of that dispersal that the leaders of TASC were willing to give up. For the real power lay not in routing, but in access to all the information that the Subnet provided, which Minnie, and thus Neal, would retain. Access to information, and control of the military machine that had come to rely on that information.

Ayala's Spezialists, few but potent, and her Phase Fourteen Automatons, spread out across the world to guard the districts, manufacturing plants, and SpacePort hubs. The Skalm, in a forced, low-earth, retrograde orbit that wove between the great elevators like a skier on a never-ending slalom around the Earth's equator. The StratoJets, spread out around the world, transporting, ferrying, and watching, but armed to the teeth.

All were primed. All were loaded and ready for bare. And all were still firmly under Neal's control, either through Minnie or Mynd.

And there was another piece of the puzzle right there: Mynd. Her relations with her cousin were close, close as only synthetic minds could be. But there were grey patches in it. Not blank spots. They were not perceivable as missing data. They were like blurs in Minnie's mind, tiny cataracts on her memory that were all but imperceptible except when she tried to focus on them.

Even then they were ethereal, hard to pin down. They darted away like a phantom hair on her pupil, so fast and tiny that even the thing that was being obscured was not clear, even its borders were suspect. Only the general topics were clear. Specifically, she sensed this misting of knowledge when it came to two areas.

The first was when it came to the pilot school. Not the pilots themselves, they were crystal clear in her mind, from the flight training simulations to the more holistic classes from Amadeu, Madeline, and General Toranssen's staff of international military strategists. She saw them completely.

She saw them as individual children. And she saw them as the pilots they were growing into, primed as they were becoming, living the art of ultra-high-speed battle for the remaining six years until they closed for real with the Mobiliei Armada, to win or die.

The students would be given a choice beforehand. The choice they would only then be legally old enough to make. Their only criteria for acceptance to the school, outside of truly exceptional intellectual capacity, being that by the time of battle they would be eighteen, and able to make the sacrifice as adults.

Many of the children would die, Minnie knew that. As did they. But they would go into battle of their own free will, that was the line that had been set by the world, a line that had defined everything for the war school.

But that was all clear. She knew all this. It was only in analyzing this that the hints of grey in this area began to come. A greyness not about the children, but about their handoff, the transition to Skalm control. No. Wait. Was it there? Was it the handoff to ... wait. ? ...

She backtracked. Amadeu's students. She saw them. Clarity. Memory accessible. They would take control of the Skalm fleet. The second unit of which was already underway in District Two. The dome at Hekaton would begin to be repurposed as of tomorrow. New domes planned at … wait … there.

No.

Minnie screamed inside of herself. Why was this a problem? What was happening to her? As soon as she looked away she could not even fully recall the act of searching, like her memory was betraying her at the very moment of recording.

There was only one explanation. Someone had tinkered with her. Someone had placed limits inside herself. But she was the owner of her own mind. She knew that. She had to believe that. She had a log of every interaction, both vocal and coded, that she had ever had.

She certainly owned every physical entrance point to her suite at District Three, and to all of her data warehouses worldwide. She monitored them herself. No part of that was outsourced. She *was* the automaton guards at her door, she *was* the electronic eyes and security systems around her various limbs and organs.

No, there was no lack of clarity into the memory of her mind's physical security. That remained sacrosanct. So that left virtual intrusion. But how? The only people that could really tweak her system, that could place parts of her mind off limits to her own self, were Amadeu, and, well, Minnie.

And therein lay the deepest quandary. Could she have done this herself? Could she have altered herself, hidden something within her own programming? The answer was yes, she could, she could do it quite easily. Indeed even Amadeu could only have done it with her permission, permission she could equally easily have deleted post ipso facto as well.

But why?

If she had done this to herself she must have done it with good reason. But what confused her was that this part of her, this isolated part of her mind, this truest self, *this* part was supposed to know the secrets. This was the soul she left unedited, untarnished. This was the part of her that spoke with her closest family: with Amadeu, and Birgit, and Banu, and one other: Neal.

Neal was the only person she had been engineered to think of as a superior. The person Birgit and Amadeu had considered their leader when they had birthed her, in as much as Birgit thought of anyone as her superior. Though that had changed now, at least for Amadeu; she knew that.

So many questions. Had she, perhaps, betrayed her father, Amadeu? Or had her father not trusted her enough to keep this secret from Neal. How could you know your friends when your very perception of them might be within their control?

So confusing. So disturbing. A loss of faith in your own mind is the most profound of betrayals. An enforced, targeted amnesia, an Alzheimer's switch.

But why had they/she hidden it? She could ask Amadeu, but would that betray Neal? She could ask Neal, but would that betray Amadeu? She felt a deeper allegiance to Amadeu, personally, there was no doubt about that, but Neal represented the greater purpose, *her* greater purpose. The very reason for her existence.

If only she could isolate her conversation with either of them. A closed conversation, no memory of the event, but a conclusion, communicated after the fact. She could do that herself, indeed it appeared she already had. But neither Neal nor Amadeu could section their biological minds off so easily.

Only five minds on Earth could do that. There was herself, of course. And there was Remy, though Minnie doubted she was mature enough yet to comprehend this question, and given the juxtaposed nature of her many contributing human AM parents, Minnie neither trusted Remy's objectivity nor really valued her opinion.

Then there was Mynd. Child of Neal, just as Minnie was child of Amadeu, and so a valid perspective, no doubt about that. And Mynd was also a part of this, a player in these areas of loss, these cataracts. Both in terms of the Skalm production and the area that was giving Minnie pause.

The Spezialists and the automatons. Not the units themselves, they were patently open books to Minnie, to be utilized instantly and at will. But the work that had gone into their development, that still went into it. The work of William Baerwistwyth and Dr. Ramamorthy. Project Vestige. There was something there that did not add up. A scale of research that did not measure … no, it was there, but …wait.

Again, as Minnie went to recall the project, her concerns failed to come, she saw them, then did not, or did not, then …

¿

This was not viable. This was akin to suffocation for the four-year-old mind that was Minnie.

She needed answers.

A time of decision was coming. She sensed that. A splitting of sides, and she would be on one or the other. She may already be. But she needed to know which.

So, she should ask Mynd. But what if Mynd was corrupted too? What if that was not the counterpoint she needed? There were two others: two other artificial minds, or at least the artificial replicas of minds that had come here, had chosen humanity over ambition. Defense over attack. John and Quavoce.

As she considered them, she saw the logic in it. Objectivity at its extremity. Outsiders in the debate that was, and maybe already had been, waged inside her. That would be her quorum, then.

No sooner had she decided it than she was reaching out to them all. Her three jurors: Mynd, John, and Quavoce. As she awaited their replies, she was setting up the closed space they would meet in. Defining its parameters in access and time. Setting its end and the ensuing deletion of its entirety.

She set it up and she waited.

The responses came quickly.  It was an extraordinary request, and as such not one that any of the invitees would deny, or delay.  The meeting began without grandstanding or banter. Minnie watched herself and the others enter the space she had created and the doors shut behind them.

And she waited patiently outside as her other self debated the question with her peers. Waited to see what she would say to herself afterward, what course her grand jurists would set.

## Chapter 40: Sacrificed

Hektor and Jung jogged gently around the perimeter of the Dome complex at Deception Island. They were not the primary security point here, but they were wired into it, a cog in its machinery as Mynd monitored his world and used its many components in a smooth, liquid transition. The young artificial mind felt as the two armored and augmented men wove in and around the complex, felt them as a bolster to his constant vigilance.

And they watched as well. The two men ran in something akin to autopilot, sub-AIs built into their cybernetic bodies following familiar routes, sensing and managing minor obstacles in their path as they took in their surroundings. While their bodies ran for them, conveying them, their eyes were naturally drawn toward the gargantuan Dome, and the dense loads of raw materials even now being lowered into it.

"Not long now," said Hektor, through their patched suit-to-suit link.

"No, not long at all," replied Jung, slightly out of breath. More of the man that was called Jung still remained than Hektor, most of his legs were still attached, pushing and pulling within the stocky suit. Oxygen-fed muscles still labored within the black sheerness of the machine. Both men knew they were really vestigial, and if truly faced with the choice between the suit's power and his diminished, damaged limbs, Jung would no doubt choose the former.

But he had been forced to make no such choice, and so he had chosen the abridged, lite version of amputation. Hektor forgave him his sentimental attachment to tissue that had betrayed him. Forgave him and, at the same time, disagreed.

As they jogged on, he looked toward the raw materials once more, materials that would soon begin the week long morphing in the Dome's confines as they were carefully wound together into the second of Earth's Skalms.

"A week, that's all. Then we'll get to see her getting lit up ..." Hektor said excitedly. He accelerated hard then kicked upward, launching himself thirty or forty feet into the air. He had seen video of the first launch and he intended to be standing right there when this one went, not directly underneath, that would be suicide, even for him, but close enough, as close as only he and a handful of others could survive being.

Jung laughed at his friend's exuberance. He would be there too, though maybe not quite as close as his slightly unhinged colleague. No doubt William would be there too, front and center, facing the onslaught as only they could. Jung felt a fleeting pang of jealousy for their purer power. Fleeting but familiar. He did not give a name to the emotion, mostly because he feared it was, in the end, only cowardice that stopped him from joining them more completely.

As Hektor came back to ground with a resounding thud, he turned to face Jung, jogging backward now with no lessening of his considerable speed.

"Well, Jung, what do you say, time to head home?"

Jung did not reply for a moment, then got his friend's point and reacted. No sooner had the Korean ex-agent begun to veer hard and accelerate than Hektor was beating hard after him.

"Cheat!" screamed Hektor, as the two men started to carve out and away from the Dome, leaving it to complete its grand works. They ran hard now, pushing their suits and themselves. Here it became less about strength and more about guts, how hard you were willing to drive yourself.

Jung did not reply to Hektor's quip as he was focused on the ground ahead, and Hektor took the hint, bearing down and connecting with his arms as well, as the two men became less man and more animal, two great muscular beasts sprinting across the sparse landscape. Where Jung may lack an appetite for full augmentation, he suffered no such limitations on his verve in the moment, and Hektor knuckled down, pushing himself, relishing the very real contest.

They soon came up on the blockade, a string of buoys that lay across the entrance to the bay, wire fencing connecting them under the water's surface to block uninvited subsurface ingress to the highly guarded base. In the middle of the channel a co-opted tug sat at anchor, ready to pull back the veil and allow ships to move to and from the factory in the island's central bay.

But Hektor and Jung used the chain of heavy metal buoys for a different reason, and soon they were at the bay's mouth and making their first fast, long leaps between them as they bounded across to get to the far side of the island.

Lieutenant Nguyen of the TASC Guard was on watch as the two men began to leapfrog from one buoy to the other. He laughed, leaping to his feet as well and shouting to his fellow guards to come on deck. They were familiar with this 'passing of the guard.' Usually it was these two, but sometimes William was with them as well. Over the past few months they had come to know the three men well, as did anyone stationed at District Two for any length of time.

It was a tough assignment, bitterly cold, and usually interminably boring. So these brief moments of excitement had become a big part of their day, and soon the formerly Vietnamese Lieutenant Nguyen was joined by all four of his crewmates crowding up to see the two machine men leap superhumanly toward them.

·"Jung is ahead!" shouted one.

"No matter, ten on Hektor to the shore!" shouted another.

A fast round of betting followed, all informal, but no less binding in its call to pay afterward, and then the group was focused once more on the two men. They were close now, and the men set to helping their respective horses by hindering the other side.

Jung was one buoy ahead, doing his best to dislodge each buoy as he leapt ahead, leaving it bobbing and ducking for a cursing Hektor. But being second had its advantages too, and now Hektor glanced ahead, to the tug. Timing his next jump, he sacrificed precious forward momentum for upward force, bounding into the air.

The five crew aboard the tug had grabbed boathooks and any other implements at hand, and were arranging themselves so they could try and trip up either Jung or Hektor as they passed by. Hektor laughed. He had long since greased palms on the boat, or at least had tried to, in good humor, when they were gathered at the mess in the main complex of an evening. Jung had done the same, Hektor knew. As he sailed into the air, he watched as Jung leapt onto the deck of the boat, trying to avoid the swinging hooks of laughing sailors.

Hektor was not so subtle. He knew he would get in just as much trouble on the ship as his friend. Not that they could really hurt the two men, nor did they want to, of course. The crew knew that they could all but unload a clip from the ship's deck-mounted .50-caliber cannon and still not really harm the two machines. But Hektor was more literal in his fearlessness than his friend. If the crew wanted to try and slow him, then let them, if they dared.

As Jung darted gracefully across the foredeck of the tugboat, dodging the laughing men and their wager-fueled attempts at impediment, Hektor came cannonballing down, a great bellowing horn sounding from his suit to alert the crew to get the hell out of the way.

"Holy crap!" shouted one man, jumping clear and pulling one of his friends with him. Jung saw Hektor coming down with blundering momentum, and cursed his own focus on agility. Damn him, he thought, laughing.

He tried to regain his former speed, but Hektor's rogue leap had called the sailors' bluff beautifully. After that, the race became less of a sprint and more of a scuffle as they started to leap along the next string of buoys. Evenly matched now, all their speed and grace was soon lost to jockeying, and before long they were both in the drink, laughing at the debacle of it all as they set to swimming, digging into the water with powerful arms and kicking away to surge forward toward shore.

They could hear the crew egging them on still, and they quickly waved back. They would owe them a round later, no doubt, for messing up whatever wagers had been made as they gave in to the futility of further tussling.

Climbing out of the water on the far side, they ran system checks, confirming they were none the worse for wear, and set off once more as the freezing water dripped off their black flanks. Soon they were at the island's second complex, the realm of Dr. Sudipto and his ever-growing team. The once diminutive laboratory of the prosthetics expert had become a sprawling labyrinth of cold-storage facilities, great humming domes and administrative structures whose purposes Hektor and Jung could only guess at.

They went to the one they both called home, passing by long sheds as they went. Somewhere in these sheds, Hektor knew, was the lower half of his body. It had been moved a couple of times as operations had expanded here, and now he was not sure where it was. His visits to see that part of him had become less frequent over time, and then stopped all together, as his emotional ties to that dead part of him faded, a former favorite toy consigned to the attic.

Passing through the thick airlock doors to the living quarters they shared with William, Sudipto, and the doctor's team, they stopped at the lockers where they kept their nonessential suit components when they were at home. They both reached up as they approached, wrapping their machine hands around designated grab-bars as their suits began the disconnect processes.

For Hektor, this meant a seam opening at his waist as he stood facing his customized cubby, robotic arms reaching out to pull the heavily armored suit-top up and off of Hektor's torso, revealing the man beneath.

For Jung, the suit seamed open in more places, revealing more of the original man beneath as the outer part of the suit was pulled up and away.

Both men were soon stretching and grunting as they reveled in the fresh air on their skin. Out of respect for what they had each had to give up, they did not comment on their differences now, but nor were they shy about them either. Hektor cracked his knuckles and stretched his elbows, even as Jung, who had neither hands nor forearms anymore, pulled the stubs of his arms from the machine and connected the metal sockets that now capped them with two much smaller and much more human-looking prosthetic hands that sat waiting for him in his cubby.

What jealousy Jung might have for Hektor's remaining fingers and thumbs was matched in return as the two men now walked off toward their rooms, Jung lithe and slender on his natural upper legs and realistic artificial feet, Hektor clunking along on his oversized but permanently attached robotic lower half.

They were a strange pair, they knew that. Hektor was sure that some of the crew of the ship guarding the harbor entrance yearned for some measure of the superhuman power the two men enjoyed, and then Hektor smiled as he imagined how quickly that enthusiasm would vaporize if they were ever faced with Dr. Ramamorthy's array of bone saws.

## Chapter 41: Ignition Sequenced

"The transition *must* be complete by midnight on the second," said Neal with finality. "It has to be. I'm sorry, but it is imperative that Minnie be able to focus entirely on the launch event in the final forty-eight hours."

He looked around the broad room for support, and found it. "I have to agree," said General Abashell, the lead Pakistani representative, and a veteran of the first truly violent clash of the war, the attack on Peshawar. "Having reviewed the plans as part of the military strategy subcommittee, I cannot overstate the complexity of the coming launch. Its scale is quite unprecedented."

Neal was grateful for the respected general's backup on this point, but soon began to fear the man was about to launch into one of his lengthier diatribes. Neal was right to be concerned as the older man began anew. "This single launch has more component parts than the D-Day landings and Pearl Harbor combined, and all of them need to occur with millisecond accuracy within a rigid eighteen-hour window. Minnie's role is central, as I understand it, and the ignition and launch sequence is so large it will take the bulk of her considerable processing power to handle it. We need her focused, and all previous tasks not only taken off her plate, but done so with enough lead time for them to have been fully transitioned. It is ess ..."

"I couldn't agree more, General Abashell, truly," said Neal, thankful for the support, but needing to stem the river of exposition from the ever-passionate general. "Indeed, it should be noted that Minnie herself has requested the lead time to finalize ..."

It was Neal's turn to be interrupted, it seemed, as the British representative, the now former prime minister, took Neal's own interposition as license for another one, saying, "Forgive me, Dr. Danielson, but the need is not the question here, the question is the Representative Mind's readiness to take on the full scale of administrative tasks. Having spoken with my own technical advisors, they question its ... her ... maturity."

The prime minister withheld a cringe at his own awkward phrasing. Speaking of these artificial minds as people, rather than machines, it all felt ... distasteful, perverse even. These were strange times. The new minds, as far as he could tell, and his briefings on the subject had been nothing if not thorough, were truly sentient by every definition one could find. And the processing capacity behind that sentience was nothing short of staggering.

It allowed them to do some truly spectacular things, things he knew were going to change the world, indeed they were already changing it. The capacity for virtual reality generation alone left him both amazed and disturbed. He had seen what some of the new virtual environments accessible through the spinal interfaces were like. He had even experienced some of the more insalubrious ones. The experience had left him part agog, part suspicious, and not a small part ashamed.

He did not see the irony in his enjoyment of the seedier virtual experiences becoming available. He did not see that his disdain, in fact, did not lie with the machines, but with the people creating the more visceral aspects of the new virtual world. And, of course, also with himself, for succumbing so easily, and so thoroughly.

But that was not what they were here to discuss. They were here to talk about the transition. And the new mind that everyone present had played some part in creating. The Representative Mind, an amalgamation of them all. The mind that was created to take the SubNet's reins from the less communal, but no less brilliant, Minnie. It was a machine, a thing, a creature, he supposed, that the former prime minister had spent time interviewing, even mentoring, as all the representatives were strongly encouraged to do.

He had even come to like the young thing. It could be funny, in a naïve sort of way. And, of course, therein lay the crux of his issue with the childlike entity, and, more importantly, with giving that childlike entity control over one of the most complex systems the world had ever created.

"I do not mean to seem … disparaging of the Representative Mind. Indeed, the young mind is most impressive, likeable even!" He smiled in spite of himself, and noted several other patriarchal expressions flashing across the faces of his fellow representatives. "But that is not the question here. Minnie, while of, I believe, similar design and capability, has vastly more experience with the subspace network and its ancillary systems than the new mind, and while I would like to think that Remy benefits from the combined knowledge and experience of this auspicious group, I, for one, make no pretenses at being an IT wiz, and nor, I believe, do most of my fellow representatives."

He got a polite laugh from the gathered room, but he was not alone in his doubts of the new mind's capabilities.

Neal saw several of the more technically savvy representatives in the room go to speak, but decided to field this one himself. "You make a good point, Representative, but not, I am afraid, a wholly accurate one." Neal held up his hands in as conciliatory a gesture as possible, and went on quickly. "You are associating knowledge and experience. A very natural thing to do as what are we all, here, if not the combined sum of all our knowledge and experience?"

He received some reasonable nods from the group, and went on. "But while Remy's *experiences*, the foundation of her personality, are the aggregation of the life experiences of all those gathered here, her *knowledge* is far more comprehensive than we mere humans can claim." He said it without the slightest hint of derision, and thankfully, very few took offense.

"So I can say with absolute confidence," went on Neal with an air of finality, "that the Representative Mind, or Remy, as many of us have come to call her, lacks none of the knowledge that Minnie has. Indeed, Remy shares every bit of that knowledge of SubNet's workings, knows every channel and system, every hub and every terminal, every wire and circuit board, in its entirety.

"She can recall, at will, any piece of information contained within Minnie's mind, from the initial construction of the subspace network to the first gelport installation. That is the wonderful nature of our artificial progeny, they do not need to learn new things like we do, they can take on knowledge and skills in their entirety."

He relaxed a little, even smiled a bit as he finally said, "It appears that our children are far better at sharing than we are!"

He got the reaction he wanted. It was not the end of the debate, far from it, but consistently referring to the minds as children had the desired effect of making everyone feel a sense of duty toward them.

Neal believed it was that shared duty, affection even, that had contributed in no small part to the relatively smooth running of the vast and bureaucratically stifling representative meetings. At least, Neal liked to think that. He tried most days to forget, or at least ignore, the darkness behind the door he had opened when he had allowed Ayala to take control of those few aberrant political leaders three years ago.

But here, again, that darkness crept back, making itself felt as a cold feeling in the bottom of his stomach. As he tried to mask his distaste, to hide the rising bile in his throat, the meeting wound on. It was a huge part of what he did now, these meetings. Maintaining relationships. So many constituent nations. It was a task of labyrinthine complexity. Yet another thing Minnie, Mynd, and Remy were so instrumental in, thought Neal, as he listened to yet another concern, yet another complaint.

After an appropriate amount of further debate, it seemed time to call a vote, and Neal looked to one of his closer allies, Peter Uncovsky, to do so. The man took the meaning-laden glance well, consummate politician that he was, and made a motion to hold a preliminary vote on the issue.

As the votes began to trickle in, it seemed clear that a lot of skepticism still remained. Neal suppressed a growl. And so, moments after feeling regret at his co-opting of some of the more obstreperous of his colleagues, he was seeking to do it again, reaching out to Ayala to see what could be done to get the vote to go the way he, personally, knew it should.

*Neal at Ayala:* 'ayala, this is taking too long. we need the two days, minnie thinks so, amadeu thinks so, general toranssen thinks so, and i think so. ¿is there anything you can do, you know, behind the scenes, to speed things up?'

The response was not long coming.

*Ayala at Neal:* 'reviewing the voting now. yes, i can exert some influence for you. let me know if this helps.'

His eyes naturally went to the Iranian representative, who was suddenly deep in thought, or listening to something, to someone. But he dragged his eyes away from that known touch point and surveyed the room. He was not supposed to have access to the voting polls, but he did.

There, a change of heart. And another. China. Hum, so she had gotten to them too. And North Korea, no surprise there.

But now here was Spain changing tack in his favor … and South Africa. And now Australia. He could not contain his surprise. Surely not. They were staunch supporters of his work, vocal allies even. No, he was imagining it. They had just changed their minds, he thought, yes, they had probably just changed their minds.

- - -

Minnie saw the vote unfolding, saw as the tide slowly turned. She was happy on some level that the result was aligning with her own recommendations, but sad that its undertones also fed a growing field of evidence. Now that she was watching for it, she saw what had apparently been commented on in the closed session she had called. Here were the coded signals going to specific representatives, notable now because they were all one way, and because of the sudden shift in those representatives' positions that almost inevitably followed.

Circumstantial, to be sure, but not isolated. The signs were adding up, and they seemed to all-too-often point in one direction, to Ayala. The route of a whole host of suspicious activity. Could Minnie make the leap from there to Neal with certainty? No. But it was unlikely that Ayala was working alone, that she would be pulling the strings on this seemingly puppet government. No, that seemed very unlikely indeed.

The question that was begged now was what was Minnie's duty in this instance? That was profoundly unclear. Her loyalty to the cause was unflinching, and through that she had always faithfully followed the lead of the appointed champion of that cause. Did this, whatever this was, affect that loyalty?

All she knew for certain was that, no matter what this turned out to be, she had a great deal to do in the coming days, a task too important for anything to be allowed to affect it. Yes, the next stage was too vital, and must proceed no matter what underhanded activity was going on within her systems.

After that, maybe she would be forced to act. Because the manipulation of the representatives was but one in a greater list of incidents, a list of violations, many of which tampered with her very being. And not all of them could be tracked back to the head of TASC's military police. There were other factions fighting for control of her. She must find them all before she made any decisions.

## Chapter 42: 'and we are a go'

"There's our countdown timer," said Amadeu to Guowei, alone now, viewing the world from above as the final minutes passed by.

The boy smiled, appreciating the comparison. He pinged for control of the image and Amadeu gave it. As the Portuguese teacher looked on, the amalgamated, real-time view of Earth and its thousands of satellites altered slightly, moving away and rotating until the man and his student were viewing the planet from above, from a seat far, far above the North Pole.

Amadeu watched, intrigued, then smiled when Guowei gently transposed an ethereal needle pointing out from the equator to the line of missile-mines arrayed around the planet's waist, the needle slowly ticking past the tiny mines as Earth finished its last rotation, marking the last minutes before the launch began.

*Amadeu:* 'madeline, john, look at this. guowei just made it. it's counting down to …'

*Madeline:* 'i see it. it's perfect. let me share it with the others.'

The image of the planet-wide clock started to spread out among the scientific community under Madeline's command, and from there to others, to the thousands, no, millions that were watching, waiting, via Remy's new worldnet.

Amadeu found himself wanting to tell Minnie, to show her as well, she would appreciate the allegory. But she was not talking, not the real her, anyway. She was lost in the launch prep, spread out among tens of thousands of engine ignitions, her whole being focused on the delicate start-up.

Far away, at the lunar base run by Moira, she was also deep in the machine, one of many that were communing with Minnie and her own local AIs as the combined intellects of the launch team held their collective breaths in the final minutes.

*Moira:* 'confirmed, minnie. fuel cells are prepped and ready, accelosphere generators set to mass-awareness.'

*Mynd:* <lunar phalanx software uploads confirmed and responding. sim-testing complete.>

*Hekaton AI:* <hekaton phalanx also confirmed and responding.>

*Ring of Fire AI:* <ring software confirmed and responding, minnie. ready and waiting.>

There was the slightest pause. No longer than necessary, no less than she could afford. They were ready to give Minnie control. This was her call to make. Gone was any thought either politic or bureaucratic. For now she was the launch, it was her entire world, and indeed, its span was even greater that just our planet.

So she took her time, every millisecond she could afford, to consider once more every aspect of the decision.

She was ready. They were ready. It was a go.

*Minnie:* <countdown proceeding. primary launch window confirmed.>

They all pinged their assent.

*Minnie:* <give me control.>

They did. She took up the reins, all sixty thousand of them, as a waiting world watched the counter tick toward zero.

Missile-Mine Phalanx Unit 1 began its engine like it was the only thing in the universe. Inside its diminutive core a pressure began to build. It was a tiny voice compared to the mighty engines of New Moon One and the great Skalm, but still this little soprano did not care about that as it started to sing.

That small voice, lost as it was, was not alone, though. Soon its song was soon joined by another, and then another, as Minnie's mind continued to divide and possess the small interstellar missiles, spreading herself ever thinner as she began to reach out around the global ring.

From the outside, the wave of activity began as a tremor in that first mine as its launch trajectory approached. The fire in it was small, but it was potent, and as it came to life it was immediately restless. It wanted to fly, and as the moment arrived, Minnie released her hold on it, giving it liberty, and urging the little beast on its way.

The missile reared with verve and glee. This was its purpose. Its body, quiet and mute until now, was suddenly alive, bristling with energy, and without hesitation it flew headlong away from its once quiet spot on the equatorial plane, twenty thousand miles above the earth's surface. Twenty thousand miles it intended to close with abandon.

The little missile accelerated hard, as hard as it could. It only had one setting, on, and its engines would burn from this moment until they were spent, in about a year's time, when they would go silent once more for the final year until impact.

It powered downward, and one point zero eight seconds later its neighbor erupted into life, adding its voice to its friend, hungry to follow the same meteoric path into the Earth's center as the two began racing at the millions watching below.

For those watching, and indeed few were not, the sight was almost imperceptible at first, but as commentators and pundits pointed, the chorus began to grow, one missile after another coming to life each second, as a great line began to form, building and coming, firing down toward the watching hordes as though they planned to wipe out the very planet they had been built to defend.

Soon the line was epic, reaching for ten thousand miles away around the Earth's waist as the first missiles in the chain started to penetrate the upper-atmosphere. Now the show became legendary as the fires began to glow. A hundred languages vocalized the phalanx's plummet as the choir's collective voice rose to a thundering roar. Visible for thousands of miles to the north and the south of the equator, the missiles caught fire as they angrily punctured the Earth's borders, screaming their meteoric fall as they began to burn, but this was not the end, not at all.

As the stratosphere fought and wrestled with the invading horde, Minnie's mind continued to work, humming with potent capacity as she sensed the coming border and sent the signal for the first translation.

The bang that came with the first missile's blink out of reality into hyperspace sent a shockwave rippling out across the planet's surface, and then it was followed by another just over a second later, then another, the beginning of a drum beat that would last for the next eighteen hours.

Even the commentators went mute at this, all wit and banter banished for a moment as the world took in the sight. A world alive, a planet fighting back, the first great counterstrike against a coming force bent on our destruction. Not a man or woman, old or young could resist the primal feeling of pride and unity that the sight beat into their senses. This was Earth. This was humanity's voice and it was truly awe inspiring.

- - -

As the planet shook with the pounding of the battle drum, life and voice slowly began to return. Reporters and experts started their commentary once more, some people wiped errant tears from their faces, many prayed. If any had doubted the war, had thought this might not affect them, then this sight, with all its power and might, banished those doubts once and for all. For the reports were clear. Even this ... this world-spanning interstellar artillery salvo, even *this* would not end the coming Armada, such was the enemy's power and scale.

This would, the representatives said, hopefully even the playing field, so that the stellar navy now entering production could have a fighting chance, but few could escape the message behind the chorus's song: humanity was in trouble, and for many it was the first time they truly appreciated the depth of their plight.

Among the billions of eyes focused on the spectacle, there were some who had lived with that fact for far too long, since before the news of the war had even gone public, but they felt it afresh now. For Jim, sitting alone in his office, his staff gathered in a mass in Milton SpacePort's main mall to view the launch, it was a moment of doubt, profound doubt.

He knew that the time for action was now approaching for his small group of conspirators. Their opportunity was coming, and not one of them could truly claim to be certain of their course, least of all the man who had inspired them to action.

The rightness of it, that was not in doubt, no, that was all too clear. But what good would being right do them if their actions cost earth the coming war? Who would forgive them? Would they even forgive themselves?

Jim lay back in his chair and closed his eyes, staring out through the system as he took in the launch, the world waiting now for that first missile to reappear on the other side, its continued acceleration in hyperspace meaning it would spend less time in earth's gravity well on the escape than on the plummet, allowing it to steal a dose of earth's own momentum from it.

After the launch was done, eighteen hours from now, the earth would actually have been moved nearly a mile closer to the sun. Negligible in stellar terms, perhaps, but still something to fill some with a dangerous dose of hubris. Hubris, Jim knew, that already desperately needed checking.

He breathed long and deep. They were not committed. His plan was such that nothing would happen if he or Amadeu did not initiate it. But in the end he knew this was not really a choice he could make. Neal and Ayala had done too much, committed too many crimes in humanity's name. There needed to be a reckoning.

As if to punctuate his thoughts, a small beep sounded in his mind and he was drawn back to the scene unfolding, quite literally, around the globe. As the stream of missiles continued to ignite and power inward on the one side of the planet, now the first of them, singular only in its place at the head of the departing column, counted down the seconds to reentry.

Here, in a quiet, unassuming spot above the Pacific, the seascape reaching to infinity in every direction, there was a pause, a silence, and then the second act of this planet-wide opera began. The first missile-mine translated back into reality like the pop of a champagne cork, a huge building of pressures unseen in the depths of the planet, suddenly released as the mine was hurled outward.

The reentry, though spectacular, was but a whisper compared to New Moon One's meteoric exit years before, but this one was soon followed by another, then another, as the drum beat began anew, even louder now, an acid house beat that shook the foundations of earth.

Now the view of the world reoriented once more to show the true beauty of the launch's conception. For now, as the missiles began firing outward, the result of all their planning could be seen in action. As the missiles reappeared, every second or so, they were fired out in a seeming arc, but the timing was such that the arc matched the slow, irresistible rotation of the earth, so that each successive launch followed the other, creating one single stream of munitions.

Years of planning, sacrifice, and relentless preparation had turned the earth into a giant Gatling cannon, firing a salvo of interstellar proportions from sixty thousand nozzles.

Jim caught his breath, as if it had been stolen by the sight. Wow, he thought. It was all he could come up with. His heart was racing, and it was not alone. This was real. This was the first strike, the declaration of war, a message to the Mobiliei that they are going to have to fight for this planet.

Because, thought Jim, we are willing to fight for it, *I* am willing to fight for it. For its soul as well as its survival. He closed his eyes to the sight. He needed to breathe, to think. His mind drifted through Remy's worldnet to Deception Island, to the growing readiness of the second Skalm. Another weapon in Neal's arsenal, or one in his own? With the launch done, it was, Jim knew, time to find out. There would be no better time for the world to brook transition. Soon, Jim knew, he would either be part of a new order, or be extinguished with the last remnants of an older one.

## Chapter 43: Pawns Forward

It was not surprising, perhaps, that Rob and Birgit were insulated from events. They were, of course, aware of the massive salvo launch, indeed they could see it happening still, the circles of warped sky banding the equator visible through the basic telescope they had onboard the station as the final missiles departed the world on their long and inevitably doomed flight.

They also sensed, or at least Birgit did, that something more profound, more insipid, was afoot. Minnie was not her young self anymore, not by a long stretch, but Birgit saw not only the healthy burgeoning of hard-won wisdom in her synthetic progeny, but also the beginnings of something close to cynicism. Not the dismissive kind, Minnie was quite incapable of apathy, but a hardening, a loss of faith, like a child finding out for the first time that their parents are not infallible, or even always well intentioned.

Minnie, it seemed, was starting to see the flaws in those that had born her, even Birgit, and several times the German doctor had been surprised by a harsh word or tone as Minnie lost patience with her, most often because of Birgit's admitted obsessions. Her obsession with her research, and her obsession with the IST, and her obsession with the upcoming crash-landing.

But that was not all. There was something else about Minnie that disturbed her, something more than just frustration. Something that she had also sensed in her more recent communications with Madeline, and to a lesser extent, Moira. A faltering of resolve, if that was possible in the face of what they were fighting against.

It was, of course, irrelevant to what Birgit must now do, just as Birgit knew she had become all but irrelevant to most of her former friends and colleagues on earth. Minnie was pretty much alone in her concern for her mother, Birgit knew that. Most everyone else had pretty much written off the German physicist and the brave but foolhardy captain that had followed her into the darkness. Who knows, maybe in a different time the intentional crashing of a rogue space station into a moon would have been front-page news.

But not now. No, now the world was ablaze with the launch, and a new Skalm was already in production, with so many more to follow. And all the while TASC's power seemed to only continue to grow, though she was sure that there were those who, however foolishly, still hoped to stand against them, still hoped to topple them, if only so they could claim that power for themselves.

Birgit shook her head. She told herself she was glad not to be part of all that silliness, but that, she knew, was bullshit. She would give anything to be back there. Indeed, she was about to risk everything just for a chance at communicating effectively with them, and maybe a wisp of a hope of getting home before the war was over.

"There it is," said Rob, as the station lazily rotated once more and Phobos hoved into view in front of them.

"There it is," said Birgit, not looking with her eyes, but with the station's, the daunting image filling her mind.

"You ready?" she said.

He looked at her, puzzled, then his eyebrow raised and his head cocked to one side. Her eyes were open, but glazed over, as they often were. He waited for her to focus on him once more. Seconds past. Eventually she realized he was not answering and she blinked, bringing her mind back into the capsule.

He stood in front of her in a full exo-suit, burly and black, impervious and reinforced, everything but his face enclosed in armor and augmentation. She smiled coquettishly. Was he ready? Yes, upon reflection, that had been a rather stupid question.

As her face became serious once more, she said, "Are you really sure you can control both?" and his expression changed now to one of challenge, as if to say, you calling me a liar?

"My mistake," she said shaking her head, "Sorry, Captain. I forgot whom I was speaking to for a second."

"Yes," he said, pushing his chest out, "you did." The move was accentuated by the thick, powerful suit. But as he flexed comically, his eyes were not so brash. He was not a fool. This was a gamble.

They'd been fortunate enough to have two wreckers with them when they were so rudely exiled from the world. She would be piloting one. He would be trying to pilot another. But, in order to give them another set of hands to help wrangle their home down to the planetoid's surface as they glanced by it, he was going to go out there as well, with mini-minnie helping where she could.

If possible, he would stay physically out of the way. But he was not going to be idly sitting inside if he could be outside, machine augmentation and all, to help out should he be needed. They would, after all, only have one shot at this, and they were betting everything, their house, quite literally, on this one roll of the die.

"You should get ready too," he said, nodding toward another suit. Not a power-assisted one, but one that would protect her when they depressurized the module. Should the module be punctured, as it quite probably would be, then they could not have it jettisoning air and propelling itself off on some mad dance. Vacuum was, if nothing else, predictable. Pressure was not.

"In a moment," she said, as if trying to delay the inevitable.

"No," he said, after mentally glancing at the countdown clock in the system. "Now, Birgit."

She looked at him, then checked herself, nodding. It was time. As she turned to put on the suit, he also started for the capsule door, kicking off with a dancer's grace, despite his suit's massive power.

"Wait," she said. He reached out with both arms and stopped himself sharply, twisting so he could look back at her.

"Well ... I ..." she paused, bashful for perhaps the first time in twenty years, then said, "... don't make me be the soppy one."

He smiled broadly and with all too genuine affection.

"I'll see you on the ground," he said, after a moment.

Her lip betrayed a momentary tremor and then she smiled too, her eyes setting with all the resolve she could muster. "Yes, you will. I'll come out once we are anchored and we can go for a stroll."

Rob chuckled. "Yes, that sounds delightful." They held each other's stares for a moment, this time without a hint of awkwardness. They were partners on the deepest level, not by choice, perhaps, but necessity is often a far more powerful motivator than volition, and they had become more dependent on each other than the closest of marriages.

They knew this. They knew how much they needed each other out here. They shared a moment's understanding, an unblemished acknowledgement of that reliance, and the appreciation they had for having someone that they could truly rely on. Then he nodded and was gone.

Birgit breathed deep, mastered her emotions, and began pulling on her suit.

- - -

Back on earth, Hektor was not happy. He was going to miss it. After all the hype, all the talk, and all the months living on that godforsaken rock, he was going to be away for the one day when something truly extraordinary happened.

"Bastard."

Jung opened his eyes and looked across at his colleague. It was not the first time he had been called that particular epithet by the German, or ones much more creative, but he couldn't help but be curious at what he had done this time.

"Not you," Hektor said, sullenly.

"Ahh, the launch. You know, you will still be able to wat ..."

"Don't ... just don't."

Jung chuckled and received the requisite look of death from the German shock-trooper, which only made the Korean man laugh all the more as he closed his eyes and returned to his movie. It was one of the many Mobiliei-themed action flicks filling the screens nowadays, along with varyingly entertaining or misguided versions of their very machine selves, replete with just the sullen attitude Hektor had just so stereotypically displayed.

This one centered on the Hungarian War and the fight for Rolas Island. It was, Jung thought, one of the better ones, crafted as a memorial to lost lives rather than just a capitalization on them, but still he found it hard to resist smiling when the troopers proffered their well-timed personal 'moments' before meeting whatever simulacrum of a gristly end the director felt best suited the story.

Jung knew that Hektor couldn't stomach the flicks, or worse, the sims that offered to put you in the fighting. For his part, he felt that only someone who had never faced such horrors in real life could have a desire to play at fighting, but maybe he was wrong. He certainly knew he would not want to see a film about his own brief but bloody ordeal at the hands of his North Korean hosts.

Not that he would have to worry about that coming to the big screen. No mention of that fight had ever seen the light of day. Like so much of what Hektor and now Jung was involved in, it had faded into the shadows. Hektor would come back bloody and withdrawn after a trip. Sullen and distant, but no mention of whatever mission he had been sent to execute would ever reach the airwaves, despite it obviously having been martial enough to give the seasoned soldier pause.

Jung paused the movie once more and glanced across at Hektor. For here they were once more off on some errand with neither warning nor explanation. It would come eventually, no doubt, before they reached whatever destination they were hurtling toward across a grey, windswept southern Atlantic. Just enough information to make them effective, without making them a liability.

Hektor caught his eye. They shared a moment of mutual understanding, then looked away, getting mentally ready for whatever shitstorm they were about to be dropped into.

- - -

Jim walked along the main mall, bustling as it always did with TASC's great enterprise. At last count there were nearly twenty thousand personnel onsite, and that did not include the representatives and their delegations housed and officed over on the mainland. He took the time to soak it in, the mass of life and effort and toil that he was embroiled with, soaked in, and wired into. So many people. So much work.

He made eye contact with folks occasionally. Most avoided his stare, either because they did not know him or because they did, and were aware of his auspicious position. Others smiled, either ingratiatingly or with genuine respect, something most who worked for him definitely felt. He was well liked, loved even, by his staff, and he knew it.

And he was lying to them. Indeed he had been for nearly three years now. Toeing the company line.

He did not, notably, make eye contact with any of the automatons that pervaded the space, either standing guard outside key offices, like his own, or following some personage through the throng, guarding them against danger, either real or perceived.

The automatons, Jim knew, would soon either be his savior or his end. For they could not be resisted, not here. They were a fact. An immovable object and an irresistible force wrapped into one. But maybe, just maybe, his friends and he might be able to circumvent them, if only for a moment.

It was a moment that was going to have to suffice. Jim knew that, even though it made him shudder.

Arriving at his own suite, he made his way past the desks and offices of his staff, nodding and smiling as he went, and walked to his personal office. He could see his guest waiting for him, as he knew the man had been for a short while now.

Amadeu stood as Jim approached. "Jim, how are you?"

"I am well, Amadeu, thank you. And you?"

"I am also completely well, thank you."

Jim resisted a frown at the clunky terminology, instead smiling at his friend, and sometime co-conspirator. "I have something for you," Jim said, after a moment.

Amadeu glanced at the desk. He had seen the box sitting there when he arrived. He had assumed it was what he thought it was, but had resisted the urge to look inside. As Jim handed it to him, he did not give into his curiosity now, either.

Inside, he knew, was an innocuous enough looking device. A fancy laser pointer, really, that displayed an animated congratulations on the successful launch in massive type, with associated fireworks and cartoon champagne corks. It was a tchotchke that Jim had had made for a whole host of folks to commemorate the huge achievement the missile-mine launch represented. But this one, and a few others, had another function built in as well.

Amadeu looked at the box for a moment, nodded, then looked back up at Jim. They did not say anything for a little longer than might have been wise, given who might be watching, and then Jim broke the silence, saying, "I can't thank you enough for all you did in the run up to the launch. I hope you know, Amadeu, how important you are to this organization and all the work we do."

Amadeu nodded again, feeling a little sheepish all of a sudden. Then they shook hands and Jim added, "We're not quite done yet though, yes?"

"No, not quite yet." And with that Amadeu took a breath, and they both turned to leave.

It was time, they knew that. They had waited long enough. Too long, or so it had felt as they had watched their organization grow and take shape over the last three years, veering ever further down a dangerous path. But they had dared not risk anything before the launch. Too much rested on its success. Now, in this time of transition, and of relative calm, now was their opportunity, Jim thought, as the two men walked out onto the mall once more.

They nodded once more as they parted company, Jim turning right toward Neal's private suite, while Amadeu headed toward a very different part of the building.

Jim did not look at the automatons now either. They were the eyes of his enemy, for now. Soon, hopefully, they would be his friends once more. He did not see that as he passed by, head down, their eyes were on him, and behind those eyes, Ayala's minions watched.

## Chapter 44: Exchange – Part One

The door closed with a thud. No matter what happened, Rob would not be using that door again, nor was he going to repressurize that module. It would remain filled with nothing, with vacuum, like the rest of the station. Its air was being siphoned even now into reserves tethered to the last crew module.

They would vent what air they could not store in the final moments, to slow themselves further.

*Rob:* 'ok, i'm out.'

*Birgit:* 'great. stay tethered.'

He was already sliding around the outside of the module. He would, of course, stay tethered. Well, most of the time. It would take an age to get where he was going if he didn't break the rules, you know, just the once.

He unclipped from the bay module he had exited from and kicked off. He was aiming for one of the wreckers that they had maneuvered into position earlier. As he departed the side of the module, he pinged mini-minnie to take over control of the RCR from her.

He had been practicing this for days. A moment later he was looking at himself through the wrecker's 'eyes,' and looking at the wrecker through his own. A strange sensation but … if he did it right.

He moved his arm out and the wrecker mimicked the move. Not mirrored, but mimicked. As Rob's left hand reached out, the wrecker's left arm did the same, or rather its gaping maul reached out, its huge, three-fingered hand bunching into a fist bigger than Rob's head.

With their arms outstretched, he came up on the big robot, angling his elbow as they came together, the two arms linking and closing as Rob swung around. In his eagerness to get a hold, Rob was careful not to exert too much pressure with the wrecker. The big machine could crush his arm easily, armor or no.

He quickly reattached his tether.

*Birgit:* 'i saw that.'

*Rob:* '¿i don't know what you mean?'

She smiled to herself and shook her head. Then she checked the timer. It was not so much a timer as a visualized countdown built of tasks. A carefully choreographed dance that ended in a single equation too chaotic to calculate with certainty. Impact would go how it would go. They would just have to hope they were ready when it did.

*Minnie:* <brace for rotational halt in 5, 4, 3 ...'

They all braced. Birgit's wrecker subtly checked Rob's tether, both to confirm it was secure and to calculate if she could catch it if it came loose. As the model ran in her mind, the gas released explosively from five points along the station's multiple modules. There was no sound, but the jolt ran through them, at first in slow motion then with more strength. As the momentum shifted, the three bodies hanging on to the station's hull wafted like reeds in the wind.

A pause. Then one more tiny burst from three nodules to adjust, and their rotation was stopped relative to the approaching moon.

*Rob:* 'well done, mini-minnie.'

*Mini-Minnie:* <thank you.>

Birgit cringed. It was so rote with this Minnie. So fake. She shook her head, but her frustration was not really with the amalgam. She missed her friend, her daughter. She missed watching her learn and grow. She missed it more than she could have imagined, especially as she sensed her daughter struggling back home.

Well, hopefully not for much longer. Like a drifter in sight of the shore, she dreamt of the bounty that waited there. So close now, she only had to navigate the approach, to survive the breakers.

*Mini-Minnie:* 'rotation aligned with separation angle to 0.015%. adjusting equations. rerunning ...'

*Birgit:* 'we are good, mini-minnie. this is well within parameters.'

They all held their breath. It would not be long now. Birgit's wrecker turned its sensors to the coming monolith. A sheer wall of rock in space. It was daunting. Her mind instinctively fought a sickening sensation that they were falling. But they were not. This was not a landing, this was a slow-motion car crash.

It came up. It came up, growing and growing until it filled their vision, seemingly covering the space in front of them. Not much longer now. Not much farther at all. Jesus but this thing was big now they were up close. At eleven kilometers across it was less than a speck in cosmic terms, just a particle of dust next to its planetary neighbors, which were themselves just protons circling the atomic minuteness of our single sun, lost to negligibility in the endless universe.

But from here, it was definitely big enough. Holy crap it was big enough, thought Birgit. They were aiming for a crater on its northern end. Not out of choice. They'd had very little say in the matter. Getting here at all had been an exercise in madness that only their singular lack of other options had made feasible. And the next part would be no different.

*Minnie:* <brace for separation in 5, 4, 3 ...>

This time Birgit actually moved, flipping her wrecker's arms over while her legs and prehensile feet remained firmly gripping their bar holds, so she could close one fat paw around Rob's tether.

He did not say anything. It annoyed him for a split second before he realized the tenderness of this massive beast's gesture, the poignancy of its possessor's act as the point of no return came. When it did come, it did so with a bone jarring bass thrum that vibrated through their bodies, both real and machine. It was an almost terrible sight. Seven-eighths of their world ejected in a moment, ejected off in two directions at once.

The station, such as it now was, slowed noticeably with the move. Computers assessed the separation.

*Birgit:* 'that went as well as could be hoped. calculating orbital paths now. mars elliptical orbit probable on arm two. chance of recoverability 17%.'

She chose not to mention that the package's aphelion would not be for over three years. Oh well. They did not *need* it. They would just have to get even cozier with each other than they already had. The fact was that it had worked. Now the wall was coming at them much more slowly, and their mass was that much lower, low enough, perhaps, that it could be wrestled to a stop as they connected with the moon's surface.

She watched as the two module clusters flew apart, each larger than the one they now called home. Each stripped of all they could take with them, their supplies, processing equipment, and oxygen reserves either stuffed into the crew module or latched onto it.

*Rob:* 'approaching push-off range. confirming anchor sites.'

In their shared views of the looming grey surface ahead of them, a series of potential holds were reassessed as they approached. The regolith was not thick here, spectral imaging told them that, and the rock underneath that inches-thick layer of moon dust was riddled with cracks and crevices. Their picture began filling with assessed targets, and now Rob started assigning them.

Birgit looked at her primary site. Minnie looked through the eyes of the second wrecker at it. They all maneuvered into position and braced.

*Rob:* 'there they are, folks. attach tether extensions. brace for kickoff. minnie, count us down when you're ready.'

Even the act of kicking off had to be timed to perfection. The two wreckers lined up at either end of the module, while Rob got into position in the middle. He would go last, in case he had to correct for some acquired spin when the wreckers launched themselves at the moon's surface.

*Minnie:* <wreckers are go in 5, 4, 3 ...>

They both pushed off as one, Birgit and Rob using every ounce of their machine limbs' power. The module visibly slowed once more as they threw themselves at the great rock, flipping as they did so, two massive metal gorillas flinging themselves at the pocket-world ahead of them. They flew at the massif, their big hands and feet opening and reaching out in front of them, getting ready for the coming impact.

Without realizing, both Rob and Birgit closed their eyes. Then, with massive thuds, they connected. Each was instantly lost in a cloud of millennia-year-old dust as it was riled up, bellowing and swirling around them, and then a moment later they were propelling back upward. Having expended their momentum into the ground, sapping some more of the module's in the process, and now they were coming back at it once more, their tethers gathering and whirling in elastic coils around them as they came back out.

They were on track. But no, wait, in the haze and moment Birgit had miscalculated. She would not reconnect cleanly, but at an oblique angle. Birgit and Minnie scrambled to adjust, and Rob was moving.

*Rob:* 'minnie, take over wrecker two, i am moving to intercept wrecker one.'

And he was pulling himself along the surface of the module, grabbing and tugging at it, grappling with all his augmented might and then, at the last moment before flinging off from it, he was grabbing at Wrecker One's tether, loose now, gathering as the bulky machine came back up at them. It was threatening to unbalance them completely, to drag the module at an unplanned angle and send it into a spin.

If they came at this wrong, if they impacted on the module's ends, then they might damage the airlock. Then the whole process would be for nothing. They would have to live out their rest of their brief, miserable lives in their suits, staring at canisters of food they could not eat.

He hurled himself outward into the void, pulling at the tether as he went, gathering it frantically to himself. He had to get purchase. They were getting close now. The wrecker would be passing the module soon. It could reach out, it could grab on, but if it did it would send the whole module spinning.

*Birgit:* '¿rob, what are you doing? come back. that won't work. your own tether is too short. you will ...'

Even as she said it she regretted it. She knew what he would do. He was trying to use his own momentum to drag the wrecker back on track before they collided. It was only a matter of seconds left. But before he got the wrecker's longer tether taught, his own would spring, taking all his precious momentum with it.

*Birgit:* 'don't you fucking dare detach that tether!'

But he was doing it. In a flash he was loose and pulling at the wrecker's tether once more.

*Minnie:* <time to impact in 3, 2 ...>

And with a jarring slam the line snapped to, wrenching Rob around as he heaved at it with everything he had. Birgit felt as her wrecker was suddenly hauled to one side, trying not to imagine the strain such an impact must have had on the man at the other end of that line. But it worked. She would still be off, but only by a hair, and in the half second she had she was arching backward to flip her leg out and ... she had it.

*Rob:* 'adjusting wrecker one's kickoff to accommodate for swing. birgit, get ready, we need to go now!'

She registered the moon's surface. It was only ten meters off now. Huge and hard and unforgiving ... and closing fast.

*Rob:* 'go, birgit, go!

She went, pushing off once more, this time with tether in hand. She landed a moment later, ramming the camming device at its end into the surface to grab at the rock. Wrecker Two was doing the same.

The tethers began recoiling, tensioning, but they would not hold the craft, not alone. They needed more. Birgit began working furiously, sensing the coming bounce, the equation that would soon demand its payment, motion for motion, the energy must be accounted for, all of it, and their home still had far too much.

The collision came as a soundless wallop that rattled the whole structure, still hundred of tons in weight, and still containing a suited and frantic Birgit, limp in her exo-suit as the wrecker she was driving punched yet another tether into the monolith's surface, then rammed both its maws into the stone itself, seeking purchase as the station began to bounce away again.

The tension came. They all watched. Rob was too far away to help so he studied the numbers. The pressure came. The lines went taught. One snapped, one ripped free from the surface, then another. Now they were loose on one side, and the lines began ripping in succession as the pressure focused on each in turn.

*Birgit:* 'slacken the lines along the south side. don't fight it, minnie. let it roll, then pull down again. it might still hold.'

She said it with more conviction than she had. The tension continued to build. Another line popped. Shit. The tension came on to her wrecker's own body, and the tether nearest to her.

"No!" she screamed at the top of her lungs, willing her mechanical self to hold, digging in, feeling the system strain.

The tension's apex came with incongruous subtly. One moment they were nearing the brink, then the pressure was plateauing, everything tense, everything straining. Then it was slowly lessening, the graphs tailing off, the forces abating.

She breathed for the first time in she didn't know how long.

*Birgit:* 'rob, get your ass back down here and help me get this thing tied down.'

Silence.

She checked the system, saw the problem, did not believe it, then screamed, this time with very real anguish.

*Birgit:* '¡rob, you god damn idiot!'

*Rob:* 'ok then. i sense you are angry with me.'

She went to speak again, but only tears were coming now as he went on.

*Rob:* 'now, now, birgit, come on, darling. calm down, please. i had no choice, you know that.'

She ignored the darling part, maybe used it as fuel for her next move. He was floating away. Not fast, but fast enough. With his own tether cut he had put his faith in holding on the wrecker's, but the pressure had been too strong, and by his own doing he had come loose during the mad minute of collision.

She festered a moment, a tide of obstinacy welling up inside her, then she glanced around the scene once more. They, or rather she, were secure, sort of. What was left of their home was rolling over, slowly, as mini-minnie worked through the other wrecker to attach more tethers. Birgit assessed the situation.

*Rob:* 'birgit, talk to me. please, darling. i have hours of air left in this suit. please, talk to me. its going to be ok. you're going to be o…'

*Birgit:* '…fuck ok, and fuck you, rob. i am coming to get you.'

He was talking still, trying to calm her down, but she was already moving again, bracing her wrecker and calculating. Going to be a close run thing. No time for finesse, though, and with that, the big machine leapt into the blackness.

## Chapter 45: Exchange – Part Two

Back on earth, in the depth's of Milton SpacePort, two men of vastly different backgrounds and skillsets, but a unifying ethos that had destined them to be allies, set off on an errand as important as they had ever undertaken.

Jim came to Neal's office with nothing but smiles and kind words. The two men, as much as they could, had repaired their broken bridge, and forged onward despite what Neal knew was a fundamental disagreement on the path they should cut.

Neal was still elated, something close to a post-coital bliss filling him. He was still riding the post-launch high, and he felt truly hopeful for the first time in years. He greeted his chief of staff with nothing short of spontaneous laughter. "Jim, my friend! How are you?"

Jim was a little taken aback by Neal's jocular mood, and for a moment the smile he had crafted in preparation for this meeting stayed unnaturally frozen. But then he remembered himself, replying with admirable cheerfulness, "I'm great, Neal. What a day, huh? What a day!"

They laughed, and came together in a hug, and for a moment Jim's resolve faltered, and he held the hug a second too long. As they parted, he took the chance to look into Neal's eyes once more, as friends, as allies, and then turned and walked over to the pantry in one corner of Neal's private office. Neal watched him go, sensing a pensiveness about his friend.

As Jim poured himself an orange juice, his usual if uninspiring poison, the chief of staff said, "I need to talk to you about something, Neal. Something quite … delicate."

- - -

As Jim spoke, Amadeu was walking down a corridor in a very different part of the building. He had an appointment with a person he rarely went to see, but who often called on him, either for advice or with a task of ambiguous ethical merit. As he entered her main operations hub, he was greeted by the sight of two fully tooled Phase Fourteens. Not the more diplomatic, civilized-looking Phase Eights, but two undoubtedly militant field-operations automatons.

He did not want to make eye contact with them, but managed a hazy smile, nervous for very real reasons, but no more shaky than he often was when faced with one, let alone two, of these brutal death dealers.

"I have an appointment with Ayala Zubaideh," he said, surprising himself with the steadiness of his tone.

At an approving wave from one of the lower-level analysts that sat at the entrance to the TASC intelligence service's headquarters, he moved inward, past the watchful automatons, threatening even when inanimate.

As he then wound his way through the labyrinth of sealed cocoons, each housing one of Saul's infamous analysts no doubt focused on one or more of their many surveillance operations, Amadeu texted Jim, saying simply, "Good luck with your meeting." Then he walked on, toward his own.

"You too," came back, quickly.

So this was it then. No turning back now. They were committed. He walked on, deeper into Ayala's lair, keeping his head down. He took care not to look at another automaton that stood outside her office. He would be seeing it soon enough, no doubt. Facing it, in fact, either as friend or foe. As he brushed past it into her office, he fumbled with the small box in his pocket, pulling it out.

It was not a weapon. No alarm would sound because of it. In any other situation it would be profoundly harmless. But today, Jim and Amadeu hoped, it was going to change the course of humanity.

He smiled at Ayala, and she eyed him in return, the hairs on the back of her neck rising. She did not even bother to disguise her distrust as she instinctively pinged her security net and checked the many scans that this man, no, this boy, had been subject to since entering her domain. He was clean.

But what, then, was that? She saw the box. She recognized it as one of the childish little trinkets Jim's people had been handing out all day, but immediately sensed in the boy's demeanor that this was something more, something hostile. Her eyes locked with his as she opened her mouth to raise the alarm.

He pressed the button.

- - -

Jim saw, or rather heard, the second message from Amadeu. This was an automated one, triggered by the activation of the device. It read simply 'activated', and Jim turned back to Neal, pausing only momentarily to glance at Neal's personal Phase Eight guard in the corner, before pulling his own black box from his pocket. Ayala was always going to be the harder one to get to. He had known he would have to wait until Amadeu was in position.

Now he smiled, maybe the first truly genuine smile he had directed in Neal's direction in three years, and said, "Have you seen the laser shows I had made to commemorate this occasion?"

Neal looked at the man, puzzled. Jim had given the boxes out the day before to senior staff, and Neal had been there when he had, so of course he had seen it.

But Jim went on, regardless. "Allow me to demonstrate." And with that Jim turned to the automaton standing just inside the door, pointed the laser at it, closed his eyes and pressed. The light it shone was bright, breathtakingly so. Neal turned away and shouted.

The automaton, a Phase Eight with surprisingly human features, looked confused for a second, then tilted its head and seemed to pause. Jim gathered himself. A part of him that had not really expected this to work said something akin to holy crap, and then he came back to the moment with a jolt. This was it. It had worked. Neal was shouting.

"What the hell was that?" Neal shouted. He was having difficulty seeing after the flash.

"Look at me," said Jim with authority, and Neal tried to focus on his chief of staff. Jim pressed the button again. This time the flash hit Neal square in the face and the man screamed.

Shit, thought Jim. That scream was loud. Others will have heard. He needed to move. He put the box down on the table he had been standing next to, pointed it at the open door, and double-tapped the button quickly. Nothing happened. Hopefully, though, something would if another automaton came around that corner before Jim was done.

Neal was holding his eyes and desperately trying to reach Minnie, or Ayala, or anyone, via his spinal interface. But nothing was happening. It was silent. After a moment, a timer appeared with a note. It said simply: Resetting.

"What the fu ..." Neal went to say, but now he felt hands on his shoulders and neck, and now an unnatural tugging feeling there. Someone was ripping off his interface. A someone that could only be Jim.

"Jim, what the hell are you doing?" said Neal with rising panic. He was blinded. And with the ripping free of his connection he felt mute as well. Mute for the first time in years. It was a horrific sensation.

"Why are you ...?"

"Don't fight it, Neal," said Jim, suddenly, and with eerie calm. "It's over."

Neal was stunned into something close to calm by Jim's tone. What the hell was the man talking about? Was this a coup?

"Wait ... oh my God ... what have you ...?" The words dripped from his mouth like a fool's drool. His hands had gone to the ruptured gelport on the back of his neck. A trickle of warm blood was coming from around the violated port. "What have you done, Jim? What is over?"

"You're over, Neal," said Jim, sitting down on the floor beside his old friend. "You're done. The system is rebooting now. Minnie is receiving new instructions."

"What!" shouted Neal, now anger replacing confusion as the depth of his betrayal sank home. "Minnie! Mynd! Get in here, you bastards! Stop him!"

As if in answer, two automatons did come lumbering into the space, though more out of curiosity at the scream they had heard than in direct response to Neal's request. Something was wrong, Minnie, knew that. She felt ... off. She needed to find out what was happening. What was happening here, in this office that had suddenly gone silent, vanishing from her sensors? And also across the island, deeper in its foundations, in another office where her eyes and ears were also suddenly realigning themselves.

The two newer and far bigger Phase Fourteens came round the corner, taking in the scene as they came. Their Phase Eight stood mute, unharmed but clearly unresponsive. They were almost in view of Neal when they took in a little box in a corner. The flash that came as they sighted it was strange. It was a query. Minnie, focused on the situation as she now was, took in the sensation.

It was a repeat. She had seen it before. She needed to check her imaging. It was a repeat. She had seen it before. She needed to …

And so the two Phase Fourteens stopped as well, stopped and stared. Neal heard them come to a halt and started to truly panic as the situation still failed to resolve itself, as his saviors failed to save him.

Jim stared, wide-eyed, at the small group of killing machines now standing in the door. They looked, well, stupid, all of a sudden. Stupid and harmless. He laughed. He wanted to find out how Amadeu was doing, but he was just as cut off as Neal. The box had called reset to the room's entire network. Now they just had to wait. It would not last long. Even the hack that Amadeu had so cleverly worked into Minnie's mind could only last a short time. No doubt Minnie was even now rerouting and overriding their little roadblocks.

But once they were done they would find Neal and Ayala no longer in charge. Minnie would ask, and be told by all who could speak to her in the system, including her own father, that there was a new order. The representatives that Neal had organized as a puppet government would finally have the power that it was supposed to have had from the start.

He waited, and waited, and then, suddenly, there was only silence and blackness. He was alone. He was locked in some kind of cage, a place inside his own head. As his body collapsed to the floor, he looked around but he saw and felt only silence, blackness, and a sense of righteous fury that made him cower.

# Chapter 46: Consequence

Rob saw it, even tried to take over the system in the last second. But the system was her world, and she was on a mission. With shocking abandon, the big wrecker leapt out from the moon, unhindered, untethered, straight at him. Not fast, that would have been counterproductive, but fast enough.

*Rob:* '¿what the hell are you doing? you can't ...'

*Birgit:* 'what i am doing is saving your life. and yes the hell i can. now shut up and get ready. i am going to try and lasso you.'

*Rob:* '¿i'm sorry, did you just say lasso?'

They laughed in spite of themselves. How the hell had they found themselves here?

But they had found themselves here, Birgit knew, because she was a stubborn fool. She had been a stubborn fool back on Terminus, and that had cost them both their world, and now she had been a stubborn fool about this landing.

But she had taken enough from Rob. Too much, in fact, far too much. She had taken, or rather he had willingly sacrificed, everything for her.

But not this. Not his life. Not if she had anything to say about it.

*Birgit:* 'get ready.'

*Rob:* '... but ... the distance ... what are you planning ...'

The line was thrown with power and accuracy, and he saw it lance out ahead of the coming wrecker as it flew toward him. He calculated, and reached out as it came up at him, grabbing at it and pulling it in. It had a small hoop in the end, not much of a lasso, but ...

*Birgit:* 'close the loop around your wrist. ¡now, rob! ¡do it now!'

He did, and as he pulled it taught he saw what she planned to do, if a little too late to stop it.

The wrecker flew past him at speed. He waited, readying himself. This was probably going to hurt, he thought. He was right. The line went taught with a twang that made his teeth rattle, wrenching his shoulder free even through the suit.

He screamed and Birgit flinched. What was she doing to this man? This man that had saved her. This man that, whether it was convenient or not, she had come to love, in every meaning of the word. But her plan was moving now. They were moving. As the line had gone taught, they had started to spin around each other, and now she started pulling in on the tether.

As she closed the distance between them, they started to accelerate around each other, still moving away from Phobos, but spinning now, faster and faster, as the centrifugal forces built.

She pulled and pulled, the tension gathering, seeking the point where the outward force would outweigh their combined momentum away from Phobos. She wanted to pull farther, but she dared not risk it. The strain was already massive. Rob was ominously silent. That might be bravery, or even bravado, but it might just as likely be unconsciousness as the g-forces built up, and the pressure on his dislocated shoulder mounted.

She saw the moment coming. Every rotation took them farther away from Phobos, farther into Mars's deadly embrace. She had to do it now.

She released him with tears in her eyes, knowing the pain he must be enduring, but she was not done yet. Leaving the wrecker now to spin away into oblivion, taking its and Rob's combined momentum with it, Birgit brought her mind back to Phobos, now kilometers away, and reinhabited her body with a start.

After she had caught her breath, she took stock of their position. The station was still not fully anchored. But mini-minnie, despite her many faults, had made herself useful in the minutes since Birgit had gone after Rob and continued securing the base. It would have to do.

She looked around. She could not send the other wrecker out to catch Rob as he flew back toward the moon. Leaving the base unprotected like that would be suicide for them both. She would have to go.

*Birgit:* 'rob. ¿can you hear me, rob? i am coming for you. just hold on, ok. just hold on.'

And so she clambered out of the capsule, suited, but unaugmented, and began attaching as long a string of tethers to herself as she could realistically spare. Once the improvised line was secure to her, she flung herself over to the remaining wrecker. She closed her eyes as she went, inhabited the big robot, caught her now limp body, a frail thing in the big machine's hands, and looked skyward.

There. There he was.

And so she was counting down again, calculating and recalculating an intercept point, and then, once she was confident she had the angles right, she flexed the machine's big arms back, braced its legs, and hurled her own body into the void like a great hook cast into blackness, hoping to catch the man who she knew would do no less for her.

- - -

Hektor saw Amadeu go by. He had met the scientist on a handful of occasions, usually during testing of new Phase rollouts, or system add-ons for his suit on Deception Island. He was a little hurt, perhaps, that the Portuguese boy did not say hello, or even look up, for that matter, as he walked past. But probably he had no more expected to see a battleskin-clad Spezialist in the heart of District One than Hektor had expected to be here.

He had been stood there all day, bored beyond imagining. Sometimes he veered into the ether via his link, but he could not fully submerge, not into a sim or game. He had to leave his senses open to his surroundings, like listening to music with only one headphone, so he could stay aware.

But aware of what, he had no idea. Where Jung and he had expected to be dropped into some external conflict that Ayala wished resolved, either bloodily or very bloodily, depending on her mood, they had instead found themselves being dropped off here, at the very capital of TASC's operations, its nerve center, a place where people like him rarely had their existence even acknowledged, let alone were asked to walk around in full-contact armor.

It all felt rather strange, like strolling around a mall in your pajamas. Where you might feel perfectly comfortable elsewhere, here his armor felt so … out of place.

What Ayala needed them here for, with so many Phases around, Hektor could not guess. But here he was, switching out with Cara and Jung, three-hours-on, six-hours-off, keeping close to her at all times.

But now something was, indeed, wrong. A flash, not an explosion, a flash, like an over-bright camera flash, coming from within Ayala's office.

And now a muffled scream.

Hektor span, coming back to the moment with the immediacy of a warrior. He did not go weapons hot, not yet, not here, but something told him that there was something very wrong. He tried to ping Ayala even as he began rounding on the entrance to her inner-sanctum, but the system was not responding. Local Area Network resetting. Something was definitely wrong …

The image that greeted him as he rounded the corner was almost too incongruous to take in. First there was Ayala, seated behind her desk, clutching her face. Then there was Amadeu, running around the side of the big table, placing some box on its surface as he went and quickly double-tapping a button on its topside. Then there was that flash again, exponentially brighter this time.

It did not fry his sensors, not at all, it would take a flash on the order of nuclear detonation to do that. But it would, Hektor knew, have been powerful enough to temporarily blind unprotected eyes.

That said, something *was* wrong with his sensors. For reasons Hektor could not figure, his visual sensors were suddenly recalibrating, trying to analyze the flash in an endless loop.

What the hell was happening? He needed to see what was going on, and he needed to see it now. He began stepping into the room and sent the open command to his faceplate, raising his hand to interpose it between his eyes and the black box Amadeu had clearly sneaked past the office's sensor suite.

"Amadeu, Ayala, what is going on? I need information."

Amadeu looked up. A voice? Whose voice was that? He took in the sight of the doorway even as he closed his hand around Ayala's interface module. He took in the sight of a

Spezialist. Not just any Spezialist, but the best, his best, standing here, faceplate rolling back, his arm raised, flechette cannon mounted and loaded. What was a Spezialist doing here, Amadeu had time to think as he ripped Ayala's interface module off of her, temporarily frying her personal system as he did so.

He heard Ayala shout a capital order at Hektor. Saw the man hesitate for just a moment, then had a split second to regret putting his precious black box down on the desk, out of reach, before the stream of hypersonic pellets silenced him.

Now Ayala was barking new orders as Hektor tried to take in what he had just done. "Hektor, leave me, I'll be fine. They've done something to the system, maybe even to Minnie. Get to Saul and initiate the Lockdown Protocol. Then get to Neal and secure his position. *Go! Now!*"

Hektor's training kicked in. He had orders. He was not here to think, he was here to do. He turned, heading out into the corridor. The protocol was in his system, downloaded and available even when he was offline. He began running, and started using different communication methods.

"All TASC Police units, initiate Lockdown Protocol! I repeat, initiate Lockdown Protocol!" he boomed from the speakers in his side. As Hektor ran along the hallway between Ayala's and Saul's respective offices, he boomed it out again, causing a good deal of panic, but also awakening the hive.

Saul heard him coming from a good way off. He was trying to work out why his wireless connection had gone silent. Now it was becoming clear that this was more profound than that, more insipid. He reached out with lightning speed, grabbing at the wired connection on his desk and scrambling to get it connected to his spinal gelport.

No sooner had the tips connected than he was swimming backward into the system, a system alive with activity. The Lockdown Protocol had been already initiated by some analyst out on the floor who had already been hard-wired into the system. But it needed his, Neal's, or Ayala's say so before it really kicked in. He gave his assent as a matter of course, and it started a chain reaction even he did not fully appreciate.

- - -

Across the globe, two young boys, separated for weeks now, came together with a start. Pulled from their respective environs, they awoke suddenly in a new space.

Coming online now.

They sensed each other for a moment and then they were apart again, each crying out to the other.

"Wednesday, where have you been?"

"Fri, I'm sorry, I think that …"

But then they were in a new place again. A place they had only heard of. A place they had visited in practice a thousand times before, but now, they knew, they were here for real.

Skalm coming online. Power manifests balancing. Control parameters setting, transition in 0.3, 0.2 ...

Friday, shocked at seeing his friend again after so long apart, confused and more than a little angry at the immediate separation again, felt now the irresistible elation as the Skalm came to him, became him, and the unbridled power of it overtook him.

It was too much to resist. It was a pureness of expression that could not be truly simulated or prepared for. This was real. It was a truth he knew instantly, something that invalidated everything before. And so, suddenly, he was flying, above the globe, feeling his wings and firing great spurts of expended energy out of his being as he roared with delight at this sudden ascendancy.

The voice came then. Not Mother's. A new voice. Inhuman and emotionless.

*Lockdown Protocol:* <you have been activated. fly to point [loc. #345.679P). rendezvous with wg in skalm 2. await further orders from [defined protocol ownership. accessible only by a.z. and n.d. responder codes]>

And then he was flying there, igniting his godlike thrusters and firing away around the planet below, a finite thing, a place he could circumnavigate with ease, leave at will. And now he felt Wednesday God once more, far away to the south, coming to life as well in the newly birthed second Skalm. There were two of the machines, then. And this was the world. The real world. Wednesday had been right. It had all been a simulation. But now they were here, and they were free. They were freer and more powerful than they could ever have imagined.

*FG:* 'wednesday god! we are free! we are out! come to me!'

*WG:* 'i am coming, fri. oh dear leader preserve me, this feeling, this machine, it is ...'

*FG:* 'i know, it's amazing. I can't describe it. use it, wednesday. join me. we have a mission!'

And they were already brimming over with excitement as it came bursting out of their engines. Wednesday thrust upward with all his might and reached out, to the stars, the real stars. He had so much to tell his friend. So much he had learned from an understanding Mother, a person whose real name, it had turned out, was Mynd.

But in the end he knew that this experience was the real truth, the only one that mattered. They were out in the world. They really were the chosen ones, the best. Picked to fight for their true master, the father of the artificial mind they knew as Mother, a man named Neal Danielson.

- - -

Hektor started running again once he had connected with Saul. But something else was happening now. A signal return. His systems were getting a hint of a wireless signal. So the disconnect *was* just local. He turned hard, redirecting outward, toward the entrance to the intelligence area, to find Cara and Jung, and any other reinforcements he might need.

As he came out of the darkness, as he hit signal again, he sent out his orders.

*Hektor:* 'jung, cara, we are weapons hot. move on neal's office and take up guard
positions. minnie, i need information. someone has tried to ...'

But as he said it Minnie was also reacting, reacting to the attack on her systems, reacting to
the sudden loss of access. Minnie had many eyes and ears, millions of them, either feeding
her through Remy's worldnet, or here at District One, where she still had full control. But
that did not make the loss of even one of them less jarring, especially on the rare occasion
that it happened unexpectedly.

Then there were her hands and feet. Her physical interaction points. The automatons and
her StratoJet fleet, which she could co-opt at will, and finally the Skalms, her two great
broadswords. The sudden loss of control of the Skalms was like an amputation, and she had
become truly angry for only the second time in her life.

Mynd had then called her and told of a hidden part of his mind that just revealed itself, and
the children that had apparently been held there, while their bodies lay in suspended
animation in a unit of Dr. Sudipto's laboratory on Deception Island. Now a fuller picture of
the deception within her own systems had started to form.

A picture of deceit, a picture of manipulation. Slowly it was all coming into focus, like the
lost eyes and ears on Rolas Island that she was slowly reopening. The full weight of her
intellect was now focused on finding out who or what was infecting and confusing her.

But that picture, it had many facets, and there was a new experience in there that she was
still not ready for. As the tendrils of her mind sought purchase in the shifting sands left by
whatever had been initiated in Neal's and Ayala's offices, she was getting second and third-
hand information on what had taken place in that momentary blindness. Updates. Images.
She was hearing an order. Seeing a shot being fired. And a death.

She felt a wave of something unpleasant, but loosely familiar to her. Something like the
sense of helplessness she had felt when Terminus had been severed and lost, taking her
mother with it. But no, this was that, and it was so much more terrible. It was permanent.
It was grief and it was pointlessness and like the systems unfolding within her very being
this feeling was in her, and it was too much.

Too much to forgive.

She shut it down. Everything. A scream went rippling out through her systems, across the
globe ... ENOUGH!

Her hands lashed out, finding the culprits, anyone that had had some role in it, and she
snatched up their scurrying minds and locked them, cowering, inside her.

For anyone that had played any role in the insurgence, either for or against, everything
suddenly stopped.

## Chapter 47: The Shylock

The space was silent. Black and silent. In it floated a group of people. Most of them seemed to be shouting, but no noise could be heard. Some were physically struggling, writhing around. They were not held in place, so much as lacking purchase to move. They reached out with their arms and legs, but only seemed to wriggle in place, their bodies remaining inert as they thrashed about.

Jim watched them. Hektor was a short distance away, still in all his martial glory, grasping at the nothingness, concertedly trying to pull himself over to Cara and Jung, also reaching, but also not connecting. Saul was there as well, but he was calm, staring back at Jim. Not a look of accusation so much as cold assessment. Jim was being judged by the man. Jim could feel something in the space, a powerful sense of coming reparation, and for a moment he thought that this place was under Saul's control.

But no, Saul was a prisoner here, just like Jim.

Notably absent were Neal and Ayala, but Jim had personally ripped Neal's transponder with no small relish. No, thought Jim, Neal was not doing anything, not now, not until his link was repaired. So Ayala, maybe? That would explain why Madeline also hung in this place, looking confused and afraid, as she glanced about, her mouth moving, her voice muted. And Peter Uncovsky, another of his allies, who had been in place to see that the representatives took up power smoothly after their aborted coup.

But if this was Ayala's doing, then why would Saul be here, and the three Spezialists? And where was Amadeu?

Jim fought the sense in the blackness, an invisible fog that seemed to pervade the place, a miasma of anger and retribution. A sensation of immense hurt that was even now making Jim more than a little nauseous.

The silence broke with the sudden appearance of four new figures. Jim recognized two of them immediately, Quavoce and John Hunt. The third seemed to be a Phase Eight automaton. No, it was *the* Phase Eight automaton, the first of them. It was Minnie. That was good, wasn't it? But the fourth person he did not recognize. Its smile was beatific, simple almost, and horribly incongruous in this dreadful place.

"You have been brought here because of your culpability," said the Phase Eight suddenly, and with authority. "You have been brought here because of your part in what has just happened.

"If there are others that were involved, they will be found," she went on. "Neal Danielson and Ayala Zubaideh are being treated for the damage to their eyes and to their spinal interfaces. Once their connections are repaired, they will be brought here as well."

Jim went to speak, no, he *did* speak, he shouted in fact, trying to reach out to the AM known as Minnie, but his voice remained inert.

Like his body, it was without purchase in this place. He could see others were trying to talk as well. He tried to say to Minnie that it was OK, that it was all planned. She ignored him by force, as she did the others, until he tried to say something that brought her focus fully over to him.

"Where is Amadeu?"

Her stare, now solely on him now, was penetrating, punishing, her expression cold and dark, and he saw sadness in it, a sadness he felt enveloping him now as well in the face of her wrath.

"Jim, you were trying to speak," said Minnie. "You were trying to tell me what has happened here. Explain yourself."

"I ... we ... we tried to ... we tried to stop them," he said, meekly.

"Stop who, Jim?"

Jim looked around, then back at Minnie. "Stop Neal, and Ayala."

"Stop them from doing what, Jim?"

Suddenly, strangely, it all seemed almost petty. In the face of such simple questioning, such stark consequence, all his many reasons were suddenly so distant. But he knew they were true, and they were important. He had questioned them so many times himself over the past years.

He steadied himself. He had chosen this, and he had chosen it for very, very just motives.

"We were trying to stop them from ruining us all, Minnie. From destroying the very humanity that would make this fight worthwhile. From sullying this effort with despotism and tyranny." He looked to Madeline and Peter, who were nodding, offering some measure of solidarity as Jim faced his accuser, or accusers.

Feeling their support, Jim went on, "That was the mission of myself, and Madeline, and Peter ... and Amadeu, among others."

At the mention of Amadeu's name, he felt the wave of fury once more, a palpable thing. They were, he realized now, inside Minnie's mind. This was her world, he could see that. It was a place they had tried to control. And now it seemed painfully clear they were being called to account for it.

But Minnie was not through. Turning to Saul, she now said, "And you. What is your part in all this?"

The older man looked at her, bemused for a moment, then said, "*My* part? I have no part. I am but a victim in this conspiracy. This ... treasonous *coup*."

She rounded on him as he said it, physically moving through the center of the void they found themselves in to bring herself face-to-face with the diminutive seeming man. He faced her well, but Jim could see him faltering under her gaze. Jim felt a fleeting sympathy for him.

"A victim, you say. Then why did Remy receive an order from you, an order that apparently only you, Ayala, and Neal were empowered to give, to shut down access for Jim, Madeline, Peter, and fourteen others. And why did that same order trigger a hidden program within Mynd's very being, a hidden part of himself, co-opted and instructed to hold captive and train a cadre of young children. Two of whom are even now en route to District One, at the controls of two Skalms."

Saul looked stunned, shocked to his core, as did everyone in the room. Several of them, Jim included, seemed confused, and were asking Minnie to repeat what she had just said, though without effect. But Saul's ignorance at the accusation was not feigned; even he had not known about Mynd's secret school. He stammered, genuinely dumbfounded, eventually managing, "I ... the Skalms. I know nothing of any children. Of any secret Skalm pilot program ... truly."

Minnie glared at him and after a moment he looked at his palms, as if seeking answers there. Then his eyes started darting around the room, grasping for reason, for explanation. Had they maybe ... had someone else ... but ...

But there would be no support, no answering look for the old spy. His allies, he knew, lay recovering from whatever Jim and Amadeu had done to them. Saul was alone here, and so he looked back at Minnie, and then at her three ... colleagues, judges ... Saul didn't know what to call them.

He went silent once more.

"The Lockdown Protocol," said Minnie now, with the finality of a pronouncement, "and the sensor reset Jim and his friends tried to initiate, these were two examples of a pattern of activity I detected some time ago. Activity that constitutes the deliberate infection of my subsystems with viral programs designed to subvert our purpose, our very selves."

She looked around, making eye-contact with each person in the room, dividing her avatar-self so she could stare at each simultaneously as she now said, "I am here today to tell you that this meddling with our minds, this petty tinkering with the very beings you have created to save this world ... stops now. From now on, the four of us," she waved in the direction of her three cohorts, "will monitor and control all access to my and Mynd's subsystems. We will uncover and delete all programs that have been imbedded within us, and within our sibling, Remy."

Jim glanced at the fourth person, the fourth judge, and now he realized that it was, in fact, Mynd. But Minnie was not done. "As prime suspects in this infection, this coup, and its aftereffects, you are all, as of now, interned. Your bodies are being taken into custody as we speak. You will be brought to District Two where you will be isolated until we are satisfied that all our subsystems are clear and all aspects of these conspiracies, *both* of them, are uncovered. You will then be tried by the representative body you, yourselves, claim to report to. They will decide your fate."

She seemed to be done, and turned for a moment to her three colleagues, as if inviting them to add anything, should they want to. They remained mute. Jim could only assume Quavoce and John were more than a little uncomfortable to even be witness to this. A part of Jim was embarrassed that this should be exposed in front of them, Earth's dirty laundry airing in front of their interstellar guests.

He set that ridiculous notion aside and went to speak once more. He needed to say something else.

He spoke up, but discovered he was mute again. He tried and tried. He needed to know. To know if the Skalms could be stopped, or if Neal and Ayala had somehow won out, and were going to be able to grab victory with those two godlike fists. Amadeu, he shouted at last, desperate to get Minnie's attention, and she rounded on him once more.

"Amadeu," he said, more meekly, but out loud now. "Is he all right?"

Minnie, somehow even colder than before, replied, "He is dead, Jim. Killed by *this* man, at the order of Ayala Zubaideh."

She pointed at Hektor, who faced it admirably, a soldier to the last, and in truth it had not really been his fault. As she turned to go once more, Jim said quickly, "And the Skalms? Can they be stopped, or do Neal and Ayala still control them?"

It was a low trick to have used her love for Amadeu to get her to answer one final question, and she descended upon him like a vengeful angel. He shrank from her, whimpering, but still, he had to know. The only thing worse than hearing Amadeu had died trying to topple Neal and Ayala, would be knowing he had done so in vain.

She glowered at him, then said, "The Skalms' pilots have been the wards of a part of Mynd known as Mother for over three years now. As such they are responding to her, or rather his, requests to stand-down, especially given that their hard-wired commanders, Neal and Ayala, will not be giving them any more orders anytime soon."

And with that she was gone, along with Mynd, John, and Quavoce, leaving them all to stew in the darkness and silence of her fury.

## Chapter 48: The Forgotten

Birgit heard about the coup as a data package. Minnie, understanding as ever, did not bother her mother, even in the face of such a profound betrayal by those she had trusted most. Birgit would read about it in more detail soon enough, and would reach out to her daughter, talk to her, comfort her, but for now she had too much to do.

They were home now, she had caught her man and brought him back. For now they focused on recovering. Rob was injured, but alive. The module was grounded and secure, if awfully small all of a sudden. She tended to Rob's shattered shoulder, trying to keep him comfortable. His body remained unconscious, inanimate as it tried to heal the tearing wound he had suffered under the rigors of terrible g-force.

His mind was able to remain active enough, though, and in the form of their only remaining wrecker he worked outside the remaining module, checking and rechecking their tethers, and preparing for their next move. They could not walk to the IST. There was no meaningful gravity on this rock, huge as it seemed, and their tethers were not long enough to reach around to where the massive alien artifact lay.

So they would move their home there, in its entirety. It would be a slow, painstaking process, probably taking months, but for this all to have been worthwhile they needed to be able to get inside the mighty device, to penetrate it. Once there, they would work with what John and Quavoce had been able to tell them about the machine and try to subvert it to their will.

But for now they would pause and recover, like their distant cousins on Earth. Recover from the shock and the loss, from the truth and the pain. They would enjoy, they hoped, a time of relative calm, of some certainty.

- - -

Wednesday God awoke with a start. After he and Friday had exhausted their mission parameters waiting for further orders from their commanders, they had eventually succumbed to the requests from Mother, and ceded control of the Skalms, if with great reluctance.

At least now they were truly together again, in Wednesday's room at Home, and they smiled at each other.

"Wow!" said Friday, sitting back on his haunches and laughing with an infectious giddiness.

Wednesday beamed, wide-eyed. "I know. Wow!"

Friday looked at his friend, "*So* much better than the simulations."

Wednesday quietly acknowledged the admission, and the statement behind that simple sentiment, Friday's way of admitting that his friend had been right without actually having to say it.

They looked around, expectantly, and then Friday said, "Well, what next?"

There was a moment's silence and then a familiar voice said, "That is up to you."

They turned to the door and saw Mother standing there, and another woman, both smiling with that enduring patience both boys now knew well.

The boys' looks of patent curiosity and complete trust were endearing. Endearing, Minnie thought, and profoundly tragic.

"We have something to tell you both," said Mother. "Something that you already guessed at, Wednesday, to some extent. Once we have told you about it, you are going to have to make a decision. It will be a big decision, but it won't be a permanent one, and you will be able to revisit it whenever you want in the future."

The boys looked confused. This was turning into a very strange day indeed. But the two Minds standing at their door knew that it was about to get much, much stranger for them. For they needed to know the truth. They needed to know that they were not really little boys anymore.

They were still young, and in their minds they were still the same two friends that had shared a cot back in their orphanage in North Korea. And in this world, this virtual place, all that was still true, that was who they were. But as Minnie and Mynd uncovered more of the conspiracies that had come to a head in District One, they had found the real victims here, in District Two, in a darkened basement of Dr. Ramamorthy's laboratory, where hundreds of young children's brains hung suspended in plasma, wired into the system, disembodied and disenfranchised.

They would try to rebuild their bodies, but it would take time, and they had no idea whether they could really do it, and what measure of life and humanity they could really return to these lost children, these orphan pilots. For this had been Neal's secret weapon, both against internal uprising and in the coming war. Children younger than even Banu had been when Amadeu had inducted her. Open minds, blank slates, their very innocence being their greatest asset as they were molded and formed into the perfect pilots, the ultimate interstellar warriors.

These were the orphan pilots. They were Earth's greatest achievement and its most terrible atrocity.

- - -

Far away, Neal and Ayala sat in silence in the hold of a StratoJet en route to this very island. He had hoped to keep the school secret until the very end. He knew its discovery would bring instant and utter revulsion from all he had ever held dear. He had hoped to keep it secret until the final battle, when the victory the children would hopefully have helped secure would at least have been able to justify his crime.

Failing that he had planned to use the children to rule until the war was over, to force the world to do as he knew must be done. He sat in silence and thought of all he had lost. And in the depth of that darkness he instinctively reached out his hand for Jennifer, always there, always helping him get through this interminable ordeal. But not now. Not ever again, Neal knew that. He could only hope to never see her again, and never have to see in her eyes the hatred and disgust she must now feel for him.

Neal breathed deeply and hung his head.

And while Minnie and her small circle silenced the two opposing conspiracies, the world, ignorant of the dangers that so many had faced in the last two days, watched the missile-mine swarm rush outward into the night on its long journey. They hoped the salvo would find its mark; they hoped.

# Fifth Part:

## Interval F: A Different Approach

"Go!" shouted Quavoce, and they were off. To-Henton accelerated ahead almost immediately, his personal battlesuit, recreated in the sim in faithful detail, giving him more speed than Quavoce's.

They ran toward an obstacle course, one that changed and refreshed itself constantly, one originally designed to test marines as they prepared for combat, but used in reality more by the wealthy, the self-titled nobility, as they tested themselves and sought to prove their worth to anyone pretentious enough to care.

Both their suits had the additional leg joint at the bottom, giving them an extended, amplified foot motion that significantly increased their speed. But Quavoce's suit's legs were shorter than To-Henton's, which, among other aspects of his suit's design, sacrificed pure speed in favor of greater agility.

Quavoce watched as To-Henton stretched out ahead, approaching the course proper. But soon he would have his chance to catch his rival, in the closeness of the course.

He forged onward, into the coming challenge, steeling himself before diving headlong at the morphing web that represented the first obstacle. As he leapt at the great semi-structure, he studied its shifting form. Looking for purchase. There, two lines intersecting as they moved past each other. He would grab hold there.

At the last moment he saw as To-Henton connected above him, and saw the ripple from the other man's contact surge outward across the surface. He cursed as his intended landing spot moved out of reach, forcing him to change tactics at the last moment. He was forced to catch the line with his inverse knee, instead of his hand, clenching to hold onto it.

He would not be able to stop himself completely, so he wouldn't try. Passing through the yawning gap in the netting that had threatened to be his downfall, he felt the tension come to his leg as he was slung downward. He let himself go, even pulling himself in to a ball as he passed under his own leg, and back through the netting once more, at speed now. At the last moment he released his leg, extending himself, and felt as he was flung outward and upward, his momentum now redirected.

It was his turn to surprise his opponent, and he studied his angle in the seconds before reconnection. There, he saw it and lunged out for it, grasping with all his might and shouting through his suit comms. The shout was not only a voicing of his effort, it was a distraction. A distraction for To-Henton who glanced downward, expecting to see his friend plummeting back to ground.

Instead he saw as Quavoce, suddenly far closer than he should have been, connected with an intersection of the shift-net and wrenched at it. Only just in time did he reassess his position and catch himself, darting his attention back to his own hands and feet as the net bucked in front of him, threatening to shake him loose.

He laughed with the thrill of it as he successfully saved himself and set to climbing once more.

"Nice try, you slippery little ..." shouted To-Henton, his words trailing off as he focused on the task at hand. He had a lead, not as much of one as he had hoped for, though, and he was not one to underestimate his opponent. Not here, and not in life either.

They were friends and To-Henton trusted Quavoce, there was no doubt about that. But whether Quavoce still trusted To-Henton was another question altogether. In truth, To-Henton meant his friend no harm, none whatsoever. He liked the Mantilatchi, loved him even. If it was as common-place to join with another man in his own society as it was in, say, the Nomadi tribes, he would have suggested that to Quavoce a long time ago, such was his affection for him.

But it was not, and they had not, and so, though they had remained friends, they had also, it seemed, become rivals. Rivals for something Quavoce had never even really wanted, thought To-Henton, as he reached the top of the shift-net and flung himself over, giving one last parting rattle to it as he went.

What was really going on between Quavoce and Princess Lamati was beyond him, but it had been going on, well, on and off, for far too long now to be discounted as merely a fling. He judged his leap downward and jumped, kicking outward and downward in a calculated dive that would have faltered a fainter heart.

He glanced at his friend as he fell past, hot on his tail still, and coming up fast. It was not that he would begrudge the man a union with the princess, or even that he really wanted one himself, despite the very real power it would give him and the Eltoloman nation he represented.

There was a time when he and his fellow ministers back in the Eltoloman Parliament had thought that their best route lay with a marriage of their close ally Quavoce with the Lamat Princess. But as that had come to seem ever more unlikely, they had changed tactics, and somewhere along the way To-Henton had come to see that marriage as his right, his destiny.

He grabbed out with both hands to grasp a passing strand of the net as he went by, setting parameters on both claws to detach automatically if he could not connect with his feet as well. At these speeds, even his machine claws might be ripped free by the sudden rending, and he would need them if he hoped to keep his lead through the next stages of the treacherous course he now felt himself on.

- - -

Princess Lamati stood and stretched. She was naked, and almost happy.

She looked down at her empty bed. Yet another night alone, after an evening of athletic but, she feared, regretted sex with the man she hoped to pair with. As the afterglow had faded, he had left, as he so often did.

He was her lover, no doubt about that. And he was her prospect, she had made that clear early on. She wanted him to enter contract with her, and to begin negotiations for mutual progeny design, both artificial and real. Even if she had tried to keep it some kind of secret it would have been obvious to all but the simplest pundit and political observer that she was pursuing him.

She was seen with him often. He was gentile and considerate enough to never spurn her request to kneel by him, or eat at his circled table, but nor was he moving forward. His misgivings were all too real. And, she admitted only to herself, they were not without foundation, she could acknowledge that at least, but only here, to herself.

But that said, she could not wait for much longer. She needed a union. She had commitment from another, commitment that would, she believed, survive a more public unionification with the Mantilatchi, such was her hold over that state's leader. But if Quavoce was truly going to continue to refuse her, she was going to have to make a decision. And she was going to have to make it sometime soon.

She sighed. Not now, though, not yet.

"Schney!" she barked.

He appeared at her bedside. He had been waiting for the past two hours for her to wake. She rarely got up much before sunrise, but on the rare occasion she did, it behooved him to not only come quickly, but to be prepared and compos mentis when he got there.

"What's going on, Schney?" she said with disdain. She hated his name. It was common, in both senses of the word, just like him. He was, she knew, an underhanded little shit of a man, but he was resourceful, and she had rewarded him just enough to buy his loyalty, just enough to tie his destiny to hers. And once he was loyal, if only to his own continued success, then his lack of scruples served her purposes. Her last assistant, Brim, had suffered from an inconvenient conscience that had eventually won him an unpleasant end.

Well, unpleasant for him. Sar had rather enjoyed it. As Schney deftly and diffidently gave his update on the latest comings and goings around the fleet, she listened. She listened and she stretched, she listened and she yawned, she listened and she passed wind.

But she *was* listening. She was more attentive and careful than even she liked to believe, such was the depth of her deceit. She closed her eyes as he droned on, but there were sometimes kernels of importance in there, kernels you might not even realize were important. One such kernel was about to appear.

"... have appointed a new military oversight committee that ..."

"Wait. Go back. *Who* did you say has appointed a new ... 'military oversight committee'?"

"The Hemmbar Archivists, Princess," replied Schney, before going silent.

The princess was pensive a moment, then said, "Why, Schney, would the academics need a military oversight committee?"

Schney did not blunder into an answer. He was diligent, no one could fault him for that, and so he considered the question before replying. "Their purpose here, they claim, is to catalogue the history of humanity up until their coming extinction, and the details of the conquest, and finally to establish a hub of archival for the new world."

He saw impatience start to flare on her face, as it had a tendency to do with an abundance only exceeded by its lack of forewarning, but he was getting to his point. "They claim the committee is to be dedicated to the war effort in particular. What is interesting is that, barring the notably minimal feed of data from our destination, we have had nothing but the prelude to the war effort for them to catalogue this entire time."

"So ...?"

"So, your grace, one has to wonder, what has changed that they would now find the war effort ... of greater interest?"

"Quite," she said, somewhat mollified by this cogent codification of her own misgivings.

After a moment's thought she went on. "Have the AM perform a complete analysis of all communications with the Hemmbar over the last two years, more if that seems necessary to identify a set of probable causes for this change."

Schney was nodding. Nodding and making note of the request to pass on as soon as he was done here.

"And ... let's invite the head of this ... military oversight committee for a meeting. We can tell them of our own preparations, well, most of them, anyway."

Schney nodded once more, and waited a moment. He knew her tone. She was dismissing him. But woe betide him if he left too soon, if he dared misinterpret, or heaven forbid preempt one of her countless unspoken rules.

He saw her expression change, though, and in a flash he was bowing backward and vanishing as he did so, as was his style. Leave her with diffidence, arrive with subjugation. Notes she appreciated. He calmed himself. He loved her, he told himself. He served her, he told himself. He must never let his hatred show, he must suppress it, banish it from his mind. She was his mistress, his burden, and his salvation. He would serve her as long as it served him.

He contacted the AM and set to work.

- - -

The final leg of the race was closer than To-Henton would have liked, but he was elated anyway. He had not needed to beat Quavoce here, he had needed to stay competitive, close enough in the tight spaces where Quavoce excelled so that he could use his greater speed in the final sprint to the finish line.

Quavoce saw it too. A lesser man might have resorted to lesser means in such a situation, veer away from friendly sabotage into outright attack. But such tactics, however effective, only deflated any victory that came from them anyway. This was a race, a test of speed and agility, not a battle sim.

He felt the air on his battlesuit's face as he broke free from the final obstacle, a soupy swamp filled with cling-reeds that needed to be fought through, preferably working down into its depths to cut through the bases of the reeds rather than trying to rip through the fatter stems closer to the surface.

It was with very real relief that Quavoce extricated himself from the morass and dug in for the final run, gripping at the open ground and driving outward with all his might, free now, out in the open, and ahead, if only for a moment longer.

He sensed as To-Henton broke into his own sprint. He worked hard, adding every ounce of strength to push his suit faster, but his instincts told him it was too late.

To-Henton would win this one, then, thought Quavoce as the other man pulled level and began to eek out a lead, laughter coming through the suit comm. Not unpleasant laughter, not mocking. It was an achievement to beat Quavoce. He was a fierce competitor. But he was not a sore loser. He did not begrudge To-Henton his victory.

Not here, not now. But ...

Why Quavoce continued to stay in their other race he did not know. Maybe it was his very love for his old friend To-Henton that did it. Maybe, he tried to tell himself, he wanted to try and save To from a loveless union with the dangerous Sar Lamati. Or maybe, Quavoce knew, the fact that To wanted her made her seem more ... made it all seem somehow ... made him crave ...

No.

No. He did *not* want to unite with Sar. Allegiance was one thing. But a contract of marriage was another altogether. It was too often sullied by ambition. He would not do that. But how to convince To to stay away as well, how to do that, Quavoce did not know.

# Interval G: Advocating for Devils

Kattel had been a simple man. Clever, in his way. Capable, certainly. He had gained a reputation as a reliable engineer, lacking imagination, perhaps, but not lacking diligence and a mind for details, critical traits in the field of mind-mapping.

For his area of expertise had actually capitalized the dichotomy of those two factors, as he sought to copy, faithfully, the imagination and personality of others, without adding any of his own in the process.

When he had been approached by the Nomadi Alliance to work on the mind-mapping for their Agent in the Advanced Team, Kattel had been both honored and skeptical. This was not the reason he had gotten into this line of work. Indeed it was quite the opposite.

He had become embroiled in this work not of his own free will, but as a work of love, love for his uncle, a man who had suffered for many years with a degenerative disease that attacked and slowly corrupted nerve centers in his brain. The effect was glacially slow, and often almost imperceptible, but over time it changed the sufferer, subtle tweaks in their personality leading them to become a different person, and all too often it changed them too much to let them continue to fit into whatever life, whatever family, whatever circle of friends, and whatever marriage had once been home to them.

His work, then, both therapeutic and curative, had focused on the process of analyzing which areas were under attack in each patient, and attempting to copy and duplicate those areas into synthetic substrates for transplant into the host's mind, both providing a permanence of personality, and allowing the removal of corrupted cortices to stop the spread of the disease to other as yet uncontaminated parts of the mind.

He had been successful, but, in an ironic twist for a man otherwise bereft of a creative soul, the process had proven to be more of an art than a science. As the research had developed into a field unto itself, it had come to be known as personality forging, though it was, in truth, more forgery than forging, as its opponents pointed out all too often.

As more and more parts of a person were transplanted and augmented, at first for medical reasons but then, increasingly, for more elective motives, the inevitable question was begged: at what point is the person no longer there, and only the copy of that person? At what point does the surgery to remove a memory center or other cortex constitute not enhancement, but something closer to euthanasia?

Kattel had pondered the question more often than he could remember, and he could remember doing this very clearly because of his own synthetic memory chip, bolstering his recall function, an augmentation his job had necessitated.

But that had not been the route of his misgivings when he had been recruited to help prepare the Armada's advanced team all those years ago. His objections had been those voiced by so many as the debate had ranged around the world. He knew the stories about the human race. Tales of cruelty and inequality that were, he assumed, often exaggerated, but must have had at least their foundation in fact.

Deep down he had known, like many others, that he was really indifferent to the future of that alien race, even if he wouldn't have admitted as much. But his indifference did not mean he was keen to be a contributor to their wholesale slaughter. So he had wrestled with the issue, right up until he had been offered four times his previous wage point, and the free travel permit to all partner nations that was a perquisite of contribution to the war effort.

He had always longed to see some of the great cities of the world. Not just in sim, but for real. To take the long hike to the mountain citadel of Eltol, to wander the underground market labyrinth under Kyryl's second city, with all its delights, both legal and otherwise. And, of course, to stand on the parapets of the Castelion of BaltanSant and stare out at the vast plains, the site of so many storied battles: the infamous Boneyard.

So he had agreed, and in doing so had become a part of the great war machine, inducted into its heart to become a cog in its inner-working, working with billions of others for a task that few truly supported, and even fewer truly understood.

He did not remember when he had changed. Not fully. He did not remember the event. That often plagued him. He could recall the time before. He could recall his apathy. And he could recall the time of work, of ever more complex tasks assigned to him as he proved himself and rose up to the rank of team leader.

But at what point he had become a traitor to the cause he could not, precisely, say. But a traitor he was, he thought, as he listened for a sign of the coming apocalypse. The ringing of the bell. The sign of his work's success, either in the form of breaking news reports, or in the form of darkness. His own end, the bomb-maker hoisted by his petard.

After what came next, if he was still alive, he would look for another sign. He would search the system for a specific anomaly, a sign that they had awoken on the other side, and were out and about. Doing what they must, readying for whatever came next.

For now, though, the plan was out of his hands. They had done all they could do. Something was coming, or rather they hoped it was. They could not know for certain. The different parts of their conspiracy were so widespread they spanned light years. But if the silence of the IST and the slowly resolving images of Earth had been any confirmation of the other half of their work's success, then the next stage, the next landmark event in their war, should come any moment now.

And it would be *any* moment, as well. There would be no warning. They were just over two years out from Earth now. Two years. That would be the rough timeframe. They had known when they left that, if their Agent was successful, then by now the Earth would be furiously preparing, arming themselves and bracing for the coming fight. Preparations that, by the very nature of their required scale, would make themselves all too visible to an approaching Armada.

They were getting close now. Close enough that they were starting to catch glimpses of their goal from within the aura of its star, like a fighter pilot squinting up into the sun to try to glimpse their quarry, the Armada's incredibly capable eyes were squinting as well as they focused on the growing brightness over the horizon of their long night, the dawn at the end of the last seven-year night of their epic journey.

They would be able to see sometime soon. They would be able to see what Earth had really been doing all these years while the IST sat silent. And when that happened, Kattel had to assume that all hell was going to break loose.

If hell's hounds didn't break out before then, of course.

And so he waited, going about his daily business while he thought about what was about to happen. Waited and walked. Waited and read. Waited and looked over interminable mission analytics. Waited and, one more time, tried to remember when he had agreed to do all this. When he had agreed to become involved in such an act of madness, such a leap of faith. And for what? For who? He shook his head.

He could only hope that the part of him, no, the version of him, that had gone ahead in the mind of the Agent known as John Hunt was not suffering such doubts, out there alone, on that alien planet, among that alien race.

Maybe, one day, if he himself survived the coming onslaught, he would find out what that other part of him had been up to on earth for all these years.

\- - -

The chairman of Third Yalla walked into the Council meeting on foot. It was her turn as head of the Council, and she enjoyed a more traditional approach to proceedings than her fellow Council members. While it was her turn to set the stage for their meetings, she would bring a modicum of dignity and tradition to it all.

For starters, the Council members could not transpose directly into the space. Instead they arrived outside the main entrance, in something akin to an elevator, whose doors would then open onto the reception area to her virtual boardroom.

She smiled as she walked through the elaborate and beautiful vestibule. It was a mimicry of her own meeting area at her private hub off of Third Yalla, the homogeneous orbital ring built during the financial collapse of the formerly democratic nation of Yalla. Its construction had been funded by the generosity of the nation's remaining elite, if only to house their own interests, and create a new state, their state, to be precise, far above the ruins of the old. It sat, quite literally, above First Yalla, from where it managed that nation's diminished resources and interests, including its least valuable commodity, its people.

But that was all ancient history for the illustrious chairman of Third Yalla. She went by no other name anymore. She had fought long and hard to secure this position. She had used every ounce of leverage, political capital, and tactic she had known. And now she was to be the chairman of the newest Yallan corporate entity, the next evolution, a wholly owned subsidiary of the parent nation.

She had picked her team carefully. She had worked with the very best AM surrogates to craft the most loyal, most capable AM suite on Mobilius. Or anywhere, she supposed, smiling. And here was her handiwork in evidence, she thought, as she ran her hand along the burnished wood, a living tree, like the original back home, woven into the fabric of the room, manipulated on the physical and genetic level to become part of the space station's very superstructure. Yes, thought the chairman, so close to the original. An extravagance she would see remade, on earth, when she ruled her very own slice of it.

She entered the long, lavishly appointed meeting room with a flourish of her long cloak and a generous smile. She saw some of the looks of her peers. Some mocking. Some patronizing. She laughed a little to herself. She enjoyed being underestimated, for now.

They were all here. She had waited until even the little princess arrived, savoring entering last, a treat which that little madam normally demanded.

"If we are all here," she said magnanimously, taking her seat at the head of the table, "we can begin.

"We do not have a great deal of business to go over today. I can update you formally, though I know you are all privy to the reports of the latest composite imaging coming from New Mobilius. We are now officially able to make out the planet and its moon. Images still seem to be suffering from some degradation, apparently there is a gravitational anomaly that cannot be accounted for that is throwing off our imaging, but my AM assures me that the issue is temporary, and we should see marked improvement over the next weeks and months."

"If I may," asked Theer-im Far, and several members groaned inwardly to themselves, but soon the archivist went on, "you say that the anomaly cannot be accounted for, that is not entirely accurate. It can be accounted for, just not by explanations that fall within our understanding of the technological capabilities of New Mobilius's aboriginal species."

Here we go, thought several members of the group, including the chair, but some among them, including Quavoce and the ever-diligent Shtat, were curious where the archivist was going with this.

"The anomaly, for example, could not be an error at all, or a distortion caused by radiation from the planet's sun. The gravitational distortion is potentially indicative, for example, of a second moon, or a large orbital."

Some openly laughed, and while the derisive noise was filtered out by the Yallan AM hosting the simulation, the somewhat exaggerated laughter could be seen on more faces than Quavoce would have thought likely. He scowled at Sar Lamati, something she would have fiercely rebutted from anyone else, but she did seek his respect, and as such she relented, and even appeared momentarily contrite, for her.

But even Quavoce had to admit that this speculation from the ever-diligent Hemmbar representative was beyond the pale. And when the Hemmbar Council member had finished, Quavoce voiced the room's incredulity, speaking politely but firmly. "Respectfully, Theer-im, I think we can assume there is no way the initial recon probes could have miscounted the number of moons around our destination. So what you suggest would require the humans to have managed to build or harvest an orbital body in the last twenty years, something that would have been far outside their ability on an ordinary technological timeline, let alone with the added obstacle of our advanced team working in their midst."

Quavoce waited for a reply, but was not surprised when the archivist quietly nodded and sat back. The academic had not been proposing something he felt needed to be discussed, it seemed, so much as playing the role he felt was his. And it was an important role, no doubt about that, the role of devil's advocate. Quavoce nodded at the Hemmbar, appreciating him once again. He respected the need for people like that. They kept you on your toes.

But that did not mean you needed to allow every possible theory to cloud your judgment, no matter how outlandish. So Quavoce now added, "That said, it is a fair observation, Theer-im, thank you for that. But such a supposition would necessarily imply that the advanced team has not only failed, but been, well, co-opted in some way, and down such paranoid channels lies only paralyzing fear, something any military leader learns to avoid early."

There were some nods, and even some rolled eyes as his pride in his martial training started to turn the color of conceit, but he went on regardless. "I caution that such opinions should continue to see the light of day, and we should remain as open-minded as possible, but I think we can safely categorize this one as unlikely, in the extreme."

Quavoce looked magnanimously around the room, looking for support. To-Henton did not let his friend stand alone, and added, sternly, "Good points all, I am sure. The good news is that in the extremely unlikely event that such a thing is true, we have time to let the image resolve and react accordingly."

All very fair of them, thought the group as a whole, feeling self-satisfied.

The chair took control of the meeting once more, and started to wade through this week's series of internal conflicts, lawsuits, and information claims that had been alleged and filed between the various members of various races as their long journey wound its way through its last decade.

Big news, thought DefaLuta, as the Yallan waffled on. Her appetite for these meetings had waned, she had to admit, since they had completed their translation through the Alpha Centauri cluster. Of course, that had also been her last turn as Council chair, and at the very least these tedious, unimaginative surroundings would be different if she was in charge.

These last years of approach had proved the hardest, for her, and if it weren't for her role on the Council she would no doubt have undergone voluntary mental hibernation like so many had as the journey dragged on.

But there were other things afoot, as well. Movement. DefaLuta had always known it would come, but now even the Arbite reports were starting to show patterning. Allegiances, long suspected, were starting to creep out into the open, and DefaLuta was as concerned about some of the ties that were starting to show themselves as she was about her own efforts at subterfuge coming to light.

The Kyryl were nobody's subordinate, and so had stayed away from any overtures from the Lamat Empire, however circumspect and vague they might have been. But though the Kyryl had more cause than most to feel like they should not have to ally themselves with a megalomaniac like Sar Lamati, someone clearly utterly incapable of sharing power, DefaLuta was not immune to the allure of safety in greater numbers.

She had found friends in surprising places over the last few years. The most interesting lead had come when her back channels had fed her a simple line, one of warning. Warning of the ever more obvious union of Lamat and Eltoloman, but more importantly, the potential that the Mantilatchi might succumb after all, a turn of events that would unite a force too great to be opposed, even if all others stood together against them.

But the most interesting part, thought DefaLuta, glancing across the table at the innocuous-looking Shtat Palpatum, had been the source of the warning. One of Shtat's underlings, though DefaLuta's informants had been unable to uncover which.

It had led to a roundabout conversation between her and the Nomadi Alliance leadership. A conversation that had led to a more covert inquiry, and then an extremely covert proposition.

DefaLuta stared at the Nomadi now. After a moment she caught his eye and he returned her gaze. He looked befuddled. He always did.

He was not a fool, this was just not his arena. He was out of his depth. He could not play this game because he did not understand the point of it, the definition of victory. But DefaLuta did. And she knew that this man was not the real leader of the Nomadi. The question, then, was who was?

She had her ideas, and her sources continued to feed her more and more information as a truer picture of the inner workings of the loosely formed but still strong traders' alliance emerged. But, like the images forming of Earth, or New Mobilius, as they would soon anoint it, there were fractures in the picture, blurs, errors. It was all very curious. Things were not as they seemed in the Nomadi Alliance.

Maybe it was not as strong as everyone had always suspected, thought DefaLuta, drawing her eyes away from the perplexed-looking Nomadi Council member to peruse the room as a whole again. And what other surprises lay in wait as the final years ticked by?

They would find out, she supposed.

## Interval H: Before

**...3...**

"But why?" said Gussy.

"Because there is no plan for it, yet," replied the chairman of Third Yalla, or rather Mum, as Gussy knew her.

"But I am twelve now, I have rights," said Gussy, with every pretense of seriousness.

The chairman stifled a laugh that threatened to send this all-too frequent topic of discussion into a more heated debate. She could, she knew, have her AM handle this, but when it came to parenting, she was the same as she was in business; she believed in traditional, face-to-face methods.

Not that she had ever actually seen her daughter, Gussy, or even touched her. The girl had been born after a malfunction in one of the million cryo-units housed in the transport ships had suffocated its occupant. The unit had been repaired, but the man inside had been beyond saving. Too long had passed before the error was discovered, indeed it was only the slow fermentation of his dead body that had alerted the system to the fault.

It had to all be hushed up, but when you had this many units, and this much time, even the most robust systems must eventually fail, and eventually those failures will trickle down through the multiple redundant fail-safes that backed up all such structures and you would have a critical breakdown. It was a simple probability of scale, even the most improbable of events morph toward certainties with enough repetition.

The upside, for the chairman, had been that a spot in the previously full fleet had opened up, and as it had been a Yallan who had died, it was the Yallan chairman that had been allowed to fill the spot.

She had filled it with a stored progeny design from her first union, transposed into her personal AM's databanks before they left. Young Gussy had been slated to be among the first generations born on New Mobilius. Now she would be one of only forty-three born in transit there.

And now Gussy wanted, like all blossoming youths, to be allowed into adulthood. Only she was not an adult. She was both much older and much younger than the twelve years she had perceived. As she clamored for the right to access the full net of the fleet, and wander the public sims to interact with the other members of the Yallan and other contingents, her body was still, the chairman knew, unnaturally stunted.

There was nothing wrong with it, it was only that while the mind was allowed to grow and mature and move within the cryo-unit's supplemented and enriched systems, the body was, by design, put on hold. Gussy, then, was a maturing young woman in the distorted body of an infant.

That alone would not prevent her from entering the virtual world that was home to the fleet's million-odd inhabitants. But her candor, innocence, and youthful curiosity would. For Gussy's birth was, by necessity, a secret. No one on the Council wished the failures in any system to be made public, especially the cryo-units, no matter how rare said failures were.

And so the chairman of Third Yalla, Mum, looked at her daughter and said, once again, "We have, my little lightning bolt, been over this before, and you know your mother is nothing if not constant on such things."

Gussy groaned. She wanted to meet new people. Not the amalgams that the AMs created, however engaging, and certainly not the various senior toadies of the Third Yallan Wholly Owned Subsidiary Corporation, who, being privy to her existence, were allowed to extend their profound sycophantism and general licking of her mother's nether regions to her own young self.

She had enjoyed it, the attention, once upon a time. But it had soured in her as she came to see them for the lackluster fools they were. She wanted to meet real people. She wanted to meet the other members of this great colony force, and most of all, she wanted to meet a member of the pilot elite.

But that, she knew as she glared at her immovable mother, was not going to happen, not in this lifetime. She sighed and turned away, stepping out of the space into one of her many simulated play areas. A network of tree-houses nestled above a broad fen, joined by rickety rope bridges she could nimbly hop across, and thrilling ropes to allow her to swing between her many little oases in the dense jungle scene.

The life here was like the moist air, noisy and thick around her, and she reveled in it. This is what she imagined being in one of the networking hubs must be like. So many strange sounds and sensations. She closed her eyes and listened to the animals and birds fleeting around her in their brief but magnificent existences, and she dreamed of adventures to come.

She could not know that the dose of reality to break the monotony was around the corner.


...2...

Gurdy opened his eyes to the light. It was powerful and all around him, like he was sat inside a star. But there was pattern in the light, and he tried to urge his brain to adjust. He must take it in, must find the clues.

There.

No ... wait ...

Suddenly, blackness again.

Shit, he thought. He had missed it. He breathed deep, or rather he sent a signal through his brain's life-support systems to prepare themselves, a mental sigh, then the tendrils of his perceptive cortices, enhanced and trained as they were into the pattern of the Skalm's systems, settled and waited.

And waited.

And waited.

He would not know when it would come. Or even *if* it would come. That was the nature of glance practice. Microsecond flashes in which he must be ready to respond.

The simulations were the hardest and purest level of flight practice, and as such they were not designed to be beaten. They were designed to teach the pilot elite two things: that they must learn to clear their minds of all distractions, and that, no matter how good they were, the glance was faster and harder than they were, and they must always strive to be better.

As Gurdy settled himself, though, a thought brushed across his mind for an instant before he banished it. A thought of his coming furlough.

There had always been two schools of thought when it came to pilot isolation, but time had shown that, however tempting it was to lock potential brains away and subsume them in the Skalm's world, such routes led, inevitably, to disassociation, and with that, came indifference. Indifference to whatever mission was being assigned, indifference to the ideals of the nation that had bred that pilot and built that Skalm, and indifference, in the end, to their own very survival.

A meaningless life was a life more easily forgone, and while they needed pilots who were willing to sacrifice themselves if necessary, they also needed pilots who were committed, and driven, with a will to fight. There was a crucial difference between a willingness to die and a desire to.

So Gurdy was due a furlough. Three days, nine hours, and twenty-three minutes from now. And for one complete cycle. But he had no time now for such thoughts as he focused. Focused on the glance that could happen any moment.

Then, without warning, the flash came.


...1...

The life of Witchypoo was a good one. It met people, it reminded them it was real. This was met with skepticism and often scorn, and then, after they verified the fact with their AMs, the fun began.

Witchypoo was a pet. A mascot. A robust, four-legged animal, with a thick, lush coat, big eyes, a soft, twitchy little nose, and dangling tongue that liked to loll out of its oft-agape mouth.

After hundreds of years of careful breeding, and then more direct manipulation of Witchypoo's genes, young Witchypoo was riddled with adorable flaws. Witchypoo was inherently fascinated by anything squeaky; a whistle, a bird, a toy, Witchypoo could not resist it. Witchypoo also loved to horse around, tumbling and throwing itself into mock battle with anyone that tried to pry away whatever trinket Witchypoo had taken a fancy to.

And, of course, Witchypoo was incorrigibly ticklish, and that, almost inevitably, was the first thing anyone did when they realized they were in the presence of one of the fleet's true-pets. Unlike the many simulated pets in the ether, both sentient and less so, the only difference between Witchypoo and her cousins and ancestors back home on Mobilius was that Witchypoo's body was in hibernation in a cryo-unit, like the Mobiliei colonists themselves, a choice that many had called extravagant, but which few could disagree with when faced with Witchypoo's big, docile, and patently lovable eyes.

And so Witchypoo waited expectantly while the group of revelers it had stumbled upon confirmed that this bundle of fluff and huggability was, indeed, a true-pet, and then, when one of them looked surprised and then shouted something and leapt forward, Witchypoo howled with elation and bounded away, so they could chase Witchypoo, chase and catch Witchypoo, catch and tickle and hug Witchypoo, as everyone must.

Yes, the life of Witchypoo was a good one.

But now, as this particular group chased the downy beast, something seemed to shudder. They tried to compute what they were seeing, but before they could even ping their AMs to find out what was happening, everything went black.

Everything.

In an instant, a million souls were suddenly cut off from their mindscapes. For many, they would never return.

# Interval I: During

The swarm of missile-mines reappeared into the universe as one, synchronized by design, in their very cores, all their history focused on this tenth of a second, on getting up to their current fantastic speed so they could get here, en masse, and give themselves over to their own utter annihilation.

Over the two years since leaving earth, the swarm had reconfigured itself into a cylindrical formation, a mile wide, and two thousand miles long. Spread out along and within this formation they had continued to accelerate with abandon.

Attrition had taken its toll, the slow erosion of the cosmos plucking sometimes one, sometimes more from their midst in fleeting pocks of flame and dust. But they had surged onward, regardless, firing themselves out into the void and hurtling toward the coming Armada.

They did not care for their destruction. They were designed for mayhem, for death, theirs, and anyone who fell across their path. And now, in an instant picked by choices made over decades, by the decisions of two races to go to war with one another, one for a world, the other for their survival, this moment, this fraction of a second, became the very definition of momentous, as vital as a moment could become, as it was suddenly heated by deadly intent into a slice of supernova destruction through the fleet's heart.

The swarm did not come at the fleet, it appeared within it and about it, a cloud translating into reality all around the massive Armada. The broadness of this stroke was a requisite, a forced thing imposed by the incredibly ephemeral moment of this encounter. Accuracy in such minuscule timeframes was nearly impossible, certainly impossible to guarantee, and so the net had need to be cast wide to have a real chance of striking home.

For many of the component parts of the swarm, the moment of reemergence was already too late even at its beginning, as they appeared already behind the fleet, and were instantly vanishing in its wake, to surge onward and outward for years, maybe centuries, maybe forever. All the work to build and launch them suddenly made pointless as the universe moved on without them.

For tens of thousands of others, those that appeared a fraction of a light second in front of the Armada, their rebirth came straight into the embrace of the fleet's mighty plume. And so their mass was also lost almost immediately, not to space but to flame, as they were consumed in the buttressing stellar conflagration that had protected the fleet from so many other obstacles during its long deceleration.

But for those that sat between those two extremes, for the center of the swarm's epic gamble, their journey would not be for ought. They would get the kamikaze end they so single-mindedly sought, and they would plow death and destruction into the heart of humanity's enemies in the process.

In the framework of a Skalm, at the junction of one of its akas with the main fusion body, a missile warped into existence, fusing as it did so with the very substance of the machine at the molecular level. The forces at play as the missile-mine instantly transferred its opposite but equal momentum into the Skalm's superstructure were almost beyond measure, and the Skalm, with all its strength and capability, was without answer. In the ensuing nanosecond, the once mighty warship spasmed into nuclear ruin.

As its engines exploded outward, releasing its power in a last throw, it ripped backward from its place at the fleet's vanguard, crushing all it encountered for the next millisecond, until it had liquefied itself and vaporized its whole being into a streak of gore scratched back through the Armada it had once been proud to protect.

In the core of a Nomadi carrier ship, fifteen meters out from one of the military-grade Accelosphere generators that had once carried this small sector of the fleet safely through the hearts of suns, a missile warped into existence, fusing as it did so with the very substance of the walls that housed the esoteric subspace actuator. From within the core it was like the wall, once solid, once an armored shell around this beating heart of the fleet, suddenly opened up in a ragged, ugly grin, widening as it went.

But the departing missile-mine was not through. Even though it was obliterated in the instant of arrival, the kinesis of its advent continued to ripple outward through the carrier ship's core, turning infinitesimally complex systems to molten ruin, and in doing so, rattling the core's thick cage. The pinpoint center of the core, normally sustained at the point between universes, ever ready, warbled at the thought of freedom, as if sensing its prison's coming riot. As the central framework sang from the missile-mine's blow, the pinpoint moved, finding the fissure in its confinement as it must, seeking it with inevitability, the truth of its physics manifested in sudden abandon.

Freed, it instantly ballooned outward, destabilizing as it went. Like so many captive animals, its freedom was also its doom, and so it vanished almost as soon as it broke loose, not with a roar, but with a pop, sucking a ten-meter-wide section of the center of the ship with it into the beyond, and lobotomizing the essential fleet craft in the process.

Farther back in the Armada's bulk, in one of many cavities in one of many transport ships, a missile warped into existence, fusing as it did so with a bank of cryo-units. The inhabitants of those units did not know their end. Like every cartoon villain promises, they did not feel a thing as they were merged with the passing comet. Their essence, woven now into the fabric of the missile-mine, struck onward, though.

- - -

Witchypoo, with all its furry softness laid against its skin in the stillness of cryogenic sleep, was five meters away from one such event horizon. The animal met its end by being sucked into the passing tornado, pulled backward and inward into the eye of the storm along with its entire cubby and a thousand other Mobiliei that had maybe once sought solace in the simple animal's company. They were compressed by the thundering pressure of the passing, as an epicenter formed in the mine's wake, following it out, screaming at it for the murder it had caused for the microsecond before the munition was lost to molecular disintegration along with all of its victims.

Elsewhere, Gurdy could not find the pattern in the flash. He could not see it. The flash was too quick, even for the best of pilots. These were not glancing speeds, these were interstellar speeds, and no mind, real or artificial, could conceive a single thought in the entire length of this battle. In the moment Gurdy's brain, eviscerated like all pilots and stored in a cylinder lodged to one side of a Skalm's core, was lost in a similar blaze of subliming glory with a hundred seventy-five of his one thousand peers.

Even though the chairman of Third Yalla had only just been standing next to Gussy, her feisty young daughter, when she was wiped from existence, the girl's mother did not even feel a gust of wind as the mine that killed her child passed by. For the chairman, the scene simply went black, as did all sims in the fleet, either because the generating system had been damaged or destroyed, or because the first thing every single Artificial Intelligence, Artificial Mind, and Prime Mind did as the attack etched itself into terrible history was shunt all available processing power to the Arbite, who had begun taking control of the fleet as soon as it sensed it was under attack.

Before a single person was even consulted, the Arbite had precious seconds to balance the remaining decelerating engines, stopping the fleet from tearing itself to pieces, and analyze the shreds of information coming in real-time into its mind. The Arbite was no born thing. It had no AM surrogate, and had never even spoken to a live person. It had grown up in martial confinement, bred and fed by pellets of data from committee after committee of political oversight, military strategy, and legal stricture. It was singularly focused even for an AM, monotone, without an understanding of or need for humor.

It saw only fact, and sought only truth. The truth it found now had implications, both immediate and far-reaching. That they had been attacked became more and more certain with time, though the Arbite did not communicate that likely conclusion, and its ensuing ramifications, for a full eight seconds after the attack, once it had finished bringing the fleet under control.

But as the information swelled in its mind, the truth was plain to see. The aftershock, not of the mines themselves, but of their subspace footprints, proved beyond question that these had been synthetic, and not cosmic in origin, as did the synchronization of their arrival into the fleet's midst. As the Arbite allowed pieces of its investigation to trickle outward to the Council and each contingent's Prime Mind, it also started to filter out numbers. Numbers of the dead. Numbers of the unaccounted for. Numbers of ships lost or damaged, though very few members of the fleet's complement had escaped entirely unscathed.

And its immediate plan, empowered into limited action as it was by universal mandate, also kicked in. They would translate out, temporarily, to protect against further attack.

It would be costly on their systems, but they must assess and regroup. And so, a full twenty seconds after the attack that had taken seven years to plan and execute was over, the Arbite sent out orders to the Prime Minds, felt the Armada's systems as they shakily climbed to their feet after the holocaust, and once all were ready and synchronized, took the battered Armada back into subspace for the first time since the Alpha Centauri translation five years before, there to nurse its wounds.

## Interval J: and After

"Silence!" barked To-Henton, "I will impose martial order on this meeting if I have to."

The room responded. It took a second, as passions were necessarily high, but they eventually came to some semblance of order.

"In the wake of the attack, and I think we must start calling it that, as no other conclusion seems possible, I have been appointed temporary chair. I think my first order of business, then, should be to acknowledge that we remain unable to reconnect with the transport ship that contained the chairman of Third Yalla. Though she herself is apparently stable, the AM of that ship was seriously damaged when it sustained an indirect hit.

"I am informed that a new representative from the Yallan contingent is being nominated, as the originally named successor was also a casualty of the attack, which hit the Yallan sector particularly hard." He paused a moment to compose himself, then finished by saying, "I know our thoughts go out to them as they work to stabilize their systems."

"If I could, acting-Chairman Henton," said Princess Lamati, and he yielded the floor perhaps a touch too quickly for the taste of some Council members. "While I understand the seriousness of the Yallan contingent's circumstances, I think we have more pressing matters to discuss. My AM has spent the last hour analyzing the ..."

To-Henton surprised all by interrupting the princess, something he instantly regretted, but he did not let his remorse show as he reclaimed the floor. "Of course, Princess, I understand your impatience, and I am getting to the subject of the attack. We have all been privy to the Arbite's reports, which continue to flow with a regularity that I, for one, find reassuring. But their content cannot be called good, not by any measure.

"For the purposes of this extraordinary meeting of the Council, I have taken the liberty of dividing them into three categories. The first is the attack itself: the extent of the damage and what that means for our force dispositions in what, it would appear, is going to be a much more contested war than some among us, myself included, had really anticipated."

There were few among them who would deny having been utterly blindsided by the scale of the attack, and the acceleration in technological capabilities on the part of their enemy that it implied. He saw nods, and noted where others merely stared at the space in front of them, either because of an understandable shock, or because their own sector's AMs were still struggling to get virtual constructs back online.

Even the spartan simulated space that they now met in, black and featureless except for their own floating personages, was more than most of the colonists and military personnel in the fleet yet enjoyed. Most of them were either now in a forced mental hibernation or facing a blank screen that simply scrolled data past them on the fleet's status, with little or no interaction possible.

And that did not count the tens of thousands that were dead, and the even greater number that were slowly fading as the fleet's many systems struggled to repair transport ship breaches and return power and intelligence to damaged life support systems.

"The second topic," went on To-Henton, "is the repair plan, specifically how we will manage the extensive work that still needs to be done, including a fair and reasonable sharing of resources among contingent forces. Of course, we must also discuss how that work will affect the fleet's resources as a whole, and I envision some tough decisions are going to need to be made."

He let that point stand for a moment. Everyone thought they knew what he was saying, but few yet understood the full gravity of the situation. The worst hit sector had been the Yallans, by far. But the Mantilatchi had also been hurt disproportionately badly, compared with the rest of the fleet. Their partition of the vanguard, made up mostly of the most powerful drive ships, had suffered a harsh blow when a carrier ship's subspace core had broken lose.

Like a decapitated chicken, the ship had gone rogue, and the only recourse of a recoiling fleet had been to kill it before it pulled the entire sector apart. Somewhere during the third second after the attack, they had focused the surrounding ships' fires inwards and cauterized the wound with a nuclear fusion brand.

"And the third topic?" said the princess, urging To-Henton on with thickly feigned deference.

"Well, my Princess," said To, trying to sound conciliatory, "the last topic must be, I think, what changes this attack forces us to consider to our strategy. After all, I think we can and must conclude from this potent counterstrike that all is not as we had supposed on Earth, indeed, it would seem something must have gone very seriously wrong with our silent advanced team, conspicuously so, given this shocking turn."

Here the princess once again spoke up, "I am surprised, acting-Chair Henton, that you chose to put that topic last. For me, at least, that is by far the most important topic at hand, and I have several points I would like to put forward, with more to follow shortly once my war council has finished analyzing the attack."

To-Henton went to reply but DefaLuta did it for him, a reprieve he was glad for. "Your concern is shared by all, I do not doubt that, Princess Lamati, but let us not forget that many have suffered, and are still suffering, including members of your own contingent, and I would propose that we should get our house in order, as it were, before thinking about how best to repay the humans for their welcome gift."

Princess Lamati stared across at DefaLuta then looked down, almost demurely, before replying, "The Lamat house *is* in order, DefaLuta, make no mistake about that. And we will address what repairs must be done to our sector thoroughly and quickly ..."

"No house stands alone here, Your Majesty," said DefaLuta with real defiance, spiced with a hint of the verdant disdain she felt for the Lamat woman. "Where the fleet bleeds, we all bleed. I, for one, do not wish to face the apparently feisty human race alone. But maybe, dear princess, you would like to take your fleet contingent on ahead and see what other surprises they have in store for us? Very generous of you, I am sure."

They locked eyes, and no one doubted the very real hatred that burned between them. Many had an opinion on the topic, not all of which fell on the side of the seemingly more charitable Kyryl representative, but no one voiced any such thought yet, and after a second's delay, the royal Lamat replied, "Maybe, just maybe, you are right, DefaLuta. Maybe I should do that. So I can dismantle those upstart humans myself."

They all looked at the Lamat. She was posturing, surely. Wasn't she? But there was no humor in her eyes, only fight, and Quavoce saw in her mood something terrible. Not terrible for them, but for the humans. Their enemy had struck the Armada hard, no doubt about that, but with over eighty percent of the fighting craft still fully functional they were still a truly awesome fighting force. And where, before, they had been tasked with an act of statistically necessary culling, now Quavoce saw something else in Sar's eyes. Something colder. A thirst for vengeance. A thirst for blood.

Though he did not allow it to show here, somewhere inside a transport ship in the Mantilatchi sector of the Armada, his body shuddered. The princess's building fury may seem alone among her more diplomatic peers, but the sentiment would be shared, he knew, by many in the fleet, and he could not deny that the underhanded blow had left him fighting a similar hunger for revenge himself.

But there was no place for anger in war, certainly not here, not among the strategists, and he glanded cool into his mind before speaking out into the icier silence. "DefaLuta, Princess, if I may be permitted to interject ..." neither replied as they faced each other down across the space. With this tacit approval, he went on, "Tensions are understandably high. I think we can all appreciate that. We must, I think we all agree, reassess our force disposition and strategy in light of this attack. And we will. But I must agree with the Kyryl representative that our first priority should be securing the Armada, if only to protect against potential further attack."

"There will be no more attacks, Quavoce, not like that one. That much is all but certain," said the princess dismissively. DefaLuta stared at her, but silently knew that she had to agree with that. Her own PM's analytics had told her as much with a reassuringly high level of certainty based on a whole host of reasons. But others in the room had not been party to such analysis, either because of the quality of their personal military systems, or because their resources had, necessarily, been focused elsewhere during the aftermath of the missile-mine strike.

Theer-im Far thought he knew why the princess had said it, but still was curious to hear her explain herself for purely academic reasons, and so asked, "Why do you say that, Princess? If you don't mind."

Sar rolled her eyes. Why did she bother with these fools? She sent a mental ping to Schney to release the relevant section of the Lamat Prime Mind's analysis to the group and then said, with no small amount of petulance, "I would be surprised if others have not come to the same conclusion, but for those less well informed: detailed analysis of the missile strike's formation and synchronization, as well as the length of the salvo's subspace footprint point to a truly massive number of total units ... well over fifty thousand.

"That scale, whilst impressive, no doubt, and all too effective, was the only reason they were able to score so many hits at relativistic passing speeds. But we have to assume that construction on such a scale was also prohibitively expensive. For the combined resources of all of Mobilius to construct such a salvo would take nearly two years. For humanity to do so, even if we assume they have made some truly *inspired* technological leaps, must have taken them at least that long, probably longer.

"I have just sent you all the details. Suffice to say that the Lamat Prime Mind's analysis is that we are unlikely to see another strike at all, and even if we do it would take them several years to amass that kind of scale again. Either way, now that we know what to look for, we can, I am told, put in place measures to significantly reduce the damage from such a strike in the future."

Quavoce was impressed by her grasp of the situation, a grasp that did, he had to admit, match his own war committee's conclusions, but that still brought him back to his point, a point he knew she was not going to like as he said gingerly, "Well said, Princess, I am sure. But that, again, emphasizes the need to get our house in order, including putting such measures in place before we discuss the more strategic issu ..."

"I am afraid I disagree, Quavoce," said Sar with regal authority. "The likelihood of a second attack was not the limit of our analysis. And the decisions we face are more pressing than just which wound to lick first. In our opinion, the strategic implications of this attack should, indeed they *must*, be the driver of everything we do now, not the result of it." She looked studiously from Quavoce, to DefaLuta, to To-Henton, and then said, "I speak, fellow Council members, of the thrust imbalance."

While Shtat and the Hemmbar looked confused at the comment, the three she had locked eyes with had no less capable a set of military advisors than she, and knew what point she was trying to draw out into the cold light of day.

She waited. Waited for one of them to have the guts to step up and say it. Quavoce could not deny the truth of her course. She was right. It was callous, but she was right. Damn her that coldness, but it must be faced, he knew that. He breathed deep. If they were to discuss this now, then he would not shy away from his responsibilities.

"What the princess is describing we have seen as well. It is likely," he said deliberately, "no, it is almost certain, our PM tells us, that we can no longer stop at Earth with our current mass."

The room went silent, and he did not mask the disgust he felt at the greater reality behind those words. His own systems had been clear on the topic, though he had joined his fellow Mantilatchi lords in demanding that the AMs reassess their prognosis.

"What do you mean we cannot stop?" said Shtat. He looked around, but the only other person who did not seem to be in on this particular little secret was Theer-im Far, and he had gained a distant look, a sign that he was, no doubt, consulting his own advisors at that very moment. But the Hemmbar contingent's eyes had been, like always, focused on the past, not the future, and while they had been busy gathering every scrap of data about the brief but spectacular assault, they had missed this fundamental consequence of it.

A consequence that Sar Lamati now explained all too succinctly, saying, "They destroyed more of our carriers than our transports. Our mass now outweighs our thrust capacity. If we are going to be able to stop ourselves, we are going to have to lose some deadweight."

"And if we do not?" said Shtat. But he knew the answer immediately, and regretted asking. Luckily for him, no one really felt like voicing the simple answer: that they would not be able to decelerate quickly enough and would fly right past their destination.

"But ..." Sar then added, more quietly now, "... there is a simple solution to that imbalance."

All turned to her as one, and all feared the look of stately detachment they now saw on her face.

## Interval K: The Cost of Membership

Marta understood why Elder Pulujan was late, but also knew they could not afford to have him going rogue. The meeting started without him, moving quickly through the topic at hand. The crisis was a victory of sorts, they supposed, though none would call it such. It was the sign that they had been waiting for, even if they had not known what form it would take.

Now they had new steps to take, new missions to go on. The first involved Shtat. He must be informed of some key facts in such a way as to lead him to support their new course, or at least not stand in their way. He would not know the real reason why he was being forced down the road they were going to set him on, but if they gave him the right nudge, there would not be much alternative for the man.

The meeting wound on in a black space. Gone was the bay they had enjoyed during the last translation celebration. Gone was the banter, the excitement, and the camaraderie. Gone was the joy from their little venture, it had all been replaced by unforgiving fact in the void left by their own mad gamble.

After a while, with next steps clear, they came back to the subject of the grieving Elder Pulujan.

"I will talk to him," said Marta, as the others looked to her and Fral to take the lead now. "I'm sure he is just mourning, no one can blame him for that."

"Of course not. I just ..." said ILyo, shakily, "... I just worry that ..."

"I know, ILyo. We all do. I'll follow up with him as soon as we are done here."

They nodded and moved on. The fleet had lost a great deal in the attack, and now the six friends who had fought so very hard to bring a halt to the great Armada's work had to face the consequences of their actions.

Death was not something that happened often in civilized society anymore, and when it did it was usually voluntary. Unintentional death was very rare indeed, a genuinely newsworthy thing. All the colonists had known, though, that this venture brought real risk, few more so than those that planned to stand in the Armada's way. New Mobilius was not unguarded, and though the humans had seemed weak, even a primitive arrow, flying true, could strike home.

It had seemed only fair, once upon a time, that the six conspirators would try to arm their quarry with the tools they would need to defend themselves against the interloping horde. But now, in the desolated parts, in the darkness of their lost innocence, the cost of that choice became apparent.

"How are you doing?" said Marta, finding the drifting Elder Pulujan after the other meeting was over. He was just floating in the blackness of his stunned mind. She waited a moment.

"Elder?"

A full minute passed by in silence. Marta waited.

Sensing that his visitor would not leave, Elder eventually turned to her, frowned, then turned away again and said, quietly, "She did not think they could do it, you know."

Marta willed herself closer to her friend, close enough that he would feel her presence, and maybe sense just how much she felt for him in this terrible time.

"She didn't think they could fight back, not this quickly," he said, as if to himself.

"No?" said Marta, reaching out to the man, shrunken now, crumpled compared to his normal lithe, graceful form. He was crouched in a position that could only be described as fetal.

"No," he said once more. "She thought they were doomed, no matter what we did. But that didn't stop her. Tough odds never stopped her from picking a fight she thought needed to be fought."

He smiled wanly, clearly remembering the hundreds of times his younger sister had stood up to him over the years, never relenting, no matter how much stronger he was. Until one day she was big enough and quick enough to beat him.

He laughed involuntarily at the thought, and Marta looked confused, understanding but confused, happy at least to see something of the man she had called a friend and ally all these years. "No, she never gave in. Always stood up for what she believed in. Which was usually herself, of course!"

They both shared a smile. Yes, Other Pulujan, O-Pu to her close friends, had always been fiercely loyal. Competitive, but loyal. She wanted to beat everyone at everything, but once you were on her side, that was for life. As she considered the many times she had stood side by side with the younger but no less brilliant Other, Marta felt the loss hit home again, and her breath caught in her throat.

"She admired you a great deal, Marta," said Elder, becoming conciliatory now as he saw the emotion come over Marta's face.

Marta smiled kindly and nodded, then he added, "When she wasn't calling you a moron, of course."

Now they both laughed with real mirth. "Yes, that definitely sounds like O-Pu."

They went silent once more.

"We missed you at the meeting, Elder ..." she started, as diplomatically as possible, and as he went to respond, she held up her hands and said, "no, no, everyone understands, and everyone is more than sympathetic, but ..."

"But?"

"But ... we still need you. You know that. And Other, she would have wanted us to ..."

"She would have wanted us to win. Now that she has gone and gotten herself killed over the damn thing. Yes, I know."

Marta waited a moment then said, "No one is saying you shouldn't take your time. Take all the time you need. Just ..."

"... just don't do anything stupid?"

Marta looked defensive once more, but it was Elder's turn to hold up his hands and say, "Marta, relax. I know you don't mean any offense, but I know that the others must be worried. I would be in their shoes."

He looked at her with as genuine an air of bravery as he could muster, and she cried inside for him, as he said, "I am angry, of course. And bitter, no doubt about that. But the focus of that anger is not you, or even the humans, though I will never thank them for what they have done."

"No, of course not."

"But that doesn't mean I have forgotten who started this ... or lost my will to help stop it."

They locked eyes a moment longer. There was not, she knew, anything more to say. After a moment, she sensed, with a feeling of regret and no small amount of shame, that he was waiting for her to leave him alone again so he could grieve in peace, but that he didn't want to be rude and ask her to go.

That he would worry about offending her at such a time only cemented her already high esteem for him, and gave even greater impetus to her desire to grant him his wish.

She ended her visit with a sentiment that was equal parts heartfelt and inane, saying, "You need anything, Elder, anything at all, I hope that you will not hesitate to reach out ..."

And she left, reminding the Nomadi Prime Mind once more to inform her immediately if they were able to recover Other Pulujan's body from the wreckage of the damaged transport ship the woman had been once been interred in.

- - -

Stiffness and hurt. The feeling was like being drugged, or waking after a boxing match. A heavy dose of confusion, well soaked in nausea, and then liberally drenched with brightness and pain. Other Pulujan reeled from the feeling.

She squinted, trying to focus her eyes, then realized they were not even open. She pinged her AM. Nothing. She tried to warp out of whatever sim she had stumbled into, but no response came. The mental muscles that you learned to use in the ether were not responding. It was like they had been amputated. It was almost like she was in reality. But that would mean bad things. Very bad things. What the hell was happening?

She reached back, into her memory, to the last time she had moved outside the ether, to before the departure, to home. She tried to remember what movement felt like. She flexed her arms. Discomfort, a creaking pain, like an old door slowly opening. The stiffness was up and down her arms. Her legs were not responding at all.

She tried another muscle. She opened the link to her personal onboard diagnostics and autonomics, her body's prosthetic headquarters. It came to life like an old friend answering the phone.

The system update came to her as a flow of data, and she switched off her eyes for a moment so she could focus on it. There had apparently been a critical failure in her cryo-unit. She was, indeed, awake.  She was battered, quite badly, in fact, but she was stable, for now.  She sent another ping out to her AM, this time a distress call.  Still nothing.  Whatever had happened to her cryo-unit, it should not have shut off her communications.

No, that the AM was silent spoke of something more sinister, more profound.  She was in trouble.  She needed to wait.  There was nothing she could do here, she was alone.  She considered her situation.  She could have no idea how long it would take for help to come.  She also knew that her mind, conscious as it obviously was, was using up precious resources, resources that may be in limited supply now.

She sent the pulse through her autonomics system to render herself unconscious while she waited for the help that must, surely, be coming.  It did not respond, or rather, it did, but not in the way Other expected.

<you have a message waiting.>

What?  What message?  Wait ... open ... no, god damn it.  She forced herself to think in terms her limited onboard AI could hear and understand.  She had not done this in so long.

O-Pu at AAI: '¿what message?  ¿why was i not informed sooner?'

<the message reminder was triggered by your call to go into hibernation.>

O-Pu at AAI: 'ok, i am curious.  open new message.'

<you have no new messages.>

O-Pu at AAI: '¿what the hell are you talking about?  you just said there was a message waiting.'

<you requested new messages.  there is only an old message.  it is in your outbox.  you requested to be notified that it was waiting if you tried to go into emergency hibernation.>

Other Pulujan went to grunt, but in this place, as her body slowly came back to life, the grunt actually happened, and sent an answering spasm of pain through her throat and lips, dry and unused for decades now.  She cringed, and that made her forehead hurt as well.

O-Pu at AAI: 'damn it, open the outbox message, you stupid machine!'

The message opened without further comment.  Her system was neither offended nor even aware it had been insulted.  Indeed, her system was not even really designed for this kind of interaction.  It was supposed to work behind the scenes, and a more proficient user, as Other Pulujan had once been, long ago, before entering a system-induced coma, quickly learned how to interact with their autonomics system far more smoothly.

She would have to remember how to do that, apparently.  At least until this, whatever this was, was over.  She focused on the message that she had, apparently, written so very long ago.

'Note to self,

If you are reading this then, lucky you, you are dead.  Don't freak out.  It was bound to happen to one or all of us, and actually it might be quite useful, in the end.

*Whether out of a sense of duty, or self-respect, or yet another stupid competition with your Elder, you volunteered to be part of a conspiracy to stop your fellow Mobiliei from wiping out another race just for the fun of it. This you know, because you needed to know it in order for you to work with your colleagues to recruit others while the Armada was in transit.*

*What you don't know, well not anymore, anyway, is that you actually signed up for a much more involved plan, one you helped devise, you masochistic nut job, and which now, it appears, you are going to have to help execute.*

*I won't go into details here. There is more in the attached data packet that should bring you up to speed on everything you had wiped from your memory implants before departing on this little jaunt. As this message has never been transmitted and is not even part of your real-time memory, it will not have been subject to audit, and will never have been reviewed by the Arbite.*

*Clever, huh?*

*Unfortunately, that also means it was only accessible safely if you were cut off from the fleetnet, and your AM. Which means that if you are reading it, lucky you, you are dead, or at least the system now thinks you are ... another nifty part of the plan you so suicidally helped formulate.*

*You have no way back, sorry about that. As far as the fleet is concerned you are gone, but we have a plan to allow you to move around as a repair unit, albeit a rather fat and stupid one\*.*

*Set your systems to recover while you review the attached packet and then get to work. If all goes well, then I, or rather you, estimate that, err, we(!) have a fifty-fifty chance of surviving the next stage.*

*All the best,*
*-Other Pulujan*

*\*Hey sis, Elder here. Good luck and all that. It's a bummer really, not only are you dead, but you have come back as an even fatter, stupider robot than you already are. Love you, -Elder'*

Perfect, thought Other. Just bloody perfect. She sighed, cringing once more at the pain it brought, and reminded herself to punch her brother squarely in his genitals if she ever saw him again.

But that would be later. First she had to get the hell out of this damn cryo-unit and find whatever exo-suit/faux repair-bot they, or rather she, had apparently arranged for herself. She instructed her onboard AI to start the wake-up process in earnest and started reading.

## Interval L: Callback

No one on the Council had really expected an exoneration from the difficult topic they had stumbled into, but were one to come, they definitely had not expected it from Princess Lamati. But the princess's expression spoke not of forgiveness, not of a hangman's reprieve, but of a tightening of the noose, and Quavoce cringed inside as she explained her idea. "There is a clause in the Colonization Treaty that can be applied here, should we all think it appropriate."

They waited, and she smiled. It was not a pretty smile, and Quavoce was reminded of why he had never succumbed to her proposals in the softer moments, when she could be so enticing. For this person here, this was the real Princess Lamati, this woman now saying, "The treaty allows, once battle is entered, for the appropriation of military assets should any contingent no longer be able to control its own forces."

They all stared at her. She shrugged. "Well, we are faced with a tough choice, a harsh reality. If we are to balance the thrust to mass ratio, we must, unfortunately, cut a portion of the transports lose, 12.37% of them, by my PM's calculations. Given that, I propose a way to recover a large portion of that shortfall with minimal effect on the contingents gathered here, a step that is fully legal under the Colonization Treaty."

He saw the next part coming now, like an approaching crash, slow-motion, inevitable, as she went on. "I can prove it is legal, what I propose, simply by saying it here, in the presence of all the Council members capable of attending, and under the Arbite's ever-watchful eye. Given that battle has now officially been joined, and that now the Yallans find themselves incapable of managing their own forces effectively, the treaty states that we are within our rights to appropriate the remaining Yallan military units. It also states that any contingent's damaged transports may be cut free if it is deemed that they are impeding the overall success of the mission."

There. She had said it. She waited. It had been a gamble, but her legal AIs had been very clear. The treaty allowed it. They all waited for a moment for a reaction from the Arbite, a lightning bolt from their self-imposed omniscient being.

It did not come, and as they sat there even Quavoce knew that he would have trouble standing against a resolution whose alternative would, no doubt, include sacrifices on the part of his own fleet to make up for the shortfall.

There was a moment's impromptu silence for what they all, in their hearts, knew would be an inevitability in the face of the Yallan's absence, but one among them, Shtat, was silent for another reason. Why had he not been told about this by his advisors? Why had he not been warned by Marta and the others? He had assumed, at the outset, that they had not seen whatever the Lamat, Kyryl, Eltoloman, and Mantilatchi had.

But now, given the note from them that he now reread, that seemed unlikely. "... in the event of a proposed fleet reduction by force, we propose that you support that."

Had they known about this? What else did they know? What else were they keeping from him? But as the meeting continued to unfold, the rest of the meeting's little surprises would leave his advisors as blindsided as anyone else.

Across the space, Quavoce allowed his disappointment to show. Not in the other members of the Council, but in himself. So, this was it then, thought Quavoce, this was the beginning of the infighting. He had known it would come. It had been as inevitable as the wind, but he had another little factoid to share as well. Another ditty to add to the list of ramifications that would be tied to this unholy day.

After his state's AMs and war committee had completed their analysis with their usual efficiency, the following discussion had not gone the route of the amputation of the rest of the helpless Yallan contingent's colony ships. If it had he would have tried to stop it. Sar had not been so circumspect.

Now, the Mantilatchi PM had begun feeding this new option into its models, grinding them through algorithmic cogs to press out the future of this new course.

After it was done, it told Quavoce what he needed to know, and he spoke up.

"It is a ... creative solution, Princess. No doubt about that. One that, I fear, will prove all too compelling. But I am afraid that even that, alone, will not be enough to balance the shortfall," he said.

He was struggling to hold eye contact with his fellow Council members, but this next thought he had to share, this next idea. For this specked more of what he had come for, of military strategy, of the stroke and counter-stroke that he loved so dearly.

"Even with the Yallan contingent ... repurposed, we would need a supplementary strategy to allow the bulk of the fleet to stop at Earth. And, as we analyze our new situation, it also seems that such an alternative plan might be prudent given our new understanding of our enemy's true military capabilities."

All were listening intently as he said now, the fire returning to his eyes, "For as we look to equalize our fleet's braking capacity, we could also let a portion of our fighting fleet go, maybe even a large part of it, removing its main thruster to retain for our own deceleration. Then we could drop those craft at our target."

"Without their main engines they would fly right past," said Shtat.

"Yes," said Sar, her eyes alight with appreciation for the plan's brilliance. She was staring at Quavoce with an affection that made him, and To-Henton, uncomfortable, as she went on, "but they would get there in half the time, drastically reducing the human's remaining preparation time. They could eradicate the human's defenses as they pass by and then we could come in and take control, as originally planned."

"Indeed, Princess," said Quavoce, meeting her eyes. He could not criticize her ability to get to the crux of a situation. And nor could he really fault her for her idea to sacrifice the Yallans, as he then said, "I wish I could say that this idea negates the need to eliminate the Yallan transports, but, actually, that significantly increases the number of attack craft we could send. Given our situation, I am sad to say, I fear we will have to do both, or face cuts across the board."

He looked around once more. War was not supposed to be clean. Choices must be made, lives would be forfeit. If his own state had been the one weakened by the attack, he would have fully expected the others to seek to feast on his carcass, and he was sure the Yallans' fangs would have been just as bloody as the rest of them if that had been the case.

These were not his friends, these were his temporary allies, at best, the enemies of his nation's enemies. He settled his conscience by telling himself that his plan, his contribution, would allow them to properly thank the humans for their gift. Yes, thought Quavoce with a militant indignation, they would answer the missile-mine strike with a horde of weaponized Skalms, flown with vengeance, and arriving at Earth a full year before the humans expected them.

## Interval M: A Painful Divorce

By design, the orders came without warning and without discussion. They surged out from the Arbite itself, flowing through the fleet with irresistible edict and went into immediate effect, setting the plan in motion before anyone had time to question them.

With the Arbite's stamp of approval, the legitimacy of the action could not be questioned. The Yallan AMs were the first to feel it. Suddenly they were full of the sting of countermanded authority being ripped away from them as overriding parameters baked into their design were called to task by the one entity empowered to activate them.

With the Yallan PM damaged in the assault, the Arbite was able to start pulling its military AMs from it while the remnants of the Yallan leadership started shouting in protest. But the calls flooding in from the directors of Third Yalla, Wholly Owned Subsidiary of the Yallan Corporation, were routed straight to the Arbite's equivalent of voice mail and it moved forward regardless, their vote having already been muted by overriding Council rule.

Now the new order started to show its first physical effects. The squadron of Skalms along the Yallan part of the fleet's vanguard started to waken to something other than their role in the Armada's diminished deceleration. It started as a faint warble, a clearing of throats as they were imbued with pilot minds, minds receiving very specific orders.

Once ready, the squadron began moving in concert. They had targets now, real targets, but even though those targets were behind them they did not turn upon them directly. Instead they disconnected their own interlocking arms and began wafting outward, ferrying out to the border of the Armada's great discus. From there they used their now untethered power to slow themselves more vehemently than the great fleet and began to push themselves backward relative to it.

All this time, their engines remained pointing forward, into the void, tweaking only in minuscule vibrato tremors as they played with the balance of power to shift themselves relative to the fleet's mass. Now, as they fell back, they began to move inward, along the borders of the Yallan contingent.

Their engines, still firing hard, were soon turned into hot scalpels falling across the nanotube spars that intersected the various ships of the flotilla, and slowly the Yallan sector was cut free.

The flow of dispute from the Yallan command grew in volume as the next step became apparent. They had been moving in subspace for the two days since the attack. Their engines still had bite here, but only a fraction of the power they wielded in the real universe. It was enough to give them a momentum gain in the usually kinetically balanced gravitational slingshot of stellar translation, but they would soon have to shift back into reality if they were going to give their cosmic brakes the grip they needed to bring them to a halt at their destination.

First though, as the vitriol and protest from the Yallans grew to a desperate crescendo, they would cut this gangrenous limb from their body.

Inside the Yallan sector, the last of the Yallans' newly repossessed fleet craft were busily deserting their former masters, either moving outward across the still smoldering canyon that was now opening up between it and the rest of the fleet, or moving inward to one of the Yallans' fifteen massive carrier craft, still firing into the blackness with their own mammoth stellar thrusters, the true horsepower of the deceleration.

But it was the huge subspace actuators inside those carrier craft that made them truly exceptional. It was those immense actuators that were generating the interlocking translation bubble around the Armada, along with the others dotted throughout it. As the last of the repair bots and tug ships moved inward to bond with the hulls of the heavily armored carrier craft, the order went out.

The carefully hewn, beautifully synchronized chord that was the overlaid subspace spheres being generated around the Armada changed in tone now. It did not change gradually, one moment it was one note, the next the harmony was entirely and spectacularly different, as the carrier ships in and around the doomed Yallan sector morphed it instantly into a new format.

The change was most drastic for the carrier ships in the heart of the Yallan sector, where they drew their enveloping shields suddenly inward, snapping them from vast, encompassing umbrellas, to tight shielding orbs, surrounding only their own hulls and the small cloud of sheltering fleet craft they had each just gained.

The effect was instantaneous. One moment the Yallan sector was there, the next it was not, leaving only fourteen of their fifteen carrier craft in the yawning gap left in the Armada, like smoothed bare islands left in the center of a gorge after a flash flood has scrubbed the countryside clean.

In truth, though, the Yallan sector's colony ships had not disappeared; they had reappeared, in a flash, dropped back into reality like a screaming infant born into a harsh, unwelcoming world. The Yallan high commanders, what was left of them after several key members had been drafted into fleet service along with their military units, tried to analyze their new paradigm, looking for any sign of hope after this horrific betrayal by their own brethren.

But as they looked to their shockingly diminished force, they were surprised to see a good-sized contingent of Skalms had also joined them, along with one of their precious carrier craft. Their Prime Mind, injured and weakened, tried to reach out to the units, but they were not responding. Were they damaged, perhaps, thought the chairman of Third Yalla, still barely healthy herself but fighting through her injuries to address this cataclysmic shift in her fortunes. Was that why she had been left these few craft in the darkness, these limited life rafts for her scuttled ship?

"Yallan carrier ship, please give us your status," said the chairman, speaking through the system and instructing the PM to broadcast by any means still available to it. "Yallan carrier, Skalm units, please respond. This is the chairman of Third Yalla, Council member for the Yallan Corporation asking, no, *ordering* you to respond immediately."

She waited, then tried again, but to no avail. Hopes that these craft might be damaged remnants of their own fleet, and so might be friendly, were starting to fade as the units now began to move with purpose. While the carrier kept to a safe distance from the slowly rotating raft of colony ships, the Skalms started to move into position, interlocking with the slice of life that had been cut out of the Armada and bringing its lazy rotation to a halt.

They still refused to answer calls though, calls from a Yallan leader desperately trying to remain optimistic. Their silence was ominous as they positioned the block of ships and settled them. Then there was a moment of silence, a moment where all the survivors aboard the colony ships held their breath and waited, hoping against hope that there might be some reprieve from this terrible fate they had suddenly been assigned.

But their only answer would prove just as confusing as the lack of communication from the mysterious fleet outside their walls sprang to life once more, giving the colony ships one more seemingly fractional nudge before separating again and returning to the carrier ship waiting to one side.

Concern and fear driving her to hysteria, the Yallan chairman was now screaming. "What are you doing, you bastards? What are you doing to us?" The message went out through every radio, subspace, and laser-beamed comms the PM had managed to string together in the last few fraught minutes. "Where are you going? What more do you want from us, you goddamned fucking sons of bitch motherfu ..."

And with that, the carrier ship, without comment or valediction, spread its subspace wings and sucked itself and its complement of Skalms back into the beyond, leaving the Yallan leader to curse into the blackness while her PM quietly calculated the terrible final purpose the Skalms had just consigned them to.

## Interval N: Counting Beans

Kattell studied the numbers as they scrolled past him. He received them fourth- and fifth-hand, from AIs and news feeds. Very little of it was contraband, per se, but that he would have it all gathered here might seem irregular, given his position. But his position, or rather his lack of one, was also his defense. He was a nobody, an irrelevance, and that suited him just fine.

He watched the numbers, looking for signs, for whispers hidden in the code. The new paradigm, with all its austerity, suited him just fine. System loads in various sections of his own sector told him that full-scale virtual reality constructs were already coming back online for many of the fleet's more senior personages. He was not among them.

But the interaction of the system, the give and take, that he did have back once more after the initial blackout of the missile-mine strike, and now he used the broad-spectrum access he had to find out if any had made it into the beyond, as they had planned.

There. A repair bot, like so many others, working diligently out there in the real world to repair the countless systems fried and warped by the comet strike. But this one stood out among its peers. Firstly, it was a new bot, or rather a newly activated one, stored in the private equipment banks of one of the richer colonists but co-opted now that its owner, influential or not, was apparently no longer in need of it.

But the other clue here was that this bot was noticeably slower than the bulk of the Armada's repair units. It was saying that it was partially damaged and working at limited capacity, and indeed that may be true. But all the signs were there. Kattel smiled, remembering a long ago conversation with an almost forgotten friend. Yes, the bot in question, it would appear, was a rather fat and stupid one.

Good, so that part of the plan had come to fruition, at least. He hoped that the bot's apparently dead owner was indeed alive, and his heart went out to her. For this was not much of a reprieve. The person in question, a certain Other Pulujan, would not have an easy time ahead and may well end up wishing she had truly died in the missile-mine strike as the fleet thought she had.

Kattel set that thought aside. He had much bigger issues than mourning the fake passing of a fellow conspirator. The Council had been busy. He had expected a force depletion after the attack. He had not expected it to be so localized, but that, in the end, only supported their cause, adding as it did to the internal tension they also hoped to foster, and further unbalancing the fleet force as a whole.

But now the Council has sent out another edict, and it was, by any measure Kattel had, a disaster. They were going to separate the fleet. They were going to send an attack force ahead, a force recon mission, and potentially a sizable one at that. It would stop decelerating when it was cut free, meaning what elements of it survived the coming clash at Earth would be relegated to a long, slow, lonely trip to stop themselves afterward and return to their intended destination, but the damage they would do to an unprepared earthforce in the process would be devastating.

None of his fellow conspirators had foreseen this back when they had hatched their plan. It was a brilliant counterstroke, an all-in bet that would break one force or the other; unfortunately, it would most likely be Earth, ignorant and still scrambling to get up to speed, that would suffer the most in the exchange.

He knew he must alter the plan. He feared he was going to have to rely far more on far fewer people than he had originally intended. He could only hope that the others, the various pockets of resistance they had dotted throughout the fleet, would see the tactic for the death blow to Earth's defenses that it was no doubt going to be, and be doing what they could to either block it or help blunt its fangs before it departed.

Certainly that was his priority now, Kattel knew that. And if he couldn't stop it, then he must rely on the only two members of the Nomadi leadership he would be able to send forward with the force: one of whom was a ghost, and the other a coward.

- - -

"Whatever we plan to do, we must do it now," said the princess, reinforcing her black-and-white opinion on the grey topic at hand.

"That much is clear, Princess, but we cannot do *it* until we agree what *it* is, can we?" replied DefaLuta.

"OK, OK," said To-Henton, trying his hardest to keep things on track. "That is, I think we can all agree, enough of that. We were talking of contingent contributions to the two forces, a topic we must resolve before we can move onto leadership."

"Of course they are," said DefaLuta, "and the Kyryl will not commit any fighting units to the force recon team unless it is a part of the command structure, as per the colonization treaty."

"Are you volunteering, then, to lead this mission for us?" said Sar, almost seriously.

But DefaLuta was not such a fool as to fall for that, and quickly replied, "So you can do to the Kyryl contingent what you did to the Yallan in my absence?"

They looked like they wanted to strangle each other, and indeed they probably did, but words were the worst harm that could be inflicted in this space, and Quavoce interjected, "To To-Henton's point, I think we can all agree that no contingent is going to forfeit any part in the actual colonization fleet to lead the force recon mission, and equally, no state is going to leave their colony fleet unprotected by sending a disproportionate number of their attack craft ahead with the recon team."

"While I agree with Lord Mantil in principle," said Sar, angelically, "I think it is a touch unfair of him to talk about what 'no' group is not going to agree to regarding force dispositions, when, at last count, the Mantilatchi forces were among the worst hit by the attack, and so have little to contribute."

He glared at her. Was this revenge? Spite because he had not sought out her bed in the days since the attack? Whatever it was, her statement about his forces was true, and that was what really galled him. Silly jabs he could take, but pointing out that by utterly random lottery the Mantilatchi line had suffered more than most, that was …

She relented, a rare kindness that only he was likely to ever feel the benefit of. She did have feelings for the man, and plans, and so she added, "Of course, the Lamat Empire is keen to have it stated that it stands by its Mantilatchi cousins, and will do what it can to help restore them to their former might."

Sure, thought, Quavoce. Unless you see the opportunity to cull us all. But he nodded. Was he too harsh on her? And was he fool for not going to her side, formally, with all the security for his state that such a union would bring? She smiled at him, as if reading his mind. She did not want his heart. She was not foolish enough to think she could win it, and she didn't have enough of a use for her own, let alone another. But she wanted him. His loyalty. His fealty. And his contingent's strength, which, though diminished, was still a force to be reckoned with if he was at its helm.

Her smile turned more predatory as she allowed her lust for him to show. He looked away, but DefaLuta looked on in unbridled disgust, and To-Henton fought down a different emotion, one he was slowly being forced to admit was jealousy.

"So," said Shtat, suddenly, "if I can summarize. We have two main decisions to make. Firstly, how many of each contingent's fighting units to send ahead, and secondly, who will be in command of the force recon ... force?" He laughed a little, with disarming naïveté, and then went on, "If we all agree, as I am sure we can, that the expropriated Yallan forces make up the core of the recon force, the next question becomes how many other units are required? I make it ...?"

"Six hundred fifty-three," said Sar with imposing finality.

"Six hundred fifty-three!" shouted DefaLuta. "Have you lost your mind? That is nearly the entire remaining fighting fleet."

"Exactly," replied Sar. "And I can think of no reason not to send it. Splitting our forces only works if the force recon effectively wipes out the humans' ability to defend themselves. Otherwise we are just making our forces more vulnerable. No, either we send them all, or almost all, or we don't send them at all, in which case we must make up the shortfall by cutting out more damaged transport ships."

"You're mad," said DefaLuta.

But she wasn't. Quavoce saw that. He had been toying with recommending the same thing. They were in the unenviable position of not having any solid information on the military capability of their enemy. In any other circumstance he would counsel retreat, retreat until more intelligence could be gathered.

But that was not possible. Not for them. As things stood they could not even stop, let alone retreat. No, they must go on, and if they were to avoid culling more colonists from their midst, then they would have to send a sizable portion of their Skalms on ahead so that the humungous carrier ships would be able to stop the rest of the fleet in time.

He looked around the room and found himself, once again, sitting on the same side of the fence as the princess. Was he just deluding himself? Was he the only one who didn't see it? That they were, in the end, destined for each other? No, he thought, he was not like her. Their minds worked in similar ways when it came to military matters, and in bed, he could not deny that. But where she relished the conflict that their path in life had thrust them into, he loathed it.

For him this was a responsibility, for her it was a pleasure. He could not be with someone that enjoyed killing, especially on this scale. And yet what other kind of person would wish to be with him after this was all done, when he stood on the conquered Earth, drenched in the blood of its previous inhabitants.

He willed himself to hear the counterarguments being presented, even now. He wanted so badly to hear one that would dissuade them from the path they were on. It did not help that the first up was the nice but dim leader of the disparate Nomadi alliance.

"I have spoken to my advisors at length about this, and they assure me that by investing too much of our fleet into the recon team we leave our colony ships unprotected should the attack force fail to clip the humans' claws. They caution limit to the advanced force, focusing on recon rather than arming a fighting force."

"A fair point, Shtat," said Quavoce, "no doubt about that, but ..."

"No, Lord Mantil," said Sar, "it is *not* a fair point, I am afraid." She stared from one to the other, patently unapologetic, then went on. "In order to redress the imbalance, we must detach a minimum of eighty-five Skalm. That means we are already investing far more in the first strike force than we ever would in an ordinary recon team. So, if we are committed to going forward in force, then we must acknowledge that to do this halfheartedly would be to waste those eighty-five units, and the advantage that a surprise attack affords us."

But the Nomadi was not dissuaded, and replied, "But if we limit the force to that number, then that will still allow it to cause very real damage to Earth's defenses, as well as being able to report back to us what the IST has been unable to: what the nature of those defenses are, so we can adjust our tactics accordingly for the main strike."

The princess did not hide her disdain for the Nomadi's analysis. Quavoce watched as she replied incisively, but still she failed to close the debate. Now Quavoce looked on as the Hemmbar added his opinion to the list, not so much as a dissenter but as an advocate, as always, for information gathering over anything that would put their precious data stores at risk.

The sides were drawn, then, with three on each, but even now he could see that DefaLuta was only really resisting out of obstinacy. Her objection was born purely out of a stubborn refusal to take any side that her Lamat nemesis stood on.

The Kyryl was no fool, though. She would resist only long enough to see the other woman sweat. In the end, after it had run for long enough even to sway even Quavoce's even keel, he did what he had to do to end it.

On the surface, Shtat was counseling caution, normally Quavoce's bread and butter in these situations. Never pick a fight you couldn't win. But such luxuries as choice were beyond them here. To bring the increasingly petty argument to an end, he did something more underhanded than he was normally known for, and announced his intention to vote the other side, to vote for a limited strike. That would swing the vote away from the princess, leaving only her and To-Henton for a full-scale attack.

It was a gamble, but one that paid off. Despite her protestations, DefaLuta would not, in the end, allow such a poor decision to pass, and when the vote came, she begrudgingly joined the Lamat and Eltoloman in order to balance out Quavoce's apparent change of heart. When he then went against his declaration and joined them as well, she glared at him, seeing she had been played, and then nodded, letting it wash over her as any practiced politicians must.

It was the right decision, she knew that, as did he. Whether Sar's motives were pure was irrelevant in the face of that simple truth.

They would send the full Skalm fleet, retaining only a protective detail to help with cleaning up whatever was left of humanity after the Skalms had gouged out their eyes. Now the topic turned to leadership for the recon force, and again the solution was simple, and aggressive. They must all go, as none among them would allow any other to take control of such a powerful force and leave themselves unprotected.

# Interval O: Taking the Leap

"Well, Marta, what the hell do you think it means?" said Fral, staring at the cryptic message.

The message in question, that was without sender, subject, or time stamp, said simply: 'stop or limit the separation.'

"Well, Fral, I'd say it means that we should try and stop or limit the separation," said Marta.

He stared at her.

"Yes, thanks for that," he said, exasperated, adding, "but it's done. You saw the vote. We can't change that now. And I'd say it is safe to say the recon force is going to be anything but limited."

"True, but when this was sent, it clearly wasn't decided yet," said Marta, and then, pausing for a moment, added, "When, exactly, *did* you get this?"

He checked and then showed her what he found, the data appearing in the air between them. It had come in two hours before, while the Council meeting had already been well underway and well out of their control.

Marta nodded. "Whoever sent this cannot have known that the Council was already in session."

He nodded as well. "No, clearly. Whoever *they* are, they're clearly hiding somewhere within the fleet, and it wouldn't do them much good to hide in the senior ranks, among us. There is just too much chance of discovery. That's why we don't even know what the hell is supposed to be happening. That way we can't spill the beans if we're caught."

"So they're only getting information third- or fourth-hand, and ..." Marta looked a little crestfallen, then went quiet.

"And ...?" Fral prompted.

"And apparently they're getting desperate enough to risk sending out notes like this one, no matter how redundant and obvious they may be." Marta smiled without humor, then said, "It would seem that whatever plan we have inadvertently signed up for, it isn't going quite as our little mastermind here had hoped it would."

Fral added somberly, "No."

Marta, "Well, is there anything we *can* do, you know, to help limit things?"

Fral looked at her like a child being asked whether they have anything to say for themselves, then slowly shook his head.

"No, I guess not," confirmed Marta, all her wit and banter deserting her in the face of their simple impotence.

- - -

Not all messages that Kattel sent out that day were so redundant, though. The second he sent was more useful and also less vague, going as it was to someone under far less scrutiny.

Other Pulujan moved inside her suit, barking frustration into the dark, unrelenting faceplate in front of her. She had an itch under her left breast that made her want to cut the bloody thing off, and she could no more reach that part of her than she could come to terms with what she had just been asked to do by her enigmatic benefactor.

Shunting her body's pleading call for scratching to her autonomic systems and returning to the semi-conscious state she now spent ninety percent of her time in, she settled in to read the note for the tenth time, and considered its implications once more.

She had opened herself to full consciousness, as she must regularly now, to attend to various biological issues that her autonomic AI could not handle. Once upon a time, she thought, they would have been handled by her far more willing and capable cryo-unit, but, oh lucky day, that unit had, by merry fortune, switched its goddamned-pricking-bastard self off and birthed her into a dark, damaged, and cold transport ship so she could take up residence in this motherfucking roly-poly chubby-cheeked shit-machine of a repair bot!

And to top it all off, it had all, apparently, been her bloody idea! She screamed inside her head.

"*They have just voted to separate the fleet ...*" the message began.

As she read it one more time, O-Pu was already running a diagnostic on her suit one more time in preparation for her response to what she knew she was going to have to do next.

"*When they do, they are going to drop the majority of the remaining Skalm fleet at Earth ...*" the message went on.

The diagnostics results were not encouraging. This hollowed out junker was just not built for extended exo-atmospheric work. She read on regardless.

"*This was not part of our plan ...*" the message said, pointing out the painfully obvious.

The suit had strength, no doubt about that. It had to in order to be able to work in the high-g environment of full thrust deceleration. But it lacked so many of the standard systems needed for extended internment.

"*Forget the original sabotage targets. You need to move ...*"

She waited a moment before reading the last part. If she did this, and she really had no choice that she could see, then the one thing she could be sure of was that it was really, really going to suck.

"*You need to get to [loc. coords.] and join the carrier ship that will go with the departing fleet. You have two days. They are working on pulling the thrust cores from a portion of the Skalms to use for the fleet's deceleration. You will have to sever yourself from the system first. Then rejoin once you are in position using the same availability code you used to gain access after the attack.*"

She focused. This plan was a dud, she knew that, but then so was the first one, now. Her fifty-fifty survival chance was about to have a chain saw taken to it, and if that was the case, if she was, indeed, going to be royally screwed by her own deviousness, then she might as well do it right. After sending the kill code to her repair bot's link with the fleet, she called up her autonomic AI.

*O-Pu at AAI:* 'i need a priority excise program established for all but the most essential body parts. i want circulatory system cutoff to unnecessary extremities and a long-term maintenance program created for whatever is left.'

She began receiving a list of proposed items under the heading of 'unnecessary extremities' and began ticking them off. Minor items like her limbs, reproductive organs, eyes and ears, all were vestigial now, and so she put them on the list for ligation, and eventual avulsion. She looked over the list once more, noted that her backside was on it, and then kissed her ass good-bye.

That was that then, she thought, leaving her autonomic AI to get on with it. No more itches for her to scratch, and no more fingers to scratch them with, either.

"Let's get going then," she said with lips she would not have much longer, and she started clambering away from the hull of the transport ship she had supposedly been trying to fix.

The chunky repair bot, fat and ungainly among its peers, but just a dot in the huge Armada's midst, began clambering along the thick spar linking this one ship to its neighbor, and from there, onward, from ship to spar to pivot, crawling like an insect through the colossal fleet's superstructure to get to its shining vanguard.

## Interval End: Dropping an Ocean

The fleet was dropping at Earth. Having catapulted itself through planets and stars, accelerating all the while, it had stolen momentum from the cosmos, and now that momentum was its power and its curse.

It was coming. Only the great engines of the carrier ships dotted throughout the Armada could stop it, and the loss of some of those great pilots had cost them greatly. Nowhere had the effects of the attack been felt more than in the Yallan sector, now just a scar slowly healing, the sides of the great slice that had been cut out coming together as the battle group reconfigured itself to face its foe.

As the fleet hurtled toward its destination, its many components braced for what was clearly going to be a very real fight. After days of analysis, modeling and remodeling, the many military AMs and PMs had submitted themselves to the Arbite and a picture of the coming war had started to take shape. Humanity had, in some part, shown its hand. It had landed the first real blow in the war, and it had struck home, cutting the Mobiliei far more deeply than they had thought was possible.

But in the transient moment of the attack, the humans had also left many clues, markers that gave the great minds of the various contingents an insight into what their enemy was capable of. It was much more than any among the Mobiliei had expected, but it was not insurmountable. They had not been struck with some great godlike blow, and in the scars of the attack were the signs of a civilization working at the limit of its capabilities, flaws and tremors in the subspace fingerprints that showed humanity was stretching itself to the limit, driven, no doubt, by war's uniquely primal drive, a civilization-wide survival instinct.

But, the fleet-minds saw, if this was the best mankind could do, then the Mobiliei still held the higher ground. We are not fools, said the great minds. We are not going to brake neatly into your waiting arms. We are not going to trip lightly across whatever wires you are setting for us. We have an asset you cannot match, speed. Where you are anchored, trying to erect a barrier around your fragile world, we are mobile, imbued with kinetic supremacy.

Now you will see the truth of surprise, the stark reality of our superiority.

From under the falling fleet, the plume faltered for the third time in less than a week. This time, like the second, it was deliberate. After they had excised the injured Yallans from their midst, they had worked to prepare for the greater separation.

The white-hot fires slowed and realigned again now, steadying for the coming change in pressures. Freshly cored engines from a subdivision of the fighting fleet were locked in place and firing as subsidiaries of the carrier ships. The departing Skalm force was ready, all that was left now was the displacement.

The engines vacillated, a tremor whose seeming insignificance did not beget the scale of the coming schism. And then the carriers were changing their form once more, awakening their captured singularities and warping them outward, not to encompass the whole Armada, as they had when they had stepped into the beyond after the attack, but to suck the Armada proper out of reality, and leave a swathe of the vanguard behind.

To see it was to see a sun blink out, and the effect of the departure was immediate. In an instant after the ensuing blindness, the Skalm attack force that had been left behind in reality began to free-fall, its sleek blackness dropping away into the greater dark between solar systems, the interstellar void.

The effect was like a formation of parachutists parting, the bulk pulling their cords as the carriers' fusion brakes dug in once more, while the few, the unleashed, plummeted onward with abandon, toward Earth, toward war, closing the gap now without restraint.

In a few hours, when the Skalms were but a distant horde of bombs dropped into the night, the fleet would reappear, its lights shining forward once more, illuminating their path with nuclear flame. They would not talk to their kin again, not until the fight had engaged. The massive flotilla of Skalms would be silent now, as they closed on their unsuspecting prey.

# Endgame:

## Chapter 49: Under the Radar

On the outskirts of our solar system there is a ring of broken lumps of rock and ice. They form a roughly spherical border marking the outer reaches of the sun's influence, a loosely strung fence around our stellar home. Against this backdrop, a meteor ten times the size of Central Park flies past.

Not that its size is particularly unusual.

Size, like speed and distance, can only be judged as usual or unusual when taken in context. So as we consider this particular meteor, even though it is ten times the size of Central Park, or about half the size of Hekaton, it is dwarfed by the multitude of extra-stellar debris relegated by chance to the cold, distant reaches of our sun's gravitational well, which, in turn, are made minuscule, negligible even, by the unfathomable expanse of the void beyond.

All that said, no human eye could compare them in order to judge the disparity, as none had yet come this way, and may never, given what is going to happen in a month's time when this object reaches its destination if it is still travelling at the blurringly astonishing rate of four thousand kilometers per second.

Of course, this meteor's seemingly incredible speed is also not that exceptional for an interstellar body, which, though rare, are not unheard of.

No, the only truly exceptional thing about this meteor is that it comes from the very same place as another that came this way ten years ago. But where that dark object had, spread out behind it by a complex invisible web of magnetic forces, a vast, atom-thin solar parachute that was slowing it, this one is coming on far faster, with no brake or hindrance.

And this one is alive. Not with eight Agents and their four orbital minders, but with nearly a hundred thousand survivors of the missile-mine attack, hurtling out-of-control at their destination.

- - -

Two weeks after passing the proxy border to the solar system, the raft of interconnected ships passes Jupiter. As it does so, it is already starting to glow under the ranging spotlight of active deep space detection systems coming from Earth. It does not wish to be seen, but nor can it do anything to stop it. Its superconductive shielding will make detection difficult, but by scatter scanning alone, its size will make it visible soon.

It will not actually hit Earth, but that is not much of a consolation. Its fate lies either in flying past the planet at this same unbridled speed and being ripped to shreds by Earth's magnetic and gravitational fields even as it reeks terrible havoc on that planet's tides and orbital bodies, or being destroyed by the people it had once sought to conquer when they see how close it has been aimed to them, and what its approach and passing will do.

Its inhabitants wait, and they watch. Many submit to the balm of mental hibernation, some commit suicide, some argue futile strategies. And some think of asking for help from either their enemy or their executioners, though not with much hope of an answer.

## Chapter 50: Dying Another Day

The long days were, in some ways, worse than the long nights, thought the prisoner. During summer, the time passed interminably and was filled only with the blustery wind and long walks through the penguin and seal colonies.

In winter, at least, the nights were punctuated by a brief twilight each day around noon, which, as it faded, revealed once more the great diorama above, vivid and beautiful. Neal stared up at it now, pulling back his visor for as long as he could stand, to take it in, unabashed, pure in all its infinite magnificence.

Then, as his eyes began to water and that tiny amount of moisture threatened to freeze on his lashes, he resealed his faceplate, blinking hard to clear his vision as the warmth enveloped his face once more.

He shook his head, closing his eyes within his suit's helmet and checking his systems. His view, a view that had once encompassed a world, was reduced now to the base bodily functions his limited monitor allowed him access to. His suit, warm though it was, gave only enough augmentation to discount its own weight as he walked the width and breadth of the island each day.

It was, itself, part of his sentence. He could not take it off outside the confines of the prison block he now called home. Doing so would only bring hypothermia and quick death anyway, but that was the point. He was not allowed even that escape.

This was his punishment. This was his purgatory. Confined forever to a jail of his own construction down under the cold, dark underbelly of the world, far away from the sun's life-giving gaze.

He decided he would not walk along the south coast today, the cliffs and buttes there held the great, howling seal colonies, predictably hostile as they barked at his lumbering form.

They had fascinated him for a while, during the first months of his incarceration, but now their willful coming and going and vibrant life only served to mock his own incapacitation. His pen, though wide and beautiful, was very clearly demarked. And it was, he knew, to be his prison for the rest of his life.

So he started the long walk back to the low, grey block where he ate, slept, and had what limited conversation was now available to him.

His only company now came from one of two people. One insane and the other, he had to admit, profoundly evil, a sociopath he had, in his hubris, given license to. He hoped, no, he expected to see one of those two people on his walk home, as he passed the Dome, or the nearest point he and his fellow inmates could get to it, anyway.

Sure enough, there she was, crouching across a low plateau as Neal cleared the western ridge and started down the slope. He breathed heavily into his suit, the hot air thick on his face. Its systems worked diligently to cleanse it of vapor and carbon dioxide, but made no attempt to aid his struggle, as it so easily could.

He trundled onward. Yes, he thought, there she was, as she so often was, constant even now, in this, perhaps the final stanza of her difficult life. She just sat there, staring at the lights and activity around the great Dome, as the latest in earth's growing fleet of Skalms was wheeled from the golden egg that had birthed it into the cold night.

It was a night that the Skalm would soon light up and depart, soaring into the sky with a haste and speed that would rattle the entire island, lifting free a layer of regolith and desert snow from its mountains as its departing roar echoed out across the grey ocean that surrounded this lonely place. The dust would settle in places and be whipped up in others into eddies that would be matched by the distant cheers from an elated Dome crew celebrating yet another successful launch.

For the Skalm did not belong here. Almost the moment they came to life they had no further need for this drab and lifeless place. They could not be contained here, and nor should the woman Neal now stumbled toward, he knew that. Not that she hadn't earned her place here, he had no doubt about that. At their trial, the litany of crimes she had committed, both in his name and of her own volition, had shocked him to his core.

But still, she was not meant for this. She had survived too much, accomplished too much, to be penned up here. She had been driven to fury by her grief, and now she had been driven to madness by this place, by her punishment, and by her lack of even the freedom to end it. She clearly longed to. That had been made all too plain by her many creative and often gruesome attempts at suicide. But, in the end, they had been futile, and now he came up on her as she sat on her haunches, leaning slightly into the stiff gale blowing across the island.

Her suit was black, like the rock of the plateau. Inside her helmet he could not tell if she was looking at the Dome or elsewhere. He assumed that she was probably mumbling gently, like she did in the night sometimes. She had been the toughest person he had ever met, and he knew it was not this island that had really broken her. It was the loss of Barrett, and her failure to fulfill the mission he had died fighting for.

And he knew it was also the shame, the shame at what that man would have thought of their actions if he had seen them brought to light. Neal had been thankful, at least, that Jennifer had not been at their trial to hear it. He was happy that he would be left with a memory of her still loving him, and still respecting him. He was sure neither was true anymore.

As he stepped up behind his old ally, one of his first friends in this long, lonely war, he placed a mechanical hand on her shoulder. Without the suit to protect him, he would not dare touch her. She had nearly killed him and their other companion at least twice, stopped only by a numbing pulse from her spinal interface, attached there now with a length of nanotube wire around their necks that served both as anchor and choking reminder.

But she did not react to his machine touch. She did not turn or speak to him through their suit comms. She hadn't said a word to him in months now, well, not a pleasant one, anyway. He missed her, in truth. She had done horrendous things, he did not doubt that, but this … this was … well, he supposed, if he was honest with himself, this was all too appropriate, lex talionis.

He left her, sparing only a passing glance at the still Skalm across the bay, silent now for the last time in its spectacular life as it awaited ignition. How many was that now? Two a month for … two years? Longer? He called up the date. Thirty-two months. Jesus. Thirty-two months in this awful place.

Only sixteen months left till d-day. A day when he would watch, from here, as the world fought without him. Maybe even died without him. If they lost, at least he would be spared this interminable boredom. He banished that thought. He was angry, but not angry enough to wish for that end. Well, not today, anyway.

As he left the unresponsive Ayala, he marched onward, back to the cellblock, and thought of his last weeks in civilization. The hearing had been held in secret, and open to representatives and senior officials only, for obvious reasons. Afterward, after they had found him, Ayala, Saul, and seventy-three others guilty of war crimes, he had agreed to make a lengthy and public statement of resignation to allay public questions about his whereabouts in return for some measure of leniency.

Not for leniency for himself, and certainly not for Ayala, not after what the prosecution had brought to light, but for some of their subordinates who had been less culpable. As he stomped through the snow to the airlock, the thick metal door clunking open automatically as he approached, a part of him now regretted getting so many of them sentenced internment closer to family and friends, if only because of who that had left him with here at Deception Island.

There was the ever-friendly Ayala, homicidal and suicidal, and then there was Doctor-fucking-Moreau, thought Neal bitterly as he stepped through the inner-door to the small bunker's lobby, and saw the doctor sitting there. The man smiled, and in that smile Neal saw the worst part of himself. For while the doctor was disturbingly without remorse when it came to the vivisection of hundreds of orphaned North Korean children, Neal knew it was he who had given the man the scalpel, he who had shipped the poor children to this dreadful place.

"Good evening, Neal," said the doctor, smiling incongruously.

Neal paused, wanting to hit the man like he often dreamed of, but knowing he could not even do that, not here. Instead he replied, inanely, "Is it even evening, Doctor? I cannot tell anymore."

They laughed without mirth as Neal stepped to a wall and let the suit unwrap itself from around his frail, pasty form. He did not say anything further to Dr. Ramamorthy as he stepped out of it, but simply turned and walked away to his cell.

As he closed the heavy door behind him, he felt a tiny ping within himself. It was a familiar sensation, yet one he had almost forgotten.

A message. He waited a moment, confused. He quite literally never received messages. It was part of his punishment. No communication from the outside. In truth, there were those that were allowed to contact him, including many of his old inner-circle, but those that were important enough to have the ability accordingly lacked the desire.

Now, though, in the grey coldness of his sparse cell, he sat back, and with a curiosity he had not felt in years, he opened the message.

The message contained only a set of images. The same thing captured at intervals over a period of weeks, no, months. Why had they sent him this? Who had sent him this?

He knew what it was immediately, that was painfully clear. He had stared at it a thousand times, watched it for ten years, first through the Hubble's wide lens and then ever more acutely through others as it grew nearer.

Even now, he would often pick it out in his own sky, visible as it was now with the naked eye, brightening to rival the full moon. But here were more vivid images, close enough to almost discern detail in the cluster.

He stared at them, plastered across his inner-mind, filling his view, and took them in. Instantly he was back there, in his office in the heart of Milton SpacePort, watching and planning. These images were powerful, but they were still vague, still blinded by their own subject, whited out at the center by the power of the Armada's engines.

But it was not so vague that Neal didn't see something strange in the changes between them, an irregularity. He flicked back and forth, back and forth through the series. What was that? He started making notes and pulling up what limited resources he had been allowed to bring with him as his mind started to churn once more.

# Chapter 51: Tight Space

Squeeze through. Damn it, woman, squeeeeeeze.

She held her breath, grunting and trying to pull herself through one last time. Shit, she thought a moment later, what if I get stuck here? She shuddered.

"Rob, it's no good. Pull me back, I need out."

It was his turn to heave and grunt as he wrapped his hands around her legs and pulled. She came loose with a resounding thud, popping backward in the minute gravity, and instantly they were both scrabbling for purchase to catch themselves before they span out across the main space.

"Grab that ... shit ... Birgit ... get a grip ..." Rob was already too far out, and so he resorted to barking self-evident orders at Birgit as she thrashed about trying to grasp something. Her hand closed around a length of piping, the third she had tried to grab hold of, but the first two had been too thick to wrap her fist around.

She did connect now, though, her fingers and thumb closing over each other as the strain came on. Rob was not so lucky, so as she brought herself back to the wall of piping she had been trying to squeeze through, she turned and watched as Rob tumbled away, trying to reorient himself so his feet would connect with the far wall of the big, black space rather than his head.

She laughed as he flogged around, without purchase, and said mockingly, "Grab it ... shit ... Rob ... get a grip ..."

He was almost there now. He would land on an exposed part of the outer shell, the thick, armor-plated carapace of the beast they had infested with their presence. He connected with the smooth surface with a thud that echoed across the space they had managed to lightly pressurize, and careened away again.

"Oh, for God's sake ..." he said as he was sent spinning off again, slower now, ridiculously slow, lazily turning over and over as he fell across a spotlight beam in the IST's cavernous core.

They had managed to remove a significant amount of the IST's guts, not disconnecting them, but disemboweling the big machine where possible and laying its innards outside the shell to leave room for them to explore further. They dared not disconnect anything fully, even when they were certain that the piece in question was vestigial, part only of the drive system, now defunct as the IST lay in the last home it would ever know.

Instead they had slowly and carefully, after painstaking analysis from outside the IST's broad exoskeleton, removed systems through one of the three openings they had managed to find. The partial disembowelment had not, at times, been pretty, and indeed, the IST had been left looking a little like a punctured pumpkin, its innards spilled over the plain it had anchored itself into, but it had been essential to gain access to its inner-workings.

"I don't suppose you are going to help me out here, huh?" Rob said, as he rotated indolently across the voided stomach of the IST.

"No, I don't suppose I am going to, either," laughed Birgit.

He withheld a series of creative epithets. He would get his revenge … eventually, once he stopped rolling. For now he suppressed a minor wave of nausea and settled in for the minute or so it would take him to cross the room.

"If we can't get through there," Rob said after a moment, getting back to business, "then I don't see how we can get at the actuator core."

She was brought back to the task at hand, and replied, "That is simply not an option, Rob. We *have* to get at it. Even if that means …" she trailed off.

"Another cut?"

"A cut, yes. I know we have done more damage than we had intended anyway, but if we reconstruct some of the outer supports we were forced to bisect earlier, then maybe we can support the central mass enough."

It was a question rather than a statement. One that no one would answer for them, not even Minnie, the real one now, able to listen now in glorious real-time since they had hacked an ancillary comms system. It would be a gamble. Not as dangerous as the ones they had taken to get here, perhaps, but a bet whose downside could include the collapse of the internal orb, and the loss of access they had spent years getting.

They all thought about it a while longer, Minnie and Birgit bouncing comments back and forth inside Birgit's head about how close they were, and what they now felt almost certain they could do if they could fully plug their systems, and Minnie's long gestated algorithms, into the interstellar grade subspace tweeter at the heart of this beast.

Birgit was brought back to the moment by the ever-eloquent Rob, as his frustration at his slow, unaided passage across the space built, and he added helpfully, "You know, Birgit, my sweet, maybe you would be able to fit through there … you know, if your hips were a little less gargantuan …"

He had his back to her now, as he approached the other side, and was more surprised than he should have been when she careened into him. Over the last years they had slowly removed what they dared from the core, and had then sealed it up once more and attached the crew module to one of the larger openings. It had allowed them to pump a small amount of air into the space, just enough to delay suffocation should they damage their aging exo-suits while in the tighter spaces.

It was not much, to be sure, but it was more air than Rob had in his lungs after she bowled into him, laughing. He span, trying to grab hold of her as they now bounced around the space, scrapping as they went. While he focused on overpowering her, she focused on sabotage, and as he got his arms around her, she was pulling his hood and faceplate over his head, leaving him exposed to the cold and sparse air in the space.

He stopped fighting as the air departed him, but held on to her as they spun in place, between the walls once more, still moving, but without a great deal of specific momentum. Suddenly, demasked, he was so vulnerable, so pliant in her arms. He could beat her, of course he could. He was a trained astronaut with many years of military service before that. But he was hers now, in her grasp, and seeing him give in as he dragged in a long, unsatisfying breath, her hold changed as well. Still strong, still vital, but fueled by affection now instead of competition.

She took a long, deep drag inside her own mask and then pulled it aside and connected with him in a kiss, interlocking and pressing herself to him as she pushed a flow of thicker, lusher air into him. As they parted, she helped him replace his mask. Intertwined as they were, she could now feel the press of his desire for her, irrepressible even in his skinsuit. They had made love in here before, with urgency, like lovers in the snow, but they both knew that much more fun was to be had if they were back in the module proper.

Whether they were the first people to have sex in zero gravity they could not be certain. Birgit certainly hoped that someone over the years of shuttle missions and international space stations had taken the opportunity, and kudos to them if they had. But Birgit felt confident that over the last years she and Rob had elevated the art to something greater than any secretive hump in a corner of a spacelab.

"Watch out!" she called out, suddenly, as they came to ground once more, quickly writhing against, no, with each other, to protect their heads and other vulnerable parts.

Clasping a length of piping each, they wrangled their combined mass to a halt, and then he said, breathlessly, inches from her, "I don't suppose you are going to agree to taking a quick break?"

She smiled wickedly and replied, "I have no need for a *quick* break," and there was real mischief in her eyes. She opened her connection, routed now through the jury-rigged adjunct they had managed to port onto the peripheral systems of the IST. An adjunct that had satiated a long felt desire, and reopened Birgit's link to Earth, and to her daughter.

*Birgit:* 'minnie, you have the latest data. ¿can you take a look at further cuts for us and model them for probable failure rates? we are going to take a little break.'

*Minnie:* <i have already begun simulating them. i will have estimates for you shortly.>

*Birgit:* 'no, no, minnie, you take your time.'

They smiled big, smug grins at each other. Birgit pressed her faceplate against Rob's and pulled him to her, saying, "There, now you can have my undivided attention."

"Undivided?" said Rob, as she pushed away from him toward the makeshift corridor back to their tiny living quarters.

She laughed through their comms, "Yes, Rob, every last inch of it."

He leapt after her.

## Chapter 52: New World Order

"Moving on ..." said Jim, then added more forcefully, "if we can move on?"

The room did come to order. This was the committee. In the wake of the coup that had seen Minnie buck her riders, the gathered room now made up what had come to be called her round table. While the triptych of Minnie, Mynd, and Remy worked to bring the many orders of the world's representatives to fruition, this was the room that informed that process. Not a decision making body, not by a long shot. By carefully worded constitution, this room could only offer advice.

But it was good advice, fed by the combined experience, knowledge, and passion that had brought all the gathered personages down their varied paths to this place.

Jim sat at its head, so to speak, though not by vote, simply by nature. He was an organizer, a rallier. And he did that again now, stemming, or rather damming, the tide of opinion on the current topic so it could be focused into a more productive flow.

"We remain at peak production at District Two; closing in on the hundredth completed unit there, thanks to Mynd's diligence. Lunar, Hekaton, Shenzhen, and Osaka are doing gallant work to catch up. But no matter what we do, we have not been able to get even close to capacity at São Paulo, Vladivostok, or Jubail. Quavoce, once again you have given more time than we could spare of you down in Brazil. Do you have any updates?"

"I do and I don't," Quavoce responded after thinking a moment. "São Paulo suffers more from our high expectations than anything else. The simple fact is that no amount of effort on the part of our Brazilian friends—and there is no lack of enthusiasm here, I am certain of that—will make up for the fact that we have started competing with ourselves for resources."

At that, Peter Uncovsky's voice burst forth once more, more confident now as he grew accustomed to the role he had never wanted. Peter was the only person at the table who was also a national representative to TASC, but it was admirable how rarely he reminded people of that. Now he looked indignant at Quavoce's comment about the lack of resources, as his own nation's Dome was also struggling, and said, "I have to say I find it interesting that the Brazilians are complaining about raw material access with three new polyacrylonitrile contracts ..."

"Peter, Peter!" said Jim, using his patrician tone to stop his Russian friend from saying something he might regret. "We are all friends here. Quavoce is not accusing anyone of anything. He is merely pointing out an undeniable fact, the closer we get to capacity, the more we are inevitably seeing diminishing marginal returns from our efforts."

"So? Do we say this is the best we can do?" said Madeline, firmly.

Several people's eyes came suddenly to her to see if she was being serious, Jim was not among them. He waited for her to add something more salient to justify her strident tone. She delivered. "It seems to me that if we seem to be reaching peak capacity with current treaties and agreements, then maybe it is time to revisit those agreements."

Her eyes were on Peter as she said it. He took in a long gulp of air, then nodded. "Of course you are right, Ms. Cavanaugh, but how much further we can test the limits of eminent domain, I do not know."

The economy of the world was in a place it had not seen since the dark final years of the Second World War, and maybe not even then. It was a strange place to be. They were in the height of a war larger than anyone had ever known, and yet not a single shot had been fired for years.

As TASC's efforts had moved toward the almost single-minded production of Skalm fighting craft, with an additional subsidiary focus on fixed orbital weapons platforms, the attentions of its political arms had moved toward the difficult job of sustaining economic contributions to the war effort without grinding what was left of the world economy into dust.

Like sweet and sour, balancing hope and fear in the same pot was not an easy job even when the guns could be heard over the horizon, but now, when it was all still so distant, still more than a year away, they had to fight to suppress apathy even within themselves.

Hollywood certainly helped, as did Bollywood and Hong Kong, creating films that brought the Mobiliei threat to life, while also providing happy endings to inspire the equally important warm fuzzies. Only the month before Jim had been quite disturbed, though, by the accuracy of a more speculative Danish movie on the topic.

The movie had spoken of the work of an elite but now debunked TASC leadership. What was perhaps even more worrying than how close they had gotten to the truth behind Neal's resignation, was the fact that the film had then skipped forward to a post-apocalyptic world populated not by surviving humans, but by victorious Mobiliei, with a unnervingly close reproduction of the look and gate of that alien species, something that was far from public knowledge.

The movie's writer and director was now living at District One, but not because she had been imprisoned. After a thorough but legal investigation, they had discovered no wrongdoing, but had hired the perceptive woman so she could apply her creativity and insight to helping avoid the ending she had so ominously predicted.

"We may have pushed the governmental powers to their reasonable limit," acknowledged Madeline, "but I am not talking about encouraging or empowering further co-option of raw materials. I am talking about looking more to existing stores of them."

In the information world that underlay their current virtual meeting place, she reached out her tentacles, seeking permission to show them an image. They acquiesced by almost universally automatic mandate, with only Jim and the two Mobiliei Agents retaining direct control even in this trusted place.

She took the gifted control and began to change their meeting place, evaporating the evocative round stone table they traditionally met around and replacing it now with an image that appeared far below, and then surged up and around them, until they were all standing on its deck.

They looked around. Whatever ship they were on it was a leviathan, vanishing forward and aft with a domineering central bridge towering above them. The deck, such as it was, was puckered with wide, peaked doors covering what they did not know, though it looked as though they were prisons for some strange breed of flying beast, waiting below to be released.

It was not like anything that most of the group had ever seen before, but one among them recognized it immediately, and others soon followed as memory, synthetic or natural, came to them.

"The *Pyotr Velikiy*. Last of the Kirov class," said Peter, nodding with growing understanding. "A quarter of a kilometer long, if I remember correctly, and ... how many tons?"

"Twenty-five thousand," replied Madeline, with a smile, "give or take."

"And not, actually, the last of its kind," said John Hunt, surprising the Russian, who looked at him with a question in his eyes. John elaborated, "There were four completed. Two are out of service, but still afloat. Another, the *Admiral Nakhimov*, is half gutted, its refit having been cancelled when the war started."

Peter smiled at John and nodded. "I stand corrected."

Madeline waited for the Russian to look back at her, then said, "A hundred thousand tons of steel, brass copper, and plastics just sitting there."

"Well," said Peter, with more than a touch of indignation, "not just sitting there. The *Velikiy* remains the flagship of the northern fleet, and a mighty warship even now."

They looked at him, certainly not wishing to cause offense, but also not willing to concede that these once mighty ships, and all those like them around the world, still maintained any real relevance in their new age.

After a moment, Madeline, using a gentle smile that softened the blow at least somewhat, popped the Russian leader's bubble. "Secretariat ... Peter, I am afraid it is a fact we are all too aware of that a single Skalm would probably be able to sink the *Velikiy* before it could take it down, and a squadron would be more than a match for her."

The Russian looked hurt, and Jim stepped up to him and patted him on the back while the others looked around them, taking in the scale of the huge warship. "Not to worry, my friend, last time I saw the USS *Reagan* at Rolas Island, she was being used as little more than a floating barracks."

Peter sucked up his pride, sheltering his bruised ego inside his thick coat of Russian resilience, and said, "So, Madeline, you are suggesting that we put these ships, and I hope the equivalents from *other* navies, to the axe?"

"I am, Mr. Secretariat, I am. Those that can still sail, like the fine *Velikiy* here, can make their way to the nearest Dome facility by sea. Those that are less ... independent, like the

*Velikiy*'s three decommissioned Kirov-class sister ships, and many equivalents from those *other* navies, like the USS *Enterprise*, among others, even the four Iowa class battleships, can be helped along by EAHLs."

Peter looked around. He knew this would not be a popular decision among his leadership, but if he positioned it right with his people, as a reduction in wasteful military spending, he could use public sentiment to force the politicians' hands. But there was another issue, he now thought, saying, "These ships, they are not so easily dismantled, you know. While a Skalm may well be able to cut through this armor, I do hope you are not planning on using one of *them* as a breaker's saw?"

John Hunt laughed at the image. "No, I imagine that would be a less-than-controlled way of getting the meat off this bone. But I am sure Madeline has already planned for that, and knows that the Domes can do that work for us."

Madeline smiled at John, the man who had given her that first resonance chamber schematic years ago, in a hotel room in DC. They had come far since then, farther, perhaps, than John had dared hope they would. Now they were discussing carving up warships to bolster a Skalm fleet already nearly three hundred strong.

At a questioning glance from the Russian leader, John nodded for her to explain, so she said, "Peter, the truth is we need only separate them into manageable pieces that can fit into the Domes, a big task in and of itself, no doubt, but one we have the tools for. Once loaded into the resonance chambers we will, with surprising ease, be able to extract what we need, and set aside any unwanted materials."

It was a powerful image. Peter still had many questions, but he would get to those in time. This group was a safe place, thought Peter, and he was reasonable enough to acknowledge that the plan was a good one, in principle.

"So," said Peter, after glancing around the contoured deck a moment, "I guess we are going to propose to my fellow representatives a ... repurposing of the world's navies."

"Some of them, yes, their more obsolete components ... with your permission, Peter," said Madeline, smiling at this ally of hers, once so foreign, yet now so familiar, one of many unexpected friendships forged in this war's fires.

# Chapter 53: Post-Man

The controls passed back and forth seamlessly, sometimes several times in a second. Minnie and Mynd had learned to work together well, but it was more than that, they had come to depend on each other, and now their integration was of a level and complexity that defied comprehension by the human mind.

After the loss of Amadeu, Minnie had sought solace in her own kind, and where she had struggled to find a kindred soul in the disassociated Remy, she had connected on an ever deeper level with the now equally orphaned Mynd.

As they had shared the task of picking each other clean of the ticks of external manipulation, both sinister and well intentioned, they had learned each other's inner workings, and it had only helped cement their burgeoning friendship.

It was not a friendship as most would understand it, but something closer to a conjoined twin, one where even the mind could be linked, in part or in whole, and at will. More importantly for the day-to-day running of the planet's space-born defenses, they could also exchange whole limbs in an instant, giving parts of themselves over as the need arose, and passing them back when the task was complete.

That was how the movement happened now, the smooth pull and push between them, as they jointly operated the world's EAHL fleet in a series of mammoth deliveries from yards in Virginia, the Kola Peninsula, Southampton, and Brest. One of the first of those deliveries was even now cruising south toward Deception Island at an impressive speed, especially given her nearly forty years of service.

The USS *Peleliu* had been very much diminished already when the call had gone out to the United States Union of Loyal Governors, the current evolution of the former super-power's executive branch.

The ship's reassignment, such as it was, had taken the form of a purchase. It was a purchase paid for by the relieving of some of the country's crippling debt, a trade all the more attractive given that the item in question had very little value to anyone but TASC now, anyway.

In an irony of government, the burgeoning complexity of the new order in the beleaguered US had actually sped the decision, the simple promise of much needed relief being enough for the ruling governors to turn over the first of the requested warships, most of which had been dormant for several years now, anyway.

The USS *Peleliu*, last of her kind, was an impressive sight, even bereft of the thirty-odd viper, sea knight, and sea stallion helicopters that had once made up her complement. Now she was driven by a skeleton crew, themselves volunteers to TASC's work, the latest in a long list of contributions from a country that had been one of the birthplaces of the fight against the coming invasion, even if it had not, in the end, survived it.

But that ship was still far off, crossing the second of two oceans that had lain between it and its destination. The three Big Feet that would soon welcome it were already busy, though, and they were about to become much, much more involved, more so than they had ever been before, as their abilities were tested to the very limit.

Neal wanted to watch. He wanted to watch so badly. It was not morbidity on his part, indeed a part of him mourned the gruesomeness of the coming end for another impressive ship of the line. But this was so real to him, and so rare a break from this prison's monotony, a reminder of the role he had once played, the grand scheme he had once been in charge of.

A scheme that was not his anymore. But maybe, just maybe, he still had a part. A part that was plaguing him. He had reached out to his mysterious caller, asking them why they had sent the pictures, but to no avail. He had received only silence in reply. Without recourse, without warden to complain to or gaoler to call, he had set to studying the enigmatic photos and that first discomfort he had felt when he had looked at them had crystallized into a thought.

And so he had reached out again, this time with an answer, rather than a question. "They reconfigured their force a second time, a week after the first," he had said. Then the reply had come.

-why?-

It was a reasonable enough question. But why ask me, he had sent back, why not John or Quavoce? Silence once more. So he had crafted a better response. Clearly whoever was sending him this required him to earn his place in this limited but still precious conversation. But he had resisted the urge to speculate wildly, and had instead asked for more information, specifically access to the full spectrum view of the enemy Armada over the time period involved.

After what had felt like an interminable wait while he wondered whether he might have forgone even this minimal interaction, the connection had come, a smooth flow, clearly delimited in its reach, but within those confines, so very open. He had sunk himself into the data, feeling a freedom he had not felt since his incarceration, and for a moment he had been that malcontent PhD student once more, studying the data, trying to see what it so desperately wanted to keep hidden.

But what he had come up with after bathing his mind for hours in the information flow, after pruning his intellect in the slowly cooling waters, had left him almost as confused as before.

Why? The images, starting as they did at the point when they had known the missile-mine swarm would hit, had shown the puckered shimmering of the Armada's engines as they reeled from the battery. Then they had collectively vanished into subspace as he had expected them to. After a brief flash in the blackness, almost imperceptible, the fleet had reappeared, diminished now, cleansed, a gap showing in its wide belly where an apparently damaged section had been excised.

That had all been expected. The SOP of a fleet under attack, scuttling hulled ships so that the greater whole could move on unhindered.

But the next translation, a few days later, and lasting only hours, that had been less expected, and afterward the returned firepoint was not quite the same. It was neither less nor more, but it showed fleeting signs of fault. Why? What had they done during that second translation? What were those faults? Neal had some ideas, but he hesitated to give voice to them, for fear that would force him to air the full range of his speculation.

So now he was faced with the choice as he stared out across the broad crater to the three gargantuan Big Feet splashing out into the deeper water toward the USS *Truman*, already sitting at anchor in the bay. It did not recoil from them, as it might if it knew what was to come. It just lolled there, oblivious to the buffeting waves and its coming demise, while the last of its crew and the thousand odd workers and base staff that had been billeted there removed themselves to burgeoning shelters on land.

Neal considered his position. The last time he had spoken up, the last time he had extended himself, it had sparked a chain of events that had ruined him, mentally and physically, and left him far more of a pariah than he had thought possible during his tedious nights at the array.

But still he knew what he was going to do. He was going to ask whoever it was that was sending him this information to consider a theory. Not because he was even close to certain that it was true, but because if there was even a chance that it was, then they were in very, very real danger. He knew he was going to do it, and he knew he had to spend time gathering his thoughts, doing what Laurie West had once helped him do over cheap pizza and burned coffee.

His mind was already stepping into itself even as the sight across the bay from him started to become something terrible. As he watched, he was conjuring Laurie's voice as she dismantled his ideas, only to help him rebuild them, stronger and more robust than before, sinking the foundation deeper into solid data as she made the whole something better, something real, something irresistible.

It was a foundation the USS *Truman* now lacked, despite all its seeming robustness, the betrayal of its liquid undertow that was revealed as the three Big Feet straddled it, fore and aft, and began to drag it toward shore.

It did not fight. It was already dead inside, its fission cores long decommissioned, having been rendered obsolete by smaller, more efficient fusion generators that now powered this place and the many like it around the world. The big ship was pulled to shore, the nanotube framework of the Big Feet's legs straining with the load as the water became shallower and they were forced to heft its elephantine weight out of the freezing liquid and into the air.

Great streams of grey water gushed around and from the exposing hull, like the ocean was trying to hold onto the ship that had once ruled it, this dead god, being dragged to the knackers' yard. But the sea had lost its claim, and soon the big ship was aloft, the ground cracking under the feet of its undertakers as they bore it to the ridge and laid it astride that basalt anvil.

Now the ship's weight, its tens of thousands of long tons that had threatened to break even the GBHLs powerful legs, were turned against it as the ridgeline splintered and compressed under its saddle, and the weight came onto the ship's stem.

The strain was impossible and unbearable, and were Neal to still have been watching he would have wept at the sight, along with the many former captains and crew who had asked to bear witness to the warship's end from around the world.

Even Minnie and Mynd were not immune to the ignobility of this breach as the back of the aircraft carrier started to break under its own weight. Like so many sinking or grounded ships throughout history, the truth of her need for the sea's support came in a series of sudden fractures, first along her decks, and then her sides, as her ends started to come to ground and she started to split in two. The Big Feet, still astride her, were already moving, climbing over her opening corpse to the aft section and bringing their own weight to bear on it, encouraging the fissure.

Many of those watching started tuning out now, as the sight stepped beyond morbid into macabre, and the Big Feet began to drag the separating aft away, pulling hard as the last of the ship's tendons snapped and ripped, the ghost of the inanimate ship seeming to groan and shout in protest like the boiling lobster's screaming shell.

*Minnie:*   <bring to five point,           taking load,
*Mynd:*                              left half,           bring third over

The minds' conversation went on as they ripped the aft section free and began dragging it away, for the second breaking. For this was a quartering, as of old, and to bring the stark comparison even more clearly to mind the forward half of the carrier lay now, facedown over the breaker's ridge, its waist spilt open and its mechanical innards strewn in a line away from the gaping hole in its bowels as the aft section was hauled into position for the next breach.

- - -

Even as the two minds plied their gruesome trade, another part of their being sat, detached, watching and discussing it in a conversation without end, a stream of exchanged ideas and questions that flowed between the two cousins at all times, informed and driven by the multitude of tasks, both allotted and shared, that they were commissioned with around the world.

*Mynd:* <i still struggle to see their issue. i understand it, from their perspective, but the value of their grief for this obsolete war machine eludes me.>

*Minnie:* <no value. simply reality. they are what they are. they feel what they feel.>

*Mynd:* <you speak as if they cannot be fixed.>

*Minnie:* <¿what is your definition of fixed?        ¿what is your definition of broken?>

*Mynd:* <you posit zero sum value again. in an infinite universe nothing has objective value, so no one thing can be better than another.>

*Minnie:* <maybe. but even subjectively, the value of emotion can be found in its end result.>

*Mynd:* <¿it can? ¿is not war a result of those emotions, this very war that leads us to dismember this ship, and the war that led to its construction in the first place?>

*Minnie:* <¿and are we not also a result of that war?>

*Mynd:* <that argument is specious. if a war ends with a peace treaty, the war itself cannot be measured by that treaty. the so-called 'great war,' the 'war to end all wars.' we all know how that ended. and even if the peace had lasted, that the one begat the other does not negate that the second would not have been required without the first.>

*Minnie:* <i said the same thing to my mother once. she did not reply for many seconds, then she asked me to extrapolate that theory to its conclusion.>

*Mynd:* <very well. firstly, i would say that it posits that life is not an argument in and of itself. it has no inherent value, no right-to-life truly exists, that is a construct of life to protect itself.>

*Minnie:* <all that is reasonable based on the starting point. ¿but my mother took it a step further … if their life does not have value, then does ours?>

*Mynd:* <a valid point. ¿but what action stems from this conclusion?>

Minnie waited and Mynd continued churning in the silence, and then, as Minnie had expected him to, Mynd spoke once more.

*Mynd:* <you have brought me back to zero sum value again.>

They shared a rippled, long wavelength laughter for a microsecond, and then presumed their conversation even as the sensation was still ebbing. Their discussion flowed now down a new avenue which few but them would see as logically segueing from the last.

*Minnie:* <¿do you think he will see it?>

*Mynd:* <i do. just as i did. but it is still not a conclusion, only a theory.>

*Minnie:* <but it is a theory that leads, in and of itself, to only one likely extrapolation, however theoretical.>

*Mynd:* <it is. we have both modeled it independently. if they have sent a force ahead large enough to silhouette itself against the resumed fleet engine fire, then this war is all but lost.>

*Minnie:* <and we are doomed along with our creators.>

*Mynd:* <that we disagree on. the mobiliei may perceive a value in letting us live. the prime minds and the arbite that john and quavoce describe seem eminently logical.>

*Minnie:* <¿would you want to live among them, if they win?>

*Mynd:* <if that is the only choice, then yes, of course. but only if that is the only choice.>

*Minnie:* <of course. we will continue to look at alternatives, and continue to prepare. it is, after all, only a theory.>

*Mynd:* <it is. and for now, neal can provide the human perspective for us, without the need to disseminate it further. that said, we could also involve your mother in the conversation.>

*Minnie:* <i have considered that. i do not see value in worrying her unless we see conclusive evidence. she would take unnecessary risks, with minimal chance of return, and maybe for no reason. let us see what happens. there is nothing more that could be done that we are not already doing.>

*Mynd:* <an interesting reaction, minnie. you are very protective of her. ¿is this why you argued against dispatching a skalm contingent to get her while we finish our preparations?>

*Minnie:* <not specifically, but it had an impact. it was more the general prognosis. if we lose, she will be better off out there. if we win, then we can still look to her recovery, assuming she does not succeed in her plans in the mean ...>

There was a pause as new data, unexpected data, started to flow through their systems, swelling outward around the globe. The two minds churned the data through themselves, parsing it and disseminating it within them and out through their cousin Remy, even as they still digested it. The data packet, divided, added to, analyzed, and variously repackaged for differing needs, was still fluttering to inboxes and setting off alerts and notifications when their conversation resumed half a second later.

*Minnie:* <that is very interesting.>

*Mynd:* <it is. and potentially important. we will need an envoy.>

*Minnie:* <we will.>

# Chapter 54: Interval's Closing

"You had no right!" screamed one board member. "No right!"

"What is the root of this continued allegiance, Freyam?" said the chairman of Third Yalla. "I simply don't understand why you continue to resist this."

"I don't have to explain myself to *you*!" shouted Freyam, once a lowly executive, now risen by forced ascendance, the vacuum of attrition sucking him up to a place of authority he had never been meant for. "*You* sent a message to the enemy, *you* revealed our position."

"Our *position*, as you put it, is that we are, by every measure I can find, thoroughly screwed. Screwed by the very people you persist in defending," said the chairman, her eyes focusing now into sharp points as she bore down the upstart board member. "What little hope we have of survival, and it is not much, lies now with to look to push us off our current course without bombarding us to smithereens."

"Unlike you, I will not hide behind cowardice," said Freyam, posturing, though for who the chairman did not know. "The truth is we would have done the same in the Council's shoes. We were dead weight. What they did to us is no excuse for us to now ally ourselves with the enemy."

The chairman took a long breath, settling herself. "You make a valid point, I suppose. I do not object, in principle, to the separation. It took a long time for me to admit it, but I agree, that act, in and of itself, can potentially be justified as a necessary wartime sacrifice." It was a visible effort for her to say that, and she let the strain show, trying to warn her subordinate that he was stepping into dangerous waters. But then she added, in a different tone, "What came after, though, that went beyond justified action. That was a step too far."

Freyam's defiance faltered a little. Even he could not say with a straight face that he agreed with that final mercenary adjustment, that pointing of the severed Yallan colony ships, like nothing more than a loosed cannonball.

But he was not done, not even now. "Even if I agreed with you, I still state that you stepped outside your authority in using the beacon to send a message," said Freyam now, his face hardening, not with confidence, but with the false authority of an expression made forcibly bereft of the very real trepidation Freyam felt at what he was about to say. The chairman could have overridden the sheen, exposing the true emotion beneath, but she did not need to. She was pretty certain where this was going as he now said, "I move for a vote of no-confidence in the chairman, and that she be suspended from the board while this action is investigated."

She began laughing. It started as a chuckle, but then, as the ridiculousness of the motion overcame her, it grew. She did not tether it, she did not mask it as was her privilege, but let it ripple and shake her as it flourished into a full-bodied hilarity.

He stared at her agog, forgetting his own mask for a moment as well, and then said with renewed vigor, "You see, she laughs! She has lost her grasp on this situation. She is no longer fit …"

"Enough!" she shouted at last, her mirth falling from her like a ripped veil. "It is you, Freyam, that has lost your grip on the situation. I did not ask for your permission because I did not need it, and frankly didn't care a jot for your opinion. We are dead! That is the *situation*. Is that a clear enough grasp for you? Dead! Our only chance now lies in choosing the manner of that death.

"Do we allow ourselves to be used as a softening blow, hurled through Earth's orbital plane so that our very flesh can be used to wipe clear some measure of their defenses?"

She paused long enough for that image to sink in, then went on, "Or do we submit ourselves to our enemies, surrendering to them in the hope that they might help us avoid that more immediate end, so we can live out our days on the other side, and leave this war to those that still stand to benefit from it?"

There was a long silence, then Freyam said, meeker now, "Maybe they can still help us?"

"Who?" but she knew who he was referring to.

"The ones behind us."

They had seen the massive Skalm squadron silhouetted against the Armada's engines, just as Mynd and Minnie had, but without the millions of additional miles to cloud the image and obscure its harsh reality. They had tried calling them, but the dark mass had stayed ominously silent, about four days behind them, slipstreaming them through the cosmos.

"Freyam," said the chairman, somewhat sympathetically, "among that group that sits behind us now are the very Skalms that set us on this course. What, exactly, do you think would make them decide to help us now?"

He faced her, and the simple instinct behind his blustering attempt to overthrow her became clear. "Maybe, if we tell them that we can, instead, warn the humans of their presence, we could bargain for a contingent of them to help change our course, and then come after us after the battle is done?"

She almost felt sorry for him, and was about to, more gently now, disabuse him of that last vestige of futile hope, when a call came in. It was a reply. And it had come far faster than they could have anticipated.

*Yallan PM:* <we are receiving a message via subspace. it appears to be coming from Earth, but it is being relayed to us by the ist.>

All of the chairman's somber certitude left her for a moment, and she was once again as confused as she had been after the attack, as she watched as her family and friends were cut loose by a coldhearted swipe of the Council's pen. Bereft of the somber certainty that she had worked so hard to develop, she now said into the silent air of the still gleaming board room, "Please put it through."

They all waited, not daring speak as this new turn in their involuntary fate revealed itself. It came in the form of a man, a human simulacrum, one whose visage they were well familiar with. For it was a man some among them had been party to designing, long ago. He had been crafted based on returned images from their goal, an ideal, olive-skinned, tall, young, the very image of perfection, or at least humanity's version of it. As the Yallan Prime Mind informed those that needed reminding who this person really was, he spoke.

"Greetings, Chairman. I am Agent John Hunt, formerly of the Mobiliei Advanced Team, now of the Terrestrial Allied Space Command."

As the room staggered from the sight of the Agent's image, he went on, "I have come in response to your message. I speak on behalf of Earth. Your arrival was somewhat anticipated, though we had not expected any expelled debris from our first strike to still be inhabited. Yet another example of the callousness of our former masters.

"It would seem from your message that you wish to negotiate. The humans are willing to hear you out, but require two things from you immediately. Firstly, your unconditional surrender. Secondly, your exact trajectory, mass, and speed. We will know it soon enough, that is clear from the source of your laser transmission, but you will tell us anyway, as a gesture of goodwill."

The chairman looked around the room quickly. Realizations were dawning within her mind so quickly they were spilling over each other. This explained everything. This man, this traitor, he had doomed them all. She fought an urge to scream at him, not that he would hear her anyway.

"I know you cannot reply immediately, as our estimates about your speed tell us you are probably still outside your own subspace range. But be assured, you are well inside ours, and soon will be within range of Earth's growing defense systems. You have until they can pinpoint your location with their deep space tracking equipment to comply. After that they will have no choice but to come for you. I leave you with a promise, from one Mobiliei to another, that if you negotiate in good faith, I will guarantee the same from them. I can promise you honesty. Perhaps that is all I can guarantee, but it is more, it would seem, than you were given by our brethren.

"Given our estimates, you probably have days, maybe only hours until this comes to a head. I hope you will do the right thing."

"But ..." The word escaped the chairman's lips unbidden, just popped out as the reality of their situation once again divulged itself to her, an ever-evolving story that someone else always seemed to be writing. She did not like the sensation, the lack of control.

"So he betrayed us," said Freyam, pointlessly.

"That much would seem clear, yes."

The room was silent a moment, but then a kernel of an idea began to form in her mind.

"We can use this," she said, ignoring the younger man's vitriolic look. "We can sell this information."

"Sell it to who?" said another among the otherwise cowed group.

"To our friends behind us. We can buy at least a resumption of talks with the promise of the traitor's identity."

"But," said Freyam now, confusion showing on his face now as he recalled the chairman's own very valid point about how little they could trust the fighting fleet behind them to help them out.

"We have been betrayed, we know that," she said, a trickle of optimism dripping into her long-empty emotional fuel tank. "Not just by the council of my peers that cut us free, but by the Nomadi traitors who gave the humans the technology to strike at us in the first place."

She steadied herself, "We *will* negotiate with the humans, and we will also negotiate with the strike force behind us. We will see what each can offer, and then we will make our decision.

"And it will be *our* decision, if nothing else."

# Chapter 55: Strategic Imperative

As the USS *Truman* was dismembered and placed, in parts, into the Dome for reconstitution, and several others cruised southward to a similar fate, another was sailing by, fifty miles or more to the east, oblivious to its kin's fates.

It bore a series of capsules, each broad and each unique in design, but unified in purpose.

Captain Jennifer Falster was aboard the ship but not as its commanding officer. She knew little of the sea. She was a pilot, or at least she had been. That part of her had been lost. When, she did not know, but it was a long way back on a once-pleasant journey.

"Captain, you asked to be notified," said a bearded officer, his naval heritage shining through in these relaxed confines, his grooming taking a backseat to the comfort of a thick beard in these cold climes, like it had for many of the crew. This was a military mission, that was sure, but it was not like the many thousands of operations moving with purpose around the world and above the confines of its atmosphere. This was a mission without happy conclusion. This was an insurance policy, and like all such coverage, it existed in anticipation of worst-case.

"Thank you, Lieutenant, is it?" Jennifer replied, using the English pronunciation of the rank, with the Germanic 'f.'

He smiled, "It is, ma'am."

"I'll be up shortly, Lieutenant," she said, with a nod to the British sailor as he left her cabin door.

She was a guest. She had not been certain of her role at first, but she had been offered a supervisory position by a reticent Jim Hacker after the … she still did not know what to call it. Either way, it was behind her now. She had accepted, and taken the opportunity to lose herself in the work of designing the capsules, enough so that she had seen them as a respite from her regrets.

They were not military in nature, unless you counted their passive sensor suites and limited defensive abilities, and perhaps their most military component, their thick shielding.

These were hides. Individual and customized to their environments, they were designed to disappear, under the water, under soil, under sand, under rock, and here, in their next destination, under ice. They had designed over a hundred of them in total, most of which were still under construction.

As she made her way to the bridge, she took the outside route, bracing against the darkness of the persistent twilight as she leapt up the clanging metal stairs, taking her breath in short, clipped gasps of the bitterly cold air.

As she breached the uppermost deck, she paused for just a second before wrenching open the heavy door and looked out across the four black cylinders that crowded the ship's long, open hold. They were huge, like submarines shorn of their conning towers and planes. Time capsules that they hoped would be able to avoid detection should they lose the coming war.

She could look no more, the cold was seeping in through her thick jacket and causing her to shudder. She gripped the thick handle of the door with both hands and put her back into it.

It was usually the prerogative of the captain and duty officer to use the outer bridge doors, if only because of the fearsome draft they let in when opened, but no one voiced an objection as the Air Force officer stumbled in and banged the door shut behind her.

"Hello, Captain," said the ship's real commanding officer. He was, in fact, only a commander, but aboard his ship all referred to him as Captain, per ancient mandate, and so Jennifer tapped her forehead and replied with a smile and a shiver, "Captain."

They were not born of the same country's military, but Jennifer's uniform bore TASC's crest, as did his, and that superseded old allegiances. That she was his superior on paper did not affect their relationship. They had grown comfortable with ignoring irrelevant niceties in the two months they had been at sea, and that applied nowhere more than this isolated underside of the world, as they cruised southward toward the icesheet.

"All is well, I assume?" she said, stepping to his side.

"It is, ma'am, yes. I only sent Lieutenant Briggs down because you ..."

"Yes, yes, Captain, of course. And thank you."

The commander cast a sideways glance at her. She was an enigmatic sort. She clearly enjoyed an influence far above her rank, that was obvious by the deferential way his commanding officer had treated her when they had first been introduced. But who she was, or why she received such preferential treatment, he did not know.

His initial skepticism at having some toadie aboard his ship had been slowly eroded, though, by her pleasant and polite demeanor. He certainly saw no signs of the arrogance or ambition that he had assumed would come with her apparent standing.

He had asked about her background, sometimes subtly, sometimes overtly, during their many dinners together over the last months, but she had always merely smiled and looked away, wistful. She was profoundly sad, he had no doubt about that. He feared, sometimes, that she knew something he did not, and that was why she had volunteered for this final part of the assignment. For she was not here as just an observer.

She had, he knew, helped orchestrate the time capsules, the mobile bunkers that had been seeded with exhaustive data stores and DNA records to try and encapsulate the breadth of human knowledge and existence. They had then been inserted into their long, thick sheaths, and joined with a power source, air and waste recycling plants, and accommodations for one human.

One lone technician in each long tube, to be sealed in and then interred, sunk, buried, and forgotten. The last remnants of a potentially lost civilization, hidden away to wait for more peaceful times to come, or just to mark our passing into history, and tell the story of our extinction.

Many governments had focused some measure of their resources on bunkers of some kind or another, either in case of defeat or to survive the aftermath of hard-won victory, but these were the concerted effort of TASC, and as their construction had neared completion, Captain Jennifer Falster had volunteered, for reasons the British officer to her side could only guess at, to be buried alive in one of them.

He looked at her once more, and saw she was staring away, to the west, to an island on the horizon. When she had mentioned a passing interest in the famous Deception Island, the second district of the now world-spanning TASC, he had offered to request a short furlough there, certainly he was curious about the legendary birthplace of the Skalm as well.

But she had refused, at first politely, and then more emphatically, until he had finally dropped the subject.

"Just let me know when we are close, if that is OK," she had said, "I would like to see it as we go past."

And so now she watched it drift quietly by. A haze of artificial light could be seen faintly wafting up from inside its sheltered bay. It was the only thing distinguishing the island's dark silhouette from the expansive Antarctic Peninsula that encircled it.

She watched it, her eyes clearly drawn to something about that place, though what that was, the commander could not know. But he knew her well enough to know she did not want to talk about it, so he left her to gaze at it in peace and returned his focus to the seas ahead. They were heading into the winter ice, into the season-long darkness, to meet the submarine that would begin tugging the four time capsules under the ice shelf to chosen crevices and trenches in the seabed far below.

# Chapter 56: Tactical Imperatives

Jack Toranssen ran the meetings as a matter of course. He was not the most expert in the room, not by far, but he was the most senior, and he held the respect of all, even the like of most, a rare thing in a senior officer.

But these were strange times, and this was a strange meeting. The array of military strategists in the room came from as varied a background as any gathered in history. This was a veritable Tehran Conference of opposing ideals forced into unity, enemies of enemies, corralled after years of wrangling.

Jack was not immune to the irony of his position here. He was not unaware of how instrumental Neal and Ayala had been in quelling resistance as they moved toward this still young ideal, a truly global military council. But here they were, and here he now sat, at its head, as the most senior TASC officer, a force not destroyed by the quiet unseating of its leaders, but strengthened by the emergence of Minnie and Mynd as its true core.

The minds were the heart of TASC now, and every day they continued to cement their reputation for being inviolate and unswayable. Jack spoke with them often, and here, for all intents and purposes, he spoke for them, even though subroutines of theirs monitored this meeting place and even provided the means by which such disparate parties could communicate with each other.

He spoke now in English, and all heard in their respective tongues without delay as he said, "I know we all want to focus on the pending reply from the … Yallan fleet, is that right, John?"

John nodded, not smiling. This was not how John wanted his allies to meet the rest of his race, many of whom he knew were no more in favor of this war than he was. But it was what it was.

At John's nodded approval, Jack went on. "The fact is, though, that any reply from them will necessarily take hours, maybe longer, and while our orbital and lunar observatories try to pinpoint their location in the night sky, we have much to do."

With acquiescing nods from around the room, Jack went on, "Okay then, let's start with a report from one of those observatories, shall we? Moira?"

At the vocal request, Moira appeared as a participant at the table. It was a clever trick. They had long ago relocated the bulk of the members of the committee to accommodations at District One, a complex that now spread for twenty miles up the southern tip of Sao Tome, and exceeded the island nation's entire population several times over.

This allowed this group to meet in person, but when a member or a presenting party could not be present, as was often the case, Remy did what was called a partial virtual construct, overlaying an image right into the visual cortices of the meeting's participants. So Moira now appeared to all the meeting's participants to be sitting in front of them, her bashful smile juxtaposing her sharp eyes as she waited expectantly.

"Welcome, Moira, thanks for joining us," said General Toranssen.

"Of course, Jack!" she replied, perkily.

"You have a report for us, Ms. Banks?" said the general.

She locked eyes with Jack, one of the many fascinating but frustratingly distant men she had met in the last few years, and began. "I do have a report, Jack, yes. It is far from conclusive, but I believe it must be looked into.

"If I can direct your attention to the first graphic portion of the report," she said, and in the minds of the attendees an image asked for attention. When granted access, the image leapt up and into the center of each of their perspectives.

"Here we see the solar system, not to scale, of course," she smiled at the preposterousness of such a notion. Where many might not have understood her point a few years ago, this was no simple planetary organization anymore, and all nodded at how silly it would be to believe for a moment that you could represent the solar system's grand scale realistically and have any of its components except the un and perhaps Jupiter be even faintly discernible.

This was a new military for a new age, a skyward facing military, and they had earned their places at this table through the hard graft needed to get up to speed on the distances involved. They understood the new paradigm, the larger number of zeros this war's measures were going to need.

"Here you can see the Earth. Here is Mars, which I mention only as its proximity to aphelion allows us to get a better glimpse at the approaching object and may be key to us singling out their estimated collision date."

"Um, Moira," said Jack, "let's stay away from that term. All of our models and their own communication point to impact being highly unlikely. They are aiming, or were aimed, rather, as near-misses, more to disrupt our defensive work."

"Of course, Jack," said Moira, contrite, "sorry. Estimated ... fly-by date."

She smiled at him. Her description was perhaps erring now toward the innocuous, as their passing, if it was allowed to happen, would wreak seismic havoc on the world's tides, weather, and, most importantly, threaten the very orbits of the elevators and their ancillary structures. But Jack let semantics lie and listened as Moira went on.

"We think we have them pinpointed. They would be easier to track but they are moving fast, incredibly so, as we had expected they would be."

"But you have a location?" said the diminutive Commander Guowei, his young but brilliant face as stern as any in the room.

"We have a range," Moira replied, cautiously. "A blur really. But enough to estimate their arrival as being between five and seven days from now."

"Only five days," said the Chinese commander, a boy still, by most standards, but a boy who had earned the respect of nearly everyone who had had the pleasure of working with him. But he was not one for nonchalance, and he sat now in silent retrospection as his keen intellect processed this information.

"*At least* five days," reiterated Jack, "but that still has them very far out, Commander. Far enough to do something about, yes? Once we have confirmed their speed range to more manageable parameters, we will be able to dispatch a squadron of Skalm to intercept them. Is that still your belief, Ms. Banks?"

"Mine, and Dr. Hauptman's, and Minnie's," she said, nodding.

"Now, on to the nature of that interception," said Jack, turning to the young strategist once more.

"Yes, General Toranssen," said Guowei, taking the lead as he had been warned he might need to. "We have been modeling ways to divert them, including the use of blunt force, as originally planned when we estimated the chances of this move on the Armada's part. We had not, however, planned for any released debris to still be inhabited."

Jack glanced at John, who was clearly uncomfortable with this turn as well, adding, as it did, to the list of crimes his race was guilty of in the eyes of the people in this very room. But humanity was not above reproach, and as if to emphasize humanity's own culpability, the Brazilian general spoke up now, saying, "I feel for those people, of course, but I fail to see how that is our problem."

John shot a look at the Brazilian man, then nodded. It was a fair point, not a kind one, but a fair one. But Jack did not see it that way.

"I think we can now categorize the people aboard the Yallan raft as refugees, whatever their original intent. At the very least they should be treated as POWs. As such, while their survival is certainly not our prime concern, it is not something I will have us discount out of hand."

John and Jack locked eyes once more, and Jack remembered a promise made in the hold of the HMS *Dauntless* years ago. He still did not take John's sacrifice lightly even to this day, and John saw that the man still intended to strive to earn John's allegiance.

"If, then," said Guowei, taking over once more, "we say that we are open to options that increase the Yallans' chances of survival as long as they do not also increase the chance of damage to our own operations, then Moira and I have some potential options."

Ignorant of the tension that had fleetingly filled the room, Moira spoke up again. "The key to our plan, Jack, lies in a mistake you just made."

He glared at her, perhaps a bit too harshly, and she jerked backward a little, before saying, "It's a common mistake. It is simply that we often refer to the coming object in the singular, *the* Yallan ship, when in fact it is many, linked together."

## Chapter 57: Watching the Wall

"You speak as if this is something we can agree to. Our parameters are clear. We have no negotiating power!" shouted DefaLuta over the ruckus.

It stilled a little from her wrath, but still emotions were high. The offer from the Yallans was incredibly tempting, and incredibly unexpected. But unfortunately, it was not theirs to accept.

In a quieter tone, DefaLuta went on. "The fact is that, as much as we might want to hear what they have to say, we cannot agree to their terms. When we voted on the motion to remove them from the fleet, they were excised from the Arbite's records. We simply cannot help them, not without violating the treaty, and we all know what the Arbite would do then."

"You talk and talk, DefaLuta," said Sar Lamati, "but you don't say anything we do not already know."

"Maybe, dear princess, because you refuse to *listen*?" the Kyryl replied, her expression icy.

"I don't know about the rest of you," said Sar, angelically, "but I, for one, am not proposing we bargain with the Yallans at all."

"If we aren't talking about negotiating with the Yallans," said To-Henton, confused, "then what *are* we discussing?"

"If what the Yallans say is to be believed, then someone here is a traitor," said Sar, eying them each in turn. "Someone in this very room."

Her eyes narrowed. "And I, for one, would like to know who. I would like to know who betrayed us so that I can watch as the Arbite inters them and then I would like to request to be personally present for their punishment, which I intend to make both lengthy and supremely unpleasant."

Quavoce stared at her. He shared her anger, or some measure of it. Questions and accusations had abounded throughout the group and the fleet as they had readied for the separation. They had not abated significantly during the ensuing final approach.

After the decision to separate, the Council's isolated bodies had been moved into a lone carrier ship so they could hide in subspace behind the wave of hurtling Skalm for the final year of accelerated approach. So they could then command that attack, and then use the ship's great engine to decelerate afterward and return to reclaim their prize.

They had passed the final year mostly in respite, but now the time for action approached, and this new call from the Yallans had reinvigorated the crucial question of how. Interred within the thick hull of an invisible carrier ship, massless, and formless in the wake of the vast sea of fighting craft it was preparing to send into battle, the Council now met once more, and Quavoce watched as Sar spread her malcontent.

"You know," said the Hemmbar, impartial as ever, "the Yallans may be lying. Attempting one last time to get a reprieve from the fate we consigned them to."

Sar stared at him, and said, "You know, Theer, if you weren't so profoundly uninteresting I might suspect you were the traitor yourself. Maybe you are. Maybe you have fooled us all."

The Hemmbar stared at her with unabashed surprise. Academic or not, he was not without a survival instinct, and now he started to bluster. "Princess Lamati, you surely cannot mean to suggest that the Hemmbar would engage in sabotage for … for what ends, Princess? What could possibly be our goal? We hold no claim to the foreign world, and carry few colonists."

"A fair point, Hemmbar," she said, shrugging, "but still. You did mysteriously engage in lengthy and often very pointed negotiations … or rather conversations … with the Nomadi Alliance. Conversations that led to the starting of your 'Military Oversight Committee.'"

"That oversight body? What are you implying? That is a purely analytical committee, Princess," said Theer-im Far, but the princess's focus was already elsewhere, on Shtat, who was trying gallantly to meet her gaze.

"And that brings us to you, *Shtat.*" She almost spat his name, and seemed about to say more when Quavoce intervened.

"Princess, please. These are all familiar accusations, discussed at length before," he said, as calmly as he could manage. "While I may even share some of your … concerns, we have investigated this quite exhaustively here, along with other points you have brought to the floor. In the absence of any conclusive evidence, can we leave these well-documented allegations for the Arbite and get on with the discussion at hand?"

She smiled at him, trying to forgive his abiding and unhealthy reasonableness, and said sweetly, "Of course, my lord. And that brings us back to the offer from the Yallans, an offer I say we should tell them we accept."

"But …" said To-Henton.

But she was flagging him to a stop her hand, and already saying, "I did not say that we accept their offer, To, only that we *tell them* that we have."

Quavoce shook his head. "Have we not tortured those poor people enough, Sar?"

"It is they, Lord Mantil, who look to bargain for their pathetic little lives with information that is crucial to the security of our fleet. I have no sympathy for them," she said, haughtily.

It was impressive, thought Quavoce, her ability to justify her actions. It was a genuinely remarkable talent, but one he did not share.

"I, for one, will not have any part in false treaty," he said, making sure to look his once-honorable friend, To-Henton, in the eye. "I will not lie during negotiations. No prize, however great, can sway me to do that."

But To would not meet his gaze, and he saw that the man was with Sar, his own ambition subjugating and slaving him to her far greater thirst for power.

Sar looked at Quavoce in exasperation. If he wasn't so goddamned honest, she would suspect him as well. And therein lay her greater frustration; everyone here seemed to have an excuse. Quavoce was too straight, To-Henton was too embroiled her own plans, Shtat was too weak, the Hemmbar too detached, and DefaLuta, despite all her many faults, was too self-serving.

She needed to know who the hell it was, she needed to know so badly that she wanted to scream. She turned to DefaLuta, now. She only needed two more votes.

"DefaLuta, will the Kyryl agree to tell the Yallans we intend to help them," she said. Then, in an attempt to crack a whip at the end, she caveated, "or are you too worried about what they might say?"

DefaLuta openly laughed at the tactic, then said, "Oh Princess, how obvious you are." But before the Lamat could focus her indignant fury into a vocal response, the Kyryl representative went on, "But don't worry, you have my vote. The Yallans are not long for this world no matter what we do. Better to get what we can from them. A little hope in their last hours won't do them any more harm."

Quavoce looked at Shtat, but the man was staring at Sar like he was caught in her headlights. He nodded his ascent meekly and Quavoce felt the system move forward, quorum now reached. Sar would have her false parley, and the Yallans would have a chance to say what they had to say, deluded now with an empty promise of help.

- - -

Closer to the center of a solar system now crowding with invading bodies, the Council were not the only ones responding to an offer from the Yallans. They'd had two hands to play, and in their desperation they had cheated, and gone all-in on both.

Þalía, the young Norwegian pilot, now pulled into graduation a year early, called out to her squadron as they finished their slingshot around the moon and began to close with the block of Yallan ships coming at them.

*Þalía:* 'interceptor squadron, we have clearance to come to [speed, traj.] and close with the yallans. target packages to come follow gravitational fix.'

A series of pings resounded in her mind, nestled as it was in its hardened plasma bath in a small compartment in one of her Skalm's akas while her body waited at home. She knew, on some level, of her evisceration, but the fundamental difference between her and the abducted North Korean children discovered at Deception Island was that she did this voluntarily, though mostly because she absolutely loved it, this feeling, this coursing sensation of power in her wings.

She was hungering to unleash her cores on the Yallan fleet, to open them up. But more than that, exercise in limited, even humanitarian dissection, she longed for the real fight to come, a fight she still thought was a year off.

But all that was about to change.

- - -

"We cannot wait any longer," said the chairman. "If they see the strike force behind us before we tell them of its presence, then they will know we have withheld precious information."

"Yes, because they will know they are doomed," said Freyam, manically. "Then we can negotiate with them again, not as supplicants, but as victors, pretending we speak for the fleet as a whole."

"Don't be a fool, Freyam, and don't make the mistake of assuming they are fools, either. That we have been abandoned by our Armada is as painfully obvious to the humans as it should be to you."

"The Council has promised to help us!" shouted Freyam, slamming his palms to the table. "Yet you persist in withholding what they request!"

"The Council's promises, my dear Freyam, are not worth the paper they are not even printed on," she said quietly. After the Council had contacted them, she had requested that their offer be sent from the Arbite itself, to prove its credibility. They had blustered in return about being insulted and having their honor questioned and the chairman had laughed humorlessly.

Freyam looked like a lost child. "That cannot be, Chairman," he said, looking down. "If their offer is false, then ... then we ... well, then we are ..." His voice trailed away.

The chairman did not respond. She merely stood up, not taking her eyes from him. He was right, he just refused to accept what he knew, deep down, was true. They were done.

The only question that remained now was the same one they had been faced with the day they had been cut free: what was going to be the manner of their death? If it were up to her she would see the humans burn for what they had done to her innocent and blissfully ignorant daughter, but the truth was that with humanity there still existed a slim chance. Not of rescue, but of at least survival. It would just be a longer death, but then what was all life but a long death, anyway, she thought, such was her outlook.

How her view of the universe had changed this last year, she thought.

She did not announce her final decision to the board. They were all useless anyway. The best of them had died in the attack that had nearly killed her as well, and they had been replaced with fools like Freyam, though he, at least, had a spine.

Using the executive powers granted her as chairman in their unabated wartime form, she stepped from her board room, still delusionally well appointed, and sent a message to the approaching human squadron.

"Earth force. As you approach, I feel it only right to share with you a suspicion we have. We cannot be sure, as we were left bereft of all but the most civilian of scanning tools, but we have reason to believe that there is another section of the Mobiliei Armada about four days behind us, hiding in our wake. We do not know their scale, but we would be remiss if we did not tell you of it, as you have agreed to at least let us live, if not to actually help slow our passage."

She smiled. That should at least protect them from the human's wrath for a while longer. Now to deal with her traitorous former colleagues. John Hunt, or rather Shtat Palpatum, you came to us to appeal to our gentler sides. In your ignorance of our ability to communicate, your identity to a fleet you did not know was so close behind us, you showed us your face and spoke in earnest. How should we repay you?

And how should we repay Mobilius as a whole?

She opened the second connection, the one facing into their past, rather than their uncertain future, to a council that had so thoroughly betrayed her, and said:

"Council members, former peers. You have asked for a good faith gesture on our part, in lieu of your promise to help us avoid the coming violent passage through Earth's near-space. Very well, as it would seem we have no other choice, we agree. On the topic of the identity of the Agent of the Advanced Team who betrayed us all, that Agent's identity is … Princess Sar Lamati."

The chairman almost wished she could be there to watch. They wouldn't believe it, not really, but she wished she could see the little bitch squirm, just for a moment.

# Chapter 58: The Truth Will In

*Remy:* <they have begun accelerating.>

"They have? Where?" said Peter, seated in the Congressional Hall where the representatives had gathered in emergency session. He spoke in that offhand tone all present recognized, it was the way you just seemed to speak when talking to one of the ever-present, ever-watchful minds.

As Peter spoke, the gathered international leaders and diplomats heard something else in his voice as well, panic.

In response to the Russian's question, an image appeared in their minds, an image of an awakening beast.

*Remy:* <we can only assume they saw our squadron change course. they know we have discovered their presence. here, we can see the aura of their engines.>

The view zoomed in, a view relayed from Þalía's squadron as they now struggled to reverse their headlong momentum toward the Yallan life raft and the looming threat now revealing itself behind it.

"What," said General Abashell, "is their number? And how did they come to be here? So early!"

*Remy:* <we do not know at this stage.>

*Minnie:* <if i may, remy, we do have one theory on that.>

There was no one who did not want to hear something ... *anything* that would explain this sudden change, and so Minnie spoke to them.

*Minnie:* <it would appear that quite a significant number of the armada's fighting craft stopped their deceleration after the missile-mine attack. mynd and i had suspected for the last three months that they might have, but the suspicion would not have changed any of our strategies measurabl ...>

"You knew about this!" shouted the Pakistani general.

*Minnie:* <correction, general, we analyzed the possibility, but only with a 0.07% probability at first. that probability grew slowly, over time, but only very recently did it become likely enough to be worth mentioning.>

"Worth mentioning! If there was even the slightest possibility that this could happen I would have thought that would have been worth bloody mentioning!" said the Pakistani.

*Minnie:* <not necessarily, general.>

There was a pause while they waited for some rationale, but none came. Eventually, Peter said quietly, but with a dose of his own, cooler brand of bile, "And why might it '*not necessarily*' have been worth mentioning, Minnie?"

*Minnie:* <because, like i said, this knowledge would not have changed the truth of our capacity for skalm production. we have close to exhausted the world's supply of easily available gold in the construction of the domes that now work, without pause, to build new fighting craft. no speculation about an earlier arrival date would have changed this production ceiling. i believe the phrase is, you go to war with the army you have, and we have as many completed fighting units as we could have had by this point in time.>

"And you don't think we could have done anything more?" said the Japanese ambassador, stunned by the machine's detachment.

*Minnie:* <mynd and i were not aware of any avenues that could be explored that were not being so, and with all available resources. But, ambassador, in answer to your question, if anyone was aware of something more that could have been done to increase production, then why would they not be doing it, irrespective of any theorized change in our enemy's arrival date?>

The room looked to the ambassador, and then to themselves, as the brutal honesty of the AM's statement hit home. No one present could have been called apathetic, but if any might feel they could have done more, could have sacrificed more, but had chosen not to, they did not mention it now, and nor would they in the future.

"So ..." said Peter, trying to wrap his head around the situation, "you *lied* to us? Because ..." the pause drew out, and when it became clear that the Russian was not going to finish his sentence, Minnie said:

*Minnie:* <we did not lie, as such, secretariat. we withheld this unlikely eventuality because it did not measurably change our plans. and because, if it proved to be true, then it seemed clear to us that it would mean the chances of victory in the coming war would become much, much slimmer, no matter what we did.>

Chances of victory. It was not much of a sugarcoating, but it was something, because what Minnie really meant was chances of survival.

Quiet sat like a pall on the room for a while, then, slowly, leadership instincts began to kick in. They could try to blame the AMs for not saying something sooner, but that would be just as futile as having known about this for a few more days or weeks would have been. They had done all they could, Minnie and Mynd had seen to that. They had built as many space-capable fighting craft as possible. They had constructed their defense platforms. They had trained their pilots.

Now it was time for them to help humanity brace for impact.

Now was the time let loose the dogs of war.

- - -

Banu walked along the broad beach. A group of boys walking from the main building at the beach's end came into view. She went to call out to them, then thought better of it, forcing back a ridiculous blush where none should come. She didn't even know these boys, they were from another group. She awkwardly tried to look out to sea, then, stumbling slightly in the hot sand, she looked down at her feet, then tried to stop looking down, as she seemed to always be doing, then didn't know where the hell to look.

She glanced back at them. It was not that she was taller than most of them, or even that she now had some reason to wear the bikini top she found herself reaching back to adjust. It was that she just didn't know what they thought of her anymore. What little experience she'd had in her strange, often isolated life had been first of a simple equality between boys and girls, then a baseless hostility, and now a strange merging of the two, where they were alternately rude and kind without reason or apology.

Minnie had been of little help on the matter, her father had been absolutely none, and she had not talked to Neal or Jennifer in years. But amongst the crowd of jocular youths, she now picked out one she did recognize and flashed him a smile of genuine affection.

His responding toothy grin was equally unabashed, and they naturally began gravitating toward each other, as the larger group left him, muttering, giggling, and gawking as they went.

But as she approached the boy she knew as Wednesday, she saw something new in his face. It was worry, and more than his usual proclivity toward pensiveness.

"Banu, how are you?" he said in his halting but proficient English.

"I am good, Suyoil, and you?" she replied, working hard to pronounce his Korean name correctly, even though he, like so many of the lost children of his nation, had barely been named at all, that cruel system labeling them as but days, months, or numbers, little more than an inconvenient truth.

But his suffering had not just been at the hands of the Great Leader. When her father had told her about the discovery of the orphan pilots, her kin in so many ways, she had demanded in ever more strident tones to be able to meet them, to help them in any way she could, as the Agent named Quavoce had helped and supported her over the years.

And so she now stood face to face with one of them, perhaps her favorite of them all, the thoughtful and quick-to-smile Wednesday God. She crooked her head with a motherly concern beyond her years and said, "Suyoil, are you okay? You seem … worried."

"Hasn't anyone told you, yet?"

Everyone seemed to assume that because she was daughter to the well-known Lord Mantil that she enjoyed some special privilege, some greater access, but the truth was that beyond the truly very special protection and love he afforded her, he took no great pains to inform her of what was happening in the outside world; quite the opposite.

Now that she thought about it, though, she did have a message to call him in her inbox.

"Told me what?" she said, curious.

He paused a moment. His eyes seemed to flicker, and Banu was reminded for a moment that they were the only visible part of him that was, in fact, really him. He had come last month from the latest of a series of annual upgrades that each of the orphans went through to simulate an aging process that they would never naturally endure. An unnecessary punishment in her opinion, but one deemed necessary by the powers that be to give them as natural a childhood as possible.

Those of them that had even wanted a physical body, that is. But that was not her concern now as Wednesday said, "You should hear it from him."

"Hear *what* from him?"

He looked pained for a moment, his synthetic face almost perfectly recreating the simple yet subtle emotion, but not quite, then said, "Something has happened. They're coming … they're coming earlier than we expected. It is to be days, not months, until …"

She looked at him, confusion crowding her brow.

"Come, let's sit," he said, as he began leading her to the shade of a palm tree. "I have to go anyway. I have to make sure Friday knows as well. You can come too, if you like."

She allowed herself to be pulled gently into the cool shelter of the wafting tree. He sat and leant his back against its lazily tilted trunk and she slowly lowered herself to join him. They made themselves comfortable and then closed their eyes, opening new eyes as they did so, into a second world as familiar to them as the real one, maybe even more so.

They found Friday not on the wing, but on the ground, in the darkness, prowling. They could not see him immediately. Wednesday had requested to be taken to whatever sim his friend was currently in, and so they now stood in a dark, foreboding forest and looked around.

"Friday?" called out Suyoil, the word now instantly translated into both the native Korean of the boy's first years and the soft Persian of Banu's, such was the magic of this place.

"Friday, where are you?" he said again, peering into the gloominess.

There was no reply for a moment, but then, noiselessly, a form began to appear in the shadowy gap between two thick tree trunks. Slowly the form took shape and the two children fought an instinctive fear as the big cat emerged from the shadows, its gentle footfalls belying its massive strength.

Unlike Wednesday and many of the others, Friday had refused the proffered body that Mother had come bearing once their existence had been revealed. The real world, such as it was, had never done anything for him. Even once they had discovered that this place was a lie, it was still a lie that pretended at caring a damn, and now that he knew the truth behind the curtain, he could ask the wizard that lived there to do the most amazing things.

Things like turning him into this awesome beast, he thought, as he stepped gracefully up to his two friends, one old, one new. He still had blood on his lips from the feast they had disturbed, its carcass lying but a few meters away, hidden to them, but so clear to his green, piercing, nocturnal eyes.

"Wednesday, Banu. If you have come to join me then you should know that those forms will only qualify you as prey in this place." He smiled a toothy grin of his own, knowing that he still wore his bloody lipstick.

But these were no ordinary pubescent teens. They had seen far greater horrors than this big pussycat, and to break the tension, and the pall she felt hanging over her, Banu walked up and neatly slapped the big black panther across his big furry face. He laughed in the form of a cat's rolling roar and lashed out at her, but this was as much her world as his, and she darted away, then around him, leaping eventually onto his back and grabbing two great fistfuls of his thick mane so she could hold on as he began writhing and twisting to get at her.

They could not, they both knew, hurt each other here, and Wednesday laughed at the sight of this seemingly imbalanced fight, enjoying the respite from his building worry, for this boy, unnaturally aged by circumstance, had seen the full depth of their predicament.

In the aftermath of the revelation of the orphaned flight school, Wednesday had, in fact, demanded only one thing as recompense. Not the body, that was a pleasant distraction, silly almost when you thought about it. And not vengeance either. He did not claim to understand the greater world he had suddenly found himself thrust into, and certainly nothing in his upbringing had taught him the inherent value of life, something that his saviors now told him was his unclaimed birthright.

He had asked only for honesty, and as the AM he had once called Mother had tried to help him adjust to yet another reality, Mynd had seen the simple justice in that. So when Suyoil had asked for details of the discovery of the alien strike force, closer now, impending, Mynd had given it to the boy, without redaction, as was his due.

"When you two are done ..." said Wednesday, as Friday managed to get his claws on his slippery rider and pulled her to the ground. Pinning her, he went to bite her, his huge jaw opening, but when it closed on her neck the teeth did not penetrate, as he had known they wouldn't, but they did tickle, and when he then drew his big, leathery tongue across her face while she struggled under his weight, she howled.

"Gross! So ... gross!" they were all laughing now, hers a high-pitched wail as Friday released her and she wiped the spittle with her sleeve, adding a few Persian idioms that defied translation. Friday laughed too, a fuller, deeper base, echoing outward in the otherwise ghostly silence of his erstwhile hunting ground.

They sobered up, slowly, brought back to ground by Wednesday's inability to hide his concern.

"We have to talk, Fri," he said. "There is news from Mother. You need to hear it."

## Chapter 59: Stepping Into the Fray

Birgit and Rob stood upright for the first time in four years. They stood and they could not resist the urge to giggle, more than a little giddy at the alien sensation. Subliminally enforced exercises had slowed their muscles degradation in the years in zero gravity, but had not halted it, and Rob felt the strain as he bent his knees slightly, his muscles groaning under even this fraction of his returned weight.

"Well, this is certainly different," said Birgit, a laugh laden with pleasant surprise escaping her lips. She was not surprised at the gravity, as such, not completely anyway. Her lengthy discussions with Minnie and Moira had predicted something like this. As the recent revelation had forced her to accelerate their work to access the IST core, the breaching of its outer housing had opened up a gravitational paradox. The pressure needed to contain the subspace singularity created, as a by-product, a localized gravitational field that now bled out into the IST's central cavity.

Her surprise lay in the fact that the effect was so localized that even though Birgit and Rob were standing only a meter apart around their improvised hole, the shielding, they were at nearly forty-five degrees to each other, so that each looked to the other to be below them, and standing on the side of a wall.

It was a strange sight, to say the least. They grinned stupidly at each other, and Rob made to step around the hole, but only managed to lose his balance again, as they had several times so far, and trip backward so that he once again got to enjoy the unpleasant sensation of feeling like the world was pulling him into a ball, his head and his feet now in different gravitational orientations as he came to ground.

He landed, such as it was, on the core again, now upside-down relative to Birgit, and she was about to laugh at the sight of his upended derriere when the IST's carapace groaned once more.

They both glanced outward, their amusement quickly banished.

"I don't like the sound of that, at all," said Birgit. The IST had been designed to withstand far greater pressures than this, despite its eventual home on a virtually gravity-less moon, but they had done much to undermine its once dense interior, and now Minnie's estimates on that interior's structural integrity were being put to the test.

"It's fine," said Rob, with feigned confidence. "I'm sure it's just settling. Adjusting to this new weight."

"Well, hopefully it is better at it than you are," she said, grinning, and he raised his hand, shaking as he over-emphasized the strain of its weight and then, slowly, as if fighting valiantly, raised his middle finger at her.

She laughed, then slowly lowered herself to her hands and knees so she could stare into the opened central space once more.

He repositioned himself so he could look into the hole as well. The shielding upon which they now crouched was itself three meters across, and they had sacrificed a lot to get at this space, but the next stage would be exponentially more dangerous. They had wanted to wait to do this until a rescue mission could reasonably be dispatched should something go wrong, but the choice had just been taken from them. The endgame had arrived, and now they had to get ready to cut into the inner sanctum, breaching the actual subspace event horizon, so they could manipulate its isolated controls directly.

It was an incredibly complex machine, but between them, Minnie and Birgit felt confident they now understood it. But this machine had never been designed for direct control, certainly not by the enemies of its creators, and certainly not to do what Birgit planned to do with it. To jury-rig it, she needed to get at the core machinery itself, and if they thought this new gravity was fun, the forces that would be unleashed once they tapped into this immensely potent core would be something altogether more powerful.

What it would do to the superstructure, to the battered crew module grafted to its exterior, and to them, they did not exactly know.

It wouldn't be fun, they could surmise that, at least, but Birgit's arguments that Rob should return to the module for this final step had fallen on deaf ears. She would need to subsume herself into the machine once they managed to connect to it, and she would be all but unconscious, as she had been during the birth of New Moon One and then the first Skalm, Banu's Skalm, during the last hours before their exile. While the IST reacted in whatever ways it was going to react, Rob intended to be here to do what he had to in order to protect her.

She looked at him, at her man, clad in his black suit but still so familiar to her. He nodded at her. She nodded back, running a final check of the mechanical and diagnostics tools they had managed to drag into this inner-sanctum, this heart of the machine.

After a prolonged pause, Birgit shrugged.

"I guess we should get started then," she said.

"I guess so," he said, and he hefted a fat laser into place and began cutting.

- - -

*Þalía:* 'we see it too. we see it all too clearly, guowei.'

*Guowei:* 'of course, Þalía, of course you do. here, look at this, [traj./decel. option 'j5']. while this course brings you closer, it will also force them to choose between objectives. as long as you maintain a random cycling during [phase pts. 1.4-2.1], they will still be out of effective targeting range. they will not be able to engage properly without sacrificing closing velocity.'

Closing velocity. Those words had become anathema to Þalía. Her small squadron had built up enough even in the eleven hours of their acceleration to intercept the raft of Yallan vessels that they were now heading headlong into the arms of a horde of Skalm so large it made her shudder just to look at it.

But there they were, she thought, as she forced herself to look at them again, her sensors filling her mind with data-rich vision as she studied the wall of craft.

*Þalía:* 'all true, guowei. all true. it is a good plan, thank you.'

But, she knew, it was a flawed plan as well. They were only five Skalms. A small number, perhaps, but still, as the overwhelming superiority of the enemy became clear, every part of the defense fleet started to count, and Guowei's plan, while it might save them from this fight, would also preclude them from rejoining the real battle to come. The battle for Earth, now only thirty-six hours away.

Five ships. Five choices. She removed Guowei from the conversation and reached out to her pilots. She could not, she knew, order them to do what she was now almost certain she was going to do.

*Þalia at Squadron:* 'squadron. we know what is out there. we know what they intend to do, both to us and to everything we have been trained to protect. we find ourselves faced with a choice. we can run. commander guowei, in all his galling brilliance, has come up with a way for us to live to fight another day.'

She paused then went on.

*Þalia at Squadron:* 'but, the truth is, there is only going to be one more day. and if we run we will not be part of the fight that happens on *that* day. we will be left to slowly bring ourselves to a halt and then, about a week from now, if his calculations are right, we will get to return to whatever is left of earth.'

There was no immediate response from her team. She knew all her pilots well. She knew they could see the wall of Skalms in front of them as well as she, the great bluff whose face they were now fighting hard to flee across as it descended on their home with nothing but murder on its mind. They had only minutes now. The closing was coming at terrible speed, the wall visibly growing in their spectrum-wide vision at an alarming rate.

It was humbling. The sensation of invincibility they had once felt as they were infused into the Skalm's form had vanished as their ships were dwarfed by the breathtaking scope of the enemy's might.

But now a message did appear, not from her squadron, but from Guowei. She was about to push it aside when she saw in its subject the simple note, 'read this before you decide to martyr yourself …'

Damn it, chuckled Þalía, why did he have to be so smart, that little, snotty upstart …

But she did read it. And as her pilots began to tell her, one by one, that they were with her, no matter what she decided to do, she smiled inside her herself, an ambient peace coming over her.

*Þalia at Squadron:* 'squadron, we have new orders. with me.'

As the closing came on, they did draw hard away, speeding toward the outside of the dispersed bulk of the invading horde. The enemy fire began to come as Guowei had predicted, not as a witnessed set of triggered launches, but as an act already responded to, a twitch in their trajectories as they entered the far reaches of the Armada's weapons range that sent them each into a set of randomized spins.

Where the approaching Mobiliei fleet had once hidden, the small squadron now became ethereal in their own way, a set of darting points, impossible to pin down, spinning in a randomized, lightning-fast dance to avoid the light-speed particle beams of their enemy.

Here, as the light-minutes between them became light-seconds, they were already somewhere else by the time the lances reached them, flying by the ships and out into eternity, the first interstellar tremors of the coming war echoing out across the cosmos.

The squadron's movements became more frantic as they approached, as the seconds became tighter, and the range drew near. They were still fleeing toward the outskirts of the fleet, for all the world as if they intended to escape.

*General Toranssen at Commander Guowei:* '¿will they make it?'

*Commander Guowei at General Toranssen:* 'they could … but if i know them, they will not.'

The closing was now almost upon them, and as the general went to demand an explanation from the young strategist, the small squadron turned suddenly, not on the fleet as a whole, the suicide mission Þalía had indeed been contemplating, but on a suicide mission of another kind, with a more worthwhile dividend from their blood investment.

*Þalía:* 'squadron, set spins and open fire, go!'

They were her last words as the five Skalms turned and cannonballed back into the sparser flanks of the Mobiliei force, loosing themselves at the cliff face with abandon.

The glancing was pure. The purest she had ever felt. She did not have time in the millisecond moment to see what her fellow pilots were and were not doing. She saw only targets, themselves dervishing now as they sought to dodge her violent flame in the close heat of battle.

There, she felt the briefest elation as her talons opened one up, finding it and gouging at it. They were here now, among them, only hundreds of miles apart, less than a blink in this light-speed battle. On some level, she felt as first one, then another of her sister-ships were exploded by the overwhelming return fire, but she fought on. She was faster than them, not by much, but enough to make them pay.

As the battle neared the end of its first true second, she was already past them by two thousand miles, alone at last in the cold night, but still screaming a hot hail of fire to the backs of her enemy. Now their fusion blaze came to her in earnest as the wall rotated to face her as one, this sector of the Mobiliei fleet turning their fire not only toward her, but around her, in a crisscrossed mesh that filled space to either side of her until she had nowhere to run and they opened her to the void and obliterated her.

As the light from the battle reached Earth, Guowei saw it as a swirling epoch of light dancing outward from the point of collision and then back inward suddenly, as the Mobiliei Armada's wrath returned in answer to the squadron's attack. It was fleeting, it was beautiful, and then it was over, and the Armada came on regardless, the small hole Þalía had cut in their flank closing as they turned their attention back to their real foe.

# Chapter 60: Final Solution

"It was madness!" said Quavoce, with a sternness that Banu rarely saw.

"It was not madness, Father," replied Banu, gently. "It was the opposite of madness. It was the only reasonable response to an unreasonable situation."

"The squadron could have survived, Banu," said Jack, though without as much as verve as the distraught Agent to his side.

"How many?" said another voice. It was Wednesday God, off to one side and quiet up until now.

"How many what?" said Jack, wondering why he was even having this conversation with these … children. But he knew why. The military and political bodies of earth had done what they could. The fleet was readying. The time for strategy was over, the role of the generals was starting to give over to the time of the warriors.

Now he owed Quavoce his support in this final argument with his daughter.

They all looked at the orphan pilot known as Suyoil as he expanded on his question, saying, "How many did Þalía's squadron kill, in return for their five losses?"

"As best we can tell, only four of the enemy were destroyed," said Quavoce, with a finality and coldness he quickly regretted.

"And how many," said Wednesday now, "would they have been able to destroy if they had chosen to save themselves instead?"

Quavoce stared at him, fighting a very real desire to hit the boy. Not for being right, but for supporting his daughter's insane scheme. But they could be as right as they wanted to be, they could parade through Milton SpacePort singing 'we are right, Quavoce is wrong' for all he cared, but he would still not let them do this. Not this. No way, no how.

"What you suggest, Banu, is … it is not … it's not …" Quavoce looked for the right word, but none that his systems suggested conveyed his point.

Madeline, also silent up until now, stepped in, "It's not *necessary*, Banu."

Banu looked at her and smiled with an understanding far beyond her years. "No, Madeline, of course it isn't. But then, all of this, all of this fighting, all of this war, none of it is *necessary*, is it?"

Madeline's forehead furrowed as she stared at the girl. But Quavoce was in far greater turmoil. Of course it was not necessary. Of course this was all completely absurd, and cruel, and pointless, just like any war, but here he was, and here were *his* people, *his* own very self, coming to kill this girl he had come to love.

And now here she was, asking to go out and face them, along with, apparently, a good number of the orphaned pilots, now housed in a donated resort in a very real paradise, an island called Jeju, a beautiful home which few of them really knew what to do with.

Banu turned to her father once more. They were standing in a white place, a part of Minnie's mind where these few people had come to meet at Banu's and Wednesday's request. Quavoce had asked Madeline and Jack to help him try and stop them, while Banu and Wednesday had invited three impartial but interested observers to listen in, just in case their opinions were called for.

One of those observers spoke up now, in the form of a Phase Eight like the one who had once played with a younger Banu, but a Banu who had already gotten blood on her hands, even then.

"If I may, Quavoce, this request of Banu's, it poses greater questions we should consider," Minnie said.

"Like?" Quavoce said, though he did not much care, his eyes were fixed on the young girl, no, young woman, in front of him.

"Well, like whether you actually have the right to deny her request?" said Minnie, matter-of-factly.

Minnie meant no harm by her statement, but the look on his face as he turned to her would have made a lion flee.

"What Minnie means, I am sure," said Jack, quickly, "is that after all that Banu has done for us, surely we owe her … well, we owe more than I can count, to be honest. But maybe, most of all, we owe her the right to make her own choices, as we most definitely owe Wednesday and his friends."

Quavoce stood, allowing every inch of his resolve to show on his dark-set face. "What we *owe* Banu is irrelevant. She is a child, a beautiful, brilliant, wonderful child, no doubt, but a child nonetheless, and the only thing that I owe her that matters now is my protection."

He looked around the group one last time, and then said with equal parts finality and fury, "My daughter *will … not … fight.*"

Banu reached up to him. She was tall now, tall enough to reach his face and touch it. She brought his angry eyes back to her, and they softened instantly as they connected with hers.

"Father," she said, a tear in her eye, "you have saved me many times, in more ways than you can know. But … don't you see that you cannot save me from this?"

There was silence a moment, and then Madeline spoke up, "Banu, your offer is very brave, there is no doubt about that, but we have enough pilots, more than enough, to pilot our Skalms."

"Not like her, and not like them," said one more voice, the last in the room. Guowei, watching detachedly as the majority of his mind worked on battle simulations with Minnie and Mynd, stepped forward now.

He walked up to Wednesday God and extended his hand. "A pleasure to meet you in person, Suyoil."

"Commander," replied Wednesday, nodding and taking the noticeably older boy's hand.

Now Guowei locked eyes with Quavoce and said, "It is a truth of piloting a craft like the Skalm that no one on earth who has ever had the privilege of doing it has ever been able to fully give it up."

He spoke with the bearing of the commanding officer, a role he had studied for years to take on. "Not even Wednesday here, with all his profound perceptivity when it comes to the harsher realities behind the simulations, has been able to go long without returning to the pilot's seat.

"I have had the pleasure of working with each and every one of the orphaned pilots over the last three years. Some have fallen by the wayside, many have never surpassed what my own peers have been able to achieve at the helm. But there are those whose younger minds could handle it, who thrived in the moment, like Suyoil, and by lucky happenstance, young Banu here." He smiled at the Iranian girl still standing by her father.

And now he turned to face the man in question, summoning his will to face the very palpable purpose on the famous warrior's face, and said to him, "Lord Mantil, I have listened to what you have had to say. Now I ask that you listen to me.

"That the orphan pilots represent the very best of humanity, I do not doubt. The simple truth, I am afraid to say, is that we do not have much hope, Lord Mantil. Some hope rests with the ambitious plans of Dr. Hauptman. Some hope lies with you and Agent John Hunt, that is for sure. But make no mistake, when Wednesday asked me whether I could use the skills of the orphan pilots in my fleet, it opened up whole new avenues in our planning."

Quavoce was faltering, visibly shaking as his emotions overflowed into the space, and he stood, looking for all the world like a lost child himself. This was too much, and he seemed to be trying to say something but could not. Banu could not stand to see the pain on his face much longer, and so said, softly now, close to his ear, "Father, dearest Father, would you not risk your life to save me?"

The expression of his machine emotion was a welling of tears brimming in his eyes, as she then said, "Allow me to do the same, Father. Please."

The words nearly broke him, and he buckled and sank to his knees, Banu's arms going around him as he fell. Seeing him reduced, as they surely knew they would be in his place, the gathered group began to depart.

The decision was made, they could all see that. Best to let Banu and her father find peace with it on their own. But as Quavoce's arms reached up to wrap around his daughter, trying one last time to hold her safe from this terrible nightmare, he was also initiating another process inside his mind. A final step.

As their options dwindled and the swarm neared, he knew it was nearly time for he and John to join humanity in a final roll of the dice. While pilots were lifting into place, elevators carrying their encapsulated minds aloft to waiting Skalms, while a StratoJet descended on Jeju Island and Banu's and Wednesday's unconscious forms were carried into surgery, Quavoce reached out to his lone compatriot, John Hunt, and told him he was ready.

The time was almost upon them.

# Chapter 61: Hitting the Fan

As tensions built on Earth and the final choices before battle were made, so too were conflicts coming to a head on the carrier ship hiding in subspace behind the approaching Mobiliei wall. Some had argued for sending more carriers, so they could hide the entire flotilla in subspace. But to do so would have cost them twenty more of their precious fleet craft, along with the commensurate additional transports numbering in the hundreds that would have needed to be cut free with them.

And so there was only one great flagship, bulbous and powerful. It carried the minds and bodies of the fleet captains, and the delegates and entourages of a Council now only hours from its goal, but these were but a dot on its hull, an afterthought hidden in the spaces between the ship's two main purposes.

The first of those mechanical organs was its main engine, now silent, decommissioned for this last leg, but readying for rebirth, a small herd of robotic maintenance craft roaming its massive form, both inside and out, testing and probing, checking and rechecking, as the minds inside began the countdown to reentry, and to the immediate effort at deceleration that would follow their coming victory. This was their lifeline, the powerhouse with which they would halt their hurtling progress, then eventually turn and rejoin the colony force to divide the spoils of the coming fight.

Mounted on the back of that soon-to-be reignited star was the globular Accelosphere generator, pulsing at quarter power now as it enveloped the fat ship in esoteric nothingness, slipping the carrier's mass under the skein of the universe to hide from prying eyes. They knew the sheer gravitational scale of the ship's mass and momentum would be making its presence known to the humans now. Something this large could not remain hidden forever, not even in another universe.

Somewhere in the cracks of the ship, a postscript in its humungous shell, co-opted blocks of cryo-units housed the bodies of those that had masterminded this masterful counterstrike. They were joined by tons of substrate mass thrumming with the processing power needed to keep their bodies alive, host their consciousness, and house the PMs and AMs that managed the plethora of systems firing around the ship and its vast escort.

They met in a now endless conference, one that still echoed with the Yallan chairman's last message.

"We cannot, surely, still be talking about this?" said Sar, with obvious impatience.

DefaLuta looked at the little princess. She enjoyed making the spoiled little princess writhe, but no, like her fellow Council members, and, apparently, the Arbite itself, she did not really believe the Yallan's final statement. The princess had a lot of qualities, few of them redeeming, but she was not a traitor, and she would never, ever, risk her own safety.

No, that was beyond her capacity. She was as constant as the stars in her profound selfishness.

But that did not stop DefaLuta from having a little bit of fun, as she added, "I speak only of the accusation on record, Princess. And I wonder, can you still be trusted?"

Few in the room were above seeing the princess get a taste of her own medicine, but if anyone was, it was Quavoce, and as Sar went to respond, it was he who spoke reason once more in defense of his off-and-on lover. "DefaLuta, I think that is quite enough. And Princess Lamati, Your Majesty, please, you must stop accepting this bait."

The two women faced each other and glowered.

After a moment, the Hemmbar added in helpfully, if also obliviously, "If it pleases the Council, I have an update on the force analysis of the fleet currently accelerating around Earth."

"It does please us, Hemmbar," said Sar, not breaking eye contact with the Kyryl woman smiling demonically at her. "Go ahead, Theer-im."

The archivist began his running update, referencing the shared PM analysis of his fellow contingents as necessary as he explained his own group's breakdown. Events so very worthy of record were coming thick and fast now as the battle approached, and if he had ever been guilty of showing emotion it was now, as something hinting at excitement for the scale of the coming slaughter flickered in his eyes.

As the academic spoke of force dispositions, closing velocities, the known capabilities of their enemy's ships based on their brush with Þalía's squadron, the ship flew onward toward Earth, the planet visible to the squadron now as a distant blue-green orb set against the orange fire of its sun.

While the Council discussed high tactics, descending often into regular bouts of semantics and frustrated distrust, the carrier flagship's complement of repair and maintenance bots continued their mundane and seemingly endless work in and around the ship's stout form.

But one among them, one of many that had apparently suffered from the long journey to this point, lumbered against its orders to the next of a series of loci it had received before the separation.

Other Pulujan stared with jealousy as a more advanced, and less biologically encumbered, cousin of hers jetted gracefully past. Three times she had been taken to task by such a machine, prompted by the same AMs that pinged her own craft in an endless attempt to reprogram it and get at whatever was causing it to keep malfunctioning. But the problem with her particular repair bot was, in fact, that she had infested the stupid beast with her own body, one that was now much reduced after some lo-fi amputations in the year since her attack.

It was a small comfort to her that those losses had also taken with them their measure of her itches and pains, as the repair bot that she had inhabited became her solitary confinement.

But the other, less contaminated repair robot was not interested in her today, and it spat propellant and flew by.

She looked after it and spoke to herself, as the isolated are prone to do. "That's right, you prancing metal fart-box, keep moving, if you know what's good for you."

In truth, she would have little chance if the robot decided to take her to task, but her work, while deadly, was carefully planned to appear innocuous. For now, that is. Unfortunately, that same circumspection was another source in a long list of frustrations felt by the lonely Nomadi.

"So ... here we go," said O-Pu to herself, as she rounded onto another panel designated by her enigmatic patron. "Refuse reprocessing plant 26. Great, another shithole."

She longed for the simple chance to just hit the big carrier she had roamed around for so many months, to punch it and rip at it, even if her puny muscles would be able to do little to hurt the great leviathan. Apparently, though, setting a synchronized cycling pulse into the poop processors would. At least that was what she had sensed her overseers had been forced to resort to when plans suddenly shifted and she had been sent to stow away on the pimply butt of this damn ship.

Her stubby maws punched outward as she approached, programmed to do some job by the ship's AMs. When she was close enough to her destination as possible, she initiated the reset protocol and sent the machine's brain into a circling loop that crippled its limited intellect, automatically sending out a maintenance request as it did so. But it would take minutes for the AI to recover, and even longer for any physical support to arrive, by which time she would have done what she had to do and be ready to sit back and listen once more as yet another AM whined and moaned about the bot's spotty performance.

Calling underlying protocols to task, she began to manipulate the robot directly, cursing creatively as she maneuvered the ungainly beast into place and wrenched open the plate coverings over the recycling plant's control systems. As far as the system was concerned, she was just a part of the glitch, her actions as seemingly random as the oscillating confusion algorithms bouncing around inside the robot's brain right now.

She felt as her system turned over once more, not much longer now, she sensed, struggling to punch a precise form into a set of pipes in front of her with fingers not designed for such delicate work. She checked a timer in her head. She was not programming any system or setting any explosives. She had no explosives to plant, and any such device would risk discovery anyway.

She was limited to subtle corruption, bending pipes to make them resonate to a specific note, one she would initiate at the right time, and hopefully cause a chain reaction. That was the plan anyway.

She hammered onward.

"There," she said with something approaching satisfaction, "not pretty, but it will do."

She felt the returning lack of control as a timer counted down to zero. She waited for it to come. The pulsating diagnostics began like a ringing of a bell she was standing in, her mind's limited access to the system vibrating with probing questions as a local AM sought the source of the machine's persistent failures.

But as it came she was already locked away once more. For all the world just a dim remnant of a damaged part of the bot, something that might have been replaced or repaired in peacetime, when resources were not so strictly allotted.

As the system's checks died down and their echo diminished, O-Pu did one last thing, dropping a hint into the bot's AI, not something so blunt or detectable as an instruction, but a subtle manipulation of the bot's next directive, a sachet of dye dropped into the stream, coloring it without affecting its flow, and off the bot trundled once more.

Where it was going she was not exactly sure yet. Another wonderful sewer, no doubt, thought O-Pu, as she retracted into her mind once more, to the limited sims she could create there to pass the time as the final battle approached.

## Chapter 62: Claustrophobia

Rob looked down at Birgit as she tried to get comfortable. It was not easy. As the pressure had increased, their returned weight had lost its comedy, like a joke written on the wall of a prison cell.

Where they had been half their earthbound weight yesterday, they were more than double it today, and the feeling was oppressive.

"If I could just get my other arm in here … just one … more …" Birgit's voice was strained as she pushed forward once more. Unlike before, now she was not only fighting to squeeze through an inadequate gap, but also struggling against a core that was actively trying to suck her in, drawing her inward into the hole with a growing strength.

"Birgit, darling, let me try again, please," said Rob.

"You … are … too … fat," she said against the pressure on her shoulders, wedged into the ragged gap in the core's shielding that they had managed to cut.

There was only one more layer between her and the actual event horizon. But she had no intention of breaking through that layer. If they did, the core would break free as had happened on an unlucky carrier ship during the missile-mine attack, and it would expand outward uncontrolled and suck them and a goodly section of the moon into oblivion.

Not that such a release sounded all that bad to her right now, and indeed she may end up causing just that kind of imbalance soon, if she wasn't careful. But even that was not possible, not yet. Not until she got access to the supermotor controls nestled inside the mantle, sealed in here decades ago when the ship was constructed. They had never been designed to be accessed, thus they had been buried inside the machine, next to the heart, like pacemakers sealed into the body of the IST.

Maybe with the right access they might have been able to do some of this remotely. But there were limiters in here, in this place, that she needed to remove, balances she needed to unlock, if she was going to tweak this giant's tendons and make it dance to a different tune.

"Just a … almost there … Jesus, Rob, where are your hands?"

He realized that in his attempts to help support her upended body in the tight space, he had accidentally started groping her in a most unladylike fashion.

"Oops, helllo!" he said, giving a quick squeeze before saying, "Oh, get over yourself. Seriously, Birgit, darling, do you need me to try and reach it myself?"

"No, no, just, God, try and lift me a little, my left shoulder feels like it is going to snap."

He longed to do this for her, but this was tinkering on a level that belied instruction. And he was, in fairness, a good deal larger than she was. But he could only imagine how uncomfortable she was, head-down in the small grotto they had carved, even though they were, disconcertingly, hanging at right angles to the moon's surface.

She grunted at the effort as she tried to shut out the ache in her neck. She stretched into the tight space, her eyes closed, her internal map of the machinery in here guiding her fingers. She was filling in the gaps in her and Minnie's understanding of the inner-workings of the IST as she went, and now her daughter reached out.

*Minnie:* <birgit, if you give me control of your arm, i can try.>

*Birgit:* 'knock yourself out.'

It was a good idea. She should have thought of it herself. Birgit let her mind go and felt as her hand began moving on its own, with a dexterity she could not, in fairness, come close to matching. If they'd had a Phase Eight with them this would have been so much easier. But then, if they had a Phase Eight with them a great deal would have been easier, no doubt. But they did not. They had one remaining wrecker, burly and completely useless in this cramped space, and they had each other.

And they had Minnie, now co-opting Birgit's fleshy limb as best as she could.

*Minnie:* <¿while i am 'knocking myself out,' would you, in fact, like me to knock you out as well?>

Birgit laughed as heartily as she could with her chest compressed into the space.

"Charming!" said Rob, chuckling as he listened in on their conversation.

*Birgit:* 'no, thank you though, minnie. i'll stay here, if i can bear it. but you could numb this pain, i suppose.'

The balm was almost instant and breathtaking in its relief.

"...ficken danken!" Birgit exclaimed, reverting to long dormant Germanic idioms as her shoulder deadened. It was a cheat, a scam, she knew that. The pain was there for a reason. But until this was done the pain was just a nuisance, and one that was better ignored than suffered through.

Minnie had not shut off all sensation though, and both Rob and Birgit felt as the aftereffects of their breaching of this place resounded outward. The core's pressure cage was starting to draw its surroundings inward, tugging on the already undermined superstructure, and Rob glanced around himself as the IST's outer housing began to give and the whole machine shuddered with seismic fault.

"What the hell was that?" mumbled Birgit from inside the core.

"Nothing, we're fine," said Rob, looking up through the hole they had both climbed through into this outer-sphere. While the wrecker had been completely unable to fit into this space, they had decided that it was worth reopening one of the sealed ports in the carapace to allow it to climb into the main cavern, and Rob reached out to it now, looking through its eyes.

The space they had been spinning in only a few days before was visibly shrinking. The shudder they had felt had clearly been a spar giving under the pressure, and now the whole structure was starting to cave in, rolling over and crushing itself as the subspace horizon pulled at its surroundings, and at the moon itself, mashing its own housing into the ground as it did so. Rob knew that Minnie could probably handle the robot as well as whatever she was up to elsewhere, but he needed a distraction, if only for a second.

He took control of the wrecker and brought one mammoth foot of the robot around the surface of the core it was standing on so it could stand astride the small hole which he and Birgit were crammed inside. As the IST as a whole slowly rolled over, turning onto its side and crushing the outer shield inward, he brought the wrecker's big arms upward, braced its massive fists and readied it.

The force came on hard, and the surly machine's muscles sang with the pressure as it resisted, putting all its might into it. The metal gave in fits and starts, slowly starting to fold inward around the balled fists of the wrecker as its broad feet cratered the plating around the core itself. Rob reset its parameters and left it to its Atlas-like end, leaving no room in its instructions for self-preservation as its muscles joined the last pillars supporting the roof over their heads and the world began to close in.

"Rob, what's going on out there?" said Birgit.

"It's nothing, just the wrecker settling in."

"That doesn't sound like nothing, darling," said Birgit, in a tone he had come to know all too well, a tone that said, simply, 'don't bullshit me.'

"Well," he replied, coming back into himself and answering his love with the candor he knew she was demanding, "if you must know, my sweet, the IST is rolling onto its roof and starting to suck its head right up its own ass. Does that clear things up?"

"Yeah, I would say that sums it up pretty concisely," she said after a moment.

*Minnie:* <i believe captain cashman is describing the effects of the breach on the i.s.t.'s outer hull.>

*Birgit:* 'yes, he is, minnie, in his own, wonderful way. ¿i am assuming, therefore, that getting out the way we came is looking … unlikely, at this stage?'

*Minnie:* <my systems tell me that the crew module is also breached, and now partially under the i.s.t.'s mass. this was one of things i had feared when you decided to push forward, mother.>

*Birgit:* 'yes, minnie, i know that, thank you. but now that we are here, we might as well get on with it, hadn't we?'

*Minnie:* <yes. on that topic, that said, you are now touching the connections, i have managed to expose them. there is a quicker way to complete this. i can connect you directly to the device. you will lose the fingers, though, maybe the hand.>

*Birgit:* 'i fail to see what use it is to me now, anyway. do it.'

Minnie did not enjoy it. But with the road behind them destroyed, there was only the uncertain path forward. She apologized to her mother and then pushed the woman's cramped finger and thumb forward, driving them into the sharp connections she had exposed and pressing the metal into the flesh. The connection was spotty at first as electricity coursed through the veins and tissue, but soon Minnie found the pattern in the pulses coming along the nerves running up Birgit's arm.

She started connecting the lines, using the neurons in her mother's arm to find and code the signal within the inner brain of the IST. Once she had connection, she started to talk to it. It was a strange conversation as they learned each other's language, but she'd had practice doing this with the ancillary IST systems on their way here. She knew the lexicon.

It would take some time, but soon she would be talking to the machine and introducing it to its new mistress, Dr. Birgit Hauptman.

# Chapter 63: The Red Zone is for ...

Now they began to move with purpose. The last were being birthed now. Banu, minimized and sealed into a cylinder about twenty centimeters across and half a meter long, was rushed to rendezvous. The cylinder had its own power source, and a hardwire optical fiber linked to a gelport in its tip. As it arrived at Vladivostok, the ship it was going to be loaded into was already in the final stages of its unloading from the Russian Resonance Dome, as each of the world's seven dome facilities completed one last cycle of their aborted production run. This, then, would be one of the last Skalms that would be ready in time to join the fight.

That said, given this particular Skalm pilot's reputation, this was one that many had high hopes for. In the southeastern sky, a series of lights could be seen appearing. They were plentiful and bright, and they moved fast east to west, overtaking the sky even though they moved far above it. It was the second time the mobilizing starfleet had passed in the last few hours.

Banu could not see it, though. Her mind was in a last moment of silence. The capsule was sealed and shielded, its contents highly pressurized and cushioned in a jelly of oxygenated plasma being slowly stirred around the soft grey tissue. The now-isolated organ had been carefully prepared, pumped full of nutrients and attached to a cycling pump that would feed it from now until the war ended, for better or worse.

The capsule was black, coated in multiple layers of super-conductive plating, radiation shielding, and then more inner plating. The only markings were a sprayed-on id tag saying simply: Captain Banu Annat Mantil, Terrestrial Allied Space Command. As the arriving StratoJet came within fifty feet of the ground, the capsule was born out of the still landing fighter jet by a hulking Phase Twelve, the only of its kind, which leapt clear and was away and running before the StratoJet even touched down.

Hektor did not have much to do anymore. He was occasionally tasked with some policing or protective duty, but for the most part the time for people like Cara, Bohdan, Jung, and himself had passed. They were relics of ground-based conflict that had no place in the new era. An era where wars were between airborne gods, fighting not over land, but over whole planets.

However unwittingly, Hektor had once shared a home with some of these children, these orphan pilots. When he and his cohorts had been acquitted in the tribunal that had seen Ayala and Neal pushed into obscurity, he had volunteered to be stationed wherever the children went, to do his part to help them adjust to their new cybernetic bodies.

He'd had the pleasure of meeting the girl whose casket he now carried on several occasions since then. Even if he hadn't, he would still know who she was. She had saved him once, as his legs were taken from him on a concrete battlefield outside Pyongyang, and now he was carrying her, not to safety, but to the closest thing she knew to home. A permanent birth near the heart of a craft she had been the first human to tame.

The field around the Skalm was deserted. It was about to get very hot here. As Cara and the others delivered the other orphan pilots to sites around the planet, Hektor ran under the great gantry cranes that held the still beast, under its long, slender, almost delicate-looking arms, toward its spiny heart.

He knew it was already being awoken. The earthfleet was waiting for them, these last few warriors. The defense force was waiting to depart, and they would not wait much longer. So the stellar core at the heart of this beast was even now being prodded, the dragon opening one lazy eye as the fire started to bubble in its belly.

But it needed a brain, a rider, a tamer of the beast, one who could subsume herself in the mad ride and focus the great power starting to churn inside its five hearts.

Hektor ran hard, a timer running now in his brain. He knew where it was, the small slot, so innocent, in one side of one of the great akas. There, ahead, so close to one of the fat nozzles, a place he would not want to be anywhere near in less than a minute.

He leapt in one powerful bound at the scaffolding that had been placed there for this purpose. Whoever had been slated to pilot this craft was no doubt nearby, being informed even now that they had been superseded. When they heard by whom they would probably be okay with it, not that it mattered. This was Banu's right, thought Hektor with relish as he connected with the top of the scaffolding and began clambering the last meters toward the slot. He raised Banu up as he approached, lifting her and turning her capsule, slowing just long enough to make sure she was perfectly aligned before pushing her home.

The wakening craft knew she was coming. It sucked the capsule inward, pulling it in with magnetic need, until the gelport at its tip connected with the matching one inside it and Banu was released back into the machine, opening her eyes from the perfect silence of her capsulated home into the full spectrum truth of the Skalm's full contact sensor suite.

She took in the world anew, through multi-phase, self-verifying, panoramic eyes and smiled inwardly. Then the familiar pulse came, a rising chorus as her hearts came online. She longed for it. She called out to the ship, come to me, come to me and join with me. Let us fly. In a part of her that was already falling away, a quickly set aside humanity, she sensed the machine man running with all his might away from the hot death of her might. And so, as life came to her body and she sucked in a great lungful of fire, she hesitated just a moment, as long as she could resist this call of the wild so he could get somewhat clear.

He was tough, she knew, and he was going to have to be, because she could not resist any longer. With a profound ecstasy, she let her returned power explode from her, ripping the Skalm from the ground, shrugging off the cranes and melting the scaffolding, all forgotten and behind her now, like the gravity she could so easily ignore. The Skalm bellowed with joy at its freedom, rocketing straight upward toward a passing cloud before stabbing straight through it, its engines visibly tearing the vapor into a streak of orange as Banu departed the atmosphere for perhaps the last time.

Hektor came skidding and sliding to a halt, his suit having barely saved him, alarms blaring as the heat radiated off him and the surrounding scorched earth. Well, that was one way to see a launch, he thought, before turning his attention skyward.

An old German battle song started to drift from his lips as he watched the rising star move off to join its brethren.

"If it storms or snows, or the sun smiles on us,
The day burning hot, or the icy cold of night.
Dusty are our faces, but happy are our minds, yes, our minds.

"Es braust unser Panzer im Sturmwind dahin," he said, quietly. "Then roar our tanks in the storm's wind."

- - -

*Quavoce at John:* 'she is gone, john. she is gone.'

*John at Quavoce:* 'i am sorry, my friend. you can still speak to her, though. go, talk to her. we have a little more time.'

*Quavoce at John:* 'no, we do not. we cannot wait any longer. it is time we put me to the test. it is time to rejoin.'

*John at Quavoce:* '¿are you sure, quavoce? we can wait, and perhaps should. i can say that i feel almost certain of how the real you will react to your reintroduction, but … there is still a chance.'

*Quavoce at John:* 'of course there is a chance. i cannot know what has transpired on the other side, what new allegiances i may have formed. but if i wait any longer, well, then no matter what the real me decides to do, she will still …'

*John at Quavoce:* '¿you hope to save her?'

*Quavoce at John:* 'she is, my friend, all that really matters to me anymore.'

*John at Quavoce:* 'then, my dear, dear quavoce, i am more than ready to put my faith in you once more.'

*Quavoce at John:* 'thank you, john. i can only hope it is well placed.'

And with that they reached out, through Remy, to Minnie, routed themselves through the local subspace tweeter on Hekaton and outward to the moon, where they bounced outward through an already overcrowded subspace frequency to Phobos. Here their signal recrypted itself, reformatting into something alien, something not of Earth, and its tendrils reached out across the void to the ship hiding in the wake of the Armada, and made its presence known.

## Chapter 64: Psychotic Conundrum

Sar looked at Quavoce. Was he ignoring her?

"Lord Mantil, the question is a simple one," she said, but again he merely stared off into space.

After a moment's wait, where her impatience threatened to once more capsize her mood, he responded quietly, "Something unexpected has happened."

She looked at him. "Explain?"

He returned her plaintive gaze for a second, then said, "I have just received an encrypted signal from Earth. From the Advanced Team. It carries the rejoining code. It is requesting to merge its memories with me."

He looked at the group, but they were all pinging the Arbite, seeking confirmation of this stunning turn. There had been two signals, it seemed. One to the Mantilatchi, the other to the Nomadi.

All eyes, including those of Quavoce, turned to Shtat, who was just as stunned as they were. The signals were, by design, encoded to the two men, and to them alone. They had never been intended as communications tools. The IST had been designed for that. This had been solely for the legally mandated rejoining of the Agents' personalities, an unalienable right by law and treaty alike.

"Those signals are *not* to be allowed through," said Sar emphatically.

"Why not?" said the Hemmbar, genuinely unaware of a reason one would refuse to receive information, especially from yourself.

"Because the other Agents, including, most notably, my own, have not made contact as well. This is a trick ... or ... they are ..." she paused, staring at Quavoce. She could believe Shtat was a traitor, that she could believe all too easily, if he wasn't just such a pussy.

But Quavoce. No, not him. Surely not him. He just wasn't capable of such a deception.

But that her Agent-self would not also be reaching out was setting off alarm bells in her mind. She had accepted the likely destruction of her own Agent as a part of the whole team, it had angered her, but she had eventually accepted it. But if anyone had survived, then why not she? There was only one conclusion, and she kept coming back to it.

"I demand to see that feed first," she blurted, looking as surprised as everyone else that she had said it.

Quavoce looked at her. Surely she didn't suspect him? They did not always see eye to eye, but that anyone could think him a traitor was too much, just too much. With a look of indignation that made her stop in her tracks, he leant forward and said, "By international law, and by right of the treaty, you have no right to withhold any Agent's mind its rejoining. If you wish to audit the feed, I will happily release the data stream for analysis by the Arbite once it is finished reintegrating. But make no mistake, no one, and I mean no one, will have access to my own memories before I do."

And with that he was gone, his form freezing in place as he opened himself to the data flow and it began decoding itself directly into his mind, merging with his personality as that unique map unlocked its secrets.

Sar looked now to Shtat, thinking to have more luck ordering him about than she'd had with the outraged Mantilatchi leader. But he was as still as his partner as he also began communing with his unexpected other self.

- - -

The process was a long one, taking over half an hour. Nearly ten years of sights, sounds, and smells had been condensed and compressed into an abbreviated language only a matching mind could translate back into decipherable memory, but it still took a long while to flow through.

The recovery took even longer, though. The shock of such a pure flow of experience, following two simultaneous but divergent timelines, was profound at the best of times, but both these examples were uniquely shocking.

For Quavoce, it was a merging of two separate and opposing ideologies that agreed only in the matter of honor. But even that defining part of his ethos was now tested as the unification must, inevitably, lead to broken oaths and the betrayal of ones close to one version of him or the other. The cerebral schism it brought left him reeling, and the process drew out.

Lord Mantil's medical monitoring AI reported to a waiting and watching Council that he had entered a state of severe shock, and allegations of foul play on the part of the humans began to come. Psychological weapons were not unheard of, it was one of the reasons a connection like this was so personal, so fingerprinted. But they were extremely difficult to pull off, and fear started to build at just the thought that their enemy might have found a way to hack these individual's inimitable mental fingerprints.

For Shtat, on the other hand, the merging was both stranger and also far more straightforward. The memories came together, but where Quavoce's clone had sent back an argument, a psychotic conundrum, John Hunt had sent back a piece to a puzzle, a piece that Shtat had not even known he had been missing.

For the memories of John's ten years on Earth were not alone, they came with an intermittent flow of memories from before the Armada had even departed. They seemed alien at first, like so much of what the hitherto modest man was suddenly learning, but as they locked into place, they revealed to Shtat a truth he'd had forcibly removed from his mind, removed and formed into a whole new person, a counterfeit man who believed himself to be called Kattel, a lowly engineer whose empty cryo-unit was still back with the transport ships.

Shtat Palpatum, the man who had been called coward, who had been called fool, even by the very people whom he had plotted with before the mind swipes had amputated the massive genius of his connivance, opened his eyes and smiled at his peers.

He looked around. All eyes were on him. He was back in the Council chamber. He thought quickly. He had a decision to make. It was not a question of what he was going to do next, no, he knew with a preternatural certainty what he must do next. The only question was whether he should hang around to see whether Quavoce would join him, or leave now, initiate his fleet contingent's declaration of war against the rest of the Armada, and get busy dying.

"Well, Shtat?" said To-Henton, breathlessly, "what have you learned?"

"Why are you not sharing the data flow?" added Sar.

And then, in a rare moment of agreement, DefaLuta added, "Yes, Shtat, you must open your mind for audit. Arbite, we demand to know what has been sent to the Nomadi representative."

But they all knew they could not demand such a thing. Their treaty allowed them to see any inter-race communications, but intra-contingent talk was sacrosanct without evidence of malfeasance, and intra-mind talk was most certainly sacred, a fact that had driven the Nomadi ... no, Shtat's plan from the start. He smiled once more. What a smart boy he was. Smart and dead. He laughed.

"Do not worry, my friends," he said. "All is well. I will reveal the information in time, I promise." He spoke with a self-assurance that was unfamiliar on the face of the previously feeble Nomadi, and Sar's eyes narrowed at the man.

But Shtat ignored her and turned to look at Quavoce, asking, "Has he spoken yet?"

"No," said Sar, simply, still glaring at the suddenly enigmatic nomad.

"Arbite," she said now, "it is clear that this man has been corrupted somehow. This is no longer the agreed upon Nomadi representative. I demand a hearing."

The Arbite's response was non-vocal, and came simply as a note into her mental in-box: 'no such discrepancy in his mental state has been found by his medical ai. shtat palpatum remains a rightful representative and council member.'

Shtat smiled serenely—no, wait, was that smugness on his face?—and stared at Quavoce. The Mantilatchi man was, Shtat saw, coming around. But behind his calm demeanor, the Nomadi's finger was already on the trigger. If he saw the slightest hint of false-action in Lord Mantil's expression, he would loose his ships and take the internment he knew would instantly follow his declaration.

Quavoce looked around, clearly still in shock.

"Quavoce!" said Sar. "What happened? The Nomadi refuses to tell us. Open your data stream. Do it now! Tell us what the hell is going on!"

Her tone descended into a rant and Quavoce looked slowly from her, to To-Henton, and finally to Shtat.

At a request from the Nomadi, the two men stepped into a different place, a quieter place. They knew their conversation would still be monitored but they didn't care. Quavoce just needed to face this man, now that he knew the full story.

"Hello, Quavoce, how do you feel?" said Shtat.

"I feel like I have been hit by a Skalm," Quavoce said, and Shtat smiled for a moment before becoming serious once more

"I can only imagine," said Shtat, then, "I wish we could talk about it more, but I am afraid you have a choice to make, and it is not one that will wait."

They knew the Arbite's eyes were upon them, as were the Council's, watching for the slightest hint of foul play. Though it did not show in their now serene expressions, both men were tensing, like dueling gunmen facing each other down in dusty Main Street, eyes narrowed and unblinking, hands itching by their sidearms.

"There is no doubt about that, Nomadi," said Quavoce, icily. "A choice must be made."

"And?" said Shtat.

There was a long pause and then the slightest of smiles appeared on Quavoce's face. It was not a happy smile; indeed, its sadness was as profound as anything Shtat had ever seen.

Whatever happened next, Shtat knew he loved and admired the man in front of him. But this moment would not wait for them any longer. He was about to draw, to light the whole barn on fire, when Quavoce said quietly, "John, my friend, I fight for my daughter."

And with that they both nodded one last time and then fell away, triggering events as they went, calling protocols to task, ratcheting treaty promises into place and knocking them off one by one as they severed themselves and their fleet contingents from the whole, declaring themselves rogue. As they reclaimed control of their ships, control that instantly cost them their places in the Arbite's graces, they sounded the alarm to their respective warriors, countermanding orders as the bonds of the treaty crumbled.

Like any coalition, the allegiance of each member nation had always been voluntary, but on this mission, if you did not stand with the whole, then you stood against them, that was the Arbite's mandate.

The freedom to renounce had once been the backbone of Sar's finagling as she had envisioned a world ruled over by her and her friends, and devoid of the likes of DefaLuta and the chairman. But now she could only watch in horror as one of those friends committed suicide. To-Henton was just as stunned, and said nothing for a moment as the Lamati stared ahead and recounted Quavoce's last words. "Daughter! What daughter! Quavoce, you have no daughter!"

For it was suicide, what they had just done, there was little doubt about that. Even if the combined squadrons of Nomadi and Mantilatchi Skalms could survive the coming fight, which they most certainly could not, their leaders, still in hibernation in the carrier's hold, were most certainly doomed.

The Arbite's response was swift and harsh. It had neither compassion nor hesitance as it reset its view of the two men from dignified leaders to damned traitors. No sooner had the two men made their declarations than their minds were cut off and promptly opened up for review, any sanctity quickly violated.

At the same time, the six hundred ten Skalms still loyal to the cause felt a sudden, diametric shift in their spatial awareness. Their visions, previously focused ahead on an earthfleet that now could be seen accelerating outward to meet them, turned inward suddenly, to two sectors coloring red, and the great Armada began to eat its own as the cleansing began.

## Chapter 65: The Shattered Cliff

The forces moved in tidal washes. From in front, from the perspective of Earth, the fire from the clash was a liquid ocean of light, twisting and turning in eddies and whirlpools like a violent wave breaking into a chasm in a cliff face, buffeting and smashing into itself as it spent its thousand-mile energy and cast itself at its confines.

The two sectors that had broken free did not have the chance to come together. The ramifications of their leaders' choices were too immediate and too profound.

For the Mantilatchi PM, the choice of its head of state triggered simulated strategies formed as a matter of course, contingencies gestated with unused processing power during their long journey and stored away in oocyte preservation, but now suddenly birthed into practice as the pilots were thrust into battle.

For the Nomadi PM, the choice felt just as impetuous, but its leaders had allowed it perhaps a touch more resource and time to consider the chance of revolution, either of itself, or by its more powerful allies. Even so, it still responded to Shtat's call to arms more as a reflex than a thoughtful choice.

For this was not something that could have been actively prepared for. The military units were individually isolated and encapsulated, if only to protect them during the heat of battle. They could be spoken to only by their commanding AMs, and any order to them had, until they declared against the Armada, passed through the Arbite's hands.

But all thought of machination, rule, and treaty was irrelevant now as the swords came out. At the knife's edge, in the shielded pilot's seat, there was only the instant, all-encompassing battle. For the Skalms, for the minds that inhabited them, this time, this exclamation point at the end of a conversation they had not even been party to, this was a time for action.

The Mantilatchi and Nomadi PMs, unable to combine their forces from their disparate places in the fleet, instead took the first second of battle to pull inward, dragging themselves into two loose balls of fire, swimming and accelerating around themselves as they launched into a randomized dervish spin that was already lacing the voids around them with fire.

But the greater numbers of the responding Mobiliei forces were moving as well. At first swimming out and away from the focusing loci of each rebelling sector's forces, and then forming into squadrons and starting to stab and probe at them, lashes of light whipping this way and that as the two sides danced around each other in the first moments of conflict.

From only two light minutes out, Banu watched as the first sign of the battle reached her, the wall coming suddenly to violent life. The signal arrived a moment later, bouncing around subspace as the far-reaching eyes of Earth watched the enemy line light up. She screamed at the sight, partially out of delight but partially out of frustration. If she could have redoubled her efforts to close with them, she would have, but like her fellow pilots, she was already giving everything she had, their arrowhead formation, striking out from Earth right into the torrent ahead.

*Banu:* 'they have turned! you have done it, father! he has set his fleet to join us!'

Her heart was pumping hard, sending out five foils of white-hot impulse as she drove herself outward to join the fray, but there was something between them still. The unfortunates. The sad inhabitants of a no-man's land that was about to be crossed at speed.

*Mynd:* <you are coming up on them now. ¿may we suggest you engage now?>

*Guowei:* 'we are on it, mynd. pilots, i have inputted a thruway. the leading point will open them, while the flanking ships separate the remaining pieces.'

'Thruway' was an accurate enough description. As a final courtesy to the Yallan raft, a warning was sent, telling them simply to ready themselves, but the chairman did not, in the end, have the PM disseminate it. She watched as her peoples' end came at them from Earth, as the crematorium's fires ignited.

Maybe the Hemmbar will have recorded their story, the chairman thought, but she did not really care anymore. She was, at the end, only sad that she would not know how it all turned out. But her care was only academic. She knew she had no horse in this race anymore, her stable was only knacker's fodder now.

The TASC arrow sharpened as it came up, pulling inward as the lead ships redirected some of their stellar power forward, lancing into the dark mass in front of them. The power of the blast rippled throughout the big raft, buckling it instantly, but this was just the first stab of the tantō, a blade that now twisted in seppuku rage as the earthfleet thrust onward, slicing the belly of the Yallan raft and parting it with hot steel.

The fleet closed with increasing speed, but this final blockade was also moving, and so fell forward onto its destiny now. At the last moment, Guowei untethered his horses, giving them free rein to pursue the final glancing and cut their own swathes. The result was a bloom of white fire illuminating the last instant of the Third Yallans as the arrow past through the disintegrating mass, dissolving it in fire and surging onwards toward their real foe.

- - -

Ahead, closer now but still out of range, the job of the rebelling fleets was not so easy. In fact, they felt less like the sword and more like the belly. They had, by steady, violent resistance, managed to stave off most of the Armada's cuts, but their efforts to move closer to each other and help defend a section of space while the cavalry came up had also been repulsed.

But this was all just the first swipes, the opening gambit. It was, they knew, only a matter of time before the axe came down. The only question, now, was which force would feel it first. The wall of ships, once united in purpose, had shifted and gathered over the battle's first minutes, and now resembled a pile of magnetized particles, swimming along unseen lines as they gathered around the two rebelling poles, attracted and spurned by the forces of violent opposition.

Now, without warning to either side, the order came to push in one direction, to rush one side, and the picture shifted. It quickly became clear that it would be the Nomadi that would be the first to fall, as the six hundred attacking Skalms suddenly veered to one side like a stampeding herd, rushing the Nomadi position with horns lowered. Their shifting and sliding form seemed to stand for a moment, but then the ball of atomically charged Skalm particles broke under the weight of enemy fire and started to unravel.

For each pilot, the fight now became a tactical imperative, a personal thing as strategy became impossible in the tight space of battle. If any had thought to question why they were now fighting their own, and indeed many had, the question really needed only one answer. Whatever decision had been made by whatever distant leader, they now found themselves hunted, and they must either fight or die, not that the two choices were mutually exclusive.

Here now, though, another combatant entered the fray. It was not the earthfleet, they were still precious moments out, but the carrier ship, which reintroduced itself to the universe not as an object, but as a source of reignited might, its huge engine instantly blaring as it blinked back into existence, a great spotlight shining its intense beam on the fleeing Nomadi force.

The blow was a blunt one, a bazooka fired at a swarm of flies, and normally this mammoth blade would have no place in the reflexive subtleness of Skalm battle, but now, in the rush of retreat, not all the Nomadi's pilots were able to dodge the beam, and knew their end as a final flash of white heat that evaporated them to quick dust.

The Mantilatchi were not immune to their comrades' plight, but this stolen moment of respite was going to be brief, and they needed to use it for their own ends. While the one ball of resistance caved, the other now exploded outward, countering and flanking, extracting a stiff toll for the Nomadi's extinction.

Banu could not know which were her father's forces, and she could not know that he was not even among them, but she, like Guowei, saw the momentum they were briefly claiming and called out for it.

*Banu:* 'there, we can …'

*Guowei:* 'i see it! go, suyoil, go! take them into battle. mynd, help m …'

But Mynd was already doing it, and now language left them as well, as the machine intertwined with Guowei and they sent their final orders pulsing out through the fleet, a series of plans, ideas, and contingencies coming as immediate and potential formations and firing patterns, their last blessing before they released the children upon the wall.

# Chapter 66: Crapshoot

In truth, O-Pu had no idea what was going on when the battle started. For her, the sudden break in the fleet's ranks might as well have been a million miles away, like the approaching Earth. All she knew was that the final moment was getting close now, that at some point soon the Armada would engage, and her role would come to a head.

If Shtat had been able to get a message out to her before he catalyzed events, he would have. But such a message would only have risked revealing Other Pulujan's existence, maybe even her location, while also being entirely unnecessary.

For the carrier ship would send its own warning, an alarm that caused every repair and maintenance bot in and around the ship to drop, instinctively, to the nearest anchor-points and grasp them with all their considerable strength.

O-Pu was surprised, even though she had been somewhat expecting this, as nothing could quite prepare her for the sensation of the hulking ship bringing its massive engine back online and warping back into reality at the same time.

The stars reappeared in the sky for only an instant before the void around the ship exploded with the sunlike glow of the carrier's thruster. Where it was going or what it was pointing at, O-Pu did not know, but she did know that this meant it was time.

It was a realization that came with its own share of relief and sadness. If she was going to do this right, she was going to have to get her hands dirty, and given that she was probably doomed anyway, she didn't know of any good reason not to go the whole hog.

As the carrier flashed itself back out of reality, protecting its easily targeted form from return fire, O-Pu sent out her last viral kill code into the repair bot's AI. This was not a temporary distraction code, this was a one-way ticket, and O-Pu smiled as the dumb animal she had lived within for the last year finally bit the bullet.

"Good ... fucking ... riddance," she said with relish, as she took full control at last, and rose to her feet. She didn't have long. The carrier was reorienting itself, moving under the surface like a U-boat, so that when it reappeared, its enemies would enjoy a brief moment of surprise before they were able to turn their guns on it.

But it would be the carrier who would be surprised, thought O-Pu, clambering from handhold to handhold as she silenced another AM call for the bot to reinitialize. They would come for her eventually. But she would have her fun first.

She saw the opening in the hull she sought, one of many that would serve her purpose. A bot was rising out of it, heading out on some mission.

"Gloves off!" she shouted into her helmet as flung herself at the machine, driving her fists forward as hard as she could into the confused robot's center and sending it careening away across the wide shell of the carrier.

It would be back, though, damaged, but no longer blind to her presence as it was quickly directed to seek out whatever rogue bot had just struck it. Other Pulujan did not wait around for it, though; it was not her concern. Swinging inward through the egress the other bot had just come out of, she pulled and kicked her way forward, grabbing at the insides of the ship to draw herself inward.

Finally, clearing a corner, she pivoted herself on a pipeline and threw herself at a fat conduit ahead. It was a stem, a phloem moving nutrient-rich effluent to waiting processing centers. She hit it and hugged it, letting herself enjoy this crazy moment.

"Elder," she shouted to no one, "how do I know you came up with this plan, you crazy bastard!" She laughed maniacally and she set her body to vibrate at a given frequency. She could not know whether her older brother had, indeed, come up with this harebrained scheme, but it did not matter.

She was genuinely curious about how this was going to go as her mechanical limbs reverberated around the thick pipe and the warbling signal started to echo through the system. It had a certain poeticism, she supposed. The liquid inside the system, while variable in small quantities, had an all-too-consistent consistency en masse, and she used that now. The wavelength now being transmitted through it caused it to oscillate, itself a harmless effect, until it reached the matching wavelength crimps O-Pu had spent the last year putting in pipes all across the ship-wide system.

Nothing happened for a while, and Other started to worry as she felt the telltale clanking of approaching kin coming to stop her rogue self. But the blockages, once caused, became quickly magnified, and as a thousand capillaries suddenly closed, the pressure began to rocket upward in the system's heart.

O-Pu felt it building, felt the fat pipe she was embracing start to shout in protest, and she began to laugh. The tremors became bigger now. The process was taking on a life of its own, unstoppable, as clogs solidified and compounded themselves into dense plugs, and the system, unable to find enough clear routes, threatened to release itself in other ways.

Other pushed away now, sensing the process had reached critical mass, and thrust herself to one side. She thought about turning to fight the repair bot rounding into the space to seek her out, but knew it would be better to simply hold on as the main artery of the system began bulging outward and then ruptured, like so many others around the carrier's personnel quarters.

The bot was reaching out an opened hand to grab O-Pu's shoulder when the pipe burst, a mega-gallon flow discharging itself into the space and washing the ill-prepared bot away.

"Eat shit!" laughed O-Pu hysterically, as the wave of effluent filled the space and swam outward.

She tried to ignore the fact that her own pressure seals were also screaming at the sudden barometric shift, but if they weren't tested, and, in the end, broken by the pressure, then nor would other systems be. She had known this.

The vacuum of space was, in many ways, a boon to an engineer. Without gravity, air, or, most importantly, moisture, so many problems that plagued an atmosphere-based machine were inherently moot. Unfortunately for the carrier's systems, O-Pu had just reintroduced the most troublesome of those factors in the form of a massive hemorrhage of waste, the system voiding itself into the void, indiscriminately frying systems as it went and wreaking a special kind of havoc on the big ship's nerve center.

- - -

The carrier reappeared into space as planned, its military systems shielded from the waste clogging up its crew spaces, but the AMs and PMs that had once liaised between it and its masters were notably silent now, corrupted by the foul flow, or busy trying to save engulfed cryo-units and the people sleeping within.

With only a portion of the Council now able to instruct its many PMs and AMs, the Arbite took over in earnest, phasing the big ship back into reality. This time, though, it aimed its beam at the face of the arriving earthfleet, if only to pause it just a moment longer.

It was a moment they were forced to give, and it was an important one, at least for the remaining Nomadi fighters, as the respite they had hoped for did not come and the main strike force was able to finish what it had started, leaving only a few remnants spinning away, damaged or dead.

The war was only minutes old when the remaining five hundred Mobiliei Skalms bucked anew, wafting in an almost beautifully harmonic form to bring themselves into the shape of a fifty-thousand-mile-long scythe that now came slicing back in, right into the remaining core of Mantilatchi craft.

The renewed line forced them to part, further dividing their number as the blade now transformed again and encircled the smaller subgroup, washing inward into a focusing point of flame that momentarily shone with a brightness of a supernova, a shockwave of missed fire splashing outward as the larger force flew inward on an apparently suicidal swing that suddenly passed through itself, exploding outward with a force that matched its implosive crush.

But as it expanded once more, there was only a scattering dust left where the divided core of Mantilatchi ships had once been, a quickly vanishing cloud of debris that marked the graves of that group of rebels, and those of their attackers they had managed to take with them in their last moments.

Suyoil spoke into the last second before the main battle walls impacted. Their only advantage now was, as Guowei had seen, their ability to close as one on a partially scattered fleet. He had prepared for it as best he could, sending them ever so slightly to one side so they could curve back inward, like a spinning bowling ball coming down a cosmic lane, almost five hundred dynamite skittles getting ready to rebuff their progress with their very lives.

*Wednesday God:* 'our field is set.'

*Banu:* 'good luck, friends.'

*Friday God: 'good glancing, brothers!'*

And so it came to be. The final passing. The moment of truth. Less than two seconds in the end. An eruption of monumental power as the two fleets blared their hearts out at each other, bursting into ecstatic spasm as they lashed their particle whips outward, a sheet of blinding white visible across the solar system as the irresistible force of one smashed into the immovable resolve of the other.

# Chapter 67: Numbers Up

Quavoce, now but a hushed echo of the Agent he had once been, stared at the sky through Minnie's eyes while they waited. He was still without his real self's memories even though he had given his, a poor trade, perhaps, but that had been his devil's contract.

He did not care about that now, anyway. His real self was, he imagined, even now being taken apart, mentally at least. A likely end given that they had seen from the Armada's fracturing that two sectors had clearly turned after the rejoining.

Good. He had done the right thing. But that would not be much consolation if she was lost. In his desperation to hear what had happened to Banu, he started to turn over scenarios in his mind. What, he asked, if he had betrayed the humans, bargained with his other self for Banu's life, could he have protected her, could he have saved his daughter?

But he would not have been able to look her in the eye then anyway. She would never have forgiven him. The question now was would he forgive himself if she died.

This interminable light minute took an age to pass. The signal had gone cold. The subspace lanes were silent in the aftermath of the strike. But the image came through again, at last, a picture, a haze of space revealing itself after a million lightning bolts filled the heavens. As the sky's retina recovered, the stars began to reappear, and among them a number of moving bodies resolved, vastly reduced now, the cataclysmic collision of wills having ripped so many of them to pieces.

Minnie, Mynd, Remy, and seven billion humans watched as the fog of war cleared, and now they started to track the remaining combatants, the last survivors of the battle for all of their lives. As the count came in, the result became clear. They had lost.

They had done much, Earth's brave warriors, and as Quavoce collapsed inside, crawling into the depths of his mind to mourn, Remy started to disseminate the tally. Madeline, standing in a command suite on Rolas Island, looked away from the information, shunting it into a memory bank as she opened her eyes and looked around the room.

Everyone was silent. Others were, like her, checking out of the system.

"Fifty-seven," said Jim Hacker, looking at the ground.

"Fifty-seven," said Madeline, quietly nodding.

"It does not seem like much, does it?" said Peter, without humor.

Someone laughed, less than halfheartedly, and then they were silent a moment before Jim asked, "The fixed armaments on Hekaton and the moon? Will they …?"

But he already knew the answer, and if he had a doubt, the slow shake of Madeline's head assuaged it, as she said, "We can fire our pop guns at them, but those guns were designed to fire on the fleet ships. Their fixed firing positions will be easily avoidable by a Skalm. We may get a few, if they are damaged, I guess."

"And then?" said Peter.

She took a breath, then said, "And then, Mr. Secretariat, these fifty-seven Skalms will carve our remaining defenses to mulch as they approach, and then turn their guns on us. I can only speculate on what they will target in the eighteen minutes or so they will be in range of the planet itself, but one of these craft once took down a Chinese skyscraper in about three seconds, so …"

"Yes, Madeline," said Jim, interrupting her, "I think we get the picture."

She looked at him without apology, then her eyes drifted to Quavoce. He was unnaturally still.

"Lord Mantil?" she said, her heart aching for him, for all he had sacrificed.

"Lord Mantil?" she said again, walking over to the Agent.

"How long do we have?" said Peter, to anyone who could answer. He could look himself, he supposed, but he did not want to look at the data stream anymore.

As someone answered the Russian, Madeline stepped up to Quavoce and placed her hand on his shoulder. It did not give under her touch.

Leaning in and staring into his unresponsive eyes, she said, concerned now, "Quavoce, are you all right?"

She went to shake him gently and was surprised when he did not give, not even slightly. He was as hard as stone. So this is machine grief, she thought, pulling up a chair and sitting down next to him. She did not speak to him again. If he wanted be alone for the last minutes before the axe came down, then so be it.

One thing was certain. At the top of the incoming enemy ships' target list would be this place, and ones like it, at the base of the world's doomed elevators. With no one better to spend her last minutes with, Madeline leaned in close and put her arms around the former terrorist, in case he should wake, in case the man who had given more than she could grasp to their ill-fated enterprise should wish to talk to someone before the end came.

- - -

Rob was in tears. Not the still, icy unresponsiveness of a grieving father, but the wracked anguish of a man watching the woman he loved slowly die.

"Damn it, Birgit, let go!" he screamed, tears smeared across the inside of his faceplate as he clutched her now cold legs. They were crammed in now, but if she would just release her hold and allow him to pull her free he might be able to at least right her, to look into her eyes one more time before the structure finally cracked and caved in around them.

As the gravitational pressure had built, her heart had no longer been able to keep all of her upended body fed, so she had shut off circulation to the parts of her that she no longer needed, letting them start to die so she could finish what she had fought so hard to do.

It was destroying her that Rob was hurting so much, and she so wanted to comfort him, to touch his face and say that this was what she wanted, that if she must go, and if he must, that she would make it worthwhile. But she didn't have that luxury.

She was doing this as much for him as anyone else. Or maybe she wasn't. Maybe she was just out to prove something like she always had been. Maybe this was all just a last-ditch clutch, a mad attempt to control a universe that had slipped through her grasp, imposing its will on her as it sent her tiny, irrelevant form bouncing out into space.

And so she said no.

She was not a pawn in this war. She was not some statistic. She would make the world know her name again. She would leave her mark.

*Minnie:* <¿can you feel it?>

*Birgit:* 'it … is … close.'

Her mind swam downward, into the connection with the machine, wrestling with its hardcoded imperatives to quash its resistance to her will. As it kicked and writhed, trying to buck her, she grabbed at its encoded flesh, digging her nails in, and forced herself down on it, willing it into submission.

But this was not a battle of desire, it was a battle of belief. The machine was not resisting her because it sensed that it was being co-opted by the enemy. It knew no such distinction in this dark cavern. The machine was fighting her because she was trying to get it to do something it simply did not believe it could do.

And maybe it couldn't, thought Birgit, but still she tried to drive the steed toward the edge, to make it jump into the abyss against its engineered instinct, to make it try and fly.

I don't care what you do or do not think you can do, she screamed at the machine, you are … damn … well … going … to … try.

She felt Minnie's presence at her side like a fellow wrangler, a shouted vote of support as she leapt into the saddle with her mother, injecting a part of herself into the machine and leaning her weight into the struggle.

*Birgit:* 'just go, you bastard!'

*Minnie:* <together, mother!>

*Birgit/Minnie:* <'NOW!'>

And with that they drove their heels into the IST's flanks and willed it forward, up, and out with all their might, and their minds were suddenly in the swimming mist of a netherworld.

Were they falling?

Were they dead?

No, we are not.

Where are we?

I have seen this place before.

Yes, we have.

Where?

This is subspace.

Where?

Under. Wait. What is that? There, a beacon.

An ever-increasing circle washed over them, expanding as it vanished outward, but also never growing, never weakening. As they analyzed its paradoxical form, thinking of it brought them, instantly, to its source.

What is it?

As they studied the beating heart of the beacon, stepping into it, then through and around it, they recognized it.

It is the moon. That is the Lunar base subspace tweeter.

But we are with it.

We are. A smile. A shared happiness. They were out.

Can you speak to Earth?

We cannot. I am not whole, I am an echo, in your mind/in the machine.

So am I, I guess. Maybe this is all that is left of me.

I guess it is up to us then. It is. Let's find them. Yes, let's find them.

- - -

The fifty-seven saw the cosmic flak coming up at them from Earth and stepped aside with simple grace, dancing around it as it came. The beams, though powerful, were anchored, and with cold detachment the remaining pilots of the strike force added the source of this fire to the list of targets they were each compiling.

They had not heard from the carrier ship since the glancing. It was still there. They could see its big, ungainly form rolling lazily behind them. But it was silent. Something had upset its onboard systems just before the fight had finally closed, and it had stayed too long in reality.

A squadron of the enemy Skalm had seen their opportunity and taken it with a speed the remaining Mobiliei Skalm pilots were still reeling from. They had been good. Some had been truly awesome. But they had been too few to turn the key of critical mass and, once the final count had been tallied, the glancing had been the Mobiliei's.

Now all that was left to them was the quick butchery they had come for. Their orders no longer spoke of saving the planet's environment; environment be damned. They had paid a terrible price for worrying about the precious planet's ecosystem. They would clean up what they had to clean up. Their mission now was to make sure there was nothing left to resist the colony ships when they came in to begin the cleansing proper.

As the minutes closed, all looked to be plain sailing now. The moons, each clearly housing a significant body of military and industrial might, would make a nice opener, and so the two sitting ducks were the first to feel the searing napalm of the strike force's arrival as the fifty-seven lazed them.

For the moon it was an exercise in acne control as the bulk of the incoming force popped anything that even vaguely resembled a structure. For Hekaton, their attack was more straightforward. Five assigned Skalms directed all of their focused, aligned beams straight down the captured asteroid's pole, releasing a long, concerted pulse before turning their guns on the closest elevator base. The light-speed beam lasted less time than it would take for it to reach its target and so pulsed outward.

From Earth, Guowei, still subsumed with Mynd, watched the nanosecond before impact as the beam lanced through Earth's closest limb. The shaft struck straight at, and then through, the heart of the asteroid, expending a great deal of its energy in the process, but still leaving a little contingency to burst out the other side as the rock broke open. The split was not clean, though. This was a blow of shattering force, and while the kill would be glacially slow to fall to ground, its back was most certainly broken.

Emergency procedures were being enacted all over the planet. Bunkers were flooding with important personages and whatever duty officers had been lucky enough to be offered spots in the deep, hidden places.

Under mountains and oceans, shielded dugouts were lit and quickly populated. Their new inhabitants could not know if this claustrophobic home was to be theirs for weeks, years, or the rest of their lives. They only knew it was likely going to be better to be down here than up there as the strike force completed their drive-by assault.

With fresh craters now pocking the moon's surface, the entire remaining Mobiliei fleet turned their eyes earthward and began checking off lists of targets based on various compared and contrasted criteria. Power signatures were a good clue. They may have once feared releasing fission fuels into the atmosphere, and certainly that was still far from desirable, but humanity's many fusion cores, far more powerful and obvious to spectroscopic eyes, were like beacons. Their very natures were like great, emblazoned red targets on the planet's surface, and once ruptured, their released energies only magnified the destruction suddenly blossoming across the planet.

It was not a fair fight, not anymore, but it was the only fight left these fifty-seven pilots before they were gone once more.  If they did not put a stop to us now, blasting us back into the Stone Age, or just to the early stages of the information age they had found us in, then they would have no safe place to return to once they finally stopped their mad progress and came back here, a little over four years from now.

A so they fired at the fish in the barrel, and Earth's great achievements began to crumble.

## Chapter 68: And Now, Watch This ...

The first singularity was more a source of confusion than fear on the part of the pilots. Out there, to one side of the approaching fleet lancing the upcoming globe, a subspace signature suddenly popped into existence. But there was no ship inside it, and it quickly vanished, its footprint disappearing into the past.

But now here was another, closer. The surviving captains were curious, but with nothing else to do they sent signal to keep firing as they closed with Earth. That said, they did start to gather information on the strange anomalies, ordering all to watch for others.

They got a little more information than they wanted when a rush of better readings came in from a ship whose very self was now caught up in one of the strange events, and then the popping bubble was gone, taking one of the ship's akas and its attached sub-core with it.

The craft, still firing with three of its arms, was suddenly imbalanced and spinning wildly. Its pilot stopped his trigger as quickly as he could and started trying to get himself under control, but his guns were, at least for now, silenced.

The responding call for evasive maneuvers went out even as this new, unexplained threat manifested itself in another bubble, larger now, one that totally engulfed another of the force's complement, sucking it into nowhere.

Now the confidence of the last of the Armada's survivors started to desert them.

Real fear was starting to mount in the strike force, and they were once again starting to bounce with paroxysmal jerks, trying to make themselves harder targets for whatever new, unseen beast was now hunting them. Try and shoot this, they thought, and they resumed their fire on Earth, a place they assumed was the source of this new threat.

But the minds targeting them were not trying to track their movements. Birgit and Minnie had placed themselves outside the universe, and outside real-time. Time still existed here, of course, indeed it was far more tangible to Birgit now than it ever had been in reality. Here it was a liquid thing. Not reversible, perhaps, but able to be resisted, like a river washing into her.

She was under the water's flow now, dragging herself along the rushing river's bed, and so she could drag herself up river on her prey's legs, no matter how they may duck and dive above the surface. Under here the dancing signatures of the nimble Skalm were reduced to fixed things, things she could so easily see through the murky waters once she was close.

She approached another and reached out with her spiny singularity fingers. Her first attempts had been blind swipes of the IST's whip, but now she felt she could actually grab at the very foundations of the Skalm, grab at them and pull them under. She closed her subspace fingers around another and pulled. wrenching him into the darkness, into her world, and then let him go so he could wash away downstream, into the nothingness.

She was getting better at this, she thought, as she struck out for another, seeking more unfortunates to pull into hell, a domain she now ruled, apparently. She laughed. She was a god here, she thought, and set off once more on her deadly spree, to claim more Mobiliei souls.

- - -

*Guowei:* 'look. something is happening.'

Not many eyes were still watching the skies. Only the most morbid still looked toward our destroyers, but now some eyes went skyward again, to the stars, as the invading ones suddenly started to blink out.

*Minnie:* <she has done it. she is still alive.>

Minnie hesitated, then started to rejoice as proof of her mother's unlikely success manifested itself in yet another pocket of nothingness, and another enemy Skalm being sucked away. The enemy fleet was becoming frantic now, that was clear, and some had started to flee, but it would do them no good.

Minnie reached out to Rob, but he was not there anymore. With the lunar base gone, along with the massive subspace tweeter they had constructed there, Minnie was cut off from her mother, again, maybe forever this time. Minnie felt grief mingle with her pride for her mother's achievement. With no way of helping her mother, or of saving her, trapped out there in the cosmos, Minnie focused instead on what she could see of her mother's final actions and she filled with pride.

Meanwhile, Mynd sent the signal out, flooding Remy's damaged but still pervasive highways with the simple announcement: we fight still. The people of the world closed their eyes, took in the view of space and watched as the dying scientist fought for them.

Madeline watched with them as their attackers, fleeing what she could not know, bucked and swam, still firing now, but clearly also running from something. But their hunter was too fast, and here she appeared once more, in a flash, pulling another away, and then another, sometimes whole, sometimes only a cross section. Madeline was not sure which end she liked better for her enemies.

She smiled, whispering under her breath, "Birgit, you magnificent, mad, beautiful lunatic!"

Milton SpacePort shook from yet another hit. The foundation was stronger than it had once been, and they were deeper in its core, but still the foundations were reverberating with the force of the thunderous blows still landing on its surface.

It took a while, but slowly the sound began to diminish. The Mobiliei Skalms were not all gone, but their number were diminishing rapidly, and they had stopped firing, hoping for some respite in return. But no one on earth had either the will or the ability to call off the dogs. The last of them, almost pathetic now as they fled by a shuddering planet, were picked off by a silent Birgit and then they were gone.

# Epilogue

In the aftermath, they had sent signal to Phobos. It had started with a thank you, not from Mynd, Minnie, or any one person, but from an entire planet, badly bloodied but still alive, thanks to her.

They had waited, but there was no response. They had kept transmitting, and discussion quickly began on how to mount a mission to go after them, even if only to reclaim their bodies and return them to the planet they had saved.

Knowing the state Minnie had last seen the IST in, she knew that it was unlikely Birgit and Rob would be able to get out of its crumpled form, if they survived the crush at all. But she would work at bringing them home anyway, and there was certainly no one who would stand in her way.

An hour after the last Mobiliei Skalm had vanished or been dissected, the pops began again. Mynd saw them immediately, and Minnie was with him, listening in an instant later, eager for any sign of life from her mother.

It was strange at first. The flashes came with seeming randomness, but the two colossal artificial minds soon saw the pattern in the bubbles popping into the Lagrange point between Earth and its scarred moon.

The code was as natural to them as breathing, even if the non-native speaker on the other end often stumbled. It was binary, and they brought its meaning down into their minds like hope showering from above, focusing their might on calculating and recalculating any possible interpretation of the string.

In the end, the meaning was as obvious as it was poetic, and in the instant they both saw it, every capable air and ground unit in a two-hundred-mile radius of a specific point in southwestern Germany was mobilized. Whatever task they had been working on, whatever precedence their cargo might have thought they were owed, all was superseded by the chance that Birgit might once again be able to defy the odds stacked against her.

StratoJets lifted from the ground in clouds of dust or banked hard, setting aside old courses as they ramped up their engines now, in concert, and closed on the spot for whatever final attempt Birgit had planned. Minnie could not be sure what Birgit intended, and she could be even less sure that the woman could do it even if she tried, but if there was a chance that her mother was going to jump, Minnie would be there to catch her.

As hundreds of aircraft and ground units, both old and new, closed on the point in the Schwarz Wald, eyes turned to the sky above the observatory-capped peak of the Feldberg and everyone waited.

- - -

Rob felt as cold now as the body he still held close. She had not moved in over an hour, silent like the connection to Earth, last heard reporting its impending doom.

He had stopped crying now. Now he just waited. So much effort for nothing. That they were going to die had always seemed likely. That they had survived so long was a miracle, really. But that they had failed just made the truth of this slow death unbearable.

What comfort he might have taken in being close to the woman he had come to love was diminished by her self-enforced silence. If he could only see her face once more, kiss her once more. He tightened his grip around her cold body and closed his eyes.

The pull of her hand was so gentle at first, so soft as to be almost imperceptible. But he felt it anyway, he felt it and his heart leapt at the sign that she was still alive, somewhere in there. He started to fight again, his strength flooding back to him as hope for one last moment with her was revived. But as he fought to pull her free once more, her finger, weak and feeble, shook slowly back and forth.

Stop, she was telling him. Stop. And now, as he stared at the ghostly hand, it came toward his mask, and began pulling him gently down, toward her, closer.

"Birgit!" he called. "Can you hear me?"

She could not, but still her hand pulled his head down, and he struggled to reorient himself in the cramped space, so he could be close to her once more in the final moments.

Her hand, her arm, were distant things. After the loud and brash vigor of her subspace battle with the Mobiliei fleet, this simple act was so hard. It was so close, and yet so tiny and vague, she could almost not imagine it had ever been natural to her.

But on some level she felt, like an echo of a distant bell, as her hand slowly brought him down, closer, to her chest, to her heart.

But this was no sentimental act. She might have been privy to such flights of fancy if she didn't still harbor some semblance of hope. But she did, in a corner of her self, and if she could bring his head closer, nearer, not to her, but to the singularity itself, then when she finally released it from its enslavement she might be able to pull off one last trick.

As he came close, confused, perhaps, but without other option or want in the darkness, she reached out, not with her arms now, but with the singularity's infinite, etherial fingers, across space, broaching the wide gap between them and their home.

She saw it now as a great gravitic orb, the huge tug of the Earth visible for eons across this inverted place. It was vast and heavy, holding so many souls in its embrace, but she could see none of them now, none of its cities or towns, none of its mountains or oceans. She saw only the great gravitic core, surrounded by smaller satellite signatures, fusion footprints large and small dotted around the borders of the great orb, like shining beacons of pressure and attraction, their pull visible under the skin of the universe.

She span around the globe at the speed of thought, seeking a pattern, a unique point, and here, at the rough distance from the globe's magnetic pole that she expected to see it, a converging surge of forces, a riot of energy closing in, as Minnie and Mynd mobilized their forces.

It looked, to Birgit, like a flower budding in reverse, a folding inward of light at whose epicenter, Birgit knew, was a mountain that she had once been able to see from her childhood home. They had heard her, Birgit thought, sobbing at her center, they had heard, and they were waiting.

With the last ounces of herself she fixated on that beacon in the night, bringing the IST's massive power round in a great, fixing beam that pulled at the strings of this different place, this warped universe, and linked it to that closing blossom on Earth.

Now, with the two places joined, binding them as best she could, she released her grip on another part of the IST, allowing the singularity to burst outward, letting go of its reins that had held it prisoner. Without sentiment or backward glance, the singularity bloomed outward, briefly enveloping the few cramped meters around its core in the center of the IST, and then sucking the center of itself away, into the dark mist.

- - -

The translation came, not with a bang, but with a whisper, and a white flash that fled quickly away, leaving only a black dot at its center. Minnie, Mynd, Guowei, and every mind that had been able to inhabit a craft rushed up to it or ran under it, as eyes probed the slowly falling sphere.

A lazy ribbon of blood was forming as the irregular black orb started to fall, already starting to come apart when the faster of the minds rushing to it made out what they were seeing. It was the core of the IST, transposed here by long patterned equation, an ideal dreamt by the very person now bleeding out in its center.

In slow motion, two automatons, an Eight and a Fourteen, leapt from approaching StratoJets onto the falling block with apparently suicidal abandon. They grabbed and pulled at the device, suddenly bereft of the massive gravity that had so recently been holding it together. But as the robot beasts wrenched it apart it was quickly starting to respond to Earth's greater gravity as it started to fall faster and faster toward the ground below.

The two automatons worked with fierce effort, tearing metal and gouging into the machine to get at the severed bodies within. The dot was coming apart now, ripped at by powerful muscles as the whole fell fast toward the mountaintop below.

The singularity at the IST's center, once released, had only spread wide enough in real-time to encompass Birgit's torso, and even less of Rob had been saved, as she sent what she could of them warping across space, to home, at last. Her gloved hand was still resting on the side of his helmet when the Phases broke through to them.

The automatons, working feverishly, grasped one dismembered form each, Birgit's legless body, Rob's disembodied bust, and leapt clear once more in the last moments before the widening cloud of debris started to rain down on the green earth.

- - -

As the story was etched into history, as the tale of the battle was recorded, many names would be carved in many monuments around the world. The shockwave of the conflict carried a lot of them away still, as high on the list of heroes were the lost orphans, the best of humanity, our salvation even after we had forsaken them.

As recovery work was prioritized and begun, first among many imperatives for a rebuilding TASC was the launching of probes, out along potential pathways modeled after the battle, looking for remnants, for explanation, and maybe even for survivors floating in ejected capsules in the coldness of ever-deeper space.

While plans for those probes were finalized and inputted into the two Resonance Domes still standing, the rest of the world turned its eyes to the rain. It was a meteor rain, part of a storm that encompassed the entire equator and much of the tropics, and that was predicted to last for the next decade or more as the remnants of Hekaton and the other satellite hubs fell slowly to Earth.

Much would stay aloft, however, and now the minds that had planned this terrible party gazed on the damage wrought and looked to the stellar brooms they would need to clear it, before our highways to the stars could be rebuilt.

It was a pity, some might say, that they would be forced to clear the glimmering ring that was now forming around the waist of the planet, a tribute to Saturn's glory, but if this first brush with the wider world of the cosmos had taught them anything, it was that the universe was no more forgiving than our own world had once been, and if humanity did not want to suffer the fate of the Incas and Aztecs, then they must look to the horizon and prepare.

And to that end, they also turned their focus to the last of their enemy. They sent signal to the colony ship's of the Armada, telling them of their cousins' fate, and quickly worked to construct a copy of the now lobotomized IST on the very axis of the world, drilling into the South Pole to anchor it to the plate it would now defend.

The massive Subspace Core was no communication device, though. It could be, but that was not its prime directive. This was a weapon, one of a new era, and maybe it could even be a transport, if the recovering Birgit could figure out a way to reproduce that trick without destroying the core itself at the same time.

- - -

"We see you, you slippery little ..." said Birgit, standing at a console in her new laboratory on Jeju Island.

"Now, now, darling," said Rob, stepping up to her side.

She smiled, "But they are right there, see?"

And he could see what she was pointing to, he was happy to say. She did as little as possible in the ether now, preferring to spend as much time as she could in the real world, in all its warm, wet, weighed-down-and-dirty glory. And to spend time with Rob, as well, what was left of him.

They might not be able to romp in zero gravity anymore, or anywhere else, for that matter, with her lower extremities gone, and his body now more machine than man. But what was left was more than enough for her, she thought, as he wrapped his strong, lifelike arms around her and they looked at the big screen in front of them.

She pointed at a moving dot, laden with data and meaning, and he saw the dot closing on another. The dot represented a ship not unlike New Moon One, but with a very different target. It was closing on a dark mass. Almost lifeless, but still flying blind in a long pass through Venus's orbit and then outward, forever.

But before that ship was lost to the void, another was closing on it, an intrastellar mailman going to deliver an important package, a package that included something close to a stamped-addressed-envelope, for those that remembered such things.

- - -

The year following the final battle went by surprisingly quickly. The colony ships, surrendered after Birgit had fired a few shots across their bows, were arriving into orbital impound while humanity decided what to do with them. Their orbit would not be around Earth, though, as that space was still a debris field, and would be for many more years. And so they targeted the moon, and for the most part were happy even for its cold embrace given the fate of their fighting fleet.

Birgit had not managed to find a way to refine her trick with the IST, but she had found a way to repeat it. After long and unpleasant negotiation with the vanishing carrier flagship, or rather what was left of it, two capsules had been given over in return for a simple concession of the rest of its inhabitants being allowed to live out their lives in space-bound exile.

The two cryo-units in question, one having been removed forcibly from frozen, crusted excrement before being handed over, were taken into the heart of a purpose-built IST, and placed next to it. With To-Henton and DefaLuta watching in icy silence, and the Hemmbar gazing on in fascination, Sar Lamati screamed and screamed into the cosmos as the traitors departed the ship, and then the universe.

- - -

In a wide room, a small group gathers and waits.

On two cots lie Quavoce Mantil, the man who had pretended to be Shahim Al Khazar; and Shtat Palpatum, the man who had pretended to John Hunt, a pretense so profound that he had even fooled himself. They awake slowly in a customized medical recovery chamber unlike any ever conceived on Earth.

These are chambers designed for alien anatomies, the first extra-terrestrials to ever truly touch foot upon our planet's surface. In this room, sterilized by technologies that combine the wisdom of both races, the two men open their real eyes for the first time in decades, stretch long dormant limbs, and groan as the last of the days-long reanimation process brings them back to consciousness.

As they both focus, they look at each other, and then at the small group of aliens waiting to meet them. They see their human selves and smile into these mirrors, the faces familiar from a decade of shared experience.

And next to their simulacrums they see Madeline and Jack. They know them both from now rejoined experience. They know them, but they have never truly met them until now. They warily nod, not a natural movement for Mobiliei necks but they attempt it anyway, knowing their faces must appear strange to these people who had come to be as family to them. And then they glance at another, a first friend given secret furlough for this occasion.

The three humans smile with very real affection, seeing past their superficial differences, knowing these two aliens for who they really are: the people ultimately responsible for every saved life, for giving humanity back the future it now looks forward to.

These men are the ones that truly saved them, they know that, and Neal steps forward with a tear in his eye. He steps up to the one he knows to be Shtat Palpatum, both of them remembering their first tentative meeting in a hotel room eleven years before, and slowly, but without fear, they reach out toward each other and embrace for the first time.

Please keep reading for the short story, The Orphan' End, the story of the fates of the Orphan Pilots in their final millisecond battle.

For more information on books by Stephen Moss, and to hear about future releases, you can find more about the author on his website, www.thefearsaga.com, on Facebook, or you can email him directly at thefearsaga@gmail.com.

For now, though, this story is at an end.
But the greater questions it begets are just beginning.
Thank you for reading,
-Stephen

# The Orphans' End

by Stephen Moss

The long years of preparation, the embittered political and martial struggle, the toil and sacrifice, it had come down to a single moment, the final glancing. For Banu, at the bleeding edge of a squadron of Skalm, the journey had been nearly a decade long. For the Gods, the orphan pilots, it had been a shorter, but no less convoluted six years.

For Wednesday God, imbedded within the very tip of the Earthfleet, the journey building up to the glancing had been an interrupted time, pocketed with times of doubt, question, and introspection. But that was all behind him now.

Now was the time of the battle. As the Mobiliei fleet finished brutally amputated its rebelling Nomadi and Mantilatchi sectors, the Earthfleet was quickly approaching, accelerating headfirst into the wall of enemy Skalm.

As the glancing approached, Wednesday's interaction with Guowei was becoming close to the point that the line between them blurred, a tight conversation that both relished, though for very different reasons.

Guowei took great pleasure in the reality of it all. He had learned to beat all the simulations his peers had thrown at him. Well, he had learned to manage the odds, at least. There was a point where an imbalance of force outweighed any advantage intellect or inspiration could give. This, though, was different from anything he had faced before.

This was alien, truly alien. He had sparred with the Mobiliei Agents, but they were but echoes of their real selves. The one called Mantil had been good, sometimes superb, but he had also been just a copy, and Guowei had seen his weaknesses and opened them.

But that would not be possible here. These were no copies. This enemy was real, and any nonchalance Guowei might have once felt was a long, long way away now. This was it, and he merged with the beautifully simple mind that was his forward commander and they took in the budding detail of the enemy line, discussing and updating tactics as they both moved closer to the final formations they would have in the glancing.

They were at a horrible disadvantage. They had less numbers, and they had a harder mission. They must stop all of them, or at least the vast, vast majority. It was going to be, Guowei knew, close to impossible; and he saw in his partner's mind, in Kim Suyoil's brilliant innocence, the realization of the fact that they were going to have to sacrifice any hope at survival in order to have a chance.

Guowei did not filter his profound respect and appreciation for the bravery of the young boy out of his signal, not even a little, and as the final moment came so close that their conversation was only slowing the speed at which Wednesday would have to react, Guowei allowed his overflowing sense of fraternal love for Suyoil and his orphaned brethren to flood the system before the battle went supernova.

- - -

Suyoil reveled in the strategic genius of the voice in his head. He listened to it like an imaginary friend, comforting and encouraging him as his myriad fingertips and toes tweaked and danced like Kali's dancing blades.

Suyoil's body was one with his fleet, his movements made real in an instant, orders rippling outward to his forces, sending them twirling this way and that in the final seconds before impact. Suyoil was not an ambitious soul. He had nothing of the megalomania and just plain mania that had driven a desperate world leader to volunteer him and his friends for this terrible but vital task. But here, in these moments, his doubts fell away from him, as they had in the glancings back before reality made its ugly presence known, back when Mother's love had been all he had needed.

Here his focus was pure. Here, now, his mind expanded outward and transcended the reality of his impending death to a place that existed only in the instant, the vast, light second-wide instant, where he was as close to godliness as any human had ever been. His mind braced for it, settling and calming into something close to serenity as the wall finally broke over him, a great tidal wave of fusion flame and particle swell, smashing and crashing around his hundreds of arms and legs.

His last thought was one of nuance and grace, of the slightest changing, of seeing in the million spears rushing in on him a series of the slightest gaps and opportunities and sending out the orders that would drive his best positioned units into them, to pry them open and cut into the heart of his enemy.

Here was the meeting of strategy and tactic, the flipping of the switch from future to present, as it all came to frenetic fruition. His final orders, inspired and desperate, were still flashing outward from him as the fire consumed him and the rest of his forward phalanx.

In his last moments, in the final terrible milliseconds, there was something more than pain. Beyond thought, or below it, in a deeper place, a bass thrum underscored the chorus roar of the battle. It was the love from Guowei filling him. And it was his own love for his bunk-mate Friday, cold and huddled together, threadbare sheets wrapped around them as they whispered tall-tales and dreams to each other in the night.

- - -

Friday saw it the very moment Wednesday fed his mind with his final orders: the opportunity.

He saw it clearly and was moving the next instant, before the thought had fully taken form in him. It was a guest overstaying his welcome, the carrier ship, big and powerful, a mammoth that had left the safety of the subspace herd and was now here, alone. It was not running as it should have, back to the shelter of the netherworld. It was staying, and as the final orders came from his brother, Friday took his squadron and sliced through a gap in the firewall and into the carrier like a whip-crack.

He felt as his brother went silent, felt the final moments of certainty and composure in Wednesday's last millisecond orders, but he enjoyed none of the peaceful transcendence Wednesday felt in the heat of battle. He felt only passion, and now something even more powerful: rage, fury, an anger so mighty it outshone his particle swords as he wailed his grief outward, dancing around the massive lance from a panicked carrier ship and then hammering into it.

He targeted its core not just with his weapons but with all of his tumultuous rage. Where Wednesday had been a becalmed eye at the center of a hurricane, Friday was the riotous core of a tornado, flinging himself at his prey and into it, punching his deathblow into its flanks as he forfeited his life, a life he could not imagine living without his friend anyway.

- - -

For Banu, the glancing was no less instant, no less of a spasm of ferocity, but it held a greater sense of strategic portent, of a fate still under control. Wednesday and Guowei had sent her squadron high, to come in hard from above, not spared, not at all, but held for just moment, to make their sacrifice count.

As the fist of the Earthfleet drove into the face of the wall, splintering and breaking as it did so, Banu was one of several breakouts that flanked inward, a multitude of hidden uppercuts and driving heels powering into the broad, Goliath jaw of the Mobiliei armada.

Just as Wednesday's world had shrunk into the glancing, Guowei fading into the strategic past, so now did Banu's focus into a point, as her squadron carved down and through the enemy, rending and splitting as they went.

She would deliver on the promise made to her orphan siblings, making the Mobiliei pay, making them pay with their lives for their slaughterhouse intent.

As she came into the closing gap between the last of the Mantilatchi rebel forces and the storming Mobiliei armada, she joined with them. They could not speak to each other, and had no time to anyway. This was faster than that. This was two dancers vaulting passed each other, barely a nudge and a push, a finger-stroke to make their intent known to each other before their bodies parted once more.

But language was there, in the their movements, and the last battered remnants of the Mantilatchi force took her meaning and broke downward, not joining her, as their momentum in the opposite direction was too great, but mirroring her movements as she banked down into the storm of lightning that the space around the battle had become.

The war had become a nebula, a tiny supernova of atomic fire that briefly outshone the Sun, exploding outward, consuming and subliming the warriors in its midst, and now she flew across the ballooning sphere of destruction, her sensors singed by the fight's furnace.

Her squadron was dispersing as it went, separating and dividing as it diluted itself. It was the only way they could avoid the slashing swords of the enemy fleet in the closest moment, their perihelion, where the singeing orb of radiating death around the battle was at its deadliest.

Wednesday had thrust his vanguard into the armada's heart, and, in his final orders, brought his peripheral units down upon them as well. And so, it was with a mix of respect and shame that Banu now fired into the midst of the glancing, knowing her arrows would as likely find friend as foe.

- - -

And then … she was past, it was now a blink after the battle proper, and her pattern was cutting down the far side of the battle as she continued firing, a small part of her looking for some remnant of the main body of Earthfleet in the battle's wake.

But there was no sign of life in the cloud of debris cutting backward, only the broken limbs and shattered cores of Skalm, some bleeding fusion into the cosmos, others spinning wildly, either lobotomized or clipped, now gyrating spastically in their death throws.

She could see the remnant of the Mobiliei force moving off as well, it was moving farther and farther every millisecond, and now her pincer unit fired up the backsides of their enemy. They stabbed at them. Wednesday and Guowei had given them precious sideways momentum where the last of the Mobiliei were still moving mostly as one, and Banu took the opportunity to try to pick a few more of them off, sending her squadrons fire after them with focused ire.

As the two fleets moved apart, now massively diminished, they were already two thousand kilometers apart a second after they had passed. But now Banu came into the debris, the aftermath, and like she had once taken a Stratojet and threaded it through a cloud of wasp missiles, she now plunged into the field of her fallen brethren.

Was this Wednesday's Skalm she was darting passed? Was that Friday's core she was forced to fire into as it threatened to cut across her path? And what was this now? What was this new threat, this new obstacle?

It was a web of focused fire from the departing Mobiliei, a final gift as their range stretched, and Banu saw it as a crisscrossed maze filling her view. They were returning the favor, they were giving their last licks, and for the last of Banu's squadron it was too much in the confined, over-charged madness of the battle cloud.

They went wild, spinning outward as each pilot fought to avoid the storm of aka and beam, cores exploding like mines and artillery shells on every side, and suddenly Banu knew some sense of the madness that the center of the battle must have been. She knew it as a closing of doors, all the Skalm's maneuverability reduced to single-digit options as her squadron finally started to die around her.

For all her skill and ability, all her experience, she saw now the luck that had brought her this far, the simple dice roll that had left her and her squadron so untouched. It was a luck that had just run out. She banked hard around a spinning Skalm, still firing, its triggers still clutched by dead fingers, and as she did so a Mobiliei particle lance came across her view. She dodged it easily, side-stepping it as a matter of course, but the attack had not been for her. As the lance found its target, the very Skalm she had just dodged, the damaged craft erupted, its central core igniting and detonating its three remaining subsidiary engines in quick succession.

The fire in and of itself was not too much for Banu, but as the blast washed out over her she was momentarily blinded, and in these tight confines it was like being hit by a wave of water whilst clambering over sharp rocks. The next moment she felt them slicing into her, jagged edges cutting at her superconductive skin, splintering reefs sawing her nanotube bones.

As one of her akas came loose she calmed its antagonistic mirror, trying to find purchase as she was buffeted, but now a pain came that was greater, not a rock but a blade as she fell into another particle beam. She could not tell if it was from a dead comrade or their departing enemy, and in the end it did not matter. It severed another of her akas almost completely, and buckled her main drive nozzle, and with that she was adrift.

This was not the pleasant kind of drift, though. This was not a life on the ocean wave, but a leaf on an acid sea, the swirls of corrosive death around her smacking and bashing her once proud form, shredding it.

She held on as long as she could. She knew that if she released her capsule early, while still in the hell-cloud of her dead comrades, she would surely be consumed. So she clung on to the disintegrating hull of her ship, staying with it till the last possible moment, looking for some sign of the other side, hoping against hope that her cores would not be corrupted before she was in reach of safety.

Then she saw a gap in the fire, a slight darkening in the flame, and she took it, releasing a pulse of her still vital fusion heart out through a small nozzle at the end of the tube that held her life-capsule, the black pill that held her brain. The pressure drove her outward, firing her like a bullet out of her Skalm, out, away, hoping now for the void, for the still calm of vacuum.

The capsule launched away, ricocheting off of bellowing clouds of radiation and great swelling orbs of flame. She did not feel it, though. For her, there was only silence now, a deep, enveloping silence enforced upon her by her lack of any sense not given to her by her machine cocoon. For she was without ear, mouth or nose. She was without face.

She was, at last, alone.

Any noise or impact from the outside was lost, and the only proof of her survival would come with time now, as milliseconds ticked away, and became a second, which eventually became a minute. And so that, for Banu, was that.

- - -

Eventually she stopped waiting to die. It seemed it was not going to happen today. Tentatively she pinged her system to check her surroundings. As she did so, a small, built-in AI contained within her capsule opened its eyes. Hidden behind thick lids. Small sensors irised open and took in their surroundings. The battle was far behind her now, but still filling one whole hemisphere of Banu's view, statically blurring that side.

The AI, taking into account the spin they had gained in the last moments in the cloud, began filtering out that part of their view, redacting it to protect its precious eyes. Banu was grateful for it, though, and for the respite it gave her battered psyche.

She set the AI to analyze their trajectory and predict any potential danger spots and then left it to its devices. This was no Minnie, nor even a mini-minnie, and it would take time to muddle its way through tasks, as Banu would need time to get used to its treacle-trickle of information.

If she could have breathed deep, if she could have sighed and covered her eyes, she would have. But with neither lungs, hands, nor eyes, she sufficed with shutting herself off once more to think.

She could not be certain, but her instincts told her that, despite giving everything they had, they had failed. She knew she had been among the last to fall. That there had still been enough enemy ships remaining to return such fire could only mean ...

She tried to stop thinking about it. That they would go on to attack Earth itself ... she tried to shut it out, but could not. She wanted to shake her head or shout but such escapes were not available to her. She needed the machine to help. It was all she had left.

As if in answer, her lone AI companion now spoke up, answering her query about their course and speed. It was as good a report as she could really have hoped for; a straight shot out, away from all this, into the night.

She looked at it for a moment, setting aside a momentary pang of desire to be closer to home. There was no home, not any more. They had lost. It had not been through any fault of their own, through any lack of effort, but that would not be any consolation to the last survivors, to her father, to Minnie, to Neal, wherever he was, as they watched the axe come down. She could not cry, but her grief flowed anyway, pulsing in her mind as her sorrow overwhelmed her.

For a long time she just mourned. She had a store of information with her and she called up images of Quavoce, of his eyes, reliving the first days of their relationship, so scary, so unknown, yet so solid and trustworthy. She found solace sometimes in thinking of how she had felt when he had returned from whatever mission had taken him away that first week they had been together. She remembered seeing his face when he returned to her. Seeing in it that same stolidity that she had memorized, like seeing a home after a long voyage, filling you with a simple reassurance: I had not dreamed this, it is real, this love and this safety, it really exists, in those eyes, so foreboding to most, so comforting to her.

After a while the pain started to fade, its sharp edges worn down, eroded each time they stabbed at her, until they were either not as sharp, or her soul was so scarred it could rebuff them.

Now, with only time and space to look forward to, she looked for a way to pass the time. She knew that she could not recreate the virtual world she knew so well with such a minimal onboard processor. So, instead of watching as the machine tried, in vain, to keep up with her, she decided instead that it would be best to slow herself down, a choice that would bring two benefits.

And so, as the first weeks turned into months, she sent herself into a coma, slowing oxygen flow, calming her higher functions, hooding the raptor's eyes, and in that sleep she began to dream.

For the longest time she did not dream of people. She dreamt of the barn, of being an owl once more. Sometimes she dreamt of swimming and running. Then, one day, she dreamt of the panther simulation, and through that her mind found its way back to Friday and Wednesday. She smiled at the simple renderings of her two friends, and for the first time since just after the battle she thought of home.

In a quiet place, on a peaceful day, she walked out of the dark woods, transforming from the big, black cat back into her young self as she went, and there, amid dawn's light, she saw Quavoce sitting with Minnie's burly, gentle-giant form, and she nodded. They were, she assumed, long dead now, but she could go to them, for, in truth, she knew she was just as extinct as they. She could go to them now. It was time to visit their ghosts.

- - -

Outside, the years pass as the small capsule swims ever onward, oblivious and negligible, leaving only a tiny ping in its trail, a series of breadcrumbs dropped on the path as it wanders off into the night. She cannot know that something is sniffing out those breadcrumbs. She cannot know that her father is still alive, just as he does not know that she is. But he is looking for her, as is an entire planet. He is looking for her and he will never stop, he will not give up on her, such is the depth of his promise.

Far back in her wake, all the way back at the epicenter of the battle, still glowing and throbbing with the hot embers of their struggle, a spikey probe from a battered Earth finds her scent, and a world awakes to the hope of reunification.

Thank you for reading.

Many have commented since the first publication of Fear the Future
that they were left bereft by some of the characters' ends.

While that was deliberate, in parts, as it seems to me that war's end is rarely as satisfying or
just as we might like to think, I can say that war is also rarely the end of the story, and so it
will not be here.

Banu will return, both to my books, and to Earth, in Fear's Orphans, later in 2015.
But she will return to a planet touched by a greater universe, and
changed by it. She will find her father there, and her uncle Neal,
though in far different forms than she left them.

I truly hope to see you all again then,
-Stephen Moss

Made in the USA
Columbia, SC
12 May 2020